The Mark Lee Masters Collection Vol. 1

Mark Lee Masters

ISBN:	Hardcover	978-1-4257-8844-5
	Softcover	978-1-4257-8839-1

This is a work of fiction. Names, characters, places and incidents either are the product of the author's imagination or are used fictitiously, and any resemblance to any actual persons, living or dead, events, or locales is entirely coincidental.

This book was printed in the United States of America.

To order additional copies of this book, contact:
Xlibris Corporation
1-888-795-4274
www.Xlibris.com
Orders@Xlibris.com
44536

CONTENTS

Who's Got a Taste for Killing?

Who's got a Taste for Killing?

This is the original 1st edition

Published by Xlibris

Printed in the United States of America

First printing: April 2008

CONTENTS

Acknowledgments

My heartfelt thank you goes to my teachers who have instilled in me the desire to write. I would also like to thank my proofreaders and the many readers who reinforced my feeling that this book was interesting. I thank my patient wife, who made it possible for me to find the time to write. My greatest respect and admiration goes to my readers who make writing worth while. Thank you to my father, who made writing something that I could afford from a financial point of view.

Chapter One

Fishing from the Gulf in Florida, 1966

On a clear warm morning at the beach in Venice, Florida, a beautiful young blond woman is found at the waters edge. Her throat had been ruthlessly cut, so that she instantly had bled to death without letting out a cry. What led up to this vicious murder and more murders to come? Come with me as I guide you through the events that lead up to each murder.

Tall lush palm trees were waving in the breeze, as Jim rode along the beach south of St. Petersburg, Florida. He was sixteen years old, and was on a Christmas vacation trip with his father Jake, his brother Bartholomew, and his two grandfathers. His dad's father was named Everett Sellers and his mother's father was named Howard Martin. They had driven straight through from Warsaw, Indiana. Grandpa Howard had driven much of the way. He loved to drive fast, and his quickness made the long trip shorter and more bearable. Throughout the trip, Jim had been the main lookout. He used his farsightedness to advantage by watching a full mile down the road for police cars. He was better than a fuzz buster. The adults always showered him with praise when he spotted another "bear". Jim was even diligent about watching for the terrible "bear in the air". "Bear in the air", meant police watching for speeders from an airplane. Thanks to Jim, no one got a ticket on the entire trip.

All that worry was behind them now. They drove slowly, and watched the palms and beach go by. The smell of the salt water was in the air. The sun was shining brightly at high noon. The beach looked bright, and almost white as they drove by. Grandma Sellers and Grandma Martin had driven down the week before. They were getting the house ready, and preparing food for the guests. Soon the men and boys would be in Venice. They could all get rested up and start thinking about fishing. Jake's father, Everett, was sponsoring this fishing trip. He didn't want to be outdone by Howard, who had paid for the last trip up to Canada. Everett was arguing playfully with Howard about who should pay for what. Everett finally won. It was agreed that Everett could pay for everything except the gasoline. Howard was persuaded to go along, when Everett said he could use the money he saved for his favorite charity. Howard was generous with charities to a fault. He couldn't resist the thought of more money going to one of these charities. Everett knew how to get what he wanted. He was a shrewd businessman. He had worked and saved hard all his life. Now that he was a millionaire from his stock investments, he still seemed like everyone else. He didn't try to act elite or snobbish. Everett was still just a hard working farm boy who had made it good. Now he had a small stylish house in Venice where he spent several months each winter. He looked forward to having some of his family there to enjoy it with him.

Jim and Bartholomew were complaining about being hungry. Everett knew of a restaurant in Venice that specialized in fried chicken. They stopped for lunch when they found the place. It was a small restaurant, but the chicken was delicious. For dessert there was pecan pie. Jim loved pecan pie so much that he had developed a rating system for them. Depending on the taste and texture of the pie's filling and crust, it would receive a rating of one through ten. Of course, no pie ever received a ten unless it was his mother's pecan pie. She was the best pecan pie baker in the world. Today's pie received a nine and one half. That was the highest rating any restaurant pie had ever received since any of the family could remember. The whole family enjoyed the anticipation of finding out what the rating would be. It was a family tradition.

Jim's Beatle haircut made him look quite handsome as he sat there at the table finishing his pie. He was slender at sixteen years of age. His grandfather Martin was always saying how Jim resembled him. Bartholomew looked like his father when he was younger. Now Jake was bald. That hid the resemblance. Bartholomew and Jim looked a lot alike. They could have been mistaken for twins if their ages had been closer together. There was one thing that they all had in common. Their cheeks sagged slightly around their chins. Especially when they grew older. The whole group of men looked a little like bulldogs. They were a mixture of Irish and British, so it would be difficult to say where the look came from. Grandpa Martin was mostly British, while Grandpa Sellers was mostly Irish. At least those were the ancestries that they bragged about. It's certain that they had ancestors from other places as well.

After they finished their meal, the two grandfathers argued over who would have the privilege of paying for the meal. They did this, in spite of the fact that they had agreed that Grandpa Martin would only pay for the gas. It was another family tradition. When they left the restaurant they headed straight for the White Sands Motel. It was right on the beach, in Venice. Everyone quickly moved their luggage to the motel room. The two boys and Jake had a room on the ground floor. The view from the room was wonderful. There was a large sliding glass door that faced the gulf. The glass was so big that it nearly covered the whole wall. The water's edge was close enough that the waves came within fifty yards of the motel.

After unpacking, Jake and the boys dressed in their swimsuits and lay out on the beach. Howard went with Everett to see his house. They would return at 6:00 P.M., to pick up Jake and the boys for the ride over to the house for supper. Grandma Sellers was an excellent cook, and they were all looking forward to the evening meal. In the meantime, the sun did its best to give the newcomers a Florida tan. The sand was hot, and it wasn't too long before the boys were swimming in the water. Bartholomew had brought a scuba outfit with him. He eagerly chattered about what all he was going to do under the water. Jim lost interest after awhile. None of the equipment fit Jim, and he knew that he wouldn't be allowed to use the stuff anyway. Besides that, he didn't know how to scuba dive yet. He spent the rest of the day walking up and down the beach looking for shark teeth. They were black, and had turned to stone after many years of lying on the ocean bottom. Venice was one of the few places where shark teeth would wash up on the beach every day. Jim found about forty of them in that one afternoon.

The smell of the salt water was something new for Jim. He breathed in deeply several times. It smelled like the freshest air he had ever breathed. He ran along the water's edge and leaped in the air many times. Then he ran as fast as he could for almost a mile. He was running on the track team in high school. It felt good to get his exercise in, after the long ride cooped up in the car. When he returned to the motel, his brother had the scuba gear spread out all over one of the beds. For a little while Jim handled the large shark knife. It was part of the outfit his brother had bought for only one hundred dollars. As he handled the knife, he wondered what it would be like to battle a ferocious shark, deep under the surface near some beautiful coral reef. Then he pictured his brother fighting the shark.

What if his brother got eaten by a shark? His brother had been rough on him when he was younger. Some of the old resentment came back to haunt Jim from time to time. Bartholomew was jealous of any recognition that Jim got from their parents, especially from Jake. Jim sometimes felt that Bartholomew wished Jim had never been born.

Jim asked Bartholomew if he could use the scuba outfit for just a short time. Bartholomew said that he could try on the equipment. Bartholomew then left Jim alone while he went back to the beach. The swim fins were way too big for him. He would never be able to keep them on. He tried on the wet suit. Surprisingly enough, it was too small. He tore a piece of the wrist off the jacket as he tried to pull it on. He was worried about what his brother would say when he returned. To his surprise Bartholomew was not upset. He said, "It's too tight for me too. Don't worry about it." Jim was greatly relieved. Then Bartholomew said, "I'm sorry, but you can't go scuba diving. I don't have time right now to train you. It's a dangerous sport. You have to know what you're doing."

The doorbell rang, and it was Grandpa Martin and Grandpa Sellers. Jake was with them too. Jake had been walking around looking at the neighborhood housing. He got back just as the grandfathers pulled in. It was time to go to the house for supper. They all piled into Everett's new 1966 Cadillac de Ville, and headed for the house, which was only a few miles away in the suburbs of Venice. When they got there, Grandma Sellers came out to greet them. She hugged and kissed the boys like she always did. They were embarrassed like they always were. She said, "I miss you boys so much when I'm down here." She almost started to cry. Grandpa Sellers jumped in, to save the boys anymore embarrassment. "Let's go in and start eating. The food will get cold." With that, they all moved into the house. Grandpa Sellers said the prayer, and they all started to eat a fine meal that was much like

Thanksgiving. There was roast beef, mashed potatoes and green beans with bacon. Grandma always made excellent coffee. They all loved their coffee. And, as usual, there was a freshly baked pie. That evening it was apple pie.

After the meal, they all went out to look at the house. There was also the boat to look at, and the canal that led to the Gulf of Mexico. The house was made of cement blocks and was covered with a layer of bright white sand. It glistened in the evening sun. Jim stared at the house from various angles. For the last couple of years, he had been interested in photography. The sparkling of the sand crystals in the sun, made him think of his camera. He got it out of the back seat of the car and took a few shots from positions that maximized the reflections of the sun's light. After he felt he had enough pictures of the house, he took a couple pictures of the family in front of the front door to the house. They all clowned around and made faces like they always did on such occasions.

Then they all went over to the canal. The boat sat there in the setting sun. It glistened from a fresh wax job. The main color was white, with a few stripes of light blue that went over the length of the cabin. There was a fighting chair mounted behind the cabin. The words "Shark Stalker" were written in large letters across the back end of the boat. Bartholomew asked Grandpa Sellers, "How did you come up with that name for your boat?" Everett said, "I don't like to go miles out after tuna and marlin. There are big sharks in closer to shore that give me all the fight that I want. You'll find out about that. Besides you always hear about sharks stalking humans. That's why I don't feel sorry for them. I enjoy sinking the gaff into them. But I've told you many stories of my fishing expeditions. I'm glad that I'll get a chance to show you exactly what I've been talking about." The eyes of the two boys got bigger. "You mean we get to catch a shark ourselves?" asked Bartholomew. Everett said, "Yes, I think you will each catch one. There are so many of them around here that we're sure to find plenty of them. And what's more, they're always hungry."

Everett saw Jake and Howard looking at each other. "Yes," he said, "each of us should be able to catch at least one shark. Of course if we have engine trouble, I wouldn't recommend trying to swim to shore." Everett chuckled as he spoke. "That's what the radio is for. But the boat is a new one. We shouldn't have any trouble at all." "How much did the boat cost?" asked Bartholomew. Everett said, "I got it for about one third the retail price, but I won't go into the details. We're here to fish, not talk money."

"How fast will it go?" asked Jim. Everett said, "With those two 350 Chevy big blocks in there, it will move out at sixty miles an hour. But I never push it that hard. Usually the waves force me to keep the speed down to about three quarter throttle. About forty to forty-five miles per hour is plenty of speed for me. When the waves are high, I slow to about thirty or thirty-five. You have to work with the weather conditions, just like you do when you're driving a car. "Why don't we climb aboard and have a closer look?" asked Jake. "That's fine with me," said Everett. The whole group climbed on board. Even Grandma Martin got in. "For a thirty-one footer, it handles like a much smaller craft," said Everett. "I had a custom reversible thruster installed on the front of the boat, so that I can make the sharp turn arounds in this canal. It cost some serious money to have that done, but its tax deductible. I use the boat mainly to entertain business associates. I find that they can relax better on the boat. I've only had the boat a few months, and I've already made enough good business deals on it to pay for ten just like it. How do you boys like the boat?" Bart said, "It's a cool boat, grandpa!"

Jim said, "Can I steer it some tomorrow?" "Once we're out away from shore you can," said Everett. Jim and Bartholomew examined the instruments at the helm of the boat, while the adults went down into the cabin to have a look around. There was a nice sized kitchen at the bottom of the stairs. It was all finished in teak, as was the rest of the boat. The head was off to the right when you got to the bottom of the stairs. It was small but adequate. There was even a shower in the head. The cabin was air conditioned and had a large king-size bed in the bow. When they got to the bedroom, Everett had to make one of his remarks that would embarrass his wife. "Mabel likes to prime the pump in this room," he said with a chuckle. Mabel elbowed him in the ribs, but couldn't hold back a little giggle.

"It's a honey of a boat," said Jake. "Sometimes I wish I could be on a boat like this all the time." Everett said, "Everyone who sees this boat feels a little like that. You aren't getting tired of farming are you? You know I want us to keep the farm in the family. Our ancestors settled that farm in the 1800's. It would be sad to see it leave the family. There are too many memories tied up in that place. We wouldn't want to have to ask strangers if we could look at the buildings. It's better if we own it." Jake said, "No, I'm still devoted to farming. It's just that sometimes I get tired of working eighty hours a week." Everett said, "Well, I could give you a business that would take less of your time, and make you more money, but I don't think you would be as happy. If you want to rent out the farm for a year and bring Lois down here, it would be fine with us. Maybe you need a long vacation." Jake said, "No, I'll stick with it. I'll feel like a new man after this week of fishing. I'm going into the house for a minute. I want to call Lois and see how she's getting along. She isn't used to feeding the cows by herself." "Okay," said Everett, but come back out. We want to watch the sunset from the boat."

Howard said, "I could use a boat like this. Would you mind if I buy that empty lot across from yours? Maybe you would let me buy into the boat. I could entertain clients on the boat." Everett said, "You can use the boat anytime for business or pleasure. I would recommend, however, that you buy your own. There are some nice tax advantages to having your own boat. You want to be able to tell your clients that it's your boat, too." Howard said, "Yes, you're absolutely right. I'm not a tax lawyer, but I think you're right. Maybe some of my current tax shelters aren't quite right for me. I'm thinking about shifting some of my assets. But that's enough about business for now, let me have a look at the engine compartment. I've been eager to see the power plants."

Everett said, "For your pleasure I had both engines fully chromed out. I also had turbo charging added. I know Bartholomew will enjoy all that, being a mechanic and all." Bartholomew was impressed. He jumped down into the engine compartment and started reading the labels. "Looks like you're running Mobile 1 for lubricant. A good choice, I think. I don't use the same oil filters as you have here, but I suppose they are the ones that came with the boat. I think you should switch to oversized Fram filters at your next oil change. I like the bypass mechanism they use." Jake said, "Bartholomew, you're starting to sound like Jim. You both get too technical for me." Bartholomew said, "All I said was, I think Fram is better because they won't allow dirt to eliminate oil circulation." Jake said, "Well I'm proud of you. I'm glad you're excelling at something. Don't let me bother you. Check out the rest of the engine. I just want to hear it run."

Everett started up the boat. "That sounds great!" said Bartholomew. "Can I bring up the "Rs" a bit?" Everett said, "Sure you can bring up the "Rs", but what are they?" Bartholomew said, "I just want to speed up the engines and hear what they sound like at different speeds." Everett said, "Okay, take the throttle. Don't run it too fast without a load on it. The dealership said I should break it in for a while. I forget how long they said. I wrote it down in the glove box. We can check it out later if you like." Bartholomew leaped for the throttle. Carefully and slowly he increased the r.p.m.s. He loved the sound of it. It was a little like hearing two 'Vettes warming up for a drag race, only these two engines did exactly the same thing. They were linked together so that they would take up equal amounts of the load put on them. Bartholomew asked, "Can you run with just one engine if you want to?" "Yes," said Everett. "You can switch off one engine when you want to idle slowly through the canal. It saves on gas."

After a few minutes of revving the engines, Bartholomew shut them off. "Thanks, Grandpa Sellers. I can't wait till tomorrow when we go fishing in the boat." "Me too," said Jim. Howard said, "Lets all sit and watch the sunset now. Then we'd better get some card playing in, so we can get to bed early. We'll be getting up early to fish in the morning." Jim said, "Can we play cards in the boat?" "Sounds good to me," said Everett. He dug a deck of cards out of the boat's glove box, and they all went back down into the galley. "Shall we play rummy or hearts?" asked Howard. Jake said, "Hearts would be the best, since there are so many of us." "Okay," said Howard, "hearts it is. I'll deal." They played cards till about 9:00 P.M. and then went to bed.

Back at the motel, the surf was beating hard against the beach. It was a windy night. Jake wondered whether they would be able to fish in the morning. If the wind kept blowing, they would have to wait for a day. Things would calm down by then, he thought. Jake and the boys fell asleep in no time at all. It had been a long trip. Their bodies and minds wanted sleep more than anything right now.

First thing in the morning, Jim was out on the beach looking for shark teeth. The strong wind had blown up several unusually large specimens. Jim snatched them up eagerly. He felt like he was gathering up golden artifacts. The teeth seemed unbelievably precious to him. Just when he thought he was alone with his treasure, there on the beach, he felt a presence behind him. He turned and saw a young girl standing right behind him, looking over his shoulder. It was obvious in an instant, even in the dim light, that she was incredibly attractive. She was about his same age, sixteen years old. "What are you doing here?" asked Jim. She said, "I come out every day before sun-up to run. I don't want every one to see me. I saw you running on the beach yesterday. It looked like you were in pretty good shape. I thought possibly we could run together. I have my swimsuit on under my jeans." Jim was already in his swimsuit. He had goose bumps all over from the cool December breeze that was blowing. "That would be great!" exclaimed Jim. "I'm running the mile on the high school track team, and I want to keep in shape while I'm down here."

"If you're going to run in your suit, do you mind if I lay my shark teeth on your jeans so they don't get lost. I need to hide them. There's an elderly woman, that I met, who comes down here every day to gather teeth in the morning. This morning, the waves brought up some nice big teeth, and I don't want her to get them." The girl asked to see the teeth. Jim held out his hand. As she took the teeth from him, her fingers touched his. Just this small touch caused Jim to take a deep breath. Her skin was warm as a kitten, even in the cool breeze. "My name is Lillian," she said. "I'm here on Christmas vacation with my mother, father and older sister." Jim said, "My name is Jim. Jim Sellers. My family is here on vacation too." Jim watched with interest as Lillian slowly worked her tight jeans down over her hips. He thought he was having a dream for a minute. He pinched his leg hard. *No*, he thought, *I'm actually awake. This is real*. Jim said, "How old is your sister?" Lillian said, "She's nineteen. Why do you ask?" Jim said, "I have an older brother who is eighteen. Maybe we could introduce them." Slowly she unbuttoned her blouse from the top down, as she talked some more about her family. "My mother was hoping that I would meet someone down here. I've been going with a boy back home, but she thinks I need to date around and get more experience with men. She says I'm too young to settle down to just one. I know she's right. Seeing me with you will make her happy. I hope you'll come over to our bungalow after we run. I want you to meet my family." Jim said, "I'd be glad to. I'll have to tell my dad first. I don't want him to worry about where I am. But I can do that after we run. I always head out to the south. If you go north you run into the public access. It isn't as nice down there."

"Okay," said Lillian, as soon as I can get this blouse off. The buttons are so tight! Could you help me with them Jim?" Jim eagerly reached out and helped her to the best of his ability. His nervousness made him rather clumsy. To his surprise, she didn't mind a bit. In the dim light he could see that she was well built, for a girl her age. Her bathing suit top was bright yellow. It contrasted nicely with the dark tan that she had a start on already. He stared involuntarily at her breasts. Lillian said, "I can tell you haven't been dating much. I'll help you get used to being with girls. First of all, look in my eyes more. I'm flattered that you like my figure, but you can't just be after a girl's body. It doesn't make for a good relationship, my mother says."

"You're right," said Jim. "I don't know how to act around girls. You're so confident. You say just what's on your mind." "My mother taught me to be that way," said Lillian. "If you don't stick up for yourself, people will take advantage of you. Come on let's run," she said. Off they went at a brisk clip. As they ran along, just skirting the water, they talked animatedly. "I'm a cheerleader," said Lillian. "Exercising is a big part of my life right now. In physical education, I got an "O" for outstanding so far this year. I really like to go all out with things. Later today I can show you my stretching exercises. Don't tell my mom though. She says that I shouldn't do them in front of boys." "Don't worry, said Jim. I won't tell her."

They were about one half mile down the beach when Lillian stopped suddenly. "It's going to get light soon. Let's go for a quick swim before the sun gets up." They both jumped into the water and swam a long way in the cool salt water. When they finally stopped swimming they could touch bottom and just barely keep their heads above water. Lillian and Jim held hands there in the water, and let the waves lift them gently off the bottom. "The wind is starting to die down, said Jim. I could stay out here forever. I love the water."

Lillian said, "I'm starting to get pretty cold now. Let's get back to shore, quick!" They swam as fast as they could. In no time they were back on the beach. "I'll race you back," she said. "You're on," said Jim. Away they sprinted, unable to talk because of their labored breathing. In no time they were back to the place where they had left the clothes and shark teeth. "I'll come up and meet your dad," said Lillian. "Then we can go to my place. I'm really glad you want to spend some time with me. I know we'll have lots of fun."

Lillian said, "Jim, you're better than the boyfriend I have at home in lots of ways. I can tell already. If you'd like, we can keep in touch after this vacation is over." Jim said, "I'd like that a lot, Lillian. Where's your home town?" Lillian said, "I live in Columbia, Ohio. It's right on the border of Indiana." Jim said, "I live in Warsaw, Indiana. I've already got a car. When I become good enough at driving, I can drive over to see you." "I'd like that," said Lillian. "At the very least we can write to each other. My boyfriend back home is becoming a jerk. I went a little too far with him once, and now all he wants is sex. He can't make conversation like you do, Jim. I think I'm going to be able to trust you to not start thinking of me as a sex object."

"Let's go see your dad, so we can get over to my house," said Lillian. Jim said, "Oh, I forgot to mention it, but I might be going fishing today if the weather dies down. This is our first day here and I wouldn't want to miss it. We might not be going today anyway. There will be plenty of time for us to be together." "Good," said Lillian. "I can wait till you get done fishing. I like fishing too." Jim said, "My Grandpa Sellers has a thirty-one foot cruiser. I'm sure he'll be glad to take us out, after the family gets done going out together. Maybe he'll even let us have a date on the boat." Lillian said, "That would be wonderful, Jim. I feel like a nymph when I'm out on the water. Like in those old Greek myths." Jim said, "Yes, I know what you mean. There were nymphs and satyrs. They were always chasing each other, or something like that." Lillian said, "The nymphs liked to play in the rivers and streams. All they wore were long thin veils that you could see through."

As they spoke the sun started to rise. It was a luxurious red sunrise. Jim said, "Dawn stretched her red fingers across the sky." "What's that from?" asked Lillian." "I'm not sure," answered Jim. "My dad and Grandpa Martin say that, when they're out fishing and the sun comes up. It's something out of literature. I'm going to ask them about it today when we're out on the boat. They think I'm going to study literature when I go to college. I like stories and poetry." "I'm like you in that," said Lillian. "I love stories. I like being in dramas. Let's go see your dad now." "Okay," said Jim, "He should be up by now."

When they got into the motel room, Jake was gone and Bartholomew was sitting on the edge of the bed. "This is my brother Bartholomew," said Jim. Bartholomew and Lillian waved at each other. "Bartholomew this is Lillian." Jim said, "Are we going fishing this morning?" Bartholomew said, "Dad went over to Grandpa Seller's house for breakfast. He said he'd be back soon to tell us if we're going or not." Jim said, "Tell him I'll be back in about thirty minutes. I'm going to Lillian's bungalow to meet her parents." "You'd better be back in time to fish, or dad will be mad," said Bartholomew. "Don't worry," said Jim. "I just want to see where she lives so that I can find her when we get back." With that said, Lillian and Jim went outdoors. They headed over to her place.

"I'd better not go in till I get back from fishing," said Jim. "It's too early for guests. We might come back late, so wait up for me. I promise that I'll come over." Lillian said, "I'll be waiting for you." She kissed him briefly, and said, "I don't want to distract you from your fishing" "You're right," said Jim. He turned quickly and ran back to the motel. When he got there, his dad was waiting for him. "Where were you, Jim?" asked Jake. "I met a girl on the beach this morning. I just came back from seeing where she is staying." "Good, said Jake, I'm glad to see you're doing better with women. The wind has died down. Your Grandpa Everett says it will be a great day for fishing. We saved some food for you boys over at the house. You'll need it for a big day of fishing. Get your brother, and let's get going as soon as we can. I'd like to be on the road in five minutes." Jim ran to get his brother. In no time, they were in the car driving to Grandpa Seller's house.

On the way there Jim looked at the palm trees as they blew in the gentle breeze. "They sure are beautiful trees," said Jim. "The whole state of Florida is beautiful." "Your new girl friend is beautiful," said Bartholomew. "Of course she's a little young for me." "She is too young for you, Bartholomew," said Jim. "She's only fifteen." He lied in an attempt to keep his brother away from her. "How did you meet her?" asked Jake. Jim said, "We both run on the beach early. That's how we met." Jake said, "I'm sure Grandpa Everett would like to take her with us out for a cruise tomorrow. Maybe she could even catch a shark, if it's a small one." Jim said, "She could probably land a pretty good sized one, she's very athletic. She's a cheerleader." Jake said, "That sounds good. I hope you two can make some memories that will last a lifetime. You'll write about these days in your autobiography, Jim," "I'm not quite ready to think about that yet," said Jim.

When they got to the house, Grandpa Everett was in the boat getting the engine warmed up. They all went up to the boat. "What are you doing?" asked Bartholomew. "I need to make sure that we don't leave anything behind. I've got a checklist to go through. We need enough fishing rods, life vests, and especially the chum. I've got some more in the garage. Jake can help me carry it. You boys go eat so we can get started." The boys ran into the house and each gave Grandma Sellers the usual hug and kiss. They gulped down their food as quickly as they could without offending grandma. She liked things to be gentlemanly. In a few minutes they were running back out to the boat.

"Unfasten the lines boys. Throw them to me," said Grandpa Sellers from the bow. Grandpa Martin was at the stern. "I'll take one of the ropes from here," he said. The ropes were taken in quickly and coiled neatly on the deck. The boys watched as Grandpa Seller's moved a long chrome lever to the left. It was mounted just to the left of the helm. Slowly the front of the boat swung around almost one hundred and eighty degrees to the left. Next Everett pushed forward on the throttle. The boat surged forward. Everyone stepped back a step to regain their balance. "I'm still getting used to all this power," said Everett. "Soon I'll be able to move off without knocking everyone off their feet." They moved down the canal at about seven miles per hour. It was the legal speed for the canal. There were only a few other boats getting ready to leave that early in the morning. Everyone that was on their boat, waved to them as they went by. Everett was friends with everyone along the canal. He loved people and could tell jokes well. When he wasn't fishing, he spent time talking to his neighbors along the canal. Sometimes they would fish together. They all kept in touch with each other on C.B. radios. Weather information would be exchanged, and they never ceased talking about the fishing. Even when Everett wasn't talking directly to other people, he could hear all the other conversations in the area. The boys were new to C.B. radio and they found it fascinating. Everett used the name of the boat to identify himself on the air. As he guided the boat down the long canal, he turned on the radio and started to use it. "This is Shark Stalker to any fisherman on the Venice canal. Do you have your ears on? This is Shark Stalker. Do you copy?" An answer came back. "This is Poseidon, good buddy. I copy." Everett said jokingly, "I told you before, Poseidon, I'm not your good buddy. Now stop that trucker lingo and give me what you've heard on the weather."

Poseidon was Everett's nearest neighbor to the south. They knew each other well. Poseidon said, "We are supposed to get some more clearing. The wind is supposed to die down completely. Lots of sun and little wind." Everett said, "That sounds good to me. I've got a boat full of landlubbers, and I don't want them getting seasick. We're reaching open sea now. The waves are already down to two feet high. Get back to me if you catch any fish, Poseidon." Poseidon responded, "10-4 on that, Shark Stalker. I hope you bring back some nice sharks today. Don't fall overboard. I'd hate to see those sharks get revenge on you for killing so many of them." Everett said, "I'll be careful. This is Shark Stalker, over and out." "Over and out," said Poseidon.

The Shark Stalker and its crew headed straight out from the canal. Everett said, "I think we'll find the sharks just past the reef that lies in front of the canal. They like deeper water where they can maneuver better." Jim looked back at land as they headed out into the gulf further. The palm trees that were everywhere grew smaller as they left the beach behind. The boat was planed out. It was doing about forty-five miles per hour. After a few minutes Jim turned to watch the sun rising over the water. It was now well into the sky. He liked the way the light glistened as it reflected off the water. Then it occurred to him. He'd better put some film in his camera and get some shots of Grandpa Sellers driving the boat. Grandpa loved to be photographed with the family. He often paid for Jim's film. Everett had an excellent camera of his own. If fact both grandparents loved to take pictures. Jim's camera was just a Kodak Brownie, but he knew how to compose shots well. The camera did a surprisingly good job, considering how inexpensive it was. Now, as he loaded the film, he started to think about the shots he wanted to take of Lillian. Her beautiful smile filled his mind's eye, like a portrait in a museum. He could remember every detail. She was like a work of art to him.

He carefully wound the film around the spindle and closed the camera. It was ready to go. "Everyone get as close to the helm as possible. I want to get some pictures," said Jim. They obligingly gathered at the helm. "Now say cheese," he said. He took a couple pictures and then passed the camera to Grandpa Martin. He took two pictures, with Jim in them and gave the camera back to Jim. "It was a good idea to bring the camera, Jim," said Grandpa Martin. Jim said, "I never go anywhere without it." Jim was still thinking about Lillian in the back of his mind. He said, "Grandpa Martin, what is that saying you always use when the sun comes up red. Remember when you said it in Ontario?" Howard thought back to the fishing trip in Ontario, two years ago. "Oh, now I remember, Dawn stretched her red fingers across the sky. That's a loose paraphrase of a line that is used several times by Homer, in *The Odyssey*. Why do you ask?" Jim said, "I was just wondering. There are lots of red sunrises here in Florida." Howard said, "You're right about that, Jim."

The boat started to slow down. Bartholomew asked, "Why are we slowing down here?" Everett said, "The depth finder is starting to read two hundred feet deep. That's the depth I usually fish at. There are bigger sharks further out, but the ones around here will be plenty big enough for starters." "Oh boy!" shouted Bartholomew. "Can I start fishing now?" Everett said, "You can start getting the rods out of the compartment. Jake, why don't you throw a bucket of chum overboard? Be careful not to get it all over the boat." "I'll be careful," said Jake. He moved to the stern and grabbed a bucket of chum. "What is this stuff?" asked Jake. Everett said, "It's fish that the crab fishermen bring in with their catch. They catch the fish with their drag nets. The fishermen call them 'junk fish'. The unwanted fish come up with the crabs in nets that are drug along the bottom of the gulf. The nets pick up everything in their way. Some of the high quality meat and game fish, that are too small for market, are set free. The less desirable fish are ground up for chum, and sold at the fish market."

"You sure are learning lots of things about fishing, now that you have this boat," said Jake. Everett said, "Well, the neighbors and I talk every day about this sort of thing. Some of them are retired. They spend the whole year fishing. They supplement their social security with fish sales. Some of them take people out charter fishing. You have to know all about big game fishing to do that. I don't need the money, so why bother." Jake threw the chum overboard and said, "Why don't you retire and fish all year round." Everett said, "I need variety. Even this kind of life style would grow old if that was all you did. I like surprises. Every time I research a new investment possibility, it provides excitement for me. I always set new goals for myself. I want to have a certain amount of wealth accumulated by a certain time. That's what keeps me young. If I would retire, I would probably die soon after. Keep working till you drop, that's my advice."

There was a sudden splash in the water to the port side of the boat. Everyone went over to look. There were several sharks gobbling up the chum that was floating on the water's surface. "Let's get a chunk of fish on your hook, Bartholomew," said Everett. He reached into a bucket and pulled out a slab of shark meat. "This shark meat is the cheapest bait. They don't mind eating their own." He forced the large hook into the meat and threw it overboard. A fourteen foot shark took the bait into its mouth immediately. Bartholomew let out a yell and yanked back on his rod hard, setting the hook. "Oh boy, Grandpa Sellers, this is going to be fun!" Grandpa Martin cheered him on. "Hold on to the rod tight, Bartholomew. That shark will take out some line, now that he knows he's hooked."

Just as Grandpa Martin had said, the shark dived deep and took out line. It also was heading out from port. The reel's drag was set just right. It put lots of pressure on the fish, but didn't allow the line to break. "Keep the rod tip up, Bartholomew," said Grandpa Sellers. "A shark that size can break your line in a heart beat if you don't keep the rod tip up. The drag can't do all the work for you." Now they grew silent for a minute and listened to the reel sing, as more line went rushing out. After about three minutes, the line stopped. Grandpa Sellers said, "You're about out of line. Let me tighten the drag a little." He did so in just an instant. He said, "I'll drive toward him. You reel in fast so we don't lose that line. We won't qualify for a record if we use the engines to get closer to the fish, but we're just practicing now."

The engines roared, and they all lost their footing for an instant as Everett swung the boat around. Bartholomew reeled wildly as the boat closed in on the fish. Now he had to bring the fish up from the depths. He pulled back with his rod till it looked like it would break. "Now reel back down to a straight out position," said Grandpa Sellers. "That's the three o'clock position. Just like on a clock face."

Bartholomew did just as he was told. "Pull back up to the twelve o'clock position." Bartholomew strained so hard he was turning red in the face. He kept that routine up for about thirty minutes, till the snapping jaws of the shark became visible above the surface. When the shark saw Bartholomew looking down at him, he took off again. This time he stayed near the surface. They could see its dorsal fin as it swam off, splashing its tail behind it. Bartholomew lost about three hundred yards of line. "I didn't know it was going to be this hard," he said. Jim said, "It takes stamina Bartholomew. Stick with it." Bartholomew said, "What kind of shark is this, Grandpa Sellers?" "It could be a tiger shark or a black shark," said Grandpa Sellers. "To tell you the truth, I still don't know how to tell them all apart. Tomorrow I'll go to the library and xerox a copy of the pictures of sharks with labels from the encyclopedia. Then we'll know what we're catching for sure." Jim said, "Sure you will." Grandpa Seller's dry humor was never lost on Jim.

Poor Bartholomew was obviously worn out, but he wouldn't let his brother take over. That would have been too humiliating. He called to his dad, "Dad would you reel him in for a little bit. I've got to go to the bathroom and also get a drink." Jake said, "Sure son. You'll get another chance to land one all alone." Jake took over for Bartholomew. Jake said, "Hey, dad. Why don't you strap me into this fighting chair? We should be doing this professionally! "You're right," said Everett. "I was afraid the boys would be more likely to lose their hold on the rod if they couldn't lunge forward when they needed to. That's how they absorb the shock. Just sit down in the chair. I'll strap you in right away."

After strapping Jake in the chair, Everett swung the boat around and kept the engines running. He said, "I'll keep the boat maneuvered so that you can have the shark out behind the boat. That will make it so that you can bring him in best. We don't want the line breaking off on the boats deck trim." Jake said, "What pound test is this line?" Everett said, "It's forty pound test." Jake said, "I'm going to set the drag tighter." He adjusted the powerful front drag in just a few seconds. Then he leaned back and started reeling in line. His powerful arm muscles bulged as he pulled the rod tip up to the twelve o'clock position. You couldn't see his right hand when he reeled in line, down to the three o'clock position. His hand moved too fast for the human eye to follow. Jim said, "Now he's giving up line. Bartholomew tired him out. This is going to be a piece of cake."

Bartholomew came back from the head and said, "You can bring him on in, dad. I want to harpoon him." Everett said, "I think this one is small enough that we can use the gaff on it. I brought an extra one, Bartholomew. We can both gaff it." Jake kept on reeling hard and fast. His T-shirt was drenched with sweat. Jim said, "You'll need those gaffs soon. Look at that dorsal fin! The shark is only about twenty yards out now." In less than ten minutes Jim had the shark near the stern. Howard unfastened the straps that held Jake to the chair. Jake jumped up and started to pull the shark along to the port side of the boat. Bartholomew let out a yell and threw his gaff into the middle of the shark. It flopped its tail wildly and tried to swim away. Jake put all his strength into the rod and turned the tired shark back around towards the boat.

Everett decided to let Howard try his luck. He said, "Howard why don't you gaff this one?" Howard said, "I think I'd better watch you the first time. I'm eager to gaff one, but I've never even seen it done by an experienced person." Everett said, "Very well. I'm sure you could have done as well as I will." Since Bartholomew had lost his grip on the gaff, and it could not be reached, Everett tied a length of rope to his gaff. When the shark was once more along side of the boat, Everett made his move. He silently thrust the gaff into the back of the shark, just behind its head. The gaff's razor sharp edges sliced through the cartilage of the shark's spinal cord. It quivered in the water, and ceased moving its tail. It was paralyzed. "I got lucky that time!" shouted Everett. "The last one I gaffed jerked the gaff out of my hand, just like this one did with Bartholomew's gaff. That's the reason I carry more than one gaff in the boat now."

"When we get good at this, we'll move to deeper water and harpoon a two hundred pounder. We'll have to build up more endurance first. A big shark like that takes stamina to land. We can't team up on the fish anymore. Only one man reels it in, or we cut the line and let it go. It's only sporting. I use regular steel leaders. In a few weeks they rust away and the shark can live a healthy life, eating human swimmers. Ha! Ha!" Everett didn't usually laugh at his own jokes, but he liked that one especially well.

The boat was equipped with a hydraulic hoist on a boom. Everett said, "I'll swing the hoist around, and we'll haul this shark up on the deck. I'm still fairly new at this, but I'm getting better. Remember, that shark is only paralyzed from the head down. It can still snap its jaws. Once I have it up high enough out of the water, I'll shoot it in the head with a 12-gauge deer slug. That way we won't be taking any chances. Howard, when the cable loop gets close enough to the tail of the shark, use that aluminum pole with the hook on the end to fasten the loop around the tail." Howard said, "I can do that." He grabbed the pole and deftly positioned the loop around the tail fin. The hydraulic pump whined as it labored against the heavy shark. The shark hung for a minute, with its head just above the gunwale. That's all the longer it took for Everett to get his shotgun.

They all covered their ears before he blasted the shark. The shark was jolted by the blast, but it didn't move on its own. The shot echoed out across the water. All the gulls took off from the water, startled by the sound of the gun. Red blood poured from the head and the two gaff wounds in the shark. Everett said, "We'll leave it there for a few minutes till it bleeds out. The blood will bring more sharks to us." Jim said, "Come on, all of you. While it's bleeding, we can take some pictures. I'll get the camera." He went to the cabin, and was back in a second with it. The group was already posed in front of the shark. Jim snapped several shots. Then Grandpa Martin took the camera and got a picture of Jim with the group. He also took a picture of Bartholomew and Jake with the shark, since they had worked together to catch it.

"Now let's swing it aboard," said Everett. The hydraulic motors whined again, as the boom raised the shark higher. Then the boom moved the shark around to the stern. Everett then lowered the shark to the deck. Everett said, "When we have four or five sharks, it may get a little crowded. We'll get a picture of them all facing the camera with their teeth showing. Hey Jake, we'd better get another bucket of chum in the water." "I'm right on it," said Jake. He was quick on his feet. His adrenaline was pumping from fighting the shark. He threw the chum with a mighty heave. It spattered far out from the bow.

"Who wants to be next?" asked Everett. No one volunteered. Everett said, "Why don't you go next, Howard? That way Jim can have a better chance to learn the right technique." "I'd be glad to," said Howard. "I want to use the fighting chair. I can see that it has its advantages." He sat down in the chair, and Jake strapped him in. Everett cut a hunk of meat off the shark, and thrust the big hook through it. Then he threw it off the bow. Almost immediately a shark gulped down the bait. It started to move away from the bow with its dorsal fin visible above the water. Everett said, "Set the hook, now!"

Howard pulled back hard with the rod. "I've got it hooked!" he said. The battle was on. The shark made a run that took out over four hundred yards of line. Howard kept the rod tip up high like he was supposed to. His arm muscles bulged as he strained against the pull of the shark. His face looked determined as he held the rod tightly and watched the rod's line counter. It told him exactly how much line was out. Finally the shark decided to turn. Howard started to reel in line as fast as he could. He said, "The line is slack, could he have gotten off the hook?" Everett said, "No, he's swimming back toward us. Keep reeling as fast as possible." Suddenly there was a loud thump, and the boat shook. Everett said, "That crazy shark attacked the boat. I'm going to shoot that thing twice with the shotgun when we get it out of the water." But the shark got the line tangled in the propeller and broke it off. The end of the line came up out of the water with nothing on it. Howard said, "Well at least I got some exercise. I'll try again later. Let's see what Jim can do." Jake took off the straps that held Howard to the chair. Jake said to Jim, "Do you want to try the chair, or will you lose hold of the rod?" Jim said, "I'll take the chair. I know that I can hold on."

It took Everett a couple minutes to tie on another steel leader and hook. He wasn't mad about the shark anymore. It was all in a day's fun. "You know," said Everett, "I don't actually hate sharks. I just don't like the fact that you can't control them. Sometimes people can swim with them around and the sharks won't bother them. Other days, those same sharks will tear people to pieces. One thing I can tell you for sure though, Jim, if you fall in amongst them when there is chum out, you're done for. They even bite chunks out of each other when they're in a feeding frenzy. I don't think I have to tell any of you to stay out of the water. We all have that much sense. Right?" "I believe you," said Jim. "I'm ready to go. Throw my bait in the water, please."

Everett threw the bait off the bow and apologized, "I'll save my lectures on sharks for after you catch your first one. I didn't mean to make you too impatient." Once again a shark was ready to give them the fight they were looking for. Howard was watching closely over the bow of the boat. He could see which shark took the bait. "It's a smaller one," he said. "It's about three fourths as big as the first one we caught. It should still be able to give Jim his money's worth." Everett said, "Set the hook, Jim!" Jim pulled back on the rod as hard as he could. The rod gyrated wildly as the shark angrily shook its head. "Let it run now," said Everett. "Remember to keep the rod tip up."

The sun was up high in the sky by now. Jim could feel the pleasant warmth of the sunrays beating down on his body. He watched the rod's line counter intently as it read out the amount of line in the water. One hundred yards, then two hundred yards of line went out. In no time at all, three hundred yards of line was out. The counter started to slow, finally. Jim started to crank the reel, but he was still losing line. "Don't crank anymore until he stops running," said Everett. "The drag will stop him. I'll tighten the drag some for you." Everett went over and adjusted the drag. Everett said, "Point the butt of the rod toward the shark. That will cause more friction and help the drag." Jim could feel the added pull on his arms. He was glad that he had been working out with weights for the last year. He could nearly press his own weight now. "He's starting to turn," said Jim. "The counter has nearly stopped." Jim started reeling in line with all his might. In the sun's heat, the effort caused him to sweat profusely. Howard grabbed a beach towel and wiped away the perspiration. "I'll keep the sweat out of your eyes," said Howard. "You just keep on reeling the shark in. I'm going to shoot this one with the shotgun, myself." Everett said, "Now that's the spirit. Each of you can blast one of those toothy beggers. I brought along plenty of ammunition."

Just when Jim thought he was getting off easy, the shark turned away from the boat again. The reel sang loudly as the line pulled and made the drag slip. Jim grinned and said, "I'm not tired yet. Just getting started." He waited for the reel to quiet down and then started watching the line counter. When it slowed almost to a stop, he started reeling again.

The shark made several more runs before it tired. Finally after about forty minutes of fighting the shark, Jim managed to bring it in close to the bow. It was lying on its side, flopping its tail slowly. Several times it tried to right itself, but it rolled back over on its side, soon after each try.

Jake released the straps that held Jim to the chair. Jim jumped up and moved to the bow. He kept the line tight and slowly pulled the seventy pound shark to the side of the boat. Howard gaffed the shark like an expert. He managed to hold it still, while Jake slipped the cable loop around the shark's tail fin. Everett ran the hoist and lifted the shark up to a good height for shooting. Then he passed the gun to Howard. Howard said, "This will be a pleasure." Without hesitation he pumped several rounds into the sharks head. After they let it bleed awhile, they loaded the shark onto the deck with the other shark. The fishing started to go like clockwork. By supper time each of them had caught at least one shark.

Jim took pictures of the sharks alone, and then got pictures of the family kneeling beside the sharks holding their fishing reels. As usual, Howard took the camera and got some shots of Jim posing with the family and sharks. They all agreed that it was time to head for home. All the struggling with the sharks had given them big appetites. They were ready for supper. Everett opened up the throttle and pointed the boat towards the Venice harbor. After a little showing off, he slowed the boat and let everyone take a turn steering the boat. They all enjoyed their turn at the helm. Boating was in the family's blood, just like fishing was. Everett said, "You boys watch closely now and see how I bring the boat up to the dock at the fish market." They watched as he slowed the boat well in advance of reaching the dock. He pulled over so that he was sideways to the pier. "This is kind of like parallel parking," he said. Next he pulled back on the throttle and threw the boat into reverse. The boat came to a neat halt. Both Jim and Bartholomew jumped out and tied the boat to the pier.

The proprietor of the fish market came out to look at the catch. As he looked at the sharks he said, "You brought in some nice fish today, Everett." Everett said, "The whole family helped catch them. If you can unload them for me, we'd like to walk around a little and see your place. Oh, I forgot. This is Bill. He owns the fish market." Then Everett introduced his family to Bill. Bill said, "I'll have my helpers unload you and weigh the catch. Feel free to show your crew around. I'll have your check ready in about twenty minutes." Everett said, "Sounds good to me. We'll go in and have a soda. We can look at your collection of pictures. He's got pictures of all the record catches here for the last thirty years." The family followed Everett into the market. There on the walls were enlarged pictures of people with their marlin, sharks, barracuda, permit, bonefish . . . The pictures were endless. They all drank their sodas and looked at the pictures. In no time, Bill was handing Everett his check. Everett showed the check to the boys. It was for $100.00. "You boys can split this money," he said. "Here I'll give you the cash now." He got out his wallet and handed them each a $50.00 bill. Jim and Bartholomew thanked Grandpa Sellers and then went running over to the souvenir shop. Jim bought some pictures of the record fish catches. Bartholomew bought a shark knife that was much larger than the one he had back at the motel.

The boys ran back to the boat, after they paid for their souvenirs. The rest of the family was already on board. Bartholomew said, "Now I'd like a turn at steering the boat." "Okay," said Grandpa Sellers, "but you have to keep your eyes open and not run into other boats. Bartholomew said, "I'm sure that I can keep from hitting them. You'll help me, won't you grandpa." Everett said, "I'll back you up. Here's the helm. I'll run the throttle." Everett pushed forward on the throttle and, as usual, the boat surged ahead. They were all knocked a little off balance, but no one fell down. "I guess I should let you take complete control, Bartholomew," said Everett. "I still haven't learned to ease that throttle forward." Everett was doing the throttle surges to be funny, but he never let on. "Here, Bartholomew you drive the whole boat. Just keep it under seven miles per hour. If you get in a tight spot you can use the bow side thruster. Here's the handle. It won't do you much good if you're going over one or two miles per hour."

Bartholomew steered the boat proudly. "This is fun!" he said. He kept the speed down to about four miles per hour. He successfully steered the boat over half the way home. Then he saw some girls out sun bathing in bikini bathing suits. He said, "You can steer now grandpa. I want to take some pictures." He begged Jim for the camera. Jim said, "Don't get so excited that you drop my camera overboard." Bartholomew shot up about ten pictures of the girls. The girls were older than Bartholomew, but they waved to him. He noted their figures carefully. "They're gorgeous!" said Bartholomew. Jim said, "You know, Bartholomew, my new girlfriend has a sister that's 19 years old. I could see if she wants to meet you." Bartholomew said, "Jim, if you can pull that off, you can use the scuba equipment anytime you like." "You've got a deal," said Jim. They both smiled from ear to ear.

"What does she look like?" asked Bartholomew. Jim said, "I don't know. I haven't seen her yet. Lillian says that she's good looking. Lillian is intelligent, so I suppose her sister is probably smart too." Bartholomew said, "I'm not too concerned about brains. I just hope she's good looking. This is only for the week you know. I'm not looking for someone to marry." Jim said, "Lillian and I are going to write to each other. I feel like I'm in love with her." Bartholomew laughed, "Ha, Ha. Everyone feels that way when they're your age if they meet a girl they like. It's just infatuation. That's what dad told me, and he was right. It only took me a month to split up with my first girlfriend. The best thing you can do is have several girl friends, so they get jealous. They'll treat you better if they know that they can't take you for granted."

Jake said, "Bartholomew, don't be so cynical. Your brother already feels strongly about this girl. If he's in love, then don't ruin it for him. I know I told you that you were just infatuated when you were sixteen. Jim's sensitive. He'll have to work this out his own way. If he wants to write her after this week, then I think he should. At the very least, it will help his penmanship." Jake had to chuckle a little at his own humor. Jim said, "She's more beautiful than the girls back home. She says that she really likes to be with me. I'm not used to real good looking girls showing this much interest in me." Bartholomew said, "Okay, be in love. Just remember that I told you so. Don't cry on my shoulder when she doesn't write back and forgets all about you." Jake said, "That's enough Bartholomew. I said don't be cynical."

Everett said, "I'd better speed up the boat a little. I want Jim to get back to the motel so he can spend some time with his girl this evening." Howard chimed in, "Yes, they need some time together so they can get to know each other. Sometimes the first love, of a man, becomes his only love. It's nothing to take lightly. At the very least, it's a time that will be remembered for a lifetime." Everett was now steering the boat at the speed limit. As he drove, he talked on the radio to his friends along the canal. "This is Shark Stalker to Poseidon. Have you got your ears on? Come back Poseidon." The radio crackled a little, and then a clear voice came over the radio. "This is Poseidon.

How'd the fishing go?" Everett said, "We each landed a shark. One weighed over one hundred pounds." Poseidon responded, "Good job Shark Stalker. You're getting to be an old hand at this shark fishing." "Thanks," said Everett. "We try our best. It was a lot of fun. That's the main thing." Poseidon said, "You got that right! You going back out tomorrow?" Everett said, "If the weather holds, we'll be right back out there. This is a tough crew, and they want some more action." Poseidon said, "I hear that! I'll see you tomorrow then. This is Poseidon, over and out." Everett said, "This is Shark Stalker, over and out."

He hung up the receiver and asked if anyone was hungry. The adults were hungry, but the boys were for heading back to the beach quickly. Jake said, "Since we'll only be here for a week, I'll take you two back to the motel as soon as we get to the house. It will be good for Bartholomew to spend time with a nice girl. If Lillian's sister is as pretty as she is, I'm sure there will be two very happy boys on this vacation. Yes, I heard you two boys talking about Lillian's sister. The only thing I'm concerned about is Bartholomew trading the sister for a scuba outfit. Try to be a little less calculating, Bartholomew. Your goal should be to win a friend. Don't think of a girl like she's a good trade for scuba gear." "Okay, Dad," said Bartholomew. "I know the lecture by heart. A girl is not an object. You must not take advantage of a girl. Don't cheapen the relationship by being too physical." Jake said, "I'm glad that you've been listening to me. You'll realize the wisdom of my sayings when you're a little older." "I know," said Bartholomew, "I'll follow your advice, I promise."

"Can I drive the car over to the motel?" asked Bartholomew. Jake said, "You'll have to ask grandpa Sellers, it's his Cadillac." "Grandpa said, "It's all right with me if Bartholomew will promise one thing. Promise you won't drive all over town with the girls in the car. That's too much distraction for a young driver. Promise you will only drive over to the motel, and then leave the car." Bartholomew said, "I promise." Jake said, "I'll have someone bring me back over there when I'm ready."

Everett brought the boat up to the pier at his house, and the boys jumped out to tie the boat to the pier. They were getting good at it. Grandpa Sellers praised them for their seamanship. "You boys are starting to get that rope tying down real good," he said. The boys beamed with pride at the sound of his praises. Bartholomew said, "Don't forget the car keys, Grandpa Sellers." "Here you go Bartholomew," said Everett, "and don't forget your promise." The boys ran quickly to the car and got in. Bartholomew drove slowly and used caution on the drive to the motel. He wanted to be able to use the car again soon.

Chapter Two

The First Date

When they arrived at the motel, Jim ran into the room to put on some fresh Hai Karate aftershave. He wanted to smell good to Lillian. "I'll go meet her parents and see if I can get her sister to come down here with us," said Jim. "Good thinking," said Bartholomew. "I'm going to take a quick shower. I'm sure I'll be done before you get here with the girls." Jim ran as fast as he could to Lillian's bungalow. When he got there he rang the doorbell and waited. Lillian's sister answered the door. She was a tall slender blond who wore a little too much make-up, but still looked great. Jim thought, *for as slender as she is, she sure has nice breasts*. Then he felt a little guilty and tried to think only of his new girlfriend. "Is Lillian home?" asked Jim. The tall blond girl said, "I'm her sister Carol. Lillian's inside, I'll get her. You must be Jim. Lillian's been telling me about you." Carol disappeared into the bungalow, and in a minute Lillian appeared. "Come on in Jim. I want you to meet my mom and dad. You already met my sister, Carol."

Jim went in and walked straight ahead into the kitchen. Everyone was sitting at the table having supper. Jim said, "I forgot it was suppertime." Lillian's mother said, "Why don't you sit down with us and have a little bite to eat?"

"Thanks," said Jim, "I'd be glad to join you." He pulled up a chair next to Lillian. Lillian's mother introduced herself. "I'm Lillian's mother, Ingrid Tahkala. This is my husband Leif." Leif stood up and reached across the table to shake Jim's hand. Jim said, "I'm glad to meet you, Leif, and you too Ingrid." Leif said, "We're glad to meet you. We've been hearing quite a bit about you. We already like you more than Lillian's boyfriend back home. I hope I don't embarrass you. We all speak quite candidly in this household. You can say whatever is on your mind. We love openness."

Jim drank some milk and said, "Lillian told me she had an older sister. I told my brother and he'd like to meet her. We'd like to double date tonight." Ingrid asked, "A blind date?" Jim said, "Well it's not really a blind date. Lillian has met my brother." Leif said, "Well, we came here so that the girls could have a good time. You have my permission, if it's alright with their mother." Ingrid said, "Just so they get home by midnight. I don't want them to become night owls." Carol said, "Don't worry, don't I always come home on time?" Ingrid said, "Yes, you're pretty good about coming home. That's why I'm letting you stay out so late tonight."

Carol said, "It will take us till 7:30 to get ready. Bring your brother then, and we can walk down to your motel. Lillian said your brother's name is Bartholomew. Is that right?" Jim said, "Yes, the family calls him that. After I introduce you though, you can call him Bart. He likes girls to call him that." Carol said, "Thanks for the tip. Bart. I like that name. Finish eating and talk to our parents, we're going to start getting ready." The girls left the table and went to a bedroom in the back of the bungalow. Jim finished the meal of fresh fish and French-fries. Jim asked, "Did you catch these fish yourself?" "Yes I did, said Leif. I brought my nineteen foot fiberglass boat down this year. I went out at noon and caught these sheepshead. They're about as good to eat as anything that swims down here. I think so anyway. How do you like them?" Jim said, "They're great."

Jim said, "Your name sounds Scandinavian. Where are you from?" Leif said, "We're Finns. That is we're from Finland. I came here with my family four years ago. I started a charter fishing business on Lake Erie. My father was a commercial fisherman. Fishing has been part of my family for hundreds of years. I made this move so that I wouldn't have to spend such long periods of time at sea, away from my Ingrid. We are both more happy now." Jim said, "That's quite romantic. You must love each other very much." Leif said, "Yes we do. We planned to move to America before the girls were born. When they were born we gave them American first names so they would fit in better here. They like their new home."

Jim said, "My grandfather took me shark fishing today. We probably used the same canal that you did, at least the last part of the canal. There were a lot of channels on it." Leif said, "We probably did use the same canal. So your family fishes too." Jim said, "Yes we do. My grandfather would like Lillian to go with us tomorrow. We plan on starting at 5:00 A.M. We'll fish all day." Leif said, "It's fine with me. That is, if Lillian and you can stay up till midnight and then wake up by 4:30 the next morning. I was young once myself. I'm sure she'll want to go. But, don't bother asking Carol, she isn't a fisherman." Jim said, "Well, if she and my brother like each other, they can spend some time on the beach. My brother isn't into fishing as much as I am. He's more into cars. That's his thing." Leif said, "There's nothing wrong with that. Mechanics have to be smart nowadays. Cars are getting more complicated every year." Jim said, "I know. My car isn't too complicated though. I have a 1940 Hudson."

Leif said, "Oh, so you're an antique car buff." Jim said, "Yes, I guess. The car belonged to my great grandfather. The family wanted it to stay in the family, so they sold it to me for twenty-five dollars." Leif said, "Hold on to that car. It will be worth a lot of money some day." Jim said, "I think you're right. My brother helps me keep it in good shape."

Ingrid had been listening while she washed the supper dishes. Now she said, "I love to listen to you and Leif talk, Jim, but shouldn't you get back to the motel so you can tell your brother to get ready for a date?" Jim said, "You know, Ingrid, you're right. Your husband is such a good conversationalist that I forgot the time. I'll go right now. We'll come back at 7:30 to get Carol and Lillian." Leif said, "Nice to meet you. I'll take you out on my boat soon." Leif shook Jim's hand. Jim waved goodbye to Ingrid, and went with Leif to the front door. Leif said, "I wish we had nice boys like you in Columbia." Jim said, "Don't worry Leif, I plan on staying in touch with Lillian. There's something special about her. Part of it is the way you've taught her to express herself. She's very confident." Leif said, "Jim, you're starting to speak your mind just like we do. I feel like you're one of us." Jim said, "Thanks Leif. I'm looking forward to that fishing you spoke of. See you soon."

Jim ran back to the motel and told his brother the good news. Bartholomew said, "Oh boy! This is going to be great! How did Lillian's sister look?" Jim said, "She's a knockout. Just like Lillian, only she's a blond." Bartholomew said, "Great! I like blonds the best. How is she built?" Jim said, "Like I said, she's great." Bartholomew started slapping Jim on the back. "You're the best brother there has ever been." Jim said, "I told her to call you Bart. She thought that was neat." Bartholomew said, "Good thinking. You'd better start calling me that too. Why don't you start right away, so she'll think I'm cool?" Jim said, "Sure, I'd be glad to. Hey Bart, can I borrow your comb?" Bart said, "You can borrow anything. You're my wonderful brother."

Jim got into the shower and took his usual long time soaking up the steam. He loved hot showers. By the time he was done showering and had dressed himself, it was about time to pick up the girls. He combed his hair carefully and headed for the door. "You come with me, Bart. You can meet their parents. They are both wonderful people." Bart said, "No, it would make me nervous. I'd rather meet her first. I'm not planning on marrying her. I just want to have a good time." Jim said, "Suit yourself. I'll have them back here before you know it."

Jim walked as slowly as he could. He wanted to run, but he knew he would get there too early. Besides he would mess up his hair. His heart was pounding. He admired the palm trees and flowers as he walked along. There were orchid bushes growing in several of the yards that he passed. Everything looked more beautiful than usual to him. Jim stopped for a moment to smell one of the orchids. Its sweet smell filled his nostrils. He felt like he was in love. Then he walked on, singing his favorite love song. He remembered all the words. He had listened to them a thousand times. Now he would be holding a beautiful girl, a girl that was having a profound effect on him.

Jim finally reached the girl's bungalow at exactly 7:30. He rang the doorbell and waited. In no time, Leif Tahkala answered the door. "You're punctual, Jim, that's for sure," said Leif. "I like that very much. The girls are ready. They're coming to the door right now." Jim could hear the girls giggling as they made their way to the door. They were dressed in blue jeans and tank tops. Lillian wore a yellow top. Jim thought, *"It must be her favorite color. She looks good in it."* Carol wore a bright red top. It went nicely with her bright red lipstick. Jim thought they both looked incredibly beautiful. "We're ready," said Carol. "We have to be back by midnight, so we'd better go." Jim said, "That's just what I was thinking. It's not far. Come this way."

As they walked, Jim pointed out the flowers to the girls. "Aren't the flowers beautiful?" he asked. Carol said,

"Yes, they're wonderful." Lillian said, "They make me feel like I'm floating on air." She swooped forward with long graceful strides, with her hands reaching out into the air beside her, as though she were gliding along, up in the air. Jim and Carol laughed and ran to catch up with her. "She's a bird!" said Carol. Jim laughed and said, "She's a seagull!" In no time they were back to the motel.

They rang the doorbell and Bart appeared at the door with a smile on his face. He had the intense smell on him of a fresh overdose of Jim's Hai Karate aftershave lotion. The girls liked the smell. Carol said, "What's that wonderful cologne you're wearing, Bart?" Bart said, "It's Hai Karate." Carol said, "Oh yes, I've seen the commercials for it." She took a karate stance and acted as though she was about to attack Bart." Then she laughed, "I'm Carol. We haven't been properly introduced." Jim said, "I'm sorry. You two locked into mortal combat so quickly, I had no chance for introductions. Bart, this is Carol Tahkala. You've already met Lillian. Carol, this is Bart, my older brother." Carol and Bart shook hands. Bart pulled her hand up to his lips and kissed her fingers elegantly. He said, "I'm honored to have such beauty as yours, in my presence. May I offer you something to drink?" Everyone laughed. "Bart is in rare form," said Jim. Carol said, "I'd like some orange juice thank you." Bart said, "And for you, Lillian?" She said, "I'll take some orange juice too."

Bart got the orange juice, and they all sat down on the sofa to watch the gulf waters washing up on the beach. It was still seventy-five degrees out. Lillian said, "We have our swimsuits on under these clothes. Why don't we catch the last bit of sun before it gets too low in the sky." Bart said, "That sounds great to me." The girls pulled off their tops and jeans right there in front of the two boys. They watched intently as the sunburned slender bodies of the girls appeared from under their outer clothing. Jim was staring at Lillian's tummy. "You sure don't have an ounce of fat on you, Lillian," he said. Lillian said, "You should know that already. You checked me out pretty closely yesterday." Jim blushed a little. Carol said, "Go get your suits guys. We'll wait out on the veranda." The girls trotted out to the veranda while the boys went to get their suits.

Bart whispered to Jim. "I can't believe it. Carol's a knockout. What a set." Jim said, "I'm not at all displeased with Lillian's appearance. Her yellow two-piece sure makes her skin look nice. What a tummy! I've never seen one so firm. She must be in great shape!" Bart said, "Who cares about being in great shape. Did you see how they stripped in front of us? They aren't shy at all." Jim said, "They came from Finland. People aren't as shy about their bodies over there." Bart said, "That sounds great to me. Jim, why don't you take Lillian for a walk down along the beach as soon as possible? I'd like to be alone for awhile with Carol here in the room." Jim said, "That'll be fine, but I can't take her past her folks place, or they'll know you're alone with Carol." Bart said, "You said they're from Finland. They shouldn't mind. Everybody in the world likes to 'make out'. I just need a little privacy."

Both boys hurried back out to the veranda where the girls were waiting impatiently. "What took you guys so long?" asked Carol. "Let's take some towels or a blanket down by the edge of the water." she said. "I love the sound of the waves up close." Bart said, "Sounds good." He went back inside and returned in a minute with a blanket. They all ran down to the edge of the water and stretched out on the blanket. The sun still felt warm on their bodies. They intently studied each other for awhile. The surf had a calming sound. There was little breeze, and the waves weren't very high. Jim said, "I've been reading about the sea. People who stop to study the ocean say that every seventh wave is twice as big as most waves." Lillian said, "That's interesting. What else do you know about the sea,

Jim?" Jim said, "The book I read said that after several thousand waves, one comes along that is twice as big as the seventh waves." Carol said, "That's incredible! I'd like to read your book sometime. Write down the title and author for me when we get back inside the motel." Jim said, "Sure, Carol. Your father said that your family has fished the ocean for hundreds of years. It's only natural that you would be interested in the sea. Jim went on. After thousands of more waves pass, I forget how many, maybe two hundred and fifty thousand, a wave comes that is four times bigger than every seventh wave. So if the average wave is twenty-five feet tall, the biggest wave will be one hundred feet high. That's why so many large ships mysteriously disappear at sea."

Carol said, "That's fascinating! Do you read a lot, Jim?" "Yes, said Jim, I like to read. Bart reads a lot too. He reads mostly about hot rod cars." Bart perked up when he heard this cue. He said, "Yes, I'm a car lover. I'm rebuilding a '57' Chevy now. It's got a 350 cubic inch big block with a four barrel Holley carb in it." Carol said, "That all sounds like the space program to me. What did you say?" Bart said, "I have a powerful engine in the car that will beat anyone else's car in a race." Carol asked, "Do you race very often?" Bart said, "Whenever someone challenges me. We usually race the back roads for twenty dollars. My Chevy's a sleeper. It doesn't look as mean as it is. That way more people are willing to race. The name sleeper means that it looks asleep, and then suddenly becomes awake and wins the race. It fools people." Carol said, "That's very clever of you, but isn't gambling against the law." Bart said, "That's the kind of bet they'll never catch us at. The cash gets passed from car to car out in the country. No one has gotten caught yet." Carol said, "That's good. I don't want to worry about you. I already feel like I've known you for a long time. I'm concerned about you. Why don't we go back to the motel room and leave Jim and Lillian here to talk about the sea. We can talk about race cars."

"Great!" said Bart. He and Carol took each other's hands and ran for the motel.

Lillian said, "We won't be seeing anymore of them till midnight!" She giggled. "My sister likes cars, but she won't waste much time talking once she gets your brother on the sofa." Jim turned to Lillian and said, "He's used to that kind of girl. I just hope they don't crash heads rushing at each other." Lillian said, "I'm no saint myself, but I think I've learned some important lessons this year. I learned to not let myself get carried away with physical stuff. You know what I mean?" Jim said, "Sure, I've never done much of anything myself, but I hear that people can get into trouble if they just let themselves go." Lillian said, "That's exactly what I mean. I find you very attractive, but it would be stupid to make the same mistake that I made with my boyfriend back home."

Lillian said, "Let's go up beside the motel where there are no windows. We can have some privacy." Jim said, "Sounds good to me." He grabbed the blanket and they sprinted up to the motel. They spread the blanket out in the sand and lay down beside each other. Lillian crawled right on top of Jim and started French kissing him eagerly. He could feel her soft pointed tongue moving over his tongue. Then she moved her tongue in circles around his. Lillian was quite creative. She slowly moved the tip of her tongue so that it traced his lips. Her hands started to tremble ever so slightly, as she repeatedly passed the tip of her tongue between his lips. Finally she said, "I've waited for this all day." Then she kissed him some more. Jim experimented with licking her tongue and lips the way she did him. When he moved his tongue repeatedly between her lips, she started to breathe deeply and pressed her lips passionately against his. He pushed her away just a little.

Jim said, "Lillian, I'm starting to get real attached to you. You're very affectionate. Let's take our time and talk a little more. We've got till midnight, remember." Lillian said, "Jim, I love it when you get assertive with me. At first I thought you were a little too much of a pushover. You don't need to be diplomatic with me. Just tell me what you want. I'm flexible." Jim said, "It feels good for you to be lying on top of me like this, but I feel a little awkward about it. Let's just sit beside each other for awhile." Jim put his arm around Lillian and gave her a squeeze. "I've never dated a girl as good looking as you before, Lillian," said Jim. "Sure, I stare at your body sometimes, but that's partly because you're so new to me. I really want to memorize your shape. We don't have that long together. I want to be able to see you when I close my eyes." Lillian said, "Jim, that's a nice thing to say. I hope you can have someone take some pictures of us. That way we can be sure of remembering." Jim said, "You're right. I'm going to do that tomorrow when we go fishing."

"We can write each other every day. That will help us get to know each other. It's about a hundred miles from my place to your home. Once I get a little better at driving, I'll come to see you." Jim said, "Lillian, I just never dreamed that you would get this excited about me so soon. The good looking girls back home just want to be friends. They don't want to kiss at all." Lillian said, "I love the way you make me feel. You make me feel like a lady, not a girl who is too fast."

They held each other's hands and looked into each other's eyes for a long time. Then he kissed her some more. They held each other tightly, and kissed till the sun started to go down. Jim felt better about making out with Lillian, now that she had expressed long term interest in him. He couldn't believe that a girl this good looking was this wild about him. She had said before that she wanted to write to him, but he hadn't quite believed her. Now he was convinced. He lost himself in her kisses. She was like an angel carrying him off to heaven. He felt like he was floating on air. She kept running her fingers through his hair. Jim had never kissed a girl with this much enthusiasm. He felt like she loved him already, even though he knew it was too early for that. Finally he quit thinking and just kept kissing.

Then he saw the sunset starting to get red. He pulled back from Lillian and said, "Lillian, I asked my dad about that quote you wanted to know about. He said, Homer is the author of that phrase I used yesterday to describe the sunrise. Remember? Dawn spread her red fingers out across the sky. That was a close paraphrase of the phrase used several times in *The Odyssey*. We'll have to read it. Then we can compare notes about it." Lillian said, "I'd love to read it, Jim. I'll read it several times. I'll write you several pages about my opinion of the book. Now will you please kiss me some more? You're ruining the sunset. I love the sunset. It turns me on." Jim dutifully said, "Alright Lillian, your wish is my command." He pushed her down on the blanket and kissed her around the neck and lips. He still didn't lie on top of her. He didn't think he should.

Lillian stopped kissing Jim for a moment and said, "You know Jim, I have dreamed of a young man coming into my life for years. The dream always has him taking me fishing. We kiss and talk and pull in fish over the edge of a boat. I love that dream. I suppose it has something to do with my father being a fisherman. I can't wait for us to go fishing tomorrow. Jim, there's something we really should do. Let's sleep with each other out here." Jim said, "Lillian! I really don't think we're ready . . ." she cut him off. "I don't mean sleep together that way. I'll just lay my head on your lap and fall asleep. We can ask my sister to wake us up. Maybe we'll save them from going too far if we interrupt them." Lillian giggled. Jim said, "I guess it will be alright. We do need our sleep, and I love being close to you."

Lillian got up and went to the motel door. Carol and Bartholomew were watching television from under a blanket. They smiled and laughed when Lillian came in. Bart said, "How are you and Jim getting along? I hope you're teaching him something about girls. He's pretty slow, you probably discovered." Lillian said, "I found him to be just right. We want to get some rest out there under the stars. Would you wake us when it's time to go home?" "Sure", said Carol. "We'll wake you two lovebirds. You two must really be getting along well. I'm happy for you. Bart and I are having a great time. Don't worry about us." Lillian said, "I won't." She turned and went out the sliding glass door. She found Jim out in the dark. There was enough moonlight that she could see him lying there on the blanket. She said, "I'm back, Jim. Do I get a goodnight kiss?" Jim said, "Come and get it." Lillian lay down beside him and kissed him gently on the lips. She didn't want to get him worked up. They needed their sleep for the big fishing expedition at 4:30 A.M. After a few more kisses, she laid her head on his stomach and looked up towards his face. She watched as he slowly fell asleep. Then she fell asleep as well. She dreamed for hours of kissing her new beloved friend.

When Carol woke up the two lovebirds, they felt like they had known each other forever. The closeness of sleeping together had made them feel a bond forming, one that would never break. It seemed like they were married. They were on a honeymoon that they hoped would never end. Carol said, "It's 11:45. We have to head for home right away. If we're late, mom and dad won't let us stay out this long again." Lillian said, "We're coming. Just wait in there for three minutes." Lillian went back outside. Jim said, "I think we'd better spend our three minutes wisely." He pulled her tight up against him and kissed her passionately. She ran her fingers through his hair affectionately as she gave him all the kisses she could muster in that three minutes, which seemed like only a few seconds. Reluctantly they relaxed their hold on each other. Each of them let out simultaneous sighs. They turned slowly toward the motel door and walked over to it, holding each other's hands. They gave each other one final kiss before they went inside.

Bart said, "Let's all walk down to the bungalow together." Jim said, "Sounds all right to me." Carol said, "Yes. Let's go quickly." Lillian said, "We mustn't be late. My mother will be waiting up. She always does." The group left quickly. They skipped and ran all the way, occasionally stopping briefly to tickle each other or grab a quick kiss. In no time they were back to the bungalow. They each had a goodnight kiss, and then the boys turned and ran back to the motel. Jim said, "What a girl! I'm in love." Bart said, "Carol was more fun than I expected. I love Finnish girls." When they arrived back at the motel they went inside and got ready for bed. It had been a great evening. Now it was time to rest. Jim set the alarm clock for 4:00 A.M. He fell asleep as soon as his head hit the pillow.

Jake came back to the motel shortly after midnight. He smiled when he saw that his boys were sound asleep. Quietly he got ready for bed. He crawled into his bed and went to sleep. He was thinking back to his own youthful days as he fell asleep. He knew that his boys were having a great time.

At 4:00 A.M. the alarm went off. Jim jumped up and turned it off. He woke up the others, and they all got ready to go fishing. They drank lots of coffee to help them get going at that early hour of the morning. Over at Lillian's bungalow the same type of scene was going on. She woke to her alarm, and started drinking hot coffee as soon as she could make some. She slipped on her favorite yellow two piece bathing suit, and pulled her Levi jeans on. Then she scrambled into a T-shirt with a sweatshirt over it. She wasn't even tired anymore, after she had that first cup of coffee. She was excited about getting back together with Jim. His family would be fun to meet. *It should be an exciting day*, she thought.

At 4:30 sharp, Jim was at her door ringing the doorbell. Lillian rushed to the door and let him in. The rest of Lillian's family was still asleep. Lillian hugged him, and they kissed for several minutes. "You little nymph!" he said. Then he laughed softly. "I'm taking a nymph fishing. For me at least, you're real good bait." They both laughed softly. Lillian knew about fly-fishing from her father. She liked the pun that Jim had made. She squeezed him tighter and said, "We'd better get going. Your father will be waiting." They went to the door. "I'll race you there," he said. They scrambled out the door and ran as fast as they could to Jim's motel. Jake and Bart were waiting in the car. "What took you so long?" asked Bart. Jim said, "We had to say good morning to each other." Lillian giggled and blushed a little. They got in the car and away they went.

When they arrived at Everett's house, he was out in the boat with the engine running. Howard was carrying the last of the chum buckets over to the boat. When Jim and the others got over to the boat, he introduced Lillian to them. "Lillian, this is my Grandpa Sellers and this is my Grandpa Martin. Grandpa Martin, Grandpa Sellers, this is Lillian Tahkala. She's from Finland." Grandpa Sellers said, "You can call me Everett, Lillian." Grandpa Martin said, "And you can call me Howard. We're glad that you could come along today. I'm sure you'll enjoy it." Lillian said, "Thank you very much. It's a pleasure to meet both of you. I'm looking forward to this day of fishing a whole lot." They all climbed on board and headed for the gulf. Lillian smiled at the sound of the engines. They reminded her of her father's boat. She felt right at home.

Jim told the family about Lillian's father being a fishing guide on Lake Erie. They were all impressed with that.

Lillian was quizzed for quite a while about Lake Erie fishing. She spoke knowledgeably about every aspect of it. Jim's family was starting to like her. Of course they liked her quite well when they first saw her. Everett asked her, "What's the name of your father's boat?" She said, "He has two boats. His twenty-four foot boat he calls *Caroline,* after my older sister. His nineteen foot boat he calls *Lillian* after me. He brought the nineteen footer down with him. He said he'd take Jim out fishing sometime this week. Yesterday he caught quite a few sheepshead. We ate them for supper last night. They were delicious weren't they, Jim?" Jim said, "They were excellent! I'd love to catch some."

The boat's engines started to slow down, and they knew that Everett had brought the boat to a good place to fish. "What's the depth?" asked Lillian. Everett said, "We're right at two hundred and ten feet. I think this is about where we were yesterday. We had great luck then." Lillian said, "Jim told me all about it. I can't wait to catch a shark! I work out a lot, so I think I can handle one if it's not huge. I don't know what I'll do if I hook a three hundred pounder." Everett said, "One that big would give anyone a rough time. We see mostly sharks in the seventy-five to one hundred and fifty pound range here. If we hook anything over two hundred pounds we just cut the line. There's no use in losing a rod overboard."

Howard said, "Lillian, why don't you fish first. All of us caught a shark yesterday. We'd love to see you get initiated into the shark club." Lillian said, "I'd be glad to. Just tell me what to do." Jake said, "How's your grip? Can you hang onto the rod if we strap you into this fighting chair?" Lillian said, "I'm strong in my hands. I like to do rope climbing at school. It builds up your grip. My father says that a good grip is important if you're at sea. It can save your life in bad weather." Everett said, "Your father is a wise man. I hope we never have to go through a bad storm at sea, but it pays to be prepared."

Jim strapped Lillian into the fighting chair, while his dad threw a couple buckets of chum overboard. Everett gave her a rod and put a large hunk of shark meat on her hook. Then he threw the baited hook over the bow, where Jake had thrown the chum. There were several sharks swimming around in the morning's early light. Their dorsal fins were visible as they swam back and forth past the bow, eating as they went. Finally one took the bait. Lillian held the rod tightly as the line went whirring out. She could barely see the line counter. Jim fumbled around in the boat's glove box and found a small flashlight. He illuminated the reel for her so that she could see how much line the shark was taking out.

Her feminine arms showed their true strength as she kept the tip of the rod up, even though the shark was pulling hard against her. Jim watched her intently as she struggled. He admired her confidence. She watched the line counter intently. After about three hundred and fifty yards the line slowed to a stop. Lillian said, "It's stopped." She started to reel the shark in. It gave some line back to her for a little while. She gained about a hundred yards, but then the shark turned and made a hard run for about two hundred yards. Lillian said, "Oh nuts! This must be a big one. I can get it though. Don't cut the line!" Everett said, "You've got eight hundred yards of line, so you're not in too much trouble yet. Stick with him! He's probably starting to get as tired as you are."

Lillian straightened up in the chair and steeled herself for a long fight. The shark finally stopped again. She started reeling in line as fast as she could. She didn't want to give the shark a chance to change its mind again. Sometimes she had to slow down. "He's trying to turn!" she would say. Then she would pull up hard on the rod and start reeling harder than ever. She pulled up to the twelve o'clock position, and then reeled back down to the three o'clock position. She knew how to fish. That was certain. She was the daughter of a professional fisherman! A Finn!

After about forty minutes of struggling with the shark, the sun started to send a little more light across the water. It was still not visible on the horizon. The shark's dorsal fin could be seen about thirty yards off to port. Howard and Jake each grabbed a gaff as the shark drew in closer to the boat. Jim unstrapped Lillian from the fighting chair. He patted her on the back and said, "You're doing great! Keep the line tight." He could feel the warm sweat all over her back. She moved to the port side of the boat and guided the shark along to where the men waited to gaff it. They sank their gaffs in with pride and held the shark till Everett could swing the boom around. Bart positioned the cable loop onto the tail of the shark. The hoist whined as it raised the shark up above the gunwales. Everett got his shotgun and got ready to shoot the shark in the head. Then he stopped. He waved to Lillian to come over. She moved quickly to his side. He handed her the gun and said, "If you can land a shark like this one, you deserve the honor of shooting it." Lillian took the gun and pointed it close to the shark's head. Lillian shot the shark several times. Her father had taught her to shoot when she was much younger. She didn't even mind the sharp kick of the 12 gauge.

Everett said, "You can be proud of that shark. It must weigh one hundred and seventy pounds!" Lillian said, "Thanks Everett. I'll always remember this moment." Jim went for his camera. He got Howard to shoot some pictures of him with Lillian and the shark. The camera's flash attachment brightened the dimly lit deck, as that moment was recorded for posterity. Lillian was so excited that she forgot herself and gave Jim a big hug and a kiss. Then she got a little self-conscious. Howard said, "That's all right, Lillian. It's okay to show affection around us. We already knew that you and Jim are fond of each other.

She jumped up and down a little and gave Jim another hug. This time they didn't let each other go so quickly. The whole family just looked and smiled, except for Bartholomew who was looking a little jealous.

Everett said, "Well, who's next for fishing? We can't stand around and watch them hug all day." Jim said, "I'll go next. I've got the adrenaline pumping from watching Lillian land that big one, I might as well put it to good use." Jake threw more chum overboard. Lillian strapped Jim into the chair. She whispered in his ear, "I love you, Jim." He smiled a big smile. Everett baited the hook for Jim and threw it overboard. In no time a shark swam off with the bait. It made the reel sing loudly as it pulled out four hundred yards of line. "This is another big one," said Jim. Lillian watched his arm muscles bulge as he tried to turn the shark. He kept the rod tip high. Lillian massaged his shoulders as he started reeling in line. He loved the reminder of how tender and sensuous she was. He reeled hard for forty-five minutes, gaining and then losing line. Finally the shark came up close to the bow. The sun was now rising with a rich red color that reflected off the waves. Lillian thought, "*Dawn stretched her red fingers across the sky. I like this family.*" Then she said, "Good job, Jim! It's about the same size as mine was." She could see it clearly through the water. Quickly she moved back to Jim and removed the straps from him. As she removed them, she sneaked in a couple of caresses on his leg. Jim loved having Lillian along. She was good at fishing, and she was also affectionate.

The shark was quickly gaffed and raised out of the water. Lillian, once again did the honors, and shot the shark several times in the head. "I got him for you, Jim," she said. She gave the gun back to Everett and ran to Jim. They had some more hugs and kisses. Howard took lots of pictures of the two lovebirds together. He knew they would want lots of pictures to remember each other with. He also got pictures of the family with Jim's shark. Its tough gray skin glistened in the early morning light. Blood was dripping from its wounds.

Everett said, "Who's next for fishing?" Bart yelled, "I'm ready!" He jumped into the fighting chair, and Jake strapped him in. While the rest were getting ready for the next shark, Jim and Lillian slipped down into the boat's cozy galley. Lillian said, "Being down here reminds me that I'm a little hungry." Jim said, "For me?" He drew her against him into a long hug. He French kissed her eagerly. Lillian responded to his advance. She kissed him back with great enthusiasm. She held onto his hips and pulled him ever tighter up against her. Then she loosened her hold on him. She said, "I don't want to get caught doing that, in case one of your family should come in. I meant to say earlier, before you so delightfully interrupted me, that I am hungry. I didn't have any breakfast. Let's see if there's a big cast iron skillet in this kitchen."

They dug through the drawers and cabinets till they found a nice twelve inch cast iron skillet. Lillian said, "I like to cook on cast iron. It distributes the heat better so that you don't burn things. Jim, would you please go and cut some meat off the shark I caught. I want to have the pleasure of tasting that huge brute beast." Jim said, "I'll be right back with some shark meat." He grabbed a large butcher knife from a drawer and went up on deck. Jake said, "What are you going to do with that knife?" Jim said, "Lillian wants to cook some of the shark she caught. I'm going to cut off a few fillets." Jake said, "Good idea. See if she'll cook up enough for all of us. We all skipped breakfast this morning."

Jim went back to the stairs that led to the kitchen. Lillian was at the stove melting some butter in the frying pan. Jim said, "Lillian can you cook enough shark for all of us?" She called back, "No problem. Just hurry, the butter is about melted." Jim said, "Just give me three minutes." He rushed back to the shark and cut off enough meat to fill the skillet. In no time he was back at Lillian's side with the meat. He said, "I wasn't sure which shark was yours." She said, "That's okay." She took it from him and soaked the meat in milk. She said, "The milk is supposed to help remove some of the strong flavor. My dad used to bring home a shark occasionally when I was a little girl in Finland." Jim said, "We should go visit Finland someday." Lillian said, "I'd like that very much, Jim. You're starting to include me in your future. I'm flattered." She leaned over from the stove and gave him a kiss on the neck. She said, "Stand behind me while I cook. You can watch. You might learn something." He leaned up against her backside as she laid the meat out onto the skillet. He kept nibbling at the back of her neck while she cooked. She giggled coyly. She enjoyed his attentions.

After about thirty minutes, the shark was fully cooked. They heard the blast of the 12-gauge shotgun. It told them that another shark was being loaded onto the boat. Jim went up on deck to tell the others that the shark was ready to eat. Everett said, "We'll be down in five minutes. You can go ahead and set the table." Jim set the table for six. In no time the whole crew was gathered around the table to eat. Howard said the blessing. "Dear Lord, we thank you for the food we are about to eat. And we thank you for this wonderful time that we can spend together. Bless us all as you have in the past. Keep us safe, in this tropical paradise you have prepared for our enjoyment. Amen." The rest of the family said, "Amen."

They grew silent as they ate the shark. They were all hungry, and the shark tasted great. The real butter augmented the robust flavor of the meat. Finally Jim broke the silence. "There is nothing else that tastes like shark." Lillian said, "I had almost forgotten what it tastes like. There are no sharks in Lake Erie." They all laughed. Howard said, "At least we haven't heard of them yet." Then they all laughed a little more.

Everett said, "This is the first time we've had cooked shark on this boat. Lillian, you haven't met my wife, Mabel yet. She doesn't like shark meat. It tastes too strong for her. I don't ask her to cook it for me. I know she doesn't even like the smell of it. Personally, I don't think it smells bad at all." Lillian said, "It sure tastes good to me. Especially after I had to work so hard for it." Everett said, "Yes, you did work hard. You're like my mother. If some of the field hands got sick, she would go out to the fields and work side by side with my father. He couldn't talk her out of it. She was a determined woman. I admire that. You're my kind of girl, Lillian. Jim is lucky to spend time with a girl like you. Yes, he could have done much worse." Jim said, "You have a way with words, Grandpa." Everett said, "Well you know what I mean. I guess I was trying to tell Lillian that I like her. I'm glad she's here." Lillian said, "Thank you, Everett. It's wonderful to be here. I'm having a great time. You're all so friendly!" She laughed a little. They all echoed in with a little laughter of their own.

Howard said, "Lillian, why don't you tell us a little about your country. You must remember lots of things about it. What was it like to live in Finland?" Lillian said, "Yes, I do remember many things. I was twelve years old when we left. I hated to leave all my school friends. However, I was glad to think about having my dad around more of the time. That cheered me up. I remember the terribly cold winters that went on forever. The snow would get much deeper than it does here. There were more trees. Mostly pine trees. We all learned to tell stories around the hearth."

Jim said, "What's a hearth?" Lillian said, "It's the fireplace. We all huddled around it to keep warm in the evenings. We didn't have many interesting television channels like you have here in America. That's why we told stories. My dad was the main storyteller. He had many experiences out at sea to use in his tales. I am sure that he exaggerated at times, but that only made the story better. My mother would tell stories about our relatives . . . about the times before I was born. Her father was a medical doctor who spent many years working in foreign lands helping poor people. She could talk about his life for nights on end. I called him Grandpa Borg. He was a big man, who looked a little like you, Howard. He had broad shoulders and no hair on top of his head. No one in the village could beat him at arm wrestling. For relaxation he would cut wood and split it. That is what he did all his life in his spare time. It made him stay strong.

Unfortunately he died at the age of fifty-five. He contracted sleeping sickness in Nigeria, where he was running a new hospital. He made it as modern as he could, but the walls were made of mud. He didn't know how to control the mosquitoes in his area. One that carried sleeping sickness finally bit him. He died not long after that. While in Nigeria, he shot many leopards and had them stuffed. My mother still has them. She brings them out often to show guests. My grandfather also sent home large python skins, which were given to him by the natives. There are dozens of ebony woodcarvings in our house in Columbia. Grandpa sent them all home while he was still alive. He wanted to be able to remember Africa when he left. All the things he sent help us to remember him, and the example he set of serving other people."

Howard said, "You have inherited your mother's gift of storytelling. Your Grandfather Borg was a great man. You are right to be proud of him. We tell stories too. Most of our stories are about fishing, or old stories about the farm life we knew when we were young. Everett, tell her about the buggy wreck that your wife was in." Everett said, "That one again. Don't you ever tire of it? Well, okay. My wife was driving the buggy past the Baintertown schoolhouse one night. When she pulled the horse to a stop at the intersection, the horse behind her couldn't stop in time. Its head came bursting right through the back of the buggy. They had the horse right in the cab with them. It was the most alarming thing my wife Mabel can remember about that time of her life." They all let out a chorus of laughter. It was an image that they all enjoyed.

Lillian asked, "Your wife actually used to drive a buggy?" Everett said, "Yes. It doesn't seem like that long ago. We take cars for granted now. They make life much easier, but life was more relaxed back then. Now everyone is in a hurry." Lillian said, "My grandparents drove buggies too. The whole world has changed. If we want to relax, we have to take a vacation." Howard said, "Luckily we have enough money to take vacations. Some people spend their whole lives working almost every day." Jake said, "Yes, I know all about that. I wish my wife Lois, could have come along. Someone had to watch the cows though. I don't have anyone else trained to take care of them. If she wasn't with them, I would have worried during this whole trip. I talked to her last night on the phone. She said that everything is going great. She said not to worry. At least now, Jim won't say that I just work all the time. He's always asking me to go fishing with him. I finally got the chance to go with him. And Bart is along too. I'm really enjoying this."

Bart said, "Talking about fishing, shouldn't we get back to fishing. It's already past 10:00 A.M. and I haven't caught my shark today." Jim said, "Why don't you all go up and fish. Lillian and I will stay down here and clean up." Bart said, "Sure you want to clean up. I know how fun cleaning up can be with a beautiful girl." Everyone chuckled as they got up from the table and climbed up to the main deck. It was starting to get warm out. Some of them shed a few clothes. Down in the galley, Jim and Lillian were starting to do the dishes. Lillian washed them and Jim put them away. Lillian said, "This hot dish water is making me warm." She pulled off her sweatshirt and proudly modeled herself for Jim. "Do you still like what you see, Jim?" she asked. Jim stepped back and looked at her flat tummy. Then he raised his gaze to take in her yellow swimsuit top that hid some of her best feminine attributes. Jim said, "I approve completely. How could my mind change about the beauty of a goddess?" He moved up close to her and put his arms around her.

Lillian said, "You aren't very shy anymore, are you, Jim?" Jim changed the subject, "I love that suit. I want to get a picture of you in it. Stay here, I'll be right back." In a minute he was back with the camera. Lillian put on a show for him. She puckered out her lips like she was getting ready to kiss him. Then she made her tongue pointed and licked her teeth, like she wanted to French kiss. Jim loved it. He shot several more photographs.

Then he said, "Let's get some more pictures up on deck. You'll have to keep it cool though." Lillian said, "I understand." She climbed up to the deck and walked around the boat casually striking modest poses that wouldn't surprise the family. Jim shot up another roll of film. Then Jim said, "Let's sunbath for awhile on the bow." Lillian said, "Sounds good to me." They went to the bow and lay down on a blanket that Jim had retrieved from the cabin. They both shed the rest of their warm clothes. They lay there in the sun looking at each other and wishing that it would never end.

After a couple hours, they realized that they were getting too burned by the sun. They grabbed the blanket and headed for the cabin. Jim took Lillian by the hand and led her to the bow where there was a bed. The bed was shaped to the curve of the bow. They lay down and fell asleep there, in their favorite position, with her head resting on his tummy. Lillian glanced down at him as she lay there. She played with his chest a little before she fell back asleep.

After about an hour had passed, they were awakened by the sound of the boat's engines starting. They looked out the window, and the sun was setting. The family was getting ready to head for the shore. Jim and Lillian got up and went topside to watch the sunset. Jim said to Everett, "Please take your time driving back. We'd like to watch the sun go down from the boat." Everett said, "I think that can be arranged. I'm glad to see that you two got a little rest. You have both been burning the candle at both ends. I wouldn't want either of you to get sick." Jim said, "Thanks Grandpa, we'll be careful. I think we'll grab some orange juice from the icebox." Everett said, "Yes, drink lots of orange juice while you're down here. It's cheap here, and it's good for you."

Jim and Lillian held hands on the deck of the bow and watched the sunset. It was beautiful to see. They loved Florida. Jim said, "We'll come back here together someday. Maybe your folks will let you come down with my family next year." Lillian said, "That would be almost too good to be true. We can at least hope for that. I'm going to write to you every day." Jim said, "I'll write to you too, every day." After the sun went down the couple spent a little more time kissing. They never seemed to get tired of it. The family left them alone at the bow of the boat. They were busy measuring the sharks, and recounting the events of the day.

The engines slowed as the boat pulled up to the fish market. Jim took Lillian into the building and showed her the pictures he had seen the day before. She marveled at all the trophy fish she saw. They held hands and caressed each other's fingers as they walked along looking at the pictures. Jim pointed out his favorites to Lillian.

She loved the sound of his voice as he explained all the pictures to her, as he understood them. Lillian said, "I enjoy seeing giant fish. The trees, flowers and animals are so different here. I think I would like to study biology down here. It would be great if we could both go to college here." Jim said, "That's a long time from now. You think ahead a little more than I do. I suppose it's a good idea to think ahead. I'll give it some thought." Lillian gave Jim a hug and then they started looking at more pictures. They came upon a picture of a man holding a fish that looked like a silver carp. Lillian read, "Record bonefish for this county." Jim said, "Fly fishing for bonefish is a growing sport. I've been reading up on it. There are wonderful fishing resorts all around the Caribbean and the rest of the world, that cater to bonefishing affecionados." Lillian said, "What's an affecionado?" Jim said, "It's Spanish for someone who likes something very much. I forgot to tell you, I'm studying Spanish in school. Lillian said, "You'll have to teach me some words in Spanish."

Jim got back to the subject of fishing. "Key West is supposed to be a good place for bonefishing. There are also many island resorts in the Caribbean. Some day I want to see as many of them as possible. The pictures I've seen of those places are unbelievable. The sandy beaches are glistening white in the tropical sunlight. The waters are shallow and sandy for a long way out from the beach. You can wade forever, casting shrimp imitations and other tropical flies to the bonefish. I've heard there's one called a Crazy Charlie that works well. They also fish for bonefish with miniature crab imitations. I'll show you some of my resort brochures tonight when we get back to the motel. You are coming over again, aren't you, Lillian?" Lillian gave Jim a hug and a kiss. "Of course I'm coming over. I want to dream about us being on one of those tropical islands fishing for bonefish. I'm excited about the thought of it already."

She occasionally squeezed Jim's hand tightly as they walked on to the next picture. It was a picture of a man with a record winning tiger shark. It measured eighteen feet two inches long and weighed one hundred and sixty-five pounds. Lillian said, "Our sharks must not have weighed one hundred and seventy pounds. They just seemed that big after all the work we put into landing them." Jim said, "We'll find out in a minute. The fish market workers are weighing our fish right now. Let's go watch them." Jim led Lillian by the hand to the weigh scales. One of their sharks was on the scale at the time. The worker using the scales read out. "One hundred fifty-one pounds, four ounces." Lillian said, "That's still a very big shark. It looks like the tiger shark in the picture." She asked the market worker, "What kind of shark is that?" He said, "It's a tiger shark. He's a nice big one. Who caught it?" Lillian said, "We're not sure any more whether that one is Jim's or mine. We each caught sharks that were almost identical. We don't need to be recorded anyway. I wasn't trying to win a record. I just got that big thing on the line, and I had to bring it in. It was a terribly big effort, but a lot of fun too."

The worker said to Jim, "That's quite a little lady you've got there. I'm sure this is a record breaker for women in this county. Let me get her picture with this shark. We'll put it on the wall. It will challenge the women in this county to get out here and catch some sharks for themselves. They usually just focus on the smaller fish. This is remarkable!" He ran and got the company camera. He took several shots of Lillian with the shark. "We can get it developed in just a couple days," he said. "There's a local photographer who does the enlarging for us. He's quick with his work. You can see yourself on the wall with the shark, if you're still here in a couple days." Lillian said, "We will be. I'm looking forward to the experience." The worker said, "My name's Pete, I'm glad to meet both of you." He shook their hands. Jim said, "I'm Jim and this is my friend, Lillian." Then Pete asked, "What line weight were you using? I want to write that along with your picture." Lillian asked Jim, "What line weight was that, Jim?" Jim said, "I'll have to ask Everett." In a minute he returned from the boat where Everett had been and said, "It was forty pound test line." "Okay," said Pete. "I'll put that down along with the picture. Oh, Lillian, I almost forgot. We usually put down people's last names too. Could I have yours?" Lillian said, "It's Tahkala. Lillian Tahkala." Pete said, "It was great to meet you two. Now I have to get back to work." He walked rapidly away from them, and went into the building.

Jim took a couple pictures of Lillian beside the shark as it hung there from the scales. It was a great moment for both of them. They climbed back onto the boat, and waited for Bill, the market owner, to bring Everett the check for the fish. In about ten minutes Bill came with the check. It was for one hundred and thirty dollars. Bill said, "The sharks were bigger today." They thanked Bill for the check and headed back to the house. On the way they talked excitedly about Lillian's new fame in the fishing world. It was a great day.

During the ride back to the house, Jim asked his dad if he could spend the evening with Lillian on the beach. Jake said it would be fine with him, just so Jim came back to the motel by midnight. Jim was delighted. He told Lillian right away. "My dad says I can spend the evening with you again if you want to." Lillian said, "You don't even have to ask. I'll ask my folks. I'm sure they won't mind. They really like you, Jim." Jim said, "That's great. We can sit down by the water's edge, and watch the stars. It will be real nice out tonight." Lillian squeezed his hand and whispered in his ear, "I can't wait to be alone with you again. I'll never get enough of that." Jim smiled and held her close to him. He whispered in her ear, "I love you, Lillian." Lillian started using her toes to play with his toes. Their bare feet were warm from the deck that had been in the sun all day. She whispered in Jim's ear, "I love you, too." They stood together silently and watched the palm trees go by.

When they reached the house, Everett asked Lillian if she would stay for supper. She said, "Thank you for the offer, Everett. I'd better go home for supper. I'm going to be out late with Jim tonight, and I don't want my family to think I've deserted them." Everett said, "I understand. But at least come in for a minute and meet my wife, Mabel and Howard's wife, Ethel." Lillian said, "I'd be glad to meet them." Everett said, "Good. I'll take you to see them right away. Then you can be on your way. It was great having you with us. I hope you can come along again soon." Lillian said, "I hope so too." They tied up the boat and went up to the house.

Ethel and Mabel had seen them coming, and were at the door to meet them. Mabel reached out to shake Lillian's hand. She said to Lillian, "You must be Lillian. I've heard about you. If you're a friend of Jim's, you're a friend of mine." Ethel said, "I'm Ethel, and I feel the same way. It's good to have you here. Can you stay for supper?" Lillian said, "I'd love to, but I haven't been with my family all day. I really have to get home for supper. I'm sure that I can stay another evening." Ethel said, "I'll consider that a promise then. We'll all be looking forward to that time." Lillian said, "You're very kind. I'm looking forward to it also." Jake said, "I can take you and Jim over to the motel now. I know you don't want to be late for supper. Jim can find something to eat in the motel room. The refrigerator is full in there." Lillian said, "I'd like him to eat with my family tonight. It will give my dad a chance to make plans with Jim for their fishing together. They already discussed it yesterday. We'll probably fish for sheepshead. That's what my dad likes best." Jake said, "That sounds like a good plan. Let's go."

Jim, Lillian and Jake climbed into the car and headed for Lillian's bungalow. It only took a few minutes to get there. Lillian and Jim thanked Jake for the ride and went into her place to see about supper. Her family was already sitting around the table. Lillian said, "Is there room for two more?" Her mother said, "We always have room for more. Sit down, both of you." Leif asked, "How did the fishing go today?" Lillian said, "I caught a record breaking tiger shark. It weighed one hundred fifty-one pounds four ounces! It took me forever to reel it in. Jim caught one about the same size. We couldn't even tell them apart." Leif said, "That's wonderful Lillian. I hope you took some pictures." Jim said, "I got plenty of pictures. Also, the fish market is going to put up an enlarged picture of Lillian with her fish. They took some pictures with their own camera." Leif said, "I'm proud of you Lillian. Now you two eat plenty of food. You'll need it after all that exercise. Drink plenty of orange juice. It will keep you healthy."

Carol said, "I'll take some more orange juice. Hey, Jim, how did your brother do today?" Jim said, "He caught a nice shark. I think he'd like to see you tonight." Carol said, "Yes, we talked about that last night. He didn't know when he would get back." Lillian said, "Jim and I would like to sit out on the beach tonight and watch the stars. Is it all right with you, dad?" Leif said, "It will be fine. Just come in when it's midnight. You can stay together longer in here if you want to. Maybe play some cards." Lillian said, "Thanks, dad. That will be great. We'll keep an eye on the motel, Carol. When Bart gets back, we'll show him how to get here." Carol said, "That would be great. I'd like him to meet mom and dad tonight. I guess he was too shy last night."

Lillian said, "Dad, can you take Jim and me fishing tomorrow. Mom and Carol could come too." Leif said, "That's a great idea. But I don't want to get up at 4:30 in the morning. This is vacation. How about 8:00 A.M.?" Lillian said, "That sounds great." Ingrid said, "I'd love to go. How about you, Carol?" Carol said, "I'm not that wild about fishing. You can all go. I'll walk on the beach. I'm collecting shark's teeth like Jim does. I've got about a hundred already." Ingrid said, "All right, Carol. We'll go without you. Try not to get too sunburned." Carol said, "I'll be fine. I might see if Bart wants to watch television with me."

The family spent about an hour talking with Jim, and asking Lillian more about her shark. Finally when they had asked all the questions they wanted to, Jim said, "Well, the stars are out. I guess Lillian and I should go out and watch them. Do you folks have a blanket we can use?" Ingrid said, "Sure I have one for you. I'll get it right now." She left for a moment and then returned with a nice heavy blanket. "You can use this one," she said. "It's been in our family for years." Lillian said, "Thanks, mom. We'll take good care of it." Jim took the blanket and walked with Lillian down to the beach. There on the water's edge, they spread out their blanket and lay down on soft sand. It was still warm from having the hot sun beat on it all day. Lillian laid her head on Jim's stomach and watched the stars. Jim silently played with her hair as they watched for shooting stars and constellations. Lillian asked, "I wonder where the Big Dipper is?" Jim said, "I don't know where any familiar stars are down here. When I'm in Warsaw, I can find the Big Dipper easily." Lillian said, "I never was very good at finding constellations. Why don't we strip down to our swimsuits? I want to see a little more of you, Jim." Jim pulled off his shirt and pants. Lillian did the same. Then Jim lay back down on his back and let Lillian lay her head on his stomach like they were before.

Lillian said, "When I look at the stars like this, I am reminded of a painting by Vincent van Gogh, *The Starry Night*. I found the picture in my mother's art encyclopedia. Her father gave it to her before he died. The moon in the picture is painted with a deep luxurious yellow. I love that color. It gives me a warm feeling inside. When we go inside I'll show you the art book. I practically have it memorized, especially the art from the Renaissance era. I think those artists were the most brilliant artistic geniuses of all time. I can see their works in my mind, even without opening the book."

After awhile Lillian rolled over on her tummy and looked closely at Jim's stomach. She playfully ran her fingers through the hairs that were growing there. She said, "I can't get over how much hair is on your belly."

She giggled a little as she stuck her tongue in his navel and moved it around in circles. Jim laughed, "You're tickling me Lillian." Lillian asked, "Do you want me to stop?" Jim said, "I want you to be happy. I don't mind. Just don't go in circles. That's too much! It really tickles."

Jim reached down and caressed her face with his fingertips. Her face felt soft and silky to him. He could see her clearly in the moonlight. She smiled warmly at Jim and kissed his fingers. Then she started to lick his navel some more, only now she reached up and massaged his hairy chest with her right hand, as she slowly let her tongue venture further and further down towards his swimming suit. When she reached the swimming suit, she comically tried to burrow under it with her tongue. Jim wished he could see what she was doing better. Lillian reached into Jim's suit and untied the cord that held his suit up. Jim thrilled at the feel of her soft hands working that low on him.

Then suddenly a wave, much larger than most, washed up over their blanket. It nearly covered them completely with water. They laughed and flopped around on the blanket, grabbing for their wet clothing. Lillian said, "I guess you were right when you said some waves are much bigger than others." Jim said, "Yes, if only we had thought to apply that knowledge. They straightened out the blanket and lay back down beside each other. Jim held her tight and ran his hands along her sides, savoring the curves of her body. Then Lillian saw the light come on at Jim's motel room. She told Jim, "There's the light in your room. We'd better go show Bart how to get to my place." Jim said, "Yes, lets get that done so we can be alone some more." "You're starting to be addicting to me."

They put their clothes back on and walked up to the motel. Jim tapped on the sliding glass door. Bart was nearby and let them in. Jake was in the shower. Jim asked Bart, "Do you want us to take you over to Carol's house? She said she'd like to watch television with you tonight."

Bart said, "That would be great! She told me how nice her folks are. I'd like to meet them. Let me tell dad first." Bart went to the bathroom and told his dad where he was going. Then the three of them walked to the bungalow. It looked cozy when they got there. The lights were all on, and some festive yard torches were burning by the door.

Bart followed Lillian into the house. Carol was already watching television. Bart sat down beside her. He said, "So this is where you live. I'm glad I found you tonight. Did Jim and Lillian tell you about the shark I caught?" Carol said, "They sure did. You're quite a fisherman. Let me see that arm muscle of yours again." Bart proudly flexed his muscles for her. Lillian said, "We're going back down to the beach. You two have a good time. Maybe we can all play some cards at midnight when Jim and I come back in the house." Carol said, "We'll be waiting for you. Don't do anything I wouldn't do." Carol giggled a little at her own joke. Bart smiled knowingly at Carol. His thoughts were on her body. Carol asked, "How did you two get all wet?" Lillian said, "A wave caught us a little too close to the water's edge. We'll get something dry to wear later." Jim and Lillian walked back to their blanket where it lay on the beach. It was wet, and didn't look as inviting as before. They decided to walk along the beach for awhile.

Part of the time they walked in the water. It felt cool and refreshing. They would stop every so often and kiss. They never got tired of kissing. They talked about what the Caribbean Islands must be like, and how fun it would be to fish together there. Jim promised to take Lillian there someday. He said that he would take her all around the world, to all the best fishing resorts. Lillian thrilled to hear him planning a future with her. She said, "It's fun to make fantasies like this. I'll dream about these fantasies for years. You have a wonderful imagination, Jim." Jim said, "I mean every word of it. I know we are young, but when you want something bad enough, you find a way to get it, don't you Lillian?" Lillian said, "You may be right. If you are that sure of yourself, then who am I to argue with you? I hope you are right. I would like to be with you in all those places." They walked for hours and talked more about fishing in beautiful tropical paradises. Finally they arrived back at the bungalow. Lillian said, "We'd better go up to the bungalow now. It's almost midnight." Jim said, "You're right. We'd better be on time. I want your folks to let us come out again tomorrow night."

They walked slowly up to the bungalow. There were several patio torches burning on the porch that faced the gulf. The low roof of the dwelling made it look cozy and warm. There was laughter coming from inside. Every light in the place was lit. Lillian went in first and explained the wet clothes to her mother. Then she brought in Jim. Ingrid said, "Don't be embarrassed. It takes time to get used to the ways of the sea. Similar things have happened to Leif and me. We love to get as close to the sea as possible. We found too, that if you get too close, it will take you with its power. It is good to love the sea, but not too much. I think I've finally won some of my Leif back from the sea. He used to be gone so long at sea. But I am talking you to death. It runs in my family. Come in and sit down at the table. I'll get you and Lillian bathrobes. You can play some cards for awhile or talk at the kitchen table."

Carol and Bart were in the other room watching television. They came into the kitchen to see what was going on. Carol said, "You two must have been wading in the water. You are still dripping water all over." Lillian said, "Yes the water felt good. We walked for a long way in the water just at the edge of the beach. It was fun. You should try it sometime." Carol said, "We're going to watch the rest of our show. Do you want to watch with us?" Lillian said, "No, we'll sit in here and play cards. Jim and I want to be able to talk." Carol said, "You should be good at that!" She laughed and went back to the television with Bart.

Jim went to the bathroom and dressed in the bathrobe that Lillian's mother had given him. Lillian went to her bedroom and put her bathrobe on. They met back at the kitchen table and sat beside each other, facing the window that looked out on the gulf. Lillian said, "Mom, will you bring us your art encyclopedia? I want to look through it with Jim." Ingrid said, "Of course Lillian, I'm glad you and Jim share a love of art." She left for a moment and then reappeared with a large red book. It was quite tall and wide, but was only a little over an inch thick.

Lillian turned the pages and found the picture of *The Starry Night,* by van Gogh, that she had mentioned out on the beach. Jim said, "Those are nice tones of yellow in the moon and stars. His brush work looks like he painted with cardboard match sticks." Lillian said, "Yes, you're right. I never thought of it that way before. Your ways of looking at things are quite interesting. Let me see what you think of the Renaissance artists. They are further to the front of the book." She turned the pages eagerly till she came to the Renaissance era.

Lillian's mother said, "Your father and I are going to bed now. Don't stay up too late. You'll need your rest so you can fish tomorrow." She kissed Lillian on the forehead and told Jim that she would see him in the morning for fishing. Then she left them alone at the table. Jim said, "Let me see your favorites first." Lillian turned the page. "Here is one of my favorites. It is *Primavera* by Sandro Botticelli. Jim was taken by the beauty of a young woman holding a basket of pink and white roses. There were three attractive young women dancing in a circle. Their veil like robes were translucent. It seemed almost as though they were nude. A cupid was taking aim at a young man who was picking an apple from a tree. The idea of what might happen next in the scene amused Jim. He laughed and said, "I can see why you like this painting, Lillian." She squeezed his hand and gave him a kiss on the cheek.

Next, she kissed him on the mouth for a little while. Then she backed away a little and said, "You understand art, Jim. I knew you would."

Lillian turned the page. She said, "This picture is by Leonardo di Vinci. See here. It is called The *Condottiere*. I like the determination in that military man's face. He reminds me of you, when you are reeling in a big shark." Next she turned to page one hundred and fifty-four. "This is Michelangelo's *Creation of Man*. See how majestic the face of God looks. Only a great master could capture such greatness!" Jim said, "Yes, I see what you're talking about. It is a great painting. His sculpture work is excellent as well." Lillian turned the page to number one hundred sixty-three. "I especially love this picture by Giorgionee," said Lillian. Jim looked intently at the picture of a beautiful woman named Laura." Lillian said, "The picture is named *Laura*. The artist captured her beauty perfectly I'd say."

Then Lillian asked, "Am I as beautiful as she is?" Jim looked over to the right where she sat. She was mimicking Laura's pose in the picture; her robe was folded back, revealing her stunning right breast. Jim was surprised, but at the same time pleased. He stared intently at her beauty and said, "Lillian, you are more beautiful. And I'm not saying that to flatter you. It is the absolute truth." Lillian held his gaze with her beauty a little longer, and then gave him a big hug. "You're the greatest, Jim. We're starting to get to know each other better."

Jim sat there and looked at the pictures in the art book, while Lillian went to the bathroom. She returned to Jim's side and looked at the pictures with Jim for a long time. They held hands and kissed occasionally.

Finally when they started to grow tired, Lillian kissed him on the cheek and said, "I'll think about you all night. Even in my dreams. Maybe you'll dream about me." Jim kissed her with intensity on the mouth . . . then said, "You can count on that." They walked slowly into the next room and found Bart and Carol sleeping in front of the television. Jim woke up his brother. Bart said, "Give me a minute to say goodbye to Carol." Carol and Bart kissed each other goodbye for several minutes. Jim went into the bathroom and put his wet suit back on. The two boys went to the door and each gave a parting kiss to his girlfriend. They walked dreamily back to the motel. It was 3:00 o'clock in the morning. Jim kept singing his favorite love song.

When Jim got back to the motel he took a quick shower and went to bed. He fell asleep almost instantly. In his dreams he saw the beautiful works of art that Lillian had unfurled before him. Most of all he saw the painting of Laura and then the unveiling of his Lillian. She had showed him that she trusted him to love her even though she was a different person than he was. She had taken a chance, and shown him her most passionate nature. He would cherish that forever. He floated up into a beautiful forest in the air. There he saw the dancing maidens. Then the girl holding the basket of beautiful roses became Lillian. She was offering him the beauty that she held next to her breast. Cupid had shot the arrow, and it had found its mark. He was now hopelessly in love with Lillian. He lost himself in an ecstatic embrace of his beloved new lady. His love flowed out to her as he held her tightly in his arms. He slept the peaceful sleep of a man in love with a beautiful loving goddess.

Chapter Three

Fishing with the Tahkalas

The early morning sun was bright enough to wake Jim by 6:45 A.M., before his alarm went off. He took his shower and got dressed for the day. Jake was awake already. He was used to getting up early because of the cows he took care of regularly. Jim said, "I was asked to go fishing this morning at 8:00 o'clock. Is that all right with you, dad?" Jake said, "I'm happy that you and Lillian's family are getting along so well. Sure it's all right. When will you be back?" Jim said, "I'm not sure. They'll probably want me to stay for supper. I'll try to get back here before midnight." Jake said, "Just so you don't get sick from too little sleep. You came back here at 3:00 o'clock last night. That's pretty late, even when on vacation." Jim said, "I'll catch a little sleep out on the boat if I get tired. Thanks for being so understanding, dad. I think I'm really in love. Lillian is a wonderful girl." Jake said, "I could sense that, Jim. I think you two should stay in touch after this vacation is over. Even though she lives clear over in Columbia, Ohio, that doesn't mean you two couldn't find a way to keep seeing each other. I'll put some more thought into it. If you want to continue seeing Lillian after this week, I think I can help that come about. A girl like Lillian doesn't come along every day." Jim said, "Thanks a lot, dad. I'll tell Lillian you're working on something. It will make her real happy." Jim hugged his dad and then sat down to eat some cereal and orange juice. He was a happy young man.

When he finished his breakfast, Jim walked along the beach for awhile. It was still too early to go to Lillian's place. He walked for about thirty minutes. There were a few shark teeth on the beach, but not as many as he had seen his first day there. After walking along the water's edge for awhile, he returned to the place where he and Lillian had been on the blanket, just a little over eight hours before. He carefully looked at surrounding trees and buildings. He wanted to remember that spot. It was now a place of fond memories. He would never forget that night with Lillian. It had been wonderful. It was like a fantasy. How could something that good have really happened to him?

He looked up, and Lillian was coming out of the bungalow. She had on a pair of jeans and a red halter-top. She ran up to Jim and gave him a big hug. Then she kissed him hard on the lips. She said, "I see you're out here tuning in to memories of last night." Jim said, "That's a pretty good guess." He caressed her cheek and looked fondly into her eyes. Jim said, "I dreamed about you last night. It was a beautiful dream. You took the place of the woman holding a basket of roses, with young women dancing in the forest." Lillian said, "Oh, yes. *Primavera,* by Sandro Botticelli. I love that picture. I am flattered that you see me like that in your dreams." Jim said, "Lillian, with all your appreciation of art, I'm starting to think you are pretty smart." Lillian said, "Remember, my grandfather was a medical doctor. He was gifted with a wide range of scholarly aptitudes. He educated my mother in the arts from the time she was young. Grandpa's friends referred to him as a Renaissance man. His interests were in biology, paintings, sculpture and writing. That's just for starters. He was an inventor as well, and he was always working on investment schemes. That is why my family has money.

He was a financial genius who got into shipping when it was quite profitable." Jim said, "He sounds a lot like my Grandpa Sellers. He has a gift for making money."

Lillian said, "I dreamed about you all night, reliving the things we did last evening. I didn't sleep very well. You'll have to keep me awake today." Jim said, "Maybe we can sleep a little on the boat." Lillian said, "Yes, I guess we could." Jim said, "I sensed that you were intelligent, now I'm starting to think you are a genius." Lillian said, "Why, because I used a few big words?" Jim said, "That's part of it. Your grandfather was so brilliant, it could be hereditary." Lillian said, "Are you threatened by that?" Jim said, "No, I think it's great. It requires intelligence to carry on an interesting conversation. That is part of what I like about you. You make interesting conversation. You even know how to keep your brainpower a secret, so you can be pleasing to a young man that you think might be threatened."

Lillian said, "Now you're making fun of me. I wasn't sucking up to you that much." Jim said, "Well you can feel free to use big words around me. I like them. Just don't use them around Bart. He gets furious when I use a word he doesn't know." Lillian said, "I'll keep that in mind." She slowly moved her face closer to Jim. Jim said, "Do I have something in my eye?" She moved in even closer and put her arm around his neck. She lightly closed her teeth on his lower lip and pulled out on it. After staring into his eyes for a few seconds, she pressed her lips tightly against his mouth and French kissed him for a long while. Jim held her tightly and kissed her back with equal fervor.

Finally Lillian pulled back a little and said, "We'd better get going. It's time to go fishing." Jim said, "I'd like to jog a little first." Lillian said, "We can jog a little. Let's go." Off they went, down the beach. After about ten minutes they ran back to the bungalow and went inside.

They entered the house through the back door, which faced the gulf. Ingrid was in the kitchen drying the breakfast dishes. She said, "It's good to see you, Jim. Have you had your breakfast?" Jim said, "Yes, I had a bowl of cereal and some orange juice." Ingrid said, "That won't last you very long. Why don't I cook you an egg while Leif is loading the car and boat." Lillian said, "Go ahead, Jim. You will need your energy." Jim said, "Thank you for the hospitality, Ingrid. I think I will have that egg. Can you make it over easy for me?" Ingrid said, "Of course. I'll make some toast, too." Jim said, "You are very kind." Lillian talked about fishing with Jim while her mother cooked the eggs. Finally, Ingrid came over from the stove with Jim's eggs and toast.

While Jim ate, he listened to Ingrid talking about art. She couldn't resist giving her views on the renaissance. She said, "Each artist had a special genius, and the fortitude to use it for great accomplishments. It doesn't do any good to be a genius if you don't use what you have for good causes. The renaissance was a time when brilliant people drove themselves mercilessly. Their creations were in their minds, crying to be released." Jim said, "I see why Lillian knows so much about art. You obviously love art intensely, Ingrid." Ingrid said, "You're right, I love to go to museums with Lillian. We are planning a trip to Rome, Italy next summer. There we can see much of the Renaissance work for ourselves. Leif will be too busy fishing, but Lillian and I will have a great time. Carol may come along too, even though she isn't as excited about art."

Jim finished his eggs and toast and continued to listen, as Ingrid told him more about art. She obviously loved the subject and could talk all day about it if she wanted to. Leif came in and said, "It's good to have you with us again, Jim. The car and boat are ready to go. We'd better get going if we want to get a full day of fishing in." They all climbed in the car and headed for the marina. Leif launched his boat and told them to get in. In no time at all, they were out on the gulf. Leif had a depth finder in the boat. When he got to a depth of forty feet, he stopped the engine and lowered anchor. He said, "This should be a good spot. It's about the same depth that I fished at yesterday." Lillian said, "I'll get the spinning rods out of the compartments." She quickly gathered them up and passed them out. Then she said, "What will we fish with today, dad?" Leif smiled and said, "The usual silver spoon jig. They work well every time on sheepshead. There is already one on each line. All you have to do is drop it over the edge and jig it at various depths till you come up with a fish." Jim said, "I'm glad you know what you're doing. I don't know a thing about sheepshead." Leif said, "They are easy fish to catch. When I'm on vacation I like a nice relaxing fish like the sheepshead. You don't have to concentrate as hard as you need to with walleye. Walleye are clever fish. You need to keep your wits about you when you fish for them." They all grew silent for a few minutes while they dropped their lines overboard and gently jigged them at different depths.

It wasn't long till Leif caught his first fish. He reeled it in easily. It was a twelve inch sheepshead. He showed it proudly to the rest of them. "This is what we're after. These little babies don't fight as much as walleye, but they're fun to catch. Notice the black stripes on the fish. That is how I know they are sheepshead." Then Lillian's pole bent down. She set the hook and reeled rapidly, till her fish came into view. It was similar in size and appearance to Leif's fish. Its black and white body glistened in the morning light. Lillian showed genuine pride in her fish. She looked at it for a long time, and asked Jim to hold it. Jim took several pictures of it with Lillian's camera. He took one shot of Lillian, her mom, dad, and the fish. Then Lillian took a picture of the fish with Jim and her parents. At last the picture taking had to stop, because Jim and Ingrid both had their jigs taken. Their poles bent down considerably. They reeled rapidly until each of them had a sheepshead dangling from their pole. They all had smiles on their faces. Leif said, "We'd better keep our lines in the water and get a lot of fish out of this school. They may move on soon and we'll have to wait for the next school to swim by." They all concentrated on their fishing. In no time they had about fifty fish. Finally the school of sheepshead moved on and things got quiet.

Lillian started to get a little bored with waiting on the next school of fish to arrive. She started tickling Jim's ear and blowing in it. Jim couldn't believe she was doing that right in front of her parents. He said, "Lillian, you need something to help you pass the time. Why don't you show me the cuddy cabin." Lillian said, "That's a great idea, Jim. Follow me." They went into the cozy little cabin. Jim explained to Lillian that he didn't want to express affection in front of her folks. Lillian promised to do as he asked. They both left the cabin and started fishing again. Leif said, "I'd like to meet your father, Jim. Lillian says that he is a farmer. He makes a living with his hands like I do." Jim said, "You must meet him tomorrow. I'm sure my grandfather will want your whole family to go shark fishing with us. Only he likes to leave early in the morning." Leif said, "It will be worth getting up early for. I want to visit with your grandparents as well. It is too bad that your mother isn't along. Why didn't she come with the rest of you?" Jim said, "Someone had to take care of the cows. We don't have anyone else trained to care for them."

Jim said, "You'll meet all my family tomorrow, Leif. It's a sure thing." Leif smiled at this. He was pleased that Jim was not just a playboy. It was a good sign when a boy wants the girl's father to meet his family. Leif said, "I'm glad that you are getting serious about Lillian. I've been praying that she will find a good companion. Her last boyfriend was such a loser. He made my stomach boil." Jim smiled, "We have learned to care for each other. My father knows how I feel about her. He says he has a plan that will allow us to continue seeing each other." Lillian jumped up in surprise. She said, "Jim, you didn't tell me about the plan. What is it? Tell me now!" Jim said, "My father didn't tell me the details. He only said that he was sure it would be possible. He was very confident about it." Lillian gave Jim a big hug. "That's wonderful! I can't wait to find out what the plan is! Your father is a very thoughtful man. We would have worried about the future towards the end of this week. Now Jake has made it so we can be happy the whole time we are together."

They all started reeling in their fish again. There had been fish on the lines for some time, but everyone had been too busy talking to pull them in. As Ingrid reeled in her fish, she said, "Jim, we are happy that your father has a plan. We were wondering about what the future could hold for you and Lillian. Now we're relieved." They reeled in fish for about an hour. When they had a total of about one hundred fish, they stopped keeping the fish. They just caught and released them. Finally they were tired of fishing. Leif and Rosa went into the cabin to rest, so that Jim and Lillian could spend some time alone.

Lillian and Jim lay down on their backs to sun themselves. They lightly caressed each other's hair. For a long time they talked about the beauty of the tropics, and how wonderful it would be to see the brightly colored fish that live there, in the coral reefs.

Jim said, "My brother has a scuba outfit. He said that I could use it since I got him together with Carol." Lillian said, "You and your brother were bartering for my sister?" She giggled loudly and then said, "I am shocked, Jim." He said, "Well, it wasn't my idea. My dad told Bart not to be so calculating. Don't tell him that I told on him, or I won't get to use the scuba gear. I was thinking we could take turns using it." Lillian said, "Maybe my dad will buy me scuba gear. He likes it when I am adventurous. He had a good summer this year with the charter business. He has plenty of money. Mom has millions of dollars in the bank, but they never touch that. My dad prides himself in having us live on his income. The bank money is for his grandchildren if they need help."

Jim said, "That is the way my father is. He likes to show he can build his own fortune. He doesn't ask his dad for money very often. If he does, he likes to pay it back. Farming is not a business that makes it easy to get rich. The price of corn doesn't go up, but the price of everything else does go up. A farmer has to spend every minute thinking of ways to cut costs and expand the operation. If he expands too much, and works with a lot of borrowed money, he ends up just working for the bank."

Lillian said, "You seem to understand the operation pretty well. Do you think you will ever farm?" Jim said, "I like farm work, but my mind is always on other things. I get stir crazy. My mother says I have wanderlust. I need to be a writer who travels the world and writes for a living. It is the only way I will be happy." Lillian said, "What about your wife. What will she do?" Jim said, "She can be a writer too, or do some job that can be done on the move." Lillian said, "You have an answer for everything. I like that answer. You're just like your father. You can solve any problem."

They talked for hours about the possible ways that they could get together during their remaining years of high school. Then, they talked about college . . . where they would go and whether they would be able to go to the same school. Finally after several hours, Lillian's parents woke up. It was getting to be late in the afternoon. Leif dumped some more ice on the fish to keep them fresh. Leif said, "We'd better get home. We need to clean the fish and cook some of them for supper. If Jim's grandfather takes us shark fishing tomorrow, we will be getting up at four o'clock in the morning." Lillian said, "I know. They like to get an early start." They put away their rods, pulled up anchor and headed for shore.

By 4:30 P.M. Leif had the boat loaded, the saltwater flushed from the boat engine and the car headed for home. On the way home Jim said, "That was interesting how you used a garden hose and suction cup adapters to flush the salt out of the inside of the engines cooling system. Where did you learn to do that?" "We flush the engines on our dingies, back home in Finland. We always used oars to move the small boats, years ago. In the fifties, those of us who could afford them, started using outboard motors. It made things easier, and made it a little more likely that you would survive. You could get out of the rough seas quicker." Jim loved to hear Leif talk about the sea. He listened to Leif talk about the old country the whole way home, and most of the time while they cleaned the fish.

During supper, it was Ingrid and Lillian who did most of the talking. They talked about their childhoods, and how it had been to live in Finland. Jim soaked it all in. After supper, he ran back to the motel and called his Grandpa Sellers to see about the fishing trip in the morning. Grandpa Sellers loved the idea. The time was set at 5:00 A.M. Jim ran back to Lillian's and told them to be ready. He kissed Lillian and held her for awhile. They watched television for a couple hours, and then walked the beach for an hour so they could watch the sunset. They held hands as they walked along. They would let their hands swing back and forth as they walked. They walked further than usual that night.

Lillian said, "We'd better not get each other excited tonight. I want us to look rested and innocent in the morning, so that your dad will work out that plan for us. Go on back to the motel and get to bed early. That will make a good impression on your dad." Jim said, "You're right. He would be impressed if I got some sleep." They walked back to Lillian's place and Jim kissed her good night. He walked back home and enjoyed the smell of the orchids as he passed them along the way. He stopped to put his nose into some of them. They were pleasant almost to the point of being intoxicating. Then he went the rest of the way home.

Jake was still up. He was talking on the phone to his wife, Lois. He said, "Yes, Jim is very much in love. When we get home we'll show you a picture of her. She lives in Columbia, Ohio. They plan to stay in touch after the vacation is over." Jake talked a little longer and then said goodbye. He told Jim, "Your mother is very happy for you. She sends you her love." Jim said, "It's good to hear mom is all right. I think I'll go to bed now. We will be getting up early in the morning." Jake said, "Why so early to bed? Did you and Lillian have a fight?" Jim said, "No, she just wants me to get my sleep. She is very sensible." Jim pulled the covers over his head like he always did to sleep. Jake said, "She does sound like a sensible girl. I'm looking forward to seeing her again and her family." Jim said, "It's going to be a fine day. Good night dad." Jake said, "Good night."

In the morning, before the sun started to rise, the alarm clock went off in Jim's room. Jim and Jake woke to the sound of the alarm. Bartholomew slept on. He didn't seem to notice the alarm. Jake woke him up. Bart said, "I'm too tired, I'm going to sleep in if that's okay. I'll spend the day walking the beach with Carol. You can go without me." Jake said, "We'll let you sleep. Just promise to behave yourself with Carol. Jim is growing close to her family. You don't want to embarrass him by taking advantage of Carol." Bartholomew said, "I promise. I'll be a gentleman." Jake said, "I knew I could count on you, Bartholomew." He patted Bartholomew on the head.

Jim and his dad ate a quick breakfast and hurried over to the Tahkala's place. Jim rang the doorbell. Leif answered the door. He shook Jake's hand. Leif said, "It's good to meet you Jake. I've been hearing good things about you and your family. Welcome." Jake said, "I'm glad to meet you. I too have heard many good things about the Tahkalas.

We should go as soon as possible. Grandpa Sellers likes to leave on time." There were quick introductions and then the families got in their cars, all except Carol. When she heard that Bart wasn't coming, she stayed at home too. She wanted to spend the day with him.

In no time the Tahkalas were in Everett's boat being introduced to Howard and him. Everett wasted no time in moving the boat out to the gulf. When they reached the proper depth of two hundred feet, he shut off the engines and lowered the anchor. He explained his methods of fishing to Leif, who was interested in every detail. Jim took Lillian and Ingrid on a tour of the boat. Ingrid loved the cabin. She said, "We should buy a boat like this. It's wonderful. You could live on this boat for weeks and not get tired of it." Jim agreed, "Yes, it is a nice boat. Someday I'll get one like this. They are a lot of fun." When Jim finally took Lillian and Rosa back topside, the shark was being landed. Leif had caught it. It was a one hundred and forty pound tiger shark. Leif looked happy as he watched Everett shoot the shark with the shotgun. Jim got his camera and took pictures.

Many sharks were caught. The Tahkalas got to know Jim's family and feel at home with them. Finally Jake said, "Jim you keep the ladies company. We older men want to talk in private for awhile." Jake, Leif and the two grandparents went down into the galley and talked for a long time." Lillian said, "I wonder what they are talking about." Jim said, "I think my dad is making plans for us. Whatever it is, I think we'll like it." Finally after about an hour, the men came back up on deck.

Leif said, "We have decided that we want Jim and Lillian to enjoy the beauty of the sea some day, here in the tropics. We are going to pay for scuba lessons. You can both meet every week in Fort Wayne for the lessons. Fort Wayne is midway between our two homes. We will pay for drivers to take both of you there and back each week." Lillian jumped up and hugged each of them. She was elated. Jim thanked Leif and his grandparents. He thanked his dad too, and gave him a big hug. Ingrid said, "It's a wonderful idea." She hugged Lillian and Jim. Then she hugged Leif. She said, "Jake, you're a genius. They're such a nice couple. It would be tragic for them to never see each other again." Jake said, "You're right. Now they can see each other every week. It will be nice for them."

It was now noon, and back at the motel Carol had gotten together with Bart. They were making out in the motel room. It went on for hours. Their passions were being allowed to gallop away totally unbridled.

Back on the boat, Jim and Lillian were sunbathing at the bow. They held hands and talked softly to each other. Jim said, "It's wonderful to think of the great times we will be having. If we learn the scuba diving well, we may be able to dive down here next winter." Lillian said, "That would be fun. I hope our families can come down again. It all depends on whether my dad has a good year with the charter business. We usually don't come down here every year. The economy has a lot to do with it. When things are going well for people, they all spend more money on fishing trips." Jim said, "I understand. If business is not as good for your dad, next year, we will still have fun taking the scuba diving lessons together." They lay there in the sun quietly for a long time. With their fingers intertwined, they slept the sleep of lovers who dream of each other. There was a contented smile on each of their faces. They slept several hours.

While Jim and Lillian slept, their two families were getting to know each other. They all had lots to talk about. After the sun started to set, everyone agreed that it would be good to head for home. Everett started the motors and they headed for home. They all ate supper at the Sellers house. There was lots of story telling and joking around. Everyone had a good time. They kept talking until it was

10:00 P.M. Then the party finally broke up, but it was agreed to do the same thing the next day.

The Tahkalas went home feeling good about the new family that was growing close to them. When they got home, Carol and Bart were watching television. They both had hickies on their necks. Leif took the two of them into the kitchen and had a long talk with them. He let them know that they would be closely chaperoned for the rest of the vacation. He said, "I don't mind if the two of you express affection for each other, but biting each other in a heated passion is completely out of line. If you are going to show such lack of control, we will have to force control on you both. We are starting to be good friends with the Sellers family. I hope that you both will try hard not to embarrass either family." Bart and Carol didn't say much. They just looked like kids caught with their hands in the cookie jar.

The rest of the vacation was similar to the first part. The two families fished together every day. Lillian and Jim got to know each other quite well. They tried their best not to embarrass the families by getting too physical. They still allowed themselves lots of kissing.

Then disaster struck. A girl that Lillian had learned to know, and who was staying in the Bungalow next door; was found dead on the beach. Jim and Lillian found her when they went out for their morning jog. Lillian and Jim were both quite shaken by the murder. The girl's throat had been cut. The attack had happened right along the water. There were no footprints near the body. The dead girl had been found lying right at the water's edge. She was about Lillian's age, with long pretty blond hair. Her body was slender, yet she was well proportioned. She was incredibly attractive. Lillian cried for most of the day over her friend. Jim decided it would be best to leave her alone with her family for awhile.

The police talked to the dead girl's parents. They said that their daughter Cathy, often went walking along the beach at night. They had been told that the area was safe, and that crimes never happened there. The police told them that they would do their best to find the murderer, but it was going to be difficult since there were no tracks in the sand and the knife had not been left at the crime scene. Another thing that made the murder difficult to solve was that the victim and her family were just there on vacation. They would not have had any logical reasons to have enemies. Cathy had probably been the innocent victim of a random act of violence. Such crimes were especially hard to solve, unless the criminal developed a recognizable pattern to his crimes, or got reckless about being seen by someone. The Tahkala and the Sellers families were questioned briefly about the crime, but they had nothing helpful that they could give the police.

Both families decided to cut their vacation short a few days. The murder had taken all the joy out of the activities. The next day they all packed for the trip home. Jim and Lillian exchanged phone numbers and addresses. They were very sad about the week of fun coming to an end so tragically, but they were looking forward to seeing each other every week for the scuba lessons. They kissed each other goodbye and then the families headed off on their separate trips home.

The weeks passed quickly during the rest of the winter and spring. The couple was learning the basics of scuba diving. Their instructor was a middle-aged man named George Anderson. He was a handsome dark skinned man with a salt and pepper beard. George had a sense of humor which made the time go quickly. He was mild mannered and knew how to put his students at ease. Each week he skillfully guided his students towards a high level of competence at diving.

Lillian was a little frustrated that she and Jim never had any time alone. They were driven to the lessons by friends of the families. There was no time at all to sneak away and be romantic. She longed for Jim's physical touch. Jim also would have liked to sneak off with Lillian, but he didn't want to embarrass his family. He contented himself with fantasies that Lillian created for him in her letters to him. She would describe vividly how she would like to hold him and kiss him for hours. These letters were full of scenes that were very exciting for both of them. She called them dramas. They described step by step what each of them would do on a particular evening together. Jim couldn't believe what a creative imagination Lillian had. Lillian promised that when she reached the age of eighteen, she would drive to Warsaw to see Jim. When that day came, she said she would bring her favorite drama with her.

When summer came, Leif didn't have as much business as the previous year. Because of that, the winter trip to Florida had to be canceled. The two families got together a couple times that year for a supper together, but other than that, Jim and Lillian had to content themselves with scuba lessons and dramas.

By the end of two years, they were both expert scuba divers. They were almost ready to get their night diving certificates. They already had the basic certificate that was required in order to get tanks filled. Lillian had her own car and was a fully trained competent driver. The family finally gave her permission to drive to Warsaw to visit Jim. Jim's family invited her to stay several days, since it was such a long trip. She had not agreed to any certain amount of time yet, but she set the date for January 19, 1968. On that day at about 1:00 o'clock in the afternoon, Lillian set out on a voyage that would change her life forever. She kissed her mom and dad goodbye, and started out for the long drive to Warsaw. She had a good map with her, and was confident about her abilities.

Chapter Four

Ice Fishing 1968

Jim and Lillian had been writing every day to each other, and meeting for scuba lessons each week for two years. He had talked to her a lot about ice fishing in 1967. He told her how quiet and lonely it got in the icehouse sometimes. It was then that he missed her most, when he was alone, and had nothing else he needed to think about. His description about how private and warm the icehouse was had given Lillian some food for thought. It reminded her of the steam sauna that her family had, when they lived in Finland. Her dad was promising to build one in their home there in Columbia, but he kept putting it off. He was busy doing other things. She had longed to be there, in that private warm icehouse, with Jim. When she was writing her dramas, she would describe vividly the exact things that she would like to do with Jim there. It was always tender and romantic. It was exciting and sensual too. Lillian had decided to show the ice fishing drama to Jim after they had caught a few fish. That way he wouldn't feel like she was just after his body. Besides, she did love to fish. She knew he would be embarrassed when he read them, but that is how she wanted to introduce her ideas to him. They wouldn't feel as awkward or embarrassed if he was only reading at first. Then, they could revise the script as they saw fit. They could do whatever fit them perfectly at that time. Of course they would always stick to their rules of control. That way they wouldn't ruin things with an unwanted pregnancy.

It was January 19, 1968, when Lillian pulled her car into the driveway at Jim's house. He lived east of Warsaw a few miles on his father's farm. There was eight inches of fresh snow of the ground that day. Jim had seen Lillian pulling into the drive and went out to meet her. He could hear the snow crunching under her tires as she drove up to the house. When her car stopped, she jumped out of the car and gave Jim a long passionate hug and a kiss. She said, "Oh Jim, I've waited for a hundred years, it seems, for this moment." Jim said, "I thought the day would never come. Come in the house and meet my mom. You've already met my dad." Lillian followed Jim into the large log house that Jim lived in. His mother and father were waiting just inside the door.

Jim's mother stepped up to Lillian and gave her a hug. She introduced herself. "I'm Lois, Jim's mother. I've heard so many good things about you, Lillian. You are all Jim has talked about since he met you down in Florida." Jim's dad said, "Jim thinks the world of you Lillian. You can feel right as home with us. Think of us as family." Lillian said, "That is very kind of you both. I've been looking forward to spending some time with you. My parents said that I could stay a couple days, like Jim suggested. It's so far away that we can't drive back and forth every week." Lois said, "I'm glad your parents agreed to the plan. We thought it was for the best. It is a long way to drive. You and Jim have been writing loyally to each other for such a long time, you deserve some time together."

"You should both get down to the icehouse before it gets dark. We won't wait up for you." "Jim can show you your bedroom when you come back. Once again, I'd like to say that you are family as far as we're concerned. Jim loves you very much. You two are unusually loyal for being so young. Jim was always a little quick at growing up. I think it's because he's so bright." Jim said, "Mom, you're embarrassing me. Let Lillian decide how smart I am." Lois said, "All right, Jim, I'm just so proud of you." Jake said, "Don't forget both gas lanterns, it's about twenty-eight degrees out there. It could get down to twenty-four or lower tonight."

Jim thanked his dad for the good suggestion and took Lillian to the barn. There on the wall were the gas lanterns. He had filled them the previous day, to save time. It was close to 6:30 P.M. and everyone had already eaten supper. Lillian had stopped to eat at a roadside diner. They put their fishing gear in the back of Jake's 4-wheel drive truck, and drove down to the farm pond. There, out in the middle of the pond was the icehouse. Jim and Lillian carried the fishing equipment to the house. The snow was too deep to pull the little ice fishing sled along behind them. It was a box on runners that had a window in the front. You could use it for fishing, if you didn't have an icehouse. A lantern would fit inside the box to keep the fisherman warm. The back of the ice sled held the short ice fishing poles, and small tackle box. There was also a thermos full of hot chocolate that Lois had sent with them. Jim carried the sled, and Lillian carried the lantern that wasn't in the sled. She also had a container of extra fuel they had brought along.

It didn't take them long to get to the icehouse. The ice was safe. The weather had been below zero often during the previous week. Jim asked Lillian to light the lanterns. He knew that a Finnish girl would be familiar with them. She pumped them up like an expert ice fisherman, and lit each one with a match. The icehouse was built oversized to accommodate all Jim's relatives who liked to fish. Jim said, "I left the ice spud down here so that we wouldn't have to carry it today. It's rather heavy." Lillian said, "I see there are two holes cut fairly close together." Jim said, "Yes, I dug them yesterday for us. Now there will only be an inch or so of ice on top. It will be easy for us to get a couple good holes cut in the ice." Jim started chopping at the ice with the long metal spud. The ice chips flew all around the house. Lillian looked around at the walls. They measured about five feet wide, by eight feel long. The ceiling was only about five feet high. They had to lean over a little all the time.

After Jim had chipped away with the spud for about ten minutes, he was satisfied with his work. He said, "Lillian, there's an ice strainer in the ice sled, would you go out and get it. It's a round strainer on a long metal handle." Lillian said, "I know about them. My dad ice fishes, only he doesn't have an icehouse." Jim said, "Oh, that's right, you mentioned in your letters about that." Lillian brought in the strainer and started to dip the pieces of ice out of the holes. Jim went out and brought in the rest of the supplies. Jim said, "Oh, I forgot. I've got a blanket behind the seat of the truck. I'll go get it. It might come in handy." Lillian said, "Good, I'll have these holes cleaned out by the time you get back." Jim ran as fast as he could through the deep snow. He grabbed the blanket and ran back to the icehouse. He was puffing a little when he returned. Lillian said, "That was quick. The house is starting to get warm already! What's the blanket for?" Jim said, "We can lie down on the floor if we want to be lazy fishermen." Lillian said, "Just like a man, wanting to get the woman on the floor. It's all right though. I know exactly how you feel. It's been so long since we held each other." "I long for it too." Jim said, "I'll spread it out now so it will warm up." Carefully he spread it out. Lillian helped him make it neat.

Jim set a couple plastic buckets, which were there, by the ice holes. "One for you, and one for me," he said. Lillian giggled, "This will be cozy. Fishing side by side." The holes were only a foot apart. Jim said, "I wanted us to be close. It may cause a problem. Can you guess what that might be?" Lillian said, "Will we get too horny?" Jim laughed, "That's true, but it's not the answer I was looking for." Lillian said, "What then?" Jim paused, "We might get our lines tangled. When one of us gets a fish, the other will have to pull up their line quickly, to avoid entanglement." Lillian said, "Entanglement is what I came here for, Jim." Jim laughed, "Well, I'm all in favor of that! But, do you understand me?" Lillian said, "Jim, I understand you perfectly. It's getting quite warm in here. Do you mind if I take off some clothes?" Jim said, "Feel free. I will too." They both took off their coats and laid them on the blanket.

Jim put wax worms on each of their hooks and dropped the lines into the water. There were miniature bobbers on the lines. Each hook was about five feet below the bobber. Before Lillian could sit down, she had a fish take the bobber down very slowly. Jim whispered, "Let it pull the bobber down about three inches and then pull up hard." Lillian did just as he said. She felt the fish pulling hard on the line. Jim quickly pulled up his line, as they had agreed. Slowly Lillian pulled in the line, hand over hand. Out from the hole came a ten inch bluegill. Jim praised her fish profusely. "My parents will be very proud of you, Lillian. I'm proud of you right now."

"For every fish you catch I'm going to give you a big kiss." Lillian said, "I'll take my first one right now!" Jim stood up and held her in his arms tightly as he French kissed her just like they had kissed in Florida, two years before. Lillian kissed him back with equal fervor. Her tongue moved lightly over his, and then all around in his mouth. They started to breath a little louder and deeper. Jim pulled back a little from Lillian and said playfully, "That's one kiss." Lillian said, "I hope I catch a thousand fish if you're going to kiss like that. You haven't forgotten how to kiss!" She lightly touched the front of his jeans with her fingers, but decided to go no further. "Let's catch another one," she said. They put the bluegill in an empty bucket, and started to fish again. In about a minute, they both caught one. They pulled the fish in hand over hand. There on the ice were two more ten inch bluegill. Jim said, "You're good luck, Lillian. The fish are really biting. Let's save the kisses for ten minutes, and see how many we can store up in that time." At first Lillian looked disappointed, but then her face brightened. "I'll just settle for unlimited kisses after ten minutes." Jim said, "You've got a deal."

That ten minutes was ice fishing as it has never been known. They started to pull the fish in as fast as they could drop their lines in the water. Each time it was a nice bluegill. Lillian looked at her watch every couple minutes and told Jim how much time was left. Lillian started baiting her own hook. She got so excited about fishing that she forgot about the time for awhile. When she finally looked at her watch, fourty-five minutes had passed. They poured the fish out on the ice and counted them. There were thirty fish there. Jim said, "I've never had this much good luck." Then he paused, "I shouldn't keep saying luck. My dad always reminds me that God gives us each fish." Lillian said, "That's what my dad says. I guess that's what all the best fishermen think."

Jim said, "I guess I owe you quite a few kisses by now." Lillian said, "I'm eager and waiting." They kissed for a long time until the lantern started to grow dim. Jim quickly pumped up the lantern. Then he got down on one knee and showed Lillian the diamond ring he had bought for her. He said, "Lillian will you marry me?"

Lillian stared down at him in disbelief. Her look of wonder though, quickly turned to rapture. She said, "Yes, yes Jim, I will!" Jim placed the ring on her finger and said, "I would like us to get married a year from today exactly. Does that sound good to you?" Lillian said, "I would love that. You surprised me, Jim. I was thinking I wanted to win you, but you had already made up your mind." She cried softly and held his head tightly against her tummy. They remained in that pose for a long time. Neither of them wanted to break the spell. They wanted that moment to last for the rest of their lives.

Lillian said, "I don't want us to ever get rid of this icehouse. I want your father to give it to us as a wedding present." Jim said, "I'm sure he'll be glad to give it to us." Finally they lay back down on the blanket side by side, looking into each other's eyes. Jim said, "We won't have trouble remembering where I proposed. It was in this icehouse." They both kissed tenderly for a long time. Finally Jim broke the silence. "I want to tell my Mom and Dad tonight. They knew I was going to ask you soon, but they didn't know it would be tonight." Lillian said, "Yes, I want to see their faces. If we don't tell them I won't be able to sleep tonight. Then I'll call my parents and tell them. They will be very happy for us." They loaded up the fish and fishing gear and headed for the truck. They took one last look at the icehouse. Then they kissed for a minute in the truck while the engine warmed up. They drove slowly to the house. All the way there, Lillian caressed Jim's leg. She whispered in his ear, when they reached the house. "You have made me the happiest woman alive. I'm going to make you truly happy." Jim said, "You already have, Lillian."

When they entered the house, it was dark and his parents were asleep. Jim led Lillian upstairs to her bedroom. She put her purse inside and then followed Jim to his bedroom. They stepped inside and Lillian closed the door behind them. Lillian pulled Jim up against her and kissed him passionately on the mouth for several minutes. Then she said, "Jim I love you more than anything." Jim said, "I love you too, Lillian. Now we'd better get some sleep. I think I'd like to wait till tomorrow to tell my parents." Lillian said, "Yes, I guess I can wait till tomorrow to tell everyone." They kissed their final good night kiss, and Lillian went back to her bedroom.

Early in the morning, at 5:00 o'clock, Jim woke up Lillian. They went downstairs and found Jake eating his breakfast. Jim said, "Dad, would you get Mom. Lillian and I have some good news to share." Jake went into the bedroom and got Lois. She came out with a bathrobe on, and sat next to Jake at the table. Jim said, "I've asked Lillian to marry me and she has accepted." Lois and Jake smiled and Lois said, "We're very happy for both of you. When is the wedding going to be?" Lillian said, "We're getting married a year from last night exactly. It will be on January 19, 1969."

Jake said, "That is good news. We'll arrange for a house for the two of you to live in. I think that people can concentrate on their college courses better when they're married. You two have been yearning for each other for long enough. Now you won't have to feel like you need to sneak in a kiss all the time." Lillian said, "I'm happier than I have ever been. It will be great to have Jim next to me every night." Lillian gave Jim a big hug. Lois said, "Welcome to our family, Lillian. It's wonderful to have you join us." Lillian hugged Lois and then hugged Jake.

Lois said, "Let me cook up some pancakes for all of you." Lillian said, "That sounds good. I want to call my mom and dad first, and tell them the good news." Lillian went to the phone and called her mom and dad. Lillian's mother answered the phone. Lillian told her to get her dad on the extension phone. Ingrid said, "Has something happened? What is it?" Lillian said, "Jim has asked me to marry him, and I have accepted." Leif said, "That's wonderful news. I like Jim. He's a good man." Ingrid said, "You must both drive to our house so that we can congratulate you both in person." Lillian said, "We will come over on Sunday. I'm sure Jim will want us to come over right away." Lillian said to Jim, "Is it all right if we go see my parents tomorrow? They want to congratulate us." Jim said, "I would love to go. Tomorrow will be fine."

Lillian told her mom, "We'll be there in time for lunch." Lillian talked for ten minutes or more. She only ended the call when she was told that breakfast was ready.

Lillian and her new family ate breakfast together and talked for hours. They made the final decision to go to Atlantus College, in Wawasa, Indiana. They knew they would be close to Jim's favorite fishing spots that way. And of the colleges they had received literature from, Atlantus seemed to have the most challenging and stimulating academic curriculum. Jim had been impressed with the wide range of courses offered by the English department. He wanted especially to take British literature. Since his Grandpa Martin was of British descent, he had learned a few things about Britain's rich literary heritage already.

Lillian was eager to study biology at Atlantus. She and Jim had been comparing notes about the college, over the phone. She wanted to study marine biology. Atlantus had a special program in that. It involved studying in Florida. She knew Jim would come with her for the courses. She asked him just to be sure, "Jim will you study biology in Florida with me?" Jim said, "I'd be glad to. It would bring back memories for us of when we first met." Lillian said, "Yes, it's like a perfect dream unfolding before us. We could scuba dive together after the classes are done for the day. Of course, it might be better if I study on weeknights. I'm sure we'll find free time on the weekends for plenty of scuba diving, if we budget our time well." Jim said, "Now you're painting a wonderful picture, Lillian. I'd love to see the coral reefs. I hear they are as beautiful as anything else on earth!"

Jim and Lillian spent the rest of the day talking with Jim's parents. They went out for dinner at a nice restaurant, to celebrate. For supper they ate the fish that Jim and Lillian had caught in the icehouse. The couple went to bed by 9:00 P.M. so they could get an early start the next morning for their trip to Lillian's house in Columbia, Ohio.

They woke in the morning before the sun was up. Jake and Lois were already sitting down to some eggs and bacon when Jim and Lillian came into the kitchen. Lillian quickly volunteered to cook some breakfast for Jim and her. Lois responded, "Normally I wouldn't think of letting a guest do the cooking, but I suppose Jim would like to get a sample of your cooking. After all, he will be getting used to it now." They all laughed and Jake added, "Jim is used to the best cooking in the world. Lois will be a hard act to follow." Lillian laughed again and said, "I won't argue with that statement. I will only promise to do my best. How do you want your eggs, Jim?" Jim said, "I'll take mine over easy with some toast, but let me help you. I can at least make the toast." Lillian said, "I'll be glad for the help." They bumped and tickled each other as they worked at preparing breakfast. The toast got a little burned and the eggs were a little over cooked, but everyone was having fun.

Finally, when breakfast was over, the newly engaged couple said their good byes and went out to Lillian's car. They took turns driving, during the long trip to Columbia. When they arrived at the Tahkala house, it was 9:30 A.M. Lillian ran up to the door and rang the doorbell. Leif and Ingrid came out on the porch immediately. Leif shook Jim's hand and congratulated him. Ingrid hugged them both, and Leif gave his daughter a big hug. They all went into the house.

Lillian proudly showed her diamond engagement ring to her parents. They were delighted with how beautiful it was. Carol came downstairs from her bedroom and gave Jim and Lillian each a hug. She said, "So, my little sister is getting married before I do. I don't mind, since you are getting such a wonderful husband. I hear that you're as affectionate as Lillian, Jim. You two will make an excellent match." Lillian said, "Of course you will be my maid of honor, Carol." Carol responded, "I would be honored."

The family sat down together and listened to Jim and Lillian describe their plans for the future. They managed to talk the rest of the morning away. They all went to a nice restaurant to eat the noon meal. Then they spent the afternoon at home talking some more about the newly engaged couples plans and dreams. They ate supper at home and played cards till about 10:00 P.M.

Lillian told her folks that she and Jim would like to stay the night with them. They were delighted. Ingrid said, "It wouldn't make sense to drive all the way back to Warsaw this late at night. You can leave tomorrow, whenever you get ready. Jim can sleep in the guest bedroom upstairs next to your bedroom, Lillian. You can show him where everything is." Jim and Lillian said good night to Leif and Ingrid, and went upstairs to Jim's room. Lillian tore up the bed and whispered to Jim, "They will never check to see where you sleep. You can come to my bedroom for the night. My sister's bedroom is right next to mine, but she won't tell." Jim's heart pounded with excitement as Lillian led him to her room.

Once inside the room, Lillian said to Jim, "I've been longing for this night ever since we parted after our week together in Florida. I prepared a little surprise for you." She made Jim turn his back for a couple minutes. He could hear her opening a dresser drawer. He also heard her pants unzipping. Finally she told him to turn around and look at her. When he did, he saw that she was wearing the yellow two-piece bathing suit that she had worn in Florida, two years ago. At least it looked like it. Lillian said, "I found a suit that looks just like the one I wore when we first met. I outgrew the other one." She walked up to Jim and gave him a long passionate French kiss. Her tongue was its usual playful self. She let it roam all around over Jim's teeth. Their tongues played with each other, as their breathing got deeper and they hugged each other tighter. After several hours of passionate kissing on the bed,

Lillian said, "We need to get some sleep. We said that we wouldn't be going all the way. It's no use getting any more excited." Jim said, "Yes, I have to admit that you're right. I sure am in love with you, Lillian." They relaxed in each other's arms and fell asleep after they calmed down.

When they woke the next morning there was a light tapping at their door. They scrambled into their clothes and opened the door. It was Carol. She had a serious look on her face. Lillian said, "I didn't think you would mind if we stayed together tonight. After all we're engaged." Carol said, "It's not that. I don't mind that. It was kind of exciting when you two were making the bed squeak for so long. I can hear everything from my room. You are both really lucky. I envy you, but there's something that I have to talk about with both of you." She entered the bedroom and stood close to them. "I think you both should go to Las Vegas, and get married right away. Your passions are so strong that you won't be able to study if you aren't married. You both need to be together."

Lillian said, "I agree that Las Vegas is a good idea." Jim said, "Then it's decided. I'll call and make arrangements Monday morning. It won't hurt if we miss a week of school. Where shall we take our honeymoon?" Lillian said, "Let's go to some of the islands in the Bahamas where they have good bone-fishing. When we were in Florida you said you would take me there someday." Jim said, "An excellent choice. I was going to suggest that myself. Today I'll call Grandpa Sellers and ask him to make the reservations. He's more knowledgeable about the Caribbean than I am. He can probably do it today. He's quick about things. Once he gets going on a project he doesn't stop until it's finished."

Chapter Five

Marriage and Honeymoon

Jim called his grandfather Everett Sellers, as soon as it was daylight out. Grandpa Sellers was delighted to hear from Jim. He said, "So Jim, I hear you're engaged. I'm very happy for you and Lillian. If there is any way that I can help you, just let me know." Jim said, "That's just what I wanted to talk to you about. Lillian and I need your help."

Jim told Grandpa Sellers about the early marriage they had planned and the desired honeymoon location. He said, "I approve of your plan for immediate marriage. I could tell in Florida that you both wanted each other with a passion. There is no point in waiting. I will give you a house and assist you with your financial needs. I'm happy to see people in our family who are as happy as you two are. It makes my life happier. I'll pay for college for both of you also. It doesn't amount to much from my perspective. It won't be any problem for me to set up the Las Vegas marriage and the Caribbean honeymoon."

"I'll fly with you to Las Vegas if you'd like. That way you won't have to worry about making connections and finding your way around." Lillian said, "That would be great Grandpa Sellers. It will be nice to have one family member with us." Jim said, "I agree. It will be good to have you helping us with details." Everett said, "I'll make sure you catch your flight to the Caribbean from Las Vegas, and then you're on your own. I'll give you plenty of traveler's checks. Call me before your flight leaves to bring you back, and I'll pick you up at O'Hare field. You'll need to be here on Monday morning by 6:00 A.M. You'll want to get to Las Vegas early, so you can be sure to get the marriage done that same day. We can get breakfast on the way to the airport."

Next, they phoned Jim's house and explained the Las Vegas wedding to Jake and Lois. They had two phones, and each of them was using one. Jim and Lillian each had their own phone too. It was a regular conference on the phone. Lois was a little disappointed, but she quickly got used to the idea. She said, "Have plenty of pictures taken of the wedding. I want them for my photo album. This is very romantic, now that I start to think about it more." Jake asked, "Will you need me to help pay for some of this? I know you have a good sized savings account, but a vacation in the Bahamas is going to cost plenty." Jim said, "Grandpa Seller's said that he would like to pay for everything. He likes Lillian, and he's delighted that we're getting married. He says he'll buy us a house and college education too." Jake said, "I guess that's alright. You've already proven that you're a hard worker. There's no need to prove that you can do everything alone. This way you can concentrate on your studies in college. I want you to be the best writer there has ever been. And I want Lillian to be able to concentrate on her studies too."

Jim said, "I'm glad that you approve, dad. We'll stay in the Caribbean for a week, and then we'll come right back for school. I still haven't figured out what to tell the school. I guess Lillian and I will just have to take our lumps when we get back." Jake said, "I'm sure that your Grandpa Seller's can help smooth the school's ruffled feathers. He might even be able to help Lillian with her school. If not, then five days of unexcused absence is not going to be the end of the world. You are both good students. I'm sure you will get into Atlantus next fall.

Lillian said, "Since Grandpa Sellers is going to give us a house, it would be great if we could get one near the Atlantus campus. I already have enough credits to graduate. I could graduate now and study at the campus library till fall. That way Jim and I could live together. I want to be with him, starting right now." Jake said, "I don't blame you a bit. If I know my dad, he'll have a house waiting for you when you come back from your honeymoon." Lois said, "That sounds wonderful. You're a genius!" "This is too good to be true!" said Jim.

When Leif and Ingrid woke up Lillian and Jim told them their new plan. They were alarmed by the plan at first, but when they heard about the house that would be waiting for Jim and Lillian, they were pleased. They liked the idea of their daughter going to college early. It would give them something nice to tell the relatives, in addition to the wedding. Leif was relieved to not have to pay for an expensive wedding. He was a generous man, but the charter business had not been good that year. He was a little hard up for money. The family went up to Lillian's bedroom and helped her pack. Jim made sure that she remembered her yellow swimsuit.

Jim and Lillian decided to go directly to Grandpa Everett's house after supper. They knew they wouldn't be able to go to sleep early enough to get up a 2:30 A.M. They would have needed to get up that early in order to make it to Everett's house by 6:00 A.M. They called to let him know that they were coming. It was a lot of driving for one day, but their excitement kept them from getting tired. In no time they were at Everett's house. After supper, they went to Jim's house so that he could pack for the trip. Then they returned to Grandpa Everett's house. They were in bed by 10:00 P.M. When 5:00 A.M. arrived they were well rested and ready for the big day at Las Vegas. Jim had his camera and plenty of film. He eagerly loaded the luggage into Grandpa Seller's Cadillac.

Jim drove all the way to O'Hare airport. He watched the road carefully, but he couldn't help glancing often at his new bride to be. She road in the back, so Everett could stretch his legs better. He had trouble with cramping of his legs on long trips. They stopped for breakfast at a truck stop, about half way to the airport. When they reached the airport, they were about thirty minutes early. The gift shop gave them something to do while they waited. They drank coffee and watched the planes take off and land. In no time, they were boarding their plane for Las Vegas.

The wedding went as smoothly as clockwork. Everett took several rolls of pictures with both his and Jim's cameras. The company that provided the wedding service supplied the bride and groom with costumes to make the event look formal. Jim and Lillian read their vows from cue cards. It was like being on a movie set, filming a picture. When it came time to kiss the bride, the acting was over. Jim and Lillian knew this part by heart and they lived each second. They kissed passionately for as long as they dared. Everett gathered up their marriage license, and they all went out for a celebration dinner. At 3:00 P.M. the newly married couple got on their flight for Miami International Airport. They arrived in Miami at 6:00 P.M. They always figured their time schedule by the Indiana time zone. In less than half an hour, they were on another plane to Astor Island. It was known for its fine bonefishing flats and for the quiet isolation that one could experience there. No vendors would ruin the atmosphere. It was as pristine and pure as it had been hundreds of years ago.

There would only be a few other fishermen on the island. The expense of fishing Astor Island helped keep the fishing pressure low. Everett had picked the Island for its beauty and seclusion. He knew that the lovebirds would want privacy.

A car from the resort was waiting to pick them up. It was only a ten minute drive to the resort. It was named "La Amor del Pescador", which in English meant, "The Loved Place of the Fisherman." Porters carried their luggage into their bungalow. It was a small but luxurious building that was built to cater to the fancies of wealthy bonefishermen and their wives or girlfriends. Jim and Lillian walked around inside for awhile and noted the hot tub and steam sauna that was provided. Jim said, "This steam room will be just like our icehouse on the farm." Lillian gave him a passionate kiss. Her tongue was all over his, and probed every recess of his mouth. She said, "Let's get our clothes off. Then it really will be like the icehouse."

Jim said, "What about the porters?" Lillian said, "I tried to tip them, but they said their tips are included in the package price. It will be nice not to have to worry about that." Jim said, "I guess it would be nice to take our clothes off. I hope that we aren't going to get bored, now that we're married." Lillian gave him a playful punch to the belly. "You'd better not get bored!" she shouted. She pushed him into the steam room and turned on the steam.

Gently but efficiently, she started to take off his clothes. Gentle sounds of passion poured forth from the room. When they finally came out of the steam room, they were smiling and happy. Lillian said, "I worked up quite an appetite, how about you?" Jim said, "Yes, I'm hungry too. I'll call room service and we can eat here in our room. What do you want, Lillian?" She said, "I'd like crab legs." Jim said, "That sounds good. I'll have the same. We can have some good champagne to celebrate our marriage." He called room service on the phone. In only about thirty minutes the food was brought in and placed on their table. There was a large window facing the ocean, in front of the table. They watched the waves come in as they ate their food. Jim proposed a toast, "To many years of fishing in the tropics, and to steam rooms." Lillian laughed and touched her glass to his. She sipped lightly at her drink. She wasn't one to drink often. Jim poured himself another glass of champagne, and offered more to Lillian. She declined, and warned him, "Don't drink too much, I want to take you out in the ocean tonight for some swimming." Jim's eyes got bigger and he put down the champagne. He said, "In that case, I guess I can do without any more drinking. You're better than drink." They finished their meal and then went down to the ocean for a nice long walk along the beach. They walked until it started to get dark. They went back to their room and played some cards until the moon came up.

The moon was full and lit up the beach magnificently. Jim and Lillian walked slowly down to the water's edge. For about an hour they lay on the towel and watched the stars. They went for a long swim in the warm tropical waters. They kissed often in the moonlight. After many hours of interesting conversation and kissing, they went back to the bungalow and crawled into the king-sized bed that was waiting for them. It felt wonderful to curl up next to each other. They slept soundly until morning.

They woke when their alarm went off at 6:00 A.M. Indiana time. It was 7:00 A.M. Astor Island time. They wanted to be at the island marina in time to go bonefishing. They skipped breakfast and got down to the marina by 7:30 A.M. One of the guides was still sitting at a table on the pier. He was drinking coffee. Jim went up to him and introduced himself, "My name is Jim Sellers. My wife and I are here to go bonefishing." The guide shook Jim's hand and said, "My name is Miguel Santos. I would be glad to take you out. All the necessary equipment is in the boat. Have you ever been bonefishing before?" Jim said, "I haven't been bonefishing, but my wife and I know how to fly fish." Miguel said, "That will be helpful. I am sure you will both be successful. I can help you spot the fish. You are probably familiar with using clock numbers to tell what direction to cast." Lillian listened intently as Miguel explained the basics of bonefishing. Jim said, "By the way, my wife's name is Lillian." Lillian said, "It's good to meet you, Miguel." Miguel continued, "We can get in the boat. I'll explain the rest to you as we head for one of my favorite fishing flats.

They all climbed in the boat and Miguel started the engine. It was a modern fiberglass boat that was made especially for bonefishing. There was a 90 horse power outboard motor, and plenty of flat deck surface to make fly fishing easier. There was a six foot high deck at the stern of the boat. Miguel explained the deck to Jim and Lillian, "I will push the boat with a pole from the poling platform. The engine would be too loud. It would scare the fish away. I will be able to see where the bonefish are from up there. I'm glad you both brought good sunglasses. They are important for seeing the fish through the glare on the water's surface."

In no time at all, they reached the sandy flats that Miguel was looking for. With his expert instructions, they were catching bonefish after only a short time. They released all the fish they caught. By 9:00 A.M. the feeding activity of the fish died down. Miguel said, "We should go back to the marina now and have some breakfast. I will take you back out this evening when the fish start to feed again. If you like, you can wade for bonefish this evening. I know where there are some shallow flats that are good for wading. They are close to your bungalow." Jim said, "We would like that. We can meet you at the marina at 5:00 P.M. Astor Island time."

Miguel had a radio on the boat, which he used to call in a breakfast order. There was a restaurant right out on the pier. When he pulled the boat up to the dock, the waiter was waiting for them. He guided Jim and Lillian to their table, where breakfast was waiting for them. As they ate, they talked excitedly about the morning fishing expedition. Jim had taken several rolls of pictures. Miguel had helped him with that. He had plenty of experience using other people's cameras to record fishing activities for them.

Lillian asked, "Did you bring enough film? I hear it is expensive down here." Jim said, "I brought about twenty rolls. That should be enough." Lillian said, "I'm glad that you're such a camera nut. These pictures will mean a lot to us later. I hope we can come to places like this often." Jim said, "I'm sure we will. I'll make it a high priority." While they ate, they looked across the water at all the palm trees that lined the beach. The quaint white bungalows glistened in the morning sun. It was a warm day. Jim knew the water would be warm again for their nocturnal skinny dipping. After breakfast they walked around the island for awhile. There were nice houses that the staff lived in. All those houses were back away from the water. Most of the houses were white, but a few were light pink or a pastel shade of Caribbean blue.

Every yard had many flowering trees and bushes. The smell of tropical flowers filled the air. It was a relief that there were no vendors selling their wares at every turn. The island was owned completely by the bonefishing resort. They saw to it that the island was maintained in an excellent manner for the pleasure of the bonefishermen and their guests. After a long walk around the island, Jim and Lillian went back to their bungalow and dressed for the beach. They lay out in the sun for several hours. They ate a late lunch and then went out with a charter scuba diving boat.

For about an hour, they explored the coral reefs that lay about a half mile out from shore. Jim had his underwater camera with him. He took pictures of every fish that Lillian pointed out to him. The colors of the fish and coral were magnificent. Colors seemed brighter and more phosphorescent than anything they had ever seen. They stayed down as long as their tanks would let them. Lillian tried to get romantic down there, but Jim was too interested in his picture taking. She felt a little disappointed, but she was glad he was getting lots of pictures. She planned to get him under water at night when he was more rested. She knew she had drained him sexually the day before. She would be patient. Their airtime was about up, Lillian pointed to her watch, to indicate that they needed to go up. Jim nodded his head, and they rose back up to the boat. They climbed into the boat and removed their scuba gear. The boat surged forward and speeded for the marina. They enjoyed the scenery as the boat bounced along on the waves.

When they got back to the marina, they had a sandwich and some tropical drinks. When it was 5:00 P.M., they went back to the marina and joined Miguel for more bonefishing. He took them to the wading flats that he had told them about. They got out of the boat and waded till the sun started to set. They caught and released many bonefish in the five to ten pound class. It was one of the best spots in the world. The Crazy Charlie was the fly that Miguel had recommended most highly. They were successful with that fly. They tried other shrimp imitations as well. The fish were hungry and were not finicky. Miguel waded with them and took pictures with Jim's camera.

When the sun started to set, Jim and Lillian got back into the boat and they motored slowly back to the marina. They thanked Miguel and invited him to eat supper with them on the dock. He consented, and they had a wonderful time eating seafood and picking Miguel's brain for more fishing tips. Finally they were starting to get a little tired. They said good bye to Miguel and went back to their bungalow. They sat at their table by the window and watched the ocean. Lillian said, "I brought us each a copy of *The Odyssey*. I promised you that I would read it. Now is a good time. We have done enough physical activity, now we can read.

I want to know why your family is so fascinated with that book." Jim said, "You have a good idea, Lillian. I could use a little reading." They stayed up most of the night reading. By 4:00 o'clock in the morning they had both finished the book. They were tired, but they made some coffee and discussed the book while they drank it.

Lillian said, "No matter what great challenges came to Odysseus, he used his wits to meet the problems head on." Jim said, "You're right. The next day always brought a new dawn that would stretch her red fingers across the sky. Odysseus had a new chance to find his way back to his beloved wife and create a utopia for them. His love and longing for her was part of what kept him keen to meet the foe. The beauty of each morning can remind us that there are difficult challenges ahead, but the battle is worth it when there is a chance to return to ones loved one." Lillian said, "I think that courage and faith are important elements in the story. It appeared that the gods smiled on Odysseus because he was courageous and had faith that the gods would watch over him." Jim said, "We can learn from this book. We need to always have courage, and trust in God." They went outside and walked along the beach for awhile talking more about the book. As they walked, a little trace of dawn started to spread her red fingers across the sky.

They returned to their bungalow and slept most of the day entwined in each other's arms. While they slept there were some interesting things going on back in Warsaw, Indiana. Everett had decided to hire Bart to help manage a car manufacturing firm in Paris, France. Everett owned controlling interest in the firm. He wanted a family member to represent him, so that he would feel that his wishes were being carried out at the firm. He went to Bart's apartment in the northern suburbs of Warsaw. Bart was just waking up at 9:00 A.M. He was a little hung over from drinking too much the night before. When Everett rang the doorbell, Bart didn't have any idea who it would be. Bart invited Everett into his deluxe dwelling. Everett said, "Hello, Bart. Have you found a new job yet?" Bart said, "No I haven't. I was going to start looking this week." Everett said, "I can see why you quit that factory you were working at. You have more brains than they needed there. I have something for you in Paris, France. I want you to help manage my car manufacturing firm. I think your love of fast cars will help you stay interested in the work." Bart said, "That will be great." Everett said, "I will get you enrolled in some management classes and computer classes at Atlantus. You won't be there for most of the classes. I will arrange private tutoring at an accelerated pace. They will help you pick out the important things, instead of making the course difficult, to weed out less diligent students. I am sure you will succeed."

"I need for you to be trained quickly, and Atlantus needs my money. It will be a good experience for you. You can leave right away for Paris. I already have your plane ticket. Here it is." He handed Bart the ticket. "My associates from the car firm will meet you at the airport. They will help you understand how the firm is operating. You will need to stay there about four weeks, in order to get a good feel for the place. Then you can come home and study for a few months at Atlantus." Bart was delighted. He said, "I'll be glad to work for you Grandpa. How much will you pay me?" Everett smiled and said, "I knew you would want to know that. I will give you a generous expense account and $30,000 a year to start. When you start making money for me, I will increase your pay accordingly." Bart said, "That sounds fair to me. Can you drive me to the airport? I don't want to leave my car up there." Everett said, "I'll take you as soon as you can get packed." Bart showered and got dressed. In no time he was packed and heading for O'Hare with Everett.

Carol decided to enroll at Atlantus. She wanted to be near her sister. At Atlantus she could study nursing and help people like her Grandfather Borg had done. She was able to convince her parents to dip into their savings for such a worthy cause. They were happy that she would be with her sister. Leif and Ingrid helped Carol pack her things, and then drove her to Atlantus. Although classes didn't start till February 1st, Carol wanted to get used to the town of Wawasa and explore the Atlantus campus. She was assured by Atlantus, that her apartment on the campus would be ready for her when she arrived.

On Astor Island, Jim and Lillian woke from their long day of sleep. Lillian's thoughts quickly moved to scuba diving. She asked Jim to go to the marina with her for supper. When they got there, Lillian asked Jim if he would take her night diving. He agreed without much coaxing. They walked to the far end of the pier, where the dive office was. Jim made the arrangements for the night dive. He arranged for the crew to bring two boats, so he and Lillian could be left on the scuba diving boat, in complete privacy. They would meet the crew at the dive office at 8:00 P.M.

Jim and Lillian went back to a table on the edge of the pier. It was right next to the pier's restaurant. A waiter came and took their order. They ate a light meal, since they would be swimming soon. They talked animatedly about diving, while they ate. Jim said, "We could take a blanket with us down to the bottom of the ocean. It would be just like a day on the beach." Lillian said, "Yes, I like that idea. We could weigh down the edges with sand."

At 8:00 P.M. Jim and Lillian were at the dive shop, ready to be taken out to a coral reef that was about seventy feet down. The dive crew was friendly and professional. In no time they were positioned over the coral reef. Jim and Lillian had their blanket with them. The crew was obviously curious about the blanket, but they didn't ask any questions. The captain of the thirty-one foot boat showed them how to use the radio in case of trouble. Next, the captain and crew boarded the other boat and left the honeymooning couple alone at the dive site.

Once the second ship was gone, Jim and Lillian helped each other put on the scuba gear. Each of them put on heavy lead weighted diving belts. They took their blanket and jumped overboard. Each of them had a powerful flashlight. They swam straight to the bottom. The flashlights scanned their bodies repeatedly. Both of them were excited to see the other swimming. The scuba gear made it seem strangely exotic and wonderful. When they reached the bottom, they watched the brightly glowing colored fish that lived in the reef. All the fish came out to see the bright lights. They were curious.

Then Jim and Lillian spread out their blanket on a smooth sandy spot. They weighted it down with sand and rocks. Lillian unstrapped her tank and laid it beside her. They embraced and kissed until their tanks got low on air. Reluctantly, they rolled up the blanket and went back to the surface. They climbed onto the dive platform on the stern of the boat and went up the steps onto the deck. Once on board, they finished what they had begun deep below the surface. They took their time and enjoyed the stars. Then the stars began to move. At least it seemed so, to the lovers who had become lost in each other's arms.

Lillian rested there on Jim for a long time. They looked fondly into each other's eyes. She played with the hair on his chest. Finally they went below deck to the head and took a shower together. Lillian said, "I wish we could use this boat every week." Jim said, "We can use Grandpa Sellers' boat whenever we want to. I know he'll let us take it out alone." Lillian said, "That would be great. I would still appreciate it if we could come here and use this boat often. It will always remind me of our honeymoon. You have given me a lot to remember. I think I picked the right man to marry." Jim said, "Thanks, Lillian. I'm glad I married you. Just let me know whenever you want me to help create another memory. I love doing it." He laughed a little. Lillian said, "I could tell."

They dried off and put their swimsuits back on. For hours they just lay on the deck and watched the stars as the waves gently rocked the boat. The moon was bright and glistened across the water. At 4:00 A.M. they could hear the other boat returning to take them back to shore. As the crew boarded, Jim and Lillian smiled innocently, as though they had just been scuba diving. The crew pretended not to notice that the blanket was all wet and sandy. Jim and Lillian held hands as the boat moved through the darkness heading for the pier. They planned to get some sleep and then do some more bonefishing after supper. They slept till 4:00 P.M., and then went to the pier for supper.

After a nice meal on the pier, they went out with Miguel to catch some more fish. Both of them were gaining expertise at leading the fish just right, so that it would take the fly. They could even manage to cast accurately when there was a bit of wind. The weather had been wonderful. It was nice and warm and there was little wind. They had picked the perfect week to go to Astor Island. Jim and Lillian each caught more than ten bonefish every day. Most of them weighed over five pounds. A few were ten pounders.

The honeymooners fished and scuba dived for several more days. They also managed to sneak in some more skinny dipping. Jim took plenty of pictures with his camera. He decided to leave the camera out of the skinny dipping. On their last evening of fishing, Lillian caught an unusually nice bonefish. She held it up proudly as Jim took some pictures of Lillian with it. When it was time to release it, Lillian said, "I sure hate to let go of a big bone when I've got one." She laughed coyly. Jim said, "Don't worry. There will be an even better one waiting for you back in the bungalow." Jim had a big grin on his face.

Lillian dropped the fish and ran to Jim. She gave him a big hug. She said, "I can't wait. Let's go." They ran over to the boat and asked Miguel to get them back to the pier, fast. He made the boat go as fast as possible. When they got to the pier, Jim and Lillian ran all the way to their bungalow.

After a quick shower they went to the pier for supper. They took their time and savored every minute of their last supper on the island for awhile. They both knew they would be back. It was too beautiful to leave for very long. When they finished their meal, they walked the beach till the sun set. They went to bed early so they could get up and watch the sunrise. They were awake by 4:30 A.M. Once they had some coffee, they walked the beach some more and watched the sunrise. Lillian said, "Dawn stretched her red fingers out across the sky." Jim said, "Yes, I always think of that phrase when I see a beautiful sunrise. It tells me that a new challenge lies ahead for us. We need to be brave and meet the challenge, no matter how terrible it is." Lillian said, "I hope we won't see anything too terrible. Our lives together so far have been too good to be true. I wouldn't mind if things would stay that way. We can always escape to this island if things get too rough." They held each other and watched the sun slowly rise from the horizon. It glistened brightly out across the water. There was a red glow all over the heavens.

Chapter Six

Atlantus

When Jim and Lillian returned to Miami International Airport, they called Grandpa Sellers right away. Jim asked him to meet them at O'Hare in three hours. He said, "I'll be glad to come and get you." He sounded excited over the phone, and asked lots of questions about how the honeymoon went. He was obviously reliving his youthful days through them. Everett said, "I've got a wonderful house waiting for you. It's olive green with dark green shutters. It's a two story house with siding made of narrow boards. It needs a little paint, but it's solid and has a good roof and furnace. There's hot water heat, and it has a large screen porch that looks out over Lake Wawasee. There's a nice balcony over the screen porch for sun bathing. The house is right on the edge of the campus. There is a large gazebo close to the house. It belongs to the college." Everett seemed like he could talk forever about the house. Jim was eager to hear about it. Jim broke in, "We caught plenty of nice bonefish." Everett said, "Good, good. Can I talk to Lillian?" Jim said, "Certainly." He passed the phone to Lillian. She talked a long time with Everett about the house. He said, "I'll have to insist that you invite Grandma Sellers and me over for supper frequently." Lillian said, "That will be wonderful. We want you to come over whenever you want to. You're always welcome."

Jim took the phone from Lillian and told Everett, "We have to go now, Grandpa. They have called for our flight to start boarding." Grandpa Everett said good bye and let them go. In no time, they were at the O'Hare airport looking for Everett. He was waiting for them when they got off the plane. They got their luggage and waited for Everett to pull up to the curb at the exit. He didn't make them wait long at all. With his speedy driving, they were standing in front of their new home in short order.

Everett handed them the key, and they went inside with him to look around. There were high ceilings and nice large rooms. The big dining room looked out onto Lake Wawasee. It was big enough to entertain guests with, on the holidays. Lillian gave Grandpa Sellers a hug. She said, "This is a perfect house. I love it! It was incredibly generous of you to give it to us." Everett said, "I wanted both of you to be happy. You can study better if you aren't worried about house payments. I helped Bart too. I gave him a job at my automotive firm in France. He's over there now learning the ropes. He'll be back in about three weeks to study here at Atlantus. He's taking a special crash course in computers and business management. I graduated from Atlantus and I donate to them on a regular basis. That's part of the reason they are eager to meet my educational needs for Bart. He doesn't need a degree. He just needs some vital information quickly."

Jim said, "I'm glad you're helping Bart too. I wouldn't want him to be left out. dad was disappointed that he wouldn't farm any more, but I think Bart will try to help your business. He has a quick mind with mechanical things. A career in the automotive industry should be right up his alley." Lillian said, "We'll invite him over when he returns. He might enjoy seeing my sister Carol, again. She has a boyfriend back in Columbia, Ohio, but I'm sure she'd like to reminisce a little with Bart about Florida. My parents called me while we were on Astor Island.

They said that Carol is already here on campus. She has an apartment. There are only a few of them on campus. Most students live in the dorms. A student transferred out of Atlantus. That's how she got the apartment." Jim said, "I would come to Atlantus early too if it wasn't for the creative writing course I'm taking at the high school. I like it, and the teacher is helping me learn to write English sonnets. I can wait till fall to start studying here. I envy Lillian though. The campus is beautiful. All the giant oak trees and the lake to look at." Everett said, "You'll get to come home to that beauty every afternoon." Jim said, "Yes, that is the nice part about having this house."

Everett asked, "What courses do you plan to audit, Lillian?" She said, "I will take Abnormal Psychology, Biology, Spanish and Drama." Everett said, "That's a nice full load. You should learn a lot." Lillian said, "Yes, I'm looking forward to it. Tomorrow is the first day of class." Everett said, "I'd better be going. I want the two of you to settle into your new home." He gave Lillian a hug and shook Jim's hand. They waved to him as he climbed into his Cadillac and drove down the road.

Lillian went to the refrigerator to see if it was turned on. It was, and it was full of food. She was delighted. She made some grilled cheese sandwiches. After they ate, they went for a walk around campus. Many of the students hadn't stayed for the interim month. They would be back later that night. When Jim and Lillian got back from their walk, Lillian called her parents and got Carol's phone number. She talked to her parents for a long time. They wanted to know all about the house and the honeymoon. After Lillian was done talking she called Carol and invited her over to the house. She agreed to come over right away. She wanted to see the house and see Lillian's sun tan.

Carol brought a new acquaintance with her. She was an attractive freshman named Rose Miller. Her blond hair and slender shapely body, made her a girl who was popular with the young men on campus. Rose was a good conversationalist, and quickly won Lillian's friendship by showing an interest in marine biology. Rose and Lillian would both be taking the same biology class. They decided to eat breakfast together and then walk to class each morning. Biology met the first hour of the day. Carol said that Rose was the first person she met on campus, and that they became good friends. Rose was going to introduce Carol to some of the nicest young men on campus.

After a long evening of exciting conversation, Carol said that she had to go back to her apartment and get some sleep. She and Rose left, and Jim and Lillian went to bed. They fell asleep quickly. They had just put in a big week, now it was time to get rested up.

In the morning Jim went to his school and Lillian went to her first class. After classes were over, Lillian met with Rose and told her all about Jim. She also told her about the marriage and the wonderful honeymoon. Rose couldn't believe they were having such a perfect life. She wanted to know if Bart was as wonderful as Jim. Lillian said, "I don't know much about Bart. My sister dated him a couple times in Florida, but she never talked about him. They never stayed in touch. I don't know what he's like."

"He'll be back from France in a couple weeks. You can meet him then if you want to." Rose said, "I am curious about him. I don't want to make Carol jealous, though." Lillian said, "I'm sure you won't make her jealous. She has a boyfriend back in Columbia. I think she'll date around some, now that she's in college. Her boyfriend will probably get pretty jealous. He's real possessive. She tried to break up with him once, but he wouldn't take no for an answer. He already told her that he is going to come to Atlantus every weekend to see her." Rose said, "It will be fun to meet Bart. I won't necessarily date him. Tell me right away when he gets back from France. I'm definitely curious about him."

Jim came home at 4:00 P.M. He was happy to find Lillian with her new friend. He said, "I'm glad Lillian doesn't have to spend every afternoon alone. It's good to see you again, Rose. I hope you can stay for supper." Rose said, "Sure, I'd be glad to stay a little longer. There isn't too much homework yet." They all worked together to cook hamburgers and broccoli. They talked till late in the evening. Finally Rose said, "I have to go now. I'm not the type who tries to get by with no sleep. My apartment is only a block away from here. I can come back in the morning and walk with you to the dining hall, Lillian." Lillian said, "I'd like that. I'll see you in the morning." Rose gave Jim and Lillian each a hug, and then walked out into the brightly lit porch. As she went through the porch doorway she turned and waved good bye. Jim and Lillian stayed up a little later talking, and then went to bed.

Bart did a good job in the French automotive firm. He learned the ropes quickly. It was clear to him that he would need to study computers if he wanted to be taken seriously by the other management people. He was a little troubled by that challenge. He hoped that Atlantus would be able to teach him what he needed to know. When he had his hands on the cars, he was a master. Everyone in the plant could tell that. Whether he was truly management material, or just the owner's son, was another question that remained unanswered.

Bart was spending a little too much time worrying about whether people respected him. The new culture was a challenge for him to adapt to. Each morning he marked on his calendar how many days were left, till he could go to Atlantus. He had been told that Carol was studying in Atlantus. He had mixed emotions about Carol. Bart thought she was sexy, but he resented the way she seemed so impressed with Jim. Bart was always wishing that he could impress women with vocabulary and exciting conversation, the way Jim did. Now that he was having doubts about how he would fare in the computer world, his envy of his brother's brainpower grew even keener.

Quickly the weeks passed. Bart flew to O'Hare, where Everett picked him up and drove him to Warsaw. Once in his apartment, Bart packed a few more things and drove to Atlantus. Everett followed him. He wanted to show Bart the campus. They arrived at Jim's house at 3:00 P.M. No one was home yet, so Everett walked with Bart to the computer center and introduced him to the instructors. They were all friendly and put Bart at ease. They explained what their hours were and gave Bart some introductory material to read. Bart thanked them, and then he and Everett went to the dining hall. When Bart knew where most things were on the campus, Everett took him to his off campus apartment. It was only a block from the campus. Everett wanted it to be easier for Bart to keep his company information confidential. The dorms wouldn't have offered that kind of privacy.

Everett stayed for a few hours and talked business with Bart. Then the subject changed to women. Everett said, "I want you to do some dating while you are here at Atlantus, Bart. I worry that you don't seem to date like you did in high school." Bart said, "I knew all the girls in school. It was easy then. Now you have to think of something clever all the time, or they get bored and go talk to some other guy. The bar scene has been a real drag. I can't stand that setting. Maybe I'll do better with the college women." Everett said, "I'm sure you will. Just don't talk too much about cars. Talk about France. I know that women like men who can tell them about another country. That is your strong suit. Play it often." Bart said, "Thanks for the advice. I'll give it a try."

Everett shook Bart's hand and then left for home. Bart thought about what his grandfather had said. Everett had given Bart the phone number for Jim and Lillian. He called their house and found that they were home. He asked if he could come over. They said that it would be fine. In a few minutes he was at their door. Jim answered the door and let him in. Jim introduced Bart to his new wife, "Bart, you met Lillian when she was in Florida, two years ago. She is now my wife." Bart shook Lillian's hand and said, "I heard that you two were married, just as I was leaving for France. That was kind of sudden. I guess I underestimated how in love both of you were in Florida." Lillian said, "That's all right. It was sudden. After waiting two years to get together, we were tired of waiting."

Bart said, "I understand. I just don't fall in love that quickly. I like time alone. However, I would like to spend some time with women while I study here. It will be hard for me to meet them, except in the computer building." Lillian said, "I have someone for you to meet. You don't have to date her if you don't want to. I think she would like to meet you, though. Her name is Rose Miller. She's a good friend of mine already. She's attractive and very friendly. I think you will like her." Bart said, "I'm only going to be here for three months. Could I meet her tonight? I have plenty of time tonight, but I'll be busy with the condensed computer course starting tomorrow." Lillian said, "I'll call Rose right now. She keeps up with her studies, so I'm sure she can spare the time."

Rose came over to meet Bart. They talked for awhile at the dining room table over coffee. Jim and Lillian helped them feel at ease by making conversation. Lillian suggested that they play cards. Bart said, "That would be fine. I haven't played cards for a long time. How about a game of hearts?" Jim said, "I agree. Hearts would be a good game tonight." Jim started dealing the cards. Rose asked, "What do you work at, Bart?" Bart said, "I'm learning to help run an automotive firm in France. The plant is located in Paris. My grandfather owns the place." Rose said, "It must be challenging to learn how to lead a company in a different country. What are you doing here at Atlantus?"

Bart said, "I need to learn about computers and business management. I'm taking a condensed course in computer. Then, I go back to France for several months." Rose said, "I am more into biology and literature than computers. I know that some day I will need to know how to work a computer, but till then I'm going to put it off."

Jim said, "I didn't know that you liked literature, Rose. What is your specific interest?" Rose said, "I write poetry. I try to experiment with every form of poetry. I'm taking creative writing this semester. Jim said, I'm learning to write English Sonnets. Of course you know that I'm still in high school. My English teacher is giving me individual instruction in sonnet writing. No one else was interested."

Rose said, "I would like to read some of your sonnets. Maybe I could bring over some of my poetry." Bart was getting a little peeved at how much Jim was impressing Rose. She seemed to have forgotten all about him. Lillian could read his expression and came to the rescue, "Bart, why don't you and Rose go over to the campus coffee shop? Jim and I need to talk in private a little, and we need to get supper ready. In about an hour you can both come back and have supper with us." Bart and Rose agreed and went to the coffee shop.

Lillian said, "Jim, I really do have to talk to you. You have to try hard not to get along with Rose so well. I know you aren't trying to come on to her, but you are winning too much of her attention. Bart is getting jealous and I think a little discouraged. Tell Rose that your poetry is for my eyes only. Find some way to keep her attention fixed on Bart. If you can't, then I'll say that we need to go to bed early. They need time alone." Jim said, "I didn't realize that I was hogging Roses attention. I'll do just as you said. I'll try to keep her focused on Bart. We may need to go to bed early like you said. All Bart knows about is cars. We can let them stay together down here after we go to bed.

They can leave whenever they want to." Lillian said, "I agree. We'll leave them alone. It's the best plan."

After an hour went by, Bart and Rose came back to the house. Lillian said, "Well, what did you two talk about?" Rose said, "I found out that Bart knows all there is to know about cars." Bart said, "I found out that Rose's last name is Miller, and she likes fast cars. I'm going to take her for a drive in my Corvette, later."

They all sat down to supper. Jim did his best not to win attention from Rose, but it was a losing battle. Right after supper Bart took Rose for a ride in the Corvette. By the time they got back, Jim and Lillian had gone to bed. Rose didn't want to stay up too late, so they talked for a little while, and then Bart walked her home. Bart was quiet, and didn't kiss Rose good night. She knew she had done something to irritate him, but he wouldn't talk about it. She said good night, and went inside. Bart went to his house and went to bed. He couldn't keep from thinking about how impressed Rose was with Jim. He had trouble getting to sleep. He paced around for awhile and drank some milk. Finally after many hours of fuming about his bad luck with women, Bart went to sleep.

Carol's boy friend, Jeff Carter, came to see her on the first weekend of her stay at Atlantus. He was a tall man, with black hair and a neat mustache that came out to the corners of his mouth. Jeff's shoulders were thick from weight training. He looked strong and impressive. He took her out to a very nice restaurant that was right on Lake Wawasee. There was a giant houseboat parked on the channel. It belonged to the restaurant. They took people on cruises in the summer.

Jeff promised Carol that he would take her for a ride on the houseboat in the summer. Carol liked the idea, but she had promised herself to tell Jeff she would be dating around. She said, "Jeff, you're a sweet guy. I like you a lot. I want you to know that I plan to date around some here at Atlantus. I'm not ready to settle down yet." Jeff said, "I'm going to come to school here in the fall. You'll respect me more when you see how I can succeed in college." Carol said, "It's not that I don't respect you. I just need to think about what kind of man I want. We can date every Friday if you want to." Jeff said, "Well, I guess that's fair enough. I can't force you to love me. We can have lots of fun together. If you start to get physical with someone else, I'm going to get pretty jealous. I don't know how I can stand that." Carol said, "I think it would be best if you didn't ask about such things. Just think about what we're doing."

Carol and Jeff danced when the band started playing. The restaurant was a fun place. Later, Carol noticed that Jeff was drinking too much. He was twenty-one, but he didn't know how to limit his drinking when he was upset about something. Carol tried to get him to stop, but he wouldn't. They argued, and Carol made him take her home. She took him to Jim and Lillian's house and stayed up with him late, till he calmed down. They slept in the spare bedroom, so that Jeff wouldn't have to drive home drunk. In the morning Carol lectured Jeff about drinking. She said she wouldn't go out with him if he kept drinking. He promised to stop.

Jeff continued to come to Atlantus every Friday. He quit drinking, but he became more and more jealous. One Friday, Carol insisted that Jeff take Rose out to supper, just so he could get used to the idea of dating other women. Jeff went along with the idea, but he didn't like it. To spite Carol, he made sexual advances to Rose. Rose thought he was joking at first. Then she got scared when she realized that he was angry and was thinking of going all the way with her to spite Carol. Rose made him take her home. He did so, reluctantly. He didn't come to Atlantus for about a month. Then Carol started seeing his car. She was sure that he was following her in the evenings and at night.

On a Friday night in April, about a week after Bart had left for France, Rose decided to go for a late night walk along the lakeshore. She walked about a quarter mile past the campus property. She sensed that someone was following her. She walked faster and faster. It was dark, and she couldn't see the person who was closing in on her. Finally she started to run, but she was grabbed from behind. She tried to scream, but to no avail. A strong hand was being held tightly over her mouth.

In the morning, she was found floating face up in the lake. Her throat had been cut quite deeply. There was a pool of blood on the beach, where her blood had gushed out after her jugular vein had been cut. The police were at the scene of the crime. They measured the footprints that were in the sand, and took photos of the dead woman. Her beauty was still evident, but now a gaping wound detracted from it. Everyone was moved by the tragic nature of such a beautiful young woman, being murdered so brutally. The police examined the young woman's purse and found out who she was. Once they discovered that she was an Atlantus student, they asked around to see who her friends were. They knew that friends might be able to give them some important clues.

Detective Omar Shami, was assigned to the case. He was thin man with dark black hair. He wasn't very tall, but his arms were muscular and impressive. He wore a thin well-trimmed mustache. There was constantly a gold cigarette holder in his mouth, with a Carlton cigarette in it. Omar's irises were almost black. His eyes told those who saw him, that he was quite intelligent. His darkly tanned skin let people know that he liked the sun. His father was from Palestine, but Omar was fluent in English. Omar went to Jim and Lillian's house to find out what he could about Rose Miller, the murdered woman. Lillian answered the door, and invited Omar inside. He sat at the dining room table and talked with Jim and Lillian.

He asked, "What did Rose do during the three months that she was in school?" Lillian said, "Rose spent most of her time with me. We were good friends. She dated Bart for about two months, but Bart was jealous of the way she was interested in Jim's writing. He quit dating her about a month ago." Omar said, "Now that is very interesting. Who is Bart?" Jim said, "He's my brother. He was in France during the murder. I'm sure he wouldn't kill anyone." Omar said, "We can't rule out anything at this point. I will check to see if he was actually in France. If Bart has an alibi, he has nothing to worry about. I must consider him a suspect, until he can prove his whereabouts at the time of the crime."

Lillian said, "My sister's boyfriend has been acting strange lately. He's very possessive of her. My sister's name is Carol Tahkala, and her boyfriend's name is Jeff Carter. He got so jealous that he started stalking her instead of dating her. Maybe he killed Rose to get warmed up for killing my sister. She had him date Rose once, hoping it would make him less possessive. It just made him mad." Omar said, "I'll talk to your sister Carol, and Jeff Carter. Rose was not raped or robbed. The murderer was either a thrill seeker, who didn't care who he killed, or the murderer knew Rose, and she triggered intensely angry feelings in him for some reason, not necessarily sane reasons. She may have inadvertently made a very insecure person feel insulted, so that they would seek revenge. It is possible that the murderer has killed before, and is planning to kill again. As friends of Rose, it is possible that you, Lillian, and your sister are in danger. We can give both of you police protection, but the best thing is for both of you to not go out at night for awhile. Give us a chance to catch this evil person."

When Omar met with Carol, she told him about Jeff stalking her. She also mentioned that Bart had asked to date her, but she turned him down. She said, "Bart didn't like being turned down. When we dated two years ago, down in Florida, he got too rough with me. He held my arms so tight that he bruised them. I thought that he was a little strange, but I never said anything because my sister was in love with his brother." Omar said, "I'm glad you're being so candid with me, Carol. You may be saving someone's life. You need to stay away from Bart. We will check to see if he was in France when the murder happened. Don't go out at night alone for awhile. I need some time to get to the bottom of this." Carol said, "I'll be careful." Omar said thank you and left.

Omar called on Jeff Carter next. He found him at his apartment in Columbia, Ohio. Jeff was very defensive. He was embarrassed about the stalking and wouldn't talk. Omar got tough with him. He grabbed Jeff's collar and pushed him against the wall. Omar yelled, "Did you kill that girl? Did you kill her? She made you feel like you weren't good enough, right? Or was she just a warm up, so you would have enough guts to kill Carol? It's Carol you're really mad at. Isn't she the one?" Jeff was sweating and trembling. He said, "Okay, I stalked Carol. I'm mad at Carol, but I don't kill people. I was working on my car the night of the murder. I don't have an alibi, but you can talk to my folks. I'm a good person! I don't kill people!"

Omar said, "I want to believe you. I'll talk to your folks, but don't go near Carol till I say it's alright. I'll be watching you, Jeff. Stay away from her till we catch the murderer. If it is you, I'll put you in prison and throw away the key." Jeff said, "I'm innocent." Omar said, "I hope you are." Omar left Jeff's apartment and returned to Warsaw.

Omar called Bart, in France, and requested that he return immediately. The next day Bart came to Omar's office and talked with him. Bart had a letter from his bartender saying that he was in France on the night of the murder. The letter included the bartender's phone number. Omar called the bartender and listened to him tell about Bart being in his bar. Omar told Bart that he could return to France, but that he should stay away from Carol until further notice. Bart agreed and left.

Omar addressed the student convocation, and asked that anyone with information about the murder would come forward with that information. He assured the students that uniformed police would monitor the campus. When Omar looked at all the evidence, he decided that he would like to try to get more information from Jim about his brother. He asked Jim to go fishing with him. Jim agreed, and they took Omar's sixteen foot fiberglass fishing boat. They fished for bass on Lake Wawasee. While they fished, Omar kept asking questions. Finally he found out something interesting. Omar asked, "Does your brother own any knives?" Jim said, "He owns several large shark knives. He knows a little about scuba diving. One of the knives came with a scuba outfit. The other he bought down in Florida. I wouldn't have bought a second large shark knife, but lots of people collect knives." Omar said, "Yes, and lots of people use knives on other people. I will ask your brother to produce those knives. It will be interesting to see if he still has them."

Jim thought of something else that Omar should know, "There was a girl that got murdered while we were in Florida two years ago. She was killed not far from our motel. Her throat was cut. I had almost forgotten about it." Omar said, "I'm glad you remembered. That is important for me to know. Sometimes when you relax with people they come up with important clues."

They continued fishing for several hours. Both men caught several nice large mouth bass. Jim said, "I had fun fishing for bonefish in the Caribbean this year. I fished while I was on my honeymoon." Omar said, "Not many men could get away with fishing on their honeymoon. How did you manage that?" Jim said, "My wife loves to fish also. We had a great time." Omar said, "My wife doesn't like fishing. I wish she did. We could go on some great fishing vacations together."

When they finished fishing, Omar called Bart in Paris, France. Omar said, "Your brother tells me that you own two large shark knives. I would like to see them." Bart said, "One of them was stolen from my apartment this year. I only have one left." Omar said, "That is all I wanted to know. You don't have to bring that one to me." Omar thought to himself, *I will have to watch this one closely.*

The murder had taken place on a Friday night. The following Sunday, Jim, Lillian and Carol went to Grand Rapids for Roses funeral. They all dressed in black. Jim drove the canary yellow 1966 Chevy Impala that his father had recently given him. It had a nice black leather interior. Jim liked the looks of the car. It handled well on the open road. As they drove, Lillian and Carol started to reminisce about Rose. Lillian said, "Who would want to hurt such a kind and wonderful person as Rose." She held her hands up to her face and started to cry.

Carol said, "The murderer will receive justice. I'm confident that he will pay for this." Jim said, "Omar will find out who did it. At least we will have that consolation. The murderer will surely give himself away. Sometimes they get drunk and talk about their crime in a bar. Possibly he will try to kill again, and the police will catch him." Lillian kept on sobbing. Carol said, "We'd better stop talking about the murderer. Lillian is just feeling worse all the time." They were all silent for the rest of the trip.

They attended the funeral at a small protestant church in the suburbs of Grand Rapids. When they spoke to Rose's parents, they each said what a wonderful person Rose had been. Rose's dad said, "It was good to have all of you here. Rose would have wanted her friends to be here at her funeral. She was our only daughter. We won't know what to do without her." A tear ran down across his cheek.

Jim said, "I've been working with detective Omar Shami on the case. I gave him all the information I could think of. I'm sure the murderer will come to justice." Rose's dad said, "Thank you for your thoughtfulness. Nothing will replace Rose. She was the perfect daughter." The minister said a prayer, and the casket was slowly lowered into the ground. Jim, Lillian and Carol said their good byes and headed back to Atlantus College. They were pretty quiet. They watched the Michigan scenery as they drove on U.S. 131 heading south.

A couple months passed with no more murders. The police were no longer present on the campus. It was a hot July evening, and Carol had been longing to walk the beach. She didn't go out till the sun had almost set. She walked for quite awhile, up and down the beach. She had sensed that Jeff had been stalking her occasionally. Somehow she thought that Jeff couldn't be the murderer. She wanted to make up with Jeff, but she didn't know how. Omar Shami had told her to stay away from him. She sat down on a park bench to think things over. Before she knew it darkness had set in. She got up and started to walk towards the lake. She heard footsteps as someone approached her. She felt that it must be Jeff stalking her. She ran towards him to confront him. It was not Jeff. She could just make out in the darkness that it was Bart. Bart had a large shark knife in his hand. As he raised it up, someone grabbed him from behind. It was a big man. When he spoke, Carol knew it was Jeff. She was glad he had been stalking her. The two men struggled for the knife. Bart cut Jeff's arm, but Jeff managed to grab the knife handle and Bart's hand. He bent Bart's wrist so that the knife dropped out of Bart's hand. Jeff grabbed the knife and thrust it through Bart's heart. Bart fell, lifeless, to the ground.

Carol ran to Jeff, and thanked him for saving her. She apologized for having been so rough on him. When they got into the light, she saw his bleeding arm. She screamed for help. Someone came running. They saw the blood and ran for an ambulance. The police were called as well.

Omar Shami arrived on the scene and looked at the dead man. He asked, "Is this Bart?" Carol said, "Yes it is." Omar said, "I am embarrassed that he almost killed you. I didn't think he would try another murder this soon after the last one. He was sicker than I thought." Omar took Carol with him to the hospital, to see Jeff. Jeff was already bandaged up and looked like he wasn't in too much pain. Omar said, "Jeff, stalking is a bad thing, and I told you to stay away from Carol, but just this once, I'm glad you were following Carol." He shook Jeff's hand on the arm that wasn't cut. Carol gave Jeff a big hug and a kiss. She said, "I promise not to make you jealous anymore. You can follow me all you want to. I'm going to get Jim and Lillian to take us to Astor Island to forget about all this trouble. We can make it a four day weekend."

Jim and Lillian arrived and ran up to see if Carol was alright. Jim was shaken to discover that his brother Bart had been killed while trying to kill Carol. Omar said, "It would appear that all the women in Bart's life were more impressed with Jim than they were with him. His primitive response was to kill the person who had insulted him. He couldn't see that he had many alternatives. With his money and intelligence he could have won many kinds of women. He was so blinded by jealousy that he resorted to murder. He must have paid the bartender in Paris for his alibi. He would fly to Paris and then come back by boat so that there would be no flight record to give him away. He was a clever man, but very lacking in sanity." Jim said, "I would have never suspected my brother of that. I'm just very happy that he didn't kill Carol." Carol said, "Jim, I told Jeff that maybe you and Lillian would show us Astor Island. I think we need to get away for awhile so that we can forget about all this." Jim said, "Astor Island is an excellent idea. I'll book us a flight down there for tomorrow morning."

In the morning, at 6:00 A.M., they all drove to O'Hare and took a plane to Miami International Airport. From there, they took a small plane to Astor Island. Jeff and Carol were given a bungalow right next to the one Jim and Lillian got. They went to the pier and talked to Miguel about fishing for several hours. They all had a few tropical drinks, and then went for a boat ride all around the Island. The palm trees were magnificent. The white beaches glistened in the bright sun. Jeff and Carol loved the scenery.

In the evening they walked the beach for hours and then had a bon fire on the beach. They played cards by the fire, and talked about the many different islands that they wanted to visit. Finally they each went to their respective bungalows and rested up for another day of fun. There was a little more than resting going on. Carol had to go easy on Jeff because of his arm. After a long night of love making, Jeff proposed to Carol, and she accepted. They would be on their honeymoon soon.

By five o'clock they were all up eating breakfast at the pier. Then they went walking on the beach to watch the sunrise. They had to walk around to the eastern side of the island to get a better view of it. As the sun slowly rose and gave off red light, Jim said, "Dawn stretched her red fingers across the sky." Jeff said, "What does that mean?" Lillian said, "It means that each new day brings a new challenge. We can face each new day knowing that courage will pull us through the hard times. God blesses those who have faith and courage." Jim said, "That's just what I was going to say." They all laughed and ran into the ocean for a swim.

The End

Mary Thresher In Search of Sunken Treasures

Mary Thresher
In Search of Sunken Treasures

First Printing 2004

Printed in U.S.A.

CONTENTS

Acknowledgments

Without the help and encouragement of my teachers in high school and college, I could have never come to call myself a writer. I wish to thank them at this time. Much appreciation is also due to my proof readers who worked many hours helping to improve this book. I'd like to thank my publisher and all the many people who helped put the book into print. I give praise to my wife, who put up with my preoccupation with the book for many long days. She made it possible for me to be a writer, by giving me support and encouragement when I needed it most. I thank those who read the book and offered suggestions before the book went to print. Last of all I thank my mother, who always encouraged creativity; and my father who helped me immensely with finances.

Chapter One

New Mexico

About 10 miles south of State Road 10, on road 186, in the southeastern part of Arizona, a 50-year old childless Indian couple lived in the small town of Culebra. Their names were Betty and Joseph Thresher. Nine years ago they adopted a newborn baby who they named Mary. They adopted her from an unmarried couple in Phoenix. Bill Wright was the genetic father and Rita Benson was the mother. Bill was a busy artist who wasn't ready for marriage and responsibility. Rita was a scientist who also was too busy to be a mother. Since Rita was against abortion, she had put Mary up for adoption. The Thresher's would never tell Mary that she was unwanted by her original parents. They told her that her mother and father were killed in a plane crash. Her biological parents didn't suspect that they were abandoning a baby who would take on the world and win at roulette, love and adventure.

Today was the celebration of Mary's ninth birthday. Betty and Joseph were delighted as Mary blew out the candles on her cake and talked excitedly to her friends as she opened her presents. She got three things from her parents. A new bicycle, a computer game and a credit card with a one thousand dollar credit limit. Her friend Marsha Fowler gave her a parrot named Joque. There was a note on the parrot's cage which listed the sayings he knew. Mary read the first one. "Shiver me timbers," Joque repeated very clearly, "Shiver me timbers!" Everyone laughed. Then Mary read the next words on the card. "Ahoy maties." The parrot said, "Ahoy maties." Then Joque went off on his own. "Trim the sails! Hoist the jib. Anchors away." The whole household was in stitches. Joque sounded just like a real pirate.

Ellenore Reynolds gave Mary an instruction booklet on searching the internet. After eating second helpings of cake, Mary gave her parents a hug, and took the girls to her private computer that was in her bedroom. Mary said, "I've been hearing about séances at school. Let's try that." She entered the word into the computer according to the instructions in her new booklet. In seconds an Internet witch was teaching them. She told them to sit around a table with the lights out and hold hands. They were told to keep their eyes shut until a spirit came. They opened their eyes and the lights were flickering off and on. Lamps and pens were floating around. Finally a gentle deep voice spoke to them. It said, "One of you is very sensitive to the spirit world. We have much to tell you Mary. Your friends can come along, but you are the most sensitive. We will tell you many things. I will tell you right now that you are to be very powerful. You will be a devotee of the Jade Goddess. She will give you great powers. The lights flickered and then came on without having anyone touch the switch. The girls were amazed, and promised to return soon for another séance.

Later that night, after her girlfriends had fallen asleep; Mary did another search on the Internet. She used the topic of witchcraft, which resulted in many pages of books on the subject. The prices were listed along with each book. Mary picked out several books that sounded interesting. *Controling the Minds and Bodies of Animals, Simple Useful Spells for Beginners, Conjuring up Animals,* and *Practical*

Poltergeistic Pursuits. She used the new credit card that she had gotten for her birthday to pay for the books. Now all she had to do was wait for the books to be delivered to her door.

Five days later the books arrived. Mary rushed to the mailbox ahead of her parents. She wasn't quite sure what they would think about her new interests in reading. She knew that her parents weren't bossy or over controlling. She just didn't want them to worry. Ellenore and Marsha came over to stay for the weekend right after Mary got the new books. They went to Mary's bedroom for privacy, and started to read the book, *Practical Poltergeistic Pursuits*. They read about making an upside down small drinking glass move along a tabletop that had a film of water on it. They tried this on Mary's dresser. Mary told her friends, "It says in the book to hold your fingers close to the glass on the side you want to pull. Then concentrate on sending energy from your fingers to the glass. Caress the glass with your energy." Mary tried and tried. She wouldn't give up. Marsha insisted, "Let me try. Maybe I can move it just a little bit." Marsha got so close to the glass with her fingers, that she kept accidentally touching it. Finally after about ten minutes, she said, "I give up. I'm sure it's possible, but I just can't seem to do it tonight." Ellenore said, "I'd like to give it a try." She took a chair close to the drinking glass and held out her hand close to the glass. She said, "Could you put a little more water on the dresser top? I want to give myself every possible chance of success." Mary poured out more water and spread it all over the top of the dresser. Ellenore let out a high pitched squeal as she saw the glass move just a little bit. The other girls didn't see it. She tried some more, but couldn't make it move any more.

Finally they gave up on the drinking glass for the night. They went to the kitchen to play with Mary's parrot. He was as talkative a usual, and they laughed for hours as he slowly went through his many phrases that are used on board ship. Mary said, "Joque used to belong to a sea captain who sailed the seven seas. When he finally died of old age, Joque was willed to the captain's brother. The brother didn't want Joque and sold him to the pet store. That's where my mom and dad found him." The pet store says that he will learn new phrases if you feed him each time you say something. Then you withhold the food for a little bit until he says the right phrase. He learns on his own, if he hears you say something often enough.

Joseph replied, "I like to hear the parrot, but I'm getting hungry. Is supper about ready?" Betty announced, "You can all sit down at the table. I hope everyone likes lasagna." They all sat down and began to pass the plates of food around the table. Mary bragged, "Mother makes the best lasagna in Arizona!" Betty responded, "Thank you for the compliment, Mary. It's my mother's recipe. She got it from the wife of an Italian missionary who worked for many years in Dos Caballos." After everyone had finished the lasagna, Marsha asked, "What's for desert? I think I know. You always make pecan pie." Betty said, "You're right. Pecan pie it is. I made two pies, so there's plenty for everyone." Betty started the pecan pie around the table, and it was eagerly passed until everyone had a piece. Next, Betty started a box of vanilla ice cream around the table. She said, "Pecan pie is even more delicious with ice cream on it." Mary quipped, "I'll agree with that." She stopped to give Joque a small piece of pie. He said, "Shiver me timbers!" Then he started eating the pie greedily. Joque thought to himself, "Finally some food fit for a human! I'm tired of eating birdseed. When I saw that I was about to die, I sent me spirit out of me and into my parrot. I didn't think about how I'd have to eat birdseed for eternity. Now at least, this little witch that owns me knows how to feed a sea captain properly. I'll help her with a spell or two, so as to reward her. Maybe then she'll feed me a nice juicy piping hot steak! Her friend Marsha has been getting some steaks from some where. She's a little plump. I like me women that way. When she gets a little older I'll give her a nip on her ear. Just to let her know that old sea captains never die or lose interest in a little fun." Joque went on musing, "Hum, everyone in the room but Mary is Indian. She must be adopted. She looks real pretty with her green eyes and red hair. There's not a bit of fat on her though. There's plenty of food in the house. I guess she must work it off somehow." Joque eyed Ellenore as the group went for a second piece of pie. He thought, "She has a beautiful face, with attractive dark brown eyes and dark tan skin. She's thin like Mary." Finally he sized up Betty and Joseph, "They're both slender and good looking for their age. I'd guess they are each about fifty years old. Since they are probably from around here, I'd say that they must be Sheriguay Indians."

After the family finished eating pie, they all went into the living room and started playing a dice game called "Ten Thousand". Joque wanted to watch the game. He started calling out loudly, "Bring her about, Matie! Bring her about!" Mary said, "He says that when he wants his cage moved. I'll bring him in here." She went to the kitchen and picked up Joque's cage and moved it into the living room. "Sometimes I almost think he's human." Betty responded, "I know what you mean. He watches our every move."

The game used six dice. When it was someone's turn, they shook all six dice and threw them onto the tabletop. A 'five' gave the player fifty points, while a 'one' gave the player one hundred points. Three 'ones' gave the player one thousand points. Three 'fours' gave the player four hundred points, three 'threes', three hundred points and three twos, two hundred points. A straight was good for fifteen hundred points. If no counters were rolled, all the previous points earned that turn were subtracted from your score. You had to get at least one thousand points to get "on the board", after which the points would begin to accumulate.

Everyone but Mary was "on the board". She was having a long streak of bad luck. Joque decided to help out. He had been all around the world, and knew lots of magic. The next time it was Mary's turn, he winked his right eye just as she rolled the dice. She rolled three ones. Now she was "on the board". She jumped for joy. "Now I'm getting somewhere!" she yelled. Ellenore retorted, "It's about time. I thought you would never join us." Marsha kidded, "Yeah. You were on a long losing streak." Mary threw again and Joque did nothing. He didn't want to be too obvious. Mary got a one. She decided to stop with eleven hundred points. Everyone else had several thousand points more than Mary did. Each time she threw for the first time, Joque would wink, and she would get three ones. In no time she was about ready to win the game. She stopped and said, "I think it is Joque's bed time." She took him back to the kitchen and placed the cover over his cage. When she came back to the table it was her turn again. She only got two one's this time. Next she rolled another one, giving her three hundred points. Her next roll gave her no ones or fives. That meant she went backward three hundred points. Each time her turn came up, she lost more points. Finally it occurred to her that Joque was her good luck charm. She didn't want her parents to know, so she didn't go back to the kitchen to get Joque. Instead she let her natural bad luck take its course. She lost the game.

After several games of Ten Thousand, Betty and Joseph said they were tired and went to bed. Joseph said, "Mary would you shut off the lights when you and the girls go to sleep?" Mary said, "I will, dad. Good night." She ran over and gave them both a hug and a kiss. After the girls had watched television for about and hour, Mary said, "I want to show you something. Come with me." Ellenore and Marsha followed Mary to the kitchen. She removed the cover from Joque's cage. Mary said, "Joque has supernatural powers. Watch this." She woke up Joque and said to him, "Sorry to disturb you, Joque. I want to let my friends in on our secret. I know you're not just a parrot. If you are possessed by the spirit of your former owner, speak to us like he did." Joque said, "Not until you feed me some more pie. I hate birdseed!" The girls jumped and squealed with delight. They gave Joque a large piece of pie. He said, "I don't have great powers, but I can help you with some things. I am good with cards and dice. I can also make things move through the air." Mary said, "Can you give us each the power to make things move. We've been trying for weeks with no success." He said, "I'm sure I can. Do you promise to give me some steak and yogurt?" Mary said, "We will. You shall always have human food." "Since you've convinced me of your good intentions, I will give you poltergeistic powers." said Joque. He said, "Each of you put your face close to the cage. I will wink into your right eye. Be sure not to blink." They each did as he said. He winked at them with his right eye. They thanked him profusely and went to Mary's bedroom to try out their new powers.

Marsha said, "Put some water on the dresser, Mary. I want to try first." Mary spread the water over the smooth dresser top. Then she placed the drinking glass upside down on the watery surface. Marsha held her hand out near the drinking glass. Ellenore lit a candle and turned off the bedroom light. They could hardly keep from shouting for joy when the glass started to follow Marsha's hand. "I can do it", whispered Marsha. Next Ellenore tried. She held her trembling hand close to the glass. It shook a little, and then started to follow her hand. Ellenore said, "This is wonderful. I can actually do some magic." Finally, Mary tried. Her hand trembled a little too. She opened her eyes wide when the glass started to follow her hand everywhere it went. Then she took both hands and made the glass move up into the air several inches. "This is excellent", she whispered.

They went back to the kitchen and thanked Joque some more. They listened for hours as he told of his life on the seven seas. They heard of many things that their parents would have disapproved of. Sea captains live rough lives. Some of the stories were terribly violent and full of evil magic. Mary knew they would have nightmares, but she wanted to hear more. Joque told of all the women he had known, and how some had bewitched him. He had to pay many witches to teach him spells that would keep him free from the tricks of these women. They wanted to entrap him and keep him from the sea. The sea was his first love. Finally Joque said to Mary, "After I have given you all the power that I know about, you must promise me that you will sell me to a sea captain, so that I can travel at sea again. It is what I want more than anything else." Mary said, "Joque, you have my solemn promise. I will return you to the sea."

Joque said, "Since you are being so helpful to me, I will help you as fast as I can. Let me start with the four basics. You will need to know that spiritual power down through the ages has always come from one of four sources. It comes from earth, fire, wind and water. The friendliest one is fire. It is easy to build a bonfire and dance around it singing flattering chants to the fire God. She loves dancing, singing and flattering words. She is eager for new devotees. It is good to stick to just one of the Gods for several years. Later you may want to learn how to use the other gods to help you. You don't want to make them jealous of each other. That could cause them to turn against you. Be wise and stick to the fire God. She will bless you if you sing and dance well. Remember, the bigger the fire is, the better she likes it. However when there is little wood, she will understand. An earnest and eager heart is what matters.

It would be good if you built a fire tonight. I used the fire god's power to help you. You should thank her." Mary said, "We will do as you suggest. Come on Marsha and Elenore. There is plenty of brush around the house and there are some old scraps of wood in the garage." Mary got her flashlight from her bedroom and gathered a large pile of mesquite limbs. They used some newspapers and charcoal lighter to get the wood scraps burning. They started the fire in the back yard where the family campsite was. They loved to camp in the back yard. It was about two hundred feet away from the house. They could sing and talk without waking Betty and Joseph.

Once the flames were high enough, Mary placed the mesquite branches on the fire. It blazed higher yet when the flames hit the dry branches. The mesquite gave off a nice odor. The girls danced around the fire and sang praises to the fire god. "Oh powerful one, hotter than the sun. How generous you are. We long to do that which pleases you." They sang for hours. Finally they sat around the fire and enjoyed its warmth. They sat in a circle and held hands. They prayed to the fire god for power. "Send us your power," chanted Mary. Marsha requested, "Help us with all our witchcraft. Make us successful in all that we try to do." Elenore requested, "Power for all of us. Please make us all powerful." The flames leapt towards the full moon that hovered overhead. The fire Goddess heard their prayers and songs. She liked the sight of youthful girls dancing in her name. She quietly bestowed power on the girls. They couldn't even detect the power as it entered them. All they felt was the warmth of the fire as it slowly lost its ferocity and dwindled down to a glowing bed of embers.

As the embers died down, the girls grew quiet. Finally Mary said, "We'd better get some sleep. Tomorrow night I'd like for us to try making some animals appear from out of thin air. I've been reading about it in the book *Conjuring up Animals*. Marsha said, "That sounds good. I can't wait. The fire god will help us." Elenore said, "Sounds good to me. Right now though, I'm really tired. Let's go to bed." Mary whispered, "Be careful not to wake my parents." They all went to Mary's bedroom and got into her gigantic bed. They slept till late the next morning. They hadn't gotten to bed till about three o'clock.

They all got up and sat around the kitchen table eating breakfast cereal. Mary put some cereal with milk in a small cup for Joque. He chirped gratefully as he greedily ate it all. The girls spent most of the day gathering more firewood. Mary spent some of the afternoon reading to Marsha and Elenore from the book entitled *Conjuring up Animals*. Mary found an old barrel, which they rolled out beside where they had the bonfire. Mary said, "We can have the animals come out of this barrel. We can each make one animal. The book doesn't tell how to get rid of the animal. We each need to know ahead what animal we want. That will save time when it gets dark. Marsha said, "I want a raven. They were popular in Edgar Allen Poe's day. They are quite intelligent. One said, 'Nevermore' in one of Poe's stories."

Elenore said, "I will try to make a falcon. I just think they are neat. They look fierce and noble." Mary said, "I think I'll make a black cat. A big black cat. Maybe even a Black Panther." They spent the rest of the afternoon reading the magic books. Marsha was reading *Spells for beginners* and Elenore read from *Controlling the Minds and Bodies of Animals*. Mary read *Conjuring up Animals*.

At six o'clock, they were called into the house for supper. They hid their books in an old doghouse that was in the back yard. Ever since their last dog had been eaten by a buzzard, they didn't get another dog. Somehow they couldn't bring themselves to give away the doghouse. It gave them pleasant memories of Buddy. He was a protective dog who sometimes bit strangers, who in turn threatened to sue the Threshers. In a way the vulture may have done them a favor. They were sure to have been sued eventually. Buddy had a thick neck and small head. Those two factors made it impossible to keep a leash on him. When he heard strangers, he would slip off his leash and go bite them. Mary was sure that she could keep her magical cat under control. Just the sight of him would keep troublemakers away.

For supper they had homemade beef stew. There was plenty of homemade bread as well. Mary's mom was a good cook. Mary gave a big piece of bread to Joque. Joseph said, "Are you girls going to have another fire tonight?" Mary said, "How did you know?" Joseph said, "The neighbors called and wanted to make sure that the garage wasn't on fire. I'll call and warn them that you girls are on a campfire kick. That way they won't call the fire department. I'm glad you are cleaning away some of the brush. It's not good to have dry brush too close to the house. It's a fire hazard. Just be careful. I know you will. I've taught you good fire safety practices." Mary said, "We'll be careful. Don't worry a bit." Joseph smiled and said; "I won't worry. Just have a good time."

Immediately after supper was over, the girls went to the back yard and started the fire. They read their books until it was almost dark. They watched the beautiful sunset and talked about how much fun they would have over summer vacation. When it was finally dark, they pulled the barrel close to the fire. Marsha went first. She danced around the fire until she felt exhausted. Then she approached the barrel and held out both hands to the opening in the top. She whispered the secret words from the book, "Bestantemisanimalesapparecer". The instant that the words had left her mouth she stopped short. "I forgot something," She said. Mary coached her. "You have to tap the barrel three times with a wand. Marsha took a stick and started over. "Bestantemisanimalesapparecer", she said in a loud whisper. Then she tapped the barrel three times. Out flew her raven. She was excited beyond words. She held out her arm and the raven came and perched on her shoulder.

It spoke softly to her, "Thank you for calling me out of the darkness. I will never leave you. Whatever you ask of me, that is what I will do." Marsha said, "I am glad to have you. For the time being concentrate on not letting anyone, except these two girls, know that you can talk. I want you to keep your supernatural powers a secret. Is that understood?" The raven said, "That is a very reasonable request. I understand you completely."

Next to work her magic, was Elenore. She danced around the fire wildly and spun in circles. She stared into the stars above and said, "Oh powerful fire goddess, send me your power as well. I will always sing your praises and be a loyal friend." Then she whispered forcefully, "Bestantemisanimalesapparecer". Next, she took the stick and tapped the barrel three times. Out from the barrel flew a beautiful falcon. It flew around for a little while and then landed on the stick. It said, "My claws are quite sharp, so I won't land on your shoulder. You will need a thick leather glove for me to land on. I promise to serve you to the best of my abilities. Thank you for calling me out of the darkness. I longed to live again." Elenore said, "You must only speak in front of me and my friends here, Mary and Marsha. I don't want anyone else to know that you are a magic bird." The falcon said, "I will do as you say."

Next, Mary took the stick and danced wildly around the fire. She sang of the great powers of the fire goddess. The other two girls cheered her on as she danced. When she had danced as long as she possibly could, she whispered the magic word, "Bestantemisanimalesapparecer". She took the stick and tapped three times on the edge of the barrel. Out leapt a large Black Panther. It moved right over to her and licked her hand. Then it said, "Thank you for bringing me out of the darkness. I will serve you as long as you live. I will try to make sure that you are never harmed. Don't worry about feeding me. I don't really need any food. I will find some jack rabbits here in the desert, but mainly because they amuse me." Mary said, "You are a handsome animal. I would like to show you off to everyone. However, I don't think they would understand. You must stay invisible unless there is no one around but me and my two friends here, Elenore and Marsha. Do you understand?" The Black Panther said, "I understand completely."

The girls and their new animals sat around the fire for a long time and talked with each other. It was nice to have pets that could help them in times of trouble. And it was especially nice that their pets could speak and understand completely. Finally as the sunrise started to bring its light, the Black Panther disappeared as he had been told to do. The raven and the falcon went off to some distant bushes in the desert. There they would wait until one of them heard the call of its master.

Summer went quickly and so did the school year. Two years passed without any trouble for the girls. Then, when the girls were eleven years old, Mary's father decided to get rid of the doghouse. When he went to move it, he discovered the witchcraft books. When he questioned Mary about them, she admitted that they were hers. Joseph didn't seem to mind when he heard about the magic drinking glass. That was innocent enough. However, when Mary told him that she conjured up a Black Panther with power she obtained from the fire goddess, he was concerned. "Mary, he said. Such powers in the past were reserved for great medicine men. The fact that the gods are blessing you at such a young age means something. I'm not sure what. I would like you to spend next year with your grandfather, Cloud of Thunder. He is a powerful medicine man. He can show you how to use spiritual power without getting into trouble. He is your mother's father. If you learn the ways of healing, it will help you throughout your life.

When Cloud of Thunder dies, maybe he will ask you to take his place as the healer for the town of Dos Caballos. It is a respected position, but we will not force it on you. If you want to live in the white man's world, we will still love you. But please don't give yourself over to witchcraft and the powers of darkness. If you ask for too much power, eventually you will have to pay for that power. Nothing is free. There is always a price tag. Some things may be advertised as free, but they aren't really free. Maybe there is no charge for power to get rich, but you pay with your soul. Think about these things this week. Tell me now. Will you go to be with your grandfather for a year?" Mary said, "I will father, but I wish I could take my friends with me." Joseph said, "I know you will miss your friends. You can write them, and I think I can talk Cloud of Thunder into letting them visit once a month."

Mary said, "When will I be leaving for Dos Caballos?" Joseph said, "Tomorrow morning will be good. I will call Cloud of Thunder right away." Mary said, "Can I have Elenore and Marsha come over for supper?" Joseph said, "That will be fine. Tell your mother, so she can prepare enough food." Mary told her mother about her friends coming for supper. Betty said that she didn't mind. Mary called her friends, and their parents brought them over to the house. Mary said to them, "I have to go live with my grandfather for a year. Dad found the witchcraft books and thinks that I need the influence of my grandfather. He's a medicine man. I'm looking forward to it. He knows all about healing with plants and things. I'll be living in a teepee." Marsha said, "Will we ever see you?" Mary said, "I'll write often and dad will take you both to see me at least once a month." Elenore said, "Then that won't be so bad. I wish I was doing something interesting like that. And you'll be getting out of school." "I know, said Mary. That's one of the best things about it."

The family sat down to supper and had roast pig. Joseph had spent the whole afternoon roasting it over an open fire. It was delicious. Mary gave Joque a large portion. He looked grateful and happy, as he gulped it down. Betty said, "You will enjoy being with my father. He is a nice man. He is old fashioned in many ways. He doesn't appreciate the white man's religion. The missionary that was in this area tried to get him to quit using his medicinal herbs on the people. Cloud of Thunder will never turn away from the old ways of healing. He believes in them too strongly.

The missionary was a good man, and we went to his church. We have not told you about that religion though. We wanted you to know of the old ways first. Then you can decide for yourself what to believe. We like the new religion, but we don't want to force it on you. You must find your own way. By knowing the old ways, you will find respect amongst our people."

Joseph said, "If you are ever ready to learn about our religion, I am saving a King James Bible for you that belonged to my father. Just let me know when you want it." He smiled and then asked Marsha, "Could you pass some of that home made bread?" Marsha took a piece and then passed it on.

Joseph said, "Mary, I forgot to mention what an honor it is to be a medicine man's apprentice. A woman has never been selected before for the position. Times are more equal now and your grandfather always liked you. When I called him, he said that you must have a strong spiritual side. He said that it would be a shame to see it go to waste. If Marsha and Elenore get along with him well, they might be selected in a future year." Elenore said, "That sounds great. We can learn a great deal from Mary, but learning from Cloud of Thunder would be wonderful." Marsha said, "I would like that too. What is the best way to get along with Cloud of Thunder?"

Betty said, "He likes tobacco, but he can't afford it. If you take him a carton of cigarettes, you are sure to win his approval. He likes Marlburros and Camels. He doesn't like filters. He says that the filters rob some of the flavor. Also, don't talk too much. He likes silence much of the time. If he starts talking, then you can talk. He spends much time thinking and meditating. Don't interrupt his thoughts. If you can do that, he will think you are wise. Once he starts teaching you something, it's alright to ask questions. He expects that, and he will answer.

The girls all nodded their heads seriously. Mary said, "Can I take Joque with me?" Joseph said, "I think it will be alright. Cloud of Thunder likes animals. We will bring you plenty of food for him. We know he doesn't like bird food. We'll bring fruit and oranges. Those seem to be favorites of his." Betty said, "If you are all done eating, Elenore and Marsha can help you pack." Mary said, "We're done eating. Come on girls. Help me to not forget anything." They all went to the bedroom. There on the bed were the witchcraft books. Mary put them into the suitcase first. She said, "You never know, I might get bored with medicine and want to learn a few more spells." The girls giggled and Marsha said, "Yes, you have to keep up your powers, or they will vanish." When they had finished packing, they went outside for one final campfire together. They didn't do any witchcraft, since Betty and Joseph were there. They simply enjoyed the fire, the moon and the stars. Three pairs of beady eyes stared at them through the darkness. The magic animals would have to stay in hiding until the adults went to bed.

Finally at around midnight, Betty and Joseph went to bed. Joseph cautioned, "Don't stay up much later, Mary. We will be leaving at seven o'clock in the morning. You don't want to be tired, on you're first day with Cloud of Thunder." Mary replied, "I'll be in soon. Don't worry." After her parents were in the house, Mary called to the Black Panther. He was at her side in an instant. She explained to him, "We are leaving at seven o'clock in the morning. You will have to stay invisible, and jump into the back seat when I open the door. I will ride in the front seat with my father. Mom will stay home and give Elenore and Marsha rides home. I have decided to name you Herb. That way if my grandfather hears me calling you, I can say I was talking about herbs for healing." The Black Panther said, "I've never had a name before. Herb will be fine with me. At the car I will rub against your leg so that you know that I am in the car."

Mary said, "We'd better go in now. I don't want to be tired tomorrow. Elenore and Marsha said goodbye to their magic pets, and then went with Mary into the house. They stopped to talk to Joque before they went to bed. Mary said, "Tomorrow you will be going with me to live with my grandfather for a year. He is a medicine man. Joque said, "As long as the food is good, I'm with you." Mary said, "As soon as possible I'll get you a new home on the open seas like I promised. It's just that I don't know how to explain something like that to my parents." Joque said, "There's no big hurry. I know you will find a way soon. I like the food here, but I am getting a little anxious to get back to the sea." Mary said, "Get some sleep now. We are leaving at seven o'clock in the morning." Gently she slipped the cover over his cage. The girls all went to Mary's room and went to bed.

Chapter Two

The Medicine Man

Mary woke well before her father called her. She got dressed and went to the front porch, where she sat on the swing and watched the sun come up. Excitement filled her as she thought about her new upcoming adventure. After the sun was fully in view, she called Herb and let him into the back seat of the car. Next, she loaded her suitcases and put Joque in the back seat with Herb. She lectured them, "Now you two get along. I don't want any trouble from either of you. I want both of you to get along like life long friends. Do you understand?" Herb replied, "I don't eat birds anyway. The feathers get stuck in my teeth." Joque chipped in, "I'll be good. I could put a spell on him if I wanted to. But if he's a friend of yours, then I'll be nice to him."

Mary went into the house and told her dad that she had everything in the car. Joseph said, "You're excited about this stay with Cloud of Thunder, aren't you?" Mary answered, "I'm looking forward to it. I'm sure I can learn much from him. Should I take him some cigarettes?" Joseph exclaimed, "I would have forgotten. He would like you even without them, but it won't hurt. He's old and has few physical pleasures in life. We can get him some at the drug store in Dos Caballos.

They ate some milk and cereal and climbed into the new Jeep Cherokee that was waiting in the driveway. It was only fifteen miles to Dos Caballos. It wouldn't take them long to get there. Mary asked, "Why doesn't Cloud of Thunder come to see us?" Joseph answered, "He doesn't like our modern house. He likes things to be traditional. He's happy that you are coming to learn the old ways. He'll never change." Mary asked, "What about his wife? Will she be with us? Joseph replied, "She stays in the home lodge. It's a large teepee where food is prepared. You will spend your learning times in the sacred teepee. That is where Cloud of Thunder prepares his medicines and teaches when he is not in the desert. He has a third teepee that is for steaming people. You will learn to enjoy the steam baths. They help to relax you and free your mind." Mary said, "What do I wear in the steam teepee?" Joseph said, "Didn't you bring your swim suit?" Mary said, "No. I didn't think I would need it." Joseph said, "You can trust Cloud of Thunder. Just wrap up in a large towel or blanket. He has plenty of those." Mary said, "That sounds good. I knew I could trust Cloud of Thunder. It's just that I've never taken a steam bath before. It sounds a little weird at first. Usually such things are segregated by sex. I mean men in one sauna and women in another." Joseph said, "It is not always so. Just don't worry about it. He is an old medicine man. He's like a doctor. Just learn from him. It is his goal to help you."

Now they could see Dos Caballos coming up over the horizon. In a few more minutes, they were at the drug store buying some cigarettes. Joseph called to the attendant, "I'll take a carton of Marlboros." The attendant said, "We're out of full cartons. Is there another brand you would like?" Joseph said, "I'll take Camels without filters, if you have them." The attendant went out back. In a minute she was back with the carton of Camels. Joseph paid her for the cigarettes and put them in the car. He and Mary drove on through town and about one hundred yards out into the desert.

There on the right side of the road were three large teepees. They were about one hundred feet back from the road. Joseph pulled into the driveway and beeped the horn. From the nearest teepee Cloud of Thunder and his wife appeared and waved to them. Joseph and Mary got out of the Jeep and walked over to them. Cloud of Thunder said, "Mary, I haven't seen you for a long time. My wife, Morningstar, has been longing to see you again." Mary said, "I'm glad to be here. I can't wait to hear all about medicine." Cloud of Thunder said, "We will start today. Your father can come with us on our first tour of the desert, if he would like to." Joseph said, "No, I need to get back home. Mary brought you some cigarettes."

Mary went back to the car and got the cigarettes. She proudly handed them to Cloud of Thunder. He said, "This is a wonderful surprise. I'll smoke them tonight around the campfire. I haven't had cigarettes for a long time. He opened the carton and held a pack in his hand. He opened it and smelled it. He inhaled deeply. "Ah! Just the smell of them is a great pleasure. Thank you, Mary." He shook Joseph's hand and said goodbye. Joseph said, "I'll get Mary's luggage. He passed the luggage to Cloud of Thunder and Mary. Then he gave Mary a hug and a kiss. He said, "I'll come back every month with your friends. They can stay for the day, and then I'll pick them up in the evening." He waved from the Jeep and then drove away.

Cloud of Thunder said, "Mary, come with me. We can go for a hike in the desert. I can show you some important plants right away. I have a canteen of water for each of us. We may be gone for a long time." He went into the teepee and got the canteens. He gave one to Mary and the other he put on his shoulder. He led her away from the road and down a trail that headed west. After about thirty minutes, they were in an area that was full of tall cactus plants. Cloud of Thunder reached up and cut off a branch of one cactus. The branch had some small pink flowers on it. It was about two feet long and six inches thick. Cloud of Thunder spoke softly, "This is the San Raul cactus. Notice the eight sides that it has. You can't always tell it by the flowers. They are only there in the spring and summer. I make a potion from the pulp inside the cactus. It is only for terribly sick people. It makes them vomit. But then, about an hour after they drink the potion through their nose, they experience the god of the cactus. It hears their problems. The patient gets a strong sense of well being. After they have spoken to this god, they don't mind if they must die. There is a special animal horn that I have them drink the potion with. It gives them the right dosage. I drink it with the sick person. That way I can go on their journey with them. I help them to have no fear. Since I am a friend of the cactus god, it will bless the ones that I am with." He placed the branch of the cactus into a sack that he had fastened to his belt.

They went on several hundred yards. Cloud of Thunder stooped down and dug in the dirt around a small cactus that was only two inches high and four inches around. There were small buttons or nodules around the cactus. He put on a leather glove and pulled off all of the buttons. He went to several other similar cacti, and gathered the buttons. After about thirty minutes of this, he had a nice small pouch full of them. He said, "These are Beyo buttons, from the Beyo cactus. I grind them up and make tea from them. They help you to contact the spirit world. Sometimes you see beautiful visions and hear the voice of a God speaking to you. It allows you to see in the dark.

You can also eat the buttons, but they make you vomit. That is why I prefer the tea. I will show you how strong to make the tea and how much to drink. If you use too much, it is like being poisoned. It is not good for you." Mary said, "Thank you, Cloud of Thunder. I have never had visions before. I'm sure it will help me. How have the visions helped you, Cloud of Thunder?" He said, "The visions give me pleasure just because of their beauty. They also draw me close to the gods. When you are allowed to see what only the plant's god can show you, you learn of the power all around you. It humbles you. You know that the material things, which you might buy, are not important. Only experiencing the closeness of the gods is important. People become sick because they are separated too far from the gods. I bring the plants and the plant god, to the people." He grew silent and walked with her for a long way. They came upon a dry riverbed. He got down on his knees and scooped up some white clay, which he put into a plastic bag.

Then they walked along the streambed for about an hour. Cloud of Thunder stooped down and scooped up some red clay from the streambed. He said, "The white clay is for on the skin. It purifies people spiritually. Evil spirits are driven out when you wear the white clay on your skin in the steam teepee. You will wear the white clay tonight. I sense that you have gotten too close to the fire god. She is threatening to take you completely. I saw your Black Panther when it got out of the car. It is an attractive animal, but I'm sorry to say that it will go when you are purified. Is that acceptable to you, Mary?" Mary said, "Yes, Cloud of Thunder. Your powers of knowing surprise me. The panther can go, but please let me keep Joque. Joque is my parrot. He is possessed by his former owner, a sea captain. I promised to return him to the sea." Cloud of Thunder said, "I will arrange for him to stay with some friends of mine until your training is complete. Then you can do with him as you wish."

They walked home silently. It was time for supper when they returned. They had only vegetable soup and coffee. Mary was quiet as they sat around the fire. When the stars started to come out, Cloud of Thunder asked

Morningstar to dress Mary in a large towel and leave her back exposed. After about twenty minutes Morningstar brought Mary out to the campfire. Cloud of Thunder covered her back with white clay. Next he gave Mary a lump of the clay and asked her to go into the steam teepee and cover the rest of her body with the clay. She did as he asked and then covered up in the towel. She sat in the hot steam filled teepee and waited.

After about thirty minutes, Cloud of Thunder arrived, dressed in a towel. He spoke softly, "I will make the fire hotter so we can have more steam." After about an hour, the rocks around the fire were extremely hot. Cloud of Thunder gave Mary a pitcher full of hot water. "Pour this hot water on the rocks. Don't let the steam burn you. We use hot water because we get more steam that way. The water doesn't cool off the rocks too soon." Mary poured the water on the rocks. The steam got so thick in the teepee that she couldn't see a thing. Mary sat back down on the buffalo hide that she had been sitting on. She saw a match light in the dim light of the fire. Cloud of Thunder said, "I like to smoke in the steam teepee. I only smoke one cigarette a day. We medicine men have a saying, 'Moderation in all things.' Don't forget that. Oh, I suppose the marines have a similar saying. They will tell you that it was their idea first."`

After Cloud of Thunder had smoked his cigarette he said, "I will go now and prepare our cactus tea." He got up and left for about twenty minutes. When he returned he was chanting an old Indian chant that he had learned as a boy. He said, "I always sing as I prepare the tea. The tea makes me happy." He set the tray with the cups of tea between them and they both sat together by the fire drinking the tea. Cloud of Thunder said, "You don't have to be a medicine woman, you know. I won't hold it against you if you decide you want something else for yourself. At least give it a chance though. Few people want to study the old ways. It's easy for people to just take some pills from the pharmacies of the white man. But many of the people around here have so little money, that they must choose between medicine and food. That is why I treat them free of charge. I don't want to take the food out of their mouths. And that is why I depend on your parents to send me money from time to time. Your father doesn't mind. He has plenty of money.

When he first married my daughter, I trained him as my apprentice. He was more interested in power than healing. He is a good and kind man, but he wanted money. I sent him to another medicine man in the mountains, who serves the Jade Goddess. Your father asked for abilities to see the future in the stock market. That power was granted to him. Now he is a millionaire. It is to his credit that he still lives simply. I just wish he would live in a teepee like I do. When the missionary converted him, he lost some of his powers to see the future, so he put all his money in safe mutual funds. He will always have plenty of money. I am sure that the Jade Goddess is upset with him. I will never know whether the white man's God will be able to save him from her wrath when he dies.

Mary said, "I always wondered where my father got his money. Can I go see the Jade Goddess sometime?" Cloud of Thunder said, "It is not a thing to be taken lightly. If you turn against her, she might punish you after you die, if not before." Mary said, "Well then, I'll forget about her for now. It would be nice to have great powers like my father had." She grew silent for awhile and then said, "I'm starting to see orange and purple patterns of light all around me. The potion must be starting to work." Cloud of Thunder said, "Soon you should be able to see in the dark. These may not be great powers, but when you add all of the powers from the desert together, they are considerable." They sat in silence for several hours and watched the colors.

Mary had a vision that she told Cloud of Thunder about. "A Jade Goddess called to me from the mountain and said that she could make me invisible. She also said that I could fly without a broomstick. I could just rise up into the air and move about. She said that she is waiting for me. She will be patient, because first I must learn to heal people of illness. She knows that I want that more than money right now. She is patient. She will wait." Cloud of Thunder said, "It is not surprising that she could hear you. Her mountain is only about forty miles away. It is nothing for her to listen in on your thoughts. But you don't have to go to her. It could be dangerous. Like I said before, she may turn against you if you are not loyal to her.

Mary said, "I will stay with you for now. I don't feel like climbing mountains. I have plenty of money. Mom and dad gave me a credit card for a thousand dollars." Cloud of Thunder said, "That is a lot of money. Let's be quiet for a while now and see if there are any more visions." They sat for about an hour and enjoyed the feeling of well being that came from the cactus potion. Finally Cloud of Thunder said, "It is late. You need some sleep. Your bed is ready for you in with my wife and me." They walked to the main lodge where Mary found her bed and went to sleep right away.

In the morning Morningstar helped Mary wash off all the white clay. Then they ate some tortillas with Cloud of Thunder. After they had eaten, Cloud of Thunder loaded a backpack with water. He also brought the canteens full of water. He said to Morningstar, "We won't be back till tomorrow evening. He turned and headed down the path to the west. Mary followed him. They walked for four hours in silence. Finally they stopped in an area that was full of lush vegetation. Cloud of Thunder said, "We will stay here. I want you to learn to fast and to meditate out in the desert." I will boil some of the leaves from these poyo plants. The tea from them will help you to meditate.

Tonight you will probably be able to travel up into the stars. Your body will stay here, but your spirit will soar into the heavens, almost as high as the planets."

Mary asked, "How will I do that?" Cloud of Thunder said, "The plants will help you to fly. On another day, we will pray to the God of birds. He will help you to fly with your body. You will not have to ask the Jade Goddess to make you fly. I can help you with that." They sat together on a blanket by the fire that Cloud of Thunder made. He brewed a pot of tea from the tall plants that surrounded them. They sat quietly and drank the tea as the sun slowly crossed the sky.

When the sun went down, Mary closed her eyes. She felt herself floating up into the clouds. She rose on up high above the earth. The feeling was great. It was like being a bird, and soaring high on the winds; gliding effortlessly, able to see for miles and miles. Finally she fell asleep for awhile. Cloud of Thunder woke her and gave her some coffee. He said, "The tea makes a person sleepy after awhile. I want to talk with you, so drink this strong coffee. It will keep you awake." She drank the coffee and found that she was soon wide awake.

Cloud of Thunder said, "Last night the white clay could not purify you, because you were longing for the Black Panther. He is still here with us, though he is keeping his distance. I would be pleased if you would ask him to go away for at least a year. If you want him back after I have trained you as a medicine woman, then you can call him back." Mary said, "I will call him at once to tell him. Herb. Herb. Come here. Show yourself." At once the panther was in front of them. Mary said, "I want you to go away for one year, while I am in training as a medicine woman. Then, you can return to me." The big cat said, "I will do as you say." It turned and ran off into the desert.

"There is one more thing, Mary. I would like you to let me keep your witchcraft books for a year. You won't need them. I will have plenty for you to do." Mary asked, "How do you know about those books?" Cloud of Thunder answered, "In the steam tent my spirit entered your mind so that I could know if you were pure. I will not always invade your privacy. This time, however, it was important." Mary replied, "I will give you the books." Cloud of Thunder said, "I will take good care of them. I have great respect for books, even when they are not the type of book that I personally like."

"Mary, I can tell that you will leave me after one year and go to the Jade Goddess. Just keep in mind that you don't have to go, just because she is calling you. She is dangerous. You can live a good life without so much power. Think it over while you are here in the desert. Think about what you would ask her for, and if it would be worth the danger involved." Mary said, "I will think about it. I honestly don't know what I would ask her for. I would like to know the future, but I don't think I would like to know everything. I would like to be able to know what number would be coming up next at roulette. It would be nice to know where pirate treasure is to be found. My father was wise to ask to be able to know the future of the stock market. That's a good wish. I'm pretty sure that I would ask to be able to know the future. Then I could tell people's fortunes. That would be fun. And like I said, I could win at roulette. Las Vegas here I come!" Cloud of Thunder exclaimed, "You have a great gift for dreaming! I'm sure you will have no trouble thinking of the right thing to ask for, if you decide to go to the Jade Goddess. Now I will let you sleep. You will need your rest. Tomorrow will be a day that will require your alertness." He spread out a blanket for each of them and they slept out in the desert. As Mary slept she dreamed throughout the night that she was flying high above the desert, sometimes reaching as high as the stars.

In the morning they woke with the coming of the sun light. They walked a long distance. Every time they saw a different bird, they would stop and pray to it for the power of flight. By evening, they had prayed to thirty different birds. They could feel the power of the bird god starting to work on them. As the sun set, Cloud of Thunder reached out and took Mary by the hand. He prayed fervently to the bird god. Slowly they both rose up above the mesquite bushes and cacti. They flew slowly to the west, and then back to where they had started. Mary exclaimed, "That was fun! Do you think I could do that alone?" Cloud of Thunder answered, "I'm sure you can, but I'm afraid you might get lost. This is a big desert. We should stay together." Mary said, "I could just rise straight up and still keep you in sight." Cloud of Thunder replied, "Do as you wish then." Mary spread out her arms and prayed to the bird god. She rose slowly at first, and then went up quickly to where the air was cold. She came back down and landed softly beside her grandfather. "It was cold up there!" she exclaimed. Cloud of Thunder answered, "That is why I usually stay down lower. Also, if you go too high, people can see you from far away. It is wise to only fly at night, or far from the habitations of man. The people who are not experienced with such flight become concerned and create problems. Do you understand?" Mary replied, "I will follow your advice. I don't want people calling me a witch, or shooting at me."

Cloud of Thunder started a small fire and made some coffee. It smelled good to Mary as she sat in the moonlight and watched the stars. Her grandfather handed her a cup of the hot instant coffee. They sat quietly for a long time and watched the stars while they sipped the coffee. After several hours of quiet meditation, they spread out blankets and fell asleep. As Mary slept, she dreamed of finding vast treasures of gold and silver on sunken ships that the Jade Goddess had revealed to her. She knew where large deposits of gold and diamonds were buried. In her dreams she could win large amounts of cash at Las Vegas. She cleverly lost on purpose many times, so that the management wouldn't suspect something. Then she would make a million dollar bet on the number she knew would come up next. She did that to every casino in the town. She dreamed of having a large boat with servants to cook wonderful breakfasts and serve them to her and her friends. She played the stock market with the benefit of her ability to see the future. She dreamed that she earned billions of dollars on the stock market. She served as an advisor to the president, and became a friend of his. Finally, just before she started dreaming of being president or king, she woke up. She thought about her grandfather's warning. If she asked for too much, there would be a price to pay. Nothing is free. Mary went back to sleep. The dreams started again, but they were more controlled. The dream had her winning and earning millions of dollars, but there were no servants. Most of the money went to feed the poor and provide medical care. After that dream, she started to sleep soundly.

When she woke, Cloud of Thunder was cooking breakfast. There was a plentiful supply of crispy bacon and buttered toast. In addition there was a nice ripe orange for each of them. Cloud of Thunder said, "I was following you in your dreams last night. It is good that you have decided not to be greedy. If you use the power you receive to help the poor, I think that you will not be dealt with too harshly when you die. It is possible, though, that the Jade Goddess will feel that you have wasted your power. What will you say to that?" Mary answered, "I will tell those that I help, who provided the help." Cloud of Thunder said, "The Jade Goddess doesn't crave the thanks of many poor people. She wants to be flattered by wise and powerful people. She wants loyalty most of all. Can you stay loyal to her, even when you have power that makes you feel independent?" Mary answered, "I will worship the god or goddess who gives me what I want." Cloud of Thunder replied, "There are many gods in the world. Many of them will want to help you. They will be jealous of your loyalty to the Jade Goddess. They will each try to win you for themselves. I hope that you will not be swayed by the desires of the moment. Don't call on the god of the birds one moment and then go back to the Jade Goddess the next moment. It is possible that you would be happier with the god of plants. They are everywhere. They could help you anywhere in the world. If you only have gold, it could be taken from you. Maybe it would be wiser to ask for love or a long life without suffering. You might want to ask for a pleasant afterlife." Mary replied, "It is getting complicated. I was sure that I wanted to be able to see into the future and know what I need to know to gain wealth. Now I'm not so sure. I can't even imagine being in the afterlife. I know, however, that I don't want to suffer after I die. What shall I do? Can't you advise me grandpa?"

Cloud of Thunder said, "I can't decide for you. If it was my decision, I wouldn't join with the Jade Goddess. I think she is capable of torturing people after they die. I don't know what you would need to do to keep her happy. It is too dangerous, in my opinion. You can decide for yourself. The god of the birds and the god of the plants are gentle gods. I trust them not to hurt me or others. They have not made our people rich, but they have kept us happy. That is enough for me. The goddess of fire is also a worthy god. You could possibly gain wealth through her without having to pay the price that might come from dealing with the Jade Goddess." Mary said, "Help me tonight to decide what is right to do. Please help me grandfather." Cloud of Thunder thought for a long while. Then he spoke, "We can eat the beyo cactus tonight. It will make us more sensitive to the goddess of fire. We will build a large camp fire and dance around it, singing the ancient songs of my people. When the time is right, you can call to her and see what she is willing to do for you if you worship her. Don't mention the Jade Goddess or she will become jealous and not help you at all."

They spent the next few hours gathering firewood and collecting the needed beyo cactus pulp. When everything was ready they sat on blankets in a clearing where they had placed the fire wood. Cloud of Thunder exclaimed, "The Jade Goddess can take you to distant planets to converse with creatures more advanced than we are! I have not done it myself, but I have heard of it from others. These creatures have their advanced powers because of the god they worship. I think they may be followers of the Jade Goddess. They must have asked her for great powers of intellect that allowed them to make space ships and colonize other planets. If you decide to worship the Jade Goddess, you could ask for power over these creatures. I personally hope that you will not choose that." Mary replied, "The possibilities are endless. I think I'm leaning towards incredible wealth. I would like lots of gold and cash. I will be wise enough to ask that I will be able to keep the wealth during a long happy lifetime." Cloud of Thunder said, "That's three wishes. I think that will be more than the Jade Goddess will give you all at once, but it won't hurt to try. Tonight you could ask the Goddess of fire for those things. I won't cost you anything with her. She isn't vengeful." Mary thought out loud, "Maybe I will ask for that tonight. I want wealth and I want a long life to enjoy the wealth in. I want health too, so that I can enjoy the wealth." Cloud of Thunder said, "Now you're thinking. Health is indeed important. Without it, the wealth would seem useless. We can build a small fire now and cook some bacon. We will need strength when we visit the goddess of fire."

Mary helped her grandfather build a small cooking fire. She was hungry from all the walking they had done that day. Cloud of Thunder cooked the bacon perfectly. He made sure that it was completely cooked, but not burned or made too stiff. They let the bacon cool and then they each ate five strips of bacon. It was lean and didn't have much fat on it. The taste of it was wonderful. Mary thought she could have eaten a whole hog, she was so hungry. Next, they built the fire much bigger. The sun was setting in the west. There were some clouds on the horizon that were shining with an orange glow. The earth grew purple around the area where the sun was dropping out of sight.

Cloud of Thunder opened the jar they had filled with beyo pulp. He emptied half of it into a bowl for Mary. He put the rest of the pulp in a bowl for himself. They sat by the fire and ate the cactus pulp. In about an hour they started dancing and singing around the fire. They danced for several hours. Then Cloud of Thunder had Mary sit on the blanket and close her eyes. He told her, "Wait, Mary, and the goddess of fire will appear unto you." She closed her eyes and waited for a long while. Finally the goddess appeared in the center of the fire. The goddess asked, "What would you have me do for you, Mary?" Mary ventured, "Please answer a few questions for me. I would like to know if you could help me find vast wealth, and at the same time give me a long healthy and happy life." The goddess said, "I can tell by your question that you have already acquired some wisdom at a young age. I can tell you that such wisdom will help you to find wealth. I do not deal in cash. If you are kind to others, I can see to it that you live a long and healthy life. That is all that I can offer. You should consider the gaining of wealth a challenge that will make life interesting. If I could give you vast wealth, you would probably grow bored with it soon. My gifts are more valuable than cash or having the ability to know the future."

Mary said, "I didn't mention anything about knowing the future." The goddess said, "I have little hope that you will be a loyal worshipper of mine. You will go to the Jade

Goddess for wealth and the gift of seeing. Seeing the next number to come up at roulette is what you have in the back of your mind. I can see it there. I am disappointed. You seemed like such a precocious girl at first." Mary replied, "Is the future you see for me absolute? Are you sure that I will not worship you?" "You may worship me, but you will not be able to give complete loyalty. I know that you genuinely enjoy singing to me and dancing around the fire. For that reason I will help you when I can, but you will go to the Jade Goddess. She will trick you. You will get wealth, but at a great cost. You will see the future, but part of the future will be hidden from you. The hidden part is about the interest that you will pay for the loan of power from the Jade Goddess. She will not be a true friend. Her only delight is in showing the wisest of humans to be utter fools. The only way that you can win with her is to stay away from her. The afterlife is a real thing. You do not want an eternity of suffering. It is true that you cannot imagine such an afterlife. However, it would be clever of you to prevent such evil things from coming to you even though you don't actually believe in them." Mary said, "I have already dabbled in witchcraft. Don't you think I will have to pay for that if there is an afterlife?" The goddess said, "Such culpability is not irrevocable. Your grandfather can help you to be a good medicine woman. I was the one whom you appealed to with your witchcraft dabblings. That is not so terrible. The innocent dabbling of a child is not to be compared to the all too human grabbing for power, wealth and powers of seeing. The price is high for those three things. The Jade Goddess will see to it that you pay the price in full. Your father only asked for the power of seeing. He will pay dearly for just that one favor from the Jade Goddess. Don't make the same mistake he made. In order for him to receive his gift he had to say that all the other gods were evil. That alienated him from all possible help. I don't think that he will succeed in winning the approval of the white man's God now. He already said that all gods but the Jade one are evil. How can he go to one of them now for help?" Mary meekly replied, "I see the problem. Calling the white man's God evil is a sin that will not be forgiven by that God. Did my father know about that when he made the statement?" The goddess of fire responded, "He did not know the gravity of what he was saying. I do not know what will befall him. He is trying to make his peace with the white man's God. I am upset with him also for his lack of faithfulness to any one god. The fire leaped higher. Cloud of Thunder warned Mary, "Don't make her angry. Give her a reason to like you."

Mary pronounced, "Goddess of fire, you are powerful and wise. I want you to always be my friend. I will follow your advice for now. It is a challenge to gain wealth. I will use the gifts of health and a long happy life. They are enough for me. You are a generous god!" The fire simmered down to its pervious size. The Fire Goddess said, "You are worthy to receive my gifts. Step closer to the fire." Mary stepped up close to the fire. The goddess pronounced, "Be not afraid, for I will protect you from myself." The fire belched out and engulfed her. She glowed red like an ember. Then as quickly as the fire had come upon her, it left. She fell to the ground. Cloud of Thunder ran to her side, "Are you alright, Mary?" Mary opened her eyes, "I feel great. Does this mean that I have received the gifts?" Cloud of Thunder said, "You have received the promise from the goddess that you will have a long and happy life. She has also given you good health." Mary replied, "Those are good gifts. Possibly I should stay away from the Jade Goddess."

The rest of the year passed quickly for Mary. She had learned most of what Cloud of Thunder had to teach her. Cloud of Thunder gave her a heavily beaded leather bag to keep her medicines in. She was proud to receive the bag. It was the sign that she was a healer, fully trained in the ways of tribal medicine. On her last day with Cloud of Thunder, she called back her invisible black panther, Herb. He came running out of the desert to her side. Mary left Cloud of Thunder without saying a word. He knew where she would go. She would climb the neighboring mountain to visit the Jade Goddess and decide whether she would follow the more powerful and fearsome god. Only reluctantly did the bird goddess fly her most of the way up the mountain. Mary landed near a small cave on the western side of the mountain. A very old Indian man was roasting a rabbit over a fire. She walked up to him and asked about the Jade Goddess. He replied, "I am called The High One. It is because I have always lived at the top of this mountain. I have been waiting for you. I introduced your father to the Jade Goddess. Now I will introduce you to her. Wear this green feather in your hair, it will help to put the goddess into a good mood. Tell her that you know she is the most powerful god. That will make her want to help you. We can climb the last thousand feet to her cave after I eat this rabbit. Are you hungry?" Mary placed the green feather in her hair and sat beside the fire with The High One. He pulled a leg from the roasted rabbit and gave it to her. She ate it slowly, thinking all the time about what she would say to the Jade Goddess.

When they had finished the rabbit, her guide packed some water, bread and blankets into backpacks. They each put a pack on their back and headed up the mountain. It was evening when they arrived at the large cave. A faint green glow could be seen emanating from the mouth of the cave. Mary followed The High One into the cave. They walked slowly along a strait and narrow tunnel until it opened up into a large cavern that was as big as a large house. The goddess was only about 12 inches high, but she glowed so brightly, that it hurt one's eyes to look at her. Her voice was soft and gentle as she spoke to Mary. "I knew you would come to visit me. Like your father, you want vast wealth. It is only natural. He disappointed me by trying to turn to the white man's God for help. I know you won't be so foolish. Possibly I can insure your loyalty if I give you far more power than he had. What is it that you would like besides wealth?" "I would like to know the future and have the ability to locate pirate treasure ships that are in waters shallow enough to dive in." The soft voice of the goddess pronounced, "It is done as you wish. I know you won't turn against me when I am this generous with you. You may kiss me now on the hand." Mary approached cautiously and kissed the goddess on her hand. The gentle voice echoed in the chamber, "I will be with you whenever you call out my name. Come to visit me from time to time. Bring the herbs of the desert here and burn them with me. I like the smell of them. I was discovered as a lump of jade and formed in the desert, by a powerful witch, thousands of years ago. I like to be reminded of such places. My followers brought me here so that I wouldn't be destroyed by the followers of other Gods. Be loyal to me. I will not show you your future that will occur in case of disloyalty. I don't want you to be troubled by such things. I know I can count on you." Mary tried to speak, but her throat was dry. She thought, "I love this soft spoken goddess. She is so gentle and powerful at the same time." The goddess spoke inside Mary's mind, "I have heard your thoughts and they are good. Next time you come, remember to bring the leaves for us to burn from the desert." Mary responded, "I just remembered, I have my medicine bag with me. There are plenty of poyo leaves inside. May I burn some for you?" The cavern shuddered a little. "You'll have to excuse my excitement. Few of my followers are thoughtful enough to bring me such a fine gift on the first visit." Mary formed a pile of the leaves close to the goddess and lit them with a match. She blew gently on the leaves so that the smoke wafted into the face of the Jade Goddess. The smoke was drawn in greedily by the goddess. She glowed even more brightly than before.

"You must sleep here before me tonight. I like you. I want to enjoy your presence. Go out and get your blanket. The High One will wait for you outside tonight." She went and got her blanket and lay down in the presence of her new god. Her mind glowed with the color of jade. She could think of nothing. She felt euphoric. Her mind was one with the new god.

In the morning she was very hungry. With slow steps, she walked away from the goddess and found The High One smoking a pipe beside a small fire that he had built. Mary shared his pipe with him and ate some bread from her back pack. The High One ventured, "How did you like her?" Mary thought for a little while and then replied, "I was surprised by how gentle she seems. Her voice is soft and her pleasures are simple. She loves to smoke with a friend." The High One spoke, "She loves to smoke the poyo leaves, but there is more. You must stay a few days if you want to get to know her. I know how to get her to talk more." He reached into his back pack and pulled out a small leather purse. Reaching inside, he pulled out a small cone of black tar like substance. He exclaimed, "She loves the poyo when it is mixed like this with the poppy extracts from the orient. It will cause her to talk for a long time and possibly tell you hidden truths. You can burn this with her now if you like." Mary took the cone eagerly and returned to the goddess. She sat before the goddess and cut up the cone into small pieces. Placing the pieces into a long stemmed pipe, she began to smoke. Each time she drew some of the smoke into her lungs, she would then blow the smoke into the face of the goddess. After a few minutes, she held the pipe close to the face of the goddess. The goddess drew in the smoke for a long time. Finally, the goddess spoke, "The High One must like you. He told you how to get into my good graces. I already liked you. Now you are one of my closest friends. I would like to tell you some things that are normally hidden from my devotees. You have heard that I made your father call all gods but me, evil. I am sure that you wonder why I didn't do that with you. It is because I decided that it was only cheap insurance of loyalty. I want you to be loyal because you want to be loyal, not because you feel there is no other help to turn to." Mary said, "I will be loyal. You are exceedingly generous to me."

The Jade Goddess glowed a little more brightly and replied, "Your praise is pleasant to my ears. I would not have you deceived in any way by me, though. I want you to know that my power comes from a dark angel who rules the world of evil. No matter how much good you do with your medicine and wealth, if you accept my help, your soul will belong to that angel when you die. Is that acceptable?" Mary said, "What will the angel of darkness do to my soul? What will it be like?" "I cannot answer those questions exactly. I can only say that it will go on for a long time, and it will not be pleasant for you if you spend your life doing good deeds. If you would do some terribly evil things, your afterlife might be better in his domain. I was allowed to escape the evil treatment of the angel, because in my human life, I made poisons for arrows and guided curses against the enemies of my tribe. The angel of darkness is fond of those who have killed many mortals. Unless you too grow fond of killing, I doubt that he will be as generous in his treatment of you. Could you kill thousands of people, Mary?" Mary thought for a long time before she spoke. "If they are people bent on the destruction of my people, I think I could kill them. I might even learn to enjoy killing, as you did. However, I know nothing of poisons. I have only been taught to heal." The Jade Goddess laughed, "You only need to ask, and I will teach you." Mary answered, "I would like to know about poisons and cursing the enemy." "The High One will show you how to make the poisons, I will teach you to curse the enemy. You must make an image of the enemy on something. Take pins or knives and pierce the enemy's image in many places, after you have prayed to me for help. Another fine way to hurt the enemy, is to carve their image on a flat square piece of wood about two inches square. Glue the piece of wood to the bottom of your shoe and walk on them for many weeks. It takes a long time, but it is very effective. I will give you many more of my old curses over the next year. I will send them to you while you sleep. Do you have any more questions for me?" Mary thought for several minutes. "If I kill many of the enemies of my people, will I have a nice afterlife?" The Jade Goddess was quiet for a long time. Finally she responded, "It is impossible for me to say. The angel of darkness is harsh and cruel. I don't have him totally figured out. I only know that the odds of successfully courting his favor are not too good. I want to be open with you. Remember, you are getting unlimited wealth and knowledge of the future. It has a price!" Mary said, "It is important to me to have the gifts that you are giving me. I will pay the price. I will try to kill enough people so that the angel of darkness will be happy with me." The goddess spoke profoundly, "You have spoken well. I hope that you will receive an acceptable afterlife." The goddess asked Mary to stretch out on the ground before her with her head toward her. The cave shuddered as the Jade Goddess sent the gifts into Mary. Mary glowed with a jade colored light and rose up. She stepped up to the Jade Goddess and touched her hand. "We are bonded now, said the goddess. I will hear you wherever you are. You can call on me and I will answer." Mary whispered, "Thank you. Thank you for my new powers. I will use them often and be forever grateful."

Mary lit the pipe again, and the two smoked for a long time. Every four hours, The High One would bring Mary some bread and water. After about twenty hours, Mary rose and went outside. She spoke to The High One, "Teach me to make poisons." The High One replied, "We must go to the desert." They waited till dark and then flew off the mountain and down to the middle of the dessert. Each of them had brought a blanket in their backpack, which also had bread and water. They each curled up in their blanket and waited till morning to look for the plants they needed for poison making.

In the morning, Mary noticed that her black panther Herb had followed them. She called him to her and stroked his soft fur. He lay down beside her and they watched the beautiful gold color of the sun as it started to come up over the horizon. Mary thought to herself, "I'd like to get Joque back as soon as possible. I miss him." She watched as The High One built a fire and cooked some fresh tortillas for them. He also made some coffee. He knew that she liked it. As he handed her a cup full, he volunteered, "It is instant Folgers coffee. The Goddess told me that you like it. She has been watching you closely for a long time now." Mary nodded knowingly and ate her food and drank the coffee. After they had eaten their meager meal, The High One said to Mary, "Now if you will come with me, I will show you some plants that will help us." They walked slowly along a dry creek bed as The High One looked for poisonous plants. After they had walked for about a mile, they came to a bush that had attractive purple flowers growing on it. Mary was told, "Look carefully at this bush and its flowers. If the flowers are crushed with a little water, they give off a strong poison that will kill the largest and most powerful person in a few seconds. You can preserve the poison if you dry it out so that only the powder remains. The powder can be placed in food, drink or on arrows. It can also be blown into the face of the victim. Even if he holds his breath, the little amount that lands on his nostrils and lips is enough to kill him." They spent several days there. The High One made certain that Mary became skilled at extracting the poison from the plant. He produced some small plastic bottles from his backpack for Mary to store the poison in.

Mary loved to work with plants. She was a quick student and wanted to learn more. Herb watched her as she carefully picked the flowers and crushed them in water. She warned him, "Don't get too close Herb, I don't want you to spill any of my poison." She questioned The High One about the plant, "What do you call this bush?" "I call it the deadly beauty plant, because the beautiful flowers are so poisonous." Mary questioned further, "Does it hurt to get the flowers on your hands?" She was told, "If you have any cuts on your hands, you should wear gloves when working with the plant. If you would start to feel bad effects from one of the poisons you work with, we could call on the Jade Goddess for help. Sometimes just drinking plenty of water for a couple of days will help flush poison from the system." Mary thought to herself, "I wish I had some gloves now." The High One must have been tuned into her thoughts. He replied as he reached into his backpack, "I have some gloves for you, in case you are worried about the poison." Mary took them gratefully and put them on. They gathered a good deal of poison from that one bush.

It was late June when Mary had learned what she needed to know about the poisons to be found in the desert. She was starting to think of The High One as a second grandfather. She had fallen asleep leaning against him as they sat around the evening campfire on many occasions. She felt safe with him. One night as they were watching the fire and smoking together, she told him, "Sometimes I wonder why you are so honorable. Is it because I am not attractive to you?" The High One Said, "I know that you are a virgin and have few thoughts that are not wholesome. Even though the goddess and I are dependent on the dark side of the spirit world for our power, we do not want to anger you with unwanted actions from us. Maybe I am beating around the bush. I mean to say that the goddess would kill me if I violated you. Since I am her close personal servant I must obey all that she wants. She is watching us closely and she is pleased that I have not tried to violate you." Mary replied, "I understand, High One. Can you at least tell me if I am attractive?" "You are slender and have a nice tan from the summer sun. I am sure that your large beautiful eyes and attractive face will make it so that you can make any man long for you." Mary sighed, "That's good to know. There are no mirrors here in the desert, and I actually don't know exactly what I look like." The High One exclaimed, "This talking reminds me of one of the things I was supposed to do for you. The goddess thought you would want to visit the gambling casinos soon, since you know what will happen next with the cards and the roulette wheel. She wanted me to ask if you would like to be 21 years old. You would miss most of your growing up years. It might be difficult for you to know how to fit in as an adult. You could call on the goddess to coach you if you get into a tight spot. I could even come along if you would like, just for a few weeks."

Mary asked, "How could I become 21 years old instantly?" The High One said, "The Jade Goddess is exceedingly powerful. I can let her power flow through me and make you 21 as quickly as a falcon flies, if you would like." Mary thought a little while and then replied, "Would I ever be able to go back to being 11 years old?" "Only if it is the will of The Jade Goddess. I think that she would let you change back long enough to talk with your parents or friends. I doubt that you will want to go back to being a young girl, once you discover how much fun adults have." Mary replied, "You're right. I would only want to be young so that I could experience the holidays with my parents and friends. Make me 21 now." The High One dug around in his backpack and pulled out a jogging suit.

He said, "I don't know how big you will turn out exactly. These clothes will allow for that uncertainty. He instructed Mary, "Slip into the darkness and remove all your clothes. Come back wrapped in the blanket and carrying the bigger clothes." Mary did as she was told and returned to the campfire wearing the blanket and carrying the jogging outfit. The High One tossed some magical dust into the fire and it flashed brilliantly with an intense jade color. He raised his hands and chanted fervently. Mary felt a tingling throughout her body and she radiated the jade color of the fire. It was more than just a reflection. She was glowing from within. She knew that she was taller. The High One told her, "You must go into the darkness now and put on the new clothes." She did as he said and returned to the fireside a few minutes later. The jade glowing of her skin had gone away.

The High One said, "I will pour water into my frying pan, so that you can see your face. It is more beautiful than any woman's I have seen." He poured the water, and she looked for a long time at her reflection. The High One volunteered, "You must be 5 feet and 10 inches tall. You are still slender, but you have the shape of a mature woman. How do you feel?" Mary responded, "I feel different. It wasn't painful changing, but it is hard to get used to. I feel huge, like a giant." The High One replied, "That will go away soon. Walk around for a few minutes. You need to get used to the longer legs." Mary walked around the fire and tested her new body. She leaped, jumped and ran. It was fun being so different. Finally she tired and sat down before the fire. The High One told her, "Tomorrow you must go back to your grandfather and explain that you are leaving for Las Vegas. Do you plan to tell your parents about your plans?" Mary sighed and spoke, "I don't think they would be happy if they knew. I will let them think that I am still with my grandfather for as long as I can get away with it.

Chapter Three

Las Vegas

Mary went with the High One to say goodbye to her grandfather. She changed back to an eleven year old for the occasion. Her grandfather went to the neighbors and retrieved Joque the parrot. They had been keeping him for the medicine man. Mary told her grandfather, "I'll be going with the High One for a short while to Las Vegas. Do you know where we can get a car?" Cloud of Thunder replied, "I think your father would give you a car if he knows that you need one." Mary remarked, "I would like to keep from worrying my mom and dad. I would appreciate it if you didn't tell them that I've left. I'll be back in less than a week. I can explain it all to them when I get back." Cloud of Thunder sighed, "Very well then. I don't completely approve, but I can help you find a car. The owner of the store just as you get into town will probably rent his truck to you. He'll do almost anything to make a dollar." Mary replied, "We'll go talk to him right away." Cloud of Thunder nodded his approval. The High One and Mary walked the short distance to the store and rented an old red 1968 Chevy pick-up truck. Mary used her credit card to pay the $200.00 for seven days of rental. The store keeper filled the truck with gas and checked the oil. Soon, the High One was driving them to Las Vegas.

On the way there, they pulled off the road for a moment, and Mary turned back into a 21 year old woman. It was easier now that she was initiated into the ways of changing. She just called on the Jade Goddess to help her. The High One stood behind the truck while Mary changed into the bigger clothes. A slight green glowing light came from the truck when she made her change. Luckily there was no traffic out there in the desert. They arrived the next day in Las Vegas. Mary took the High One shopping, and they both bought appropriate clothing for the task of gambling in the casinos. Then they ate at a restaurant and rented a room for the night. Mary told the High One, "We will need to be rested. I want to win big at every casino in just one day. If we spend too long winning our money, the word will get out that I have special powers. The casinos won't let us play anymore once they get wise to us." The High One replied, "You are thinking of all the angles. The Jade Goddess will be proud of you." They bought a deck of cards and played some black jack for a couple hours. Then they slept in the two beds that were in their room. Mary had purchased flannel pajamas for both of them. She wanted to keep her appearance modest so that she wouldn't tempt the High One with her new found beauty.

As soon as the sun came up, they ate breakfast and then headed for the first casino. Mary instructed the High One, "I will write the winning number each time we are ready to win. I will pass the number to you. If I don't give you a number, just bet small and lose. That will make it take longer for them to get suspicious. I have $400 that I took out of the credit card. Whenever I give you a winning number, bet all our money. When I poke you in the back, go cash in your chips and give the money to me. I will give you a couple hundred to play black jack with, while I go back to the roulette table and win more money. When you see me leave, wait for ten minutes and then leave also. I will wait for you in the truck." The High One replied, "I will do exactly as you say."

The High One started by betting $20.00 on a losing number. Then he did it four more times. He was down to $300.00. Mary passed him the number 10. He bet $300.00 on 10 and won $300.00. He now had $600.00. After about an hour of gambling, the High One had won $100,000.00. He cashed in his chips and gave the money to Mary. As he had been instructed, he went to the black jack table and played while Mary made some more money. In about an hour, she walked away with a cool million dollars. She cashed in her chips and went to the truck. She felt secure with Herb there. He would protect the money and her. Joque was in the back of the truck. He knew what was going on and squawked, "I could buy a new ship with all that money." Mary told him to keep quiet. She whispered to him, "I will buy you a nice ship. We will be doing some treasure hunting soon. I know you'll like that." Joque chirped softly, "Ah, this will be just like the good old days." The High One emerged from the casino and they drove to the next casino. They used the same method of operation at that casino. In a couple of hours they left with well over 10 million dollars. By the end of the day they had been to 10 casinos and had 200 million dollars. They went to the nearest bank and opened a savings and checking account. They had to put it all in the High One's name, since Mary was still on the books as being an eleven year old girl.

The next day Mary had the High One buy her a set of identification cards that said she was 21 years old. Then she transferred the money into a new account in her name. They bought some investment newspapers and went back to the motel. Mary spread the papers out on the bed and called on the Jade Goddess to help her find the best high risk investment. The Goddess guided her to pick an oil pipeline stock that was available from China. Mary took the High One to a stock broker and they placed all but one million dollars into the pipeline stock. That made a 199 million dollar investment. Mary called on the Jade Goddess to help her decide where to buy a boat. The Goddess told her, "Mary, I long to smoke with you again. It is good that you are doing so well. I think you will find the best boat in New Buffalo Michigan. On Saturday morning of March 6th, you will see a young man and his girl friend buying boats. They have the desire to fish and love treasure hunting too. I think you will enjoy their company. They are currently fishing in Alaska. You can meet them this coming Saturday when they go to New Buffalo to buy two 40 ft. boats. The boy's name is Bob and his girlfriend's name is Ellen. They are both 18 years old. They will have Bob and Ellen's fathers with them. Their parents let them do what they want to do. It will be easy to talk them into treasure hunting with you. I am watching them start their fishing trip even as we speak. Why don't I let you watch in on them with me? I can let you tune in on them throughout this week, so that you are assured that things are going according to plan." Mary exclaimed, "I would like to watch them. Let me see what they are doing now." She sat in a chair and closed her eyes. She could see a boy and girl fishing at night for salmon. There was a white gas lantern glowing in the darkness. The sound of the rushing river was in her ears. Mary watched, off and on, for several days and managed to piece together the whole fishing trip that Bob and Ellen were taking. This is how it pieced together.

Chapter Four

Alaskan Fishing

Two teenagers named Bob Ellis and Ellen Morris, were night fishing on one of the best salmon fishing rivers of the Kenai Peninsula, in Alaska. They were on the north bank of the Kenai River, fishing with night crawlers and 30 pound tackle. Bob said, "We've already fished the Kasilof River, the Ninilchick River, Deep Creek and Crooked Creek; with only 30 pound salmon to show for our troubles. Now I want something big. I need a 50 pounder. We were told this is the best river. Where are the king salmon I've been hearing about?" Ellen said, "I've been having a great time. Those 30 pounders were a challenge. They fought hard. Don't forget to enjoy the scenery and the experience of being in the wilds. Your manhood won't fall off if you don't get a 50 pounder. Remember, the record is over 97 pounds for a king salmon. I suppose next you'll be wanting one that big." Bob said, "I want one bigger. I want to set the world record for a king salmon catch." Ellen said, "I hope you achieve your dream, but could we be a little quieter. I think the salmon may be able to hear us." Bob whispered, "You may be right. Do you think we should have brought the guide with us? They always help you get more fish." Ellen whispered, "We can use the guide tomorrow for our afternoon fishing. I like the chance to be with you at night, alone." She reached over and squeezed his hand gently. He smiled and gave her a hug. He said, "I'm glad we can be together too. I'm sure our dads are enjoying Crooked Creek these few extra days. They liked it so much that they wanted to stay a couple more days. It was nice of them to trust us to come on ahead to the Kenai River without them. I like moving every day or two. They liked the remote setting on Crooked Creek. Sending us ahead, gives them a chance to talk about the good old days when they were young. They love to talk around the camp fire."

Bob pumped up the white gas lantern that was starting to grow a little dim. It glowed brightly now and lit up their faces clearly. Ellen's short red hair, freckles, and green eyes were clearly visible. Bob didn't mind that she was flat chested. Her face was exceedingly cute. She had a short up turned nose and a small delicate chin. She was graceful and thin, but had strength in her lithe arms and legs. She looked for a moment at Bob's face, with his short blond hair and hazel colored eyes. He had bushy eye brows and a handsome thin nose. His ears stuck out just a little bit. She thought he was a handsome young man. Ellen whispered, "Remember when we first met? It was two years ago, when we were only 14 years old. You were launching your 14 foot aluminum fishing boat at the Wawasee Lake boat launch with your dad. Bob whispered, "Yes, you and your dad were launching his boat. I helped you and your dad with your boat so that I could get mine in faster. Then I got talking to you a little, and realized that you loved fishing almost as much as I did. We fished together that day, and we've been doing it ever since."

Ellen Whispered, "At first I thought you were crazy when you told me you were investing $30,000 on the stock market. I still can't believe that your dad trusted you with that much money." Bob whispered, "He could see that I was making money on paper, so why shouldn't I actually invest. I bought into new bottled water companies just as they were catching on. Of course I bought on leverage, which increased my earnings ten fold." Ellen whispered, "I don't understand all that. I'm just glad that you have enough money to take us on fishing trips like this one. I hope that you put most of that money in secure investments now. It would be a pity to lose most of it by speculating too much." Bob whispered, "For not understanding, you have good horse sense. I have precious metals holdings now and United States Savings Bonds. You can't get more secure than that." Ellen sighed a big sigh of relief. "You are truly gifted when it comes to money. Some people get addicted to trading stocks all the time and loose their shirts on all the brokers' fees and stock losses," whispered Ellen.

Ellen's rod dipped suddenly. She jerked up on it and set the hook. "It must be a king!" she said aloud. "Help me hold the rod, will you." Bob grabbed onto her rod and helped her hold onto it. The salmon threatened to jerk it out of both of their hands. "It must be a monster!" yelled Bob. Ellen said, "Try to keep quiet, or we won't get any more fish tonight." They held on, as Ellen cranked on the large capacity open faced reel. The drag sang out as line was being stripped from the spool. "Tighten the drag," said Bob. Ellen fumbled for the drag in the poor light. Bob let go of the rod and went to get the lantern. Ellen was pulled to the water's edge. One foot went into the water. She was glad it was the fourth of July and things were at least a little warm in Alaska.

The cold water stimulated her adrenalin. She found new resolve and pulled back hard enough to get herself back onto the shore, away from the water's edge. Bob held the lantern and she tightened the drag. She cranked vigorously and pumped the rod up and down like a pro. She pulled up to the 12:00 o'clock position, and then cranked rapidly back down to the 3:00 o'clock position. Over and over she repeated the process. Sometimes the line would come to a stand still. At other times the fish would take out more and more line, as though it would never stop. The sweat was dripping off her chin and running down her chest. Bob started wiping her chin with his handkerchief. He wiped her chest as well. Ellen said, "There's nothing there, if you're looking for something." Then she laughed. Bob said, "I wasn't trying to get fresh. I'm just trying to be helpful." Ellen said, "Could you pour some soda in my mouth, I'm getting thirsty." Bob went to their small cooler and took out a coke. He held it to her lips and she drank as best she could. Most of the coke went all over her face and on her chest. Bob started wiping off her chest. Ellen said, "I guess I'll just have to get used to you doing that. If you like it, I don't mind. It doesn't thrill me though." Bob said, "Stop accusing me of going for your chest. I'm a complete gentleman." Ellen said, "Yeah, sure sure. Hold onto me so this fish doesn't pull me back into the water." Bob stepped behind her and held onto her waist. He liked the feel of her firm muscles rippling under his grip.

Ellen felt more secure with Bob's big strong hands holding her. She reeled more forcefully than ever. Her whole body writhed with exertion. She was getting more and more line back onto the spool. Finally the big salmon jumped out of the water only 50 yards from the bank. Ellen gave it all she had and brought it in close to shore. Bob got the net and netted it for her. He had to strain to get it up on the bank. He said, "It must weigh around 50 pounds. How will we carry it back?" The king salmon's silvery sides glittered in the light of the lantern. Its blue gray back blended in with the dark grassy bank. They could just make out the small funny shaped spots on the back and dorsal fin that helped them to know that this was a king salmon. Bob said, "It has to be a king if it's this big." Ellen said, "I never could have gotten it to shore without your help." She stepped over to him and hugged him. They kissed for a few moments.

Ellen said, "Let's leave the equipment here and carry the fish back to camp." Bob said, "Aren't you forgetting that I'm a rich man. We'll take the equipment back to camp, and send the guide out to get the fish. He'll want to clean it and freeze it for us, anyway." Ellen said, "Won't they think we are rich brats if we do that?" Bob said, "Right, let's carry the fish back. I can't clean a fish this big though. I wouldn't know where to begin." Ellen said, "You can wake the guide. John will be glad to clean if for us. He will respect the effort we went to, carrying this big thing all the way back." Bob gutted the fish to make it lighter. They took turns carrying it, till they had hiked the half mile back to camp.

John Walther was in his cabin sleeping when the knock came at the door. He opened it to see that Bob and Ellen were standing there holding the giant salmon. He said, "That's a wonderful fish. I'll get dressed and clean it for you. Take it to the cleaning station. I'll be right there." Bob and Ellen carried the salmon to the cleaning station. In a few minutes John arrived carrying his large 12 inch fillet knife. He weighed the fish with the scales that hung from the roof of the fish cleaning station. John said, "This thing weighs 52 pounds. It's a nice fish, even for the Kenai River. Who caught it?" Bob said, "Ellen did." Ellen said, "I never could have landed it without Bob's help." John deftly slit behind the salmon's head. Next he cut above the top of the rib cage. He slid the blade along the spinal column and parted the fish in half. Next he did the same thing to the other side of the fish. With uncanny skill he slipped the knife along the skin side of each fillet and parted the skin from the meat. He took the meat and placed it in a plastic bag. "I'll put the meat in the freezer for you," he said. He walked over to the freezer shed and disappeared inside.

Bob led the way back to the cabin they had rented along the river. They could hear the water rippling by as they stepped inside the large log structure. Bob turned on the light and lit a fire in the pot bellied stove. Then he rolled his sleeping bag out on his single bed. Ellen rolled her sleeping bag out on the floor. She said, "My bag is made for two people. I like lots of room. They took turns showering and dressing for bed in the bathroom. It was the only private area in the cabin. The rest of it was one open room. They crawled into their sleeping bags and went to sleep.

Ellen woke first the next morning. She went to the refrigerator and got out what she needed to cook bacon and eggs with pancakes. She knew they would need a good breakfast to give them the energy they would need for a big day of fishing. It was actually about noon. They had slept late, after the long night of fishing on the river. John Walther, their guide, would take them out in the boat later in the afternoon. Ellen thought that John was an unusual man. He was about 35 years old and was quite overweight. He had long sandy brown hair and a mustache. There was a large mole on his right cheek, just an inch across from his mouth. Ellen woke up Bob, and by getting real close to his face and rubbing noses with him. He woke with a start to see her so close. She said, "I've got breakfast ready." He said, "Great, I'm hungry." They ate a nice large breakfast with plenty of hot Folgers instant coffee.

They went to the boat house and watched John getting the boat ready for their fishing trip. He was gassing up the boat with five gallon cans of gas which had to be flown in regularly from Anchorage. He said, "This is why fishing costs a considerable amount here. Everything needs to be flown in. Milk, flour, meat, propane; you name it. It all comes by plane." Bob said, "That gives plenty of pilots jobs." John said, "That's true." John said, "If you're both rested enough, we could leave in about an hour. I need to eat and finish gassing up the boat." Bob said, "That sounds good to me. Ellen and I will walk the beach till you're ready to go." Ellen said, "That does sound good. I love walking along the water's edge." John said, "I'll give the dinner bell a single clang when I'm ready."

The couple walked slowly along the beach holding hands. Ellen said, "I hope you catch a nice big king salmon today." Bob said, "I'm sure we'll catch plenty of nice fish. John's one of the best guides around. The brochure said there is a 100% success rate." Ellen said, "That does sound like the fishing is always good here." She gently squeezed his hand. They stopped and looked out across the water to the east. There was a gentle breeze blowing against their backs. Ellen had on some low cut wrangler jeans and a short top. Bob glanced approvingly at her attractive navel and exposed waist. He said, "You sure are in good shape, Ellen." She said, "It's nice of you to notice. I don't over eat and I get plenty of exercise. Of course they say it's easier to stay in shape when you're young. The faster metabolism eats up calories quickly." Bob said, "I don't want to get fat like my father. He can't move around like he used to. His feet are always sore. At least he still likes to fish with me." Ellen said, "Your father does pretty well for 55 years old. My father is only 40, and he's starting to slow down already. He makes mom mow the yard. It used to be fun for him. I think he's aging prematurely." Bob said, "Your dad isn't in that bad of shape. He doesn't get winded playing golf. He and I played 18 holes at Three Oaks. There are lots of hills there and we walked it." Ellen said, "I guess he just doesn't like mowing the yard."

Suddenly they heard the dinner bell ring sharply one time only. Bob said, "It's time to go fishing." Ellen said, "Excellent. I'm ready to go." They turned and ran to the boat garage. John was loading the cooler and the bait. Bob said, "What are we using for bait?" John said, "We'll be using cut herring with flashers on downriggers." Ellen said, "That's all Greek to me." John said, "The cut herring is bait, cut so they give off more scent. The flasher is just an orange or chartreuse board that spins and flashes its color to get the salmon's attention and bring them close enough to be attracted by the herring. The downriggers are rods that hold a weight on a cable. The fishing line is clipped to the weight so that is releases when the fish takes the bait. I can use six to eight downriggers at a time. They hold the bait at various depths and maximize our chance of catching fish." Ellen said, "That helps some. I'll just keep my eyes open and see what you're doing." John said, "I'll point out the downriggers as we deploy them. You will be able to see how the lines are attached."

They all got into the boat and headed out for deep water. John said, "I usually fish in about 200 feet of water. I set the downriggers at 75 feet, 95 feet, 120 feet and 170 feet. That gives me a wide range of depths from which to catch fish." In about 20 minutes they were at the right depth. Many fish were showing up on the electronic fish finder. Ellen watched closely as John baited the hooks and fastened the lines to the heavy cannon ball weights. John said, "Each cannon ball weighs 4 pounds. That is enough weight to keep the cable fairly straight up and down, even when we are moving at about 1 ½ to 2 miles per hour. When you hook a fish I will need to keep the boat moving, or all the baits will sink and get tangled."

He started the boat moving at trolling speed and asked Bob to steer the boat while he positioned the rest of the baits and lines. John then said to Bob, "One of you can take the first fish. Watch all the poles. When one of the tips dips down suddenly, grab the pole and set the hook." Ellen said, "Since I caught the fish last night, why don't you start the fishing today, Bob." Bob said, "Since you insist. I will. You can help me watch the poles." Together they watched the eight poles that were in use. In about 20 minutes, one of the poles dipped dramatically. Bob grabbed the pole and jerked back on the rod twice. He said, "Now the fun begins." Ellen said, "Hold on tight, Bob." He pointed the rod at the fish for awhile, and just let it work against the drag. He didn't want to break the rod. Finally, when the fish had taken about 500 yards of line out, he raised the rod high to the 12:00 o'clock position. The rod bent down and pointed towards the fish. Bob tightened the drag, and started pumping the rod and cranking in line, little by little. Sometimes he would lose line to the fish. He cranked and cranked. Ellen watched with admiration as Bob's arm muscles bulged under the strain of pulling the rod. She moved behind him and massaged his shoulders as he cranked the rod. Bob liked the feel of her touch. He tried to concentrate on the fishing. Bob said, "We'd better stop the boat. I'll never get this one in with the boat moving away." John said, "I was just getting ready to do that. You may have a record holder on the line. If you want to claim a record, you will have to net the fish yourself." Bob said, "I will try then. I would love to be in the record books."

John stopped the boat and said, "Ellen, if you touch his fishing rod, it disqualifies him. She stepped back and said, "I'd better just stay back. I don't want to make him miss winning a record." Bob kept up pressure on the fish. He cranked harder and harder. He was determined to get this fish. The salmon jumped about 100 yards from the boat. Bob reeled in the loose line and kept it tight. In about another 10 minutes, he had the fish along side of the boat. While still holding onto the rod, he netted the huge king salmon. He set aside the pole and put all his effort into lifting the great fish into the boat. Every muscle of his body was strained to the limit. Finally the fish came over the side and landed on the deck. They weighed the salmon on a scales that John had mounted to a boom. The fish weighed 102 pounds. It was a new world record. John took a picture of the fish on the scales with Bob beside it. Bob was so happy he couldn't contain himself. He hugged Ellen and kissed her on the mouth. He jumped up and down and yelled, "Hurra-a-a-a-ay! I did it." Ellen threw her arms around him and kissed him some more. She said, "This is wonderful. Let's fish all summer."

They took turns bringing in big salmon, although they weren't as big as the first one that Bob had caught. The other salmon averaged around 20 pounds each. There was one other king that Ellen caught, which weighed 55 pounds and the rest were sockeye salmon. John said, "Tomorrow you might like to catch some halibut. They are even heavier than king salmon. 100 pounders are common here and they go up to around 200 pounds. You can catch 2 halibut per day. The limit is one per day on king salmon and up to six per day for sockeye salmon." Bob said, "I think it would be nice to catch some halibut." Ellen said, "I agree. Tomorrow we could also catch another king salmon or two." John said, "That would be fine. You might want to release some of the fish. You probably won't want to eat that many salmon." Bob said, "I think it would be good to release some of the fish. We don't want to be hogs and deplete the supply here." Ellen said, "Yes, I like conservation. We can release all the fish that we catch from now on." John said, "If you want to, we can ship some of the fish to anchorage for use as food for the poor." Bob said, "That sounds like a good idea. We can send a couple hundred pounds of fish to Anchorage." John poured them some hot coffee he had brought along and they headed back to camp.

When they returned to the camp, John put the 102 pound salmon in the freezer. He said, "If you want to, you can have the fish mounted. We can ship it to a taxidermist of your choice near your home, or you can have it mounted in Anchorage. A fish this big would cost a little over $500.00 to mount." Bob said, "I think I would like to have it mounted. It would look nice over my dad's fireplace. I can have it over the fireplace at my own house when I get one." Ellen said, "It would be nice to be able to show it to people. Pictures are nice, but you can't beat a nice stuffed fish, especially when it is a world record." Bob said, "You aren't making fun of me are you?" Ellen said, "I'm serious about how nice it would be to keep the fish. I have to admit that I don't get overly excited about stuffed fish. You can't beat the real thing." Bob said, "I guess I understand. I'm excited about a stuffed fish. I'm going to have a replica made for my dad to keep and I'll keep the original for my room." Ellen said, "That sounds good, now let's go get some supper." John said, "We're having barbequed ribs at the main lodge tonight. You might as well eat with the rest of us." Bob said, "I love ribs. How about you, Ellen?" Ellen said, "That sounds good to me. We need to get cleaned up first. I'm all sweaty." Bob asked, "What time is supper?" John said, "It'll be ready by 7:00 o'clock." Bob said, "We'll be there." Ellen smiled and they walked back to their cabin.

Ellen watched Bob take off his boots and socks. She said, "You really worked hard on that fish. You'd better eat some salt or you could develop muscle cramps." Bob said, "I guess I will eat a little salt." He went to the kitchen counter and poured a teaspoon of salt into his palm. He licked it up and made a funny face. He said, "That tastes terrible." Ellen said, "Take off your shirt and belt. I'll give you a back rub." Bob did as she suggested and laid on one of the single beds. Ellen rubbed his muscles for him. She was dedicated to her work and didn't stop until she had given him a good soothing massage. He sighed occasionally. Ellen said, "I like giving you a back rub. Your skin feels so warm and soft." Bob said, "Your hands feel nice and soft. You can give me a back rub every night. I'll give you one too. We won't have enough time now. I'll give it to you after we eat." They left the cabin and went to the large building where meals were served. It was made of logs too. They stepped inside and looked around.

John was already at the table with some other fishermen. They were digging in on large piles of barbequed ribs. Bob and Ellen went to the kitchen window and selected their food from the counter that stuck out from the large opening in the kitchen wall. There was soda and mashed potatoes, tossed salad. It all looked good. They heaped up plenty of ribs and poured themselves some Folgers instant coffee. Bob led the way as they walked over to the table with the other fishermen. John introduced Bob and Ellen to the four men he was sitting with. They all shook Bob's hand to congratulate him on his record catch. The men only gave their first names. From left to right they were Bill, Tom, Joe and Phil. They were all together as a business group from Buffalo, Michigan. Bill said, "I'm the president and CEO of Buffalo Marina Inc. I recondition boats and provide storage. Tom is my vice president, Joe is the company treasurer and Phil is the office manager. We come here every year. Is this you're first time here?" Bob said, "Yes, this is the first time here." Tom said, "Are your parents here too?" Bob said, "Our fathers are fishing on Crooked Creek for a couple of days. Then they will join us." Phil said, "That was an incredible fish that you caught. Your picture will be in the paper tomorrow in Anchorage." Bob said, "That's nice. I like being in the paper."

Bob said, "I can't wait to tell my friends in Indiana." Tom said, "So you're from Indiana. What part?" Bob said, "We're from Goshen. It's in the northern part of the state. Elkhart County." Tom said, "I'm familiar with that area. It's a nice place to visit. There are lots of lakes around there. The fishing is pretty good on Wawasee isn't it?" Bob said, "We do well there. The bass are big and hungry. We like fishing for pike. The bluegill are plentiful as well." Bill said, "What do you do when you aren't fishing?" Bob said, "I do investing in the stock market. I've made enough to retire already. We plan on traveling and fishing indefinitely." John said, "Be sure to come back here often. We can always fit you in. We'll put up a tent if we have to." Bob said, "That sounds good. We'll be back often. You've taken good care of us. We like the cabins. Why don't you reserve that same cabin for us next year on the fourth of July? It'll bring back fond memories." John said, "Consider it done. You don't need to make a deposit. I know you'll come."

Bill said, "How did you make so much money so quickly?" Bob said, "Lots of people ask me that. I invested in newly started bottled water companies. It was part luck and part studying the market on my part. I'm in precious metals and United States Savings Bonds now. I am mainly interested in maintaining my current wealth. I'm not taking many risks." Bill said, "It sounds like you're playing it safe now. Where did you get the money to play the market?" Bob said, "My father let me have $30,000. He has great faith in my abilities." Bill said, "He sounds like a smart man. You made him rich." Bob said, "He gave me half the money. He is very generous." Bob said, "It sounds like he was fair with you. I'd like you to help me invest a couple million that I have that is liquid." Bob said, "I can give you free advice. The market is going to drop even lower or at least not climb. Keep your money in gold or C.D.s until you start to see market improvement. It will probably be in 2003, two years from now. People are afraid to invest now, but the government is spending to stimulate the economy. Things will start to improve dramatically. Then research the mutual fund market, and find the one with the best record for the last 10 years and for the life of the fund. You should put your money in that and leave it there for at least 10 years. You should get a nice percentage return for your money that way."

Bill said, "Thanks. It sounds like you know what you're doing. I think I'll take your advice. I might even liquidate some of my other holdings and put them in C.Ds and gold." Bob said, "I'm sure of what I'm saying, but remember that all investments are at your own risk. Don't get upset if you lose money. It's only money." Bill said, "I know. I won't blame you. It's my own decision in the final analysis. Ellen said, "I sure am tired of talking about money. It's nice to have, but let's not over do it." Bill said, "I'm sorry. It's not every day that I meet people so young who have earned a fortune. I like learning from other smart people. Would both of you like to play some poker. We could just play for small stakes." Bob said, "I like poker. I usually only play for pennies." Bill said, "That's fine with me. We may not have enough pennies. We can use beans and macaroni too." They all started playing poker. The evening flew by, but they stopped for a moment to watch the sunset. As the sun dropped into the horizon full of pine trees, the rays of light reflected off the few clouds that were in the west. Colors of deep purple and orange glowed from the clouds and sky. The light tinted everything in sight. The buildings and trees glowed with the orange hue of the sun. A black bear casually walked through the camp, as though he belonged there more than they did. John said, "We don't need to worry about the bears. They're just curious. We don't leave any food around, so they soon leave. They went back to playing cards and sharing fishing stories.

Ellen started to get tired. She yawned and stretched her arms. Bob said, "Ellen, if you're tired we can go back to the cabin and get some sleep." Ellen said, "That sounds good to me." They shook everyone's hands and walked back to the cabin. Ellen asked, "Can I have my back rub now?" Bob said, "I thought you were tired." Ellen said, "I'm not too tired for a back rub. They stepped into the cabin and turned on the light. Bob started a fire in the wood stove and left the door open so the light would shine out around the cabin. Ellen shut off the room light and lay on her sleeping bag in front of the stove. Bob rubbed her back firmly. He rolled his knuckles into her tight muscles. Then he rapidly did a chopping action with his open hands. She liked that. She said, "Keep it up, Bob. You do great work." Finally he rubbed his palms in circular motions over her entire back. Ellen asked, "Do you think we are too young to fall in love?" Bob said, "I think I am in love. We are going steady, aren't we?" Ellen said, "You never asked me officially. It's just that we never date anyone else." Bob said, "Will you be my steady girl friend, Ellen?" Ellen said, "That's nice, Bob. I'll be your steady girl. What does it mean to go steady though?" Bob said, "To me it means that I'm in love, and I don't want you to date any other guy." Ellen said, "I'm in love too. I like being with you all the time. This summer has been great." Ellen turned onto her side, and Bob leaned down and kissed her briefly on the lips. Then he said, "We'd better get some sleep. There is another big day of fishing ahead of us." Ellen said, "I know. I get the bathroom first." Bob said, "That's fine." He watched the fire as Ellen showered and got ready for bed. She came out and crawled into her sleeping bag. Bob showered and then came out and got into his bag. They fell asleep quickly.

Ellen woke first again in the morning. She made some ham and eggs with orange juice, and then woke Bob up with her usual rubbing of her nose on his. He woke gradually. She kissed him on the lips a long but gentle kiss. He woke up completely, and said, "What was that for?" Ellen said, "You were such a gentleman last night. I know for sure I can trust you not to push me too far. I have decided to kiss you more. After all, we are going steady now." Bob said, "I agree. Kissing shouldn't be a problem. It just means that we like each other a lot. It doesn't mean we are getting ready to 'do it'." Ellen said, "Exactly. We aren't working up to 'doing it'. We are just showing affection." Bob got out of his sleeping bag and joined Ellen for breakfast. They had some nice strong Folgers instant coffee with the food. Bob especially liked the coffee, and had several cups of it. When they had finished breakfast, they got dressed and went to the boat garage.

John was loading the ice chest and bait onto the boat. Bob said, "Is there anything I can help you with?" John said, "If you want to, you can carry some of the cans of gas from the back of the boat garage and put them beside the boat. Let me fill it though. I know how to avoid any spills." Bob said, "I'd be glad to help." He carried four of the cans over to the back of the boat where John was getting the funnel ready. John said, "When did you say your fathers would be arriving?" Bob said, "They should be getting here this evening. They stayed at Crooked Creek another couple days, because the sockeye salmon were biting so well. They sent us ahead, since we were tired of sockeyes. I wanted something bigger." John said, "That's the way I am. I like the challenge of a nice big fish. Ellen, are you going to be able to reel in a 150 pound halibut if you hook one?" Ellen said, "I intend to try my best. I may need a little help pulling it up into the boat. I think that I can reel one in though. I don't want to try for a record. I'll appreciate a little help." John said, "That's good to know. We'll give you a hand landing your fish. We can leave as soon as I finish topping off the gas tank. We can use herring again today. It's a great bait and I have plenty of it." He finished filling the gas tank and then started the engine. The boat was a 31 foot cruiser that was completely white. It was obviously well cared for and clean. John backed the boat out of the garage. He turned the boat around and they headed out to the west for deep water.

When the depth gauge said 160 feet, John slowed the boat and then stopped. He baited the hooks and threw them directly off the boat. He said, "We'll just fish right off the edge of the boat for the halibut. They feed on the bottom. It shouldn't take long for us to hook on to our first one. You can both fish at once. If one of you gets a strike, the other should reel in the other bait so the lines don't get tangled." Ellen said, "I understand. Do we pump the rod like we did for the king salmon?" John said, "You don't have to, but most people do. It makes it a little easier." Ellen said, "I guess I'll pump it then."

The early morning sun was just coming up on the horizon. It made the water glitter with yellow as the top of the sun appeared to be coming out of the water in the east. Seagulls were following the boat and letting out their mournful cries. They were hungry and seemed to think the boat might lead them to fish they could eat. After about 10 minutes, Ellen got a strike. Her pole bent down towards the water. She jerked hard two times, to make sure the hook was set. She started cranking the reel and pumping the rod. It was a little more difficult pulling straight up with the rod. She wasn't making much progress. She said, "Am I doing something wrong. The fish isn't coming up." John said, "You are doing fine. I think that you have an extra big fish on. They take plenty of work to get them up off the bottom. Pace yourself and work steadily on that fish. We'll help you get it into the boat." Ellen said, "That sounds good. I'm still cranking." She rested a little after each time that she raised up the rod. It got harder to do each time. She said, "How long have I been doing this?" Bob said, "You've been fighting that fish for 20 minutes. Keep at it. You have that fish almost beaten."

She continued pulling up on the rod and then cranking it back down quickly. Finally the fish splashed to the surface. It was huge. John got the net and went for the head of the fish. It slipped into the net without too much trouble, but when he and Bob started pulling up the net, the fish fought and flopped around. It was quite difficult, but they finally managed to get the fish on the deck. John hooked it to his boom and weighed the halibut. It was as big as Ellen and weighed 150 pounds. Ellen was excited when she heard how heavy it was. She said, "That is a big fish. I want my picture taken with it. Bob, you can be in the picture too." They posed and John took several pictures of them with the giant halibut. The halibut was as long as Ellen was tall. It was wide in the middle and tapered down to the tail. Ellen said, "It's an unusual looking fish. It's kind of flat." John said, "They lie flat on the bottom and wait for food to swim by. Being flat helps them to hide." John put new bait on Ellen's hook and threw it in the water. The wind was picking up just a little. Small three foot waves were rocking the boat gently.

In about 30 minutes, Bob got a strike. He set the hook deeply, by jerking hard two times with the rod. He could feel the fish struggling against him as he tried to reel it in. He pumped the rod, pulling it up high and then quickly cranking in line as he lowered the rod rapidly. Bob repeated the process over and over. His muscles were still a little sore from the previous day's fishing. As he slowly got more and more line back onto the spool, his anticipation grew. He wondered how big this fish might be. Ellen said, "You've almost got him, Bob. Keep cranking." John said, "It must be a big one, judging from the way your pole is bending." At times the reel would sing as the fish pulled out more line and tried to get to the bottom again. It took Bob almost an hour before the fish came into view and splashed on the surface. John netted it, and Ellen helped him pull the enormous halibut onto the deck. John hooked the fish onto his weigh scales and hoisted the fish up with the boom. It weighed 175 pounds. John said, "We don't get too many that big. I have seen some that weighed over 200 pounds though." Bob said, "I'm happy with one this big. I can't catch a world record for every type of fish." Ellen said, "It's a wonderful fish. It will feed lots of people in Anchorage. She gave Bob a hug and they got their picture taken with the fish.

In about another two hours, they each had their limits of halibut. They each had two. The last two were a little over 100 pounds each. John said, "You can each catch another king salmon today if you'd like." Bob said, "That sounds good to me." Ellen said, "I still have a little strength left in me." John baited the hooks and set them out on the downriggers. It wasn't long until Bob had a strike. He fought the fish for 40 minutes and finally landed a nice 80 pound king salmon. Next, Ellen got a strike. It took her a little longer to fight her fish. It kept taking out more line. It was a real fighter. Soon though, they were netting her king salmon. It weighed 92 pounds. She was delighted with it. They had John take their pictures with the king salmon. Bob said, "This has been a good day of fishing.

Our dads are going to love this kind of fishing." Ellen said, "Yes, I know my dad will really enjoy this. Tomorrow, we can just watch them fish. It will be fun to sun ourselves on the flying bridge." Bob said, "It's almost warm enough for sun bathing." They watched the wind swept water as John steered the boat back to the camp.

When they arrived at the boat garage, they watched John clean the fish. When he was done, they helped him carry the meat to the freezer building. They let John take the meat into the building. It was very cold in there. John said, "In a couple days, there will be enough meat to make a shipment to Anchorage. We usually ship once a week." Ellen said, "I feel good about helping to feed people." John said, "People in nursing homes and other poor people need the food. I feel good about feeding them too."

Ellen said, "Why don't we do a little sun bathing right now. It is almost noon. We can sun for an hour before lunch." Bob said, "I'd rather wait till after lunch. It will be warmer then." Ellen said, "That's fine. What shall we do till lunch?" Bob said, "We can walk along the shore line." Ellen said, "Lead the way." She followed him down to the narrow beach. There wasn't a very wide expanse of beach. The tree line came almost down to the water's edge. They walked as close to the water as they could without getting wet. Bob took Ellen's hand, and they walked slowly, letting their hands swing gently between them. Bob said, "I never told you exactly how much I made on the stock market." Ellen said, "You don't have to tell me." Bob said, "I want to brag a little. I had six million dollars which I split with my dad." Ellen said, "That's a lot of money. What will you do with it?" Bob said, "I am giving ten percent of it to my church. You've been there with me. It's nondenominational. They help poor families and sponsor missionaries for work in over seas missions."

Ellen said, "That sounds good. What else will you do?" Bob said, "I want to buy a couple fishing boats like the one we fished on today. I want one for Lake Michigan, and one for Jamaica. I hear that the fishing in Jamaica is excellent. It is less expensive to keep a boat there than it is in Florida. I want a place where I can fish in the winter." Ellen said, "It sounds a little extravagant, but I guess you can afford it. I wish you would get a little longer boat though. That 31 footer has such a small bed room and toilet." Bob said, "They call the toilet on a boat the 'head'. We should call it that, or John will think we don't know anything about boats. I like your idea. A couple 40 foot boats would be nice. Will you come to Jamaica with me over Christmas break? We could have a great time on the boat." Ellen said, "We'd have to take our parents. I don't think they would want us living together that long alone." Bob said, "You're right. We'll take all of them along. I'm sure they'll be thoughtful enough to give us plenty of time alone together. We can all play card games in the boat's galley. You can help me pick out a nice boat when we get back to Indiana. They have a large selection of them at New Buffalo where those fishermen were from that we played poker with. We can talk to them at lunch about it, if they aren't out fishing. Ellen said, "That sounds good. They might give you a special rate since you're a fishing pal of theirs now." Bob said, "They probably will give me a good price. We won't let them know just how much money I have. We should keep that a secret." Ellen said, "I can keep my mouth shut." They walked a little farther and stopped to embrace. Ellen said, "It feels so good to hug you. We've been friends for a long time now. I feel closer to you every day." Bob said, "I'm getting used to having you around all the time. I like it." They kissed and then walked farther down the beach. After another ten minutes, they heard the dinner bell. They turned and ran back to the large building where meals were served.

They got their food and sat next to the four fishermen from New Buffalo. Bob said, "We each caught two nice halibut today and we caught a couple king salmon." Bill said, "That sounds like a busy morning. You should be hungry." Ellen said, "I could eat a horse." She ate some of the sweet potatoes and ham that she had on her plate. Bob said, "Do you have any 40 foot cruisers that are in excellent condition, something about 10 years old? Bob said, "We have a couple nice ones. I could let you have one for $50,000." Bob said, "Can you give me a lower price if I take two of them? Bob said, "Two? What will you do with two boats?" Bob said, "I'm going to take one to a winter location, in Jamaica." Bill said, "I can let you have them for $40,000 each. That's my bottom dollar." Bob said, "We'll have to take the boats out and test them of course, but I like you and I'd like to give you first chance at making the sale." Bill said, "I'll have the boats ready in about a week. Then you can take them both for a test run. They are in excellent shape. We just need to do a little cosmetic work on them. You can come over next Saturday if you like." Bob said, "That sounds good. Just draw me a map of how to get to the marina." Bill replied, "I'd be glad to. I'll do it right now." He picked up a napkin and drew the map for Bob. Bill said, "This should get you right to our main office. I'll be looking forward to seeing you there." Bob said, "This map looks clear enough. We'll be there around 10:00 o'clock in the morning, if that's fine with you." Bill said, "That will be fine."

Phil, the office manager, said, "Where will you be keeping the boats?" Bob said, "I'll keep one at Grand Haven, Michigan; and the other I will keep in Nigel, Jamaica. I've been studying Jamaica on the internet. It looks like Nigel has the best beach and some excellent sunsets to watch. It is also close to some very good fishing currents." Phil said, "It sounds like you've figured all the angles. I'll make sure that all the paper work is ready for you to sign when you arrive in New Buffalo." Bob said, "That will be great. What's your last name, Phil? Just in case I need to ask someone to find you." Phil said,

"Anderson, Phil Anderson. I'll be in my office Saturday. You can count on it."

Ellen spoke forcefully, "No more talk about business now. How did your group do fishing this morning, Phil?" Phil replied, "We all caught our limits, but there weren't any over 70 pounds." Bob said, "We were lucky enough to get some nice big ones. One of mine weighed 175 pounds." Phil replied, "That's a fish to be proud of. We're going to try for a couple more days. Possibly we can land some that big." Bob said, "I hope you do. There are plenty of big fish out there. That's for sure." Ellen said, "I caught one that weighed 92 pounds. It felt like it weighed a ton." Phil was a tall thin man with dark black hair and bushy eyebrows. His left eye drooped a little and looked tired. The right eye looked alert though. Phil was more interested in Bob and Ellen than the rest of the group. They were talking amongst themselves about business. Phil asked, "Which location will you go to first after you finish fishing here?" Bob said, "I think we'll go to Grand Haven, Michigan first. I want to get experience steering a big boat, in waters that are familiar to me before I go international. I'll take the boat there by water from New Buffalo. The boat for Jamaica, I'd like you to ship to Key West, Florida for me. I'll steer it to Jamaica from there. Please install a 300 gallon fuel tank in it for me, if it doesn't already have one. I don't want to worry about running out of fuel. I'll find someone who is a good navigator to come along with me on the trip. I don't know much about that yet. I'm going to start studying as soon as we get back to Indiana." Phil replied, "I'm sure you'll master it. I can recommend a navigator for you if you'd like." Bob answered, "That would be great. I'd prefer someone with a sense of humor." Phil said, "I'll see what I can do. I'll give you the man's name when you come to see the boats.

Bob finished the food on his plate, which was now cold. Ellen said, "Let's go back to the cabin for awhile and drink some coffee." She took him by the hand and pulled him toward the door. They walked slowly back to the cabin. Ellen said as they walked, "How can you be sure that you can trust those men?" Bob laughed and said, "I don't really trust anyone. I just work with them and keep my eyes open. They run a legitimate business. I'm sure they will treat us fairly." Ellen said, "Shouldn't we have a lawyer look over the paperwork?" Bob said, "My father will need to sign for me. I'm not old enough to enter into a legal contract on my own. If we like the boats, I'll ask him to go up the next day and sign the papers. You don't need a lawyer to buy a car. Why should we need one to buy a boat?" Ellen answered, "I guess you're right. I just didn't like Phil's black bushy eye brows. I thought he looked sinister." Bob laughed, "You can't judge someone because they have thick eyebrows. He was the nicest one of the group except for Bill. The others pretty much ignored us." Ellen said, "I suppose you're right."

They went inside the cabin and made some coffee. Ellen stated, "I want a better tan. Let's wear our swim suits while we fish this afternoon." Bob said, "You can. I think it's a little too cool for that." Ellen replied, "Then we can just sunbath on the beach for an hour or two. We don't need to go fishing till later this afternoon." Bob acquiesced, "It'll be nice to listen to the waves and watch you tan." They got into their suits and ran to the beach. Ellen spread out a beach towel and they put their heads on it. Their bodies were in the sand. It was a bit cool, but it felt good. Bob spread lotion on Ellen's whole body. He was careful not to miss any spots. As she lay on her back, he studied her pale skin. *She really does need some sun,* he thought. He gently rubbed more lotion onto her tummy. She smiled and said, "I'll give you just 10 years to stop that." He laughed and said, "You're in great shape, Ellen." He pushed his fingers into her stomach just enough to feel the firm resistance of her muscles. She said, "I try to keep in shape. I do sit ups most mornings. They help me wake up." Bob said, "So do I. It helps me get going in the morning." He thought, "She is so slender and firm. I really enjoy looking at her." He let his eyes scan her slowly from top to bottom. Her suit was a skimpy bikini. There wasn't much of her that was left to his imagination. He could feel himself getting a little in the mood for kissing. When he leaned over to kiss her, she scolded him for blocking the sun. He fell back onto his back and said, "Then you can kiss me. Your back will still be tanning while you do it." Ellen replied, "Someone might see us. We don't know when our fathers are coming." Bob said, "We'll hear their plane when they arrive." Grudgingly Ellen raised herself off the towel and leaned over him. To his surprise though, she became more enthusiastic than he had ever experienced her. She liked being with him there on the beach. She laid her leg gently across him and eagerly kissed his lips. He let his hands become familiar with her back side. They took turns French kissing each other. It went on for a long time. The beach seemed warmer than before.

Suddenly they heard the sound of Bob's father's voice, "It's good to see that you two are fighting against homosexuality. Don't be embarrassed. I like to encourage heterosexuality in youth." Ellen quickly rolled back off of Bob with a surprised look on her face. Her father was there too. John Morris, Ellen's dad, said, "I wondered if you were a healthy girl, Ellen. Now I know that you are rapidly growing up. Just remember to let Bob be on top some of the time." Ellen said, "I just didn't want him to block the sun. I'm trying to get a tan." They all laughed. Pete Ellis, Bob's dad said, "We decided to take a boat to get here. That's why you didn't hear us come in on a plane." Pete was a short overweight man, 55 years old and blond haired. John Morris was 40 years old and had red hair and freckles like his daughter. John was thin with green eyes. He said, "I'm glad we could get here in time to fish. How did you two do this morning? I mean fishing. I trust that you haven't both been here all day."

Bob said, "I caught a 175 pound halibut and Ellen caught one that weighed 92 pounds." Ellen shouted, "Bob caught a world record king salmon yesterday. It weighed 102 pounds!" Pete said, "That's wonderful. I'm proud of you, son." Pete shook Bob's hand. "John and I will go out this afternoon and see what kind of salmon we can catch. You can both come with us if you'd like to." Ellen said, "I'd like to go. I want to work on my tan some more." Bob said, "I'd like to go too. Maybe I can catch some more big salmon. We met some men from New Buffalo, Michigan who might sell me two 40 foot cruisers. They want $40,000 each for them. I said that I'd go look at them on Saturday." Pete said, "I can go with you. If you like the boats, I can sign the paperwork." Bob said, "That would be fine. We said we would be there at 10:00 o'clock in the morning." Pete said, "That sounds good. It won't be too far away. I used to walk the beach in New Buffalo when I was younger. It will be good to see the place again." John said, "I wouldn't mind going along myself. I've never been there before." Bob said, "We'd be glad to have you."

They all went to the boat garage and watched John Walther loading the boat. He said, "I can take you out in about 10 minutes. I just need to add a couple cans of gas." He gassed up the boat and said, "I'm all ready now. You can all climb aboard." They boarded the boat and John steered the boat out to deep water. They all took turns fishing. John and Pete caught bigger fish than they had ever caught before. Their king salmon both weighed in the 80s. Bob and Ellen caught king salmon that were in the 70s. They fished till the sun started to set and then watched as the orange and purple colors lit up the sky. The sun setting across the water was always a pleasant sight. The seagulls kept calling out until it was dark. Then the birds settled down on the beach and rested. The boat slowly pulled up to the boat garage. A light glowed on the inside and helped them see `where to take the boat.

John Walther cleaned the fish and put them in the freezer. Bob, Ellen and their fathers went to the cabin. They all washed their hands and went to the dining hall. Bob introduced John and Pete to the men from the company in New Buffalo. They talked boats for a short time and then talked fishing. They all filled up on the delicious meal of perch and home made bread with mashed potatoes and gravy. They all played cards for an hour or two, and then went back to the cabin. John and Pete took the single beds, and Bob and Ellen got the two sleeping bags on the floor. Bob put his sleeping bag close to Ellen's and went to sleep with his arm around her.

They fished for a couple more days and then flew back to Chicago. From there they drove to Goshen, Indiana, where Bob and his dad lived. John drove the car to Pete's house in a luxurious subdivision just north of College Avenue in the southern part of the city. It was 6:30 in the evening and the sun was starting to get low in the western sky. As they got out of the car, they watched the sky for awhile. Bob's mother, Judy, came out of the house to greet them. She gave Pete and Bob each a big hug. She was a thin blond haired woman of average height. Her blue eyes were strikingly blue. They glowed like diamonds. She was obviously delighted to have her men back home. They all stood in the yard and watched the sun set. Pete and Bob told her all about the fishing trip. Finally, after the sun had disappeared below the horizon. Only an orange and purple glow remained in the western sky.

John and Ellen said their goodbyes and drove back to their condo on the south end of Lake Wawasee. Ellen's mother, Sandy, was waiting for them when they got home. She gave them each a hug and a kiss when they came through the door that led into the condo. She asked all about the trip. Ellen said, "Bob is buying two 40 foot cruisers this Saturday in New Buffalo, Michigan." Sandy said, "What will he do with two boats?" Ellen said, "He will use one boat at Grand Haven for spring, summer and fall fishing. The other boat he will keep in Jamaica for winter fishing." Sandy said, "That sounds like fun." Ellen said, "Bob and I are officially going steady now. He asked me on the trip." Sandy said, "I'm happy for both of you. Are you going with Bob Saturday to buy the boats?" Ellen said, "Yes. His father is going along to sign the papers. Dad is going too. It will be fun."

Chapter Five

New Buffalo

Mary thought for awhile about all that she had seen happening in Alaska. Then she told the High One, "We need to rent a car and take the truck back to the store." The High one replied, "You can follow me with the rental car. I'll drive the truck." Mary said, "I'll need to tell my parents what I've done and where I'm going. I would also like to explain things to my friends. They will understand, I'm sure. Possibly they will come with me. I doubt that they can get permission to go with me. Whatever happens, we must get to New Buffalo in time to meet Bob and Ellen." They drove to a car rental place and rented a nice Lincoln Continental. Then they drove back to Mary's house. Her parents were a little shocked to find that she was 21 years old. Mary explained her new powers that the Jade Goddess had bestowed. She also explained the two hundred million dollars. Last of all she told her parents of her plan to search for pirate's gold with a young couple named Bob and Ellen.

Mary's parents were accustomed to using spiritual powers. They gave their consent to Mary's plans. They knew how strong the urges for money and adventure were. They only wanted Mary to be happy. Mary's father told her, "Just promise me that you will give adequate time to thinking about how to avoid an unpleasant afterlife.

I've given it plenty of thought. It's important. Promise me you'll do some thinking about it. I know you'll come up with a good plan." Mary responded, "I'll give it plenty of thought. I've already thought about it a little. Of course I haven't come up with a plan yet. I know that I'll have to do some sort of payment for all the favors the Jade Goddess is doing for me. She wants me to kill many people, so that I will find favor like she did." Her dad said, "That is typical of the Jade Goddess. It's logical, but it just isn't like you. I hope you can come up with something different. I know you'll do well. There's no need for us to dwell on it now. I hope you find plenty of pirate treasure. Do you need to leave right away?" Mary responded, "I want to talk to Marsha and Elenore before I leave for New Buffalo. I know they won't be allowed to go with me, but I want to explain to them in person what I'm doing."

Joseph nodded in agreement and Mary kissed both of her parents and then turned and headed for the car. As she walked away she could hear her mom talking to her dad, "She still looks quite a bit like she did as a little girl, only bigger." Mary smiled and got into the Lincoln. She led the High One with his truck to the store to return the truck to the store owner. When they arrived, the High One gave the keys back to the owner. He asked the shop keeper to sell them a thermos of hot Folgers instant coffee and a road atlas. He paid with a hundred dollar bill and said, "You can keep the change. I did well in Las Vegas this week." He turned and left with the thermos of coffee and atlas.

Mary drove first. She drove fast through the desert. She only stopped for gasoline and restrooms. The High One and Mary hadn't been far from home before. They eagerly watched the scenery as it went by. When they got to St. Louis, Mary let the High One drive. She was tired. They traded places in the car and Mary warned, "You'd better not go over the speed limit now. We're in a part of the country with more cars and probably more police." The High One retorted, "I certainly don't want a ticket." When Mary got to sleep the High One drove even faster than she had been driving. He thought to himself, "She will use her special powers if we get into trouble with the police." After about three hundred miles they passed a speed trap. It was night time and the red flashing light woke Mary. The High One exclaimed, "I'm afraid I was going about a hundred miles an hour when this police car started following us." Mary called on the Jade Goddess, "What shall I do? The police are after us." The Jade Goddess said, "You can't allow the police car to get close enough to you to get your license number or you will lose your license." Mary replied, "I don't have a license. What can I do?" The Jade Goddess commanded, "Imagine yourself on highway 80-90 and going the speed limit." Mary did as she was told. The High One held the steering wheel while she closed her eyes. Mary could see jade colored light glowing in her mind. After a few seconds she opened her eyes and they were driving on a different road and going the speed limit. They passed an interstate road marker that indicated they were traveling on interstate 80-90. Mary thanked the Jade Goddess and decided to go the speed limit. She didn't want every police car in the nation to start looking for a black Lincoln Continental.

When they got into the area around Chicago they started studying the road map. They were both tired from the long drive. They went on past Chicago one hundred and fifty miles and stopped near Middlebury, Indiana. They pulled into Middlebury to study the map better and see if anything was open. It was three o'clock in the morning and everything was closed. Mary exclaimed, "Look at the horse manure in this street. I thought this would be a more modern city." The High One exclaimed, "Things aren't always as they appear. This may be a farming community where horses are considered more economical than cars." They studied the atlas for a long time and decided what roads to take. Mary commented, "We should take one thirty-one up to twelve. We can follow twelve all the way to New Buffalo. I can drive the rest of the way. What day is today?" The High One answered, "Tomorrow is Saturday. We will need to get a few hours sleep and then wait at the boat sales place for Bob and Ellen." Mary got into the driver's seat and headed the car for New Buffalo. She casually mentioned to the High One, "How will we find the boat sales place?" The High One replied, "There may only be one boat sales place in town. Did you say there were several employees of the boat sales place on the fishing trip in Alaska?" Mary replied, "Yes, there were several of them." The High One responded, "It must be a big operation then. Just to be safe, you might want to ask the Jade Goddess." Mary retorted, "I've got to start working alone as much as I can. We can look around when we get there. If there appear to be several places that might be selling boats, then we may need to ask the Jade Goddess for help." The High One replied softly, "That is good logical thinking. You are doing well."

Mary saw the sign for U.S. 12 and turned left onto it. They were heading back to the west. In about one and a half hours they were in the town of New Buffalo. They drove to a nice hotel on the shore of Lake Michigan and got a room with a view of the lake. Mary asked to be called at eight in the morning. They both slept in their clothes. In the morning they had breakfast at the hotel and then asked the concierge about the local boat sales places. The concierge told them, "The only place that would have two 40 foot boats for sale on the same day would be the New Buffalo Marina Incorporated. It is just south of us, next to the Yacht Club." Mary thanked the concierge and led the High One to the car. They drove south until they found the marina. Mary got out and went in to talk to someone inside.

It was nine o'clock and only the president of the company had arrived. He greeted Mary and told her, "I'm Bill

Phillips. I can help you. My staff doesn't come in for another hour yet. We stay open late. Most boaters like the evening hours better than the morning. It's usually nicer weather in the afternoon and evening. What can I do for you?" Mary asked, "Do you have a couple nice 40 foot power boats for sale?" Bill looked surprised and exclaimed, "As a matter of fact, I have several nice 40 footers. My two nicest boats were sold this week. They're forty footers. I'd love to sell them to you, but I already promised them to a fine couple that I met fishing in Alaska this week. I can't break my verbal contract with them." Mary replied, "I wouldn't want you to do anything against your principles." Bill said, "My happy purchasers will be here at 10:00 to sign the papers. You can meet them if you'd like. They're wonderful people in their teens. Their names are Bob and Ellen. Bob made his money on the stock market." Mary exclaimed, "I'm in the stock market too. It's all a big gamble, but I'm managing to stay on top." Bill replied, "I don't want to be nosy, but do you mind if I know what type of investments you're making besides boats?" Mary responded, "No, I don't mind at all. I'm invested one hundred percent in a Chinese oil pipeline company. It promises to make me an exciting return on my investment." Bill sighed, "I wish I could catch a stock like that on its way up." Mary commented, "I only bought it two days ago. I'd say there is still plenty of time to get in at an opportune time." Bill smiled a pleasant smile at Mary, "Thanks for the tip. Will you help me make sure I get the right stock? Mary replied, "I can help you." Bill opened the door to his office and invited Mary in. He turned on the internet and went to his brokerage company. Mary typed in the name of the oil pipeline company for him. He sighed, "I just didn't want to get the wrong stock."

Mary asked, "Are you married, Bill?" He answered, "Yes, this is a picture of my wife, Janet." He pointed to the picture on his desk. Mary replied, "She's an attractive woman. After they had talked for quite awhile, Bill asked, "Would you like to see some 40 foot boats?" Mary responded, "Yes, I would like to see some." They walked out to the piers and looked at boats for about an hour. When they went back inside, Bob and Ellen were there. Bob's father was looking over the paperwork for the boat purchase. Bob called into the office, "We should take the boats for a cruise before we buy them dad." His dad responded, "You're right son. Let's go for a ride. Mary walked over to Bob and Ellen and spoke somewhat shyly, "My name's Mary Thresher, I'd love to go along. I'm thinking of buying a 40 foot boat too. I'd love to see how they handle." Ellen said, "We'd be glad to have you come along. I'm Ellen and this is Bob. Ellen introduced Mary to her father and to Bob's father. Then they all went for a cruise. Bill went along and piloted the boat. He showed them how it cornered and how it cruised at top speed. It had an impressive amount of power. Bob steered the boat for awhile. He smiled as he felt the power of the boat while he adjusted the throttle. He let Bill take the boat back to the dock. On the way back Bob exclaimed, "I love this boat. What is its name? Bill replied, "You can name it anything you want to." Bob thought for a minute. Mary sent a soft and gentle message to his mind. He said, "For some reason I want to name her the Jade Goddess One. And the other boat can be called the Jade Goddess Two." Bill said, "That's a different name for a boat. No one that I know of has ever used that." Bob exclaimed, "It just came to me. From where I don't know."

They went back to the marina and took the other boat out for a cruise. It performed well and looked nice. They cruised for about thirty minutes before they headed back for the marina. Mary told Bob, "I want to buy a boat to use for hunting pirate's gold in the Florida Keys." Bob exclaimed, "That sounds exciting. I've been mainly into fishing. If I knew where to look, I'd love to find some pirate's treasure." Mary responded, "I have some good information about exactly where to look. I don't find boats that interesting just in and of themselves. They are just a way of getting me to the treasure." Bob said, "Ellen and I could take you to the treasure in our boat." Mary exclaimed, "That would be excellent. Then, I could concentrate on finding the treasure. I could work with my maps while you and Ellen worry about taking care of the boat. We could split the treasure fifty-fifty." Ellen said, "That sounds fair. I just hope the government doesn't take all the treasure after we go to the trouble of finding it." Mary said, "They will probably want a good deal of the treasure. I'm not in this for the money. I'm more after the excitement. I would be happy with a couple handfuls of pieces of eight and a gold chain or two." Ellen replied, "That sounds good. We have plenty of money too. There isn't any point in getting greedy."

Bob exclaimed, "First of all I have to get my pilot's license and learn how to pilot the boat. Ellen should learn how to pilot the boat too." Ellen said, "I'd be glad to pilot the boat. That way we could make better time on long cruises. We could drive in shifts." Bob exclaimed, "Exactly. We could find treasure in no time at all." Mary said, "How long will it take you to get you pilot's license?" Bill said, "He should be able to get a pilots license in about a month. They have accelerated programs that you can enter. You can pay for a personal tutor if you want to." Bob replied, "That would be a good idea. I'll look into it today yet."

When they arrived at the marina, Bob's dad went in and signed the papers and paid for the boats. Afterwards they all went to the town pub and ate lunch. The High One joined them. Mary introduced him. "The High One is my personal trainer. He helps me mainly with spiritual matters." Mary went on, "We left New Mexico in a hurry and didn't have enough time to bring all our clothes. We both need to do some shopping." Ellen replied, "I'll help you shop for clothes. The men can stay here and talk boats." Bob exclaimed, "Don't be gone all day. If we aren't here, we'll be back at the boats." Ellen responded, "We can find you. Have a good time." The two love birds kissed and said goodbye.

The High One followed Mary and Ellen from shop to shop as Ellen coached Mary on what sorts of clothing would be popular in nautical settings. The High One also stocked up on clothes. When the clothing got too heavy they would go back to the car and put the clothes inside. They made sure that they locked the car and then returned to the stores to buy more clothing. Mary bought her own Lincoln Continental so that the High One would be able to take the rental car back to Las Vegas. She and Ellen got talking about where she would live. They agreed that she could stay on one of the boats with her and Bob. There was plenty of room on the boat and there were a couple extra bedrooms. When they found the men back at the boats, Ellen asked if she and Bob could let Mary stay with them on the boat. Pete said, "I trust you kids. I don't know Mary very well, but she seems nice enough. If any of you run into any trouble give us a call right away." Ellen's dad said, "I don't object. You can all learn to handle the boats." The girls moved their clothing onto the boat. Ellen told Bob, "You'll need to go home and pack your clothes. I'll go along so that I can get packed too. Mary can stay here on the boat and get to know the town a little better." Mary said, "Yes, go and get your things. I'll be fine here. The High One will drive back to New Mexico tomorrow morning. Will you both be back tomorrow sometime?" Bob responded, "I'm sure we'll be back in time for supper. We'll meet you at Jade Goddess One at close to six o'clock in the evening."

They talked some more as they spent the afternoon looking over the two boats. As the sun started to set, everyone sat on the deck and watched the sun go down. The sun's beautiful golden hue reflected off all the boats and the water. The scattering of clouds in the sky were colored in regal purple. After the sun was completely out of view Pete and Bob Ellis along with Ellen and John Morris headed back for Goshen and Syracuse. Mary stayed on the boat with the High One. Mary showed him his own bedroom. He showered in the roomy boat's shower and then went to bed early so that he could start early in the morning on his long trip back to New Mexico. Mary told the High One, "You must go to my house and have my father bring you back from Las Vegas when you return the rental car. My father will take you back to the mountain of the Jade Goddess." The High One replied, "I will do as you ask. It has been fun being with you. You should send me a message once and a while, or come to see me." Mary responded, "I will talk to you through the spirit world sometimes. I'm sure we can learn to talk to each other at great distances just like I talk to the Jade Goddess." The High One replied, "Don't call to me by name. Just say, 'Listen, my friend'. I will hear you. We will know each other by the sound of our voices. Possibly in this way we can speak in private without alerting the Jade Goddess. Why should she hear everything we say?" Mary said, "That's a good point. I would enjoy a little privacy once in a while." Mary went up on deck and let the High One get some sleep.

Mary went to the car and got Joque and Herb. She took them to the boat and showed them around. She spoke to Herb, "You'll need to stay invisible during the day. I'm sure they don't allow black panthers to roam around this town. Just stay on the boat and protect us. Joque, you must be starved." She went to the galley and found some crackers. She explained, "These will have to do until tomorrow. I'll buy you a nice steak then. I was terribly busy today. Sorry about leaving you in the car so long." Joque said, "No harm done. I'm used to the heat of the tropics. At least you left the window down. This is a great boat you have here. Let me out of this cage so I can look around." Mary let him out. He went all over the boat looking at every aspect of the boat. Herb fell asleep on the deck. When Joque was done looking at the boat he came back to Mary and stood on the captains steering chair. He silently watched Mary.

Mary watched the stars and thought about her new friends. It would be nice to dive for gold. How deep would the gold be? Would it be covered with much sand? Would Bob and Ellen be good navigators? Mary decided that she would learn to navigate too, just in case Bob and Ellen weren't as bright as they seemed.

As midnight approached Mary went below deck. She went to the navigation room. There was a computer in there. She turned it on and accessed the internet. It was only natural to want to check on her stock. The stock had gone up ten percent in just one day. Mary said to herself, "Twenty million dollars profit in one day isn't too bad. After turning off the computer, Mary went to her bedroom and set the alarm clock for nine O'clock. She took a shower and then went to bed. In no time she was sleeping soundly.

The alarm went off at nine O'clock. The High One was already awake and sitting at the helm of the boat. He said, "I wouldn't mind going for a ride in a boat like this one." Mary replied, "I could take you for a little ride. I'm certain that nobody will mind." She turned the key in the ignition and the boat started up. Mary stated, "I know that this lever controls the speed and direction. I'll just pull back on it. She pulled back gently and the boat eased backwards. The boat suddenly jerked to a stop. Mary exclaimed, "I forgot to untie the boat. Would you get it for me High One?" He quickly untied the boat and got back in. Mary eased backwards out of the boat's mooring. She turned the steering wheel and the boat responded to her touch. She asked Joque, "What's next?" Joque replied, "Push the lever gently forward and steer carefully out to sea." Mary pushed forward on the lever and steered the boat out of the marina. She idled out onto Lake Michigan. The water was calm. She pushed forward on the throttle and the boat surged ahead. The High One smiled and asked, "Can I take the helm for awhile?" Mary said, "I don't mind. Don't lose sight of the marina though. We don't want to get lost." The High One pushed the throttle lever all the way forward. They roared along the coast for about a mile and then turned around and headed back to the marina. Mary said, "You better let me park it." The High One replied, "Take the helm. I've had my ten minutes of glory. Now you can drive."

Mary parked the boat, and they all went to the Yacht Club for breakfast. At first they weren't allowed in since they weren't members. Bill Phillips was finishing his breakfast and saw them at the door. He got up and went to the door. He told the doorman, "I'm giving these people a membership. Please see to it that they get everything they want." Mary responded, "Thank you, Bill." She gave him a hug. He looked pleasantly surprised. He gave her back the hug and picked her right up into the air. He set her down and said, "That stock you gave me went up ten percent yesterday. I made a bundle." Mary said, "So did I. Can you stay for another breakfast?" Bill said, "I'll make time for you, Mary." They all went over to Bill's table. Mary ordered a steak for everyone including Joque. Mary said, "My parrot thinks he's a sea captain and he likes steak and pecan pie." Bill stated, "That's an unusual parrot. Can he speak?" Joque said, "Ship ahoy, matie." Bill exclaimed, "He speaks well. How long have you had him?" Mary said, "I've had him for two years. He is always learning to say new things. Bill, I decided I would like for you to teach me navigation." Bill responded, "I'll give you a book you can start on after we eat. I'll show you the instruments on Jade Goddess One today if you like." Mary responded, "That would be great." Their steaks arrived and they all ate eagerly. Mary asked Bill, "Your wife doesn't get jealous of you teaching young women about the boats does she? Bill laughed and responded, "She trusts me." Mary responded, "I just feel that I need to know about navigation, in case something would happen to Bob and Ellen." Bill replied, "If you ever get into trouble with being lost or a storm catches you, just call the coast guard. They can find you quickly and help." Mary said, "That would be embarrassing. I hope that I can stay out of trouble like that." She watched Bill's attractive blue eyes as he looked back into her eyes. She thought he was quite handsome, but she respected the fact that he was married. She didn't want to try to be a home wrecker. Bill finally stated, "I think you'll make a fine navigator. Where are you staying?" Mary said, "I'm staying on the Jade Goddess One. Why don't you come over this afternoon around two o'clock and show me the instruments?" Bill said, "I'll be there right at two o'clock."

When they finished their breakfast, Mary said goodbye to the High One. He gave her a hug and then left in the rental car. Mary thought to herself, "I would like to meet a nice man like Bill to spend some time with while I'm here. I need to learn how grown women act. Possibly Bill will introduce me to someone at the Yacht Club." She spent the rest of the morning looking at the shops she hadn't seen the day before. When two o'clock came, she was back at the boat eagerly waiting for her lesson. Bill was right on time. Mary asked, "Could you introduce me to a nice man at the club who wouldn't try to take advantage of me?" Bill laughed, "Almost any man is going to try to take advantage of you. I mean he will test you. If you want to stay a virgin just stand your ground. Men respect that usually." Mary asked, "How did you know that I'm a virgin?" Bill said, "The way you hugged me. You still trust men." Mary said, "I guess I shouldn't rush into dealing with men. I haven't dated at all. I lived out on the dessert and there were only very old respectable men around."

Bill replied, I guess I could teach you a little about men. Why don't you put on a bikini and sun bath with me for awhile so I can give you some pointers?" Mary responded, "That sounds like fun. She went to her room and put on a very skimpy bikini. It was canary yellow.

She grabbed some sun screen lotion and went back to the deck where Bill was waiting. His eye brows raised a little when he saw how good she looked in the bikini. Bill stated, "You're incredible! A perfect body!" Mary blushed a little and started rubbing some lotion on herself. Bill said, "Lesson number one, always ask the man to rub the lotion on you." He took the lotion and started rubbing it all over her. He concentrated on her behind. He kept rubbing and rubbing. Finally he said, "I was just testing. You shouldn't let the man rub you there too long. And don't let them put lotion where you don't need any. When you have a suit like this on, a man will get excited and try to kiss you. Mary said, "You may kiss me if it's for the lesson." Bill kissed her passionately. She was surprised how hard he kissed her. She was also surprised that she let him go on so long. She kissed him back and ran her fingers through his hair. "Let me on top, commanded Mary, you're blocking the sun." She rolled on top of him and pulled off his shirt. "You should get a little sun too." she said, giggling as she flipped his shirt around. Bill looked young for 54. His hairy chest was still completely black. He had a nice full head of black short hair. Mary liked his thick dark eye brows.

Then Mary frowned and exclaimed, "What am I doing? I forgot you're married!" Bill laughed, "I just use that 'I'm married' story so that women won't be threatened by me. You have to admit, it worked quite well." Mary replied, "I'm glad you're not married, but I wish you weren't so sneaky." Mary tickled his ribs and started kissing him some more on the lips. Mary said, "What's the next lesson?" Bill said, "Since you know that I'm not married, you won't need lessons on how to get along with other men. You can simply date me." Mary replied, "I like you, but I want to be honest with you. Unlike you, I want to tell the truth." Bill said, "Oh no. Now is when you tell me you have some terrible disease." Mary laughed, "No, it's not that bad. I just want you to know that I'm after more than some passionate kisses. I want you to go with us to look for pirate's gold. I'm sure you're a good navigator. You could speed our project. We wouldn't need to study navigation for months before we leave. You could teach us navigation while we are at sea."

Bill responded, "I like you more than any other woman, Mary. You're incredibly attractive. I'd follow you anywhere, but what about my business? I make most of my sales in the summer." Mary said, "It's time you trusted your staff more. Let them make the money for you. Put them on commission. If you don't make as much this summer as last summer, I'll make up the difference. I have two hundred and twenty million dollars. Money is no problem for me." Bill responded, "Mary, don't tell people how much money you have. They'll try to take advantage of you. Everyone will charge you more for things. You don't have to promise me money. I'm not exactly poor. Being on the ocean could get pretty cold at night. Will you keep me warm?" Mary replied, "We could go steady if you like. I don't want you chasing other women every time we get to a town along the coast. I'm sure I can keep you warm at night. I just don't want to go all the way yet. Do you understand?" Bill said, "I can respect that." Mary asked Bill, "Can you think of any good way to explain to Bob and Ellen how we got so close to each other so fast? Bill said, "Leave the explaining to me. Besides being a business owner, I'm a salesman." Bob and Ellen climbed on the boat just as Bill and Mary had mentioned their names. Bill shook their hands and said, "Welcome to Jade Goddess One. I have some great news for you. Mary and I have spent the day getting to know one another, and we've come to the conclusion that we want to go steady." Ellen said, "That's wonderful. Bob and I are going steady too." Mary said, "Bill has agreed to go with us to the Florida Keys searching for pirate's gold. He is an excellent navigator and he can teach us navigation on location." Bob replied, "That's great. It will make it so that we can start searching for gold immediately. Can you scuba dive, Bill?" Bill answered, "Yes, I'm a certified instructor. I can give all of you a crash course in diving. That way we can all enjoy the thrill of finding the gold."

Bill said, "Let's talk about the treasure hunt. I think we will need to take both boats to the Keys. We need a boat for supplies and staff, and another boat for us." "Staff?" asked Mary. Bill answered, "Yes, we can't spend time cooking and cleaning. We'll need a maid, a cook and a pilot." Mary replied, "Now that you mention it. We do need them. It's a little bit like we are on a honeymoon. We don't want to be tied down with cooking and cleaning." Bill said, "Now you're getting the idea. How shall we pay the help?" Mary responded, "I can pay. Money is nothing to me." Bob and Ellen excused themselves so they could see the rest of the marina. Mary waited till they were gone and said, "Bill, I have a confession to make." Bill exclaimed, "Another confession!" Mary insisted, "This is serious. I want you to promise that you will tell no one." Bill replied, "You have my solemn promise." Mary went on, "I am a medicine woman. I was raised by Indian people in New Mexico. I went on to train as a witch under the Jade Goddess. I can't tell you much about her or she might get upset. She allowed me to win two hundred million dollars at Las Vegas. My trainer and I did it in one day. I'm a little afraid that the casinos have figured out that they were cheated. They may be looking for me." Bill said, "You certainly have a vivid imagination, Mary. Are you testing me in some way?" Mary replied, "I'm completely serious. If you don't believe me, we won't be able to stay together." Bill said, "Don't get excited. I will believe you if it kills me. I just need a little while to digest all this.

What kind of witch are you?" Mary answered, "I am trained to know the future. I know what the next number at roulette will be. I know many ways to kill people. If I don't do many evil things during my life, I will have a terrible afterlife. The Jade Goddess works for Satan. He made her a goddess because she killed thousands of people with poisoned arrows." Bill said, "You seem so nice. I can't imagine you killing thousands of people." Mary said, "Yes, I'm trying to figure a way around that. My father took power from the Jade Goddess as well. He used it to get rich off the stock market. I'm afraid he'll have a terrible afterlife. He swore to the goddess that all other gods are evil. How can he go to them for help now?"

Bill responded, "I think I can help you. Remember, I'm a salesman. We need to sell you to the Christian God. Only he can protect you if you have sold your soul to the devil. Did you swear that all gods but the Jade Goddess are evil?" Mary said, "No, the goddess was very friendly and is trying to win me with generosity." Bill exclaimed, "I'm usually not so religious. I'm trying to come up with a logical way out for you. You need to give total loyalty to the Christian God. I know enough from my childhood church going to know that God, the Father of Jesus Christ, is the only one who can save you from the power of Satan; especially if you have made a deal with him. You will need to give all your money away. Give it to the poor. I don't think you would be safe trying to give it back to the casinos. You can live off my money. I'm a millionaire too. I really do love you. I'm not just after your body. Oh, what a body!" he laughed. Mary replied, "You are a salesman. I like your ideas. Can we go ahead with the treasure hunt first? Bill replied, "Yes, I think it is safe for us to go, but you will need to keep the Jade Goddess thinking that you are still greedy for more money. Contact her every week asking for stock tips." Mary exclaimed, "That's brilliant. If she starts to suspect something, I can give the money away in just a few hours. Will giving the money away, give me a happy afterlife?"

Bill replied, "I'm not an expert on this sort of thing. I think that you would need to pray to the Christian God. You need to work through his Son Jesus. You would need to ask for forgiveness for the sins of using witchcraft and cheating the casinos. You should ask forgiveness for all your sins. You may not even know what some of them are. I've been told you need to pray for forgiveness of sins every day." Mary responded, "I must be loyal to Jesus. I feel guilty though for not being loyal to the Jade Goddess. She was honest and generous with me. After I turn from the Jade Goddess, I will send her a message explaining that I couldn't bring myself to kill thousands of people like she did. I felt that I had to tell you about all this, Bill. You were certain to catch me praying to the Jade Goddess. When I pray to her, I glow the same Jade color that she is. She glows constantly. I can hide the glow if I'm getting numbers from her in the casinos, but I forget myself when I pray in private. I loved smoking with her. We felt close and friendly." Bill whispered, "You will learn to love being close to Jesus. You can talk to him all the time if you like."

Mary said, "You sure learned a lot as a child. There is one more worry that I have." Bill replied, "You can't surprise me now. Mary exclaimed, "Wait till you hear this!" I am actually eleven years old. I used witchcraft to become twenty-one. If I give up witchcraft, I'm afraid I might go back to being eleven again. Would you wait for me to grow up?" Bill said, "I would wait." Mary went on, "If I am kind to the Jade Goddess and don't anger her too much when I leave her, she may not change me back to an eleven year old girl. She loves flattery. I will shower her with praises. She knows how unlikely it would be for me to become a Goddess like her. Satan would probably use me as an eternal sex toy, a very sick and perverted sex toy. He might have me tortured with unbearable pain or throw me into a hot fire." Bill exclaimed, "Don't get carried away on that topic. You'll give yourself an ulcer. I don't think we should tell Bob and Ellen about this, do you?" Mary said, "Not right away at least. They're quite young. They might get scared and tell their parents."

Bill thought out loud, "It doesn't seem logical that the Jade Goddess can zap people and change there age. If she had that power, she could make everyone very old and bring the whole world to an end." Mary exclaimed, "You're right, Bill. I asked to be changed to 21 years old. She probably can't change me unless I ask her to. Maybe I have nothing to worry about." Bill said, "You still have plenty to worry about. You won't dare communicate with the Jade Goddess after you become a Christian. The Father of Jesus is a jealous God and will not like you talking with another god. I think it would be safest if you would become a Christian tomorrow and never talk with the Jade Goddess again. She will be angry, but it will be too late for her to take action." Mary replied, "She is angry about my father trying to leave her. She says he swore that all gods but her were evil. Now she thinks he is doomed to a terrible afterlife. I'm afraid that I agree with her. What can he do?" Bill responded softly, "It does sound like your father is in trouble. I will call my uncle who is a protestant minister. He will know if anything can be done. I'll use my cell phone right now. I have the number on speed dial."

Joque started talking as Bill dialed the phone, "Getting a new religion I see. At least you might not have to spend eternity as a parrot like me." Mary replied, "Stop complaining. You have a nice pair of boats to ride, and we're going to Florida soon. You should like that." Joque said, "I like the tropics. I'm hungry." Mary responded, "I'll feed you soon. We're working on something important now."

Bill finally turned off his cell phone and spoke to Mary, "My uncle says that if someone causes a person to turn to Christ, it erases a multitude of sins. He says that your father must turn quite a few people to Christ. It is his only hope." Mary replied, "Can I use your phone?" Bill handed it to her. She dialed her parents. Her father answered. Mary said, "Dad, my new boyfriend here in Michigan has an uncle who is a protestant minister. Bill, my boyfriend, asked his uncle how you could get a pleasant afterlife. His uncle says that even though you are in serious trouble; if you convince quite a few people to turn to Christ, you might be saved. Doing that will erase a multitude of sins." Mary's dad replied, "I'll get started on it right away. How did you know about my problem?" Mary answered, "The Jade Goddess told me about it. She is angry with you. She didn't make me swear that all Gods other than her are evil. She knows it didn't work with you. She's trying to win me with generosity. I will soon be leaving her and become a Christian. Please be sure not to let her read your mind and discover my plan." Joseph replied, "I'll keep her in the dark. I won't even think about it." Mary asked, "Can I speak to mom now?" Joseph answered, "I'll get her right away."

Mary and her mother spoke for about twenty minutes. Mary told her all about Bill and their plans to go treasure hunting in the Florida Keys. Marsha said, "I'm glad that you're having fun. It's good to see that your friend Bill is so smart. I hope he can help you find that good afterlife. It is important." Mary replied, "I'm sure there are other benefits to being a Christian besides a good afterlife. I'm hoping to receive power like I did with the Jade Goddess. Possibly I will still be able to know the future. It would be wonderful to be successful on the stock market without owing it to the Jade Goddess." Marsha stated, "You must call often. I want to know how you are doing. We never heard from you when you were in the desert with your grandfather." Mary replied, "I will call often. I promise. Goodbye now. I love you." Her mother said, "I love you too. Goodbye."

Chapter Six

A Proposal

Mary turned off the phone and handed it back to Bill. She took Bill's hand and told him. "I want your uncle to baptize me tomorrow. I don't want to wait any longer." Bill replied, "I'm sure he'll do it. He loves to baptize people. While we have him with us he can also marry us." Mary asked, "Are you proposing on the first date? Don't answer that. I will marry you. Then we won't be tempted to live in sin. I love you, Bill." They kissed and hugged until they were interrupted by Bob and Ellen. Mary exclaimed, "Bob just proposed to me. We're getting married tomorrow!" Ellen's eyes got big, "You two move fast. I'm not going to try to keep up with you." Bob said, "I believe in love at first sight. I think you two are a nice couple. Can we come to your wedding?" Bob said, "I want you to be my best man, Bob." Mary exclaimed, "And you, Ellen, must be my maid of honor." Ellen smiled and said, "I'll be glad to do that. Where will the wedding be? Bill replied, "My uncle has a church just a mile from here. He will baptize Mary tomorrow morning, and in the afternoon we'll have the wedding."

Joque started calling for food again, "I'm hungry Mary. I want a cracker." Mary went to the galley and found some crackers. She fed Joque quietly while Bill told Bob and

Ellen about the rest of the plans Mary and he had made. Bob and Ellen liked the ideas. When they had finished talking about the plans for the treasure hunt, Mary said, "I want to give away two hundred and twenty million dollars today. Who should I give it to?" Bob said, "I think it would be good to give it to your church." Mary said, "I don't have a church yet." Ellen replied, "You could give some of it to the church that baptizes you and the rest you could give to agencies that feed the poor." Bill said, "I'll call my uncle back. He can give you a list of agencies. You'll need to get receipts or you'll end up with a terrible tax bill. You need to be able to prove to the government that you gave the money away." Mary exclaimed, "Do you have a lawyer that I could have do this. It doesn't sound like much fun."

Bill laughed, "Yes, I'll have my lawyer take care of everything. Just give me your account number and I'll have him get right on it, as soon as you convert your stock to cash." Mary said, "I can have that done in a couple hours. It will be good to have that off my mind."

Bob asked, "Could we go somewhere and get something to eat?" Bill said, "You can go over to the Yacht Club with me. I'll buy both of you memberships. I gave one to Mary this morning." Bob said, "That will be great. Thank you!" Ellen responded, "You're very generous. Those memberships are expensive!" Bill answered, "Think nothing of it. We are all on the same team now. We are explorers of the underwater depths." Mary took Bill's hand and said, "Come on explorer. I'm hungry." They walked over to the club and took a table that offered a view of the marina. Bill told the waitress that he was getting married to Mary the next day. She went and told the owner of the club. He came out and congratulated them. His name was Reggie Pfund. He insisted on providing their meals free of charge. He shook Bill's hand and kissed Mary politely on the cheek. With great enthusiasm he went on and on about how attractive Mary was, and how he wished he had spotted her first. Mary blushed as Reggie let his eyes trace the curves of her body. Bill asked to pay for some champagne, but this was not allowed. Reggie brought out his best champagne and poured it himself for his guests and then proposed a toast. "To a happy marriage with many wonderful children. And if, God forbid it, Bill should ever lose his life, I promise to take care of his wife and take her for my very own." He hugged Mary as though he would never let go. She was a little pink from blushing slightly. She kissed Reggie, and told him how sweet he was.

Their food arrived and they ate eagerly. More champagne arrived as well. Reggie filled their cups and Bill made a toast. "To a prosperous search for pirate's gold. May we have a safe journey." They all touched each other's glasses and drank heartily. After an hour of eating and drinking, a stringed quartet arrived and played for the bride and groom to be. Reggie had pulled out all the stops. He had called all of Bill's friends. They started filing in. Each of them shook Bill's hand and kissed Mary. She was surprised at how enthusiastically some of them kissed her. She decided they liked her quite a bit. Bill watched to make sure they didn't get too carried away with their displays of affection.

The music soothed Bill and Mary as they watched the sun settling down into Lake Michigan. The gold and purple colors gave them nature's congratulations on the start of a new and wonderful life. Mary thought, "I can't wait to start talking to Jesus. I'm sure he will give me even greater power than I had with the Jade Goddess. He will be certain of my loyalty. I certainly won't be able to go back to the Jade Goddess after I do this to her." She watched the sun until it had totally disappeared. Then she asked Bill, "Will Jesus give me power?" Bill replied, "He knows you will need power to resist the hate of the Jade Goddess once she knows you have betrayed her. If you pray for power every day, you will certainly get some. You could get power to heal or even power to know the future." Mary's eyes opened wide. "I would love it if I could still know the future." Bill said, "I don't think you will be allowed to use the gift for gambling, Mary." Mary replied, "I wasn't thinking of that. I would like some help with the stock market. I'd love to make millions of dollars on the stock market again. I'd want money that didn't have a great price with it. Honest money that I could be proud of." Bill said, "I hope you can do well on the stock market. You can invest my money for me. I have confidence in you." Bob said, "I can give you a few insights that I've used to make my money. We can work together if you like. I'm a Christian. There's nothing wrong with making money on the stock market. It's as American as eating apple pie!" Mary replied, "I'll be glad to hear all that you can tell me about the market, Bob." She gave him a hug.

Mary asked Bill, "What else does Jesus do for his people?" Bill said, "You'll have to ask my uncle about some of that. I've heard that people feel better. They have an inner peace. They know they are safe and protected. I'm going to get more religious now that I have you. I can tell you are going to be quite religious and I want to stay close to you whatever you do." Mary said, "That sounds good, Bill. We can pray together every day, and we can pray for plenty of children. I want many children." Bill smiled and said, "I'll do my part to help answer your prayers." He laughed and hugged his wife to be. They danced for hours and finally said goodbye to their host. Bob and Ellen went with them back to the Jade Goddess One. Bill said, "I think we should change the names of the boats." Ellen said, "I think it would be good to call them Angel one and Angel Two." Mary asked, "That sounds good. I heard about Angels from my friends in grade school, but I don't know much about them." Bill said, "I like those names." Bob said, "Good names, yes I'll have to agree."

Bill went on, "I'll have the names put on tomorrow, and I'll ship the boats to Florida as soon as the paint dries. We can buy some maps in Florida and we'll be searching for gold in just a week or two, as soon as we can hire the cook, housekeeper and pilot."

Bill asked, "Where would you like a honeymoon, Mary?" She thought for a minute and said, "I think we should honeymoon right in the Florida Keys where we will be treasure hunting." Bill exclaimed, "I like that idea! Would you mind if I make reservations at one of the best bed and breakfasts?" Mary replied, "That would be perfect, but what will Bob and Ellen do while we are there?" Bob said, "We can meet you at your bed and breakfast when you are ready to go treasure hunting. We'll stay somewhere nearby and work on our sun tans. There wasn't much sun in Alaska." Ellen said, "We can work on the internet to find some maps that will help us find the treasure." Bob added, "I know just where to look. I'll check under topographical maps of the Florida Keys or of the Gulf of Mexico. There should be maps that show water depths, from bait shops in the Keys area. We can figure that ships would have run into trouble around fairly shallow water, from ten to eighty feet deep." Bill replied, "Yes, I have heard that most treasure is found in fairly shallow water. As beginners, you don't want to dive at two hundred feet. It is too dangerous. Possibly in a year or two, after you have more experience, we could try something like that."

Mary sighed, "I'll need to send my pet black panther back to the desert. I can't have a magical, at times invisible, cat with me if I want to be a good Christian." I'll hire someone to drive him home tomorrow. He knows how to live in the desert without me. I will miss him. Herb gave me a nice sense of being protected." Ellen said, "It's good to see you're willing to give things up for your religion. I hope you and Bill have a perfect marriage." Mary replied,

"Thank you, Ellen. I know we will be happy. Bill is an affectionate person and he knows how to make me feel good. We don't know as much as some people know about each other when they get married, but I think we have quite a bit in common. We both want plenty of children and we like adventure. We don't have trouble with being shy about our bodies. I think we will be able to please each other plenty." She smiled and took Bill's hand. He squeezed her hand and added, "I've never seen a woman that I was so instantly attracted to, and attracted so intensely."

Ellen exclaimed, "I know what you mean! Bob and I are attracted intensely. We try to keep it under control since we know that we should wait a year or two to get married." Bob said, "I agree. We don't want to shock our parents by getting married too young. We're enjoying going steady. It's fun just to fish together, and we have our share of passion." Ellen complained, "Bob don't embarrass me. I'm sorry, Bob. I guess I should admit that we are practically married, but I'm not ready for children. I want some more years of adventure before I settle down to raising children." Bob said, "It's getting kind of late. Ellen and I are sleeping on Angel Two tonight." Bill said, "I need to do some packing and other things at my house." Mary said, "I'll sleep on Angel One. I'd like it if you would help me find a white dress to get married in, Ellen. Shall we meet at nine o'clock on my boat?" Ellen replied, "That'll be fine. I think we should meet at eight though, so we can get breakfast before shopping." Bob said, "I can eat breakfast with you. Then I'll go shopping for some things on my own." Bill stated, "I'll make the final arrangements with my uncle Jack, for the baptism and wedding. Meet me at ten thirty so we can go to the church for the baptism." Mary replied, "Tell Jack that I'd like the wedding in the evening, so I have plenty of time to get my hair ready and fix up my dress. I think seven o'clock would be the right time." Bill said, "I'll take care of everything. We won't need to practice. I'll ask Jack to give us a simple but beautiful ceremony. I'll call him now. It's not too late."

Bill dialed his uncle and talked for ten minutes or so. Then he handed the phone to Mary and said, "He wants to talk to you, Mary." Mary took the phone and talked with the minister for a long time. Finally she said goodbye and handed the phone back to Bill. Mary told Ellen, "We'll need to shop for the dress at one in the afternoon. Bill's uncle wants to give me some basic instructions in the faith before the baptism. He says that he needs several hours to go over things with me. I'm meeting him at nine. I'm glad he's going to teach me some important things. We'll have plenty of time in the afternoon to buy the dress." Ellen replied, "I can spend the morning with Bob. We both need to buy more tropical clothing for the trip to Florida." Mary answered, "Be sure to come to the baptism at eleven." Ellen responded, "We'll be there. Is he going to put your head under the water three times?" Mary replied, "Yes. He said they do it that way. I will just lean forward and he'll push my head down under the water. I'll have plenty of time to catch my breath before I go under the water again. I just hope the water doesn't boil or something strange happens because I've been too evil." Bill laughed, "I don't think you'll have to worry. No evil power is any match for God. He will be in control of things." Ellen said, "You don't seem so evil to me. What sort of bad things have you done?" Mary said, "I don't want to tell you now. Maybe when we get to know each other better." Ellen replied, "I understand. I didn't want to be nosey, but I guess I was." Mary said, "I'm not offended one bit." Bob said, "The important thing is that you are on the right side now. I think you will have a great life as a Christian." Mary replied, "With Jack helping me, I know I'll do fine."

Bob yawned, "I think we'd better get some sleep. We'll meet you at eleven. Where is the church?" Bill replied, "It's a nondenominational church on Main Street, across from the fruit market. It's an old fashioned church building, you can't miss it. There's a white cross in the front yard and a tall steeple on the church with a large bell in it." Bob replied, "We'll find it." Bill went on, "Here's my cell phone number in case you need to reach me." He wrote the number on a small pad of paper that he always carried in his shirt pocket. Bill took the number and put it in his wallet. "We'll see you at the church," said Bob. He took Ellen's hand and they walked back to the Angel Two.

Bill and Mary drove down to the park and walked along the beach. The waves were high and the wind was blowing steadily, howling across the water. They stopped after awhile and embraced. Bill thought that Mary's face felt quite warm in the cool evening breeze. He kissed her hard on the lips and pulled her tight against him. She ran her fingers through his black hair. Mary thought how she would love to be with him during the coming night. They had grown so much and learned so much about each other. It would be hard to say good night and spent the night apart. She knew that she had to be strong and not sleep with him on this, the night before their wedding. They climbed out on the pier made of enormous chucks of limestone. When they reached the end of the pier, they could feel the mist from the crashing waves on their faces. Mary said, "It seems like we were meant to be together. I know I'll never want to be with other men. Will you stay loyal to me, Bill." Bill replied, "Loyalty is important to me. I will never chase after another woman, I promise you." Mary replied, "I'm the jealous type. That's why I asked." Bill exclaimed, "I'm the jealous type too. I want you all to myself!" They kissed passionately and held each other close. Bill said, "Are you sure you don't want a big wedding?" Mary exclaimed, "I just want to get on with the honeymoon!" Bill laughed, "I feel the same way." Mary went on, "Besides, I don't want my parents to worry about us getting married so soon. I'll tell them about it a couple months from now. I don't want them traveling all the way out here. Beside, they can't possibly get here by tomorrow. We need to keep things moving so we can begin the treasure hunt." Bill replied, "As long as you're sure this is what you want." Mary sighed, "I'm sure about it. I just want us to be together as soon as possible."

They kissed for a long time and finally Mary broke it off. She shouted, "You're making me too excited. Let's go home before I start doing things I shouldn't." Bill said, "Yes, you make good sense. Why get carried away tonight when tomorrow night will be the beginning of our honeymoon?" They got up and carefully climbed back over the large slippery chunks of limestone. The waves crashed and sprayed them as they walked. They drove back to the marina, and Bill let Mary out. She asked, "Will you take me to the church in the morning?" Bill answered, "I'll pick you up at seven so we can eat breakfast first." Mary said, "I'd like that." She kissed him one last time and then walked briskly over to the Angel One. She set the alarm clock, showered and went right to bed. Bill went home and did some packing. He was too excited to go to sleep right away. He made a list of clothing he would need to buy in the morning. While Mary was talking to Jake, he would do some shopping. Finally he grew sleepy and set his alarm clock. In no time he was asleep.

Bob and Ellen weren't very sleepy. Pretending to need sleep was their way of having an excuse to leave. They wanted to be alone on their first night in the boat. Something about the boat excited them. They made coffee in the galley and drank several cups. Ellen said, "We should act more like we are married. I mean I think we should be natural when we are around each other." Bob asked, "I like the sound of that, but what exactly do you mean?" Ellen replied, "When we were together today, I felt close to you. I felt like we would always be together. Was I right? Do you actually want to marry me some day?" Bob replied, "As far as I'm concerned, we are married. I just don't want to make it formal because our parents would object." Ellen asked, "Can you keep secret what we do on the boat?" Bob said, "My parents never ask me about that kind of thing." Ellen said, "Don't even tell your friends, O.K.?" Bob replied, "My lips are sealed." Bob said, "We're going to be together on this boat for several years. I can't see why we shouldn't be intimate. After all we're going steady. In fact," he said, as he got down on one knee, "I'd like to propose that we be secretly married." Ellen smiled and said, "I accept your proposal. I only wish we were a couple years older so we could get married tomorrow like Bill and Mary are." Bob replied, "I'll buy you an engagement ring. I would like it if you would tell people that we're engaged." Ellen exclaimed, "I'd love that! I'm tired of being thought of as a little girl. People will realize that I'm growing up quickly." She kissed with Bob for a long time. Finally Ellen asked, "Do you think we are being sinful being so passionate with each other?" Bob exclaimed, "Now's a great time to ask that! I know we're too young to be engaged, but we are engaged! Engaged people get passionate with each other." Ellen said, "I still feel a little bit wicked. I'll be glad when we get married. Our passions are too strong for us to wait too long." Bob replied, "I agree. I think we should start working on our parents. Get them used to the idea. We can even tell them we're engaged. That should move things along a little faster. Why don't we get married next July?" Ellen said, "I think that would be wonderful. The first week in July, on a Sunday afternoon." Bob said, "It's the only thing to do. Why should we go on struggling against our bodies? We have plenty of money. The lack of money is why most people wait to get married." Ellen responded, "Bob, you are so smart. You've figured out everything." They got quiet and went to sleep.

Bill picked up Mary in the morning and took her to the Yacht Club for breakfast. They sat at their favorite table with the view of the marina. Reggie came out and talked to them. "So, today is the big day is it. I hope the wedding goes smoothly. I'm sure that it will." He disappeared for a minute and then returned with a present for them. "I hope this will make your honeymoon even more enjoyable." He whispered, "It's some excellent champagne. I'm having the chef make a nice platter of cheese selections sliced to perfection. I'll bring it out when you're ready to go." Bill responded, "You are too generous Reggie. Please come to our wedding today at seven. It will be at the church across from the fruit market." Reggie said, "I'll bring my staff too, so the church won't be so empty. I know you didn't have any time to invite guests. We'll bring some food for the reception, and I insist on providing a cake. My chef can make up a big wedding cake in no time." Mary said, "We'll never forget your generosity, Reggie." She jumped up and gave Reggie a heart felt hug. He held her hand then and spoke softly to her, "You are going to make Bill a very happy man. In all my life I have never seen a woman more beautiful and friendly than you."

They spent a long time talking to each other during their breakfast. Reggie kept bringing them more and more coffee. Each time he came with the coffee he would tell them about his life, or ask them about their plans. Before they knew it the clock said eight forty-five. They asked to pay for breakfast, but Reggie wouldn't hear of it. Bill drove Mary to the church and introduced her to Jake. Bill said, "Mary, this is Jake Miller, my uncle and pastor. Jake this is Mary Fletcher, my wife to be." Jake responded, "I'm glad to meet you Mary. I have a Bible for you to read and some devotional guides. We can go over the basics of the faith in my office." Bill said, "I'll go do some shopping and leave you two to your business. I'll be back at ten thirty." Jake replied, "That'll be fine." Jake invited Mary into his office, where his secretary was working on a computer. He said, "Just pretend Esther isn't here. Mary replied, "I'll do my best." She wished they were in total privacy, but she knew there were certain ways things had to be done.

Jake asked, "Why do you want to be a Christian, Mary?" Mary said, "I want to have a good afterlife. I don't want to be tortured by Satan when I die." Jake smiled, "That's a good place to start. Many new converts don't actually believe in Satan. He is very real, and it is wise to find a way to stay away from him. Jesus died on the cross so that you could be freed from sin. He took away the sins of all who call on Him and say that He is the Son of God and their personal savior. When he returned to heaven, he left the Holy Spirit here to help us. The Holy Spirit can convey powerful spiritual gifts to us if we pray for them. We can be given power to heal, to prophecy and do many other powerful things. Your devotional guides tell more about spiritual gifts. Start reading the New Testament first. Romans and Ephesians will tell about spiritual gifts. A new Christian needs to pray for spiritual power right away. That will prevent Satan from being successful in causing trouble for the new Christian. I will baptize you in the name of God the Father, Jesus and the Holy Spirit. You can hold your nose so the water doesn't bother you." Mary said, "Thanks, I understand. Can some Christians learn to tell the future?" Jake said, "I don't have much personal experience with that. It would come under the gift of prophecy. Do you want to tell the future?" Mary replied, "When I was following the Jade Goddess, she made it so that I could tell what number would come up at roulette and she helped me pick stocks on the stock market. I'm giving all that money away, but I'd like to be able to do the same sort of thing through the power of God." Jake laughed, "I would like to have that power too. But seriously, you can receive power from God to do almost anything that you set your mind on, as long as God doesn't think that such power would be bad for you. He only gives good gifts. Satan gave you your previous powers hoping that greed would cause your downfall. You can still work with the stock market, but pray for guidance. Don't expect that you will always make high returns every day. Even if you have a bad year, don't get angry with God. He may be testing you. He wants people who will worship him even when things aren't going their way."

Mary thought for awhile. "Will I feel any different after the baptism?" Jake said, "Wait and see. Some people can feel the Holy Spirit coming into them. They feel at peace and happy." Mary asked, "Will it be certain that I have a good afterlife?" Jake said, "Heaven is sure to be waiting for you if you stay loyal to Jesus and pray to him for forgiveness on a regular basis. Pray for forgiveness of sins every day. Be humble and pray on your knees at your bedside every night before you go to bed." Mary said, "That sounds simple enough. Tell me more about the life of Jesus. We have more time." Jake gave a summary of the life of Jesus and helped Mary to see how many aspects of his life could be used by her as examples for good Christian living. They talked right up to the time when Bill came to be present for the baptism.

Jake had notified many of the congregation about the hastily planned baptism. About fifty people filed in and took seats in the front of the church. There was a baptismal tank in the front of the church. Jake told the congregation about Mary's strong desire to be a Christian. Some hymns were sung and then Jake baptized Mary. When she came out of the water she closed her eyes and saw white light glowing inside her head. She felt warm and happy. Mary knew that the Holy Spirit was entering her. She took a chair and sat for several minutes enjoying the good feeling of being free from sin.

She changed into dry clothes and thanked Jake. He handed her the Bible and devotional guide which she held tightly as she and Bill went to the car. Bill said, "Well, how do you feel?" Mary said, "I feel wonderful. I love being free of sin." Bill went on, "I wonder where Bob and Ellen are?" Bob came up. We were talking to some people in the church. They wouldn't stop talking. Here comes Ellen." Ellen said, "Bob proposed to me last night. We're getting married next year in July. Oh, it was a nice baptism, Mary." Mary said, "Congratulations. Where will you get married?" Ellen exclaimed, "We haven't gotten that far in our planning yet. The wedding will probably be in Goshen, Indiana; at Bob's church. It's sort of my church too. I've been going there with him for two years now. We don't go every Sunday, but we enjoy it there when we do go."

Bob said, "I think I'll go with Ellen and pick out an engagement ring." Mary said, "We'll come along. Afterwards, Ellen and I can find a wedding dress for me." They went to the jewelry store and looked at rings. Bob wanted her to have something big and impressive. Ellen said, "I don't want to get mugged for the ring. Let me have something about one carat in size; a traditional round one on yellow gold." The shop keeper found her something that was perfect. They even had the right size. Bob said, "You can wear it now. I already proposed last night." Ellen put the ring on her finger and smiled. "I love you, Bob," she exclaimed. Bob said, "I love you, Ellen."

Bill said, "We need to buy some rings too." Mary picked out a two carat round diamond with plenty of blue fire in it. Like Ellen's ring it was yellow gold. Bill said, "You can wear the diamond. I'll keep the wedding band until the wedding." Mary said, "You are a wonderful man, Bill." Bill kissed her and then picked out a wedding band for himself. He gave it to Mary and said, "Don't lose this. You'll need to hand it to Jake when he asks for it at the wedding." They paid for the rings and the women went shopping for a dress.

Bill said, "Let's go to the Marine Products Store and get some supplies for the trip." Bob replied, "Lead the way. I've got nothing better to do." They walked down the block to the nearby store. Bill said, "The boats already have life vests, but we should buy some of those special vests that sense if you have landed in the water and send out a location and distress signal to the coast guard. They could save our lives. Forty foot boats aren't any too big for the Gulf of Mexico or the Florida Keys. The waves get quite high there if you get caught out in a storm." Bob responded, "I'm in favor of taking safety precautions. How much do they cost?" Bill responded, "I think they run about five hundred dollars per vest." Bob said, "They're high, but it sounds like they would be worth it." Bill went on, "Angel One should have a special sonar that will detect metal on the sea bottom. They run a couple thousand dollars." A clerk came up and started helping them find what they needed. They had a cart and it was starting to get full. Bob stated, "I think things will be less expensive here than in Florida. We should get everything we can think of." They bought repair kits for the boats, extra flares a couple shot guns to kill unwanted sharks with, and plenty of deer slugs for the guns. Bill said, "If the sharks start coming around, we can shoot a couple of them so the others will eat them and allow the divers to get out of the water. We may need to feed the sharks about a quarter mile from where we want to dive. That way they will leave us alone. We may need to hire another boat to keep feeding them as long as we want to dive. Sharks can be a real problem in the tropics." Bob said, "Just so you know how to deal with them. I don't want to swim up close with them, that's for sure."

They bought some dried food for emergency rations and bought heavy canvas bags for hauling the gold up with.

Bill whispered, "I think we'd better get plenty of bags. We might find hundreds of pounds of gold and silver. We may need to double bag. We don't want precious gold and silver ripping out and scattering all over the ocean floor." Bob's eyes got bigger as he thought about all the gold they might find. He helped load the heavy canvas bags into the shopping cart. Bill asked the shop keeper to ship the things to the Key West post office. He told Bob, "When the boats arrive at Key West, we can pick up these things at the post office and put them on the boats. We won't have to lug all the stuff onto the jets that we fly down to Florida in." Bob replied, "That's good thinking. We might as well make things as easy as possible."

They went over to the dress shop and found Mary and Ellen looking at dresses. Mary said, "I've picked out the dress, but I don't want you to see it till the wedding." Bill said, "Bob and I will go wait at the Yacht Club for you. I'm getting a little hungry." The men each kissed their woman and then left for the club. In a couple hours the women joined them. They found the men discussing the treasure hunt. They sat down and everyone ordered lunch. Bill said, "We need maps as soon as possible. That way we can decide where to look first. I think I can find some maps on the internet. We can buy some more detailed maps when we get to Key West."

Mary said, "I know you'll like the dress I picked out. It shows off my shoulders well. That's all I'm going to tell you about it." She giggled and put her hand on Bill's leg. He smiled and replied, "I'm looking forward to seeing you in it. By the way, Mary; have you ever flown in a passenger jet?" Mary replied, "No, I haven't. Why do you ask?" Bill said, "Sometimes they hit turbulence and the plane shakes quite a bit or takes a sudden dip. I just don't want you to get frightened. Jets are quite safe." Mary quipped, "I'm not a bit afraid. Have you both flown jets before?" She looked toward Bob and Ellen. Bob replied, "We just got back from a trip to Alaska. There wasn't any trouble. It took awhile to get on the plane though. They're checking for terrorists and they go through everyone's luggage carefully. All that takes time." Mary replied, "We could drive to Key West." Bill exclaimed, "We'd be so tired from driving that we wouldn't enjoy our honeymoon." Mary responded, "I guess you have a point. With all the checks you say they are making on people and luggage, it should be fairly safe."

Their food arrived and they took their time eating. Mary asked, "Do most Christians pray at every meal?" Bill said, "I often forget to. I know I should." They stopped eating and Bill said a prayer out loud for all of them. Mary said, "I want to do the right things now that I'm a Christian." Ellen said, "My parents don't always pray at meals. Sometimes our meals are more like a feeding frenzy. Everyone just grabs something out of the frig. On Sundays, they usually pray over the meal." Bob said, "My parents are the same way. They pray over the Sunday noon meal." Mary asked, "Do you two pray at night before you go to bed?" Bob said, "We're going to start tonight. It's important."

They finished eating and Bill invited them all to his house. He said, "You can all relax while I look on the internet for maps of the waters off Key West." Mary complained, "He's getting married to me today and all he can think of is maps." Bill responded, "You want plenty of gold don't you, Mary?" Mary smiled, "I want to spend more time planning our honeymoon. What will we do in Key West while we wait for the boats to arrive?" Bill said, "Earnest Hemmingway had a house in Key West. I hear that people still go to see his favorite pub and have one of the drinks that he used to drink." Mary responded, "That sounds exciting. Let's be sure to see the house he lived in. We could do some sun bathing. Is there good music there?" Bill exclaimed, "It's a place for tourists! There's bound to be plenty of good entertainment. Now I want to talk for hours about Key West, but first let me work on the net for just twenty minutes or so." Mary replied, "That's fine dear. Knock yourself out. I'm going to snoop around your house."

Bill quickly found maps of the waters just off Key West. There was a warning that it was off limits to treasure hunters. The coral reefs were being protected. He found a dive site and wrote down the phone number. With a quick phone call he found that treasure hunting was restricted to waters that were three miles out from shore. He started doing some major rethinking. "Bob, Ellen," he called. "We are going to need bigger boats. We aren't allowed to treasure hunt close to shore like I had planned. You can keep your forty foot boats, but I think we should use one hundred foot boats. We will need to look for gold far away from the shore. I can provide the boats. I have two great hundred footers that I haven't sold this summer yet." Bob replied, "You know what's best. You have more experience with the ocean than we do." Ellen chimed in, "The bigger the better. They will handle the waves without throwing us all around."

Mary came into the room and exclaimed, "You have a nice place here, Bill. I love all your paintings." Bill replied, "Thank you, Mary. We've decided to use bigger boats; one hundred footers. There are laws that prevent us from treasure hunting close to shore. We will be in water three miles from shore. We could easily get caught in bad weather. The bigger boats will handle the waves better." Mary responded, "I'll enjoy a bigger boat. The rooms will be bigger and the shower should be bigger too." She giggled and put her arm around Bill's neck. Bill looked a little embarrassed with Bob and Ellen there. Ellen said, "Don't be embarrassed Bill. When we're all on the boat together I think we shouldn't be inhibited at all about things. If you want to make some noise while you're having sex, go right ahead. We won't mind. And stay in the shower with Mary as long as you want to."

Bill responded, "Thanks, Ellen. It'll be nice to know that we can be ourselves." Bob stated, "We may make a little noise too. It's nothing to be embarrassed about."

Mary asked, "Where are these bigger boats coming from." Bill said, "I have a couple that haven't sold yet this summer. We can use them as long as we like." Mary replied, "That's generous of you, Bill. The bigger boats are probably a good idea. Just so there's a marina in Key West big enough to moor them." Bill stated, "A rich location like that is certain to have a roomy marina. I'll call down and check, just to be sure. If they have the marina space we'll rent some spaces. If not, we'll have to use Fort Lauderdale as our port of call." Mary reacted, "I still want to honeymoon in Key West, even if the boats need to stay at Fort Lauderdale." Bill soothed her, "I agree completely. We'll need to honeymoon a little longer, though. Boats that big will need to be piloted down there by water. It will take several weeks for them to arrive." Mary joked, "Do you think you'll get tired of me?" Bill laughed, "I'm sure we can keep each other busy for that long! I'll hire two pilots and get the boats on their way today. We shouldn't be with each other like this right before the wedding." Mary pouted and replied, "That's fine, I'll leave you to business. Ellen, Bob and I can go over to the church and help get the wedding planned and set up." Bill replied, "I'll be at the church by six o'clock." Mary kissed him on the lips and said, "I'll meet you at the altar. Don't lose my ring." She laughed.

Bob stated, "I'll drive. It shouldn't take long to get everything planned. We can get some supper before the wedding." Mary said, "I'm going to eat something before I put my dress on. I don't want to get anything on it." They left Bill at his house. He started calling around to hire a couple pilots. He also checked out the marina at Key West. He spent the afternoon making all the arrangements for the honeymoon. There were reservations to make and tickets to buy. He purchased the jet tickets for everyone, and hired a limo to pick them up the morning after the wedding. He knew Mary would want to spend their first married night together on Angel One. It was the only place familiar to her. She couldn't hide her enthusiasm for the boat. She had been like a kid with a new toy when he spent part of his first day with her on the boat. He retraced that day in his mind. The sun bathing. She had been so innocent; letting him rub the lotion on her behind so provocatively. She must have felt like a young girl in a doll house. She felt at home with him on the boat. He was amazed at her lack of inhibitions. When she wanted something she stepped right up and took it. She must have known all along that he would always want to be with her. She was so endearing. Her body was so tantalizing. Bill knew he would never tire of making love to her. He longed for her as he retraced their steps together."

With another phone call to his staff, he got some people busy cleaning and preparing the boats. They needed fueling and the electronic equipment needed to have last minute checks performed on them. Bill decided to take the liberty of naming the new boats Big Angel One and Big Angel Two. He didn't want to bother Mary and her new friends with such a thing while they were working on the wedding. The staff promised to paint the new names on the boats immediately. Finally, Bill decided to go down to the marina for a first hand look at the two boats. It occurred to him that Mary might like spending a little time in Big Angel One. He gave his vice president, Tom, instructions to hook up the water and electricity to the boat.

While he was at the marina the two pilots he planned to hire, arrived and found him on Big Angel One. They introduced themselves as Mark Yoder and Jim Hershburger. Mark was thirty years old and had brown hair and brown eyes. He was about six feet tall. Jim was thirty-two years old and had blond hair and hazel eyes. He was five feet ten inches tall. Bill showed them both around the two boats. They asked him some questions about insurance and payment. Bill answered their questions and explained that he had located docking space big enough for the boats at Key West. He gave each of them directions to the marina and gave them his cell phone number. Finally, he explained, I'll be sending two cooks and a housekeeper with you. Be sure to be respectful and professional with them. If both of you can stay with us for a couple months, I'd appreciate it. You would receive the same pay while down there. Both men eagerly agreed to stay. Bill went on, "The boats will be ready to move out by noon tomorrow. Push them a little, but don't take any chances on the weather. I don't want any bad news ruining my honeymoon."

In a couple more hours Bill managed to hire the cooks and the housekeeper. He explained what he was willing to pay them and what would be expected of them. The cooks were named Steve Johnson and Mike Schrock. They both had black hair and moustaches. Steve was twenty-eight and Mike was twenty-nine. They were both close to five feet ten inches tall. Both men had impressive resumes. It was the search for adventure that had lured them away from their present jobs. They each worked in local high class restaurants. That's how Bill was able to find them on such short notice. The housekeeper was twenty-one with blond hair and blue eyes. She was thin but shapely. Bill tried not to notice how shapely. After all, he had promised to be a loyal husband. Her name was Linda Wilson. She said that Reggie told her to call Bill about the job. He knew Bill would be needing a housekeeper. Bill told the new employees to be at the boats by eleven the next morning. It was six o'clock and he had to get dressed and be at the church early for last minute coaching about the wedding vows.

Putting all other thoughts aside, Bill went home and got cleaned up and dressed. He owned a nice tuxedo and had some new black shoes which he had never worn. Looking in the mirror a smile came to his face. He looked closely into his own eyes and exclaimed, "You lucky man you!" He put on some elegant diamond cuff links and headed off to the church. When Bill arrived, his uncle led him to the front of the church. The wedding vows were explained to him and he and Mary practiced them a couple times. Mary stated, "Reggie and his staff are setting up the cake and refreshments for the reception. They're in the basement." Bill responded, "I'm looking forward to the reception. I've been so busy that I forgot to eat anything." Mary whispered, "We need to come in from the basement so the guests don't see us till we walk in. The organist is going to play a traditional wedding march for us." She led Bill to the basement to wait while the guests arrived. About ninety people had learned about the wedding from Bill and Reggie. They were all good friends.

In thirty minutes the guests were all seated and the organist started playing the wedding march. Bill and Bob walked in first. They watched down the isle as Ellen walked in and then Mary came in, escorted by Reggie. Jake addressed the congregation and delivered a conventional few words about the sanctity of marriage. Next he had Bill and Mary say their wedding vows. They were nervous, but managed to get their words out correctly. Each of them found the wedding ring they needed and placed them on each other's fingers. When Jake said, "You may kiss the bride." Bill was relieved and gave Mary a long and passionate kiss. They marched out together and everyone followed them to the basement for the reception. They socialized for hours. People gave them presents. Mary thought, "How amazing that they all had time to buy gifts." She and Bill opened all the gifts and thanked each friend for the generosity. When everything was over, Reggie promised to take the gifts to Bill's house. Bill knew that Reggie would perform the traditional jokes on newly weds. He would half sheet the bed and put salt in the sugar bowl, just to name a few of the anticipated pranks.

Bill and Mary went to the marina and climbed onto Angel One. Mary asked, "How did you know I'd want to spend our first night on this boat?" Bill answered, "I feel like I know you pretty well, even though we have only been together a couple days. This is the only familiar thing we can share together on our wedding night." They carefully put their clothes away and climbed into the shower. They enjoyed each other's affections for a long time. Finally they dried off and climbed into bed. Ripples could be seen around the boat in the still water till the middle of the night, when the couple's passion for each other had fully expressed itself.

Bob and Ellen went to their boat and got ready for bed. Ellen said, "I liked the wedding. It was amazing that everyone pulled together like they did to make it happen." Bob replied, "The wedding was nice, but it made me wish we were old enough to be married." Ellen responded, "I felt the same way. I'm happy for them, but I wish we could get married on the spur of the moment like they did. Why should five years of age difference make so much difference? Ellen said, "Did you notice the ripples going out from their boat?" Bob said, "No, I missed that."

Four hours later their alarm woke them. It was time to meet Bill and Ellen for breakfast. Then they would be leaving in the limo for O'hare airport. They went to the Yacht Club and found Bill and Mary at their favorite table having eggs and ham. Bob said, "Please, don't get up." He pulled out a chair for Ellen. The waitress came and took the orders for Bob and Ellen. They also ordered eggs and ham. In no time it arrived and they ate as though they were quite hungry. Mary said, "I regret that both of you can't get married right away like we did. I know the time will whiz by for you. In no time it will be next July and you'll be married too." Ellen said, "We're enjoying this engagement period. We get to enjoy plenty of satisfaction even though we aren't making babies." Mary responded,

"I'm glad you can be so frank and honest. I am looking forward to the babies. I just hope they don't get in the way of treasure hunting. I want to get some diving in before I get too pregnant." She laughed. Bill said, "If we need to, we can send the cooks and the housekeeper down to bring up the gold!" They all laughed.

When they finished eating everyone went outside where the limo was waiting. Bob said, "Reggie promised to put my car away for me. We can all go around in the limo to pick up everyone's luggage. In no time at all they were on their way to O'hare. Bill passed out the tickets and they discussed diving techniques as they rode along. Time passed quickly and they arrived at O'hare in plenty of time to board their plane. Their luggage was scrutinized carefully and their identifications were checked. Mary had some trouble getting through the check point. Her I.D. showed that she was eleven years old. Finally they let her through. She said to Bill softly, "I think the Jade Goddess is pulling some tricks on me. I bought that I.D. with her money. That's why she was able to change it back to the original age." Bill responded, "My accountant can get you a new I.D. I'll have him mail it to us. We can have it in less than a week." Mary said, "Great. I'll be glad to get rid of this one." Then it occurred to her, "How will Joque get to Key West?" Bill exclaimed, "Don't worry! He's riding on one of the new boats. I left instructions for the cook to feed him steak and pecan pie every day until he is tired of it." Mary responded, "You think of everything, Bill. You'll make a great husband." Bill answered, "You can count on me, Mary. Don't worry about a thing."

Chapter Seven

Key West

In a few hours they were landing at Key West. Bill rented two cars and gave one to Bob and Ellen. He said, "I took the liberty of reserving a bed and breakfast for the two of you right next door to ours. Once you get to know the area you can venture out on your own." Ellen replied, "That was quite thoughtful of you. It will make it easier on us." Mary interjected, "Why don't we all meet for lunch after we get our clothes put away. Then we can part company for a few days." Bob said, "That sounds good. We'll be together plenty over the next few months. You two should have some time alone. We'll do some sun bathing." Bob and Ellen left and found their bed and breakfast. They settled in and put their clothes away.

It was warm and sunny. A nice breeze was blowing in from the west. Mary and Bill walked along the beach and talked about their future together. Bob and Ellen drove around town looking at the buildings and the people. Ellen said, "The only problem is that when she is forty-six, he'll be seventy-five. He may get too old for sex when she is still fairly active." Bob exclaimed, "Don't be that way! Ninety percent of the time it's the woman who loses interest first, or she gets too lazy to make it exciting any more." Ellen replied, "Where did you get all this expertise?" Bob replied, "I read magazines and talk to my friends at school. Just promise me that you won't get lazy once we're married. Haven't you heard the riddle that asks what food is the worst for a woman's sex drive? The answer is wedding cake. Many women just us really fun sex to lure the man in. After the wedding they get lazy." Ellen retorted, "I'm not a faker. I'm going to make you the best wife any man ever had. And when you're seventy-five, you'd better not start getting lazy. I plan on having great sex till the day I die!" Bob exclaimed, "Don't get too excited now. I was just checking." Ellen argued, "I suppose you think I'll get real fat right away, too." Bob defended himself, "Ellen, let's not argue. I know you take pride in your good looks. You know how excited your great figure makes me. I know you won't do anything like that. Let's not fight anymore. It's not like us." Ellen acquiesced, "You're right, Bob. I won't argue anymore. But sometimes you can be aggravating."

They drove down to the public beach and walked along the water for a few hours. They watched the people and listened to the seagulls. Holding hands they went a long way down the beach before they turned and came back. They sat in the sand for awhile and watched the waves. They reminisced about their fishing trip to Alaska and talked about their early years together. Finally, they knew it was about time for lunch. Bob drove Ellen back to find the newly weds. Bill and Mary were in the garden having some tea. When Bob and Ellen arrived they sat down and showed some interest in the tea. Mary rang a bell and a waitress appeared in just a few seconds. She took the requests for more tea and returned with it in no time. Mary said, "It's so nice here in this garden, why don't we eat here?" Ellen said, "That would be nice. We can see a good restaurant downtown for supper." Mary replied, "The truth is I just love ringing this bell. They come so quickly. It makes me feel like royalty." She gave the bell to

Ellen. "Here, you ring it." Ellen gave it a ring. The waitress reappeared with a smile. Bob stated, "We'd like to see some menus if we may." The waitress disappeared and returned quickly with the menus. She waited patiently as they studied the menus. She mentioned, "The shrimp is fresh from today's catch." They all ordered shrimp and baked potatoes. Bill ordered champagne for his new bride. He whispered to Bob, "If you and Ellen dump out your water I'll give each of you some of our champagne. No one will notice. I want us all to toast the great adventure that we are about to set out on. And we need to toast the first day of marriage for Mary and me." Bob said, "I agree. A toast is in order."

After the food arrived and the champagne was on the table, Bob and Ellen dumped their water. Bill filled their glasses from the bottle. Ellen commented, "That's an enormous bottle of champagne!" Bill replied, "I ordered a magnum, since there are four of us. We might as well get a little happy our first day here." They all touched glasses and Bill made his toast, "To our successful marriage and to the successful search for pirate's treasure." Bob added, "And to Ellen's and my engagement and to excellent fishing." They drank heartily to those toasts. They talked for awhile about the fun they would soon be having in the restaurants and theaters. Finally Bill refilled the glasses and Ellen made a toast, "To the never ending powerful sex drive of wives, may they never tire of delighting their husbands." She winked at Bob and he blushed quite noticeably. He replied, "I'll drink to that." They clicked their glasses together and drank to a worthy toast. Bob explained quietly to Bill that he and Ellen had been discussing whether women diminish in sexuality after marriage and that it got rather heated. He warned Bill softly, "I think possibly Ellen has had enough champagne for awhile. Her tolerance is not very high. We never drink." Bill whispered back, "I won't order any more today. I think I see what you mean." Bill was watching Ellen eat her shrimp. More than a little of it was getting on her blouse.

Ellen said, "I'm sure that I could have a baby at my age. Think about the settlers of our land. The women got married much younger than I am and they started having children right away." Mary responded tactfully, "You're absolutely right, Ellen. Our society forces women to wait for child rearing long after their bodies are ready for it. I don't understand it. I suppose it's partly because parents want their children to marry for the right reasons." Bill replied, "The divorce rates are so high, I can't imagine any generation saying that they did it the right way." Bob sighed, "Maybe I worry too much about what my parents think." Ellen answered, "I worry about my parents too. I care about what they think, but I'm tired of not being an adult. If we have our own money, why can't we just be like adults?" Bill stated, "Being adult isn't all a bed of roses. When you have children you have to care for them. It's a big responsibility. Sure you can hire baby sitters or nannies, but a child needs plenty of time with its parents."

Mary volunteered, "I'm a little scared of having kids at my age. I want to have them right away though, so they can enjoy Bill while he's still athletic. When the oldest one is fifteen, Bill will be sixty-five." Bill frowned, "I should still be athletic then. I take good care of myself!" Bob jumped in, "Now don't you two start fighting. Ellen and I had our turn today. Why don't you two just skip it?" Mary said, "Right, Bob. We need to celebrate. What shall we do?" Ellen said, "I want to search for gold right now! I saw some people on the beach with metal detectors. Let's go buy some and look for gold coins on the beach." Mary yelled, "Gold! Gold!" Bill whispered to Bob, "I think Mary is starting to feel the champagne too." Bob laughed and said, "Let's get those metal detectors." They tipped the waitress generously and asked her where they could find metal detectors. She drew them a map and handed it to Bill. Bill said, "We need a driver. We've all been drinking." She said, "I can get off for forty-five minutes. It's my lunch break. I'll drive you down there." To there surprise she had a Rolls Royce. They all climbed in. Bill said, "If you'll excuse my saying so, but you drive an awfully expensive car for a waitress." She replied, "I own the bed and breakfast. I just like meeting people and serving them. My father made a fortune on the stock market. He bought AT&T before it became so successful. He died last year and my mother has been dead for five years. I'm the only child, so I inherited plenty of money. I bought the bed and breakfast and bought stock in a Chinese gas pipeline company. I heard that some well respected money people were investing, so I got in too." Bill replied, "That's an incredible coincidence. My wife, Mary, advised me to buy that stock just a couple days ago. I made a ten percent return the first day." The waitress said, "By the way, my name is Sandy, Sandy Booth, and I'm not related to John Wilkes Booth. I plan to sell my stock in a couple years. I wouldn't hold on to yours for too long. When the big investors start taking profits the stock will go down drastically. I don't plan to stay in for the long haul like my father did. Things are changing too rapidly these days." Mary jumped in, "I plan on playing the stock market too. I was thinking of also investing in China. It's where the action is. I'll just watch for the latest development and jump in on it while it's growing in a strong way." Sandy replied, "It sounds like you have good common sense. I think you will do well. We should stay in touch, I love to talk the stock market." She handed Mary her business card. "I'll be looking forward to hearing from you." Mary replied, "I'll be sure to stay in touch."

They arrived at the metal detector store and Bill quickly bought four metal detectors. Sandy drove them back to the bed and breakfast. They all put on their swim suits and went up and down the beach looking for gold and silver coins. After hours of searching they found one small gold coin. Sandy came up in a very small bikini and said, "I don't work after three in the afternoon. I thought I'd get a little sun. You may have better luck down the beach about a mile. This area gets checked almost every day by our tourists. That area to the west is more primitive and doesn't get so much traffic." They thanked Sandy and walked to the west. Sandy was quite shapely and looked like she was about thirty five years old. Mary noticed that she was a natural blond and had stunning blue eyes. She decided to keep a close eye on her husband. She didn't want him to be tempted on their first day together.

Mary noticed that Bill was so intent on looking for gold that he didn't even seem to notice Sandy. She was pleased by that. Ellen heard her detector go off and dug down in the sand. She let out a squeal, "It's gold!" She rinsed her find off in the water and showed it to everyone. Bill said, "That proves there is pirate's gold near here. Too bad we can't search in the water close to the shore." Bob volunteered, "If one ship came this close with treasure on board, there are probably others further out."

They kept looking but only found a few small pieces of gold chain. Mary thought out loud, "They were probably trying to get to the orient to trade for silk and other goods that are characteristic of that area. They must have been trying to get past Florida so they could go further west. I'll bet that we can find other treasure near sand bars where ships might have been hung up and torn to pieces." Bill responded, "I think you are one the right track. We need to think like the explorers did. Not all the boats were pirate ships. The pirates probably knew the waters better than the traders. We should look for trading ships in the waters further out." Bob said, "Whether the ships were pirate ships or trading ships, they would have cannons on board. Those will most likely be what our sonar will detect first." Bill exclaimed, "And then we can swim down with underwater hand held metal detectors and find the place where the treasure was deposited as their ships broke to pieces!"

Sandy said, "I don't want to listen in if you want to talk business. I can tell that treasure hunting is serious business for all of you. If I can be of any assistance to any of you, just let me know. She walked briskly back towards her own beach. Bob looked as she walked away. Ellen kicked him and said, "Try not to strain your eyes, Bob." Bob turned his eyes back to Ellen and replied, "It doesn't hurt to look a little, does it. She's way too old for me." Ellen said, "If it turns you on so much I'll start walking like she does." Ellen paraded around swaying her hips in an exaggerated manner. Bob said, "You do that quite well! I don't mind if you walk like that." Ellen jumped on him and wrestled him down in the sand. She started throwing sand on him. He threw sand back. Finally they went into the water and rinsed off. They started kissing in the water. Mary knew they wouldn't be finding any more gold coins. She and Bill looked till the sun went down. They each found a gold piece of eight. Bill said, "These are worth enough to pay for our trip!" Mary responded, "We need to come out here first thing in the morning at five o'clock. The waves will have washed up more coins by then." Bill said, "We should be able to find quite a few coins by the time the boats arrive."

They all sat in the sand and watched the sun setting into the horizon. The golden glow reflected off the bodies of the girls and made them look even better to their men. The two pairs held hands as they walked back to Sandy's bed and breakfast. They ordered a late supper of pizza and chicken wings. The waitress had been told by Sandy to give them the most excellent service. She anticipated their every whim and brought them cup after cup of strong coffee. They loved the coffee there. In the nearby outdoor hot tub, Sandy was soaking in the steamy water.

Occasionally she glanced over at their table. Finally she got out and dried off with a towel. She walked over to there table and spoke softly, "At night clothing is optional in the hot tub." Mary answered, "We appreciate the freedom. We may use it a little later tonight." They all laughed nervously. Mary rang the bell and their waitress came quickly. She told the waitress, "We'd like more chicken wings and two cartons full of them so we can take some to our room." The waitress asked, "Is there anything else?" Mary said, "Please have a small bottle of your best champagne delivered to our room." The waitress replied, "As you wish. Would you like two glasses or four?" Mary said, "I think we should have four. Our friends might want to come up for a night cap." Ellen responded, "As long as it's not one of those magnum bottles. I shouldn't drink that much." Mary added, "I'll do the pouring. I can make sure you don't drink too much. Just don't start drinking out of other people's glasses." Ellen smiled, "I'll be good. I hope I didn't get out of line at lunch." Mary said, "You were funny. But you shouldn't get that wasted again. It's not good to over indulge." Bill said, "She speaks with the wisdom of the ages." Bob said, "I've heard that wine is for the poor to give them a merry heart." Bill said, "In that case we'd better drink quite moderately. We're happy enough already." Mary said, "I agree. I'm very happy. I don't need a drink. We'll each just have a little sip."

They went to the living room and lit the gas fireplace. It was a little cool out after the sun was down. Bill went to the bedroom and got the champagne. He brought the glasses down on a tray already poured. Mary proposed the toast. "May the money I gave away today bring happiness to many people and may we all be protected from evil by Jesus." They clicked glasses and sipped the champagne. Bob said, "I would like to propose a toast." They all looked at him. "To the hot tub. May Ellen and I have it first." Ellen slugged him on the shoulder. "Don't be that way. I mean,

I agree, but try to be serious." Mary said, "I don't mind. You two love birds go out and use the tub. We'll sit by the fire for awhile and talk." Bob and Ellen ran out and got in the tub. They liked the warm bubbling water. Bob stated, "This is a wonderful hot tub. It's fun." The two kissed in the tub and looked up at the stars and the moon.

Bill looked at Mary's face next to the flickering fire. He thought she was incredibly beautiful. "What was the biggest reason you married me, Mary?" Mary replied, "There are too many reasons. You are so helpful. When you rubbed that lotion on my butt it excited me." Bill laughed, "The old butt rub trick; it works every time." Mary went on, "No, seriously, I fell in love with you when I first looked into your eyes. You were so warm. I knew you wanted me, but I didn't want to take any chance of losing you. I was hoping you would like the looks of my body. I hoped you would want me around longer than just one hot date." Bill responded, "You're incredibly smart. Who did you say your parents are?" Mary smiled, "I'm adopted. I was raised by a nice Indian couple in Culebra, New Mexico. They told me that my real parents were quite intelligent, but they couldn't raise me for some reason. That's why I want to have plenty of children and raise them properly. It isn't pleasant knowing that your real parents didn't want you, no matter how good their reasons might have been." Bill asked, "What are the names of the couple who raised you?" Mary answered, "My father is Joseph and my mother is Betty. I wish they could have been at the wedding, but there was no time. I should warn you that they have only known me for one day as a twenty-one year old. They still think of me as their young child." Bill responded, "I thought of that. You should call them every day and tell them what you're doing. Don't say we're married. Just call me your friend. We can break the marriage part to them in a couple months. Maybe they will guess the truth after awhile." Mary said, "They will be happy that I have a close friend. They worried about me when I was in the desert. I couldn't contact them. I spent two years out there, learning about herbs and magic."

They talked till late and then went out and enjoyed the hot tub for awhile. They too enjoyed looking at the stars while they enjoyed the warm water. The lack of clothing made them feel free and happy. They kissed for a long while. With some reluctance each of them put on the robe they had brought with them. With quick steps they made their way to the bedroom. Mary and Bill did their best to keep quiet as their passions took over. Mary thought, "It's wonderful to be married to Bill. He's so affectionate." They fell asleep in each others arms. After about an hour Mary woke up. She realized that she had forgotten her prayers. She woke Bill and asked him to join her. They got on their knees and took turns praying to Jesus. They thanked him for allowing them to be together. They asked for forgiveness of sins and asked for protection from evil. Mary crawled back in bed. Bill asked, "Are you sure you want to look for gold at five in the morning. Can't we sleep in?" Mary answered, "Set the alarm for five o'clock. We can look for gold for several hours and then come back and take a nap. Once you're rested, who knows what will happen." She squeezed him and he sighed, "Please, Mary, I'm an old man; let me sleep." Mary exclaimed, "Don't say that! I know how to bring out that energy. Just think positive!" Bill said, "O.K., I'm a young man; just not anymore tonight." He put his arm around her and they fell asleep.

When the alarm went off in the morning, they took a shower together, dressed and went out to search for treasure. Mary said, "We can eat a late breakfast after we find enough gold." Bill responded, "That's what I like, thinking positive." They raced to their favorite spot and started sweeping back and forth with the metal detectors. They concentrated their search down by the water's edge, where waves would have deposited new finds during the night. It was a blessed day. Mary said, "I'm glad we prayed last night. I think we are being blessed." They each found several large gold and silver coins. Bill exclaimed, "I love this. It's exciting." Mary exclaimed, "I found another one." She stooped down and pulled up a long slender gold bar. Bill shouted, "An ingot! That's worth several thousand dollars. We'll have to declare these finds." Mary asked, "What will they do, take the gold?" Bill answered, "Since we found the treasure on the beach, they can't take the gold, but they can make us pay tax on it. The only way to avoid being taxed to death is to reinvest the money the same year. You can be thinking about ways we can invest our treasure. The government is dear to me and I don't mind paying taxes, but why should we give them most of the money? We can build a vast estate so our children can live well." Mary replied, "Our children will be smart enough to do well on their own. I would like to leave them some money to get started on. It takes money to make money." Bill replied, "Exactly, they will need a couple million each to get started." Mary exclaimed, "We'll need to teach them about religion and generosity to the poor! I don't want to raise a bunch of greedy children!" Bill responded, "That's a good point. We need to find a way to encourage their spiritual growth and at the same time encourage them to be aggressive investors."

They started searching for more gold. Mary thought about how they could invest their gold profits, and the profits from her husband's investment in the Chinese gas pipeline company. She tried to concentrate, but she kept finding more pieces of gold. Finally it came to her. They should make a business of starting other businesses. They could help third world countries attract contracts by setting up the basics for industry. She could feed people and make them healthy so they could work in newly developed factories. This sort of investment would eventually bring them profits. They could use the profits to start even more businesses. She told Bill about the idea. He said, "It would be better than giving hand outs. People need work to do, but you're right, first they need to be healthy enough to work. I like your ideas, Mary. At least they would give us a tax shelter. If any money ever comes back from the third world businesses, we could put it into a trust for our children. Even if there's no profit, I'll find plenty of money for our children. I've got millions in a retirement pension. That money alone will do the trick. We can do whatever you want to do with the money from this gold." Mary gave him a hug and kissed him passionately. She sighed, "I think it's time for that nap we promised ourselves. They took their gold and ran back to the bed and breakfast. They spent some quality time rubbing each other in the shower before they went to bed for a nap. Mary set the alarm so they wouldn't miss supper.

When the alarm woke them, Mary and Bill dressed for supper. They went to the front desk and notified the woman at the front desk that they would be eating in the garden. Sandy overheard them from the next room and came over to ask them, "Do you mind if I join you this evening. I'm dying to hear how your treasure hunting went this morning." Mary responded, "I'd love to have you join us. I have several things I'd like to share with you." Bill chimed in, "Yes, we'd love for you to spend a little time with us."

They walked to the garden and sat at one of the white wrought iron tables. The waitress came and took their orders. Mary ordered the Lobster with drawn butter. Sandy and Bill followed her lead. They also ordered baked potatoes and tossed salads. Bill ordered a small bottle of white German wine; it was a Rhine wine called Swartz Katz. "It's not an expensive wine," volunteered Bill, "but it is one of my favorites." As they waited for the food, they sipped on their glasses of wine and Sandy quizzed them on their gold finds. Mary said, "I found a long heavy ingot of gold. It's surprising that the waves could bring it up on the shore. The wind must have gotten fairly strong last night." Sandy replied, "There were forty mile per hour winds last night. Such strong winds are capable of amazing things. That ingot is worth thousands of dollars. Did you find anything else?" Bill replied, "We found many large gold coins. Do you know where we can sell them? Sandy replied, "I would be glad to buy them from you. Did you notice the display of gold and silver that I keep in the living room opposite the fireplace. It helps inspire my customers to return in search of more coins. Not many of them have been as fortunate as you two have been." Mary responded, "I think Bill will agree that we'd be happy to sell them to you." Bill added, "We'll sell you most of what we find here. I'm sure you'll give us a fair price."

The food arrived and they quietly enjoyed the lobster. When they were finishing their meals, Mary told Sandy, "I'm starting an investment group that will be starting businesses in third world countries. The initial thrust will be for good nutrition and health, but once a strong work force is created, we would set up production centers with the goal of making a profit over the long haul. Bill and I see it as an excellent tax shelter and a way to make a positive impact on the world." Sandy replied, "I've been looking for another good tax shelter. The taxes that I pay are incredible. It's rough on a person when you make millions of dollars each year." She laughed roguishly. Mary asked, "Then you'll join us?" Sandy said, "You can count on me for matching funds. Whatever you put in I'll match. Unless you find so much gold that your contribution exceeds one hundred million. I'm not the richest person in America you know; only exceptionally rich." She laughed again. "You two are so clever, I don't doubt that you will surpass me in wealth if you haven't already, but I'm not into competition of that kind. I only want enough money to live well and so that I can afford to be generous with the poor. I've heard that the rich will have as much trouble getting into heaven as a camel would have getting through the eye of a needle. That's why I want to be generous with the poor. I don't want to go to hell." Bill responded, "That's a prudent approach to things. I hope it works." Mary said, "I just became a Christian this week. I absolutely want to go to heaven when I die. My preacher told me it was important to pray for forgiveness of sins every day." Sandy replied, "You're good for me, Mary. I have been negligent about praying. I know I can't buy my way to heaven. I just don't get into praying very much. I pray on Sundays mainly, when I manage to make it to church." Mary said, "We could go with you this Sunday. That would help you to be sure to go." Sandy said, "I'll look forward to that. It'll be fun if some friends go with me."

They all had some mint ice cream for desert. Bill volunteered, "Mary and I will have the charter for the investment group set up in a couple weeks. When it's ready we'll let you know." Sandy replied, "I'll let my friends know about it once it's established. I think it's an excellent idea. We need to show the whole world that business is good for everyone, not just the rich. I don't see why terrorists want to blow us up!" Bill replied, "That's just politics. They don't like America helping the Jews. It's a struggle that may never end. We just need to protect ourselves. We can't let almost anyone into our country like we used to. The borders must be protected." Mary responded, "We try to alleviate suffering, and others insist on creating more suffering. It's frustrating."

They talked more about the world and events until it was dark. Sandy had some torches lit around the hot tub and they all got on their suits. They didn't want to be immodest in a group setting. Sandy had also arranged for a classical guitarist to perform for them. He was a young man in his twenties with dark black hair and a moustache.

He not only played many classical pieces for them, he played their requests as well. He could play by ear and was an excellent musician. After the heat of the tub got to be too much, they dismissed the musician and went to the living room and sat around the fire. Sandy showed them her favorite works of art from an art encyclopedia she had owned for fifteen years. She told them, "This book has given me much pleasure. The men I have dated during my life have caused me to grow tired of them, but I never get tired of this book. I have quite a collection of art books. Possible some day we can all go to a museum together." Bill responded, "That sounds great." Mary chimed in, "I'd love to go." Sandy went on, "There's an exhibition in Miami this weekend. We could fly over in my jet to see it and still be back in time for church." Bill and Mary agreed to go. They set the time for departure at Saturday morning, nine o'clock. They wanted plenty of time to see as much as they wanted to see.

The threesome stayed up till quite late playing cards in front of the fireplace. Sandy told them all about her life. Mary told about her whirlwind romance with Bill and how he proposed on their first date. Sandy was shocked. She asked, "How can you fall in love that quick? I can't find a man that makes me happy. They are either too aggressive or too lazy. Is there no middle ground?" Bill laughed and asked, "Have you ever had a man rub your butt with lotion on the first date?" Sandy replied, "I've done more than that, but what's your point?" Mary jumped in, "Bill means that we quickly developed a strong physical attraction to each other and that was immediately followed by intimate talk which let us know that we needed each other." Bill added, I was swept off my feet by Mary's beauty. Mary, please excuse me, but you seem like such a prude." Mary said, "Well, that was before I became a Christian. That same day Bill converted me." Sandy responded, "You married her and converted her on the same day?" Bill answered sheepishly, "I know it's not the ideal scenario, but I couldn't let her get away. I knew I wanted her for my own the day I first set eyes on her, but I wanted a Christian wife. When I found out she was an Indian witch doctor, I knew I had to do something about it. She was eager for a change, so . . ." Sandy exclaimed, "Wait a minute . . . Indian witch doctor? This is getting a little hard to believe!" Mary explained her training in the desert, and the Jade Goddess. She went on, "Don't say anything about the witch doctor stuff to Bob and Ellen. We aren't ready to tell them yet. They would just worry unnecessarily." Sandy sighed, "Don't worry a bit. I can keep a secret. No wonder you want to do some good deeds. You probably have many sins to make up for." Mary said, "I pray for forgiveness. That takes care of my sinning, but you weren't entirely wrong. I was supposed to kill many people if I wanted a nice afterlife. That's one of the main reasons I got out. I knew I wouldn't be able to kill people."

Sandy responded, "I really can't see you killing many people." She laughed. "I love you both and your lives are exceedingly interesting, but I'm afraid I'm going to need to get some sleep now." Reluctantly she stood up from in front of the fire where she had been sitting and walked towards the door. "We can talk some more tomorrow night if you'd like. I love the fire place in the evening when it's cool." Mary replied, "We'd like that. We can sip some of the white wine by the fire." Bill spoke sleepily, "Yes, some more wine and conversation would be nice. We'll meet you after supper."

Sandy went to her quarters, and Bill and Mary went up to their room and showered. When they got in the bed they didn't go right to sleep. The left the covers back and did what honeymooners do so well. They tried new things together. They spent several hours being typical honeymooners before they finally tired and got on their knees beside the bed to say their prayers. They finished their usual prayers and then Mary asked that the new investment group would prosper. With their prayers finished, they crawled into bed and fell asleep in each other's arms. All night long they dreamed they were still making love to each other.

The bright golden morning light woke the love birds, or they would have slept till noon. In the garden they enjoyed some breakfast and listened to the seagulls calling as they fought the stiff breeze that was blowing. Bob and Ellen dropped by and joined them for breakfast. Ellen proudly displayed their new cell phone. She said, "We should have gotten one of these a long time ago. We don't usually need one, but we got thinking. We know how to reach you, but you couldn't reach us; so we got the phone. Here's our number." She handed Mary a piece of paper with the number written on it. Ellen continued, "We wanted to know, the minute the boats arrive." Bill replied, "That was good thinking. I was wondering how to get in touch with you. The boats should be here in another week. We're going to Miami this Saturday to see a museum. Sandy's taking us in her jet. I'm sure she wouldn't mind if you want to come along." Bob intervened, "We'd like to come, but Ellen and I want to spend some more time alone. We haven't had enough of that yet." Bill responded, "I understand completely. Maybe at a later date we can do something like that." Ellen replied, "That would be great. I like art, but I agree with Bob; we need more time alone together. The beach is nice, even though there has been some pretty strong wind. At least the sun has been shining most of the time."

Mary volunteered, "We decided to start an investment group that will help start businesses in third world countries. I was wondering if you might be interested. The group would concentrate on feeding the people first and making sure they have health care. Then we would introduce factories that could work on contracts. It would most likely yield a profit eventually." Bob said, "We helped feed people in Alaska with the fish we caught. I got a good feeling from that. I think we could help you in a small way; maybe a hundred thousand to start with." Ellen said, "That sounds good to me. If we have so much money, we can at least help others with some of the money." Mary said, "Great! We'll have the group set up in a couple weeks. Bill's lawyer is working on it now. He called him last night." Bob said, "Just let us know when you're ready for the check."

Ellen said, "Bob and I will probably spend the afternoon on the beach, but why don't we all go see Hemingway's house and then see his favorite bar? Bill said, "I'll call a taxi. They know where everything is. He can lead us to the house and bar." Bill used his cell phone and called information for the taxi number. Next, he dialed the taxi. In fifteen minutes the taxi was waiting. Bill told him the plan and the man agreed to do it. He led them as they drove along in their rental car. It was a roomy Mercedes. In no time at all they were able to learn from the taxi driver where the places of interest were. Bill paid the taxi driver and tipped him.

They all looked around the house for awhile and read the many information sheets that were posted at sights of interest. There was a typewriter facing the east window. Apparently the great man liked to watch the morning sun as he worked. After they had seen everything in the house, they went to the bar that was the writer's favorite. They went inside and saw the many pictures of Hemingway that covered the walls. They talked with the bartender and drank coffee.

"At one o'clock," Ellen said, "I think Bob and I will be on our way." Mary said, "We'll drop you off at your place. Bill drove them back to their bed and breakfast. They said goodbyes and then Ellen led Bob to the bed room. They put their suits on and went down to the beach. They spread out a large beach blanket and lay down to sun themselves. They never tired of looking at each other.

Bob said, "How many children should we have?" Ellen replied, "I think two is the ideal number. If you have too many children you start having trouble with some of them not thinking they are as loved as the others. If you will spend enough time with them, I'll give you all the children you want. How many do you think you want?" Bob responded, "We have plenty of money, why not have plenty of children. Just promise me you'll keep your nice figure." Ellen retorted, "All the women in my family are slender. I could have ten children and still stay slender between children." Bob sighed, "That sounds good. There's one problem. How do I get sex when you're pregnant?" Ellen laughed, "Don't worry, I'll be a good wife and find some sexy way to keep you happy." Bob laughed, "I knew you were a resourceful woman!" He kissed her on the lips. They didn't want to make too big of a public display, so they stopped kissing after a few minutes. They relaxed and enjoyed the sun as it baked their skin. Ellen sighed, "I never get very tan. I just burn over and over again." Bob replied, "Remember how tan I got last summer. Down here I'll get a deep dark tan." Ellen responded, "I like it when you get a good tan." Bob replied, "You look real nice when you get some sun. You look flushed pink and healthy." Ellen replied, "Now that sounds like a real compliment. I know you're trying though, so thank you."

They chatted for hours while they soaked up the sun. Ellen stated, "I'm starting to feel a little guilty about not praying like Mary and Bill do. I just feel funny praying when we are always so passionate. I guess I don't really want to repent for that. Bob said, "If you feel distant from God, maybe we should go back to just kissing. Ellen replied, "We will be doing some dangerous diving soon. I don't want a shark to eat me and then go to hell because I was being too sensual and not praying for forgiveness." Bob continued along the same line, "You have a good point. I believe in hell and I certainly don't want to go there. Diving is dangerous. I'm sure Bill is a good instructor, but we shouldn't count on necessarily living through this adventure. We can pull back on the sensual stuff. We need to pray together every night like Bill and Mary do. I want to stop feeling like I'm angering God." Bob sighed, "I think you're right. It will be hard to go back to the way we were in Alaska." Ellen said, "I must have felt like I needed to compete with Mary. She got her man right away and got married the next day. I wish we could do that." Bob exclaimed, "We could get married here in Florida. I think the legal age for marriage is younger here!" Ellen reacted, "I want my parents to attend and I want the wedding in Indiana! Let's just wait another year. We can be married in Indiana with our parent's consent. I know people younger than we are who got married that way." Bob agreed, "We'll do it your way. Just so I can still kiss you all the time. Don't cut back on that." Ellen smiled and started kissing him. It was getting late and Bob was hungry. He interrupted, "We should get something to eat." Ellen responded, "Yes, there are too many people watching us here anyway. We can make out in our room after supper." They went to Mary and Bill's place and found them waiting for them, drinking coffee in the garden.

Bill shouted, "Welcome friends! Come and join us! Bob and Ellen pulled up chairs and Mary rang the bell for service. The waitress came with coffee for Bob and Ellen. Ellen stated, "I'd like something different tonight. I think I'll have some clam chowder." Mary said, "That sounds great." Everyone agreed. They all ordered the clam chowder. Bill told the waitress, "I'd like a magnum champagne, the best you have, and four glasses." By now the waitress knew that Bill and Mary were drinking too. She didn't act like she suspected they were too young. Ellen said softly after the waitress went away, "I appreciate the generosity, but I won't be drinking anymore till it's legal for me to. I've been trying to get closer to God." Mary responded, "She's right, Bill. And we shouldn't drink in front of them. It makes it harder for them to do the right thing." Bill rang the bell and when the waitress came he cancelled the order for the champagne. Bill asked the waitress, "Could you make us all exotic fruit drinks with no alcohol in them?" The waitress responded, "I can make you our house special. It has mango juice, pineapple, papaya and orange juice with seven-up and blended ice. I know you will all love it. It's on the house tonight."

She left and made their drinks. In ten minutes she was serving them their delicious treats. She handed them a drink list and said, "These are all the non-alcoholic beverages we offer. They should keep you entertained during your stay with us." The group looked over the list. Bob said, "This is an impressive variety. I guess it won't be too hard to do without alcohol. Ellen and I are serious about getting closer to God. It'll be tough, but we want to stop acting like we're married. We know we need to wait another year. Our parents would probably prefer two years, but I think they will understand. We can't wait forever. Passion is trying to tell us something." Mary added, "I guess I haven't set a very good example to the two of you. Bill and I got married too quickly. You will have plenty of fun here in Florida without being married. Bill told me he wants us to start our diving lessons tomorrow. Is that fine with both of you?" Bob responded, "The sooner the better. We want to be skilled divers." Ellen chimed in, "Yes, I want to dive as soon as possible." Bill told them, "I rented a couple hours of time at the local high school for the training sessions. I'd like us all to go to a dive shop I found and buy our equipment tomorrow morning."

The clam chowder arrived and they all stopped to eat. Bill asked, "What time would you like us to meet in the morning?" Bill replied, "I think we should meet at breakfast at eight o'clock. We can buy the dive equipment and be to the pool by eleven." Mary stated, "I'd like to search for gold on the beach early tomorrow morning." Ellen responded, "I'd like to do that also." Bob and Bill agreed as well. Mary said, "We should start around five o'clock if we want to be sure no one else beats us to the treasure." Bob replied, "We all need to get to bed early if we want to get up at four." Ellen volunteered, "We should all relax in the hot tub for a while." Mary responded, "I like that idea. It will help us to get to sleep early." They finished their meal and got dressed in their suits for the hot tub. After about thirty minutes of hot water and chatting, they parted company and went to bed early.

Bob and Ellen slept together with their pajamas on. They didn't even kiss much. Bob put his arm around Ellen and they went to sleep. Bill and Mary went to bed and said their prayers. They fell right to sleep. When each couple woke to their alarm in the morning, it was still dark out. By the time they were showered dressed and on the beach, the eastern horizon was just starting to show some signs of light. They turned on their metal detectors and started sweeping back and forth. There hadn't been much wind that night and not much new gold had washed up from the depths. They managed to find some small coins with a total value of around four hundred dollars wholesale at the time. Mary said, "I enjoy finding gold this way, but we'll never finance our investment group this way. I can't wait till we find a major pile of gold from some wrecked ship." Bill replied, "It won't be long now. We might find our first treasure ship in less than a month from now. But it could take several years. I hope we don't need to search that long." Bob stated, "I plan on doing some fishing while I wait for the big gold find." Ellen replied, "There should be plenty of time for fishing, but you'll need to do your share of diving." Bob answered, "I think I'll enjoy diving. I can see the fish while I'm down there."

Three miles off the coast of Georgia, Bill's two boats were making rapid progress towards Key West. They stayed in sight of each other and were moving along at 25 knots. Mark was piloting Big Angel One and Jim was at the helm of Big Angel Two. Linda was working eagerly at dusting Big Angel One. She was a good worker, even though she spent a good deal of time flirting. She went back and forth between Steve, the cook and Mark the pilot. She wanted to keep them company. They both appreciated her attentions. When Mark had to stop the boat so he could rest, Linda would play cards with Steve till late at night. She wore a white outfit that included a short skirt. Linda loved to let Steve caress her legs. He had initiated the practice almost the minute they started playing cards in the galley. They drank coffee together and started doing some kissing. Soon the cards were dropped on the floor and the entire time was spent kissing.

In the other boat things were much calmer. When Jim took a break from piloting, he and Mike would have a meal and both men would spend time reading before Jim went to bed. Jim needed more sleep because of the strain of being at the helm all day. Mike would stay up and read much later into the night. Mike had notice how attractive Linda was. He was looking forward to the day she would come and clean his boat. In another six hours the two boats would continue their long voyage. They would reach Key West in three more days if the weather continued to hold.

Back in Key West, when five o'clock came, Mary and Bill were already at their favorite spot sweeping back and forth for coins. There had been some wind that night and they hoped some new treasure had been washed up. Bob and Ellen arrived about a half hour later. Bob apologized, "I'm sorry we're a little late. We just couldn't get moving this morning. Ellen stated, "He would have made it on time if there had been fishing involved." Mary replied, "You should get your chance to fish soon. The Big Angel

One called last night. They're off the coast of Georgia and will be here in three days." Bob shouted, "Great! I can't wait to go fishing!" Bill exclaimed, "I've got something. His metal detector was giving off a loud buzzing sound. Bill stooped down and dug with his fingers. He was right at the water's edge. He pulled up a fairly thick chain with a cross attached. When he rinsed it off, he could tell it was pure gold. Bill exclaimed, "This is too nice to sell. I'm giving it to you, Mary. I want you to wear it." Mary came over and looked at the chain and cross in the low light. She said, "I think it will look wonderful when it's cleaned up. I'll wear it always, Bill." She gave her new husband a big hug and then squeezed his hands.

"Let's find some more gold!" she exclaimed. They all started working seriously along the edge of the water. By seven o'clock, they each had found quite a few gold coins. The small bowl Mary had brought along to hold the gold was nearly full. It was heavy now. Mary let Bill carry it. Bill said, "These coins should be worth around twenty thousand dollars wholesale." Bob replied, "Not bad for two hours work. How much an hour did we make?" Ellen answered, "Divide twenty thousand by two hours. That makes ten thousand. Divide that by four people. That makes two thousand five hundred. We each made two thousand five hundred dollars per hour." Bob stated, "I think I'll get out of bed on time next time. We need to do this every morning." Bill said, "If there's no wind at night, there won't be much new treasure on the beach. We should still try. It's a nice way to start the day."

They all went back to Sandy's place to eat breakfast in the garden. Sandy came out to wait table for them. When she saw all the gold she exclaimed, "I've never seen any group bring that much gold back in one morning. Will you sell it to me?" Bill replied, "We want to keep the gold cross and chain I found. I'm giving it to Mary. She wants to wear it. We'll sell all the coins to you. How much are they worth?"

Sandy responded, "I'll give you twelve thousand for them, it's all I have on me." She reached into her waitress apron and pulled out a stack of hundred dollar bills. She laid it on the table. "Is this enough?" Bill said, "That's a little more than we expected. We'll put it into the investment group for starting businesses in third world counties." Sandy replied, "I knew you would. That's why I paid you a little extra." Ellen said, "Do you always carry so much cash with you?" Sandy said, "I often need it to buy gold." She giggled and took their orders. They all had ham and eggs with toast. When she left to get the food, Bill said, "I suspect that she plants some of that gold for us to find. Why else would she be giggling?" Mary said, "Do you think this is her gold cross?" Bill said, "If it is, I'm sure she wants you to have it. She has a long generous streak in her." Mary said, "Why don't we ask her to be president of the investment group? Everyone would like her." Bill responded, "I like the idea. What do you and Ellen think, Bob?" Bob replied, "I like her. She would be good if she will do it." Ellen chipped in, "Let's ask her to do it. I like her too."

When Sandy returned with the food, Mary told her, "We would all like you to be the president of the investment group. Will you do it?" Sandy laughed, "I've always wanted to be the president of something. I'd be happy to do it. Just so I don't have to keep track of the money." Bill replied, "My lawyer will collect the money and channel it where the club directs him to. All you need to do is host our meetings and make some appearances for membership drives and other promotional work. It shouldn't take more than fifty hours per year." Sandy stated, "I can certainly give up that much of my time for such a worthy cause. Thank you for asking me." They asked her to sit with them during breakfast. She sat for a little while and listened to their update on the location of the boats. They also told her about the scuba lessons that would start that day.

When they had finished with breakfast and drinking coffee, they drove to the dive shop. They tried on fins and masks. Each of them bought a snorkel and air tank with regulator. Bill stated, "I'll need to buy fifteen air tanks. I need them delivered to my boat, Big Angel Two. The boat will be arriving at the marina in three days. My pilot will show you where to store the tanks. Make sure they are all full. The gold we are searching for will go to help third world countries. Can you give us a discount on our rather large purchase today?" Tom, the store keeper, answered, "I'm always eager to help out a worthy cause. I'll give you twenty percent off. Can I interest you in a couple underwater towing vehicles. They are used, but in excellent condition. These electric micro boats will pull you along at five miles per hour. The price for you is one thousand dollars each." Bill responded, "I'll take one. We'll see how we like it. I forgot, we all need wet suits suitable for one hundred and fifty feet down. We'll be searching in the general area of Key West. That will help you judge how much thermal protection we need." Tom replied, "I'll get everyone fitted with a suit right away." He led them to the back of the store and started measuring them and helping them find the right suits.

Bill paid Tom in full and the group went to the high school pool for their first training session. They all put on their swim suits and met at the side of the pool. They all climbed into the pool and Bill showed them how to clear their face masks if they got knocked around and filled with water. They all practiced using the snorkels and fins. In no time at all they were also swimming with the tanks and regulators. When it started to feel natural breathing with the scuba tanks, they went to the bottom of the deep end of the pool. They stayed down until their tanks started to run low on air. Bill wanted them to recognize when the tanks were getting low. They started needing to pull the air from the tanks. It didn't come into their lungs as easily as the air from a full tank came. Bill pointed to his pressure gauge and pointed up. They all understood him and followed him back to the shallow end of the pool. Bill asked them to all take their equipment off and lay it on the side of the pool. He put everything back into the car and they drove to the beach. Bill stated, "All of you did well today. We need to practice more in the pool for a couple days. Then we can take a charter boat out and do some shallow dives in waters not too far from shore. Each day we will dive ten feet deeper, till we get down to sixty feet. That will be deep enough for our first couple weeks of diving. We will gradually work down deeper till we all feel comfortable one hundred and twenty feet down." Mary replied, "That seems like a long way down. Will my ears hurt?" Bill reassured her, "We stop whenever the ears feel uncomfortable and wait for them to adjust. You should feel fine when you are in deep water. "I'm going to give each of you a small book that covers what you need to know about 'the bends' and decompression. Read the books carefully. I will test all of you to be sure you know everything that is important in the book."

Ellen asked, "When do we start diving from one of the Big Angels?" Bill answered, "We should be able to start diving from Big Angel Two one week from today. That will be when we all can dive to sixty feet." They read their books carefully and Bill tested them on their knowledge. Each of them learned quickly. When they weren't working on scuba diving, they went snorkeling together. They were rapidly becoming excellent swimmers.

Chapter Eight

The Boats Arrive

The boats arrived at the marina on a Saturday. Everyone was excited. They moved their belongings to Big Angel One. Introductions were made of all the crew to the divers. Bill requested that they all eat a meal together so they could get to know each other better. It was one o'clock and both cooks went to work preparing the meal. Linda, the housekeeper, helped Mary and Ellen set the table. At five o'clock they all set down to a meal of roast beef and potatoes. Bill said a prayer for the meal and then everyone started to eat. Bill announced, "I'm going to mix business with pleasure. I wanted to make sure that all the crew is willing to serve as safety workers while we are down diving. We need someone on the radio in the boat at all times. We may need a basket lowered if there is an emergency. We will need someone to run the winch when it is time to haul up treasure. Someone will need to listen to the weather radio and tell us if bad weather is approaching. Will all of you help with anything we ask you to do?" They all agreed. Linda reported, "I took good care of Joque on the trip down here. He ate well and was quite talkative."

Bill continued, "In four more days, we will start diving from Big Angel Two. We'll keep Big Angel One as living quarters. After we eat I'd like to show everyone how to use the winch and the basket. Except for meal preparation and serving in the evening, you are all free to do whatever you like for the next four days. Then we will start spending long times at sea. We may go for a month working on a good spot. We don't want to risk not being able to find the spot again. I hope that we can all have shore leave at least once a month. We will take one week of shore leave and then go back to sea." Everyone liked that arrangement. Bill took them to practice using the winch and basket. By the time it was dark they all knew how to operate it well. The setting sun spread golden and purple colors out across the water and sky. Everyone watched as the golden ball of sunshine sank down into the waters of the Gulf of Mexico.

The divers went back to their boat along with Steve the cook and Mark the pilot. They had their quarters on Big Angel One. Bob and Ellen went to their bedroom and looked it over. They tested the softness of the bed. Ellen stated, "I like the bed, it's nice a roomy." Bob responded, "The windows are bigger than I had imagined. Let's go look at the shower." They were amazed by the roominess of the shower. Bob said, "This is better than our boats. I think I'll upgrade them when I get enough money." Ellen said, "Don't try to keep up with Bill. Remember these aren't his boats. They are part of his business inventory." Bob went on, "Still, I'm going to set a goal of owning one boat like this one. We could still keep the two forty footers for fishing." Ellen said, "It's fine to have big dreams, just don't think you have to prove something to me. I'm happy with you just as you are."

Mary and Bill were looking at their bedroom and shower too. Mary stated, "This boat is good enough to live in year round. I love the big shower." Bill replied, "Is their anything in particular you would like to do in the nice roomy shower?" Mary hugged him and whispered something in his ear. He started taking off her clothes, but she said, "Not right now. Let's be sociable. We can play cards with Ellen and Bob for a couple hours." Bill agreed and they went to find their friends. They knocked on the bedroom door. Bob opened the door and asked, "What is it?" Bill answered, "Would the two of you like to play some cards in the living room?" Ellen responded, "We'd love to play. What game shall we play?" Mary answered, "I like Rook. Do you know how to play?" Ellen said, "I can learn." Mary continued, "It's an easy game to learn. We play as teams and follow suit. The ace is high and fives, tens, fourteens and aces count as points. Shall we go?" They all went to the spacious living room. It had a gas fireplace with a card table in front of it. They all sat down at the table and Mary started teaching them the game. As they played, the light from the fire flickered on the hardwood floor and all over the rest of the room. Tall oak bookcases adorned the room. They were full of the classics. Moby Dick, The Odyssey, Crime and Punishment, The Possessed; the list went on and on. When they had learned how to play the game, they started talking about other things.

Mary asked, "How are you two love birds getting along. You haven't been going to far have you?" She laughed. She loved being blunt at times. Ellen replied, "We've been quite restrained actually. We sleep with our clothes on." Mary stated, "Well I'm glad to hear it. I know you feel better about yourselves when you control your bodies." Bill jumped in, "Mary, please stop trying to embarrass Bob and Ellen." Bob responded, "It's quite alright. We like a little kidding once in a while. We long to be older like you two. It must be great being married. You can do whatever you want with each other and you don't need to feel guilty." Mary said, "It is nice. It certainly was better than living in the desert. I was raised in the desert." Ellen went on, "Tell us more about your life in the desert, Mary." Mary continued, "At first I lived with my adopted grandfather. He's a medicine man. I was his apprentice and learned all the ways of healing. I had to learn how to prepare the plants of the desert for use as medicine. Grandfather and I would eat, drink or smoke the plants so that I would understand what they did. He trained me spiritually too. I learned to know the Gods of the desert and how to please them.

When my training with grandfather was finished, I went to the Jade Goddess on her mountain. I received powers to see into the future. I could win every time at roulette, and the Jade Goddess helped me win on the stock market. Now that I'm a Christian, I have lost those powers. I'm still a little worried that the Jade Goddess will appear to me and try to win back my loyalty. It will always be a little tempting to ask for her help I suppose. She was exceedingly kind and friendly, but she admitted that her power came from Satan." Ellen asked, "So you became a witch?" Mary replied, "Don't get scared. I never killed anyone. I would have needed to do plenty of killing though if I wanted to have a pleasant afterlife. That is why I was so happy when Bill offered me a way out." Ellen went on, "It's hard to imagine you as a witch! Bill replied, "I'm keeping an eye on her. She has the Holy Spirit in her now. It will protect her from any attack from other Gods. Bob replied, "I thought once a person became a witch, they were lost forever." Mary answered, "I never swore an oath against Jesus. The Jade Goddess made my father swear that he thought the Father of Jesus was evil. That is supposed to be an unforgivable sin. My father is trying to serve penance for that sin by winning many people to Jesus. He has become an evangelist." Bob said, "I hope he is forgiven. It doesn't pay to anger God."

Mary told more about her life with the High One and how she won millions of dollars at Las Vegas. She didn't tell them about how she was changed from eleven to twenty-one. Mary asked, "I haven't scared the two of you, have I?" Ellen responded, "I trust you. It's obvious that you've made a change. Do you think you'll ever see the future again?" Mary responded, "I'm starting to pray for that. I've been reading in my devotional book that there are many powers which Christians are given. There were Christian prophets in the Bible who could see the future. I know it's asking for something exceptionally big. I should be happy with the gift of helps. I have always been a healer. I like the idea of helping people." Bill stated, "You are being a great helper with the investment group you're starting. It will help millions of people." Mary acquiesced, "I hope you're right. I want to see the future so I can do well on the stock market. That's the surest way for me to help fund the investment group." Bill said, "You don't have much faith in our ability to find large deposits of gold and silver treasure." Mary answered, "I hope we find plenty of gold, but the stock market seems like more of a sure thing." Bob chipped in, "I agree with you, Mary. The stock market is a good way to make money. Please tell me if God helps you know of some excellent investments. I would love to make more money. I want to buy a boat like this one." Mary stated, "You'll be the first to know."

Bill told Bob, "I can sell you this boat at cost. It's only one hundred and seventy thousand." Bob exclaimed, "I thought it would be much more." Bill said, It was built in 1986. Because of its age, the price is lower. A new boat like this one would be well over a million dollars. This one is in excellent condition." Bob replied, "I'll talk it over with Ellen. If we find some gold, I'll call my father and ask if he will sign for the purchase of this boat." Bill responded, "You can call the boat yours right now. I know we'll find gold and if your father doesn't want to buy the boat, you can rent it cheaply for as long as you want it." Bob replied, "Thank you, Bill. I love owning this boat. It makes me feel wealthy. I don't think it will depreciate much. It will be a collector's item in ten years." Ellen stated, "Well, your wish for a boat like this came true quickly. I can't wait for us to break it in by taking a shower together. Just kidding!" Bob exclaimed, "We should celebrate!" Bill stated, "There's some mint ice cream in the galley. Let's go get some."

They all went to the galley and opened the freezer. There was a large supply of ice cream. Bob dipped everyone a big bowl full and they went back to the card table to eat. Mary said, "I'd like to be able to use my minds spiritual power to help us find gold." Ellen said, "How would you know for sure that it wasn't your old friend the Jade Goddess leading you?" Mary replied, "She always gives off a jade glow when she comes to talk to me. The Holy Spirit causes me to see a white glow. The Jade Goddess can't come inside my head anymore since the Holy Spirit is in me. She has to stay outside." Ellen asked, "Have you heard from the Jade Goddess since you've been a Christian?" Mary responded, "Once she appeared when I was asleep in bed. She stated that she would be required to offer help when I needed it most. I will resist her. No help can be worth losing one's place in heaven." Ellen responded, "I will pray for you. I know you will resist her completely." Mary said, "I even gave away all the money I won at Las Vegas." Ellen asked, "How much money was there?" Mary replied, "Two hundred and twenty million dollars." Ellen asked, "Who did you give it to?" Mary answered, "We gave some of it to pastor Jake's church and the rest went to agencies that feed the poor." Ellen said, "That should please God."

Bill said, Why don't we all pray for Mary to be able to know about the stock market and know where gold is? Even if she doesn't receive a gift of knowing, God might be willing to help with these two things. After all, the money will go to a good cause." Bob responded, "I think it would be good for Mary to have those two things." Ellen said, "I'd like her to receive more power than she ever had with the Jade Goddess." They all held hands and prayed for a long time. Mary could see the white light of the Holy Spirit growing brighter inside her. She knew that she was receiving power. She smiled and thanked God. They all played cards for another hour and then went to bed.

In the morning Bob and Ellen went to eat breakfast with Bill and Mary. After they had eaten, Bob announced, "Ellen and I have been secretly married since we left New Buffalo. I want for us to go ahead and get married. Our parents should understand that eighteen is old enough for some people to get married." Ellen looked surprised and delighted. She said, "Where can we get married?" Bill said, "We can take the boat to Jamaica. You can get married there. Later, you can get a license in the States." Bob and Ellen looked hopeful. Bob said, "I like that idea. Let's go today." Bill said, "I'll call Mark and tell him to make sure the tanks are full. We can head out by noon.

Bob said, "I'll need to rent a tux." Ellen said, "I'll have to buy a wedding dress." Mary said, "It looks like we've found a way to defeat the Jade Goddess again." She smiled and finished her ham and egg sandwich. Ellen said, "This still doesn't explain how Mary knew about us. Mary said, "I think I've received the gift I asked for. I'm going to test it out on the stock market today. Bill has fifty million for me to play with. I'm going to put it into the Chinese publishing industry. A newly enriched land with a billion people is going to need plenty of reading material. I think the profits will be coming in quite soon. I'm going to invest on leverage, so if the stock goes up ten percent, I'll make fifty million dollars." Bob said, "I'm going to invest with you, if you don't mind." He called his bank and had his money transferred into Mary's account. Mary asked, "Do you want to be in on leverage too?" Bob answered, "Sure, I want to get as much money as I can." Mary stated, "I think we should diversify just a little. I'll put twenty-five percent of the money into the Chinese car industry. With their inexpensive labor, they should be exceedingly competitive on the world market. It's amazing how they can make almost anything there." Bill said, "I've talked with many Chinese people. They are friendly and intelligent. Their country has been a leader in the arts for thousands of years."

Ellen stated, "Once we have found all the gold we want, we could take the boat to China and stay there for a year. We could research their economy so we could make more informed and logical decisions about how to invest." Mary asked, "Don't you trust my ability?" Ellen replied, "I hope you do have a new gift. I just think it would be fun to go there." Bill said, "It will be a couple years before we find enough gold. Possibly we should fly to China for a couple weeks. You two could take your honeymoon there, and Mary and I will research the economy. I plan on writing a book about or treasure hunting. I can find out about how to work with Chinese publishing concerns while we are there." Ellen said, "First we go to Jamaica." Mary stated, "Of course, Ellen. But we need to make arrangements now for the China trip. Bill can set it all up." Ellen responded, "I'd love to honeymoon in China. How about you, Bob?" Bob replied, "I like the idea too. It will be something to tell our grandchildren about." Mary retorted, "Those grandchildren may be coming sooner than you think. You'd better buy plenty of protection if it's not too late already." Ellen said, "I wouldn't mind having a baby. People would treat me more like a woman. I guess I wouldn't mind waiting though. When I'm nineteen, I want to start having a baby every year till I'm twenty-nine." Bob said, "I agree. Let's have lots of children. They will visit us when we're old and keep us company."

Bill stated, "Let's go back to the boat. I want to use the phone in privacy. I'll get all the arrangements made for Jamaica and for China." Mary responded, "I'll drive you back and then I'll take Bob and Ellen to shop for clothing." She let Bill out at the marina and kissed him goodbye.

Then she helped Ellen find a wedding dress. They found one that showed off her bare shoulders and flattered her relatively flat chest. Mary explained, "You shouldn't feel self conscious about not being full breasted. Men are most excited by slenderness. You have that. Your breasts will be filling out quite a bit in the next couple years." Ellen responded, "That's a relief. You sure know how to build up a girl's confidence. She tried on the dress and it fit perfectly. Mary whispered, "Be sure to give Bob plenty of variety. They like that till the day they die." Ellen whispered back, "Don't worry. He won't get bored. I don't want him to ever think longingly about what he could get with some other woman." Mary responded, "Good thinking. A little prevention is worth a pound of cure." Ellen paid for the dress, and they went to the car and put it in the trunk. Bob was in the car. Ellen giggled when she saw him. She said, "We were talking about you." Bob replied, "It was good, I hope." Ellen said, "It's going to be good for you!" Bob blushed a little and smiled, "I'm looking forward to that." They took him to the tux shop and he decided to buy a tux. He would need it in China. They purchased more supplies for the trip to Jamaica. When they had everything the wanted, they headed back to the boat. Once on the boat, Mary made the calls she needed to make in order to get properly invested. They ate lunch on the boat as their pilot headed for Jamaica. The other boat waited for their return.

Chapter Nine

Another Wedding

It took them nearly a day to reach Jamaica. They powered into Montego Bay at mid-morning. A taxi took them to their motel, which was close to the marina. Bill arranged with a local church for the wedding to be in the evening when it wasn't so hot. The minister was excited about having the service. He loved to perform weddings. After assuring himself that the proper papers would be filled out and the marriage license was signed by the proper official, Bill took everyone for a tour of the city. They drove along the coast and looked at all the palm trees and the sun bathers. When they had seen enough, they went to the Yacht Club and had some iced tea to celebrate. Bob and Ellen were staying away from alcohol. Mary proposed a toast, "To a marriage full of variety." Ellen laughed at the inside joke. They touched glasses and drank to the marriage. Bill toasted, "May all your years together be happy." They all drank again.

They spent a few hours watching the boats in the harbor. It was exciting being in a different country. They dressed for the beach and did some sun bathing. Ellen sat on the sand in front of Bob and said, "I shouldn't let you see this much of me right before our wedding." Bob responded, "I don't think it will hurt anything. If you like

I can turn the other way." Ellen slugged him. "No, I want you to look at me." They rubbed lotion on each other. Bill and Mary were out in the water. They were splashing each other and laughing. Ellen rubbed lotion gently on Bob's body. He loved the feel of her soft hands on his skin. They decided to swim for a while. They did lots of splashing and laughing. It was a wonderful time.

Finally they came out of the water. Bill was busy rubbing lotion on Mary's legs. They were on a yellow blanket that was large enough for everyone. Bob asked, "Where did you get the blanket?" Bill said, "A vendor brought it to us. It was only two dollars." Ellen stated, "That's a bargain. How much was our wedding license?" Bill said, "It was ten dollars. I bet you two forgot to buy wedding bands." Ellen gasped, "Oh no!" Bill said, "Don't worry they have some good stores here that are still open. The prices are better here. We'd better go right away, before they close." They all got into the rental car and went back to the motel and got dressed. Next, they went to the jewelry store. They bought each other nice 14 ct. gold rings. Bob's had an exquisite row of diamonds across the top of it. There were eight diamonds that formed the shape of a small bolt of lightening. Mary asked, "Why did you get diamonds shaped like that?" Bob replied, "It reminds me of the time lightening struck me. It didn't even hurt me. It went through me just as I was pointing at a telephone pole. The lightening went through me and out from my hand. It struck the pole and knocked it down. I think God was trying to prove that He still works miracles in our day. I was impressed." Mary responded, "I think I'm on the right team. God the Father of Jesus Christ our Lord and Savior. He is the God I worship. The storekeeper said, "Amen, sister." He took twenty percent off the price of the rings. He said, "That certainly is a nice cross you're wearing. Would you consider selling it?" Mary responded, "No, My husband found this on the beach in Key West,

Florida. I'll always keep this." He said, "I've never seen anything like it." They paid the storekeeper and Bob and Ellen each put the ring they would soon give away, into their pockets.

They all went to a restaurant for the evening meal. It was an early meal, since they had to be dressed and at the church by seven o'clock. They ate quickly and chatted about the upcoming wedding. In no time at all they were back at the boat getting dressed. They arrived at the church in time for the pastor to go over what they would all say. The church filled completely with the congregation that went there. They were all eager to see the young American couple. Bob and Ellen took their places in the narthex and waited for the music to begin. When it was time they walked in and stood before the altar. When it was time to exchange their vows, they each said the vows without any trouble. The rings were exchanged and the pastor pronounced them man and wife. They kissed eagerly and walked to the back of the church. They were led to the basement where there was a cake and presents. The congregation all attended the reception and there was a festive mood. They all congratulated the newly weds and danced to a live band that was playing for the reception. The dancing and partying went on till midnight. Finally Bob and Ellen went back to the boat. They changed clothes and went on deck to watch the lights and stars. Mary and Bill had told them they would stay in the motel for the night. The cook and pilot were staying on shore for the night. They had the boat to themselves.

They watched the stars for about an hour and kissed in the moonlight. Finally they brought a blanket up from the bedroom and crawled under it. Bob told Ellen, "I love it when you get me excited like this. He was still watching the stars, while Ellen did interesting things to him under the blanket. He let his fingers run through her hair, as she kissed him over and over again down there. Finally, he couldn't stand it any longer and pulled her to the bedroom where they consummated the marriage. Bob made sure it was a night Ellen would never forget. She did all she could to make sure he would remember the night. Finally after hours of love making, they took a shower together. Bob said, "I've been looking forward to this shower. Now we can take showers together every day for the rest of our lives." Ellen responded, "I love the shower too. The water feels so nice and warm and your warm body is up against me." They hugged and kissed in the shower for an hour. Finally they dried off and crawled in bed. They slept together, entwined in each others arms.

In the morning they were up early and made themselves some eggs and toast. They ate on deck and listened to the seagulls. The sunrise was beautiful with scattered clouds reflecting the golden color of the sun. When they finished eating they chartered a small boat and went for a ride along the coast. There was only a little breeze blowing and the waves were small. After a couple hours of cruising, they went back to the harbor and paid the boat owner. They spent the rest of the morning looking in shops and buying souvenirs. Ellen bought many post cards and Bob found some coffee mugs with fish on them. One had a blue marlin on it. Bob asked, "Why don't we spend the afternoon fishing. We could charter a boat and see how big the fish are down here." Ellen responded, "That's a great idea." They went back to the marina and chartered a boat for fishing. They were out all afternoon and caught some large blue marlin which they released unharmed. One tuna was caught, which they donated to an orphanage. Bob and Ellen took movies of the whole event. They had purchased the camera in one of the shops in town. It was easy to operate and worked a long time before it needed recharging. Bob liked to play with the zoom. He would zoom in so close on Ellen that her nose filled the entire screen. Sometimes he would embarrass her by filming her chest up close. Ellen exclaimed, “Stop! You know I’m self conscious about that. Who’s going to see these movies?” They filmed each other reeling in fish and made interesting chat while the action was taking place. When the sun started getting low on the horizon, their captain brought them back to the marina. Bill thanked him and paid him.

Bob and Ellen went to the Yacht Club for supper. They each had sirloin steaks and baked potatoes. Ellen said, “Bill said we should spend two days on the boat alone.” Bob responded, “I’m sure we can think of something to do to occupy our time.” They enjoyed their time alone on the boat. It was fun to have some privacy. In the evening Mary and Bill returned to the boat. They asked the cook to prepare supper. When it was almost ready, they woke Bob and Ellen.

There was fun and laughter at the supper table. The newly weds told all about their fishing and shopping. They even told about how fun the boat was for having a honeymoon in. Mary responded, “Someday Bill and I would like to be alone on the boat for a couple days. Possibly tomorrow.” Bob said, “We’ll stay at the motel. Both of you deserve some time alone on the boat.” It was decided. The staff members were given more time off, and there was a new honeymoon on the boat.

In a couple days everyone was ready to get back to scuba training. The pilot guided the boat back to Key West and docked at the marina. The next morning they all went out in Big Angel Two and practiced diving. They continued diving each day until they could dive proficiently at sixty feet down. Both boats were then taken into international waters, and the search for gold began. The sonar was activated and the boats cruised over a pattern that was plotted on the global positioning system. It looked like a fish finder and showed where the boats had been and where they were at the moment. It also showed where they should go next to complete a systematic search of the area. Mary was on deck praying to Jesus for knowledge about where the gold was. She wanted to support her investment fund. Bill's lawyer would have it set up by the end of the week. It was Wednesday now. Mary wanted to find gold by Saturday night. She prayed for hours about what counties she would help first and how she would give the credit to God for the help.

The sonar went off and they stopped the boats. Mary continued praying even as she put on her wet suit. All divers went to the bottom to see what they could find with hand held metal detectors. They found some cannons, but their search only yielded a few silver coins. Mary felt extra close to God when she was under water. It was so quiet down there. She thought she heard God telling her to go further south. When they surfaced, Mary told Bill, "I thought I heard God telling us to go further south." Bill said, "We can go south then. We aren't finding anything here."

Chapter Ten

A Massive Find

The next day they went south with the sonar running. After about ten miles the sonar went off in one hundred and ten feet of water. Bill said, "I'll go down with Mary. I don't want too many people to worry about at this depth. We aren't experienced at this depth yet. The couple dove in with their metal detectors. They each wore an extra tank so they could stay down longer. They descended slowly and carefully. Bill tested the radio, "This is Bill. We are almost to the bottom. My depth gauge says ninety feet. Do you read me?" Bob was on the other end and replied, "I read you. You are coming in loud and clear." Bill and Mary swam the rest of the way to the bottom. It was a sunny day, and the visibility was good. They swam past some cannons and then spotted a couple gold coins lying on a rock. They took the coins and started their metal detectors. Bill spoke to Mary with their radios, "The current here it going north. The heavy contents of the ship should be north of the cannons. Mary spoke, "I'd like to go north. I feel that the cannons fell off first as the boat turned on its side. Then it broke apart when it hit bottom farther north of here. The hull must have been starting to come apart right here. That's why we found the gold coins."

They headed north with their metal detectors operating. After about one hundred yards the metal detectors went off. They closed in on a small mound that was just ahead of them. When they brushed aside the sand, it turned out to be a treasure chest stacked full of gold coins and jewelry. There were diamonds and rubies in the chest too. They were careful not to lose anything. Bill called to the boat in code in case someone was listening in on their frequency, "We have located some scrap brass we are sending up a location marker." He tied the twine from the marker onto the treasure chest. Next he activated the self inflating marker. It rose to the surface pulling the twine behind it. Bob saw the marker and had the pilot move the boat to the proper location. They put down the anchor slowly and carefully. Bill called up to the boat, "Send down the basket."

Ellen and Bob lowered the basket and Bill and Mary filled it." Bill called up to the boat, "The basket is loaded. Don't lose any small items like lightening on your finger." Bob understood the code. He told Ellen, "There will be small diamonds. We mustn't lose any of them." Bob told the cook, "Bring us some pans and buckets to put the treasure in." The cook hurried and brought the buckets and pans. Bob operated the hoist and brought up about five hundred pounds of treasure. They quickly unloaded the basket and sent it back down. Bill and Mary emptied the rest of the treasure into the basket. Bill called the boat, "Take her up carefully. All the scrap it loaded and we're coming up." Their tanks were almost empty, but they had to stop ten feet from the surface to decompress. Mary could feel her lungs staining to get the last air out of her tanks. Finally they surfaced and both of them gasped eagerly for fresh air. They climbed onto the boat and examined the treasure. Bill and Mary were delighted to see how nice the gold looked when it was rinsed off. There was about one thousand pounds of gold in that chest. Bill asked, "Where are the diamonds and rubies?" Bob passed him a pan full of gems. Bill exclaimed, "These gems must be worth one hundred million dollars. The gold is probably worth half a billion dollars. I think we should cash this stuff in before we get robbed. We can return in a few days and continue our search for more gold." Mary asked, "Will your lawyer be ready for this much money?" Bill said, "He is always ready for any amount of money. It will take him a couple more days to start the investment fund. We need to tell Sandy that her presidential duties will be needed now. She needs to hire a personnel director and get some people hired to start setting up health and nutrition centers. She'll need to charter ships to take the food to the centers. I know she'll like the excitement." Bill asked the pilot to take them back to the marina at Key West.

Three hours later they were unloading the gold into a Brink's truck that Bill had called. The divers all followed the truck to Mary's bank. They had the bank store the treasure for them. The bank weighed the gold and photographed the diamonds and rubies as they bagged and labeled them. Bill was on the phone to a lawyer he had hired in Key West who was familiar with the laws concerning treasure found on open waters. The lawyer said that he would arrange for the sale of the treasure. He would make sure they got a fair price and that local authorities were aware of the new income for the charitable agency. The lawyer asked, "What did you say the name of your agency is?" Bill asked Mary, "What should we call the agency?" Mary replied, "Investors and Divers for World Development." Bill agreed and told the lawyer. Bill went on, Sandy Booth is our president. She owns Sandy's Bed and Breakfast here in town. If you need more information, she can help you. Wire the money from all our sales to my lawyer in New Buffalo, Indiana. His name is John Miller. I'll give you his phone number." Bill gave the lawyer's number and then ended the call.

They all went back to the boat and gave the crew a day of shore leave and a generous amount of bonus money. The dive crew went to Sandy's place to give her the good news. They found her in the garden having some tea. Bill said, "You'll be busy this week. Mary found a half ton of gold and gems today. We need to start sending out boats of food and clothing. We need to hire people to make the agency work smoothly. Are you able to devote the extra time this week?" Sandy exclaimed, "I'll make time. I'm having a local club meeting tonight. I'll recruit a personnel director from the people at the meeting. I'll pick someone with lots of dedication to the cause." Bill responded, "That sounds like a plan. We decided to name the agency, Investors and Divers for World Development. How do you like it?" Sandy replied, "It sounds like a good name to me. I'll be proud to be president." Should we offer free dive training to others who will donate their finds to the cause?" Bill responded, "Sounds good to me, but concentrate on getting investors interested. Emphasize how low labor costs will help merchants make profitable sales and investors will win. Also point out that the laborers will have a much better standard of living, and we won't promote industry that will destroy American jobs. We want to make goods available that wouldn't be produced at all in America. We can promote labor intensive operations like clothing and crafts. Without third world competition for contracts, eventually our traditional suppliers of inexpensive labor would start asking for a larger piece of the pie. It is in the interest American traders to have competition for the contracts they make available to the world." Sandy asked, "Would you write that down for me. I'm going to include it in my speech tonight." Bill said, "I'll write it down. He pulled out a piece of paper and started writing. Mary asked, "What have you been doing?"

Sandy replied, "I've been calling people and telling them about the meeting. We're having the meeting here in the garden. I didn't book any guests for tonight. I'm having food catered in. I rented a sound system and it'll be hooked up soon." Mary said, "I wish we could attend, but we need to get back out on the water. If word gets out about our finds, there will be plenty of other treasure hunters searching the same waters we're looking in." Sandy responded, "Yes, strike while the iron is hot! Bring me enough gold to feed the whole world." Mary laughed, "I'll try.

Ellen showed Sandy her wedding ring. She said, "Bob and I got married in Jamaica a couple days ago on Wednesday, July 21st. Bob said, "We spent our honeymoon on the boat while it was in Jamaica. We went fishing and we caught some blue marlin and a tuna." Sandy replied, "Let me see your ring, Bob." Bob held out his hand. Sandy said, "I notice there's a unique pattern to the way the diamonds are set." Bob said, "I bought it because the lightening pattern reminds me of God's power to protect. I was hit by lightening once and it didn't hurt me a bit." Sandy replied, "That's quite interesting. Don't ever take that ring off. I hope I have that kind of protection during my life. So many people live in sin and think nothing will ever happen to them. Anyone can die at any time. People need to be right with God so that death isn't their doorway to hell. I know I like to swim naked, but I pray for forgiveness of sins every night. We all sin. It feels good to be forgiven. Most people would rather have some cheap sexual thrill than the assurance of going to heaven to be with Jesus."

Mary exclaimed, "I didn't know you were such a practicing Christian." Sandy responded, "I've always been a Christian, but knowing all of you has helped me feel closer to God. I love being able to help poor people like I am. You're quite inspiring, Mary." Mary said, "I got it from Bill. He was the one that asked me to become a Christian. I don't think he would have married me if I had refused." Sandy looked at Bill, "You surprise me Bill. I didn't know." Bill stated, "It's just that Mary is so excited about her new religion that she talks about it more than I do. Every time I come up from a dive, I thank God for keeping me safe. There are sharks, barracuda and air problems to deal with down deep in the water. A person can certainly use protection from harm." I always have our other boat feed the sharks a quarter mile from the dive site. That way the sharks aren't around us, but there are always sharks that are crossing the dive site on their way to the food. They smell blood and they're hungry."

They had some tea with Sandy and then said goodbye. They went to a fine restaurant and had more sirloin steaks cooked medium well with baked potatoes. Ellen said, "This is such a grand day and such wonderful things are happening, I think I would like just a little of the German white wine you like so well, Bill." Bob said, "I could use some too. It's been an exciting day." They all had a half glass of wine. Ellen stated, "I feel like smiling. Is that the wine?" Mary commented, "I think it's partially the wine and partly the fact that you're happy." Bob said, "I feel it too. I can't help but smile." They finished their meal and ordered some apple dumplings with vanilla ice cream. Bill exclaimed, "This reminds me of the wonderful apple dumplings my mother used to make." They ordered more coffee and sipped it while they ate the dessert. They talked for a long time and then returned to the boat.

Bob turned on the gas fireplace. It wasn't cold, but a strong breeze was blowing. They played rook for several hours. Mary stated, "I hope this wind dies down. Can we dive in wind?" Bill said, "As long as the wind stays below fifteen miles an hour we can dive. If it gets much stronger than that, it would be too hard to keep the boats in position. Let's listen to the weather forecast." Bill brought in the radio from the navigation room. He turned it on and they listened quietly to the announcer. The announcer reported, "Skies will be clearing tomorrow with ten mile per hour winds dropping off in the evening. A storm front is coming in from eight hundred miles to the east of Nicaragua. It is expected to reach Key West in two days." Bob stated, "We will need to work fast if we want more treasure. That storm will put us out of work for a couple days." Bill responded, "We can get in a full day tomorrow. Then we'd better stay ashore till the storm passes."

They played rook for another hour. The women were using their bare feet to play with the legs of the men. Mary gently caressed Bill's leg with her feet and gave him a look that said, "I want something you've got." Ellen was doing the same thing to Bob. Finally Mary said, "I'm tired. Can we quit for the night?" Ellen said, "We're going to bed too." They all went to their separate bedrooms and took showers together. The excitement of the treasure find made them excited about each other too. It was a night for love making. The crew was still ashore, so they didn't worry about staying quiet. Even the large hundred foot boat sent out ripples in the water that showed how passionate the lovers were.

In the morning the lovebirds woke in time for breakfast. The crew was back and everyone had pancakes and syrup. Bill asked the pilot to go back to their former position. They would keep exploring in that general area. The boats headed south. Ellen said, "When the storm sets in, I'd like to go to China for another honeymoon." Bob replied, "That sounds like a good idea. Bill, do you and Mary want to come to China to do economic research like you spoke of earlier?" Bill asked Mary, "Would you like to go?" Mary exclaimed, "Of course I'd like to go! We can have a honeymoon too." Bill responded, "I'll call my travel agent and get things set up for tomorrow. We can take off in the morning and be there in twenty hours or so. I'll get the agent to find us a package deal with flight, room and food all included." He picked up the cell phone and called the travel agent. Everything was go. He picked the deluxe package that included the best hotel with hot tub and a view of the river. Bill called his favorite restaurant and had some of his white wine sent to the hotel he would be staying at in China. He wasn't sure they would have his favorite wine in China. He called the American Embassy in China and asked them for the phone number of an agency that could give them a tour of the book printing companies and some of the best publishing agencies as well. He also asked to be shown some of the auto manufacturing. The Embassy gave him the phone numbers he would need to set up the tours and talk to developers. He called them and set up the times for the people to meet him at his hotel. The auto manufacturers asked him to come to their office. He was told that a car would pick them up at the hotel at the designated hour.

The boats arrived at the dive location in about three hours. The water was sixty feet deep. Bill asked all divers to go along. They all suited up and were in the water in about twenty minutes. The other boat was feeding the sharks about a quarter mile away. They were all in the water and heading for the bottom. When they reached the bottom, they immediately started sweeping the ocean floor with their metal detectors. From out of nowhere a twenty-two foot shark moved in and picked up Ellen by the chest. It swam thirty feet and then dropped her. She managed to keep the air mouthpiece in her mouth. The tank had protected her back, but there was blood coming from her chest. Bill took her up quickly to the surface, he ordered the crew to pull her on board. The rest of the divers got out of the water as soon as possible. Mary took off Ellen's wet suit top and looked at her chest. Amazingly there were just a few shallow cuts just below her breasts and down by her stomach. Mary got the first aid kit out and treated Ellen's wounds. Bill asked the pilot to take them back to shore. When they got to shore, they took Ellen to the hospital where she got the cuts stitched up. Ellen insisted, "I still want to go to China in the morning.

We can't scrap those plans. These are just superficial cuts. They don't even hurt." Bill said, "If you feel fine in the morning, we can go." Ellen said, "I wasn't even scared, I knew God would protect me." Mary held Ellen's hand and said, "You are learning to trust God. That's why the shark dropped you without shaking its head. God was helping you." Bob stated, "I'll admit I was a little worried, but there was nothing I could do. We're at the mercy of God down there." Bill added, "We're always at His mercy. We just don't think about it under most circumstances."

They all went back to the boat when Ellen was released. They dressed in their swim suits so Ellen's wounds could get some air. She was proud of her wounds. She showed them to all the crew and to the divers. They all made a fuss over her. Mary said, "I can't believe you didn't drop your mouthpiece." Ellen replied, "All I could think about was that I didn't want to drown. I had to breath with my stomach. The shark was crushing my chest." They lay in the sun for a few hours and then went to the living room and played cards. They ate supper on the boat and then watched television while Ellen lay comfortably on a couch. She didn't complain about any pain. She insisted, "We need to pack our suitcases. I'm definitely going to China in the morning." They all gave in and packed their suitcases. Since they had to be at the airport by eight o'clock, they all went to bed early. Ellen insisted that Bob make love to her. He was very gentle with her. She said, "I'm so glad to be alive. It's wonderful that we can still do this. She lay still and let him do everything. Bob was happy to oblige. She felt a little pain in her chest as she experienced climax, but she didn't make a sound. She didn't want Bob to stop what he was doing.

Mary and Bill were in the shower. They had decided to have all there fun in there. They were laughing and having the time of their lives. Bill never got tired of the way Mary wanted to do something different every night. She was full of mischief tonight. She wanted him for longer than usual. He was the kind of man who could go all night when he had a woman this eager. Mary was his perfect mate, he thought.

In the morning, the alarm clock went off in Bill's room at six o'clock. He woke the others and they had breakfast. The cook made them omelets. They took their bags to the car and went to the airport. It was starting to storm as they took off. The wind was about thirty miles per hour. They experienced a little turbulence, but things went well. They fly first class and played rook for hours as they flew. The stewardess brought them all the drinks they wanted, and at noon they had a hot meal. In the afternoon they watched a movie and then did some reading. Each of them had brought a couple books from the living room of the boat. Bill was reading Moby Dick. Ellen laughed, "I wonder if that was Moby Dick who got hold of me yesterday." The stewardess asked what she meant. Ellen explained about the shark. She showed the stewardess the cuts on her abdomen. The stewardess couldn't believe it. She said, "A shark carried you thirty feet? What were you doing down there?" Ellen explained that they were treasure hunters and that they gave their finds to help feed people. The stewardess said, "My name is Cheryl. If you need anything for pain, let me know. I could give you some wine too if you want." Ellen said, "I wouldn't mind a half glass of wine. Maybe it will make me sleepy. If I sleep, the time will go by faster." Cheryl brought them all a small glass of white wine. They thanked her and savored the wine. In a little while they were all napping as the plane drew closer to China.

When they awoke, they were landing at Beijing airport. A limo was waiting for them. They didn't have to carry their own luggage. The limo driver and his assistant moved the bags into the trunk. Within minutes they were at their hotel. Their suitcases were taken to their rooms for them, and they went to see the rooms. The view was breathtaking. They looked out over the river and contemplated how far they had traveled. Bill volunteered, "Let's go to the hotel's restaurant." They all agreed and went to eat. The special was seafood with fried rice and egg drop soup. They each ordered the special with some egg rolls on the side. Mary asked the waitress for hot tea for everyone. They took their time eating and looked around the room with interest at all the people there from different parts of the world. When they finished eating, they rode the limo around town. The driver explained all the sights to them and took them anywhere they asked to go. They went to an ice cream parlor and had their favorite ice creams. Next they went out of town to see the countryside. They loved seeing the friendly people. It was good to know that they all had enough food. The driver said, "In China the family ties are strong. Each family does their best to keep all relatives well fed. More people are moving to the cities. The ones who have jobs will send money to the country to take care of their relatives. Mary replied, "It's good to care about family. My real parents didn't raise me. I suspect they were too busy to be bothered with me. But my adopted parents are good to me. I call them every day to check on them and see if they are doing well." The driver smiled, "It was good of them to care for you. Do you plan on having children?" Mary smiled, "I plan on having twelve or more children. They will keep me company when I am old." The driver introduced himself, "My name is Chen. I hope that all your children are healthy and may you have a long and happy life." Mary replied, "Thank you very much. Do you have children?" Chen replied, "I have eight children. The oldest is fifteen and the youngest is two." Mary talked more with the driver as they went further into the country.

Finally the driver stopped and turned around, "We must go back. There are no gas stations out here. Our tank is only half full. It was full when we left." He drove them back into the city and filled the tank. They drove to more points of interest. Finally they grew tired and asked Chen to take them to the hotel. When they got to their rooms, they showered and went to bed. There was a long day ahead for them.

In the morning Bill and Mary were met by representatives from the publishing and printing businesses. They took them on tours and provided them with the information they needed to set up contracts with them. They were also told what stock names to look for and how to invest in the companies. In the afternoon they met with the auto company representative. They learned how to invest in that industry as well. It was all quite interesting to Mary and Bill. They knew they would be making a profit on their investment in these companies.

Ellen and Bob were spending their day around the hotel pool. They ordered plenty of fruit drinks. Ellen thought they would help her healing. They met some people by the pool and talked with them. Ellen explained her encounter with the shark. Their new friends were impressed with Ellen's courage. Eventually it was time for supper, and Bill and Mary arrived back at the hotel. They paged Bob and Ellen and went to supper with them. They all had roast duck. As usual they had sides of egg rolls. Bill stated, "One of the representatives from the printing industry suggested that we visit Tianjin on the gulf of Chihli. He said there are some nice boats we could charter there. We could see the river and the gulf. They are having a driver pick us up in the morning. Ellen responded, "That sounds nice. I feel fine. My cuts don't hurt much." Bill said, "It will be nice to see what their boats look like here." They ate duck when it arrived and talked about the trip to the gulf of Chihli. When they finished eating, they went to the lounge and played cards till late. Bill had one of his bottles of wine delivered to the table. They all had a small glass and then went to bed. The couples went to their own rooms and cavorted with their partners till early in the morning.

They got up in time to eat breakfast before they were driven to the city of Tianjin. When they arrived, they were greeted at the marina by the owner of a large hundred and twenty foot boat. He said, "My name is Sho Li." They introduced themselves. Sho Li continued, "You can stay on the boat. We'll have meals there for you and there are nice big rooms for you to stay in. We'll tour the river in a smaller boat." He led them to their rooms. The boat was new and well appointed. Everything was teak and hardwood. The living room had a black grand piano in it." They all went back up on deck and asked to be taken along the shore of the gulf. Sho Li told the pilot where to take the boat. The engines fired up and the boat started its trip along the shore line. There were small fishing villages all along the water's edge. The boat took them out into the Yellow Sea to the small town of Qingdao. They pulled into port and stopped for an early supper. They looked around town for awhile. The people didn't see tourists very often. They were friendly and courteous. The town was a mixture of farming and fishing. The group took a taxi around the outskirts of town to see all the small farms with their many animals. Down by the docks was a fish market where fresh catch was being sold. They spent several hours talking to the fishermen and the local people who were gathering to see them. Finally they had met everyone there. They went back to the boat. They stayed on the deck and watched the shore as the sun went down and the lights of the towns started to glow. The lights reflected out across the water. The boat anchored and they spent the night on the water. Early in the morning they returned to Chihli. They had breakfast on the boat and then took a smaller boat up the river. The river had small towns every five or six miles. There were fishing boats and junks all over the river. They saw many people catching fish. After several hours on the river they returned to the marina. They said goodbye to Sho Li, and the limo took them back to Beijing. They stayed the night at the hotel and left the next morning by jet. In twenty hours, they were back in Key West. The storm had passed and it was time to look for more gold.

Chapter Eleven

The Jade Goddess Returns

Both boats were taken early in the morning to the dive sight where Ellen had been bitten by the shark. Ellen was not healed enough to dive yet. Mary, Bob and Bill put on their wet suits and started the descent down to the bottom. Ellen was on the radio to help when needed. When they reached the bottom they were able to see clearly. They discovered a drop off to their north. Mary talked on the radio, "I think a ship could have been washed over this drop off. Why don't we investigate?" Bill warned, "It could be quite deep. Let's be careful." They all wore radios and kept talking as they went down over the edge of the drop off. When the reached one hundred and ten feet down, they found a ledge that was about twenty feet wide. There were gold coins scattered on the hard rock surface. The current had kept the sand washed away. They carefully searched the entire area and picked up the gold. No one noticed that Mary had developed trouble breathing. She had gone into advanced stages of oxygen depravation and was swimming rapidly into the deeper water off the edge of the ledge. The mouthpiece fell out of her mouth and she fell into a semi state of unconsciousness. She could see the color of jade glowing in front of her face. A voice told her that the main deposit of gold was deeper down. She had to swim deeper. Her depth gauge read two hundred and fifty feet. It was getting dark around her. The Jade Goddess spoke to her, "I can help you Mary. Please let me help you."

In heaven, God was aware of what was going on. He called his arch angel Michael unto him. God said, "Satan has resorted to Satanic attack on Mary. She is dear to me because of her efforts on the part of the poor. I want you to remind Satan that he cannot attack Mary when she is under my protection. If he wants to go beyond temptations and attack good Christians, he will have to deal with me. I want you to smite him on his cheek to remind him of our agreement. He cannot harm you. You have my protection."

Michael instantly appeared in hell before Satan and walked up close to him. The magnificent large white wings of Michael were impressive. Satan stated disdainfully, "What brings you here, oh pure one?" Michael spoke with a powerful voice, "You will stop attacking Christians who are under God's protection. I speak of the attack on Mary Thresher. You took away her air supply while she was diving and now she approaches death. You long to hear her call on you for help." Satan said, "Let her decide what help she wants." They listened as Mary spoke to the Jade Goddess. "You are kind, Jade Goddess, but I am forever with Jesus. I cannot ask you for help." Michael slapped Satan on his cheek. Satan sent out a laser blast of molten rays from his eyes. Michael held out his hand and the rays were repelled. Michael spoke, "I am under God's protection. You cannot prevail against me. Do as we ask and only resort to temptation of Mary, or you will be punished."

Michael vanished from hell and appeared at Mary's side. He slowly brought her back out of the deep water. He went past Bill and Bob and assured them that she would be fine. The angel put her gently on the boat and removed the water from her lungs with the touch of his hand. She started breathing and spoke to Michael, "You are my guardian angel. Thank you for helping me." Michael replied, "Continue helping the poor. We like what you are doing. I need to leave now." Michael disappeared. Bob and Bill climbed onto the boat and found Mary sitting in a chair. She was in perfect shape. Bill said, "I don't know how you got into so much trouble so fast. I only turned my back for a second." Mary said, "It was Satan trying to make me turn to him. He sent the Jade Goddess to call me into the deep after more gold. I kept going deeper and I breathed the water. Finally the angel appeared and brought me back to the boat." Bill said, "Yes, we saw the angel carrying you back. I think we should let some professional divers pull up the rest of the treasure. We can mark down our coordinates and sell the location to the highest bidder." They asked the pilot to take them back to Key West. On the way back, they examined the gold they had found. It was enough to fill a quart pan. Bill remarked, "It was a good day's work. We should make some good money from that much gold." Bob fingered the gold and showed pieces to Ellen. She stated, "Soon I'll be able to go down too."

They arrived back at Key West and went to see Sandy. She was at her usual spot in the garden drinking tea. Mary told her about the Jade Goddess and the angel. Sandy said, "I think that is the last you will hear from the Jade Goddess." She changed the subject, "I hired some people for our agency. Ships are on the way to locations all around the world, taking them food and clothing. I have people hired at the various ports to receive the supplies and distribute them. Distribution has been the problem all along. Our country grows plenty of food. No one has ever managed to raise this much money before to pay for distributing the food. We follow the food all the way to the consumer to make sure it doesn't get stolen." Mary replied, "I'm impressed with your organizational abilities." Sandy responded, "I just hire good people and then delegate responsibility." Bill asked, "Would you like to come with us to see a movie?" She agreed to go, and they all climbed in her Rolls Royce. They ate buttery popcorn and saw several movies. When it grew dark, they all went shopping. The women bought new swim suits and some dresses. When they tired of shopping, they returned to Sandy's place and put on the swim suits. Everyone made a fruit drink and went to the hot tub. They soaked for nearly an hour and watched the stars.

When it grew too hot for them to stay in any longer, they said goodbye and went back to the boat. They played rook in front of the fireplace for several hours and then ate ice cream. On that night they had butter pecan. Mary stated, "I still can't believe that an angel with huge white wings saved me from drowning. The Jade Goddess was calling me into the deeper water saying that the gold was down there." Bill added, "God must love you quite a bit if he sent an angel to help you." Mary replied, "It's humbling to be saved that way. I will always be grateful. I was thinking that it wouldn't be all that bad to be with Jesus from then on, but I wanted to spend more time with you, Bill. We just got married not long ago, and I'd like to have some children."

Ellen's short red hair and freckled skin glowed in front of the fire where she was sitting watching the flames dance around. She said, "I'm glad I didn't get killed by the shark. Possibly God saved me too. It will be nice if I can live to have some children." Bob responded, "I think that when we dive, we should have two people watching for sharks with spear guns while the other two scan for gold with the metal detectors." Bill exclaimed, "I like that idea! It would spoil our whole lives together if one of us got killed by a shark. Possibly we should train the cook and the pilot to dive and help look for sharks." Bob responded, "I think we need the cook and pilot in the boat. We may need to hire a couple professional divers who are skilled with spear guns." Bill commented, "That's another good idea."

Mary lay down on the white deep shag rug that was in front of the fire. She asked Bill to give her a back rub. He obliged willingly. Ellen said, "That looks good to me, but I'd like to get the back rub in bed." She took Bob by the hand and led him to their bed room. Once inside she took off her clothes and lay on the bed. Bob undressed too and found some lotion on the night stand. He warmed the lotion in his hands and gently rubbed Ellen's back. She moaned softly with pleasure. After letting Bob give her a nice thorough back rub, Ellen rolled over and pulled Bob on top of her. She stated forcefully but quietly, "I want some babies, and you're going to give them to me." With great determination she went about exciting him and causing him to make a good attempt at starting a baby. Ellen whispered in Bob's ear, "If there's ever anything special you want me to do, please speak up. I want to make sure you are completely happy." Bob whispered back, "I am delighted with you. I like the way you obviously want me. I don't have to beg for affection." Ellen said, "It will always be this way. I will always want you." They took a shower and held each other for a long time under the hot steaming water. They liked to watch the water run down over the other's body. Bob commented, "I like your breasts. They turn me on." Ellen said, "They'll get bigger when I get a few years older. They should also grow bigger when I have a baby to nurse." Bob laughed, "That will be fun to see."

Bill and Mary knew that everyone was in bed for the night, so they made love in front of the fireplace. They turned off all the lights and enjoyed the glow of the fire on their bodies. They spent hours fulfilling each other's fondest fantasies. When they had completely satisfied each other, they went to their room and took a long hot shower together. When they were finished, they put on their bath robes and went to the galley for some fruit drinks.

Mary said, "Will you hire professional divers tomorrow? I don't think we should dive until we have them." Bill replied, "In a town like Key West, it should be easy to find some good divers. They could help us get the gold that is down too deep for us." Mary responded, "I don't want to dive there again. That's for sure. I don't mind being in the boat while the professionals go down to get the gold." Bill assured Mary, "I can have some divers by tomorrow night. We can go right to that spot and get the treasure." They sipped their drinks and thought about the deep water. Mary said, "I wonder how much gold is down there." Bill responded, "There could be several ships that were washed by the current over that ledge. We may be there for more than a few days thoroughly searching that area." They finished their drinks and went to bed. They took off their robes and crawled into bed where they fell asleep in each others arms.

In the morning Bill called around and found some professional divers who were willing to work with them. He hired them and explained the trouble they were having with sharks. The men were expert with spear guns. They would keep the troublesome sharks at bay. One of the men was named Tim Kessler. He was about six feet tall and had black hair and moustache. The other man, Pete Miller, was also tall and had blond hair. They were both quite tan. Bill also hired two extra men to bring up gold from the deepest areas. These last two men were experienced at working at great depths. They were named Jeff Pile and Eric Williams. They both were tall and dark haired. On the next morning the new expanded crew went back to the previous dive site where Mary had been saved by the angel. The four new men went deep into the water that Mary had been lured into earlier. They took the basket with them. It held metal detectors and lights. The water grew colder and darker as they descended. They took the electric submersible tow vehicle with them. They needed its powerful lights to help them see what they were doing down there. Each man had four tanks on his back. That would enable them to stay down long enough at that depth to find most of the gold and get back safely.

When they reached the bottom, there were two ships lying there in the darkness. The men concentrated on the ship closest to them first. Its hull was broken open and just outside the ship was a large pile of scattered ingots made of gold. They were still shiny after several hundred years. The men quickly loaded up the bars of gold that weighed about ten pounds each. Next they scanned the area with their metal detectors. They found several hundred pounds of golden doubloons. They were starting to run low on air, so the made a slow and careful ascent with the basket. They stayed in contact on their radios so that the basket operators would know when to stop the basket and when to continue. By going back up slowly, the divers were certain not to develop the bends. When they reached the surface, they helped unload the basket. After several hours of rest, they put on full tanks and went back down to explore the second ship. They were pleased to find that a giant chest held all the treasure in that ship. It hadn't broken up when the ship sank. With great effort, they managed to roll it on to the basket. The chest was still closed and locked. They didn't know what was inside. Jeff, the lead diver, called on the radio to have the basket lifted. Slowly they made their way to the surface again.

The divers all climbed on deck and watched as Bill and Bob pried the lid of the treasure chest open. It took plenty of effort, but they finally managed to open the lid. To their amazement, the chest was completely full of precious gems. Most of the stones were large diamonds, but there were hundreds of large rubies as well. Bill said, "This is better than gold." We have at least two billion dollars worth of gems here!" They returned to Key West and had a Brink's armored truck pick up the treasures and take them to the bank. The divers and crew all celebrated at a local sea food restaurant where the lobster was excellent.

Everyone ate till they were full and then drank coffee and talked about the day's work. They planned where their next dive would be. Everyone thought there might be more ships that had been washed over the ledge into deep water. They would find out the next morning.

They all went back to the boats. There were just enough bedrooms for everyone. Mary invited the divers and crew to play cards with her husband and friends in the living room. She had the cook bring each one a bowl of ice cream and they played cards. One of the divers, Eric, had brought his guitar. He played folk songs for them and they all sang along on the choruses. Linda, the housekeeper, couldn't resist the large audience of young men. She did a dance for them in her bikini. They all loved watching her. When she finished dancing she complained of dry skin. She insisted that each man rub some lotion on her. They cooperated with enthusiasm. Finally, Bob and Ellen excused themselves and went to bed. Bill and Mary didn't stay up much later. They could hear the guitar and Linda's laughing till well past three O'clock in the morning. Bill stated, "Well, Linda certainly is good for the morale of the men." Mary replied, "I just hope they'll have enough energy to dive in the morning. Maybe we should wait till noon to start the first dive." Bill answered, "I agree. We don't want sleepy divers working down that deep."

When everyone finally woke up the next day, it was nearly time for lunch. They all sat down to some tomato soup and crackers. Joque saw the crackers and started asking for some, "I could really use a steak or some pecan pie, but those crackers will do for starters." Mary gave him several crackers and talked to him, "I'm afraid I've been ignoring you, Joque. I've been so busy, with the wedding and starting the agency for feeding people and giving them jobs." Joque replied, "You can make up for that by letting me out of this cage. I'd like to see the whole boat. I'd like to steer the boat." Mary responded, "As you like,

Joque." She opened the cage and let him have the run of the boat. He walked all around and tried to see everything on the boat. Mary asked the staff to be careful not to step on him. She asked the cook to make a perfect pecan pie for Joque. She felt guilty for leaving him in the hands of others so much of the time.

Once the crew had all eaten enough soup and had a bowl of ice cream, they started to get their gear ready for the day's dive. Bill announced to the divers, "I want us to explore as much of that drop off as possible. We found two ships down there, and we will most likely be able to locate several more. I think it's a prime location. Remember that two of you must be on the look out for sharks. I don't want any injuries. Now you can all suit up. Bob and I will operate the basket. Ellen will be ready on the radio. The divers got ready for the dive and all entered the water when Bill gave the order. They took their time and kept an eye out for sharks. They had the submersible tow vehicle with them and their metal detectors. When they reached the bottom, they all held on to the tow vehicle and let it pull them along the edge of the cliff that formed the drop off. The lights from the vehicle were helpful. It was rather dark down there even though it was a bright sunny day on the surface. At two hundred and fifty feet down, they would have about thirty minutes to search the bottom. They would need fifteen minutes to ascend slowly and avoid the bends. They were able to cover a long distance in the half hour. They wouldn't retrace their steps. They would go straight up and send up a flare if necessary. It was such a clear day, they knew that the boat would probably be able to see them even if they were a quarter mile away. There was no ship to be found in the area they were able to search in thirty minutes. Slowly they returned to the surface. At least they had not encountered any sharks. The boat saw them and quickly came around to pick them up. Bill marked their position on the global positioning grid so they would be able to start their search from the same position the next day.

The search went on for weeks before they came across another ship. The divers found a ship that had not broken up when it hit the bottom. They called Ellen, "We have located a ship that is still in one piece. How shall we proceed?" Ellen responded, "I don't know what to tell you about that. I'll get Bill." She found Bill in the navigation room and called him to the phone. Bill stated, "You will need to rip open a hole in the hull with explosives. I'll send down what you need in the basket." Bill loaded enough C-4 plastic explosives into the basket and also included a detonation kit. He sent the basket down. Eric was the explosives man. He positioned the charge and hooked up the detonator. He used a radio controlled detonator. He used his radio to tell Ellen that they were coming up. They slowly ascended to the surface and climbed in the boat. When they were all on deck, Bill handed Eric the radio sending device for setting off the charge. They moved the boat five hundred feet away. Eric set off the charge. The water churned visibly in the area above the blast. They moved back into position over the wrecked ship. Dead fish started to float up around the boat. The cook used a long handled net to gather some of them. He exclaimed, "We can have some nice fresh fish for supper!"

The divers put on fresh tanks and went back down into the dark watery depths. They found the ship with a large hole in its hull. The blast had done a good job. With great anticipation, they pointed the submersible into the hole. Its bright lights revealed what they were looking for. The floor of the lower deck was covered with massive gold bars and Spanish gold doubloons. There were heavy golden chains and some small gold statues. They found two chests that had not been blown open by the blast. Jeff Pile called up for the basket. It arrived in a few minutes and everyone started loading up the treasure. It took all of the men to load the heavy unopened chests. They had to work fast since they only had thirty minutes worth of air. When their air started to run low, they took what they had and headed back up to the ship. The basket got to the ship before they did. They stopped, as usual, at regular intervals so they wouldn't develop nitrogen bubbles in their blood. When they got to the surface, they all climbed on deck and examined the treasure. Bill and Bob pried open one of the treasure chests. It was full of jewelry. There were necklaces and bracelets covered with rubies and diamonds. There were other precious stones as well. They eagerly pried open the second treasure chest. It was completely full of gold doubloons. Bob stated, "This is a good day's work." Eric replied, "This is only half of it. We ran out of air. We'll need to go back down tomorrow to get the rest. We saw gold scattered all over the lower deck of the ship. It may take several days to get all of it picked up." Bill responded, "We can send the other boat back to get more air tanks. I think we have enough for tomorrow's dive." He got on the cell phone and called the other boat, "We need more air tanks. Go pick up forty more." The pilot responded, "I can have them back here by tomorrow noon." Bill responded, "That will be soon enough. We have enough tanks for tomorrow's dive."

Big Angel Two pulled away and headed for Key West. Bob had the divers put the gold in heavy canvas bags and load them safely into a storage room. When they were done, everyone showered and got dressed for supper. They set up card tables on the deck and watched the sun go down as they ate the heaviest meal of the day. There were sirloin steaks and T-bones. Baked potatoes and tossed salads. Bill treated everyone to his favorite white wine. Everyone was content as they watched the golden sun dropping slowly into the water. The purple and gold reflected off the scattered clouds that were in the sky. The color danced across the rippled water. There was little breeze. It was a perfect setting for a wonderful celebration meal.

Once it was dark, Eric got his guitar and played for everyone. Linda massaged each diver's shoulders and flirted with all of them. On popular demand, she put on her bikini and danced like she had the previous night. The men loved to see her in the moonlight. Ellen got jealous and dragged Bob off to the bedroom for love making. Mary followed suit and left Linda alone with all the men. Bill came back out at midnight and ordered, "All of you to bed now! Tomorrow I want more of that gold to be brought up." No one contradicted him. They all headed for bed. Bill went back to Mary and they finally went to sleep after having spent the evening expressing affection in one way or another.

It took four days to bring up the gold from that ship. The treasure hunters spent the whole year exploring that one long area below the drop off. It went on for miles. They found several more ships and brought up well over six billion dollars worth of treasure. When they decided to take a break for a month, Mary called her parents and had them come to Key West for a visit. They had figured out long ago that she had married Bill. Mary wanted them to see him and she wanted to see them again. When they arrived, Mary had them stay at Sandy's bed and breakfast. Bill and Mary had met them at the airport and brought them there. They introduced Joseph and Betty to Sandy. Sandy had her waitress serve them supper in the garden. Joseph asked about the treasure hunting, "Have you done as well as you wanted to this year?" Bill responded, "We couldn't have dreamed of doing this well. We will be able to feed and cloth thousands of people and give them jobs to work at." Betty stated, "I'm proud that my daughter is working to help poor people. God will bless her. I know He will. He already has. It is wonderful the way He sent the angel to save you from drowning." Mary responded, "I will always remember the generosity He showed me." Mary asked her father, "How is the evangelism work going this year?"

Joseph responded, "I gave the money that I got from the stock market to the poor. That was good advice you gave me. Now I don't owe anything to the Jade Goddess. With the money you loaned me, I started my television ministry. I have been getting letters from hundreds of people thanking me for leading them to Jesus. Television is a powerful tool for good when put in the right hands." Mary responded, "God will be generous with you. I know He will be." Betty stated, "We are hoping for that. Your father regrets that he ever got involved with the Jade Goddess."

The waitress brought out some tossed salads and dressing. They all prayed over the meal and began to eat. Bill said, "I wish we could have had you to the wedding, but we wanted to get started with the treasure hunting and got married rather quickly." Mary stated, "What he means to say is that it was love at first sight and we got married the next day." Betty said, "Well, we approve of the fact that Bill was the one who caused you to get baptized and become a Christian." Mary responded, "I certainly was Bill. He knew what I needed right away. He's a good salesman." Joseph said, "It might be good if you could appear on my television show some day." Bill laughed, "I don't really think of myself as an evangelist, but I would be willing to appear. Would you let me put in a plug for our investment group and tell what we're doing to help the poor?" Joseph responded, "I wouldn't mind at all. In fact I'd insist on it." Their steaks and lobster arrived and they all ate the delicious fare.

The next day Mary and Bill showed Mary's parents where they searched for gold along the beach near the bed and breakfast. Bill had a metal detector with him and showed them how it worked. Betty noticed the large gold cross and chain around Mary's neck. Mary stated, "Bill found it right here and gave it to me when we first came to Key West." Joseph responded, "It's a beautiful cross. I know you'll always wear it."

They walked back to the bed and breakfast. Bill said, "I'd like for both of you to see our boats. They're at the marina." Betty responded, "We'd love to see the boats. You can show us all of Key West." Mary stated, "I'll drive." Sandy said, "I'll stay here. You all have a good time." She told Mary's parents, "It was good to meet both of you. I hope you enjoy Key West. When you come back we can play some cards and talk some more." Betty responded, "We'll be looking forward to that."

Bill, Mary and her parents got in the car and went to the marina. Bill led them to Big Angel One. Betty and Joseph took a tour of the boat and then sat on the deck with Bill and Mary. The cook brought them some mint ice cream and coffee. They talked for hours and then saw the sights around Key West. At the end of the morning they went back to Sandy's and ate lunch. In the afternoon they watched a movie and visited the stores around town for the rest of the day. When evening came, they drove back to the airport and said their goodbyes. Betty and Joseph made Mary promise to come back for a visit to Culebra in New Mexico. Mary and Bill left the airport and went back to the boat.

Ellen was explaining to her mother that she had been married for a year. She wanted to have a wedding in Indiana so that her parents and friends could attend. Her mother told her father and they agreed to have a wedding for her in Syracuse. Ellen was happy that her parents now knew about her marriage. Bob had explained things to his parents, and they were supportive as well. The wedding would be on the first Sunday of July. That would be about one year after their first wedding.

There were many more treasure hunts. The oceans of the world yielded up hundreds of pounds of gold and gems. The divers took their boats all around the world to find sunken ships. Bob and Ellen had their second Wedding and everything went well. Mary and Ellen each started having children and soon another boat was needed. Mary and her family had one boat, Ellen and her family had a second boat and the supplies were kept in the third boat named Big Angel Three. Bob and Ellen went back to Michigan often to fish with their forty foot boat. They also used the forty footer which they kept in Jamaica. The investment group did well and showed a profit. The group continued helping the poor of the world with food, clothing and jobs.

In hell, Satan was still keeping an eye on Mary. He didn't take defeat lightly. With one of his favorite assistants by his side, he thought out loud about Mary, "I thought I really had her when she started winning all that money in Las Vegas. She loves money and gold. Who would think that a human being would give all that away to poor people? She really knows how to piss me off!" His assistant responded, "Don't be upset, boss. Remember, this doesn't happen very often." Satan said, "Yeah, you're right. Let's cheer ourselves by burning and torturing some lukewarm believers." They marched off eagerly towards the edge of the fiery pit.

The End

Dr. Exeeto

Dr. Exeeto

1st Edition

Mark Lee Masters Publishing

Printed 2007

U.S.A.

CONTENTS

Acknowledgments

I give my heartiest thanks to the many patient teachers who put up with my rough edges as they ardently strove to make me more than I was. I thank my wife, who provided a home climate conducive to creative activities. I'd like to express great appreciation to my friend, Tony Lala, who patiently offered timely suggestions for the improvement of this book. Thanks, most eagerly goes, to those who show an interest in my books. You, my readers, are those whom I write for. I constantly covet your attention. Undying gratitude goes to my father, for his generous financial assistance, which made it possible for me to continue with my writing.

Chapter One

Dr. Exeeto's Laboratory

We find the good doctor in his laboratory which is located two hundred feet below the surface of the Atlantic Ocean. He carefully located his underwater lair with the desire of having it where the ancient city of Atlantis was. He hoped to make the spot once again the center of all truly civilized existence. The doctor is currently walking slowly along the outer perimeter of his laboratory. The outer wall is made of clear acrylic which was designed to withstand the pressures of such depths. Dr. Exeeto is a two hundred pound man with tan skin, salt and pepper mustache and advanced baldness. He's in his late fifties. His right ear is a little lower than the left one, and the right eye droops a little with a faint scar running from that eye to the lowered ear. The abnormalities were from a mountain climbing accident when he was young and climbing with his girl friend. He's more than a little self conscious about his face and it's appearance. The doctor is currently briefing an important scientist, Dr. Smith, on his overall plan for the laboratory.

"Yes, Dr. Smith, since you have proven to be my best scientist, I'd like you to take charge of all the biological operations. I, of course, will maintain direct control of the climate altering gases. I always operate on a 'need to know' basis with my workers. You now need to know. I want someone controlling the biological operations who can agree with my philosophy for world change. Of course, if you don't agree with me, you can still work here, but in a lesser capacity. I have shared some of my ideas with you previously, and you were sympathetic, so now I will tell you more. World powers, large and small, have their fingers on the nuclear button. Each wants to use atomic weapons to gain more power and world control. Our enemy is not any one of these world powers. Our enemy is the nuclear radiation. The approaching nuclear wars will destroy the genetic pools of the animal and plant life which we both hold so dear. My plan is to make life on earth so unpleasant for humans above the sea, that they will forget about killing each other and spend all their time just trying to survive."

Dr. Smith responded, "I agree with you in principle so far, Dr. Exeeto, but how do you plan to make humans so miserable? How will making them miserable keep them from pushing the atomic buttons?" Dr. Exeeto answered, "I think I understand mankind. War is a luxury they engage in when they are bored. When they have plenty of food and things are going well, that is when they become bored and start warfare." Dr. Smith said, "I have no logical objection to your theory. You have convinced me over the last few months that nuclear annihilation is imminent without our intervention. I want to help. I'm just not sure that you have the power to stop the madness of mankind with snakes and mosquitoes."

Dr. Exeeto explained further, "I trust you more than any other human, Dr. Smith. For this reason, I will tell you the full details of my plan. Not only will we be releasing venomous snakes that have been rendered more fertile and venomous. Not only will there be malaria carrying mosquitoes and plague carrying rats. No, I also am building up a massive supply of F-12 refrigerant to release into the atmosphere when the time is right. It will destroy the ozone layer, and the earth's mean temperature will be raised to one hundred and twenty degrees. The temperature will be near one hundred degrees even at the north and south poles. There will be massive flooding. The earth will become totally tropical with terrible hurricanes over the entire globe. No one will feel like pushing an atomic button then." Dr. Smith replied, "I agree with your plan, in principle, even though I'm not totally convinced it will work. I think we must do something to avert the nuclear radiation caused destruction of the gene pool. Will the earth every come back to normal?" Dr. Exeeto answered, "In about a hundred years, the vast increase in vegetation will cause enough increase in the oxygen supply to enable the ozone layer to reestablish itself somewhat. I think the earth will be tropical for well over a hundred years. The ice caps may not reform for thousands of years. That would be the case, at least, if World War III doesn't bring a nuclear winter."

Dr. Exeeto pointed out into the sea at a whale shark that was swimming by, "There's one of my favorite creatures. It's a giant, yet it's completely gentle and harmless." Dr. Smith agreed, "It is, indeed, a truly impressive creature. What do you want me to do with the venomous snakes, Dr. Exeeto?" "I want you to make sure they are well nourished and energetic. We will be releasing them soon." "I understand, Dr. Exeeto. What takes highest priority?" "Take utmost care with the plague viruses. You mustn't infect any of us. That's why I'm having you do that work in a quarantined module. I want the infected rats ready for delivery on short notice. The snakes can be distributed as soon as you have them ready. I will release the F-12 gases when you release the rats." Dr. Smith commented, "It's a pleasure working with you, Dr. Exeeto. I sincerely hope your plan works well. The future of the world depends on us." Dr. Smith was a 5'8" man from India in his early forties. He was dressed completely in white. His skin was dark tan and his face was angular and somewhat handsome.

Viewed from just below the surface of the Atlantic, several hundred miles east of Florida, the laboratory complex looked like a cluster of glass bubbles on the bottom of the sea. Many small subs were carrying supplies to the deep sea lab. The glass domes covered tens of thousands of square feet. Dr. Exeeto obtained his funding from oil rich terrorist groups who thought he would be sending snakes and rats only to their enemies. Little did they know of the doctor's actual plans. The good doctor also accepted funding from many other powerful countries. Anyone's money was accepted. They were all funding their own demise.

One country wasn't too trusting of Dr. Exeeto. The United States of America was trying to trim on its budget for biological weapons. The C.I.A. was briefing a small crack team of agents to check up on Dr. Exeeto. The initial meeting was in one of the C.I.A.'s top secret command centers in a nuclear powered submarine off the coast of Florida. Major Donald McBride was the male agent selected for the mission. He was a lethal martial arts expert and had been a navy seal before entering the secret service. He was in his middle thirties. His counterpart was Major Sandra Ferguson, who was also in her thirties. She also had been a navy seal. Her blond good looks and McBride's handsome features made them seem like anything but highly trained warriors. Ferguson was slender with well toned muscles. She looked attractive enough to be a model. McBride was six feet four inches tall, clean shaven and ruggedly handsome with a full head of black hair and bushy eye brows. You could tell he worked out. They looked like a red hot Hollywood couple hiding from photographers. This is part of why they were selected for the mission of investigating Dr. Exeeto. They were both scientists as well. Major McBride was trained in germ warfare, while Major Ferguson was a medical doctor with special training in the area of snakes.

The C.I.A. administrative representative was General Mark Daniels. He was a gray haired man in his early sixties. He had a rather flattened nose and steel blue eyes. He was stocky and strong looking. At six feet tall, he looked like a man to be reckoned with. McBride was thinner, but also powerful looking. He had a winning smile. He looked at Ferguson and said, "I never thought I'd be working with a beautiful woman on this mission." Ferguson replied, "I hope you can see past appearances and keep your thoughts on the mission. I'm not here to entertain you!" She stared coldly into his eyes for several long seconds. General Daniels interrupted, "I hope you two can get along in a professional manner. It's part of our plan that the two of you appear to be more interested in each other's bodies than in the business of meeting Dr. Exeeto. This will put them at ease. They will think you are typical blundering idiots who are no threat to them. Is that understood? Dr. Exeeto has promised to deliver bubonic plague infested rats and poisonous snakes to our enemies. We have given him billions of dollars to finance his operation. It has recently come to our attention, that he may also be accepting money from our enemies. We need to know just what his plan is and how he intends to carry it out. Each of you will carry one of these brief cases." The General pointed to the brief cases on his desk. "They contain enough diamonds to bribe just about anyone. They are explosive enough to blow a hole through almost any door. There is a twenty second delay on the explosion. That will give you time to get to safety. Neither of you will be carrying a handgun. We don't want to alarm Dr. Exeeto and his colleagues. He has a formidable army of miniature submarines defending his laboratory. Don't do anything to let him know we're suspicious of him. Once the two of you have gathered as much information as you can get, come back to the surface and report to me immediately. We don't object to him accepting money from our enemies, we just want to make sure he's still working for us. Are there any questions?"

Sandra Ferguson responded, "How do you propose for us to discover what his intentions are?" "Find out who is his closest companion and confidante. You may need to use your feminine charm to get this person to give you what you want. If the confidante is a woman, Major McBride will need to deal with her. Don't use brute force to get the information. At all costs, I don't want to cause Dr. Exeeto to suspect that we know of his double dealing. In the front of each briefcase is a small canister of aerosol truth serum to help you get the information we want. Act like you're using it as a breath freshener. It has a nice mint flavor. The neutralizing tablets are in a bottle fastened beside the aerosol. You will want to take the tablet for neutralizing the truth serum at least five minutes before you use the aerosol. We don't want you telling your secrets. The aerosol should get you the information we want. Kissing the person you are interrogating will intensify the affect of the aerosol, but just breathing on them should do the job. The aerosol wears off in about twenty minutes and leaves no trace."

Major McBride commented, "That's an ingenious system for getting information. Do you think we'll be able to find anything on Dr. Exeeto's computer's?" "We think he's too crafty for that. He'll have everything protected with codes. Now, report to Corporal Henderson. His helicopter is on deck and will take you to Dr. Exeeto's heliport which floats above his laboratory." McBride and Ferguson looked at each other and then saluted the General and left for the deck.

Back at Dr. Exeeto's laboratory Exeeto was continuing his briefing of Dr. Smith. "We'll be receiving some guests soon from the United States. I keep agents employed on all their submarines who keep me informed of the latest plans of their C.I.A. They want to know if I'm loyal to them or not. I have some of the serum they will be using on you. I want you to practice lying while you're under its affects. Tell them that I'm only using the terrorists to get more money to finance my operation. You can tell them anything about our operation. The only thing you need to concentrate on keeping secret is the F-12 refrigerant releases we're planning. Let them send representatives with us to release the rats and snakes. They are only to divert the attention of our supporters from the refrigerant operation. If you concentrate on babbling on and on about the snakes and rats, I'm sure you can keep quiet about the F-12 refrigerant. I will introduce you to them as my most trusted doctor who is steering the entire operation for me. This will cause them to target you with the truth serum."

Dr. Smith asked, "What if I do let slip about the refrigerant?" "I won't fill you in on any details of the F-12 operation. Just don't start talking about the world warming up. I'm sure you can do that much, can't you?" "My loyalty to you is strong. If I receive the practice with the drug, that you promised, I'm sure I can plant the right information on them. When do we begin?" "Even as we speak, one of my most attractive assistants is preparing the serum. She will use every trick in the book to get you to talk about our most important plans. She is quite gifted, so be on your toes. I know I can count on you."

For hours Dr. Smith was subjected to questioning and temptation by the beautiful assistant. Dr. Smith was used to the affects of the serum by the time Majors McBride and Ferguson arrived. McBride and Ferguson met with Dr. Exeeto for lunch and discussed the progress of the biological agents. They discussed the planned cuts in funding which the C.I.A. had in mind. Dr. Exeeto explained, "You don't need to worry about expenses any more. I have tricked some oil rich terrorist nations into helping with my expenses. I'm sure that has come to your attention. Is that not the real reason for this visit?" McBride was slightly taken off guard, but he recovered nicely. "We have never doubted your loyalty to us. I assure you that we are only concerned about finances. Politicians are always wanting to show how thrifty they are. We no longer have a blank check that allows us to do whatever we please. We have to answer to the tax payers." Dr. Exeeto replied, "I'm sure you do. I'm sure you do. It's good to hear you haven't lost faith in me. I'd like you to meet my head of operations, Dr. Smith. He's my most trusted associate. I've left all the research leadership up to him. I'm too busy with finances and all the other responsibilities a C.E.O. has to deal with. We run this place like a business. I'm quite democracy minded. The damn communists don't realize the necessity of harnessing the human desire to better themselves. People won't work their hardest just for the common good. And that working for the common good is just hot air. Small cliques of communists want control of the masses. That's what communism is all about!" McBride replied, "I'm glad we're on the same page! If you need any technical support or manpower, just let your wishes be known. Money is the only problem right now." Dr. Exeeto proudly exclaimed, "I have little need for more money, now. All I need is a little more time for my scientists to finish their work. Everything is moving along as planned. Dr. Smith will give you a tour of the facility. I have some pressing work to do. You must excuse me." He rose from the table and left them quickly.

Dr. Smith made small talk with the Majors while they finished their meal. McBride said he was experiencing a bad case of indigestion and asked to be allowed to stay in the dinning room to sip tea. He said, "Dr. Smith, you can take Major Ferguson on the tour. This visit is just a formality anyway. We know you're on our side and your work is proceeding as planned." Dr. Smith responded, "I hope you start feeling better soon. I'll take Major Ferguson on the tour right away." Major Ferguson took the doctor's hand and said, "You can call me Sandy. All my friends do. I want this to be an informal visit." The doctor smiled and squeezed her hand, "You can call me Bob or Bobby." He led her quickly away.

When the tour had led them through the rat operation and the snakes, Sandy asked, "Is there a place where we can relax a bit. I'm a little tired of walking." Bob responded, "I'll show you my quarters if that isn't getting too intimate." Sandy said, "I'm not at all afraid of intimacy. Not with a man as attractive and intelligent as you are." The doctor blushed ever so slightly and led her to his quarters. He had a wonderful view of the ocean. One whole wall of his quarters was open to the sea. The apartment was elegantly appointed. He had a grand piano and crystal chandeliers hanging from a high ceiling. Bob asked Sandy, "Would you like a drink?" Sandy replied, "I wouldn't mind a screwdriver. I didn't have time for my breakfast orange juice this morning." Bob said, "Screwdriver it is. I'll have one too." He eagerly mixed the drinks and kept one eye on Sandy. She was wearing a white pressed top with a black short skirt. She wasn't wearing a bra, and Bob was more than a little interested in what he was seeing of her chest. They sat on a sofa and talked about their work and personal lives a little. Sandy asked, "Would you mind making us a couple more screwdrivers?" Bob replied, "I'd be more than happy to." Sandy went to find the bath room while Bob mixed the drinks. While she was in the bathroom, she sprayed the serum in her mouth. She had already swallowed the pill she was supposed to take, when Bob wasn't looking.

When she returned for her drink, Bob was waiting eagerly. She sat close to him and said, "I certainly admire a man with your responsibilities and intellectual challenges. Do you think you could think of me as a close friend? I'm so busy with my work, I never get to experience friendship.

McBride and I have just met. He's not as bright as you are. He'll never rise to a position of responsibility, like you have." She leaned over and kissed him. He was receptive and kissed her back with enthusiasm. After a few minutes, Major Ferguson felt that Bob should be under the affects of the truth serum. She asked, "Do you really think Doctor Exeeto is as keen on democracy as he says?" Bob replied, "He'll take anyone's money, but he prefers democracy. The communists just use people. They don't have true respect for the people who help them. They seem manipulative to him. He isn't actually too interested in power politics. His concern is with the continued existence of the world. He's always talking about how afraid he is that the whole world will be destroyed." Sandy relied, "That's a noble concern for him to be contemplating. Is that why he's helping us cause problems for the terrorists?" He doesn't tell me everything. I know he doesn't like the terrorists. They are always too loud when they come to visit. He thinks they have hormonal imbalances and they need tranquilizers." Sandy laughed, "He's quite perceptive. I like him. Tell me more about his concern for the end of the world." Bob caught himself going the wrong direction. "Oh, that's just something he said one day. I don't think he's obsessed with it. He's mainly concerned about keeping the United States happy with his biological initiatives. He's not only after the money. He longs for the respect of America. All the best scientists work for America. That's where the money is. He thinks about respect, and he wants to be on the winning side. He knows America will win."

Sandy was sure she had the truth from Bob. She repeated the questions several times more. He always gave the same answers. Finally, as an excuse not to have sex, she said the drinks had made her stomach upset. She ran to the bathroom and made herself vomit. Bob obligingly took her back to the lunch room to find McBride. He was sitting at one of the tables sipping some tea. McBride and

Ferguson took the next available shuttle to the surface and returned to the States without incident.

Back at the lab, Dr. Exeeto was reviewing a tape recording which Dr. Smith had made with a recorder hidden in his clothing. Dr. Exeeto was quite pleased. "You told them just enough of the truth to be convincing. You should get a job in the theater, Dr. Smith." Dr. Smith smiled, "I enjoyed the task. Major Ferguson is a good kisser. I just wish she wouldn't regurgitate just when things are getting interesting!" Dr. Exeeto replied, "I hope you don't mind that the next visitor is a man. You don't have to kiss him. Just let him cough on you. He'll be using the same truth serum. Iran is sending him to find out if we are loyal to their cause. If you convince him as well as you convinced Major Ferguson, I'll double your bonus this month." Dr. Smith asked, "How do you know he'll be using the same truth serum?" Dr. Exeeto exclaimed, "All countries have poorly paid janitors and cleaning ladies. They're all working for me. It's the main reason my operation requires so much money. It costs money for good intelligence."

While Dr. Smith was feeding misleading information to the Iranian representative, Dr. Exeeto did his daily walk of the facility. First he checked on the vast rat raising facility. Most of the rats were recruited from the various sewer mains of the world. France had provided the bulk of the rats. Since the money was good, no one questioned what the rats were for. The doctor questioned the shift's virologist on the readiness of the plague virus for transmission to the rats. "Will there be sufficient virus to quickly infect all the rats?"

The virologist was a professional looking Mexican woman with a somewhat attractive appearance that was only marred by a slightly crooked nose. She had been kicked by a horse when she was a young riding enthusiast. Her dark sensuous eyes and thin sensuous lips didn't go unappreciated by the doctor. "Yes, Dr. Exeeto. The virus is here in sufficient quantity to infect every rat in the world, if we had them all here." The doctor laughed, "It would take a big room to hold them all. How many rats would you say we have?" "During our inventory last week, we came up with the figure of fifty thousand rats." The virus is now concentrated in ticks which will be released onto the rats just before they are released to the outside world." "Yes, said Dr. Exeeto. Just as we planned. Every country having possession of the hydrogen bomb will receive its share of rats on June first. The plague spreads best in warm weather. That's only thirty days from now. See to it that everything runs smoothly. You'll receive extra bonus." "Thank you, Dr. Exeeto. Everything will happen as you've planned. We could release them sooner if you decide to."

Next Dr. Exeeto visited the snake laboratory. He asked the shift supervisor about the inventory, "How many snakes do we now have?" The supervisor was a short heavy man with red hair. He proudly reported, "We have three hundred thousand snakes. They are mostly the aggressive king cobras which you specified. We are also heavily stocked with timber rattlers. They are resistant to the cold climates of northern areas. Since we started your project, ten years ago, we have been able to amplify the potency of their venom ten fold. They are exceedingly lethal." Dr. Exeeto asked, "Is there adequate food supply for them all?" The supervisor replied, "That's the problem. As you know, we've been feeding them the offspring of the rat population. We can't keep up with their appetites much longer." Dr. Exeeto said, "Good, we'll release them immediately. I had no specific time schedule for their release. Since they are a little hungry, they will be aggressive when they are deposited in the capital cities of the world where nuclear buttons are located. I want people to have something to think about other than pushing those buttons that will destroy the genetic pool."

Dr. Exeeto excused himself and moved quickly to his office in the central bubble. He paged Dr. Smith to his office. In ten minutes Dr. Smith was at his door. Dr. Exeeto asked, "Were you convincing with the Iranian representatives? Let me hear the tape." The doctor listened to the tape and was impressed with Dr. Smith's deceptions. "I like your work, Dr. Smith. I couldn't have done better myself. However, my instincts have taken over. I feel a logical worry that one of our backers may become nervous and ask to oversee our work. We will load the rats, snakes and malaria mosquitoes tonight and tomorrow. Tomorrow night we will release the animals at their destinations. I have teams of transport agents who will use every mode of transportation necessary to achieve the best distribution possible. I'm releasing the F-12 gases tonight. No one can stop us now. We have the element of surprise. No one expects us to strike for a month or more." Dr. Smith responded, "I can make everything happen as you wish. I have everyone on alert to respond at a moments notice. Everything is ready." "Very well, Dr. Smith. I'll count on you for quick results. You'll have to excuse me now. I want to release the gases." Dr. Exeeto rushed from the room and made his way quickly to the gas storage module.

All the storage tanks had their own valve and pipe to the surrounding sea. Quickly the doctor started opening valves. The pipes got frosted as they released the refrigerant. Dr. Exeeto turned up the room thermostat to eighty degrees. He wanted the tanks to empty quickly. He took great pride in opening the tanks himself. There were hundreds of them. Each one holding hundreds of gallons of refrigerant. Finally he flipped some toggle switches which opened the largest valves on the tall thousand gallon tanks. They would take many hours to empty, even though they had heaters installed in the tanks. The doctor couldn't help but laugh as he listened to the gases escaping. He was thinking of the overly aggressive people of the world who constantly thought of overpowering others. He was picturing them sweating so profusely and being so overcome by heat, that they couldn't even think of mustering enough energy to engage in fighting or dreaming of warfare. He could visualize the ice caps melting. The sea was raging before his eyes as hurricanes ravaged the coastlines of the entire world. The doctor felt certain that now his sea creatures would be safe from radioactivity caused mutations.

Dr. Exeeto returned to his quarters to make final preparations for the days ahead. He was working on tow time capsules which he planned to plant in a uranium mine in the western United States and in a mine in the Ukraine. He sat in a plush white leather sofa and looked out into the sea which was visible through the acrylic wall of the laboratory. For months he had collected pictures and movie clips in his lap top computer. It was a custom made Dell with DVD burning capability. He eagerly worked with cut and paste, making sure every scene started and ended at just the right time. He had a remote which controlled a CD collection of all his favorite music. He could dub in any selection of music he liked, onto the DVD. He worked deftly and with great intensity. He thought, *If I can just warn a future civilization not to make the same mistakes we have made. The price of using atomic bombs is absolutely too high. It sets back civilization thousands of years. Are we to constantly claw our way to the top of a slippery spiral, only to be knocked back to the bottom by our own vicious hateful impulses? How long must man continue in this eternity of futility that mirrors the Myth of Sisyphus. Is there nothing more than rolling a rock up a mountain and then letting it roll back down. We are not cursed. We were meant for more than this. I am only forced to play God, by the fact that every powerful nation of earth wants to play God. Everyone wants to be the first to end the world. It's up to me to save them in spite of themselves. This graphic review of what brought the world to its knees may help a future civilization to move on and above the futile upward spiral of growth followed by collapse. At least I need that hope to help me endure my last years here on earth.*

He entered inspiring sections which portrayed man's accomplishments in art, music and architecture. He explained the delicate nature of all earth's organisms and how atomic radiation could mutate most life forms and turn creation into a hideous joke. He portrayed the affects of atomic warfare and the nuclear winter that would kill off all but the most cleverly protected of life forms. Finally he ended the DVD by proclaiming that if they have found one of his two time capsules, they were probably mining uranium. If they don't take drastic measures, mankind may totally eliminate himself from the face of the earth, just as they almost did when the time capsules were hidden.

Dr. Exeeto assigned some of his best people to hide the time capsules. He specified the location where one would be hidden in a uranium mine in the United States. The other would be hidden in a uranium mine in the Ukraine. With Dr. Exeeto's advanced tunneling machines, his people would be able to access the mines in less than eight years. Dr. Exeeto had spent much time and money discovering exactly where the best mines were located. His advanced computers were programmed to carefully plot subterranean locations.

He wanted to be able to say that at least he tried to stop mankind from acting foolishly. Dr. Exeeto was a little sad as he sent off his time capsules. He was certain that the men and women of the future wouldn't heed his warnings. They would find the capsules, but they wouldn't listen. This, he was almost certain of. Because of this cynical belief, he left his last two words for the future at the end of each time capsule's DVD. First he recorded the words in the original Pennsylvania Dutch. Next he recorded the translation, English for the America time capsule, and Russian for the Ukrainian time capsule.

After the DVD was completed, Dr. Exeeto called to his secret laboratory, which was fifty miles away, deep down into a giant fault in the ocean's floor. The fault was several hundred yards wide and allowed his supply submarines to easily slip down and out of sight into the five mile deep chasm. The doctor called his hidden lab "The Cellar". Now as he spoke on secret low frequency radio, he called to his head of cellar operations, "Dr. Marlow, this is Dr. Exeeto, do you read me?" There was a pause and the radio crackled slightly as he waited for a response. Finally Dr. Marlow answered, "This is Dr. Marlow. I read you loud and clear." Dr. Exeeto stated, "Please report. What is the status of cellar operations?" Dr. Marlow reported, "Everything is go. We are still compressing nitrogen and oxygen as planned. Storage is eighty percent full. Food storage is completed. Computers are programmed to return survivors to island destinations if conditions become right for a return to the surface. Expansion of living space is going on even as we speak." Dr. Exeeto asked, "When will you be ready for occupants to arrive?" Dr. Marlow stated, "We can accept your entire population at any time. Living quarters are more than adequate." Dr. Exeeto stated, "We'll be coming in just a few days. We've moved our biological deployment ahead to tomorrow. I have already released the F-12. We should be done with the biological deployment in three days. Then we'll immediately start moving all personnel to your site."

Dr. Marlow said, "We'll be ready for you. We can use the additional people. Adding to the living space is labor intensive. There's plenty of room for eating and sleeping, but we need much more work and recreation area." Dr. Exeeto responded, "I understand. Keep planning ahead. I'm sure you can make things go smoothly. That's all I have for now. I'll see you in two days. Over and out."

Dr. Exeeto decided to relax by watching his favorite footage of home videos. He had never married. In his early days, he had his friend, Jim, film him as he experienced the best of life. He had placed all these pleasurable film clips on one DVD.

Now he sat back and watched as he walked with an attractive blond along the trails of the Grand Canyon. Her name was Cheryl Schmucker. There were clips of them together all over the United States. They had visited Canada and seen the expansive forest lands and the northern frozen tundra. It was bittersweet for him to watch the video of them together. She had left him to marry a promising lawyer. At the time he was a poorly paid lab technician for a small pharmaceutical company. She longed for security and a prosperous future. It didn't matter how good they were together. She didn't care that he thought she was the best thing that had ever happened to him. After her leaving him, he lived with the memory of how good it had been with her. He never had seriously thought of marrying after that. He was cynical about the motives of women for marrying. The experience with Cheryl had made a lasting impression on him.

The doctor turned off the DVD and went to the kitchen for some coffee. He grabbed some blank sheets of paper and a pen as he made his way there. After microwaving some water and mixing instant Folgers with milk and sugar, he settled down to writing down his thoughts on what he wanted his future life to be like. He thought about the attractive intelligent women he had working on his team, and asked himself if it would be a sound decision to initiate a relationship with one of them.

Dr. Exeeto's thoughts turned to his virologist in charge of the bubonic plague virus. Her name was Lucia Vargas. He thought to himself that her duties would be greatly reduced once the plague ridden rats were released. She would be asked to help him with his duties as C.E.O. If she didn't find him to be someone she'd like to have as a mate, he would still enjoy working with her. He wrote down how he would present the idea to her. Then another idea struck him. Why be so circuitous. She might admire a more direct approach. He impulsively dropped the paper and used his phone to page Lucia and have her come to his quarters. Returning to his paper and pen, he wrote down some possible ways of presenting the idea of dating him, to Lucia. Actually he wanted to just start making love to her right away. He had finally decided to drop the past and his fond memories of Cheryl. He wanted to move quickly into the future. *There mustn't be any feeling of coercion,* he thought to himself. He quickly wrote some opening lines to present to Lucia. At all costs he didn't want to be guilty of attempting to seduce her.

The door bell rang, and Dr. Exeeto answered it. Lucia greeted him at the door and he let her in. The doctor apologized for calling her on short notice. "Lucia, this is more of a social appointment than a business meeting." He led her to the kitchen table and offered her a drink. She accepted some coffee. Lucia stated, "It'll be nice to get to know you a little better. I've enjoyed working with you all these years. We're always so busy. I've always longed to know a little more about you as a person, Dr. Exeeto. Dr. Exeeto replied, "You can call me John while were in private. I've admired the work you've done for me. There will always be a place for you here in my laboratories. Let me be direct and to the point now, Lucia. I have decided I want someone special to have an ongoing relationship with so as to meet each other's needs as they arise. I know this is terribly sudden, but you're a scientist and I'm sure you'd want to approach this situation logically. We'll be living soon in a cave under the ocean till the day we die. I don't want to be lonely and childless."

Lucia stated, "Doctor, your ideas fascinate me. I don't wish to be coy, but I'll need a little time to think about this. I find you attractive, and I'm not dating anyone, but this is quite a shock. I never guessed that you were attracted to me." Dr. Exeeto explained, "I usually bend over backwards not to come on to my staff. Perhaps I was a little too secretive about my feelings." Lucia winked at John and said, "I don't want to seem easy. You might not appreciate a woman that was too easy to win. Could I ask you for a drink? I know you're professional and don't want to take advantage of your staff. As you said, this is a social meeting. We should loosen up and listen to some music over drinks." Dr. Exeeto eagerly took his cue. He poured two exotic vodka filled fruit drinks and put some tasteful Jazz music on. They quickly drank their drinks as they watched the ocean view out from the front transparent wall of the doctor's living room. John took Lucia's hand and asked her to slow dance with him. They moved to the music and softly whispered their admiration for each other. After a long and touching dance, Lucia asked for another drink. She said, "Make it a strong one, I'm still a little nervous about this whole thing." John poured them more drinks and then sat down with Lucia on the sofa. He said, "Lucia, you shouldn't feel nervous. I'm not out to take advantage of you or trick you. I'm trying to be as straight forward as possible." Lucia explained, "I want to get to know you better before we make any long term commitment. We're scientists. I'll tell you frankly. I need to know if you're good for me. I only want to express my concern for compatibility."

Lucia explained, "This drink should help to loosen my inhibitions. If you are indeed serious about wanting something long term, then I don't see why we shouldn't proceed now, if there's time in you schedule. Dr. Exeeto explained, "I'm free this evening. We can go with this, where ever you want it to go." Lucia stated, "I'd like to take a shower and clean up a little. I just came from work." "Perfectly understandable, Lucia. I have a steam sauna as well. Do you like them?" I'd like to see how the sauna would be with you. Shall we proceed?"

John started up the sauna. After Lucia's shower they sat in the steam and talked animatedly. Lucia said, "I feel so at home with you. You were direct and honest. I would have felt manipulated and insulted if you had tried to seduce me." John replied, "It was tough knowing exactly how to approach the situation. We have something in common as scientists. We can discuss things logically. John asked, "Why haven't you been dating anyone here at the lab?" Lucia answered, "I've been so busy with my work. There's been no time for socializing. What about you. Why did you wait so long to start something with me?" John said, "It was my preoccupation with the mission. I was totally absorbed in being successful with the development and release of the biological and chemical agents." Lucia asked somewhat puzzled, "Chemical agents? You never told me about that." "It sounds worse than it is. I'm merely causing the earth to experience accelerated global warming with the release of massive amounts of refrigerant gases. My goal is to distract the global community so it won't be as likely to destroy the gene pool with radioactivity." Lucia said, "There's much talk of nuclear proliferation. There's no doubt that nuclear war is imminent. You're a good steward for wanting to preserve the gene pool. Where will we be if it's destroyed? It would set the world back hundreds of millions of years. The beautiful life forms we now know would quite likely never reestablish themselves. Beauty as we know it, would cease to exist." Suddenly John eagerly took Lucia's hand and led her back to the living room couch. They kissed eagerly for hours. Dr. Exeeto was capable of much passion. Lucia was feeling reassured that they were right for each other. She spoke softly, "I think our commitment to each other is a good idea. You definitely know how to please me." Dr. Exeeto replied, "I can't imagine wanting more than what you bring to the table." Dr. Exeeto laughed and said, "We'll make a good team. I'll help you move your things here tonight." Lucia replied, "That'll be excellent. I'm looking forward to settling in."

Back on board a submarine off the coast of Florida, Major McBride and Major Ferguson were being debriefed. Major Ferguson's report was uneventful and revealed that she had found nothing to raise any doubts about the loyalty of Dr. Exeeto. His most trusted assistant apparently knew nothing of any devious plot by the doctor to turn against the United States. Major McBride's report of his mission was a little more revealing. General Daniels asked him, "What, of interest do you have to report?" McBride stated, "I was able to seduce a terribly neglected virologist named Lucia. She happened to come to the break area where I was feigning illness. She led me to her quarters, where I put the serum to use. I was informed that there were enough rats and plague virus to infect the entire world. She said that Dr. Exeeto often spoke to her about his concern for the gene pool of the world and its apparent imminent destruction at the hands of world powers. She believed that the doctor was only concerned about the future of the world. He wasn't, in her opinion, the type of person who would seek riches or political power."

General Daniels asked, "What do you think we should do?" Major McBride replied, "I think we should come up with an excuse to make another visit to the laboratory. This seems to demand a little more looking into." Daniels stated, "I agree. We'll wait a few days and then send you back for substantiation of the strength of the plague virus. That will allow you to further question the virologist. It bothers me greatly that Dr. Exeeto sees himself as guardian of the gene pool. If he's not motivated by money, there's no telling what he may do. We can't have a loose canon going about blasting the world in any way he sees fit! Try to access his rat deployment schedule to see if we're on the list for receiving the pesky creatures. If he's turned against us, we'll have to take steps to terminate his organization. Is that clear!" McBride answered, "I'll do my best to see what he's up to. Should I take Ferguson along this time?" "Yes, you'll need her for back up. Be sure they perceive the two of you as people controlled by there hormones. I want them to see you as harmless pests and nothing more. I'm sending the two of you on shore leave together. I want you both to practice staying in character as people who are more interested in each other than in business. Is that clear? I've given Ferguson the same instructions."

McBride saluted the General and left to find Ferguson waiting outside the door. She said, "I guess we're on leave together. Where shall we go?" McBride replied, "I think we should go to South Beach, near Miami. If anyone's watching us, it'll be clear that we're only shallow hedonists." Ferguson stated, "Just don't get any funny ideas, now!" McBride replied, "Please, Ferguson. Stay in character!" He patted her tenderly on the derriere. She smiled reluctantly and took his hand saying, "What I won't do for my country!" Then she grabbed him and kissed him passionately. McBride broke away after several minutes and said, "At first I felt a little daunted by the assignment, but now I feel like this should more than a little pleasurable." Ferguson asked, "Your cabin or mine?" "My cabin has the best selection of liquor. Shall we?" Ferguson replied, "Lead the way." They entered McBride's cabin and had some dry martinis together. Ferguson asked, "Tell me, Major McBride, do you like this type of assignment?" McBride replied, "Since we're meeting informally, you can call me Don." Ferguson stated, "And you may call me Sandy." McBride continued, "I like serving my country to the highest of my capacity. I like the excitement of this type of work. I know I'll enjoy working more closely with you." Ferguson said, "My sinuses are a little plugged up. Do you mind if I open them up in your shower with a little steamy hot water?" Don replied, "I wouldn't mind a little steam myself!" Their clothing could be seen dropping to the floor and soon they were in the shower together."

Ferguson asked, "So how did you manage to seduce that virologist so quickly?" McBride replied, "I appealed to her motherly instincts. I said she could help my stomach problems if she'd provide me with a rum and coke and a back rub. How many women can resist an opportunity like that to help out their fellow man? Why all the interest in the virologist?" She replied, "I was just filling myself in on what makes you tick. I wanted to know your M.O., so to speak. I've found out some of what you do, but I've got a feeling you haven't spent the last round in your gun." The steam got thicker and thicker. They grew quiet as things got hotter and hotter in the cozy shower.

The next morning they climbed on board a helicopter which took them to a hotel roof in South Beach. Their bags had been packed and provided for them. They had already been checked into their rooms by phone.

In no time at all, they were in their swim suits and out on the beach catching the last of the afternoon sun. The beach was full of attractive sun worshippers, all perfecting the tan on their nearly perfect bodies. Many of the people were exposing as much of themselves as was possible without giving in to the temptation of going totally nude. McBride had known what to expect, so he was able to seem uninterested in the scantily clad nature of the women around him. Ferguson said, "It's refreshing to see so many people with little in the way of inhibitions about displaying their nearly naked bodies to the sun." McBride calmly responded, "Oh, I hardly noticed. I was too busy thinking about the mission, but we can't talk about it out here. I certainly like your body Ferguson. I can't get enough of you." Ferguson replied, "I admire your candor. Just don't assume too much. Last night might have been just a one night stand. I'm not a woman who likes to be taken for granted." McBride said, "I was only alluding to a back rub. Don't let your imagination run wild!" Ferguson retorted, "My imagination run wild! Stop thinking and put some lotion on my back." She slid over closer to him and let him lotion her entire back side. After fifteen minutes she rolled over and passed him the sunscreen. I could use a little more on my top half, in front. I'm always afraid of getting burned there." McBride applied the lotion as sensuously as he could. Then he whispered in Ferguson's ear, "I think I hear our sauna calling us."

They ran back to the room. McBride turned on the steam sauna, while Ferguson poured them some drinks. They sat in the sauna for a long time sipping their drinks and making small talk. Neither of them felt like discussing the mission right at the moment. When they finished their drinks, they slowly drew closer to each other and started kissing. McBride whispered, "I think we're getting along great socially, but do you mind if I mix a little business with pleasure?" Ferguson looked in his eyes as though trying to discern his thoughts. He glanced down and then looked warmly into her eyes. She smiled and took his cue for her to distract him as he spoke. She listened closely as he talked about the mission. It was easy for her to get his point as he slipped into her receptive mind with his misgivings about the mission thus far. He said, "Your questioning of Dr. Smith went a little too easy to be believable. It was as though he was coached to give us just enough information to make us feel he had told all. I'm wondering if they had the antidote to the truth serum. They may have the truth serum and have practiced avoiding certain topics while under its affects." Ferguson nodded and pushed McBride on. He stammered a little as he went on to his final point. "We need to question those people again, but we must push them harder on specific points about the lab and its operations." Ferguson nodded again, this time more vigorously. McBride came around to making another point. Ferguson's tenacity had drawn him out more. "We need to follow their operation where ever it takes us. If they're double crossing everyone, they probably have a secret lab where they can hide when the payback it due. They know we can strike them where they are now. We need to find out if they have a back up location." They continued discussing the fine points of the mission for several hours. Ferguson expertly drew McBride out as fully as possible.

Chapter Two

Release of the Plagues

The next day, Dr. Exeeto approved the return visit and scheduled them for the next Friday. It was Wednesday and Exeeto said he was too busy to deal with them immediately. He said he was conducting some time sensitive testing that couldn't be put off. The meeting was set for three o'clock in the afternoon. Ferguson and McBride enjoyed the extra days together and kept planning for the mission.

Dr. Exeeto was busy directing his staff for the immediate deployment of the biological agents. The malaria carrying mosquitoes were sent out first since they would attract the least amount of attention. The rats and snakes were deployed the next day with equal precision. They were dropped off at the various targets under cover of night. It was the best time for the animals to adapt themselves to their new environments without being captured.

The last twenty-four hours was spent moving vital equipment to the new lab and in the transport of all staff to that lab. The people who didn't want to commit themselves to the life in the new lab were transported back to land at the last minute, just before most of the loyal personnel were transported to the new facility.

Dr. Exeeto was in his quarters watching some international news reports about the appearance of the poisonous snakes.

The rats had still managed to stay relatively undetected since they had been spread out over a large area. As the news announcer described the many deaths resulting from snake bites, Dr. Exeeto explained to Lucia, "It's regrettable that so many people need to die. I couldn't devise any other plan that had the remotest chance of postponing World War III.

I'm sure my distractions will only work for a short time. Mankind is too bent on self destruction." Lucia replied, "At least you're doing something to protect the gene pool. I thank God you're not a racist. You're preserving a sample of the people from most of the nations of the world, as workers you've hired for your secret lab. Eugenics is so misguided. Why would God have created so many different races of people if there was no good reason for it?" Dr. Exeeto exclaimed, "Precisely. I'm not trying to alter God's creation. I'm trying to preserve it.

Chapter Three

The Chess Game

What is it about mankind that makes the majority of them want to destroy. For example, even though trees create the oxygen we breath, mankind goes about destroying as many trees as possible. Every jungle is seen as a potential cane field or golf course. Now that mankind is intensely overpopulated and can see the end to the presence of fossil fuels, he's getting desperate. Crazed by the thought of losing power to the discontented mobs, the leaders of the world point to other countries as the reason for world hardships. Universal folly will never be owned up to. Instead they all resort to the panacea of the hydrogen bomb. We won't need to wait long for the nuclear winter that will end life on land. Even the most die hard survivalists, like those living in Iron Mountain, don't have enough food and clean air to last fifty years. I hope they surprise me, though."

Lucia asked, "Why do you hope they surprise you?" Dr. Exeeto went on, "It'll be a lonely world when the nuclear winter is over. If there are survivors, they won't be eager for more hydrogen bomb explosions. They'll be peace loving, like our children will be. I can't say that I love peace, because I'm engaging in extreme forms of violence. The end doesn't justify the means. I feel terrible about all the deaths I'm causing. I'm sure though, that when it comes down to defending the gene pool, my means must be employed. It's logical. I refuse to give into the insanity of mankind. My violence has a purpose that is undeniable. Someone has to protect the earth's creatures from extermination. Mankind's petty violence is just a struggle for control. It must be determined on the battlefield, who will be allowed to rule. Everyone wants to rule, to kill their enemies and to gain riches." Lucia asked, "Why does it have to be so bad. I was taught there is a loving God who wants the best for people." Dr. Exeeto laughed. He laughed almost uncontrollably. It was an almost diabolical laughter. Finally he stopped laughing and put his arm around Lucia. He said, "I believe in God. God wants man to live in harmony with nature. But, mankind has free choice. I believe this, because if he is a robot, doing only what God makes him do, then the nature of God must be less than perfect. God is perfect, but he lets mankind make mistakes. If we want to destroy his creation and ourselves, he will allow it. He's interested in developing souls, or spirits, who have been tested in the fire. Earth is a crucible for heating up souls and separating the dross from the gold. I'm helping God, by making the crucible a little hotter."

Lucia responded, "Yes, I see your point. It isn't important how you die or whether you die. It's important that if you die, you have been tested and found to be worthy. We all end up going to heaven or to hell. Whether you die of an atomic blast or of snake bite, isn't important. You need to stay loyal to God no matter what. I used to like reading the book of Job in the Bible. He was tested by Satan. He lost everything and was still loyal to God." Dr. Exeeto asked, "Are you saying I'm like Satan?" Lucia responded, "You're doing work that is similar to what Satan does. Unlike him, I think you have a good heart and you are striving for what is good. Satan was put on earth for a purpose. He wants to prove to God that mankind is evil and that pure hearts are rare indeed. You must feel a little like Satan at times don't you?" Dr. Exeeto thought for a long time. "I haven't giving it much thought. What you're saying is logical. I suppose I'm just playing a game of chess. I want my opponent to win. Mankind is my opponent. The trouble is, he doesn't want to win. He's a big loser. My job has been too easy. Even without my plagues to trip him up, he would have found his way to be checkmated without my even trying. It's too easy to destroy the world. It's much more difficult to rebuild it once it's destroyed."

"All the terrorists who think they are winning seventy virgins in the after life, by killing people with their bomb laden suicidal bodies; they're just earning themselves a place in hell. Instead of virgins, Satan will give them giant mirrors to look at for eternity. They'll have to look at their own naked bodies and realize they have no penises. They can't possibly need virgins. If they had penises, they would find women to love on earth and they wouldn't feel so much like killing themselves. They hate Jews because they are the rejected descendants of Abraham. They are all related to Abraham's concubine who had a son for him when his own wife was barren. Then when his own wife, Sarah, had a child; she became jealous of the concubine's son and had the boy and his mother thrown out. That sort of rejection lives on for eternity. As I see it, all mankind is equally damned. Only a miracle worker like Jesus could possibly save anyone from such an unlikely crew." Lucia exclaimed, "You certainly know your Bible for one who operates like Satan." Dr. Exeeto exclaimed, "You can be sure that Satan knows his Bible. He just reads it with a little different slant than most people. He's looking for ways to trip people up. He wants to find a way to make God break a promise. God promised not to flood the world again with water, so someone is pushing fire and then freezing. I'm making the world hot, but Satan is confusing the minds of leaders of the world to make them resort to hydrogen bombing. That's what will bring the freezing.

I'm not Satan or his innocent dupe. I'm more like Noah. I have an ark full of sea creatures that I'm going to protect from the next purge of the earth. It's time for a new chess game. God and Satan have agreed to wipe the slate clean. Satan won before the flood. God won by sending Jesus. This round was a draw. I think their playing for three out of five, or something like that."

Dr. Exeeto started laughing at his own joke and kept laughing a little too long. Lucia looked concerned and asked, "Would you like me to pour you a drink?" Dr. Exeeto accepted. After a few drinks Dr. Exeeto brought up a sensitive subject. "Lucia, I know you were seduced by Major McBride when he visited the other day. Don't be alarmed. I'm not angry with you. You didn't tell him anything that compromised our mission. I just want you to promise me exclusive sexual loyalty. Can you do that?" Lucia explained, "He used some drug on me. I couldn't keep quiet about things. I'm terribly sorry. Were you recording us?" "Yes, I reviewed the tape right after he left. It had nothing to do with my selecting you as a mate. I only want to be candid with you about what I know." Lucia said, "I'll be loyal to you. No more feeling sorry for sick visitors." "Good. Then it's settled. We're a team. Major McBride will be returning on Friday. He'll find an empty lab. If his timing is wrong, he'll be blown up with the lab. We'll just have to see how quick witted he and Major Ferguson are. If they make it to our secret lab, we can plant some information on them and let them escape to the surface. It'll be rewarding to watch them thinking they're so clever, when they're really just playing our game our way. It's a form of chess I like to play, though not on as grand a scale as played by God and his fallen angel."

Lucia got up and made another drink for Dr. Exeeto. When she returned she sat close to him. She said as she handed Dr. Exeeto his drink, "John, I'm terribly glad you're so understanding about my apparent indiscretions with Major McBride. I want to make sure that if there are any hard feeling, that I can make them go away." As Dr. Exeeto sipped his drink, she started kissing him tenderly and whispering in his ear. He tenderly stroked her hair as she reminded him of why he was so forgiving with her.

The next day, Dr. Exeeto helped Dr. Smith make sure everything got moved to the new laboratory in the proper manner. Dr. Exeeto stopped working to watch the evening news with Lucia in their quarters. Lucia remarked, "I'm going to miss this place, even though I've just recently become familiar with it." Dr. Exeeto explained, "I wouldn't worry about that. I've had our new quarters made up identically to this. The only difference is the fact that there is no open view of the sea. We'll be watching a view of the underground aquarium full of my sea creatures. We can't expose ourselves to the radioactive sea water that will soon be everywhere." Lucia replied, "I understand. I'm going to miss the normal world, I think." Dr. Exeeto stated, "We'll all miss the outside world terribly. I've stored a vast library of videos to provide views of natural beauty. We'll get by. I've put much effort into making the life at the new lab an enjoyable experience."

They grew silent as the news came on. The newscaster explained, "Today saw record high temperatures all around the world. Most areas recorded temperatures that were ten degrees higher than ever before. Tropical areas are unbearable. Even in temperate zones, the temperature is hitting one hundred and ten degrees. Scientists are puzzled about this sudden warming of the earth's atmosphere. Although global warming has long been predicted, no one thought we would see a sudden warming trend like this. The United Nations has issued a statement saying that it has convened an emergency session with the intent of establishing a plan for studying the problem. There have been wide spread electrical black outs because of the sudden high demand for electricity to power all the air conditioners in the world. Most factories have needed to shut down because of the heat. Vast numbers of people are staying in their cars with the air conditioners running. It is predicted that this will soon cause gas shortages and long lines at filling stations. Beaches are clogged with people trying to stay cool in the water."

Dr. Exeeto changed the channel to get the international news. The newscaster stated, "Every country in the world is looking for the answer to this new challenge to life as we know it. Who would have guessed that this much heat could hit us so suddenly? I am switching you to our correspondent in Moscow who will interview Dr. Libyatnikin, one of that areas leading atmospheric scientists." Dr. Libyatnikin came into view with a microphone being held close to his mouth. He was asked, "What, in your view is the reason for this sudden heat wave?" He responded, "Our instruments, along with the instruments of other countries located at the south pole, confirm that there has been a sudden elimination of a large percentage of the ozone layer. Whether this was the result of gases released from recent volcanic explosions, or whether it could be an intentional destruction of the ozone layer, is at this time impossible to determine. There are certain gases which if released in large enough quantities, could have eliminated much of the ozone layer. The best thing we can do now is to find ways to stay cool while the earth reaches a new equilibrium. The increased sunlight will bring about more vegetation gradually. We must encourage the production of oxygen. Oxygen is necessary for production of ozone, which we need to keep out the intense direct rays of the sun. Trees are our best friends in this new challenge of reestablishing the ozone layer. I know it seems a little unusual, but steel production is our other best friend. During the steel production process, ozone is created. We need to push all steel producing facilities to the maximum. The steel should be used to create underground shelters against the heat. I will predict that the increased intense sunlight will cause more water evaporation. There may be areas of intense drought, and areas of flooding. The ice caps will melt completely in just a few months. This will bring about costal flooding. All people would be well advised to store a thirty day supply of water. The scientific community will be studying the problem further in an attempt to come up with a solution. It's possible that generating sun blocking particles may be possible. Until this problem is studied further, we'll need to concentrate on burrowing underground. The earth's outer crust is cool enough to keep us at a comfortable temperature for a long time. Our current projections for temperature increases indicate that temperatures will rise to one hundred and twenty degrees for most of the globe. The north and south poles will no longer be havens of cool air. Their difference in temperature from the rest of the globe was caused by the ozone layer blocking the suns rays more completely as they had to pass through the layer at an angle. Water temperatures will increase so that a dip in the local lake will no longer be attractive. Those water temperatures will reach over a hundred degrees in just a few weeks from now. The oceans contain enough cool water, and they have enough volume of water, that they will keep most of the earth from reaching temperatures much over one hundred and twenty degrees Fahrenheit. However, if we don't quickly restore the ozone layer, the ocean's mean temperatures could rise as much as six degrees Fahrenheit per year. In five years, earth's mean ambient temperatures could be at one hundred and forty degrees Fahrenheit. At such temperatures, it is certain that human existence would be impossible on the outer surface of the earth without special suits, or with the use of specially designed heat resistant buildings. Our future may depend on such insulated buildings or living below the earth's surface."

The news commentator stated, "Thank you Dr. Libyatnikin for that succinct portrayal of the problem we're faced with. Is there anything you'd like to add?" "Yes, I would recommend that everyone drink plenty of fluids. People who live in cities will experience the worst stress. If you know people you can live with in the rural or suburban areas, consider moving. There's no place to burrow underground in the city. Because there are few trees in the city, the mean temperature is five to ten degrees hotter there. Living where the wind tends to come in off the ocean is a good idea. These will be the coolest spots on earth." The correspondent said, "Thank you Dr. Libyatnikin. We'll be looking forward to hearing more from you as this situation develops. Now back to Bill at International News headquarters."

Bill Thatcher addressed the audience, "That was a sobering address by Dr. Libyatnikin. Now we have with us Dr. Boswell, the Surgeon General for the United States of America. Dr. Boswell, what can you recommend for the people of the world?" Dr. Boswell responded, "For people with access to health care, who are stressed out by the current circumstances, I would recommend the use of some mild form of sedative or tranquilizer. These medications can reduce the number of heart attacks and strokes people will be experiencing from this disaster. As Dr. Libyatnikin advised, drink plenty of water. Make sure you have access to plenty of water even though we are experiencing many power outages. Move to cooler parts of your country near bodies of water. Limit physical activities to less strenuous ones. Keep air conditioners turned on low and stay close to them. This will reduce the number of power outages. Clean your air conditioner so it works efficiently. Wear white clothing when you go out doors. White reflects light and keeps you cooler. If it's cooler outside than it is in your place of residence, stay outside as much as possible. Find trees to take refuge under. Wooded areas are ten to twenty degrees cooler than areas with no trees. Whenever possible spend some time each week in wooded areas. Such areas are relaxing and will help preserve your sanity. I would recommend that everyone join in, to plant more trees. They will help cool the entire planet if we plant enough of them.

If you see someone pass out from the heat, move them out of sunlight and place cold towels on their feet, hands and head. Call 911 immediately." Bill asked, "Is there anything else you would like to add?" "Yes. Everyone should stay away from alcoholic beverages as much as possible. Alcohol only makes you more thirsty and makes your mouth feel terribly dry at night. People will be experiencing more irritation with each other during this heat. Alcohol will only lead to heightened irritation and violence.

Bars will put a premium on keeping their places cool. This will attract many people. Be wise enough to only use small amounts of alcohol. You would be surprised how pleasant the exotic fruit drinks served in bars are even without any alcohol. Try to enjoy the cool air and the cool drinks without the alcohol. Our nation is dependent on each citizen to keep a cool head. Traffic will be crowded as people flock to leave the cities and find places to live where it's cooler. Road rage may be an increasing problem. Stay calm and get a prescription for some tranquilizers if you think they may help you."

Bill said, "Thank you Dr. Boswell. I'm sure your words will bring relief to many people as they struggle to deal with this new problem of accelerated global warming. Now we go to our correspondent at the United States White House, Phil Conners. Phil, what is the White House saying?" Phil said, "I just attended a press conference at the White House. New initiatives are being implemented even as we speak. Tunneling has begun for new underground housing projects. Steel mills are being assisted by the national guard and are going to be in full production around the clock. They will be making steel for reinforcement of the new underground housing. Aluminum production is also being stepped up. The earth's crust is made up of seven percent aluminum. There is plenty of the metal available. The processing of aluminum also creates ozone. The aluminum poles and beams will be used to stretch sun reducing meshes over farm crops and help reduce evaporation. New super insulated buildings are being designed and will go into production almost immediately. Men in specially cooled suits will build the new buildings. Mostly buildings related to transportation and agriculture will be built above ground. A new interstate tunnel system is being implemented. It will be powered by wind power and by nuclear power stations. Nuclear power stations can't work as efficiently in the new heat. Their cooling towers will need to be enlarged. Scientists are predicting that the increased heat will generate constant high winds. This, and the reduced use of areas above ground for other purposes, is making wind produced electricity much more attractive."

Dr. Exeeto switched to the business news channel. The commentator was just starting to cover the world stock markets. "We are seeing substantial increases in stock prices for tunneling companies. Steel and aluminum manufacturers are also receiving a shot in the arm. Inland Steel and Bethlehem Steel were top contenders. Each saw increases over one hundred percent. U.S. Steel peaked one hundred and fifty points higher, while Bethlehem Steel reached an impressive gain of one hundred and sixty-five points higher. Metal manufacturers in other countries posted similar gains. Mining equipment stocks also experienced outstanding growth. Agricultural products swung higher as the government announced the establishment of much larger food reserves. Bottled water firms experienced solid growth after the Surgeon General's advice that people store up plenty of water. Stocks for the major oil companies turned down substantially as the prospects for travel after people relocate, diminished. The increase in government sponsored building was not expected to offset the fact that most people are taking one final trip to a cool place. There won't be as much driving. Most factories are shut down because of the heat and there aren't nearly as many people driving to work. The recreation industry is taking a hit. Air travel is less than half of what it was last week."

Dr. Exeeto exclaimed, "I was smart to invest in aluminum, steel and mining equipment. I would say that soon I'll be the wealthiest man in the world. It isn't my goal to be the wealthiest. It's hard not to be successful on the stock market when you know what's going to happen next in the world." He started laughing like he was prone to do. He laughed so hard he started sweating and coughing. Lucia intervened, "Let me pour you a drink." She patted him firmly on the back and then brought him a tall ice water. He gulped some down and stopped coughing. Staring into the glass of water he spoke slowly, "Water is better than fine gold. Better than rubies. Even better than wisdom, when you're quite thirsty. I have thirty million gallons of spring water frozen at the new lab. In its frozen state, it will stay fresh for hundreds of years. My desalinization plants, at the lab, can produce enough fresh water to sustain a population of fifty thousand people. Although we're deep below the sea, I think everyone would have to agree that we're right on top of things." He started to laugh, but caught himself. He finished the water then went to the kitchen and made a couple of his favorite fruit drinks with a double jigger of vodka in each. Lucia asked, "Isn't it a little early to start drinking? We still have a large amount of equipment to move." Dr. Exeeto explained, "We were just getting in the way. The staff are all well trained. Everything's working like a well oiled machine. We need to watch the ocean while we still have it in its present state. Tomorrow morning we'll be going to the new lab and we'll never come back." Lucia replied, "I want this to be an evening we can remember. Are you sure no one will interrupt us?" Dr. Exeeto locked the door and turned off the P.A. system. He said, "Dr. Smith will only call me on the telephone if there is an emergency. I know everything is going well. We're alone. Let's enjoy ourselves." He slowly unbuttoned her white blouse as she sipped her drink. She whispered, "I sort of guessed this would be your next move. It's my form of chess, you might say. I took a shower thirty minutes ago. They kissed there on the sofa and experienced a new closeness.

In the morning they packed the rest of their things and went to the new lab via one of the lab's compact submarines. It carried up to ten people and two tons of cargo. There were ten submarines in all. Each of them powered by a small nuclear reactor. The new lab was fifty miles southeast of the old lab. It was about a mile down into a giant fault in the ocean floor. The fault was about a hundred yards wide and posed no serious problems for navigation. The fault was five miles deep. There was a large cave opening one mile down.

Chapter Four

The New Lab

The cave was the opening to Dr. Exeeto's new laboratory. He pointed to the cave proudly as the submarine approached. "It took us years to carve away all this rock. The bottomless fault makes an excellent place in which we can hide the rock debris from our digging. It's quite unlikely that anyone will ever find us here. When we bring the United States secret agents here, if they survive, we'll keep them blindfolded until they're in their quarters. They'll never guess they're over a mile below the surface."

Lucia asked, "When will you blow up the old lab?" "Dr. Smith will do the honors of setting the timer once he knows the secret agents are on their way. Our meeting is for 3:00 P.M. I know they won't be late. I instructed Dr. Smith to give them ten minutes exactly to get themselves captured by our guards and put on the sub. After the sub leaves, in ten more minutes the explosion will take place whether the agents are on the sub or in the old lab. It's totally up to their resourcefulness." Lucia replied, "Well, at least they have a chance." Dr. Exeeto continued, "They will also have a chance to stay with us and be safe. I'm sure their training will cause them to want to escape to the surface. I won't detain them long against their wishes. I'm not a kidnapper. I'm sure they'll dutifully report that we are the ones responsible for the heat wave. Of course most people won't believe them. Things will be so bad on the surface in thirty days, when I allow our agents to escape, that searching for us will be the last thing on the minds of our former supporters. They'll be too busy contemplating how best to conduct World War III! I couldn't reverse the heat if I wanted to! The course is set. The rudder is locked in place. No one can change course now! All that remains is for Satan to decide when to start the war by sending his demons to enter the minds of the world's leaders. Only the demonically possessed are capable of exterminating all life on a planet. I couldn't do it. It requires a depth of hatred and megalomania that goes beyond anything I would be able to muster up."

Lucia whispered, "Try not to get too worked up. You'll tire yourself. Remember, we have to initiate the new suite. You'll need all your energy for tonight. I was being easy on you last night!" The doctor smiled and whispered back, "Of course you're right as usual. I will be needing my energy." He gently rubbed her thigh as they waited for the sub to mate up to the docking plate inside the cave.

Once inside, Dr. Exeeto took Lucia to their suite. They dropped off their carry on luggage and decided to take a quick tour of the facility. They rode a monorail that took them through the agricultural caves, the desalination plants and the recreation areas.

The agricultural area went on for miles. Everything was lighted with grow lights. All the major crops of mankind were represented. There was corn, cotton, sugar cane, rice, soybeans and timber. That only scratches the surface of what was being grown. The excavation of the gigantic farming areas had taken over ten years. Millions of tons of soil had been carried to the location. The desalination plants alone took up as much room as a small city. The shiny stainless steel vats and massive condensation coils gave the area the appearance of being something from outer space.

The recreation area was almost as vast and impressive as the agricultural areas had been. The cave was as long as ten football fields and a hundred yards wide. The ceiling was four hundred feet high. The whole area was brightly lighted. There were trees everywhere. Under some of the trees were hot tubs. There were swimming pools and tennis courts. There was a par three golf course. Wild animals wandered around. Some animals were in a large fenced in park area for animals only. On one side of the recreation area was an immense glass wall for viewing the gigantic aquarium for the sea creatures.

The couple left the monorail and walked through the recreation park. As they walked through the area with the aquarium, Dr. Exeeto explained, "Since we'll be down here for at least fifty years, we'll have plenty of time to dig more caves like this. Each cave can have a different theme. One might be tropical. In one, we could imitate winter conditions for those people who might theoretically miss winter. I personally can't imagine that." Lucia laughed, "I can do without winter. I'll stay in the tropical cave! Can you simulate night time in this cave?" "Yes, the lights automatically change to stars and moonlight at night. We even have the northern lights. We can stay up late tonight and watch it." Lucia replied, "I'm looking forward to that. Could we see the dining area next? I only ate some cereal for breakfast." "I tried to get you to eat some of my eggs." "I know. I'm never too hungry in the morning. All this walking has worked up my appetite."

They went to the restaurant, which was made to look like a tropical bungalow, but on a grand scale. Everything was done in bamboo and native hardwoods. White, pink and turquoise were the colors that predominated. There were many artificial log fires powered by propane. The fires were in small fireplaces at the center of the large round tables. Lucia said, "It'll be nice to watch the fire at suppertime when the night lighting comes on." The doctor replied, "We have portable fires like these that have portable propane tanks. We can have a campfire anywhere out on the park grounds. Anytime you like." Lucia commented, "I like that kind of romantic setting. We need to do that often." She leaned over and kissed Dr. Exeeto on the lips. Then the waitress came to their table with the menus. Lucia said, "I feel like having some sea food. Is the lobster good?" Dr. Exeeto smiled and responded, "I assure you, I've obtained the best chefs money can buy. We raise our own lobsters. How can we go wrong?"

Lucia stated, "Then I'll take the lobster dinner with plenty of mashed potatoes. Make sure the potatoes are the real thing. I prefer real potatoes, not instant." "Nothing but the best for you, my dear. Rest assured we also raise our own potatoes. It wouldn't make sense to dehydrate them when they are always available fresh. Any extra potatoes we raise we simply turn into vodka or fish food." Lucia added, "Yes, vodka. I approve of that. But should we indulge this early in the day?" Dr. Exeeto exclaimed, "We're still on our honeymoon. We can drink whenever we want. Just so we don't become addicted. Moderation in all things, I always say."

Lucia told the waitress, "I'll have the most exotic fruit drink you have, with one once of vodka in it. Just one ounce. I don't want to get drunk. We're on our honeymoon and I want to stay as sober as possible so I don't forget any part of it." Dr. Exeeto exclaimed, "That's a touching sentiment dear. I'm glad you're looking forward to remembering our first times together." Lucia stated, "I'm starting to feel better and better about being your woman. You know how to treat a woman. At first I thought you'd just be domineering, but you turned out to be delightfully considerate. I've never met a guy that I liked better!"

The waitress smiled patiently. Dr. Exeeto winked at the waitress, "I'll have what she's having, only make mine a double order. I've been working up quite an appetite this week." The waitress said, "Yes, honeymoons require quite a bit of energy!" She laughed and turned to leave, but stopped and turned. "I hope that wasn't too frank." Dr. Exeeto exclaimed, "Not at all. We're all one big happy family down here. I hope you have a mate." She said, "Not yet, but I'm eager to find one." Dr. Exeeto said, "Mention something to the Human Resources Department. They're set up to do match making. You should get started as soon as possible. They'll find someone for you who has compatibility and who's attractive to you." She replied, "Thanks. I'll look into that first thing Monday morning." She left with their orders. Dr. Exeeto thought, *"Her shapely yet slender figure and flowing red hair are definite assets. Those green eyes of hers will quickly remove any doubts her date may have at first. I won't even speculate how good she might be in bed."*

Lucia elbowed him and whispered, "Stop thinking how happy she's going to make some guy. Didn't you get enough sex last night?" Dr. Exeeto laughed, "You already read my thoughts. We'll make a great couple. What am I thinking now?" Lucia blushed, "I know, but I can't say it in public. It's something about my lips and what you like about them. Is that all I am to you. Just a set of hot lips?" Dr. Exeeto squirmed and said, "I was first attracted to your eyes. Now I'm mainly fascinated by your mind. What made you get into virology?" Lucia explained, "I had a grandfather who was a doctor. I guess I wanted to follow in his footsteps. It's a challenging field and it's a little dangerous. One false move and you can be infected. It demands perfection. I like doing things precisely and giving my mind a challenge." "I know what you mean. I've received my challenge with the planning of this facility. Making it operate smoothly will be another challenge. What sort of work would you like to do within the new lab?" Lucia explained, "I think I should work with the veterinarians on keeping the animals healthy. I can also help the doctors by screening blood samples for viral pathogens. I'd like to do some teaching too. We'll need to train our replacements for when we grow old and there'll be more trained specialists needed as we expand our population."

Dr. Exeeto exclaimed, "Well said! I can see you're thinking ahead like I have to. If you have any ideas for making the recreation areas more pleasant, please let me know right away. You have a fine mind. It would be a pity to see any of your powers wasted!" Lucia whispered, "Thank you for the kind words. It did cross my mind that we might want to utilize the park in a sexual way, if you catch my meaning." Dr. Exeeto smiled, "Yes. I was thinking along those lines myself. Tonight I'll arrange for us to have some privacy under the stars of the park. Is there any location you liked best? We can't reserve the entire park." Lucia whispered, "I liked the hot tub that was in the deeply wooded area. Could you arrange for some cool breeze to be wafting over us and the smoke of some burning oak leaves? I love fall and the smell of burning leaves." Dr. Exeeto had a twinkle in his eye as he pulled out his cell phone. He said, "I love a challenge. It will be just as you have said." He dialed a number and spoke into the phone, "Is this environmental? This is Dr. Exeeto. I'm reserving quadrant forty-two for the next three days. I'd like a soft cool breeze with the smell of burning oak leaves. Ambient temperature sixty-eight degrees Fahrenheit." Lucia asked, "How can they simulate wind when the ceiling is so high?" "There are louvers that pop up as needed. The effect is convincing." "I love romantic settings like that." She giggled and pushed herself up against him. "I'm starved! I hope the food gets here soon. They held hands as they waited for their food and played footsy under the table.

Major Ferguson and Major McBride were on their way down to the old lab as Lucia and Dr. Exeeto were munching on the lobster dinner. Both Ferguson and McBride had along their exploding brief cases and plenty of tricks up their sleeves. When they got to the reception desk, there was no one around. Major McBride whispered, "This could be a trap. We can't expect them to be too happy about this return visit." McBride pushed open the door behind the reception desk and stated to Ferguson, "The office is empty. I think they've evacuated. They probably have something to do with the global warming and they're expecting a retaliation." The couple went into the office and pulled up the daily planner. It stated that evacuation was to be completed by 3:10 P.M. Ferguson exclaimed, "They must be almost finished with the evacuation. She entered into the computer the question, "What happens after 3:10 P.M.?" The computer responded. "There is no information after 3:10 P.M." Ferguson whispered clearly, "They're obviously finished with this lab. It could self destruct soon. I think we should be getting out of here!" McBride stated, "I concur. Let's go back to the surface." They went to the docking bay where they had entered, but the sub was gone. They rushed along the outer corridor of the main bubble and read the labels of the branching hallways that led to the various other facilities. They passed the snake lab and the rat areas. Next they passed the virology hallway. Finally they came to a larger hallway labeled shipping. They flew down this hallway and came to a large double door. McBride asked Ferguson to stay back. He placed his brief case at the base of the door and then ran back. It blew open the door obligingly and let them pass.

Inside the shipping area they were approached by six guards dressed in black uniforms. The guards attempted to restrain Ferguson and McBride but a battle ensued. The guards were overpowered and Ferguson and McBride ran onboard the last departing submarine. They held Dr. Smith and the captain at gun point. The sub started to move in the direction of the new lab. Dr. Exeeto called the sub from his dinner table. Major McBride answered him on the microphone at the helm of the sub, "This is

Major McBride. We had a 3:00 P.M. appointment. I don't like being stood up!" Dr. Exeeto explained, "I had to test your resourcefulness. Since you are on the submarine, it would be best if you just relaxed and let the captain do his job. The sub is programmed to explode if someone causes it to depart from its course against my will. Just sit back and enjoy the ride. The old lab will explode in sixty seconds from now. I hope you can join us for dinner. The lobster is exquisite!"

Major McBride realized his predicament and acquiesced, "Fine. We'll play it your way. You have some explaining to do. Do you think we can't locate your new lab? Why have you double crossed us?" Dr. Exeeto explained, "I hope you won't prejudge me. It will all be logical when I explain it all over a nice meal. My intentions are purely honorable. I am attempting to preserve mankind, not be a hinderance!" Major Ferguson asked, "Is cooking part of your preservation process. How can heating the planet help mankind?" Dr. Exeeto explained, "I am merely providing a helpful distraction for mankind. Left to his own devices he will surely destroy himself with atomic bombs. I'm only delaying the inevitable. Humans will no doubt destroy life as we know it on the planet. I just want to be able to say that I attempted to delay them. I want my conscience to be clear." Ferguson reacted, "How could you be sure that atomic annihilation was imminent?"

They were interrupted by a jolt as the old lab exploded. Ferguson and McBride exchanged glances. Dr. Exeeto exclaimed, "All you need to do is watch the evening news. All countries want atomic bombs. Like children with new toys, they practice exploding their atomic bombs. They practice launching intercontinental ballistic missiles. Then they miniaturize their bombs and place them on the missiles. The will to kill is already there. They only need a little more time to gain the technology." Ferguson went on, "You're logic is powerful. Dr. Exeeto, but what are you getting out of this. You aren't making any demands, or even announcing responsibility for the global warming." Dr. Exeeto explained, "My thinking is complex. I'd rather go into this in more detail here at the dinner table. I'm not a hostile person or power hungry. I merely want to protect the gene pool from mutations do to the upcoming atomic radiation poisoning of earth. Since I am relatively certain that my diversions will only temporarily protect the environment from radiation, I'm using my secret lab as a contingency plan. If and when World War III breaks out, I'm ready for anything. Always have a contingency plan. Isn't that a code that your people live by?" Ferguson answered, "It's true we always follow that Modus Operandi. It works for us. I'm surprised you know about that, but I won't ask who told you. What is your plan for us?" Dr. Exeeto explained, "That's not set in concrete. We're willing to work with you to a certain extent. Our only requirement is that you stay with us for a few weeks to assure us that our plans will go forward unhindered. It's beyond our ability to reverse what we have started even if we had the desire to do so. There's no turning back. We're hoping you'll come to realize this and stay to become a part of the team we've built. Your children will inherit the earth, so to speak. Now I hope that you will submit to being blind folded. I promise that no harm will come to you." Two of the remaining guards on the submarine blindfolded Ferguson and McBride, who went along with it grudgingly. The remaining explosive attaché case, which Ferguson had been carrying, was jettisoned from the sub.

The guards watched the marine life go by as the submarine sped for the new lab. There was a row of small round windows on both sides of the sub, at eye level. One guard said to the other one, "I like this part of the trip. You can see the marine life better since they aren't moving by so fast." The other man replied, "Yes, there's a spectacular view during this part of the trip." The submarine was slowly dropping into a deep fault in the ocean's floor. The water grew darker as they dropped deeper and deeper into the vast wide fault. They followed one of the walls down into the deep darkness of that watery pit. Steam bubbles could be seen everywhere. The invisible bottom of the fault was no doubt made up of steaming hot molten rock at a depth of over five miles down. Unusual fish were to be seen out of the port holes. Some were iridescent and their eerie bodies seemed to glow from inside in the clear and dark waters of the fault.

After about four hours, they heard a dull clanking sound as the submarine connected to the labs docking plate. McBride was thinking to himself, *we must not have traveled more than one hundred and twenty miles given the average speed of submarines and the amount of time we spent getting here. Of course there's actually no telling exactly how fast we were traveling. I'll bet we're hidden down in a fault.* Their blindfolds were removed and they were hurried to the dining facility where Dr. Exeeto was waiting for them.

Chapter Five

Guests Arrive

Dr. Exeeto greeted them warmly and introduced Lucia to them. "Major McBride and Major Ferguson, this is my new wife, Lucia. Lucia, this is Major McBride and Major Ferguson of the United States intelligence service." They all shook hands and smiled graciously. Dr. Exeeto informed them, "I took the liberty of ordering for you. Service here is a little slow. We're just getting started. Our order should arrive with yours. When I first spoke to you, on the sub, we were having a delightful lobster meal. I ordered shrimp and steak for this evening. I hope your trip was a pleasant one." McBride responded, "It was comfortable, but how long did you say you plan on keeping us here?" "I was hoping you'd stay a month or two. It's so hot on the surface. I'm hoping you'll become addicted to our nice cool climate here. It won't be long till the world powers will be contemplating how to start World War III. Then they'll have little concern for exacting revenge upon us. At that time you'll be free to leave. Even if you should be clever enough to find your way back to the surface on your own, I doubt if the United States will be finding time in its busy schedule to come looking for me. You see, I fulfilled my contract with the United States. I delivered plague and poisonous snakes upon the terrorists so they would have something to think about other than attacking U.S. interests. I just went the second mile and delivered more plagues than were bargained for. We delivered plagues to all nations who are poised to use atomic bombs on other nations. It's for a distraction. We bear no malice for any particular nation. I'm trying to protect the gene pool." Ferguson replied, "I've heard you mention the gene pool before. What do you mean when you say that? Are you trying to create a super race?" Dr. Exeeto explained, "I want no super race. I believe that all men are created equal. They are equally eager to destroy the planet. I wouldn't mind if mankind contented himself with guns and cannons. Conventional bombs don't destroy the beauty that is held in the current human genetic code. The atomic bombs which everyone wants to use, disturb me a great deal. The use of atomic bombs results in radioactive pollution that breaks up the genetic code of humans and animals alike. Luckily trees are a little more resistant to mutation. I have recruited staff from almost every nation on earth so that I can preserve the diversity of the human gene pool. I'm also planning on protecting most sea creatures. My laboratory has the capability of preserving human and animal life for well over one hundred years. Can you see the worth in what I'm doing? Is it not evident, to even the casual observer, that World War III is on its way?"

The food arrived and they all ate in silence. After dessert Dr. Exeeto took Ferguson and McBride on a tour of the recreation park. As they walked he answered some of their questions. Ferguson asked, "How did you raise the temperature of the earth so quickly?" "I released massive amounts of F-12 refrigerant, which breaks up the ozone molecules. The only way for the ozone to be replaced, is with years of concentrated effort. In time the increased vegetation growth from the increase of direct sunlight will bring back the natural balance of things. It might take hundreds of years. I'm predicting that World War III will come first and produce a nuclear winter that will all but eliminate human and animal life on the planet. Only living things in protected environments such as ours will be able to survive." Ferguson asked, "What makes you so sure about the occurrence of radioactive pollution?" Dr. Exeeto smiled, "It goes along the lines of Murphy's law. 'If circumstances are such that something bad can happen, it probably will happen.'" Too many nations are eagerly developing the atomic bomb with delivery systems. I think it's amazing that the United States and the Soviet Union managed to resist using their atomic weapons for so many years. They are nations who worship logic. Mutually assured destruction made sense to both parties. That is what kept them from using the atomic bombs on each other.

The nations that are now acquiring atomic capabilities are not so logical. Arab nations are not concerned so much about mutually assured destruction. They're concerned about virgins in the after life. All that's important is to kill the enemy. It's not important for their own nation to survive. Just so everyone has lots of virgins in heaven." He laughed a little but stopped himself. "I'm actually quite serious about what I just said. It seems ludicrous, but it's absolutely the truth."

McBride stated, "I'm sure there is some truth to what you said, but there are some reasonable people in every nation of the earth. How can you assume that the fanatics will always gain control?" Dr. Exeeto answered, "The fanatics kill all the reasonable people. Reasonable people are too soft on the fanatics. They don't realize that they need to kill off the fanatics or be killed by them. The world has boiled down to survival of the fittest. But not the survival of the morally fit. The most ruthless killers will survive, or those who use their wits and think ahead. I have planned ahead. I have plenty of food and water. I plan to sit back in hiding while the aggressive killers of the world expend their wrath on each other. Then when they have succeeded in killing everyone on the surface of the earth, they too will die from the nuclear winter. Then, a hundred years later, more gentle people will inherit the earth."

McBride stated, "I must admit that your logic is powerful. I don't approve of your destruction of the ozone layer, but I strongly approve of your survivalist tendencies. As you know, my own government has a project called "Iron Mountain". We have our own plans for surviving atomic bomb attacks. The preservation of the gene pool is a noble goal. Speaking for myself, I'm willing to stay here with you indefinitely. Since the ozone layer is destroyed, there's no turning back. I've always felt that World War III would come in my life time. I agree that the heat and plagues will only delay man's march towards his own total annihilation." He turned and winked at Ferguson who was staring at him in disbelief. She took her cue, "I agree. I've been expecting the end of the world. There are so many clues. Nuclear proliferation seems uncontrollable. To delay the end seems like that best anyone can wish for. I'll stay here. It's too hot on the surface and there's no chance for success there."

Dr Exeeto exclaimed, "I'm glad to see you're both such logical people. Your stay here will be much more agreeable when you're working with us instead of against us. We can meet frequently. I enjoy your company. I insist that both of you enjoy the same atmospheric program this evening that Lucia and I have planned. There is an open quadrant just a few hundred yards from ours. You can experience a starlit night together with a hot tub under a grove of oak trees with the smell of burning oak leaves gently flowing through the air." Ferguson responded, "That sounds wonderful. I think I can speak for Major McBride when I say, we accept."

They walked for over an hour all over the park. Dr. Exeeto explained, "You'll have complete freedom, as long as you stay in the residential, park and dining area. The other areas are off limits for the time being. When I get to know you better, and World War III is nearer, I'll start to give you more freedom and responsibility. Our facility is a place where your abilities can be of great use. The sky is the limit. Our standards of living will be at least as high as what you are used to having on the surface. Our rewards system will vary from gold and precious gems to positions of power and prestige for your offspring. Your grandchildren could be responsible for the reconstruction of entire continents. Does that fire your imaginations?" He smiled at their obvious attentiveness. He knew they were starting to get interested.

"We hope your "Iron Mountain" people are successful too. The rebuilding of civilization will be a daunting task. The United States is a noble nation with high ideals. They just got a little careless with the way they threw money around. Their lust for oil caused them to enrich people who had no business with wealth. The terrorists own words were, "If we wanted to hang the United States, they would sell us the rope to do it with." There is truth is that. Powerful nations tend to get overconfident and let their enemies have too much money. Money can buy you anything, including intercontinental ballistic missiles armed with nuclear warheads. If representatives from the United States survive the nuclear winter, I'm sure they'll be more cautious about whom they bestow power upon."

McBride said, "I'm glad to hear that you're not against the United States. There is one problem. They're going to wonder what has happened to us. We always report in every day. They'll know something is wrong." Dr. Exeeto explained, "They'll send down some divers who will discover that the old laboratory is destroyed. They'll assume you were both victims of an untimely accident. There's really nothing to worry about. Our position is terribly well concealed and the people on the surface have many pressing problems to keep them occupied. I think it's safe to say that you'll both be assumed dead." McBride replied, "Well I guess that's logical and reassuring. I won't need to worry about people wondering what's happened to me."

Dr. Exeeto stopped and pointed to the grove of trees nearby. "There's your quadrant for tonight. I'll show you your living quarters, and then you can enjoy the evening under the stars." The doctor led them to their suite which was similar to his and only a little way down the hall from his. The doctor invited them to come to the dining area at 8:00 A.M. for breakfast. Then he and Lucia went to their hot tub under the trees.

McBride and Ferguson looked around in their suite. McBride turned on all the water in the bathroom and also turned up the television. He brought Ferguson into the bathroom and whispered, "I'm creating noise to make it impossible for them to hear our whispering. We can assume our room is bugged. They won't trust us for a long time. We can make them lessen the guard on us if we appear to be going along with them." Ferguson whispered back, "I agree with your plan. What is your long term plan? What can we do about this disaster?" McBride whispered, "We need to let the world know who caused the heat. Possibly they won't blame each other and start World War III." Ferguson whispered, "I agree. That's the most important thing. People need to know who did this to them. If we can steal one of Exeeto's submarines, we could get back to the surface in time to tell the world who precipitated the global warming." McBride replied, "I think we might do well setting a charge and threatening to blow this place up. Preserving the lab is their highest priority, no doubt." Ferguson nodded.

Under the stars, Dr. Exeeto was enjoying the hot tub with Lucia. He had his arm around her and was softly telling her what he expected from their new guests, "They'll find a way to threaten us and force us to let them take one of our submarines to the surface. They are no doubt hopelessly dutiful to their employers. Military people are that way. I suppose it's commendable. I'd like to have more people with that kind of loyalty. I'll be setting out some convincing looking clay that looks like the C-4 we use in our rock blasting. We'll all look terribly threatened and let them escape. I actually want the world to know I caused the global warming. I'm proud of it! Now that all the damage is finished and no one can reverse it, I like the idea of everyone knowing that I was responsible. Most people won't believe it. And no one will want to acknowledge that they were working with me on biological weapons. I'll just be glad if a few people know the truth."

Lucia said, "I like Ferguson and McBride. I wish they'd stay with us. I hate to think of them living up there in all that heat. Can't you think of a way to get them to stay voluntarily?" Dr. Exeeto said, "I'll give it some thought. They're terribly loyal to their country. I'd have to convince them that their country wants them to stay here and monitor us. It would be difficult, but I may be able to come up with something." Lucia responded, "I really would like for us to have them stay. They seem like such a nice couple." Dr. Exeeto thought for a minute and then said, "I could ask one of our staff to pose as a traitor and grant them access to my 'lab to surface' transmitter. It operates on ultra low frequency and will transmit through thick rock. Access to that transmitter would cause them to be able to communicate with their leaders. I think they would probably be asked to stay and report on us. Since we have nothing to hide except our location, there would be no harm in it as long as we severely limit the amount of time they can spend with the transmitter. Too much time on the transmitter might allow the surface people to narrow down our location."

Lucia laughed, "I knew you could come up with something. You're so logical and creative in your thinking. Oh, good! I smell the burning oak leaves. That smell makes me horny." She reached out for the doctor and found him receptive. They crawled out of the tub and played with each other in the grass. Lucia feigned that she was sleeping and let Dr. Exeeto look lustfully at her lush lips. She pretended not to wake up as he played out one of his favorite fantasies with her. She thought to herself, *he's a little strange, but I like his enthusiasm.*

One of Dr. Exeeto's assistants knocked on the door to the suite of Major McBride and Major Ferguson. When McBride opened the door, he explained that he was to help them find their quadrant in the park. He said, "With only the moon light to guide you, Dr. Exeeto was afraid you might need a little help finding your hot tub and oak tree grove." McBride offered, "We appreciate the consideration. We'll be right along." McBride went back into the suite to consult with Ferguson. Ferguson stated, "We might as well enjoy the moonlight. I enjoy burning oak leaves. There's no telling how long we may be here." McBride offered his arm and they left with the assistant.

Once at the hot tub, they disrobed and got into the delightful warm water. The assistant had left immediately. They soaked a long time in silence and watched the moon through the branches of the trees. McBride finally stated, "Everything's quite realistic. The moon looks real. I bet they even have some bugs crawling around for realism. What would a world be like without bugs? He tapped Ferguson on her ear. She smiled and nodded. "Yes bugs are essential." Since they agreed that there were probably listening devices in the area, they just made small talk. Ferguson asked, "If we stay, how many children would you like to have?" McBride answered, "I think we should have an even number. Four or six would be sufficient I should think." Ferguson responded, "Now be serious. I really want to know." "Well, in that case, I'd have to say that two would be enough. I wouldn't want any of them to feel neglected. We'd have plenty of time to spend on each of two children." Ferguson responded, "I like that way of thinking. Let's think about doing justice to each child. There's no need to repopulate the earth all at once. What if the surface people never really get killed off? I'm not so sure I'm totally convinced that World War III is so inevitable. Possibly the heat was actually a good idea. Mankind may be so busy trying to stay cool, that he'll forget about warfare for awhile." McBride stated, "Well, the heat should slow some things down. The recreation industry will take a hit. I'm not sure how it'll affect terrorism. With all the rats, plague and poisonous snakes, the terrorists may have to admit that they've been one upped by Dr. Exeeto. He just took what they were doing and pushed it a few steps further. Now everyone's miserable. I doubt if anyone has learned a lesson though. I think the doctor's right. People have atomic bombs and they will use them." Ferguson theorized, "I wonder how many atomic bombs have to go off to cause the nuclear winter Dr. Exeeto is so fond of mentioning?" McBride answered, "New technology has made the bombs much more powerful than the ones used during World War II. I think that ten of the new bombs would definitely stir up enough dust to block much of the sun's rays and bring about a winter. Of course that's just an educated guess. I'm sure one or two bombs wouldn't do it."

Chapter Six

The Debate

Ferguson asked, "What nationality would you say Dr. Exeeto is? He's a handsome man, but I can't place where his ancestors would be from." McBride ventured, "I'd say he has a bulldog British chin, but his hair and eyes, and that tan skin, make me think some of his ancestors were from Mexico. He certainly is intelligent. Imagine how much thinking went into organizing all this. So far, the only crime he's committed is that of air pollution. Most companies in the world do that every day. Everyone does that when they buy a fuel guzzling car. If we had gone to wind power and ethanol fifty years ago, none of this would have happened. The terrorists wouldn't have financing and Dr. Exeeto wouldn't have been recruited for biological warfare. It would have set World War III back hundreds of years. Now the world is a desperate place. Who can blame someone like Dr. Exeeto, for having contempt for mankind. He's doing the only logical thing to do. Preserve the gene pool." Ferguson said, "I must admit. He seems logical and quite sane, except for when he starts laughing uncontrollably. I suppose that's just nerves. He has much to be concerned about. I wonder if he feels guilty for causing so much hardship on the surface?" McBride stated, "He thinks in big terms. Survival of mankind.

The gene pool. He probably shuts out the suffering he's causing. It would make most people feel guilty. Possibly he's been made cynical about the population of earth by the many negative people he's encountered in his life. There are a large number of unpleasant people on earth. If a person isn't forgiving and has a long memory for insults, a strong dislike for most humans would seem to be the logical result."

Ferguson added, "Yes, I think the crowding of people that has resulted from so much population growth, is bringing out the worst in people. People now see other humans as competition for limited jobs and resources. During the frontier days of America, people were more bonded together by hardship. People were spread out so much then, that it was refreshing to get the opportunity to talk to another human being. Now murder and violence is on the upswing. Rudeness is a way of life in the work place. You never know when a postal worker is going to start shooting his fellow workers. Sorting mail must be a real drag. At the end of the day you probably feel like hurting someone."

McBride said, "Don't single out postal workers. More factory workers are coming to work with guns and wanting to shoot other workers. Many of those workers deserve to be shot. Everyone wants to screw someone else's wife or see how pissed off they can make someone. I suppose most of the world deserves the global warming. I just don't think Dr. Exeeto should play God. It seems like he's trying to control the whole world. He seems to be planning out the activities for the world for the next several hundred years. Can't he just let things happen naturally?"

Ferguson responded, "Maybe he's helping God. Maybe this is God's plan. The earth's population is for the most part evil and deserves punishment. Dr. Exeeto is just a little more efficient at punishing, than most people. His mind has a genius for solving problems. If we could just get him on our side. If he wanted to, I bet he could eliminate the global warming." McBride laughed, "Well why don't you make that your special project. Get Dr. Exeeto to reverse the global warming." Ferguson insisted, "I'm serious. There doesn't seem to be anything this man can't accomplish. Don't be so cynical. Let's both work on him. He admires logic. Let's point out the logic behind not placing so much hardship on mankind. We need to find out what's making him tick. What are the reasons he has for his misanthropy? Is there anything that will make him change his mind about mankind?"

McBride sighed, "Well, you've certainly selected a big project for us. What do you think should be our first move?" Ferguson explained, "We need to plan out a debate. He knows his Bible. I caught him slipping in a little Bible when we were on the submarine. He said that our children could inherit the earth. He was twisting around a section of the sermon on the mount. He loves to play with Bible passages apparently. We can use the Bible to try to affect his thinking. McBride confessed, "I'm no expert on the Bible. You'll have to do the Bible logic on him." Ferguson said, "I think I can help him see things a little more our way. We can't ask him to leave his lab, but we may be able to convince him to help us reduce the heat a little. I'm confident our medical community can get control of the plague he's released. The snakes aren't as dangerous as the plague. People will just need to learn to stay away from the snakes. A little insect spray can take care of the malaria mosquitoes. Maybe things aren't as bad as they seem."

McBride exclaimed, "You're a hopelessly optimistic person. But there's no other plan I can think of. You work on your Bible logic, and I'll work on being nice to the doctor. I'll try to find some things he and I have in common. Actually the heat isn't such a bad idea if it weren't for the suffering it causes for the little people. Mankind does need a diversion to keep them from being so fascinated with atomic bombs. A nice volcanic eruption right under North

Korea would be an excellent diversion! They like seeing how big of an explosion they can create underground. Why doesn't God just allow them to break the earth's crust and cause the molten lava to gush up and consume them?" Ferguson explained, "We can't know the mind of God. You need to be a little more humble. We won't get anywhere if you go around angering God with your arrogant comments."

McBride explained, "I just need a little more training in the area of relating to God. You know your Bible well. Tell me some of your favorite insights. We've got plenty of time. We could be here for years!" Ferguson explained, "Humility is one of the biggest things. You need to be humble at all times. This can be backed up by many different passages from the Bible. I'll start compiling some of them for you. Next, you won't receive anything you pray for if you don't have faith. You need to believe that God has the power and desire to help you. I'll have you read the story of Jesus with the centurion. The centurion was the man who had more faith than Jesus had ever seen before. You need to read that whole story. It's only a few paragraphs long. So you see, faith and humility are two of the most important things to remember and practice. A third thing is to help other people. Give a cup of cold water to a thirsty man. Feed the hungry and help the poor and widows. If you give when you yourself are poor, you will be truly blest. I'll have you read the story of the widow's mite. I think it's also important to long for wisdom. Read the Bible on your own and search for wisdom. The Bible offers wisdom as opposed to foolishness. The Bible says to stay away from vices and to build up treasures in heaven. I'll find the passages that make what I'm saying now clear. I don't have them on the tip of my tongue."

McBride exclaimed, "You should have been a preacher!" Ferguson explained, "My father always encouraged me to read the Bible. He read the whole Bible every year. He loved reading it." "Is there anything else you can teach me tonight, Ferguson?" Ferguson replied, "You're an eager student. You'll learn quickly. Let me finish your lessons for tonight with the golden rule. Always do onto others as you would have them do unto you." McBride said, "Now that one sounds familiar." They held each other in the hot tub for a long time, kissing gently from time to time. Finally they returned to their suite and got ready for bed. McBride said, "So it would appear that Dr. Exeeto has gotten tired of rude people who don't follow the golden rule. Possibly he feels he is helping God punish an evil earth." Ferguson responded, "I'm sure it's something like that. If he wasn't angry with most of the earth's people, he wouldn't have sent those plagues on everyone. It's going to be quite difficult trying to turn away his wrath. I'm sure we'll come up with some ideas by morning." They slept a sound sleep and woke up in time to be ready for breakfast with Dr. Exeeto.

After they had started their breakfast, Dr. Exeeto asked, "Are there any questions I can answer for you? I'm sure you must be curious about some things." Ferguson asked, "What was it that made you decide to send the rats, snakes and mosquitoes on all the world instead of just the terrorists as we had agreed?" Dr. Exeeto explained, "I was actually targeting the nations that have acquired atomic bombs. It's regrettable that most of the world will probably have to deal with the plague. My goal is to delay the coming of World War III. I thought some nice distractions would keep humanity busy doing something other than engaging in war. I'm not a pacifist. Don't make that mistake. I don't mind if the world engages in conventional warfare until they have eliminated most of the population of the world. I'm against the atomic radiation and what it can do to the genetic make up of animals and humans."

Ferguson asked, "Are you misanthropic?" Dr. Exeeto said, "Not entirely. I despise most humans in existence today, but I'm willing to admit that a society raised up in a less congested world, might be capable of being at least slightly less deserving of contempt. I think a civilization raised up after World War III would be less prone to resorting to the use of atomic bombs, however there would probably be a strong tendency for history to repeat itself."

Ferguson asked, "Are you open to some discussion in which we attempt to convince you to help us reverse the global warming?" Dr. Exeeto laughed, "You must think I'm God. It was easy to produce the global warming. It would be exceedingly difficult to rebuild the ozone layer. It took thousands of years to create it. I certainly can't think of any way to quickly recreate the ozone layer, even if I had the desire to do so. But I'm curious. Go ahead and present your arguments for reversing the climate change. I enjoy a good debate."

Ferguson stated, "Although your idea of keeping mankind busy with so many problems seems logical, you're bringing suffering to millions of kindly and relatively innocent people, people you would like if you met them face to face. Many of these people have lived their lives by the golden rule and have been kind to everyone they meet. How can you justify hurting such people?"

Dr. Exeeto thought for a minute. "You are a powerful debater, Major Ferguson. I respect that. I must humbly offer the defense that I am at war with powerful arrogant world leaders who wipe out entire cities with their atomic bombs, and think nothing of it. How can I war against such people and not hurt some innocent bystanders. The only important thing is whether or not each person is right with God. Their soul is the important thing. What difference does it make whether a person dies of the heat, or dies of old age? Old age is usually a bad way to die. It often spells out prolonged suffering. My plague kills quickly. People die in just a couple days. I admit that at times I feel a little like an angel of death, but my goal in honorable. I don't want mankind to survive in a mutated hideous form. Isn't it logical to want to preserve what God has made?" Ferguson responded, "God made the ozone layer. You destroyed it. You appear to be playing God. Let God punish mankind in the ways that he sees fit. Restore the ozone layer so you aren't in the position of destroying what God has made."

Dr. Exeeto paused and smiled. "I like your logical approach to things. I'll make a compromise with you. I'll help you restore a buffer between earth and the sun, if you'll wait two weeks. I need to see mankind learning some kind of lesson. They need to be made to contemplate what it's like to have an atmosphere thrown out of kilter. World War III will cause a nuclear winter that will be a much more drastic atmospheric problem than what I've created. My plan was to warm the world by about thirty degrees Fahrenheit. The nuclear winter will cool the world by at least seventy degrees. It will end all life that isn't in an artificial world such as my lab. After two weeks, I'll radio a partial solution for the problem back to your leaders. Is that acceptable?" Ferguson responded, "At least you're meeting us half way. Can you give me a little hint about how you intend to reverse the global warming?"

Dr. Exeeto explained, "I haven't got a complete idea in my head yet. I do know that the United States has what are called "Clean bombs" They are as powerful as the original atomic bombs, but they yield very little radioactive fall out. Part of my short term fix for the problem, would be to explode several such bombs over an area with powdery soil. The resultant plume of dust would shut out enough of the sun's rays to bring down the temperature of the earth considerably. I'll allow you to radio this information back to your leaders in two weeks. I'm sure World War III will not be averted, but this action will make me feel that at least I've shown some mercy on the small percentage of innocent people who exist on the surface."

Chapter Seven

A Meeting of the Minds

Ferguson said, "I appreciate your cooperation. In return, I promise not to attempt to reveal your lab's location to the surface." McBride interjected, "I too would like to say that I have no interest in bringing down the wrath of the world upon you. I won't try to send your coordinates back to my leaders. You are showing mercy. I must admit that it was our idea about the venomous snakes and the plague. I think they will help reduce terrorism. A helpful distraction, as you are so fond of saying." Dr. Exeeto smiled, "Yes, mankind needs distractions to keep his mind off how jealous he is of everyone else. Every nation wants the wealth of other nations. Every political group wants to gain control of the purse strings. Mankind needs his problems or he would get bored. It's boring just being nice to each other." McBride responded, "I have to admit that what you're saying does seem to be based on reality. At first, I must admit, I thought you were insane, but now I can see that you just see things a little too clearly. You aren't an instrument of Satan. I think that possibly God and Satan both want the earth punished. Thank goodness it's not the flood again. That would be difficult to survive!"

Dr. Exeeto laughed, "You're starting to see the truth that I see. God and Satan are merely playing a vast game of chess. Satan was able to control things before the flood. He made people so evil that they all had to be destroyed by God. God won the second round of chess by sending in his Son, Jesus to win the game. Now this third round appears to be a draw and they want to wipe the board clean again." McBride commented, "That's an interesting theory. It incorporates everything in such a way as to be logical and convincing. I don't want to argue against such a world view, but I still wish you had stuck with our original plan of dumping the plagues only on the terrorists. Now I'm caught in a difficult position. I feel I need to help my country. How would you recommend that I best do that?" Dr. Exeeto offered, "Just sit back and wait for me to recommend the "clean bombs" for cooling off the planet. Things will work out for the best. If you return to the surface, they may press you to help them find me. What would you do then?" McBride answered, "We really don't know where you are. As long as you stay low key and don't start announcing to the world that you're responsible for all their troubles, I think the United States will be happy to forget about you. They may learn from your example and start beefing up their Iron Mountain project and make sure that it's geared up for the survival of enough people for over a hundred years."

Dr. Exeeto said, "There are indeed many things which the United States and other civilized nations should be doing now. Before, I was tempted to announce my responsibility for the heat, but now you and Ferguson have warmed my heart to the few weak and humble individuals who no doubt still exist on the surface. I'll make some suggestions to the United States if you'll suggest who would be good to correspond with." McBride responded, "I can send your suggestions right to the Joint Chiefs of Staff. I have an access code that will allow me to send them an urgent encrypted e-mail. They know that I only send them letters if it's quite important." Dr. Exeeto replied, "That's great. Here's what I would like to see done." He started typing eagerly on his laptop computer. "For any survival unit to be successful, it's important that vast quantities of air and water be stored. There must be adequate and thoroughly reliable means for recycling the air and water. I feel that one of the biggest oversights for the planners of survival caves, is that they don't provide enough recreation space. For a community to survive one hundred years under the surface of the earth, it must have good exercise and relaxation areas. Libraries must be well stocked.

Another thing to keep in mind is providing meaningful work for all your people. The claustrophobic nature of living in a cave will be more tolerable for people, if their minds are constantly focused on a meaningful goal. Continual expansion of the living space is one good goal to pursue. The staff will be exhilarated at the thought of creating new expansive recreation areas. Build wooded parks and giant aquariums. Let your imaginations go wild on these things. Your tunneling will need to connect you to important resources such as coal, metal ores and minerals. The expansion of your complex will require the input of raw materials. As the radiation starts to decline on the surface, you can send out teams to install wind generators that can push electricity to the caves and tunnels. It's quite likely that you'll be able to harness geothermal energy to provide for your energy needs. Because of the dangerous nature of the nuclear power station and the difficulty of finding places for the storage of nuclear waste products, I don't recommend nuclear power as a long term solution to energy needs.

Careful screening of the individuals you choose to have stay in the survival habitat is crucial. I personally recommend preserving as many nationalities of people as possible. This seems like a self evident good which I won't debate with you. Select people with no criminal history. Look for kind, gentle team players. People who are hyperactive and overly aggressive will be harder to keep happy in the cave environment. They will become the problem people who will start movements to push for early return to the surface. You need people who are calm, gentle and prone to stay professional at all times. You need people who are diplomatic. Avoid mean people who are liars and thrive on gossip. Extensive testing of prospective candidates for inclusion in your program will pay off in the long run. The average person is greedy, lying, overly aggressive, rude and has poor personal habits. Just keep in mind that you and your children will need to live in close proximity to all the people you select for the survival experience. Don't make your survival facility an exercise in hell. Keep out the rude and nasty people! There are bound to be some undesirables who slip through. Once these people are identified, they should be kept busy at remote sites doing work that is not likely to throw the operation into jeopardy if it is done by rebellious people.

Be sure to have an excellent system of rewards that will help keep a positive attitude in your population. Their needs to be plenty of gold and gems to inspire your population to work hard. Reward people with promotions. Remember that sometimes just a change of work duties can be a reward. Not everyone can be promoted to top leadership positions. Stay tuned in to what your people's goals are and help them reach their goals.

Recreate the best images of what beautiful things were in the world before World War III. People will want to remember the landscape and the beautiful vistas. These images can be recreated with videos and with three dimensional reproductions. Recreational rewards for people should include beautiful scenes, excellent food soft satin sheets and soothing hot tubs. Remember to keep children away from television and encourage them to enjoy reading. This will help insure that your next generation is capable of keeping the complex operation of the survival habitat going and is not a generation of violent ignorant fools."

Ferguson volunteered, "We should include that they should encourage spiritual development. The United States survival communities will be largely Christian or nonaligned individuals. Few members of other religions will be represented, because of their low amount of members in the population. They, of course will be allowed to practice their religion as long as that religion doesn't call for elimination of the survival community. The Christian members will need leaders who are not greedy for material gain. Those people will be the chaplains for the community. They will emphasize the ways in which the Bible encourages people to get along with one another. The survival community should desire to be pleasing to God. Otherwise he will destroy them or bring hardship upon them."

Dr. Exeeto stated, "I just have a few more things to add. For the immediate reduction of heat in the world, I would recommend exploding some of your 'clean bombs' in an area which will produce a maximum amount of dust. The bombs should take the dust high enough, that it will shield some of the sun's rays from the lower atmosphere. Do not use too many bombs. You don't want to start a nuclear winter."

McBride asked, "How can I transmit this to the internet?" Dr. Exeeto explained, "I have a low frequency transmitter that can send from here. It's connected to this lap top by wireless transmitter." Dr. Exeeto pulled up the transmission frame and moved his message into the proper place on the screen. He asked, "Do you see the box labeled "address"? McBride replied, "Yes, I see it." "Move the cursor to that box and enter your code. Then hit send." In seconds the words appeared in the box, "message sent". McBride exclaimed, "Now they know I'm still alive. Do you think they'll come looking for me?"

Dr. Exeeto anwered, "They have more important things on their minds.

They finished their breakfast and had one last cup of coffee. Dr. Exeeto explained, "I trust both of you a little more today. I think I'll take you on a tour of our food growing and energy harvesting facilities." Ferguson said, "That sounds interesting. Thank you for your trust."

Chapter Eight

The Joint Chiefs of Staff

A meeting was being convened in the White House of the United States, while Dr. Exeeto was giving his tour. The Joint Chiefs of Staff had just been getting ready for an emergency meeting, when the Secretary of the Navy got the emergency e-mail from Major McBride. Once the meeting started he read the e-mail to everyone present. He said, "I'll have copies of this made for each of you. This means that Major Donald McBride is alive. He was on assignment with Major Sandra Ferguson to find out what plans Dr. Exeeto has for the future. As you know, we were working with him to cause plagues on our enemies. It appears that he may have gone a little overboard. We have plague carrying rats and a dramatic increase in poisonous snakes here in the United States. We think he took money from our enemies as well and dutifully sent plagues to us. I personally would love to see him punished. The President of the United States was present and said, "We're not in a position to spend time looking for him now. There's too much on our plate. We need to get control of the heat first. Dr. Exeeto's laboratory has exploded this week. We can only assume now that he had a secret back up lab. That must be where he is now with our two agents."

The Secretary of the Air Force asked, "Why is Dr. Exeeto sending us this message in which he appears to be trying to help us?" The President answered, "We can't know for sure why he sent the message at this time, but the information sounds logical and helpful. I suggest that we use the information to the best of our ability. At least now that the snakes and rats are on us too, we can easily deny responsibility for them. We truly were not entirely responsible for them. I suggest that we explode four bombs as soon as possible. It will be easier to explode the bombs on our own territory. I suggest Ferron, Utah as the best place for the first two bombs. It's one of the dustiest places on earth. The other two bombs will be exploded in Death Valley. No one lives there and environmental impact will be low. We'll relocate the people from Ferron, Utah into some of our newest underground dwellings. I'm sure they'll be glad to get out of the heat. We should pay them handsomely for their land, which I'm sure they take great pride in. At least they always try to keep things clean in Ferron. I'll do a tour of our Iron Mountain facility to see that the right kinds of things are being worked on. We should start many more projects like Iron Mountain."

In two days, all the people were evacuated from the proposed blast areas in Ferron, Utah and Death Valley. The "clean bombs" were exploded at 6:00 o'clock A.M. The dust plume was amazing and rose up out of sight into the sky. After the explosions, there were some after shocks. Volcanoes in Hawaii erupted with great ferocity. Mount St. Helens erupted in a less ferocious manner. An entire tectonic plate was moved slightly. The whole earth was cracked, you might say.

By evening of the next day, the winds had carried the dust so that it covered the entire United States. Temperatures outdoors dropped down to eighty degrees. People were rejoicing, but in a few more days the cooling effect of the dust had moved to the east. Temperatures were now climbing again. Four more atomic bombs were set off in areas near where the first ones were. The blasts were repeated every twelve hours. After sixteen bombs had gone off, the bombing was stopped. A week later the earth's temperature had returned nearly to normal. Many nations didn't fully understand why the United States was setting off so many bombs. North Korea and Iran stepped up their atomic bomb testing, and did the testing above ground with dirty bombs. They didn't possess "clean bombs" and the United States wasn't going to help them obtain them.

Chapter Nine

The United Nations

The United Nations was in emergency session. The United States was reassuring the other nations that they were not planning any aggressive actions. The U.S. Ambassador explained, "We long ago did all the testing that we needed. Our bombs don't yield large amounts of harmful radiation. We're just creating dust that will cool the world temporarily till we can recreate the ozone layer."

The North Korean Ambassador stated, "The American blasts are geared towards threatening the rest of the world. North Korea and her allies will not be threatened. We are stepping up our nuclear programs in response to this threat." The Iranian Ambassador stated, "Jahad is clearly here. We are already at war. This is just the stage where threats are made. Soon we will engage fully! American heads will be cut off!" The U.S. Ambassador responded, "Temperatures have gone down to normal since we exploded our bombs in the desert. The dust is blocking out the sun as we hoped."

The Israeli Ambassador asked, "Who caused this vast increase in global warming? What can we do about it? And who unleashed the poisonous snakes and bubonic plague on us?"

The American Ambassador responded, "The warming was caused by volcanos and by the emission of hydrocarbons. The hydrocarbons have been building up logarithmically along with the population growth. Use of automobiles needs to be limited severely throughout the world. All roofs and streets should be painted white or silver to reflect the sun's rays away from earth. Plagues are causing a great reduction in population. This will reduce the hydrocarbon releases from individual fossil fuel usage. We have no knowledge of who might have released the plague or the poisonous snakes. No one is stepping forward to take credit for the plagues. The dead need to be taken care of in ways that will reduce the spread of disease. We are recommending that the dead be thrown into the worlds hottest volcanoes. This is the only way to prevent disease and not increase the generation of global warming from crematorium fires."

Many nations objected to the suggestion about volcano crematoriums on religious grounds. The ambassador from India stated, "If the volcano would explode, the bones would be scattered everywhere. This would not seem to be an honorable burial."

The ambassador from the Ukraine stated, "The people of the Ukraine are dying by the thousands every day. We are eager to dispose of the bodies in a hygienic manner that is appropriate given the current global warming crisis. We will send our dead to Hawaii for burning in their volcanoes. It's a beautiful country. Who wouldn't love to have their ashes floating out across an area of such beauty? We have converted all our activities to horses and mules. Anyone in the Ukraine caught driving a gas guzzling vehicle will be shot! We are even requiring that all motorcycles be under 100 cubic centimeters in displacement. Why can't you other countries follow our enlightened example?"

The British Ambassador rose and spoke, "I applaud the measures being taken in the Ukraine to lessen global warming. They are also exemplary in their attitude towards disposing of their dead. What other measure should we take to reduce heat? We can't just stir up the dust perpetually. We need to work on recreating the ozone layer!"

The German Ambassador rose, "We are told by American scientists that the manufacturing of steel and aluminum generates ozone. We Germans are proud of our excellent steel. We will be running our refineries day and night. The world will need all the steel and aluminum it can get in order to reinforce all the tunnels and caves that need to be built for underground living. The ozone layer may take centuries to recreate. Let's all work together to produce as much steel and aluminum as possible."

After the United Nations meeting, millions of corpses were sent to Hawaii where they were given their final resting place in that State's hottest volcano. Every country on earth did it's best to manufacture as much steel and aluminum as possible. Tunneling and cave building was pushed to the maximum. Dr. Exeeto was nearly forgotten during the bustle of activity. There was full employment all around the world. In two month's time the dust from the bombs was nearly settled back to the surface. The temperature started to rise again. Tempers around the world were growing fierce. North Korea succeeded in launching a test missile that landed in a rural area of California. Many threats were exchanged. Iran was testing missiles. Israel was threatening a nuclear retaliation if Iran launched any more missiles in their direction.

Only a month into the world's renewed warming problems, Dr. Exeeto had worked out a deal with McBride and Ferguson. In return for him sending millions of doses of anti plague serum to the surface, the two agents would return with Dr. Exeeto's earnings from the stock market. He had foreseen how things would turn out, and bought stock in mining equipment companies, aluminum and steel companies. His holdings were going through the roof. Now all he needed was for someone to convert the stocks into gold and precious gems. McBride and Ferguson had come to an agreement with Dr. Exeeto. They would be allowed to return to the surface and bring back the gold and gems. They could then do as they pleased, as long as they didn't give away the location of the secret lab. Dr. Exeeto had provided them with the necessary paperwork needed to sell his stocks and collect the money.

Dr. Exeeto was eating breakfast at the diner with his new partners. He stated, "It'll be wonderful to see all the gold and rubies. I do hope you decide to spend more time with us then. Life on the surface must be terrible by now." McBride explained, "We'll need to report back to our leaders, once our mission for you is completed. You have excellent food and recreation here. We may retire soon and come live with you, if the offer of hospitality is still open." Dr. Exeeto replied, "The offer is always open. You're helping me more than I can explain. I know you're bending the rules by not announcing your release the day it happens, and using the time to send me my gold and rubies.

McBride responded, "I don't foresee any serious problems. We're granted much latitude in our methods of promoting the best interests of the United States. We'll send the ant-plague serum to the proper authorities. I'm sure it'll be appreciated in the States after it's tested. There may be few other nations who are trusting enough to vaccinate their people with it. By the time they test the serum and put it into use, it may be too late for them." Dr. Exeeto responded, "Well at least I've made an attempt to help. You can give twenty percent of my stock proceeds to the Salvation Army. I like the way they feed the poor. That will ease my conscience a little. I didn't think I'd feel guilty about the affects of my plagues. I guess I was only thinking of the evil people whom I wanted to punish. I forgot about the poor and relatively innocent people of the world. Of course there are poor people who are disgusting and evil too. Life is complicated. It's hard to do anything that doesn't harm someone. I know it sounds like I'm making excuses. I'll send out some teams later to help the hungry people who survive the plagues. We have an excess of food growing capacity here. We'll send canned rice and vegetables. My chef makes an excellent stew, with or without meat. We'll can it and disperse it throughout the world by helicopter. The cans will have my easy to open tops. Each can will have some helpful saying on it about living life in a way that is pleasing to God. I want people to think about making sure their hearts are in the right place before they die. I'm almost sure they will all die soon. They need to be right with God."

Ferguson responded, "We should all pray that World War III doesn't happen. Many people need to be punished, but not the innocent poor and the innocent children." McBride said, "The world has been punished quite a bit already. I hope things will change for the better now. There certainly are many distractions to keep people busy. There's plenty of trouble for everyone. They don't need to be bored and blow up the whole planet!"

Dr. Exeeto started laughing in his diabolical way. After a long time, he regained control of himself and said, "You still don't understand. It isn't man's learning something or being adequately kept busy that matters the most. It's time for the board to be wiped clean. Nothing we do can keep Satan from sending his insanity into the minds of world leaders. He'll make the Iranians go nuts thinking about all the virgins they'll have after they launch their bombs. The North Koreans will be made even crazier by Satan. One wonders how he could make them crazier. They're almost infinitely crazy now. Who knows what sort of deformed logic drives them on? All we can do is look for the innocent poor people of the earth and try to help them out before they die."

Ferguson responded, "You may be right, but I hope you're wrong. McBride said, "I wonder what the average citizen from each country would say if they found out their country had survival caves which wouldn't include them in time of disaster. Do you think most people can accept that some people will be saved in places like Iron Mountain, while they are forced to stay outside and breathe the radioactive dust?" Dr. Exeeto exclaimed, "Now that's a happy thought! Now I feel even more guilty than before. As I said before, I think it's time to wipe the slate clean. God and Satan can't start a new game if a large percentage of the old game is left on the board. I suppose God wants to collect the souls of the innocent people so he can enjoy them in heaven. People are often taken early in their lives to protect them from the rougher times to come. I'll have my teams recruit fifty thousand innocents. They'll disappear like thieves in the night. I can use them in my tunneling operations!"

McBride said, "The people who survive the atomic blasts will fight each other for the right to loot grocery stores and houses. Mean aggressive people will thrive, while more decent people will starve. It would be a terribly grotesque world if it weren't for the nuclear winter which will eliminate the aggressive and the meek alike."

Dr. Exeeto stated, "I preferred the sixties. People were happy and carefree. Sure there was a threat of atomic warfare hanging over everyone's head, but we could forget that for months at a time. Now the news media won't let anyone forget for a month. Atomic warfare is always a threat. Not a day goes by when you don't hear of Iran or North Korea pushing ahead with their atomic weapons programs. That's why it's essential to get away from it for a little bit each day. I always listen to my sixties music in the evening. I turn off the television and try to remember how nice things were when I was young. Do you ever do that?" McBride said, "My music is more from the nineties, but I'd agree that sixties music is good. I spend most of my spare time watching old James Bond movies. I also like the "Pirates of the Caribbean" movies. I've got a huge collection of DVDs. I'll bring them the next time we come to see you." Dr. Exeeto exclaimed, "Yes! The pirate movies sound exciting. I'd love to see them. A person needs to escape from the troubles of the world from time to time. Videos and music are wonderful escapes."

Chapter Ten

Back to the Surface

Dr. Exeeto and Lucia rode the monorail with Ferguson and McBride to the submarine where they would be leaving for the surface. Dr. Exeeto applied the blindfolds. "This is for your good. You won't need to try to hide anything from your government about what you saw on the way back to the surface." The two agents rode the sub for sixty-eight hours. Their blindfolds were removed after eight hours. A helicopter picked them up from an oil rig off the north west coast of Africa. They were flown to Spain, where they landed in Madrid. In a couple days they would be able to sell the stocks and buy gold for Dr. Exeeto. They found that the rubies would take longer to acquire than they had initially hoped. It would be about a week before they would be ready to return to the lab. Dr. Exeeto had provided them with a miniaturized red transmitter that could be activated by a code number when they were ready to return. His helicopter would pick them up at a remote location which they had a map for.

It was noon on a Friday and the temperature was a scorching eighty-eight degrees Fahrenheit. McBride shipped the plague serum to the United States via refrigerated express air freight. He noted on the package that it was from a friend of the United States. He and

Ferguson watched a bull fight and then had supper in a small town in the hills near the ocean. After watching the sunset over the water, McBride explained to Ferguson. Everything is changing now. We're still on a mission, but there's no point in our maintaining our original image of two hot singles. I think we're going to be on this mission for a long time. Our country will want us to keep an eye on Dr. Exeeto. I'm asking you to marry me, Ferguson!" She paused and then said, "I'm going to need to think about this for some time." Then she smiled and kissed him. "Time's up. Which church shall we get married in?" McBride explained, "First thing in the morning we'll make quick arrangements for our wedding to be done this week." Ferguson responded, "There won't be time to have a formal dress made up. I'll buy a nice white outfit that's off the rack. Now how about some of our very last premarital fun? I don't think it would be good to go all the way on the very week of our wedding, but we can still enjoy each other." McBride smiled, "You're the bride. Whatever you say goes." That night the two lovebirds had an exceedingly long discussion. Ferguson drew McBride out on many points. McBride was quite appreciative. She never cut him off short. She encouraged him to finish what he had started. They got along famously.

The wedding was held in a small chapel close to the ocean. All the parishioners attended. McBride had found a tux in time, that fit. The service was perfect. The priest was experienced at weddings, and things went well. The couple exchanged rings and kissed to finalize their wedding. They lingered most of the day with the parishioners, eating a full course meal and enjoying the stories that people had to tell.

They spent their honeymoon in an ocean front hotel which had a nice hot tub and sauna. The hotel was surrounded by lush green trees. There were fig trees and ancient twisted pine trees near their window. The scent of pine came into their room. Most of the houses in the area were white with orange tile roofs. They wrote letters to their families about the wedding, but they didn't dare send the letters till they were on their way back to Dr. Exeeto. They didn't want to be intercepted and questioned. They asked their priest to mail the letters a week after they had left. After soaking in the hotel's hot tub for a long time and watching the sun go down, they rubbed lotion on each other as they talked about their future together. Ferguson asked, "What do you hope we do, stay on the surface or stay in a survival cave?" McBride replied, "I'm in love with that park of Dr. Exeeto's. I'd never get tired of that. His whole operation is well thought out. My patriotism makes me want to stay in America, but I'm fairly certain I'm not on the list of future occupants for Iron Mountain. It'll be too full of politicians and their families. Secret agents will be a thing of the past soon. There may be no one else to spy on; just Iron Mountain and Dr. Exeeto wondering about each other and what the other's doing. My guess is that we'll be asked to stay with Dr. Exeeto to keep an eye on him." Ferguson said, "It would be strange reporting to our country with no knowledge of how they're doing. Dr. Exeeto isn't set up to receive messages. Possibly in the future he'll set up a radio to receive messages on one of his submarines." McBride asked, "Would you be happy living in Dr. Exeeto's laboratory for the rest of your life?" Ferguson responded, "As long as I have you with me, I'll be happy." They rubbed each other with lotion some more and talked softly about all the fun they'd have in Dr. Exeeto's park at night. By now, in their relationship, they knew each other's fantasies and what made the other tick. The sauna became their steamy ship which carried them to the highest ecstasy of pleasure. Their kisses were eager and passionate as they let themselves follow their body's urges. After hours of delightful consummation, they finally went to bed for the night.

When the sun rose, it found them up early eating cereal for breakfast in their room. They were both fairly silent and engrossed in thought. Ferguson felt it was great to be a couple after so many weeks of living together common law. She was a bit wild, but she liked being respectable. McBride was happy with his choice to get married too. He knew all along that he thought more of Ferguson than that she was just a team mate. He knew he'd never grow tired of her pleasant smile and good conversation. Of course she was pleasing to the eye, but she had much more going for her. She was classy and intelligent. She was independent, yet she took great pride in making her man happy. Exceedingly happy. She rarely took things for granted, commenting often on how good the food was or how exquisite a panoramic view was. She had been professional acting and a little remote before the wedding. Now she was always holding hands, kissing and showing affection. She felt good about letting her feelings show now.

Chapter Eleven

Return with the Treasure

On the following Friday, everything was ready. Dr. Exeeto had sent six men to help carry the gold and gems back to the helicopter. The helicopter had to make two trips to haul all the gold. The couple hated to leave the beautiful beaches and tree filled hills of Spain, but they climbed on the helicopter with the last of the gold and returned to the submarine.

When they returned, Dr. Exeeto was waiting for them. He congratulated them on their successful mission. "I can't thank you enough for bringing me this gold and the rubies." He had the crates taken to his suite. There, in their presence he opened two crates and looked at the gold. It was all in 1/20 ounce American Gold Eagles, just as he had requested. One smaller crate was entirely full of rubies. Dr. Exeeto opened that crate too and examined the gems. He looked quite happy as he held the rubies up to the light. He remarked, "These should make good rewards for my loyal crew. I insist that each of you have one of these rubies. A bowl full of gold for each of you would be good too." He dished up some gold and gave it to them. The doctor was like Santa Claus at Christmas. He obviously loved being generous to people.

Dr. Exeeto asked, "How much did my stock sell for?" McBride responded. It sold for eighty billion dollars. As you requested, I gave twenty percent of the money to the Salvation Army. You now have approximately four tons of gold coins and the rest of the money went for the rubies. Here are the receipts." He handed Dr. Exeeto all the paper work. Dr. Exeeto explained, "I trust you with the money, but I want to keep an inventory of everything.

Now that both of you have proved to be so helpful I'd like to offer both of you positions with my lab. Ferguson, you could serve as my chaplain. McBride, you could be on my planning team with Ferguson and be in charge of the mechanical aspects of tunneling. You would receive pay equivalent to what my top scientists receive. Free food, housing, medical care and fifty of these gold coins every year to do with as you please. You could save them for your grandchildren who could spend them when they return to the surface." Ferguson answered, "It would be great to work with you here. We'll have to report back to the United States now. There's no telling for sure what our next assignment will be." McBride explained, "We can recommend that we be allowed to come back and keep an eye on you, but in the end we have to do what they tell us to do. We're in the middle of a tour of duty. If we don't like our assignment, we can put in for early retirement and most likely get it. Since our work's dangerous, the tours of duty are short." Dr. Exeeto stated, "I understand. I don't want to get you in trouble with your country. I'll send a transmitter with you so you can report back to me if you decide not to return. I'd like to know one way or the other. If you decide not to return, I'll change the frequency of our receiver and we'll be out of contact. I can't risk frequent communications with people on the surface."

McBride responded, "That's understandable. We should leave tomorrow. I hope we can return to spy on you. I'd like the tunneling job. By the way, you need to congratulate us. Ferguson and I got married this week!" Dr. Exeeto gave them each another ruby and congratulated them. "I sincerely hope you find a safe place to stay for the rest of your lives. Retire early if you have to. Be sure to return here soon. I firmly believe that World War III will be here in only a few short years at the most, but tonight we must celebrate. We'll stay in the dining area for a gathering with some of my staff, and then you can enjoy some of my best wine tonight in your favorite hot tub under the oak trees in the park. Wear your swim suits. Lucia and I will join you at nine with another bottle or two of wine. We can chat till late. You can leave tomorrow after breakfast if you like." McBride replied, "That sounds fine to me." Ferguson said, "I'm looking forward to the hot tub and wine."

Ferguson and McBride returned to their suite and took a nap while they waited for the party at the diner to begin. Ferguson couldn't sleep during the nap time and kept kissing McBride in various places. Finally nap time ended up becoming more than what had been planned. After a couple hours of not sleeping in the bed, they showered and got dressed for the party.

Chapter Twelve

Celebration in the Lab

When Ferguson and McBride arrived at the party, Dr. Exeeto announced the wedding to his team of scientists. They all congratulated them. A wonderful steak dinner was served with plenty of mashed potatoes and gravy, dressing, butter fried morels and excellent salads. During the meal, Dr. Exeeto had each staff member introduce themselves and tell a little about what they did.

To the left of Dr. Exeeto was doctor Irosito. He was the Japanese agronomist in charge of agricultural operations. Although short and thin, he was possessed of a commanding presence. His short black hair contrasted nicely with his immaculately ironed white dress shirt. The doctor explained, "I keep food on the table, you might say. My team of over a thousand agricultural workers and scientists manage all phases of food and timber growing. We use both hydroponic and soil based media for nutrient supply. Our capacity is currently well beyond the needs of the present community. We like to keep it that way. Extra produce is turned into alcohol for energy storage and consumption. We maximize growth in food and timber with organic fertilizers and optimum water supplies. We take great pride in our morels. It was once thought that morels could not be grown under artificial conditions.

They're grown here in massive quantities, because of how popular they are with our people. Do you like them?" McBride answered, "I would never tire of them. They've always been favorites of mine." Ferguson stated, "They're excellent. I congratulate you on a fine accomplishment!" Dr. Irosito nodded appreciatively. "I hope you can visit our areas often," he responded.

Sitting to the left of Dr. Irosito was Dr. Ubani. He was the South African head of excavations. At over six feet tall and of solid build, he commanded an impressive presence. Dr. Udani explained, "I'm responsible for all the digging that has gone on. My training is in geology. I rely on my well trained staff to work the equipment. I make the crucial decisions about where it's safe to dig large caves. At one time I was employed by the gold mining concerns of South Africa. Dr. Exeeto was able to lure me away from them with the challenge that such a large operation as his, presents. I much prefer making large caves to only making small tunnels. Dr. Exeeto tells me there is some possibility that you might help us with our excavations. Is there any truth to that?" McBride explained, "I haven't made my final decision on that yet. Ferguson and I still need to report back to the surface. Then we can find out if we will be allowed to come back to stay here. We love it here, but we need to meet our obligations to our current employer." Dr. Udani replied, "That's understandable. If you do come to work with me, I assure you there will be plenty of challenges for you. We have professional staff who are easy to get along with. You'd fit right in." McBride said, "That sounds great. I hope we can work together soon."

Dr. Antonov and his wife were sitting to the left of Dr. Udani. Dr. Antonov was a little under six feet tall and had a full head of long dark hair with a beard and moustache. His wife was blond with stunning blue eyes. She was quite attractive and intelligent looking. Dr. Antonov explained, "My wife and I are in charge of the animals and the aquarium. We're both veterinarians with advanced training in marine biology."

Next to them was Dr. Chen and his wife, of China. He was five feet, nine inches tall with short black hair and a captivating smile. His wife was short and thin with intelligent dark looking eyes and a beautiful general appearance. He explained, "I'm in charge of human resources. My wife and I will be helping our population find suitable mates, and we also have responsibility for placing people in the jobs they find enjoyable and for which they are suited. We have a large staff to help us, of course."

Next to the Chens was Dr. Clearwater. He was of native American descent. His skin was dark tan and he was tall with long black hair. Dr. Clearwater explained, "I'm in charge of culture and communications. My staff operates the library, entertainment and communications facilities. We have a casino and a well equipped library. We have our own radio station and newspaper. We also print several trade magazines and other magazines designed for literary tastes. My staff is nearly as large as the agricultural staff. I employ hundreds of people doing writing and publishing."

Several other department heads introduced themselves and then everyone took turns getting to know the bride and groom better. It was encouraging to see how friendly they all were. There was no egotism or unhealthy attitudes to be discerned. Everyone seemed professional and compatible. Ferguson whispered to McBride, "I really like these people. They're all so laid back and friendly." McBride explained, "It's a necessity here. They're going to be living together for the rest of their lives."

Dr. Exeeto ordered a round of champagne for everyone and proposed a toast, "To the certain return of our newly weds. May they join us for a better life!" Everyone clinked their glasses together and drank to the toast." McBride proposed the next toast, "To a community that knows how to party and get along perfectly together." They all cheered and drank eagerly to that toast. Most of the doctors proposed toasts. The champagne was excellent and never ran out.

At midnight McBride and Ferguson excused themselves and found their way to their hot tub out under the oak trees. There was still ever so faint of a trace of the burning oak leaves. They stripped off all their clothing but their swim suits, and climbed into the hot tub. Ferguson sat on McBride's lap and stared into his eyes in the moonlight. "We have to come back. That's all there is to it. The surface is the pits now. Everyone is struggling to be included in a good survival cave. There is so much competition between people. I don't think it's healthy." She was slurring her words just a little. She frequently indulged in alcohol, but she wasn't used to quite as much as she'd had on this night. McBride responded, "I agree with you. This is where the laid back and friendly people are. The surface has too many people. They're all biting each other's backs. Here, though, I know I'd miss the mountains and the ocean beaches." Ferguson stated, "They have a massive library with videos of those things. You'll get to enjoy the beach without the mosquitoes. You can enjoy seeing the mountains without getting winded from climbing." McBride laughed, "There you go again, being a total optimist." Ferguson went on, "When you're busy with your work and we have some children who need us, you won't be so preoccupied with mountains and beaches. We need to think of our children. We can't let them die from the nuclear winter. We'll never be included in Iron Mountain. They're the most advanced survival facility America has, and I'm not so sure they're actually adequately prepared for one hundred years underground. They're more geared towards military preparedness. They want to be able to survive a potential first strike so they can launch America's missiles as retaliation." McBride said softly, "You're right. Our children need adequate protection. I'll do whatever I can think of to get us assigned down here."

They grew silent and let the beauty of their surroundings overtake them. Gently and silently they started to know each other better as man and wife, there in the warm steaming water beneath the oaks. Their sighs mingled with the sound of the artificial breeze in the trees.

Chapter Thirteen

Return to the American Submarine

After a quick breakfast the next morning, McBride and Ferguson made the long trip back to the oil rig off the northwest coast of Africa. From there they were shuttled to Madrid where they took a flight back to Miami. In no time at all they were in the C.I.A. submarine off the coast of Florida. General Daniels called them into his office immediately. He smiled as they entered the office. They both saluted and were saluted in turn by Daniels. He ordered, "At ease." He opened, "I haven't heard from either of you for quite some time. We received the plague serum and our scientists are finding it to be acceptable for our use. How did you get Dr. Exeeto to part with the serum?" McBride explained, "We served as expediters in the sale of some of his stocks and converted them to gold and rubies for him. He needed the gold and gems to pay his staff with." General Daniels stated, "That was quick thinking. You saved many lives by making Exeeto think you were working with him. Where is he located? Ferguson volunteered, "We were blindfolded during most of our transport to and from the lab. We only know that he's less than one hundred and fifty miles from his original lab." Daniels sighed,

"Well, we may need his expertise in the future. We're following his advice about making ozone with steel and aluminum production. Did you find out if he caused the destruction of the ozone layer?"

McBride explained, "He destroyed it with hundreds of tons of F-12 refrigerant. He thinks he's delaying World War III by causing problems for the world. Especially problems for countries with atomic weapons." Daniels continued, "He must have developed some liking for both of you, if he told you that much. I'm asking you both to return to him and keep an eye on him. I don't mind if he wants to hide under the sea, but if he starts plans to eliminate us entirely, I want to know about it. Is that understood? He'll be curious about what we're up to, so I'm sure he'll let you communicate with us. He'll listen in on everything of course. At least he forced us to dig in and make survival caves and tunnels. I've been advocating that for years. Our enemies have always been ahead of us in tunneling. Now it's a matter of life our death. No one wants to be left on the surface. We're tunneling for all we're worth. It'll be interesting if our tunnels run into Exeeto's.

Try to keep us informed about where he's expanding his tunnels to. How big are his caves now?" McBride revealed, "He has a recreation park that's ten football fields long and four hundred feet high. His food growing facilities are ten times larger than that. They have a ten year head start on us." Daniels exclaimed, "I was afraid of that. What's their military capability?" Ferguson stated, "We saw no evidence of military capability. They have a couple dozen guards, but that's all we saw." Daniels said, "I think he just wants to wait out World War III. It doesn't take a rocket scientist to figure our that it's coming. The world will belong to whoever can survive the nuclear winter and the wait for nuclear radiation to die down." McBride stated, "Exeeto expressed doubts that our Iron Mountain facility is geared up for a one hundred year wait. He thinks we aren't planning ahead quite far enough." Daniels explained, "The President is working on that. Right from the beginning the President put an emphasis on beefing up Iron Mountain and duplicating its work elsewhere. I want you to get back down there right away. I don't want you to miss anything he's up to. Thanks again for the serum. You're dismissed." McBride and Ferguson saluted and left. They were flown back to Madrid, where Exeeto's helicopter picked them up and took them to the oil derrick off the coast of Africa. There a sub took them back to Dr. Exeeto's lab.

Dr. Exeeto greeted them at the submarine docking station. He was obviously delighted to see them. He asked, "Are you here to stay?" McBride stated, "For the foreseeable future. I don't have to tell you why." Dr. Exeeto smiled, "Yes, I can imagine that your commander is deeply interested about what my plans and activities are. I don't mind being watched. I'm proud of my little operation. I hope that if you work for me, you won't be considered to be aiding and abetting the enemy." McBride explained, "We aren't restrained by the rules governing the usual soldier. Since our missions are so complex and require much creativity, we're granted almost unlimited latitude as long as we're working to fulfill our mission. As long as we report back regularly, I'm sure my commander won't mind if we help out down here. He was thankful that you inspired our nation to dig tunnels and caves like we should. There was a great negligence in that area for a long time."

Dr. Exeeto exclaimed, "Yes, American's love the wide open spaces. It's hard for them to contemplate living in caves and under rocks. It's humbling. A proud nation wants to be free, but who can stay free when the board is being wiped clean. Of course there's freedom in death, to a certain extent. Ferguson, since you're going to be our religious leader, tell me, will there be beer and wine in heaven?" Ferguson laughed, "I believe so. Jesus created wine from water when he was here on earth. I'm fairly certain there's going to be wine in heaven. I don't know about beer." Dr. Exeeto continued, "Let's go to my suite and discuss religion a little longer. Our discussions in the past have made me start thinking more along those line."

They rode the monorail to the residential section and then walked to Dr. Exeeto's suite. Lucia was gone. Dr. Exeeto explained, "Lucia went to the library. She should be back before too long. We can sit in the living room and watch the aquarium. Would you like some drinks?" They nodded. "I'll make up something tropical with vodka." In a few minutes they all had their drinks. It was almost supper time. Dr. Exeeto asked, "What exactly do I need to do to make sure I'm not sent to hell for the actions I've taken against the surface lately? I feel like I've tried to help both Satan and God, by punishing mankind, but you've made me realize that I've hurt many innocent people. I don't really want Satan or God upset with me. What would you recommend?"

Ferguson explained, "I would start thinking in terms of being loyal only to God. You can't suck up to Satan. He's a punisher. You can't win with him. He'll pick you apart, condemn you and then burn you. God on the other hand, is a forgiving God, but he's a jealous God. If you try to please him and Satan both, you'll be a total loser. I want you to think about the story of Jesus dying on the cross to save you from your sins. Only if you can accept the forgiving grace of Jesus will you be saved. No one goes to heaven except by being a friend of Jesus. You're his friend if you do as he taught us to do. Love your neighbors. Follow the golden rule. Be generous to the poor, orphaned and widows. Have deep faith in the power of Jesus. He's more powerful than Satan. Jesus has the winning team."

Dr. Exeeto sighed, "That's quite a bit to think about. I'll give it some serious thought. I hope we can have daily discussions until I have a better understanding of God and Jesus. He sighed, "I feel a little better already. Can you baptize people, Ferguson?" Ferguson sighed, "I'm not an official preacher, but I guess I'm going to need to be. After I'm sure you know all the basics of Christianity, then, if you still want to be a Christian, I'll baptize you."

Dr. Exeeto exclaimed, "That's great. I'll tell Lucia when she gets back. She's Catholic. I'm sure she'll be pleased. My life has been so busy with projects and work, I haven't spent enough time thinking about religious things. We all die sometime. I could die tonight in my sleep. I can't imagine myself totally ceasing to exist. I'm happy now. I don't want to die, but I know it'll happen some day." Ferguson replied, "You've read much of the Bible. You know about the God who punishes evil. You long for the evil world to be punished. That's not all bad. I agree with you. It gives Godly people a good feeling to see evil punished. I hope you can start focusing more on the supportive and kindly nature of God. He loves people who are trying to follow his teachings. He'll provide for your needs and will take you to heaven when you die. No sin is so great that he can't forgive it. As long as you believe God is good, he will help you."

Lucia came in and greeted them. Dr. Exeeto explained to her what they had been discussing and that he was going to become a Christian. Lucia exclaimed, "That's wonderful. Now we can go to church together and you can quit worrying so much about what will happen when you die. He's always talking about death," she said looking at them. Dr. Exeeto said, "There are lots of people dying even as we speak. I caused much of it. That's a heavy burden to bear. I still think I did the right thing. Something was telling me, almost forcing me to punish the world. I still don't know if it was God or Satan." God and Satan coexist. They have games or contests, like the testing of Job. They confront each other in the persons of the armies of the world. Good against evil. Each side thinks it's the good side. Is God bored? Why must he always be in a battle with Satan and his followers?" Ferguson answered, "We can't know the mind of God entirely. We have to trust that he is good. We see his handiwork in the mountains and seas. The heavens were created by him in all their beauty. If he wants us tested and purified by fire, who are we to criticize him? The testing won't last forever. There will be adequate reward. Job was given back twice as much as what was taken from him. Apart from future rewards, it's pleasurable to read your Bible from a Christian perspective. Don't tear apart every thing. Try to understand the Bible. Pray for understanding. Read Matthew for the guiding words of Jesus. Read Proverbs for wisdom. The more familiar your Bible becomes for you, the more you'll enjoy it. Pray every day for forgiveness of your sins. That way if you die that night, you're right with God. Heaven actually exists. Angels exist. Jesus is actually waiting to acknowledge you as one of his own, and accept you into heaven. It doesn't really matter how many people on earth die on any one given day. What matters is how many people are right with God on any given day."

McBride exclaimed, "That was a good sermon, Ferguson. You should write that down and present it for a Sunday sermon." Dr. Exeeto smiled, "I record everything. I got the idea from your American Presidents who always record White House conversations. I'll have that sermon printed up for you, Ferguson. You can present it to the staff Sunday." Ferguson laughed, "That's fine with me. I might as well get started right away."

They spent the rest of the evening eating carry in Kentucky Fried Chicken. It was an identical duplication which the chef at the diner knew how to make. They also snacked on butter fried morels. The seventy-two inch liquid crystal monitor on the wall displayed for them the exhilaration of climbing steep mountains. Next they watched some of McBride's pirate movies. McBride explained, "Next week we can watch a couple James Bond movies. I never get tired of them." Dr. Exeeto exclaimed, "That sounds great!" He and Ferguson battled playfully over the last of the morels.

Finally Dr. Exeeto poured one last round of drinks. He proposed a toast. "May we all draw close to God. May we all be forgiven." They all clinked their glasses together and drank heartily. Ferguson and McBride said their goodbyes and walked back to their suite. It was past midnight, and they went to sleep as soon as possible. Dr. Exeeto let Lucia fall asleep and then watched her beautiful lips as he thought about how much fun they were having down below the ocean.

Chapter Fourteen

World War III

North Korea finally perfected their intercontinental ballistic missile systems, only a few months after McBride and Ferguson had gone to stay with Dr. Exeeto. The North Koreans managed to persuade the Ukraine to sell them one of their most powerful atomic bombs which was designed for mounting on a missile. This had moved North Korea's nuclear capabilities ahead considerably. They showed off their new power by obliterating Detroit. The murder capital of the United States was toppled completely. There was nothing left of it. America retaliated immediately with five nuclear warhead missiles, targeting the capital and suspected launch sites. Caught up in the excitement and not wanting to be out done, Iran launched nuclear warheads against Israel. Israel detected the launch and responded with its own launch of nuclear warhead missiles.

America knew from its C.I.A., that the Ukraine was the source of North Korea's atomic bombs. America launched twenty nuclear warhead missiles on the Ukraine. The Ukraine responded the moment they were aware of the U.S. launches. All major U.S. cities were targeted. China and Japan also engaged in an exchange of atom bombs. The Japanese had only recently acquired atom bombs from the United States for use against North Korea.

Most of the bombs exploded in the air over their target cities. Hundreds of millions of people were vaporized or charred beyond recognition. The people who were on the outer edges of the cities received extensive burns over most of their bodies and most were blinded by the intense light from the bomb. There was wide spread panic. Babies were crying desperately in the arms of their helpless mothers. The stench of burned flesh filled the air. People were wandering aimlessly about, in a daze.

Many people who had been lucky enough to be in basements of well built structures, during the blast, were soon out looting businesses and the homes left standing. There were no police to stop them. The whole world seemed to have gone mad. Everything was total chaos.

The temperature of earth quickly plummeted. Fierce winds and hurricanes took over. The snow fell constantly. In only ten days, the temperature of earth had fallen to twenty below zero Fahrenheit. The oceans were starting to freeze over. The snow was starting to build up at the north and south poles. Snow over the entire earth was six to ten feet deep.

People were burning demolished buildings to keep warm. Hundreds of burned and discouraged people huddled around the blazing buildings. They were hungry and tired. Most cities of the world had similar scenes of suffering. Those rare people who had food and water, were sick from radiation poisoning. It was hard to find a happy person on the surface of planet earth. Everyone's hair fell out after a few weeks. Their eyes were dark from illness and depression. Frozen corpses littered the streets and sidewalks. Those who were managing to survive, longed for death.

The digging of survival tunnels and caves over most of the world had just begun a few months ago. Progress was varied. Most tunnel complexes had no food growing capability and there was inadequate ability for recycling water. The radiation levels were so high, that it was certain death to go out to the surface. Most of the world's population was dead from the bombs or from the cold.

Deep in the bowels of Iron Mountain, General Daniels was trying to establish radio contact with McBride. Daniels was broadcasting on multiple frequencies in the long wave spectrum. There was no response. Iron Mountain had given in to human weakness or strength, depending upon your perspective. They had let more people into the facility than it was designed for. Daniels had been meeting regularly with the President, who was also in Iron Mountain. Daniels had mentioned to the President that Dr. Exeeto had enormous caves for growing food. The President had asked Daniels to attempt to buy food from Dr. Exeeto. They could connect tunnels with the President's solemn promise not to attempt to take over Dr. Exeeto's operation. The President explained to Daniels, "We only have enough food to last twenty-five years. We need to stay in here at least fifty years and preferably one hundred years. We need Dr. Exeeto's help in feeding our people." General Daniels explained, "Dr. Exeeto will never let us connect to his tunnels. He'll never trust us." The President made the point, "By the time we run out of food, he'll probably be dead from old age. Possibly the new generation will want to work with us."

After three months of listening to a silent radio, General Daniels finally heard a voice. It was McBride reporting in. McBride was on the lowest frequency of the radio. His voice was faint but could be understood. McBride stated, "All is well here. We're tunneling south at a depth unknown to me. We feel the equator will be the first area to warm up. If we ever emerge, it will be there. Our destination is Panama, for now. We'll leave a food growing cave there for you and then bury our tunnel. Dr. Exeeto foresaw that you would be short on food. Some of his staff will stay to show you how to operate the facility.

Our tunneling capability is far beyond anything surface civilizations have mastered. We will be working on the Panama food cave in about one year. You should reach the cave in less than ten years. It will be located at the eastern end of the Panama canal.

We plan to stay below ground for one hundred years. Our tunnels will run under the oceans. We do not wish to come in contact with other civilizations. Dr. Exeeto doesn't want us to be overpowered by some other civilization's military. We are free and we want to stay that way." General Daniels radioed back, "The President has promised not to try to take over your operation. We thank you for the food and good will. Hope to hear from you again soon. How is Ferguson?" McBride explained, "She's in charge or religious matters here. She's happy and doing well. We'll all pray for your survival." The radio went silent.

Digging operations for both Iron Mountain and Dr. Exeeto's team went on furiously. The advanced equipment of Dr. Exeeto made it to Panama in about a year. It took another two years to dig the expansive cave and start the food growing process. Once everything was set up and there were enough volunteers to stay and keep the operation going, the tunnel was closed. Dr. Exeeto's men pulled back one hundred miles and then built a tunnel to Venezuela. It was there that Dr. Exeeto felt they should access the surface when the time was right. They also tunneled further south and further to the north. In time Dr. Exeeto hoped to completely circle the globe. He felt it would give them unlimited escape routes should another civilization attempt to trap them. Every two hundred miles, they would build a food growing station. Food was seen as their most important asset. Water desalinization was also seen to be of critical importance. Each growing facility was linked to the sea with a pipe that would lead sea water to the desalinization facility. These systems wouldn't be used though until radiation in the ocean reached acceptable levels. For the time being water had to be piped to the various food caves from the main water storehouse at the original cave.

In ten years, the Iron Mountain tunnel workers made their way to panama and found the food cave. They immediately started transporting food back to iron mountain. Iron Mountain had succeeded in improving its own food growing capabilities, but they were still delighted to obtain the extra food.

Chapter Fifteen

One Hundred Years Later

Time went on, and Dr. Exeeto's team was nearly forgotten. After a hundred years, the Iron Mountain facility opened up and the attempt to rebuild America was begun. Everything branched out from Iron Mountain. There was plentiful electricity. They had learned to use geothermal heat to make steam to power generators. Now that they could work in the open air, it was much easier to make steel and aluminum. Everything was operated with electricity. It would be a long time before mankind would be able to get fossil fuel production going again. Manufacturing of cars and trucks was a big priority. Rail lines were still in place, so electric trains were built and set into operation. Food production was stepped up immediately. Everywhere a new town was established, a geothermal electricity plant was installed so that electricity wouldn't need to be wired in from a long distance away. With this new found source of electricity, even Ferron, Utah became a thriving community. Because of its coal deposits, it became a steel manufacturing center. Even though the steel was heated with electricity, the coal was still needed to make coke for adding the right amount of carbon into the steel.

Dr. Exeeto had passed away from old age and his great grand daughter, Jessica, was now the leader of the

Exeeto subterranean dynasty. McBride and Ferguson had also passed away from old age. They left in their stead, twenty great grandchildren. All of them were on friendly terms and most of them were top people in the mining operations. Some of them were religious leaders who followed in Ferguson's footsteps. Dr. Exeeto had initiated the use of geothermal electrical production with his operations long before the Iron Mountain people had developed it. Some geothermal operations information should be revealed at this point.

In order to control the intense heat which is present in hot rocks deep below the earth's crust, it is of critical importance to inject a controlled amount of water into the bore hole. The water is injected with a pump similar to a high pressure washer, except that the volume of water is higher. Thick walled stainless steel tubing, with an inside diameter of one eighth of an inch, is positioned inside a highly insulated collar. The one foot in diameter collar of insulation is jacketed with a strong layer of stainless steel water proof sheeting. This assembly is lowered into the bore hole, down into the area of the hot rocks. The bore hole is capped with steam harnessing two foot in diameter piping. The piping guides the super hot steam to steam turbines which generate the electricity. Such electric generating systems are quite reliable and work for decades with little maintenance. It was the geothermal steam which powered the incredibly large and wealthy civilization of Exeeto's conception.

Jessica inherited Dr. Exeeto's love for gold. Whenever her mining operations came across gold deposits, they refined the gold and coined it for currency. Every citizen of Jessica's underground nation had buckets full of gold coins which their families had earned down through the years. Gold was the motivator for industriousness. It was a status symbol and object of much pride. Most of the people were religious and had appropriate Christian values. They didn't worship their gold. The gold took the place of a nice car. It was something to be proud of. The size of a person's gold pile spoke of how industrious his family had been down through the years.

Chapter Sixteen

The Vision

Jessica was married to John McBride, one of Don McBride's many great grandchildren. They were having breakfast together at the same dining room their relatives had used for a hundred years. Jessica explained to John, as they ate their omelets and toast, "I've been having a reoccurring dream. I keep seeing the earth from several thousand miles away. It starts to glow red hot around the edges of the continents and then it's blown in half by an explosion. It splits down the middle of the Atlantic ocean and the Pacific." John responded, "Have you been using too much of your Ritalin? I know you're always pushing yourself to perform at the highest possible level. Your brain might need a rest. Why don't we take a vacation?" Jessica answered, "A vacation is a great idea, but I think this dream is more like a vision. It's not a stress hallucination. It isn't terribly frightening. The red and orange glowing earth is beautiful as it splits apart. I see it calmly. I think we're being told to stop concentrating so much of our activities on the band of tunnels we've created under the Atlantic and Pacific oceans. We need to branch out to the east and west. As long as we stay in the southern hemisphere, we won't make contact with Iron Mountain tunneling operations. I think they've gone back to the surface by now. Their tunneling will be greatly reduced. Dr. Exeeto intended for us to always remain in our tunnels. He predicted that history would repeat itself and we would once again need the protection of the earth's crust." John exclaimed, "So you think the earth is going to split in half right where our tunnels are?" Jessica responded, "That's what the vision seems to be saying. Of course it could be a thousand years from now. I feel we need to split off to the east and to the west. If the earth does split, half of us will have a chance of surviving. Possibly even all of us would survive, if we aren't blow too far out of orbit. Mankind doesn't realize how delicate earth's orbit is. If we ever make the leap of technology that brings us to even more powerful bombs than the atomic bomb, we could feasibly split the earth it half. The core is liquid, with a solid center. Only the outer crust and gravity holds it in shape. Dr. Exeeto's diary contains documentation of how earth quakes and volcanic explosions always followed the most powerful atomic bomb explosions. Those explosions were moving the tectonic plates enough to force molten lava up through the volcanoes. The earth's crust is not a play thing for earth's people to entertain themselves with. If we mess up the outer structure of earth, we're really screwed!"

John expanded on the topic, "It's kind of like a dog and its dog house. A dog knows not to move its bowels inside the dog house. If he did, things would be messed up and it would no longer be pleasant in there." Jessica laughed, "Well, that's a crude but effective analogy. Yes, the surface people tend to start destroying the wonderful habitat they've inherited. It may take a thousand years, but atomic bombs will probably return to haunt our descendants." John said, "It doesn't pay to dwell on such a vision. Just tuck it away and let's move on. You can write in your journal about it. I say we need to go on our vacation right now." Jessica explained, "I'll be able to relax better if I know the new tunneling to the east and west has begun. Then we can do as you say."

She used her emergency phone to call the head of mining operations. Bill McBride answered the phone. Jessica said, "Bill I want all our efforts to start focusing on tunneling as far as possible to the east and west of our current positions. I want this tunneling to take place only in the southern hemisphere. Is that clear?" Bill answered. I have no problems with that. I am a little curious about the reason for this decision. Do you mind filling me in?" Jessica explained, "I've had a vision. I see trouble for our current locations. It'll happen a long time from now, but we need to plan ahead." Bill responded, "That's as good a reason as any, I suppose. Maybe we'll find more gold!" Jessica laughed, "We usually do. How many buckets full do you have now?" Bill laughed, "There's always room for more. I always want more!"

Jessica hung up the phone. She leaned over and hugged John. "Where would you like to vacation?" John answered, "The tropics is my favorite. Let's go to that new one we created a couple years ago. It's just big enough to make you feel out in the open. It's about five hundred miles south of here. We could get there in about three hours on the monorail." They went to their suite and packed.

About four hours later they were on a sandy beach with warm salt water to swim in. The lighting imitated that of the tropics. A large intense sun simulator shown down upon them. The warmth felt good on their bare skin. The beach was a mile long and full of beautiful white sand. There were only a few other people close by. Everyone was spread out over the entire length of the beach. Jessica stated, "There's one thing I miss about the surface. I'd like to sun myself on a beach with real sunshine. I'd like the beach to go on for many miles, so we could walk along it until we were tire of walking." John replied, "We could send subs up for vacationing on the beaches. That way we wouldn't need to worry about other civilizations finding our tunnels." Jessica responded, "I like that idea. We'll tunnel close to the Brazilian beaches and then go up by submarine to enjoy the beach."

They relaxed and enjoyed the warmth of the artificial sunlight. Jessica had tan skin like her Mexican great grandmother, Lucia. John had his great grandfather's bulldog chin and the tan skin as well. John and Jessica were both a little under six feet tall. They were attractive people with intelligent looking dark brown eyes. John's eyes had a tint of green to them.

John raised his hand in the air, and immediately a young couple came running up to them. The girl was blond shapely and tall. Her companion was tall and tan with black hair. The young man asked, "What is it that you require?" John explained, "I think we would like some tropical drinks with plenty of vodka. Could you make that a double shot for each of us with papaya, orange juice, pineapple and peach. Lots of ice and in a giant glass with straws and parasols." The young man responded, "We'll have that ready for you in a few minutes. Is there anything else we can bring you?" Jessica exclaimed, "Yes, we'll have a couple pounds of butter fried morels. Powder the morels with white flour, please. Use plenty of salt." The young man explained, "That'll take ten more minutes. I'll bring you your drinks while you wait. Is there anything else?" John asked, "Do you have a copy of this week's issue of *Tawdry and Lewd Sayings*? We'd like two copies." The young man answered, "I'll bring it with the drinks. It's unusually pleasing this week!"

In a few minutes he returned with the drinks and magazines. On the front of the magazine was a close up picture of a woman reading the magazine with an alarmed look on her face. She was dressed in Elizabethan clothing with a plunging neckline and much cleavage revealed. A young man was looking over her shoulder. Jessica stated,

"It's so refreshing to peruse something that isn't stuffy like the constant meetings I have to attend." John responded, "I know exactly what you mean." She read aloud, "A man was away from home at a convention. He called up a prostitute and asked what her fee was. She told him the fee was two hundred dollars. He explained to her that he'd give her three hundred dollars for the worst sex of his life. She told him that for three hundred dollars, he'd get the best sex of his life. He complained, 'No, I want the worst sex. I'm not horny, I'm lonely.'" Jessica complained, "I'm not sure I get that one." John explained, "The man's wife always gives him the worst sex, and he wants to be reminded of her. It's easy to see why you wouldn't get it. You always give the best sex. You can't see that kind of logic, naturally. I'm glad you can't."

John read on, "What food ruins sex drive? Wedding cake." Jessica laughed, "Now I get that one. Often the great sex is to lure the man into marriage. Then the sex goes down hill. This magazine is crazy. Who writes this stuff?" John explained, "Many different people contribute to it. It's not just one person writing it all." Jessica blushed slightly and handed the magazine to John, "I've had enough for now. This thing is terrible. There's page after page of this stuff."

John exclaimed, "We have to maintain freedom of the press. If people like being embarrassed or titillated, who are we to judge them. I enjoy the thing. You have to admit that there's some humor there. That's something we need more of." Jessica whined, "Do they have to push things to the limit? That first joke with fornication is not something I want to read about. I want some humor, but not that kind!" John thought out loud, "Possibly we should have them split the magazine into a lewd section, and a section in the back for things in terribly poor taste." Jessica laughed, "Yes, I'll mention that at my next meeting with the publishers. You'll probably always turn right to the back pages!" John exclaimed, "Please, Jessica. Don't impugn my honor!" He laughed. Jessica asked, "Where did you get that word?" John explained, "I've been watching my great grandfather's DVDs of pirate stories. I like the ways they spoke in those days. Archaic language is becoming a favorite thing of mine." Jessica smiled, "I like the old words too.

Why don't we play some Scrabble with the open dictionary? That way we learn more new words." They called for a Scrabble game and two dictionaries. The young couple brought them more drinks and morels too, without being asked. Jessica exclaimed, "You two really know how to roll out the red carpet." She reached in her purse and pulled out a gold coin for each of them. She asked, "Are the two of you a couple or are they just having you work together?" The girl responded, "We're a couple. We've been working together for a year. The resort manager thinks that having young couples working together adds to the pleasure of the guests." Jessica responded, "Well, I guess there's some logic to that. Do you like this kind of work?" The girl said, "Yes, it's fun to help other people have fun. We live right here at the resort, so we can enjoy the beach any time we like. That's a great fringe benefit." Jessica asked, "Can you help us have fun here on the beach tomorrow too? We're staying all week." The girl said, "We'll be sure to be right here for you. I'm Debbie and this is Eric. We work till nine o'clock this evening. Just let us know if there's anything you want. We have twenty flavors of ice cream. They're all nutritious and nonfattening." Jessica ordered, "We'd like a couple T-bone steaks medium well and two more drinks." Debbie smiled, "We'll be right back with them."

The time went quickly as they continued drinking, eating and soaking up the sun. There were palm trees scattered around on the beach. They had been transported from the main agricultural area. As the hour grew late, the sun followed its program and dutifully set in the west. The moon came out in a full state, along with brightly twinkling stars. Deb and Eric carried out an artificial camp fire and placed it near the blanket where Jessica and John were laying. Eric said, "We go off duty now, but there are servers working round the clock. Here's a transmitter to call for service." He handed John a white plastic transmitter that looked like a remote phone. Then Eric and Debbie disappeared out across the sand. The artificial camp fire was attractive, with the well designed artificial logs and the propane flames dancing over them. The warmth given off by the campfire was considerable. John and Jessica snuggled up to the campfire. They kissed passionately and allowed themselves the pleasures which they could afford each other. They were both in their thirties. In their prime and both being physically fit, their passions were not quickly sated. The novel surroundings and the sound of the waves lapping up on the beach drove them to extend their love making for hours. Finally, they collapsed in each others arms. Jessica whispered, "We've got to come here more often." John answered, "I agree with that. Why do we push ourselves so hard? We've got all the time in the world. We aren't competing with the surface. Why don't we start taking every other month off?" Jessica thought a minute. "That's an excellent idea. Let's become a more vacation oriented society. We have the work force now to sustain such activities. Work is great, but I love this vacation. Let's have everyone do it."

The week of vacation went well. The mile long ocean was complete with a coral reef and live tropical fish. There was scuba diving and skiing. Nothing had been neglected in the desire to provide a memorable experience.

When they returned to their suite at the main complex, Jessica convened an emergency session with all the department heads. They met at the diner for butter fried morels and drinks. Jessica opened the meeting. "I have some good news for you. I know that we usually discuss important matters together as a team before I make a decision about major courses of action. This time it's going to be an edict handed down from me. I'm mandating that all members of our civilization spend every other month on vacation." Everyone applauded.

There was a toast called for by the head of environmental affairs, "To a healthier and happier existence." They all touched their glasses together with a tinkling sound. They drank heartily and laughed as they discussed what they would like their next vacation to be. Jessica went on, "I think the extra free time will help increase our population. We'll need more people as we push to the east and west. Free time means more fertility and more sensuous expression of affection. These are items held in high regard by our civilization.

Unlike the surface races of mankind who are fascinated with bombs. We make love, not war.

I am hoping that all of you will keep an eye out for humorists in our midst. Our magazine *Tawdry and Lewd Sayings* is in need of more writers. The magazine will be featuring a tame section in the front, and more embarrassing sayings in the back. This way, gentle readers can enjoy some humor without exposing themselves to subjects not mete for the tender sensibilities of our more gentile population. All our publications will need to be thicker and published more often. Our vacationing population will have more time to read and relax. Poetry and novels will be in high demand. The arts must be encouraged. All my goals for the future depend on increased population growth. I'm instituting a two thousand dollar bonus to each couple who brings forth a new baby.

On a different note, I'm happy to announce that we have discovered a new fault zone in the southern Atlantic ocean. Not only is it four miles deep, it has a width of two miles and is almost a hundred miles long. This trench will give us plenty of room to hide our rock debris from tunneling operations. We don't want the surface civilization to be able to determine where our tunnels are by looking for the rock debris."

The head of communications asked, "Is there any new word about what the surface civilization is doing?" Jessica explained, "There have been no explosions yet. It's safe to say that Iron Mountain retained the information on making atomic bombs. They are bound to start making them again. History repeats itself. Our scientists have discovered in our archives some plans for making a fusion bomb. Such a bomb would be nearly a hundred times more powerful than the atomic bomb and would generate temperatures as hot as the surface of the sun. It's my belief that this bomb will be developed and used sometime during the next thousand years. We need to prepare for that event. Such a bomb, or an array of such bombs, could feasibly split the earth in two.

I've had a vision in which the earth was split in two before my eyes. My vision showed the earth splitting down the middle of the Atlantic and Pacific oceans. It's my plan for us to develop both sides of the Atlantic. If my vision becomes reality, at least half of us will survive. There's no telling what sort of orbit the halves will go into if and when they separate. One half may go into the sun. It's almost a certainty that the two halves would change speed and orbit. The thought of this split doesn't need to alarm us. It's only important to be right with God. Your spirit is what's important. We can enjoy ourselves for many generations. Possibly God will bless us by exterminating the surface population. He probably stays his hand because there are a few good people left on the surface. My vision probably won't come true for a thousand years. The surface is no doubt completely occupied with rebuilding the world's sea ports and cities. It'll be a long time before the population grows back into the billions and people are bitterly struggling for precious resources.

When the first atomic blasts are detected by our seismometers, it will be time to move our people away from the oceans and block off the tunnels to the oceans. The fusion bomb won't be far behind and the splitting of the world into halves." Dr. Smith the third spoke up, "My great grandfather worked closely with your great grandfather, Dr. Exeeto. He recorded in his journals that Dr. Exeeto was a man who could see the future. He knew what would happen next. It appears that you have inherited his abilities. Can't you use your abilities to tell us whether to go to the east or the west? It seems like such a pity to lose half of our citizens because we don't know which way to go."

Jessica laughed almost diabolically and then broke into coughing explanation, "I'm sorry for my weird laughter. The responsibility for making such a decision makes me nervous, and the thought of half of our dear citizens being burned on the sun is unnerving to say the least. 'Life is just a big game of chess,' my great grandfather used to say. I, on the other hand like to play blackjack. The game exposes psychic ability more than any other game. I must admit that I win nine times out of ten. I'm not willing, however to take a ten percent chance that mankind will be totally eliminated. I like the beaches of Brazil. America is to the west along with the beaches of Brazil. I sense that America will be following us into whatever new orbit we establish. I'm proposing that we leave ten percent of our population in the east so as to hedge our bets. Most of God's favorite people, the Jews, who survived World War III, are now in America. God will want us to take them with us." Everyone cheered, "To the west. To the beaches. To America."

Jessica went on, "The Americans will not believe in my vision. There's no point in trying to turn them from the fusion bomb. We'll just be there; silently, as far below the surface as possible, so as not to disturb them. We'll be able to provide food for them again. They always forget to save back enough food. God is guiding me to help them. I despise their hyper aggression and their excessively competitive nature. Their adults fight with each other at their children's athletic games. The soccer audiences of the world kill each other in frenzied hatred at the end of games. They're mad, but God still loves them. He loves the handfuls of generous meek people who still remain there. Some of them ride around in black buggies drawn by horses. They speak Pennsylvania Dutch and wear black. There are meek and generous nuns who go around feeding people. I remember watching a video that my father made of an Amish man with his horse raring up at the sight of Dr. Exeeto with his video camera. The Amish man kept saying, 'Dumba Shiza! Dumba Shiza!' My great grandfather did much research to find a person who was willing to translate that Dutch phrase. It means literally, 'Dumb Shit! Dumb Shit!' Well my great grandfather knew he had provoked an otherwise peaceful man beyond what he could stand. My great grandfather's last words for the world were, 'Dumb Shits'. He knew that mankind was full of folly. He was only too eager to go and be in heaven. Luckily for us, we won't see the end of life on earth as we know it. That will be for relatives of ours many generations removed. Write in your journals. Explain to your future progeny about how we managed to find meaning and hope under the surface of the earth. By being meek, we inherited the earth. We would have died off a long time ago if we had engaged in warfare down here. Our environment is artificial and unforgiving. If we don't all work together, we have no light, food, air or water. We are a team, bent on survival. Part of our innate makeup is the will to survive. That's why it's so difficult for a person to drown themselves. When they actually start to slip into unconsciousness under the water, their survival instinct takes over and they return to the surface for air.

Some people succeed in drowning, but it's more difficult than it appears.

The surface people are drowning in hatred and competition. We love gold down here. We take pride in how much our families have horded over the years. On the surface they will kill for gold. Some civilizations on the surface would probably like to find us and take our gold. That will never happen. We are too clever for them. They are right though when they say in their ancient texts that the world is a place for survival of the fittest. But fit means meek and clever. Bulging muscles and excess testosterone won't save you from the fiery inferno of the sun. Pushing other people down won't save you. Letting God guide you to the right or to the left is what saves you. Letting God send you to the east or to the west."

They all spent the rest of the evening talking about the new direction for the cellar. The tunnels would be going in new directions. People would be getting good tans on the beaches of Brazil. Humor would be written that wasn't absolutely disgusting.

They drank their tropical drinks and consumed between fifty and sixty pounds of morels that were rolled in white flower and cooked in butter. The tropical fruit drinks were followed by champagne. After everyone was well lubricated, Jessica announced, "Lets all meet at the swimming pool in the park for a late night swim." They all departed and dressed in their swimming suits. In no time they were all in the pool, having more champagne and discussing everything under the sun.

Bill McBride was the tall red haired and freckled leader of excavations. He found Jessica with her husband, his distant relative. He exclaimed to Jessica, "I'll appreciate getting new direction from you. Do I have permission to order ten new tunneling machines from machining and engineering?" Jessica explained, "I want you to have as many as you want. You'll be creating the new world. Don't get to close to the surface and stay in solid rock. I know you know all this, but the earth is going to be going through some intense stress. These new tunnels will need to last for eternity." Bill continued, "I could probably do a better job if I had some mind enhancing drugs like you take!" He chuckled heartily. Jessica gave John a dirty look. "So John's been spilling out my secrets! I hardly think your work requires that kind of heightened awareness. Besides you're already a mechanical genius." He smiled, "I love it when you talk that way. I was only kidding. As much stress as you put up with, it's no wonder you crave a little boost once and awhile. Tell me a little more about what that medicine does for you." Jessica frowned, " Are you going to twist this all around for gossip?" Bill promised, "We're related. I'm not going to smear you. I seriously think I might need some." Jessica explained, "Most days I can't get going in the morning. I can't work up to my highest abilities much of the time and that's a little depressing. I have the intelligence and desire to achieve, but my body won't cooperate. The medicine just gives my body a jump start. I fine tune the buzz with coffee and other drinks with caffeine in them. I think Mountain Dew is responsible for much of my productivity. The ten mg. upper works for about six hours. My doctor said it would only work for four hours. I guess I'm a little more sensitive than most people. I take half of what they prescribe for children. No wonder the little imps are bouncing off the walls!" Bill said, "Well if it's working for you that well, I want to try it." Jessica warned, "It can give you a heart attack if you drink too much caffeine with it or take too big of a dose. You should only start out with about five mg. once a day. If you have any pain in your chest, stop taking it. Are you sure it's worth that to you?" Bill sighed, "Well, I guess you have a point. It's not worth having a heart attack over. I'll just keep doing push ups in the morning to get myself going.

How far west do you want me to go?" Jessica smiled, "I haven't given it much thought. I suppose we shouldn't get too close to our tunnels under the Pacific Ocean. I'd like us to make plenty of large agricultural and recreational areas where the crust is stabile. Stay away from the mountain ranges. They could shift downwards when all the bombing starts. I'd like the beaches on all sides of South America accessible to us. All our people will be spending half their time on those beaches. We want them to be able to spread out. We also want them to be able to retreat to the nearest tunnel when trouble starts. Each tunnel opening needs to be concealed perfectly. We don't want them to become possible access points for invaders." Bill asked, "How soon will I be getting more staff?" Jessica responded, "I'll give you all the people you want. Be sure they all get their vacation time. We aren't trying to beat the clock. It's a high priority though." Bill smiled, "Send me five hundred more people right away then. I have almost enough machine operators, but I need back up people desperately. We need electricians, mechanics, dietary help and more sanitation workers. I'll need to quadruple my staff on rock disposal. That new trench is a long way from the tunneling operations. We'll need more rail cars to haul all the rock debris that far away."

Jessica said soothingly, "Everything'll work out fine. Just stay calm and don't get frustrated if delays come. If there's a bad bottleneck that can't be circumvented, go on vacation. Your children can always finish what you don't get done in your lifetime." Bill laughed, "Yeah, I'm going to try to collect some of those bonuses you're offering for more babies. Linda was prodding me for more children before. Now I guess we'll really cut loose. Another bucket of gold under the bed won't hurt anything!" He called his wife Linda over to talk with them. She was a thin red head with green eyes and a delightfully cute face. She was well developed for being so thin. Bill told Linda, "Jessica just announced today a bonus for babies, so I guess you're going to get all those children you were wanting. They'll have to create a new world under South America when they grow up, so you'll have to raise them up right." Linda smiled and said, "Thanks for the bonuses Jessica. He hates getting up in the middle of the night, but he'll do it for gold. Our son Mark is four and he wants some brothers and sisters to play with."

Jessica said, "Considering Bill's mechanical genius and your uncanny beauty, your children should make a considerable contribution to the cellar. If you give us seven more children, I'll throw in a ruby for each one and a solid gold achievement award. You can have all the help raising them that you want. I don't want you to miss any vacation time!" Linda hugged Jessica and exclaimed, "With that kind of incentive, I think I can have fourteen children. It's not painful giving birth with our modern medical assistance. I don't mind being fat all the time." She took Bill by the hand, "We need to be getting home now, honey. You have a lot of work to do." Bill smiled, "She knows how to get the best out of me!" Linda slapped at his face playfully. "Just let me take the lead. I've read up on this sort of thing!"

After they left, Jessica stated, "Be sure to get your department moving on those new excavating machines. Didn't you say you had some new technology that would speed things up a little?" John explained, "Yes, we can incorporate the new ultrasonic technology to help loosen up the rock before the mechanical teeth attack the rock face. The laser rock vaporizing unit is effective, but we don't have technology in place for moving away the vapors without drawing attention to ourselves. We can't vent them to the surface and we aren't equipped yet to filter the gases out of the air in the tunnels. I think the ultrasonic assisted conventional boring is the best way to go. We can have those machines ready for delivery in two months. I'll put my best people on it."

Jessica whispered in John's ear, "I wouldn't mind some of that baby bonus myself. They hurried back to the suite. With total abandon he let himself give in to her charms. Afterwards, they held perfectly still for a long time. Both of them were tingling. Jessica whispered, "We need to do this as often as possible. You're so good, I can't stand it!" John whispered back, "I know." Jessica slugged him, "You're supposed to say something nice about me, not pat yourself on the back!" John explained, "I wasn't done. I meant that I know you're the best that anyone has ever had." Jessica smiled. They held each other and then fell asleep, right there on the floor.

Chapter Seventeen

A Thousand Years Later

Before Bill McBride died, He managed to tunnel under most of South America. He made all the beaches available to the people in the cellar. The tunnel dwellers were living fulfilled lives and their tunnels remained a secret to the surface dwellers. Bill's descendents all became part of the excavation team. Something about his genetic makeup was powerful, and affected all his progeny the same way. They were all diggers. They built caves more expansive than anything which had been done before. The population of the tunnels and caves had risen to over a billion inhabitants.

The cellar was presided over by one of Jessica's relatives who looked just like she had looked. She also had the gift of seeing the future like her grandmother so many generations before. Her name was Jessica. She also saw the vision of the earth being split in two. She was held in high regard by all who knew her. She led her people after the model of a democratic corporation, but her people were glad to let her make the major decisions. She rarely made mistakes. They trusted her leadership.

The surface civilizations had found Dr. Exeeto's time capsules which he had placed strategically in major uranium deposits. They were made of tuff stainless steel, and weren't destroyed when the mining equipment hit them. The world's leaders had viewed the DVDs created by Dr. Exeeto, in which he tried to convince them of the folly of using atomic bombs. The arms race was too powerful for such logic to dissuade it. Uranium was mined relentlessly. The new technology for the fusion bomb was developed. Through effective spying, the technology became available to all. By using twin atomic explosions to compress a center mass of highly refined weapons grade plutonium, a fusion reaction could be sustained long enough to create an explosion approximately a hundred times more powerful than one atomic bomb alone. No country had tested the bomb. It was being saved as a last resort. It was a final retaliation device.

Jessica had seen a vision, that during the next winter a bombing exchange would happen between the east and west. She had hidden monitors and telescopes all over South America so they would have a better idea of what was going on after they retreated permanently into their cellar.

When the winter came, Jessica ordered all people to retreat from the surface. Their seismometers quickly picked up the vibrations of the first atomic blasts. Then after a temporary cessation of explosions, there were two unbelievable blasts only seconds apart. The fusion bombs had been set off. There was a harsh jolt, and everyone was thrown against the northern walls. Light fixtures broke and glass was flying everywhere. Emergency sensors were signaling that the north and south running tunnels were flooded. All door to those tunnels automatically closed. The doors were of massive stainless steel and had been carefully designed to withstand almost anything. Explosive charges went off automatically and piled rock debris up against the doors sealing them even more effectively.

The earth had been split in two. From the surface telescopes, Jessica watched as half of the earth toppled gradually towards the sun. The eastern and western halves were slowly rotating from north to south. The other half of earth could be seen only during half of the day. The part of earth carrying Eurasia was the half moving towards the sun. Each day it looked a little smaller from Jessica's point of view. Jessica's half of the world was moving away from the sun towards outer space. It could be seen that the solid inner core of the earth was still attached to Eurasia. Jessica's section of earth was only the outer crust. Jessica felt much lighter. Two thirds of the earth's mass had left her, for parts unknown. She could see smoke rising up from America, but she couldn't see the land. There was too much curvature to the earth's surface. Earth was now on an elliptical orbit around the sun, which lent itself to many possibilities. Jessica spent the next month traveling throughout the cellar, encouraging the occupants and letting them know that everything would be fine.

There had been some damage, but the tunnels and caves had held up well. Only a few thousand people were hospitalized and there were surprisingly few fatalities. Jessica assigned a team of scientists to monitor their progress through space. Wind speed on the surface hadn't changed much. Jessica's scientists went to the surface dressed in radiation proof suits. Each man who formerly weighed two hundred pounds, now weighed seventy pounds. They bounded about the surface, jumping fifteen feet at a time, with great ease. With powerful telescopes they looked out in all directions.

The telescopes radioed images back to the new headquarters under the middle of Brazil. The headquarters had been moved there many years ago in anticipation of the splitting of earth. The rapidly decaying orbit of the eastern half of earth could be followed for part of each month. After a couple years, that part of earth was pulled into the sun. As it approached the sun, it gave off a large plume of steam. The remaining earth hit the sun hard and splattered fire in long streams in all directions. In a couple months it could only be detected as a fiery blob becoming smaller all the time as it spread out over the surface of the sun. The sun gave off slightly more heat because of the new source of fuel.

Jessica was worried that their new orbit would take them into the gravitational pull of a planet large enough to shatter them with the impact of their meeting. She prayed fervently for God to guide them and to have mercy upon them. They were not the ones who had destroyed the planet. They were humble tunnel dwellers.

God heard her prayers and answered her with a glow of white light that stunned her for several days. While in the middle of the white light, she was told they would be going to mars. When she came back to normal, she told her people to prepare for a long voyage. God had promised her they would land on mars.

It took eighty years for Jessica's portion of earth to reach mars. Jessica had been blessed by God with unusual youthfulness, and at one hundred and ten years of age, she could still see mars coming close to them. Earth caught up slowly with Mars. After the jolt of connecting with mars, they were relieved to be forced into a more stable orbit. Without the solid core of the earth, their mass had not altered the orbit of mars considerably. Now that they were part of mars, Jessica was happy. She named the new hybrid planet mirth. She laughed as she named it. It was a happy time for her. She passed on her authority to her second oldest daughter, who had the strongest gift of seeing. In a few more years, she passed away with a smile on her face. She had lived to see the evil half of earth melted away. She only hoped that America had survived the explosions of the final bombs.

Chapter Eighteen

Search for Survivors

Jessica's most seeing daughter was also named Jessica. This second daughter knew there were survivors in America. She focused her tunneling teams on building a tunnel to Iron Mountain. In two years time she reached her destination. Jessica's team broke through into some tunnels that were only five miles from Iron Mountain. Radio contact was made and a meeting was set up. Jessica spoke to the President of the United States. She explained that she would provide unlimited food. As much as they wanted. In return, she would like for them to jettison all radioactive materials into deep space as soon as they had the capability. President Miller laughed and complied readily saying, "We certainly don't need any more atomic explosions. Why are you so friendly to us after all these years? We weren't sure you even still existed." Jessica explained, "We have the same God and he loves us all. I think you've learned your lesson about bombs. If they're there, someone will use them. It's Murphy's law. Don't make any bombs. President Miller laughed some more and then replied, "Can we still play football?" Jessica replied, "Just don't broadcast it down here. I don't want my people seeing such barbarianism. Scrabble is much less damaging to your body and it develops the mind." They chatted for hours and agreed to have talks every week.

The End

Mirth

Sequel to Dr. Exeeto

Mirth

Cover art by Linda Kimpel

1st edition

Xlibris Corporation Publishing

Printed 2007 In the United States of America

CONTENTS

Acknowledgments

I give my heartiest thanks to the many patient teachers who put up with my rough edges as they ardently strove to make me more than I was. I thank my wife, who provided a home climate conducive to creative activities. Thanks, most eagerly goes, to those who show an interest in my books. You, my readers, are those whom I write for. I constantly covet your attention. Undying gratitude goes to my father, for his generous financial assistance, which made it possible for me to continue with my writing.

Chapter One

Mirth Begins

Here is chronicled the continuation of life on the new planet of Mirth. Mirth was created when half of earth landed gently on Mars. To discover how earth was split in half, one would need to read the immediate predecessor to this book entitled *Dr. Exeeto*. For the time being, let me indicate only that circumstances on earth took a turn for the worse, and earth's better half found itself on Mars.

Most people survived the sudden change in orbit and the landing on Mars. Dr. Exeeto had prepared his people to expect terrible explosions. The events were more traumatic to the surface people. Only a small remnant of them survived. Dr. Exeeto was a biological weapons scientist who initiated the plan to start a separate culture of people almost totally isolated from the world on the surface. They all lived in tunnels and caves which were fitted out with all the trappings of an advanced civilization. There were libraries, parks, recreation areas and restaurants, all miles below the floors of the oceans. Toward the end of earth's time as a whole planet, Dr. Exeeto's great grand daughter, many times removed, positioned her headquarters and most of her people under Brazil. That grand daughter's name was Jessica.

When earth landed on Mars, Jessica immediately began to have her people tunnel towards the United States of

America. She was a psychic Christian who felt it was her duty to help the Christian President of the United States. She had only conversed with him on one occasion. Earth had become engulfed in atomic warfare, and Jessica created a food growing station under Panama to give to America. She knew the Americans never planned adequately for hard times. Food was in short supply when at the last minute human compassion drove authorities to let too many people into Iron Mountain. Dr. Exeeto had developed ways of producing incredible amounts of food in his underground caves. Jessica used that knowledge to help her provide for her unseen friends in America.

Now, as her tunnelers worked feverishly to find the American's survival cave, Iron Mountain, Jessica relaxed in her plush steam sauna as she thought about her first meeting with President John Miller, of the United States. Jessica was thirty-five years old, but had a slightly younger looking face. Her long red hair flowed gently over her shoulders as she lounged in a reclining chair, eating fried morels and drinking mango juice. Her electrifying green eyes flashed with excitement as she contemplated meeting the most powerful man of the surface culture. Jessica had kept the Exeeto name, to honor her grandfather. She was quite proud of what he had accomplished in his life. Her slender body was wrapped in an over sized white terry cloth towel. The intelligent wisdom which her face always emanated, was intimidating to many men, but she knew the President would feel comfortable with her. She didn't know much about him. Her people didn't do much spying on the surface people. They had their own world to worry about.

Jessica thought, *It will be nice to have some one to help me decide how best to develop this new planet.* She spent her first months on Mirth, expanding the food growing caves. She made plans for tunneling down into Mars, and then expanding a network of clear topped tunnels over the surface of Mars, which would allow viewing of the stars. After many more months of anxious waiting for Iron Mountain to be reached, the day finally came. She was put into radio contact with President Miller. The President began, "It's good to hear from you Miss Exeeto. Your people tell me you have plenty of food." Jessica responded, "You may call me Jessica. I indeed have food enough for everyone. There is one requirement which I have, Mr. President." The President said, "Please, Jessica, you may call me John." Jessica continued, "I'd like you to promise to jettison all plutonium into deep space as soon as possible. We don't need any more atomic wars." John laughed, "I don't think we'll need plutonium here. I'll gladly comply. Is there anything else I can do for you?" Jessica answered, "Please promise not to broadcast football down here. We follow more peaceful pursuits." John asked, "What do you do down there?" Jessica replied, "We play Scrabble. We like steam saunas, eating fried morels, sun bathing and having fruit drinks." John asked, "When can I come for a visit?" Jessica responded, "I insist that you come visit me immediately. I guarantee your safety and promise to give you royal treatment." John replied, "I'm humbled by your generosity. I don't need royal treatment. The things you just described sound royal enough for me. I love fried morels. The steam sauna sounds good too. Are you married?" Jessica exclaimed, "John, you aren't coming on to me, are you?" John soothed her, "By no means. I only wondered if it might be more relaxing to discuss the future in a relaxing sauna. You can trust me to be a perfect gentleman." Jessica sighed, "Thank goodness. Now that I know you can control yourself, I'll confess I'm single and looking forward to meeting you."

John stated, "Meeting someone of your stature and confidence will truly be a pleasure. How long do you think it will take me to travel to your headquarters?" Jessica responded, "We have rail systems which hurl the comfortable cars at over a thousand miles per hour. You should arrive here in less than ten hours." John exclaimed, "That is absolutely amazing. Your civilization has done well for itself! I'll leave as soon as I can get my things together. I'm looking forward to that sauna of yours." Jessica warned, "Remember, I'm not promising physical intimacy, but I hope we can work closely together and feel at home with each other." John replied, "Don't worry even a small amount. As I said before, I'm a perfect gentleman. I love steam, because my sinuses are always plugged from polluted air." Jessica said, "You'll love it here. Our air filtration systems are as advanced as our rail systems. I'll have our best recreation facility prepare for your arrival. We love to simulate the tropics down here. We even have convincing sunshine." John said, "It's eight o'clock in the morning here. If I leave at ten, I should arrive at eight in the evening." Jessica responded, "Yes, I'll meet you at the train station. This is good-by for now. May you have a pleasant journey."

The President had his assistants pack his luggage while he went to the vault. The door of the vault was two feet thick and made of polished stainless steel. The inside of the vault was brightly lit with white fluorescent lighting. He looked thoughtfully over its contents. There were priceless works of art. Renaissance paintings were on the walls and gold sculptures were on pedestals. He lifted down a painting entitled *Lady with Ermine.* It was done by Leonardo da Vinci around 1483. The artist was the President's favorite. He placed it in a protective molded plastic case. Next he picked out a golden Egyptian artifact. It was a statue of Horus, the hawk like god. Horus protected the Pharaoh. John loved the Egyptian culture and the way they advanced humanity further into scientific knowledge by applying themselves to learning. He carefully wrapped the golden sculpture in bubble wrap and placed it in his carry on bag.

When he returned to his quarters, the luggage was packed. He took some body guards with him to carry the luggage and make sure the tunnel people were truly friendly. They sped along the tunnel from Iron Mountain to where Jessica's people had intersected with it, on an electric cart. The rubble from the penetration into the tunnel had been removed, but not all the lighting fixtures had been installed yet. The tunnel was somewhat poorly lit at this intersection. The guards used their flashlights as they led their leader into the new tunnel. Track had been fully laid up to the intersection. Jessica's train was waiting for them, just a few yards down the track. The President and four body guards entered Jessica's train and headed for Brazil.

The train was well lit and fitted with some couches and reclining chairs. There was a large screen television and a wet bar. The side panels and ceiling were done in a shiny scarlet red and there were wide oak moldings throughout. The floor was black marble, which was highly polished.

They were given plenty of fruit drinks on the train and there were full course meals fit for a king. John was in his early fifties and was six foot two inches tall. He sported a salt and pepper moustache which was trimmed to military specifications. His hair was cut short and his eye brows were bushy. His arms looked quite muscular as was the rest of his body. John's clever looking brown eyes were currently reading the latest Iron Mountain newspaper. He loved to read, and always kept some British classics with him. Among them were Wordsworth, Keats and T. S. Elliot. He also liked Andrew Marvel. The President was dressed in a dark charcoal gray suit with a black tie. His body guards were all dressed in black.

It seemed like time passed rapidly. They had just finished their second meal on the train, when it pulled into the station at Brazil. Jessica was there waiting for him to disembark. The President was led off the train by his body guards. They were put at ease by the appearance of Jessica and the absence of armed guards. The President walked over to Jessica and she offered her hand, which he kissed gently and said, "This is a deep pleasure such as I have never experienced before." Jessica responded, "It's wonderful to have you here. I hope your trip was pleasant." John responded, "I loved the fruit drinks and the fried morels. The air in the train wasn't too bad, but I am looking forward to your sauna." Jessica laughed, "I knew you'd say that! We'll be there in a few minutes." John offered her his arm, and they entered the monorail car which took them to Jessica's quarters. The Presidential body guards followed in the next car.

Once inside her residence, Jessica stated, "Your body guards can stay in the suite across the hall. It's empty. You actually don't need any guarding here, but I suppose you needed someone to help with the luggage." John laughed, "You're right. I wasn't going to carry all those bags by myself."

The guards took their cue and went into the suite across from Jessica's. John and Jessica entered her suite. The suite was quite spacious and well lit. The walls were white and the floor was an amazing mosaic of semi-precious stones. Each wall had large murals which portrayed beach scenes and scenes of woodlands and meadows. The furniture was made of oak, and styled in Victorian fashion. There were elegant antique hutches and desks. This living room type of area was fifty feet long and thirty feet wide. There were many doors, which led to other rooms.

Jessica asked, "Would you prefer to talk over coffee, or should we indulge in the sauna?" John said, "My sinuses are truly plugged up. The sauna would be fine, if that's the custom in your country." Jessica laughed, "It's not actually a custom. The sauna is where I do my best thinking and meditating. We'll feel more relaxed there." She took John to her large spare bedroom. "You can hang up your clothes here. There's an oversize bath towel over on the bed. You can dress for the sauna in that." John couldn't help looking a little surprised, "Is that what we'll both be wearing?" Jessica laughed, "Of course! There's no point of being in a steam sauna if the steam can't get to your body, is there?" John laughed too, "I know you're right. My country is so stuffy compared to yours. We're more formal. I like this though. Can you show me where the sauna is? I don't want to get lost walking around in just a bath towel."

Jessica led him to the sauna and then went to her own bed room. She got dressed in the bath towel and met John in the sauna. She had turned it on before she left to pick him up at the station. It was densely filled with hot steam. The sauna was spacious and had a patio table and chairs inside. There were also lawn chairs. Jessica sat at the table and waited for John to sit down. He chose a chair next to her. One of the walls was covered with a water proof mural of a forest. In the thick steam and low lighting, it was easy to imagine that one actually was in a steamy forest.

There were fruit drinks on the table, and Jessica was sipping at one of them. John asked, "Where should we start?" Jessica smiled and said, "I'd like to know whether you and your people can resist trying to take over down here. I think we've proven we are quite independent and resourceful. I hope your country doesn't feel this is an emergency situation and you have to be in charge." John frowned, "You've got me all wrong. I respect what you've done here below the surface. You saved us a lot of suffering with the extra food you sent us. I only want to cooperate. You are in no danger of losing any power to me. We'll respect your customs and not try to change you." Jessica smiled, "Well, I'm glad we agree on that."

John stated, "Oh, I forgot. I brought you a few presents. The painting can't come in here, but let me go get the sculpture I brought you. He left and returned shortly carrying the sculpture of the god Horus. Jessica exclaimed, "I love gold and ancient art. This is priceless. How generous of you! She struggled to hold onto her towel as she gave him a hug and a kiss. To her surprise he kissed her longer than she thought he would, and she liked it. His moustache tickled her in a delightful way. She sat the sculpture on the table. John pulled a bottle of wine and some glasses from his carry on bag. He said, "This gift isn't as expensive, but it's equally pleasurable. It's Costa de Sol, a twenty year old Portuguese wine which I'm sure you'll like. It's slightly dry and full bodied." Jessica stated, "I'm sure it will meet with my approval. The dry wines are the best, in my opinion. Do you need a cork screw?" John responded, "I have one in my case here." He opened the wine and they each sipped it slowly as they discussed affairs of state.

John asked, "Where do you think we should start in developing our new planet?" Jessica thought for a moment and then responded, "I think we need to concentrate our efforts on creating acceptable atmosphere for the planet. To do that, we'll need to cover the planet with trees. They will create the oxygen we need. We can create the carbon dioxide the trees need with our steel production work. The steel can be used to build surface tunnels which will allow our people to enjoy seeing the stars. These tunnels will form a matrix over the planet until the proper atmosphere can be created. We lost half of our atmosphere when earth split. The remaining atmosphere spread out over Mars and is now too thin to be safe. Wind will cause areas that are dangerously low on oxygen. I'd like to see entertainment centers every fifty miles. We emphasize entertainment here. People who are laughing are less likely to become sick or malcontented." John said, "I can see you've been giving this plenty of thought. You're a brainy woman. I like that." Jessica laughed, "I was hoping you'd like it."

Her hand dropped gently onto his knee as they sipped the wine. Jessica asked, "Would you feel my back for me. Does it feel dry?" John dutifully felt her back. "It's not too bad, but it could use a little lotion." Jessica said, "I'll lie on one of these lawn chairs and you can put some lotion on my back. You don't mind do you?" John exclaimed, "Not at all! I'm really starting to like you. I want you to be comfortable." Jessica found a tube of lotion and handed it to John. He applied lotion and expertly massaged her back while she expounded for hours on her hopes and dreams for the new planet. She liked the fact that John was such a good listener. He was good at massaging her too. She wanted him to go on forever. She felt her attraction to him growing, the more time they spent together.

Finally she insisted that he let her lotion his back. She couldn't help but laugh at how hairy his back was. John asked, "What's that laughter for?" Jessica said, "I just can't get over how hairy you are. I like it, but it usually means a man has too much testosterone. I'm surprised you aren't out of control and trying to feel me up!" John explained, "In my younger days, you might have been right. I've learned to control myself with will power." Jessica asked, "Yes, but do you have the desire to resist?" John explained, "As leader of my people, I need to be pure. I don't do anything that would disappoint my followers." Jessica responded, "That sounds quite noble. It's a little hard to believe, but it certainly is noble." John stated, "Don't get me wrong, I'm not a robot. My body tingles all over when your hands are massaging my back. It makes me feel close to you." Jessica exclaimed, "That's good! I want us to be close. It's good you're in control. I love being with a man who isn't intimidated by me. Our being together in this steam room and sharing our dreams, is thrilling. I hope we can get together often. How long can you stay?" John explained, "My people are well trained. They can get along well while I'm away. I'll be in radio contact with them.

I shouldn't stay longer than a couple weeks though." Jessica smiled, "Since you're so pure, we can sleep in the same bed. I've been longing for someone nice like you to cuddle with." John laughed, "You certainly aren't shy. I'd like that too, but not all night. I have to sleep alone. When I'm asleep, I don't have total control over my body. I'm sure I'd end up doing the wrong thing." Jessica laughed, "In your sleep? We could keep a cold glass of water by the bed. I could wake you up."

John explained, "It's better not to court disaster." I'm certainly happy that you find me attractive. I thought I might be a little too old for you." Jessica exclaimed, "A seasoned wine is the finest." John took one of her hands in his, "Since we're being so frank, did you ever think we might want to form a marriage alliance to cement our two countries together?" Jessica asked, "Is that a proposal?" John whispered gently in her ear. If we marry, we can sleep all night together. Will you marry me?" Jessica said, "My people know I need a man. They won't be shocked by the sudden nature of this marriage. I'm in charge. I can do what I want to do. You have swept me off my feet. I love the way you make me feel. I know I should play hard to get and wait a few months to decide, but I want you with me now. I accept. Can I have our chaplain perform the service tomorrow?" John stated, "The sooner the better. We can have our honeymoon right here in your suite." Jessica frowned, "No I want us to sleep here tonight, but let's go to one of my tropical resorts. We can sun bath and you can massage my back some more. I'll never get enough of that." John acquiesced, "I want you to be happy. More back rubs sounds good to me. Are we going to mix business with pleasure? I want to hear more on your ideas for developing the planet." Jessica answered, "Don't worry. I can't stop with these ideas. I'm obsessed with them." John asked, "Where will we have the wedding service?" Jessica explained, "I don't want us to tie up lots of time with the wedding. Let's have the service right here. I can have a camera crew here tomorrow, and the chaplain is a close friend. He'll understand. We have pressing business to attend to. I'll make all the arrangements right away.

Chapter Two

The Leaders Unite

John stated, "It's getting late, I'd better go sleep in the suite across the hall." Jessica pouted, "I want you here with me." John explained, "I told you I can't control what I do in bed with a woman when I'm asleep." Jessica whispered softly to him, "I think I know a little about controlling a man's urges. Just leave everything to me. I know how to stay a virgin, at least technically." She laughed and then kissed John passionately on the mouth. Then she said, "Let me make a few calls. We can have the marriage at noon and be at our honeymoon resort by supper time." "That sounds good to me. You take care of the phone calls while I open a bottle of champagne. We need to celebrate."

After all the arrangements were made, Jessica and John shared champagne in the shower together. They kissed for almost an hour in the steamy shower. After drying each other off, they climbed into Jessica's spacious bed. After kissing for another hour and making small talk, they pulled up the covers and tried to sleep. John had his arm around Jessica. He was too excited to sleep, and Jessica could feel it and did what she could to help him relax. She did everything she could think of for him, but she retained her virginity. John knew she was going to make his life an exceedingly happy one, full of surprises.

Finally they were sated with romance and fell asleep in each other's arms.

Early in the morning they were up eating breakfast and preparing for the wedding. Each of them had a copy of the vows they were memorizing. Jessica was trying on her wedding dress. John asked, "How do you happen to have a wedding gown ready to wear?" Jessica answered, "Don't forget about me being psychic. I had a feeling I'd soon be hearing wedding bells. Besides this was my mother's dress. I fits me perfectly." John hit his forehead dramatically, "Amazing. Simply amazing. Do you have any stock tips for me?" Jessica laughed, "We don't have stocks here. Everything is socialized. People keep buckets full of gold under their beds just for status symbols. People don't need the money. Everything is provided by our government. We're a democracy, but we take care of everyone's needs. There are no poor people here." John laughed, "That doesn't sound half bad, but I don't think my people are ready for that. They're programmed to be acquisitive. Each one tries to get a better standard of living than the other guy. That's what makes our economy tick. People always want a nicer car or a swimming pool. I can't ask my people who have acquired great wealth, to give it up for socialism."

Jessica stated, "I'm perfectly happy if we maintain separate systems. Just don't let any segment of your society become too poor. I don't want to find myself feeling sorry for them. Can you promise me you'll take care of the poor?" John explained, "We have homeless shelters and feeding programs. We won't let anyone starve. Besides, all our poor are dead now. I regret it, but there wasn't room for everyone in Iron Mountain. All my people will be gainfully employed for hundreds of years, developing this planet.

Jessica rebutted, "Well, that's a convenient solution to the problem of an imperfect political system. The poor are always left behind. Dr. Exeeto had the same problem, but he assuaged his conscience a little by recruiting ten thousand extremely poor people to work for him in our tunnels and food growing caves. At least he showed some concern for the poor!" John defended himself, "Jessica please cut me some slack. The atomic war came on so quickly, there was no time to gather up some poor people. We took in twice our capacity of people the way it was." Jessica said, "You're making a logical defense for yourself, and it's believable for the most part, but what do you really believe about poor people?"

John scratched his head, "I think they usually have lesser mental capacity and they lack ambition. Some of them are mentally ill." Jessica laughed, "Well, at least you're honest. I admire that. We are starting to find that many of our lowly agricultural workers and tunnelers have a great capacity for higher learning. They have learned to operate the food growing and tunneling operations with little outside supervision. They are allowed to promote leaders from within their ranks. We offer free computer generated course work to all our people, free of charge."

John explained, "Our society is now partially socialist in nature. We offer health care to all. I'll admit that during much of our history only the rich could afford good health care. People who couldn't afford the medical treatment were sometimes given free treatment if they were utterly poor, but people with limited means were turned over to debt collectors and such people were launched into a pauper's state by the debt collectors who were aided by the courts. I regret that past. It seems primitive as I look back on it. We still utilize credit cards which get some of our people into too much debt. They usually remain in deep debt for the rest of their lives. Our system isn't perfect. How do you deal with people wanting more than their budgets will allow?"

Jessica said, "We have no credit cards. People get special rewards of gold or rubies for excellent work.

Everyone is given all the food they need. We don't have many cars. I've heard that the love of new cars often drove the surface people to dive deeply into debt. How could your leadership allow people to lend money and charge high rates of interest? Doesn't the Bible forbid the charging of interest? Aren't debts supposed to be forgiven every seven years? John explained, "There is God's ideal way for things to be and there is the less than idea way. We never learned to be ideal."

Jessica went on, "Our way isn't ideal either. We reward our top scientists with much more gold than we give the agricultural workers. I think all types of work should be rewarded equally if the worker is showing industriousness. Of course the gold is only a status symbol with us. There is nothing in our society to spend it on. Still, I wish we could make everything equal. People only naturally become envious when they hear about others getting more for their work. Envy is a sin, but almost every human gets envious in one way or another. We have particular trouble with our young men being envious of their brothers. We had to insist that all inheritance be divided equally amongst all brothers and sisters. That helped end many of the family squabbles that were bringing unrest to our society. In the Bible, often the oldest son would receive the bulk of the inheritance. The wayward prodigal son received his inheritance though. I'll never understand why God favored Abel's animal sacrifices and shunned Cain's sacrifices of vegetables. I guess God's like most humans in that way. We all hate to eat our vegetables." God favored Abel, but not because he was the oldest. It was because God liked animal sacrifices."

John exclaimed, "You certainly know your Bible!" Jessica explained, "I'm the top religious leader for my people. I'm always reading my Bible." John asked, "Were the early Christians really Communistic?" Jessica laughed, "They held all things in common, but they weren't like any communist nation you've ever heard of. They were terribly concerned with the poor. Wealthy converts sold extra fields and the money was used to help poor people, widows and orphans. They weren't Marxist. Marx hadn't been born yet. They weren't concerned about overthrowing the rich and powerful ruling class. They wanted to do like Jesus had done. He said to 'give unto Ceasar what is Ceasar's. Jesus healed the sick, fed people and converted people to Christianity by revealing that he was the Messiah."

John stated, "Some of my people are so rich, they'll never consent to being part of a socialized system. We'll have to stay separate financially and politically. If I tried to make my people share all things in common, there'd be a civil war. I don't need that kind of trouble. Jesus said, 'You will have the poor with you always.' Maybe we're just making sure his words are true." Jessica laughed, "I see you know your Bible too. We'll have many a wonderful evening debating the Bible." John said, "Yes, and worshipping God as well. It was miraculous the way he guided us into a safe orbit with Mars." Jessica replied, "Yes, we'll always pray together. We'll make many prayers giving thanks."

The phone rang and Jessica picked it up. "Yes Stan. We'd like the service to be here at my suite with only immediate family members present and of course the camera crew to broadcast the wedding. Seven this evening will be fine. If you get here at five, we'll have supper together and run through the order of the service. I'll see you then, Pastor.

Next Jessica called the news media and asked that everyone be encouraged to watch the wedding on the evening television broadcast. John sent a message to his people encouraging them to watch the wedding which would be sent over the new cable, Jessica's engineers had been working on for the last few months. He also explained how he came to be marrying Jessica. To his press secretary he stated, "After meeting and getting to know Jessica Exeeto, it became apparent to me that she was just the person I've been looking for, to marry. Our marriage will help cement the new bond of cooperation between our two countries. Jessica is the religious, as well as political leader of her people. She believes in the Bible, just as we do. Our two countries should have no trouble working together in harmony. I will be returning to the states every week to conduct the affairs of state. Jessica and I will be working together to set goals for the development of our new planet. All input will be appreciated. Thank you."

John and Jessica spent the rest of the afternoon touring her central cave, which was named Xanadu. It was four hundred feet high, a thousand feet wide and five miles long. Jessica explained, "This is just for the administrative, educational and information networks. The maintenance, food growing and recreation areas have separate caves which we can see later." John asked, "How is such a wide ceiling supported?" Jessica explained, "Our predecessors selected cave locations carefully so the rock would be solid enough. Where necessary they reinforced with steel girders."

They visited the giant library and an art museum. Each of them told the other a little about their favorite books and works of art. They had to hurry though, because it was getting close to five o'clock. The pastor would be arriving soon. They took the monorail back to Jessica's suite and waited for the caterer. Jessica had called them before they left. At a quarter till five, the caterer arrived with generous portions of T-bone steak and fried morels. There were freshly made dinner rolls and broccoli with melted cheese. A few minutes later Pastor Stan arrived. He said a blessing for the food and they ate a leisurely meal together. At six, the caterer came and took away the dishes. Jessica's family arrived just after she and John had practiced saying their vows. John and Jessica got dressed in their wedding outfits while the camera crew set up.

When John came out, he was asked to make a statement for the television audience. He consented. "I came to this land under Brazil, to thank Jessica for her country's assistance to America. When I saw how beautiful, graceful and intelligent she was, I couldn't help but want to be with her always. Jessica knows me to be a good Christian and an honest man. She also knows that I have pledged to work with her for the benefit of both our countries. I'll be spending two days each week in America, and the rest of the time I'll be here with Jessica. I hope everyone will be as happy as we are, that we found each other. We are rushing things a bit, but there is much we have to work on together and a long drawn out courtship would only slow down our work together. We fell in love at first sight, you might say. We are exceedingly confident we are making the right decision." Jessica spoke next. "I have never been so sure of what I'm doing. Not only am I seeking my own happiness, I long to see us allied with America more closely. Join us now as we perform our wedding ceremony."

The ceremony went well, and the couple remembered their vows. After they exchanged rings, Jessica's family congratulated them and Pastor Stan McConnell gave a short sermon in which he wished the couple well and exhorted them to seek the guidance of God in all their endeavors. Jessica's mom and dad and older sister stayed for an hour and got to know John. Then they left with the pastor and camera crew. Jessica and John were alone finally. It was nine in the evening and Jessica suggested the hot tub. They undressed each other and climbed into the steamy hot tub which was at the far end of the steam sauna. Jessica stated, "I made our reservations for the best tropical resort we have. It's only twenty miles from here. If you like, we can leave first thing in the morning." John acquiesced, "Whatever you say dear, as long as I get what I want tonight." Jessica giggled and snuggled up against him. "And what might that be?" "I'll show you in due time." They grew quiet and looked into each other's eyes. They drew slowly closer to each other. With gentle kisses they teased each other till they finally gave way to things more intensely passionate.

In the morning they packed their clothes and took the next train to the tropical recreation center. The two love birds had taken a leisurely breakfast in Jessica's suite. Jessica cooked the omelets, on that first breakfast together as man and wife. She told John, "You'd better look in your coffee cup before you drink. I wouldn't want you to choke!" John looked quizzically into his cup. "What are these red things in my cup?" Jessica smiled, "You came bearing gifts for me, the gold statue, the painting and the wine. Those red things are rubies. They are our most precious stones, valued even more highly than diamonds. Dr. Exeeto collected them and brought them to the tunnels. He called the underground complex 'The Cave'. He loved their warm red glow when exposed to light. We usually present one to a person who has made a great accomplishment. I'm giving you ten as a token of my immense love for you. Don't lose them. They are great status symbols in our culture. Few people have even touched one.

Once every year, those who possess them gather at the leader's suite to view each other's rubies under ultraviolet light. That lighting gives the rubies a supernatural glow which we all find inspiring. Little is said at the meeting. The viewing of the rubies is more like a group meditation session than anything else. After an hour of viewing, we all leave quietly and whisper gentle good-bys." John asked, "Is there a name for the group?" Jessica replied, "No. It's a cultural event for acknowledging accomplishment. Everyone already knows who has accomplished what. Our newspapers constantly remind our community of the fine accomplishments of our people. The night of the rubies is more to admire the beauty of the ruby and its light. Gold has a lesser but similar function here. Families hold onto it and pass it on from one generation to the next."

Jessica passed John a cup full of coffee. She asked, "Would you like cream or sugar?" John quipped, "I had enough sweetness last night. You're sweeter than sugar." He laughed. Jessica left his coffee black and poured herself a generous portion of cream. John asked, "Why don't you just have a glass of milk instead?" Jessica laughed, "I have a sensitive stomach. I like coffee, but it makes my stomach acidic." She finished cooking the omelets and they each prayed a silent prayer over the food.

Jessica asked, "How much is that da Vince painting worth? I hate to ask, but I'm dying to know." John laughed, "That's perfectly understandable. It's my favorite painting in the whole world. It's priceless. Eleven hundred years ago, our history books say it was valued at around a million dollars. Things have been so chaotic since then, that it would be difficult to arrive at a price that would be very meaningful. We at Iron Mountain have gone back to the gold standard. Paper money isn't used anymore. I suppose the painting is worth approximately enough gold to fill a large bath tub." Jessica sighed, "Possibly I should have given you more rubies. I don't want to lessen the value of the rubies other people have. I hope you understand." John stated, "Don't be ridiculous. I love the present. I never look a gift horse in the mouth." Jessica looked puzzled. John explained, "It's an ancient saying of ours. It's hundreds of years old. It dates back to the times when horses were used more often, for transportation. They were suitable for gifts. It was considered in poor taste to complain about the quality of a free horse." Jessica laughed, "You certainly know your history. I admire history myself. I'm constantly reading about Dr. Exeeto and his early work, setting up our society. He wanted everyone to be happy. He wanted our leaders to see that everyone's needs were provided for. He knew that with little use of money, crime would be nearly eliminated. To this day, we have little crime. The biggest problem is getting the gold rewards to the people who deserve them. I should deliver it all in person, but it would take up all my time."

John munched his omelet and looked thoughtful. "Have you thought of using credit cards and backing the credit lines with gold?" Jessica answered, "That's a good idea, but it opens doors to credit card fraud which I'd rather not deal with. All my people keep their gold in their homes. Since there is nothing to spend it on, there are few attempts to steal the gold. We must keep our economies separate. Your people might want to barter for my people's gold. I wouldn't like to see the gold leave my country." John replied, "I understand. It would upset the way you do business down here. It would create a black market for gold and the things gold can buy." Jessica responded, "Yes, we don't want our people taking addicting mind altering substances which your people might bring with them. I've read in the ancient history books about the problems opiates caused in the old world above ground. Here we have perfected our medications so they aren't addictive. Even I, at times, use a mind enhancing substance to elevate creative activity and I.Q." John stated, "I could use some of that. What's it called?" Jessica answered, "I won't mention it. I don't want other people asking for it. We refined it and lessened the dosage so it doesn't cause grinding of the teeth any more. It still can cause edginess and a double dose could cause a heart attack. I don't want you using it unless you really have a difficult problem you're faced with." John quipped, "Yes, mother. I'll be careful." They both laughed.

Jessica went on. It doesn't help a bit with sexual performance. It leaves you a little worn out when it wears off." John said, "Thanks for the warning. You certainly know quite a bit about the mind and its performance. Have you ever used mind altering drugs like marijuana?" Jessica explained, "I stay away from anything but the mild mind stimulant I was talking about before. From my conversations with patients on marijuana, I would say that the euphoric affects of the drug would tend to make a person's judgment suspect. We feed cookies laced with marijuana to our elderly to treat depression and pain. It also cures glaucoma." John exclaimed, "How do you know so much about medicine?" Jessica said, "I was trained as a doctor before I moved into my leadership role. I still serve as a consultant to our hospitals on diagnostic matters. We have a few hours before our train leaves for the Bahamas. That's what we call our most desirable tropical resort, the Bahamas. Why don't we go visit the nearest elderly care facility and you can see for yourself how nice growing old is, here." John replied, "I'd like that. My people all dread growing old. It would help me cheer up about my own advancing age."

Jessica sent their bags ahead to the train station and asked that they be guarded carefully. She didn't want anything misplaced. They took an electric tram to the nearest elderly facility. As they entered, John noticed there was no foul smell. He said, "I can tell already that quality care is being given." Jessica explained, "With our health system, operating money is not a problem. Each elderly client receives a full time helper who checks on them every fifteen minutes. State of the art sensors alert the personal health worker to each and every problem as it arises. Let's visit Martha Miller. She's a long time favorite of mine. I used to do rounds at this facility. Here's her room." Jessica knocked on the door and waited for a response. A soft voice called for them. "Come in." They stepped inside the spacious room and stood beside Martha's bed. She was watching cable television with live coverage of a casino comedian she liked. Martha said, "I hope you can watch for a little while. This guy is good. He reminds me of Jack Benny. I love watching those old Jack Benny DVDs." Jessica said, "Oh, I like him too. We'll be glad to watch for awhile. This is my new husband, John Miller." Martha stated, "Glad to meet you, John. You picked a wonderful girl here. Jessica really cares about people. She's been coming to see me for fifteen years. She never misses a week. Can I offer either of you a cookie and milk?" John forgot about the cookies and eagerly accepted, "I'd be glad for a cookie. Where's the milk?" Martha explained, "The milk's in the fridge at the foot of the bed. Hurry or you'll miss this comedian. He's getting funnier every minute." John grabbed a chocolate milk and then a cookie. He had already swallowed a bite of cookie when he remembered what Jessica had said about them. He looked over to where she was sitting next to him and raised his eye brows questioningly. Jessica subtly nodded her head. John carefully dropped the cookie behind him on the floor. They watched the television with Martha quietly. The comedian was talking about being tight with money. He said, "My father gave me a gold coin for my tenth birthday. I asked him for an advance on the next year." Martha laughed and laughed. She couldn't stop laughing. She said, "I can't imagine a culture where people were so greedy for more money. Here everything's provided for you. This Joe Bucks comedian, had to study the old history books to come up with this sort of stuff. He's actually a historian. A historian of greed." Joe went on, "In the old days, inheritance wasn't divided equally like it is now. The bulk of the estate went to the oldest son. In some cases the estate went to the son who sucked up the most to his father. I knew enough about the system that my jealous brothers called me Hoover, because I sucked up so much. I really wanted that money." Martha laughed loudly and ate more cookies.

John looked over at Jessica and whispered, "Isn't she going to get an overdose?" Jessica smiled and whispered back, "The first morning cookie has the most active ingredients, the other cookies served, contain just a maintenance dose." John nodded in understanding. He stated, "That Joe is indeed a funny guy." Martha nodded and sprinkled cookie crumbs down her front. Joe went on, "When my father finally died he left me very little. I learned I had to go out and get what I wanted for myself. He always said I was his most independent son. There's one thing he could never provide for me, anyway. Wild women! My dad was quite conservative. I wouldn't have thought of asking him for some wild women. Being the poorest son, I had to learn to laugh at things. Once I became a comedian I had all the wild women I wanted." Martha exclaimed, "Oh, what a tart! His father would roll over in his grave!" John and Jessica laughed heartily.

After another fifteen minutes of visiting Martha, Jessica explained, "I'm sorry we have to leave. We must get started for our honeymoon." Martha laughed, "Don't hurry off. You don't want to get honeymoonitis. You're a doctor, Jessica. You know what that is!" Jessica blushed and said, "Don't worry, Martha, I'll keep him under control." John shook Martha's hand and so did Jessica. They left hurriedly. John asked, "What's honeymoonitis?" Jessica blushed again and explained, "I don't want to explain in public. Ask me in private, later." John nodded and said, "Oh, I see."

They visited a few other elderly clients at the facility and then traveled to their train so as to leave for the Bahamas. As the train took off at a thousand miles per hour, John asked Jessica, "What do you do on the train when there's no scenery to look at? Jessica explained, "We watch videos. As you see, each seat has a separate video screen in front of it. You wear head phones and watch your own favorite show. It's all free!" John quipped,

"Naturally it's free. You're all socialists. I guess I'd better get used to it." Jessica retorted, "It's just a different way of distributing wealth. We have no poor people and we have very few disgustingly wealthy people. You and I are the only disgustingly wealthy people, along with a few moderately wealthy top scientists. Our comedians are also quite well paid. They get more vacations than anyone else. Their jobs are stressful. They need the rest. Our comedians are more respected and admired than anyone else. My people love to laugh. The comedy routines are partially copied into our newspapers so people can catch up on the latest humor, even if they missed their favorite comedian on television. Part of the reason we give the comedians so much vacation time, is so they can work up more comedy routines. Of course some of our best comedians can improvise almost endlessly and still stay terribly funny. Let's turn on Joe Bucks some more. He's on channel 01. He cracks me up!"

John smiled, "Sure! I like him too." Jessica turned on the screens and they put on their headphones. As usual, Joe was still talking about money. He stated, "A friend of mine was helping me with my taxes this year. He said he gets thousands back each year. I did everything he said, but now I'm getting audited. I guess I got too much back. He's getting audited too. I owe two thousand dollars more than if I'd prepared it myself! With friends like that, who needs enemies?

My great grandfather started a business making wooden boats. He only gave the workers one ten minute paid break each day. They weren't paid for their lunch break. Health insurance was when you were encouraged to eat an apple every day. Pension was when you were guaranteed that you could keep all the money you saved during your lifetime. The boats were quality boats though, and the workers always had work. Once my grandfather was asked if there was anything he liked better than a good worker. He answered that he'd like two workers, just as good, who would work for half the money.

Of course most of his workers were from other countries. He said the local workers were spoiled and wanted too much money and fringe benefits. The workers from other countries started wanting more money too. That was when he started having all his boats built in China. It worked great for a while, but the Chinese have a problem with wood boring larva. Much of the wood over there gets holes eaten in it. Quality became a problem and the whole business languished. Grandpa was so eager to save on labor costs that he started adopting Chinese babies. He knew they wouldn't overcharge him on labor. After he died, his principles of business were continued except that most of the shareholders and workers were Chinese."

Jessica laughed, "He really knows how to poke fun at aggressive capitalism." John removed his headphones and Jessica followed suit. John stated, "Many of our richest men were aggressive philanthropists. I think he's being a little to rough on business and business policies. My country left many people without health benefits, but it was because health care become too expensive for businesses to cope with." Jessica asked, "Why didn't your country at least socialize medicine. You could have mandated prices. You allowed medical schools to intentionally graduate few doctors, so the price of their services could be kept high. Who is worth a thousand dollars an hour? What pill is really worth twenty-four dollars? What shot is worth thirteen hundred dollars? I've read about all these pricing difficulties, and I'm being diplomatic!" John went on, "We have few enough people now, that our health system is socialized. Everything is provided by the military. It'll be many years before a private health care system will reemerge. I hope, when it does come back, that it will utilize more restraint in pricing of medications and services."

Jessica stated, "Isn't it a little naïve to hope that greedy people will show restraint in how much money they'll take from the public? Americans were always being arrested for going to Mexico to get good pain pills. That doesn't look good to me. Millions of Americans in pain because they can't afford enough of the high priced medications. Poor people going without insulin or testing supplies. Homeless allowed to wander the streets and die in the cold. The wealthy presented the smug information that all homeless people were mentally ill. This is on some of our ancient copies of internet information."

John looked a little disappointed, "You're starting to sound like a real hardened socialist. Don't be so hard on us." Jessica smiled and took his hand, "Just promise me you'll take care of the poor and keep everyone healthy in this new world we're creating. I'm on your side now." John smiled and gave her a kiss, "I'll see that everyone is well cared for. We really do care about people." They put on their headphones and watched some more Joe Bucks.

Joe said, "I always liked the part about tithing in the Bible. It made me realize how lucky I was all those years I didn't tithe. I just take the interest on all the money I didn't tithe, and now I can afford to tithe just off the interest! It's like magic. The magic of compounding interest. When you start getting interest on the interest, then you're starting to get somewhere."

John stated, "This guy is kind of funny, in a ridiculous kind of way." Jessica gently patted his hand, "You're quite tolerant. Much of our humor makes fun of greed. It's one of the greatest enemies of any society." John agreed, "Yes, greed is a deadly sin. Jessica, your society seems so perfect. I don't want to annoy you on our honeymoon, but I sense that possibly it's a little too perfect to be true. Possibly you've overlooked something. Maybe you aren't even aware of it. People are people, no matter how carefully they've been brought up and educated. Somewhere, under your command, there are some ruthless, greedy and spiteful people. When they surface, you'll be glad for my military. You'll be glad for some rich powerful people to come and save you." Jessica exclaimed, "I'm supposed to be the prophetic one. Here you are prophesying to me!" She laughed. "What you say is logical. I've been too proud and quick to point the finger. Pride comes before a fall, and pontificating can be unattractive. I do want to be an attractive bride. Forgive me, John." Their car had been reserved for them alone and they were indeed all alone. Jessica did her best to let John know that she wanted him to be happy. After a few minutes of her sensuous teasing, John's mood lightened.

Jessica said, "I would like to discuss politics some more, as long as I don't annoy you with rhetoric." John explained, "I'll promise to be understanding of your background and training. I didn't expect you to be a Wall Street capitalist right off the bat." Jessica countered, "Right off the bat. So you're hoping to convert me! Now things get interesting! I know I may need your protection sometime. I rule over a billion people. I have no way of exercising direct control over them. Many of them are descendents of exceedingly poor Asian people whom we saved from Dr. Exeeto's plagues at the last minute. I've heard rumors that some of them are resentful that Dr. Exeeto killed their ancestors. Their religion is big on ancestors and I don't fully understand it. The Buddhist religion is quite ancient and its followers are terribly loyal. They think nothing of dying for their cause, because their spirit is transported into some other worthy entity. They are taught to think very little of their own self. Ego is shed and the devotee thinks of themselves as but one drop in a large ocean. They have a great love for plants and animals, and make excellent agriculture workers. It's the tunnelers I worry about. They are so distant from the rest of our culture. Their work is always critical and we can't always give them as much vacation as they deserve. They are the youngest people, with uncontrolled minds. They are most likely to follow a malcontented genius who might want to start some kind of revolt."

John asked, "How did you hear rumors of resentment?" Jessica replied, "It was a dying old tunneler I visited at the elderly facility. He was so touched by my visit and my concern for him that he told me there was some trouble in the tunnels, political trouble. That is all he would tell me. He didn't want his afterlife to be disturbed because of telling on his relatives." John said, "That sounds like it could be reliable information. Why don't you check it out?" Jessica whispered, "Our tunnel complexes are so far reaching and labyrinthine that I couldn't possibly bug all the tunnels. They speak in such a heavy dialect, I wouldn't understand them anyway. Often there's too much background noise from the tunnel cutting machines." John stated, "I see your problem. Will you let me put some of my people on the problem?" Jessica said, "I'll let you work on the dialects with some of my translators. We can send people in with voice recorders that look like something else. We'll say we're checking radiation levels." John said, "I like that! Place hidden microphones in their break rooms and in the rest rooms. Do you have access to their living quarters?" Jessica replied, "Yes, but I hate to go that far with this." John stated, "If they aren't plotting against you, we can remove the microphones after a few months. You want to know what's going on don't you?" Jessica acquiesced, "You win. Bring in your experts and let them bug everything. I don't want some malcontents killing everyone else off!"

John explained, "Half the world disappeared, but we still have all of Satan. He isn't going to let this new hybrid planet be heaven. It's a given, that we're going to run into trouble. I believe in planning for every possible trouble which I can think of. Then I build up a plan and a contingency plan for each trouble. We can work together on these plans." Jessica said, "I'd like that." They watched Joe Bucks on the television for the rest of the trip.

When they arrived in the Bahamas, it was supper time. Their bags were taken to their suite, which overlooked an artificial ocean. There was white sand everywhere. Palm trees were growing in plentiful numbers throughout the resort. All the buildings were painted bright white and most had red tile roofs. Their hotel had a small quaint restaurant with a nautical theme. The walls were done in bamboo as were the tables and chairs. The bar was made of a large fishing boat with a glass top added to it. Fishing poles and anchors decorated the walls. A full glass wall faced the waterfront. John and Jessica sat near the glass wall and watched the water and the sea gulls. John's body guards weren't far behind. They had been on the train cars in front of and behind the one John was in. Now they sat at the bar and tried to disappear into the woodwork.

Jessica whispered, "Do you actually think you need the body guards here on our honeymoon?" John explained, "It goes with the office. Even the President has to follow the rules." Jessica asked, "Where will they be when we're in bed?" John explained, "Two of them will be out in the hall at all times. I've instructed them to stay away from our door as much as possible. They've been carefully selected. They're quite professional and sworn to secrecy about all my activities." Jessica sighed, "Well, that's refreshing. I'd hate for the details of our honeymoon to reach the newspaper in Iron Mountain."

Jessica stated, "Let's order. I'm hungry. I'm hungry for egg rolls and fried morels." John sighed, "No more morels for me. I'll take a well done sirloin steak with mashed potatoes and peas." The waitress heard them and came over to get their orders. John also ordered a bottle of chilled Riunite Lambrusco. He said, "It's not a high priced wine, but it's one of my favorites, I'm glad they carry it here." Jessica responded, "Dr. Exeeto loved wines. He brought all his favorite grape varieties with him to The Cave when he retreated from the surface. He wanted to be sure that excellent wines survived any hardships the surface would face." John quipped, "I'm starting to like the man more and more." They both laughed.

The wine came first. They were allowed to smell the cap, which was a screw on version. The waitress laughed at her own little joke. Jessica explained, "We train our service people to strive for humor." She gave the girl a gold coin. The girl was around eighteen with long black hair. She was slender yet somewhat shapely. She asked, "Did you see Joe Bucks today? I thought he was at his best." Jessica smiled brightly, "Yes, we watched him. I thought he was quite funny today." John stated, "I prefer Jack Benny. But, I'm sort of old fashioned." The waitress winked at John and said, "Everyone knows that Jack Benny is the king of comedy. He's in our hall of fame for comedy. I've been watching Jack since I was a little girl." John laughed, "I never would have guessed." The waitress said, "My name's Wanda, by the way. I'm happy to serve you this evening. We have a live comedy show here tonight at seven. The place gets pretty full then." John said, "We'll be looking forward to it. Is he anything like Joe Bucks?" Wanda replied, "No. They're quite different. Jim Benny is the comedian. He took Jack Benny's last name. It's helped his career immensely. Everyone loves Jack Benny, and they love to be reminded of him. Jim even plays the violin badly like Jack did." John stated, "We'll be looking forward to it." Wanda left them to enjoy their wine together. They played footsy under the table as they drank. They had both slipped their shoes off.

The food came and they enjoyed a quiet meal. In no time at all, the lights were dimmed and people started streaming in to fill all the chairs. There was a drummer setting up, who would accent the jokes. When he was set up, he gave a long drum roll and thereby announced the entrance of Jim. Jim brought out his violin and played *Moonlight and Roses* after a fashion. Then he slowly and methodically put the violin and bow back in its case on top of a stand which had been installed there for that purpose. Jim looked out toward the ocean and said, "It certainly is a nice night tonight. We have some special guests tonight. I know they're going to have a nice night." He nodded knowingly. The audience roared. He continued, "I remember my honeymoon night. I didn't tip the bell hop, and he knocked on the door every ten minutes all night long. My wife didn't speak to me for a week!" The audience exploded with laughter. "Once I underpaid the paper boy five cents. He dipped the end of my paper in water all month! Jim crossed his arms and looked off to one side. Then in an indignant voice he exclaimed, "Well!" That brought down the house. Everyone loved it when he did that.

Jim continued, "I'm sure you've all heard of my servant, Richard. Richard. Come on out here!" Jim said, "I need to pay the paper boy tomorrow. I don't want him soaking my paper in water. Can you go down to the vault and get a dime out for the paper boy?" Richard said, "Boss. I don't like those alligators you got down there protecting the vault. Can't you come down there with me?" Jim stated, "That's fine, Richard. I'll come along. I'll enjoy getting another glimpse of my money." The audience laughed. Richard and Jim left the stage. Jim came back on stage and did one liners for another ten minutes. He kept everyone in stitches. He finished by playing *Moonlight and Roses* again.

After the comedy was over, Jessica and John went for an evening dip in the artificial ocean. The artificial full moon, made Jessica's yellow bikini easily visible in the clear water. She filled out a suit nicely. John said, "I could stand here, holding you in this warm ocean forever." Jessica sighed, "This is delightful." She pushed herself tight against him as she kissed him with deep passion. All her life she had been looking forward to having a wonderful husband like John. John let his fingers slowly trace her body as they moved downwards. Gently they slid over her shapely hips and onto her exquisite derriere. He pulled her even more tightly up against him. She loved the way he wanted her so much. John said, "The body guards are the only ones watching, lets make a run for our suite. I'll send one of my guards ahead to catch the elevator." They made their run for the elevator and managed to get to their suite without attracting too much attention. They showered the sand off their feet and enjoyed the suite's steam sauna for an hour. Jessica loved to tease John sexually and keep him worked up. He didn't mind too much, but finally it became too much for him. He took her right there on the sauna floor. That was what she had been wanting. She loved it when he got a little forceful with her. She thought to herself, *He shouldn't have any trouble keeping up with me. He's like a volcano. I hope we can have children soon.*

John was so excited about how good Jessica looked to him, that he kept her in various states of nudity for the first day of their honeymoon. She didn't mind a bit. She loved being thought of, as so beautiful. She modeled all her negligees for him, and her collection was rather extensive. After he had picked out his favorites, Jessica introduced them to him up close. Their romantic entanglements caused them to have worked up big appetites. They got dressed and ordered in Kentucky Fried Chicken and veggies. After they had eaten, they spent the day sunbathing on the beach.

Chapter Three

Dr. Li

While they were enjoying the warm sun and giving each other back rubs, there was a much different scenario taking place at the South Pole in one of the deepest tunnels. Dr. Li was in his morel growing cave with twenty of his most devoted workers. The cave was a thousand yards long, one hundred yards wide and fifty feet high. The cave walls and ceiling were painted in white. Everything was lit with violet colored grow lights. Dr. Li was officially in charge of this area, which posed as a morel growing facility. It actually did raise tons of morels each year. Below the growing area was Dr. Li's secret laboratory. He led his followers to an elevator which was concealed behind many stacks of skids. After having the skids moved, Dr. Li led the devotees to his hidden laboratory. The secret laboratory was a thousand feet below the morel growing cave. It was only half as big as the upper cave. The workers filed out of the elevator into the lower cave where Dr. Li had a conference table with chairs waiting for them. They all sat down and eagerly waited to hear what Dr. Li had to say.

Dr. Li sat at the head of the table which was out in the open. None of the cave was sectioned off by walls. The walls were unpainted. There was brilliant white light emanating from the ceiling. Dr. Li was taller than most

North Koreans. He was five foot eight. He was in his early fifties and had a full head of short black hair. Although thin, he looked imposing in his white lab coat, with his intense eyes, as he loomed over his new recruits. His right eye had an intermittent twitch that was somewhat distracting.

Dr. Li started, "It's good that all of you are here today. I've wanted to tell my best people what our program goal is, for a long time. I have tested each of you thoroughly and find that you are loyal and can keep secret information to yourselves. Today I am promoting you from your morel work, to more scientific work. You have all received several years of academic training in your new specialty fields. Each of you will fill important positions helping me to achieve my end goal. As you know, eleven hundred years ago our ancestors were destroyed on the surface by Dr. Exeeto. He sent terrible plagues which provoked the major world powers into atomic warfare. The atomic bombs were so powerful that they created a nuclear winter which killed most of our ancestors on the surface. At the last minute he brought ten thousand of us into his protective caves beneath the oceans. He must have had some last minute guilt about killing all the poor. He saved some poor people to do his agricultural work and dig his tunnels. For eleven hundred years, my family has been planning this revenge, which is only two months away. We have developed a multiple fusion bomb which will send the earth into the sun. By then we will have completed our self sufficient colony on Mars, which we started the moment the two planets became united. We will remove all our people who are loyal to our ancestors, before the explosion. It has taken us eleven hundred years to find enough plutonium to make these bombs. We are tired of being the forgotten lackies of the Dr. Exeeto culture. We will send them into the sun, just like our ancestors were sent there by the United States of America. The Dr. Exeeto culture and its ally, the United States, will find a similar fiery tomb to reside in. I'm placing all of you in leadership positions for the tunneling and colony establishment projects. Your workers must not be told what our final plan is. Our goal must be kept secret. Our bomb locations were carefully chosen as the best positions for the separating blasts. Earth will be pealed off the back of Mars with the simultaneous blasts. I have timed the blasts to launch earth towards the sun. It will be a gradual and painful death for them." Dr. Li laughed uncontrollably at the thought of such a demise for his enemies.

Dr. Li explained, "Initially our plan was to blow up the half of earth that remained. When we landed on Mars, we changed our plans. We now have this new plan I've described to you." He paused for a drink of water. Then he continued, "Respect is everything. We have been used and disrespected for centuries. Soon our revenge will come. Our ancestors will be able to rest peacefully, once we have exacted the revenge on their enemies. We will die with honor when each of our lives is over. We will be totally in control of our new planet." The twenty loyal workers applauded loudly and nodded their heads in approval.

Dr. Li continued, "We have secretly diverted much tunneling equipment to this location. This is where the earth's mantel is cooling the most rapidly. The North Pole is also cooling, but it is too close to the United States. We don't want them to find out what we're doing. We have tunneled through the south end of the earth to the place where it first makes contact with Mars. This was the coolest point. We didn't want the added burden of refrigerating our tunnels so they weren't over heated by the earth's core. From that point, where earth touches Mars, we've tunneled a thousand miles from the future blast site. That is where we will now finish building our agricultural caves and recreational sites. There will be plenty of recreation time for our people when everything is completed. We won't be told that our work is too important, and there is no time for us to vacation." More applause came from the workers. Dr. Li raised his hands for silence. My family lived in North Korea before Dr. Exeeto came for them. North Korea had a poor growing climate. They were poor people. They were dependent on a larger neighbor country for food. That country was called China. The Chinese were happy to do work for the United States. They had 'Most favored nation' status for trading purposes. Those two countries became wealthy from trading with each other. North Korea was left out in the cold. The United States and North Korea were always at odds. Now my starving relative's spirits will rejoice when we kill off the Americans!" The workers applauded eagerly. "Honor! Honor!" They chanted.

Dr. Li was visibly pleased with their enthusiasm. He stated, "For hundreds of years we planned to blow earth to pieces. The surface people beat us to it and the wrong half of earth went into the sun. Since the split, we've been planning to blow up the remaining half of earth. Now that we have landed on Mars, the plan has changed again. We will blast earth away from us once our people are safely on Mars. The bombs are already in place and are being wired for their new location. All that remains is for the Mars caves and tunnels to be completed. Most of the digging is done. We need to complete the setting up of operations.

Dr. Li continued, "All of you will work on developing Mars. We will need to work quickly. We want to develop our culture on Mars, before the Dr. Exeeto culture and the United States start to move onto it. If we need to, we can develop diversions to keep them off Mars. We will resort to brute force if we need to. Our machine shops are building an arsenal of guns just in case we need them. The gun making program will be moved to Mars as soon as possible. It is a top secret operation. Make no mention of it to anyone outside of this room.

Our wealthy leader, Jessica Exeeto, has married the American president. We can expect them to be cooperating extensively. The American's have plenty of guns. That's why we need them too. We have plenty of tunneling machines now. Each of you has thousands of workers now, eager to serve you. Humbly apply yourselves to reaching our new goals. Inspire your workers with your dedication. Tell them only that you are responsible for colonizing Mars. Make no mention of bombs. That information is for top leadership people, like yourselves, only." Dr. Li continued with his lecture for a long time. His eager listeners never grew tired of him.

Chapter Four

The Honeymoon Continues

In the Bahamas, Jessica was rubbing John's feet and conversing with him. She mused, "I'm overwhelmed with how many new things are beginning. An explosion is about to happen, an explosion of ideas and the spread of culture. I hope we can quickly improve the atmosphere so people can enjoy life on the surface again. Our remaining atmosphere, after the splitting of earth, spread out over Mars. Now there is little protection from the sun and the cold of outer space. We need to develop more atmosphere." John answered, "I can have my people start steel and aluminum production on the surface. That builds atmosphere. The carbon dioxide produced will expand the thickness of the atmospheric layer. What should we use all the metals for?" Jessica stated, "I think we need to build steel reinforced surface tubes to all the surface areas we'd like to access. That way we can control the temperature around travelers and make it comfortable day and night." John said, "I agree with that. It will keep our people busy for many years. We need constant meaningful work for all our people. Otherwise, they become discontented and bored." Jessica said, "Yes, everyone must have meaningful work, and we need more comedians. We've thought of cloning the ones we have, but instead we're launching talent contests to help us find our new crop of funny people. The trouble is that no one wants to hear the not so good comedians. Nothing's worse than jokes that aren't quite funny." John exclaimed, "I know what you mean. I've been watching reruns of our old talk shows from before the earth split. Ninety percent of the time the comedians aren't all that funny. Some of them are too dirty with their language. I can't see the humor in that." Jessica responded, "That's quite interesting, people trying to be funny by being naughty with their language. I hope that doesn't spread to our culture. A little naughty can be funny, but they shouldn't make a habit of foul language. It's in poor taste." John apologized, "I'll put all those videos in some deep archive where they'll never be found. Don't worry about it."

Jessica smiled, "Jim Benny is performing again tonight. I can't wait. What shall we have for supper tonight?" John yawned, "You tired me out last night. I just need a strong cup of coffee and some Viagra." Jessica laughed, "Don't take that stuff. We don't have to get it on every night. I know I'm twenty years younger than you are. I went for years without any sex at all. I'm just happy with you the way you are. Don't give yourself a heart attack!" John sighed, "You're quite understanding. I'm starting to like you more every day." Jessica laughed, "That's good. You've got quite a few more days ahead of you."

They got dressed and went to the dinning room. The drummer was setting up early. John called Wanda, the waitress, over to their table. John said, "I'd like some strong Columbian coffee. Jessica stated, "I'll take the same, but with lots of cream. Please bring us some butter fried morels for appetizers." Wanda said, "As you wish. I'll be right back with your orders." She walked briskly away to the kitchen. John said, "I'm actually in the mood for some more morels tonight. You seem to be addicted to them." Jessica replied, "It's our national food. Our national tree is the red oak. Our national bird is the pink flamingo." John stated, "I've been in Iron Mountain all my life. We have few trees. Our national bird is the bald eagle. Our favorite drink is the run and coke, with Riunite Lambrusco as a close second."

Wanda returned with their morels and coffees. Jessica asked, "Could we have some buttered white bread slices. I like to wrap my morels in buttered bread." Wanda answered, "It'll only take a minute. I'll be right back." She was true to her word and returned in a few minutes with the buttered bread." She asked, "Are you ready to order?" Jessica answered, "I'll have lobster and sirloin steak. I'd like real melted butter to dip the lobster in." John added, "I'll take the same. Make my steak well done, please." Jessica chimed in, "Well done for me as well." Wanda said, "Just as you please. It won't take long." She left hurriedly.

John said to Jessica, "I need to make a phone call about state business. It's not a secret from you. I can tell you about it later. I need to go back to our room for a minute." Jessica said, "That's fine, hurry back so your food doesn't get cold." John kissed her on the cheek and left quickly. Two of his guards followed him to the room. They stayed outside the door. The other two guards remained with Jessica. John got out his large suite case and removed the special radio which could transmit through rock. He called his secretary of state, Warren Anglemeyer. Warren answered in about twenty seconds. John said on a scrambled frequency, "I want you to get Don Meyers and Deb Sanders down here on the next train. I need them to check for possible subversive activities down in the remote tunnels. We have a tip from a reliable source which indicates there may be trouble brewing, over?" Warren replied, "I'll get them briefed tonight. They'll be on their way. Anything else?" John continued, "I need a team to bug various areas in the tunnels. They can pose as scientists checking for radiation." Warren responded, "I'll have them on their way as soon as you send a train." John stated, "I had a train sent this morning as soon as I got up. Jessica gave me authorization to move trains back and forth as I see fit. One should be there in a couple hours." Warren said, "We'll be ready for it. Is that all?" John said, "That's all for now. I'll have some people meet them at the train station. I'll give them the final briefing myself, do you read?" Warren answered, "Message received. Is that all?" John said, "Yes, over and out."

He turned off the radio and rushed back to the dining room. The food was just arriving. They ate their food and had some wine to go with it. Jessica explained, "Jim Benny likes to do Bible humor. He's well versed in the Bible. At times he's a little more like a preacher than a comedian. You'll see."

At seven, Jim Benny started his routine. He started out with some one liners and then went into a monologue. He was talking about a Bible passage. He said, "Jesus said that a man shouldn't call his brother a fool or he would be in danger of hell fire. That was in Matthew five, verse twenty-two. It takes a serious offense to deserve hell fire. I know that all sin is separation from God, but will a murderer of children receive the same punishment as someone who steals a watermelon? I personally think there will be different punishment. Let's assume, for argument's sake, that there's a rheostat on hell fire. Now I'm thinking that calling some one poop face, doesn't even qualify you for the lowest setting of hell fire. Every farmer gets a little poop on his face from time to time. There's no disgrace in that. But no one wants to be called a fool!

Suppose one were to call his brother a fool. That might rate for a hell fire at ten percent of maximum capacity. To commit murder might cause the heat to go up to fifty percent of capacity. Now we are assuming that these hypothetical sinners didn't repent before they died. Now

I know what you're all thinking. Do they ever use one hundred percent of heat capacity in hell? What does one need to do to get the hottest hell? I hesitate to mention it. As sure as I do, someone will want to do it. Don't do it. Many have done it. It wouldn't be a first, and you'd regret it for eternity. Blasphemy gets the hottest setting. Those who say the nature of God is evil. Don't even say that just joking around. You don't want to go there! Such a statement is upsetting to both supernatural powers of the universe. God is enraged because you are calling the infinitely good entity of the universe, evil. Satan is enraged because you're calling his enemy evil. Satan wants to lay claim to being the only evil one. You are trying to steal his claim to fame. So you have God and Satan both blowing on the flames to make it hotter for you. Good luck. You'll need more than luck! Blasphemy is the only unforgivable sin.

You see the heat of hell gives you pain and disgusting sweat, but you aren't consumed. Somehow your spirit is not totally devoured. You regenerate just enough to be burned over and over again for eternity. So even ten percent of hell fire is not something you want. Don't call people names. Try to be friendly and helpful. Give the thirsty a drink of cold water. Help someone who's injured. Read your Bible and follow the teachings of Jesus.

The fear of hell shouldn't be our only reason for being Christian. We should want to be closer to Christ's example because of the inspiration he gives us and because of the Holy Spirit filling us. Also remember to pray every day. I pray for forgiveness for my sins every day. I thank God that he has a sense of humor. His Bible is a very sacred and important book. When I poke fun at certain passages, I try to also clarify what the passage means. I've read the entire Bible. I like it. I think it's important. Some sections lend themselves to humor though.

How about Noah and the ark? Scholars are constantly arguing about how big the ark was. What exactly is a cubit, anyway? The cubit was a measure of length used to describe how big the ark was. Now Noah had to get all the world's animals on the ark. He also needed enough food for them. He needed bedding. He needed his own food and food for his relatives. I'd say the ark must have been almost as big as an oil tanker. Noah and his relatives all had big arms. They must have worked their behinds off to build that thing, to say nothing of throwing all that manure overboard! It's an interesting story, and I believe it. What's so hard to believe? Mankind put a man on the moon, why couldn't man build a big boat. Look at the pyramids. Big!

Now I know some of you have wondered at one time or another, why Adam ate the apple? Wouldn't it be nice if we didn't need to work, and God just provided everything for us? The apple was from the tree of the knowledge of good and evil. When they ate of the apple, they disobeyed God. We all want to do our own thing. No one seems to enjoy obeying. Of course if we were still in the Garden of Eden, there wouldn't be negligees, would there?" There was much laughter.

"The Jonah and the whale story is a little hard for some people to believe. What's so difficult to believe about a huge whale swallowing someone and then spitting them back up on shore three days later? If God has infinite power, why would that be too hard for him? Maybe God was helped by the fact that Jonah didn't bath too often. The whale was probably delighted to get rid of Jonah!" The crowd laughed heartily.

"That's enough on the Bible. Let's hear a round of applause for Jessica, our religious leader who's here tonight." Much applause. "And applause for her new husband, John Miller, the President of the United States of America." There was loud applause. Jim asked, "Can you say a few words to us, John?" John stepped up to the microphone and said, "I'm glad to be with all of you this evening. Your leader, Jessica, is a wonderful woman. I love your hospitality. I'm looking forward to spending many happy days here in your country." There were several minutes of eager applause.

Jim thanked John and continued his comedy act. "My parents are dear and wonderful people. I respect them very much. If I were to criticize them on any one point, it would be how exceedingly frugal they were. We never spent any of our monthly clothing allowance. Our clothes never wore out because we washed them in cold water with very little soap. Of course our society is socialized and there isn't much need for money. Health care, housing and household furnishings are free. If people want to save on their food credits, they can exchange them for gold. We ate macaroni and cheese for five straight years once!" The crowd laughed nervously. Jim continued, "No, don't feel sorry for us. We each had our own bucket of gold from the food savings. We also saved on toilet paper. When we needed to use the toilet in that way, we went to the neighbor's house or we went to a public building. During my childhood I saved enough on toilet paper to buy two pounds of gold. I was glad that all heating is provided by our government. I never had to be cold.

I was pushed into comedy at an early age. My parents liked the fact that comedians are well paid. We earn similar salaries to our top scientists. I had to write one page of comedy lines every day during my entire childhood. I was paid in gold for my work. My parents were generous when it came to paying for humor. They actually thought I was funny. So that's why I'm here. I owe everything to my parents. They made me be funny. They insisted on it. Let me tell you one of my early jokes. Why do ducks have flat feet? So they can put out forest fires! Why do elephants have wide flat feet? So they can put out flaming ducks!" There was a big wave of laughter. The crowd liked that one. Jim went on, "What's yellow and goes bang,

bang, bang, bang? A four door banana!" There was more enthusiastic laughter. Jim asked, "What's wrinkly and rides a horse? Roy Raisin." That joke flopped. Jim said, "I guess you'd have to be old enough to remember the Roy Rogers cowboy shows to enjoy that joke." Jim continued, "What's green and prickly and lies on the bottom of the ocean? Moby pickle." That one got a good laugh. Jim stated, "I have to save some of my best stuff for tomorrow night. That's all for tonight." He took his violin and played a slightly off key version of *Moonlight and Roses*.

John spoke softly, "I asked some of my best people to come and help us with the problem in the tunnels. They'll be at the Brazilian central train station in twelve hours. I promised to meet them." Jessica looked disappointed and then brightened. "I can ask Jim Benny to return here next week. We can catch the rest of his jokes then. We can spend a whole week here." John replied, "I agree. We'll spend the whole week. I promise not to make any more interruptions. I'd brief them with a telecommunications screen, but this is too top secret. We can't risk the enemy intercepting our communications. There's no telling how sophisticated they may be." Jessica responded, "I know what you mean. Even half the earth is so large that I can't possibly know what's going on in every part of it. Some of my tunnelers could have developed a small city that I don't even know about!" John explained, "We don't know too much about Asian religions. They could be up to anything. I've read quite a bit, though, about their culture as it has manifest itself down through the ages. They are a terribly proud people. If you show disrespect to them, you have a problem on your hands. The ancient country of North Korea used to attempt to launch intercontinental ballistic missiles at the United States. They did everything they could to undermine us. They copied our currency in large quantities. They were an ingenious people, but they focused on revenge and pride. The United States fought a war against them once. That will never be forgotten by them. North Korea couldn't grow enough food for itself because of the climate. They refused to trade with the United States. Their attitude made the prospects for their future dim. They received assistance from other communist countries. I think that is part of why they did so much posturing against the United States. They hated us in truth, but it helped them get sympathy from wealthier communist countries when they attacked us. There was no talking to them. They were fanatics. It was countries like theirs that led to the final war and explosions that split earth apart."

Jessica exclaimed, "You have an impressive grasp of history. Some of what you have described is familiar to me. Dr. Exeeto had large libraries with large history sections. We have little information, though, on what has happened on the surface in the last thousand years. You can tell me more on our ride back to the main Brazilian cave. By the way, we call that cave Xanadu. You've read Samuel Coleridge haven't you?" John stated with pleasure, "'In Xanadu did Kubla Khan a stately pleasure-dome decree.' Yes I love his writing. He had the equivalent of your marijuana cookies before he wrote that poem. It was an opiate derivative for pain. I think it was called laudanum, if my memory serves me well." Jessica smiled and said, "I'm impressed. That's correct. Without his impressive innate imagination, though, I doubt if just taking an opiate would have resulted in such a fine poem."

Jessica said reluctantly, "Well we'd better get going. We need to pack, and we don't want your people to arrive in Xanadu before we get there." They walked back to their honeymoon suite and packed for the return trip.

In no time at all, they had made it back to Jessica's suite. Soon they were waiting for the train at the station. The train arrived on schedule and Don Meyers and Deb Sanders were the first to disembark. Deb was tall and slender with long brown hair. It came ten inches below her shoulders. She was attractive, with piercing hazel eyes and well toned muscles. She looked like an Olympic swimmer with her muscle tone. Don was beside her now as they approached John and Jessica. Don was six feet four inches tall and quite muscular. He had short black hair and was clean shaven. His eyes were blue and he had thick eye brows which made him look a little intimidating.

John introduced them to Jessica and they proceeded quickly to Jessica's suite. The bugging team followed behind. Jessica asked Don and Deb if they would like a fruit drink. They accepted. John started the briefing. "Jessica has confided in me that there is possibly some organization of malcontents who are likely to cause trouble somewhere in the tunnels. I'm asking the two of you to check into it. All we have now, is a dying man's confession that there is trouble brewing. My guess is that some of the most remote outposts might be good places to start. This enemy has managed to completely stay in secret until now. It would have been hard for them to manage that, if they were right here close to the center of things. Jessica's society isn't geared towards surveillance. They've been a little too trusting through the years, it would appear. You're here to help Jessica be more informed." Jessica passed them each a badge. "This badge will allow you unlimited access to our computer terminals and their programs. If someone is creating a secret threat to me, they have probably been using some of our tunneling machines to create hidden operations centers. Possibly you can track them by following the movement of the tunneling machines. They're all supposed to be accounted for and their locations logged. If you find some missing, it will be a valuable clue."

Don replied, "That makes sense. Do you have a terminal here, or should we use one in a different location." Jessica explained, "There's one across the hall you can use. It's a large suite where the guards have been staying. You can set up operations there in a connected room off to the left. The bugging team will be staying down the hall to the right. You can use it now if you like." John explained, "We need to brief the surveillance team now. Let us know the minute you come up with anything."

Don and Deb left and crossed the hall into their new work area. John called for the surveillance team. There were ten men on the team. John quickly explained to them where the bugs were to be planted. "Each of you will be accompanied by an escort, who will help keep you out of trouble. Place bugs in the most remote tunnels. We want the listening devices placed in public restrooms, break rooms and in homes of a cross section of people. We want to listen to leaders and workers alike. We have no way of knowing who might be involved. There are only a limited number of translators that we can trust, so we'll only have each of you plant a maximum of ten bugs at a time. After a month, we'll move to a new location. Learn the language as quickly as you can. Until you do, we'll have to depend on the translators for all our information. Jessica will send you a fax of the maps you will need. We have someone working on that now. You can all go to your new quarters now. I'll have food sent over. You can leave at noon. It's eight o'clock now. You should have your maps and escorts by ten o'clock."

The surveillance team left and found their spacious quarters down the hall. There was an inner hallway which led to their individual rooms. Each room was large and generously appointed with a gas fireplace, chandeliers of fine crystal and a refrigerated wine closet. There were saunas and whirlpools. These rooms were obviously created for honored guests. After seeing their rooms, the team members went to the large central room to view an informational video lecture about their host culture.

Don and Deb were in their quarters working together on the tunnel cultures computer records. They had quickly located ten missing tunneling machines. There were hundreds of the machines, and the missing ones had gone unnoticed until now. Deb stated, "Most of the missing machines are in the southern most locations. Do you think that's where we should start looking?" Don replied, "I think that's right. Our trouble makers didn't want to take chances on making long trips with the machines. They probably took the closest ones at hand. They never thought they would be looked for till it was too late. What would a group of people want with ten tunneling machines? Two or three would be plenty to make a giant cave with." Deb said, "They must be working on something big! Don mused, "I wonder what all they're up to?" Deb responded, "We'll have to go down there and find out first hand. This computer won't be able to help us much more. We need to find where Jessica's world leaves off and the rebel world begins. There has to be a port of entry. I think we should start questioning people who work along the train tracks. They would have seen the tunnel machines go by." Don exclaimed, "Once again, brilliant. I think you're on a roll. Of course the machines may have been in crates, to hide what was going on."

They went to Jessica's suite and filled John and her in on what they had learned. John said, "It's interesting that the missing tunnel machines are all from southern locations. I agree that the rail workers would have seen at least some of the machines go past. Start looking where the northern most machine disappeared from. Work south from there. You have enough truth serum in your standard kits to get started with. I'll have some more sent down, right away."

Jessica stated, "You'll need a guide. I'll call in one of my most trusted people. She can be here in just a few hours. She's always eager to help me. Her name is Shawn Lui. Her ancestors were North Korean and she knows most of the dialects. She can help you understand what the people are saying. I'll have her here in less than three hours. When she gets here you can start your mission. We operated on Shawn's mother ten years ago and saved her life. Because of that helpful operation, Shawn is quite devoted to us. She won't sympathize with a band of rebels, even if they are North Korean.

In two hours, Shawn Lui appeared at Jessica's suite with her suit case in hand. She was only four feet five inches tall, but her bright and happy eyes conveyed confidence as she introduced herself. "My name is Shawn Lui. I'll be happy to serve as your guide to the southern regions." Jessica introduced Don and Deb to Shawn. Don said, "I'm looking forward to working with you, Shawn. Your input will be extremely valuable to us."

Jessica explained, "You can all stay at resort housing in the areas where you're working. Here are passes that will give you the best rooms available." She handed the passes to each of them. "John and I are returning to the Bahamas to complete our vacation. If something important comes up you can call us on this phone." She handed the small black phone to Don. "It uses a scrambled frequency. We use them for secret communications. John and I will each have one with us at all times. We use these radios when we talk about transfers of large amounts of gold or rubies. We don't want to tempt people to resort to robbery, even though it seems like a remote possibility here."

Don, Deb and Shawn left for their journey south, while John and Jessica helped the surveillance team get acquainted with their translators. When the team and the translators had left to start their missions, John and Jessica returned to the Bahamas. They arrived in time for the evening comedy routine by Jim Benny. He was just starting his act. John and Jessica had eaten supper on the train.

Jim played his violin, as usual. When he was done, he started another Bible monologue. "Do any of you know who the most powerful prophet in the Bible was? Come on. You should know this! First I'll tell you who the second most powerful prophet of the Bible was. Elijah was the second most powerful prophet in the Bible. Elijah could part waters by slapping the water with his cloak. He could bring down hell fire on his enemies. Even kings knew not to mess around with Elijah.

Before Elijah was taken up into heaven by a chariot of fire, Elisha asked Elijah to give him double the power that he had. Elijah said that if Elisha saw him taken up into heaven, he would receive the power he asked for. Elisha was terribly determined not to leave the side of Elijah, and was indeed able to be present and see him taken up into heaven. Elijah's mantle fell off as he left, and Elisha took it for his own. Be sure to read that story in the Bible. I find it terribly interesting. When Elisha wanted power, he asked, 'Where is the Lord God of Elijah?' That was the prayer that caused miracles to happen. Why didn't Elisha use the prayer to allow him to create a pile of gold or rubies? All he was interested in, was that God's will would be done. That must be why he was allowed to exercise so much power.

If I had that much power, it would be tempting to make just a few rubies appear in my pocket. I could ask God to grant me all the vacation time I wanted!" The audience laughed. "Imagine all the power you could possibly want. Call down fire. Part water when you want to take a short cut across a lake." He went to one of the guests who was nearby. "What would you do with all that power?" The guest responded, "I'd ask for more vacation and I'd have my own electric car." Jim stated, "That sounds good. I'm like you. I want some things for myself. Elisha wanted what God wanted. They worked together well. By the way that story is in Kings II, Chapter 2.

That's enough Bible for a little bit. Let me tell you an interesting story. Before the world split in half, there was a country called Africa. There were animals called elephants in Africa. We still have some of them in our zoos. It is said that once three blind men discovered an elephant. The first blind man said, 'The elephant is definitely like a tree.' He had taken hold of the elephants leg. The second blind man said, 'The elephant is certainly like a sword.' He had a hold on the elephant's tusk. The last blind man said, 'The elephant is surely like a rope.' He had hold on the elephant's tail. So you see, we all perceive things differently depending on what our senses happen to latch onto. Two people might read a book and each have a different opinion of it. We read and remember selectively. No two people see another person in exactly the same light.

That's just food for thought. Now getting back to elephants. People used to shoot elephants and have them stuffed. Sometimes they'd have their pictures taken with the dead elephant. I know that seems a little primitive now, but let me tell you a joke that has been around for at least a thousand years. It's about shooting elephants. How do you shoot a red elephant? With a red elephant gun. How do you shoot a white elephant?" Jim pointed to a man in front. "You can say it. How do you?" The man said loudly, "With a white elephant gun!" Jim continued, "No. You dig a hole a hundred feet deep and bury a peanut in it. The elephant comes that night and digs up the peanut and eats it. Elephants love peanuts. The next night you dig a hole two hundred feet deep and bury a peanut in it. The elephant comes that night and digs up the peanut and eats it. The third day, you bury a raisin five hundred feet deep. That night the elephant digs and digs and digs, until it finds the raisin. Elephants don't like raisins. It gets mad and turns red. Then you shoot it with the red elephant gun." There was quite a bit a laughter and applause after that joke. Jim told dozens of one liners before he was through. Finally he played his violin, which signaled that his performance was over.

John and Jessica stayed late and listened to a blues band that was playing. The lead guitarist played in the style of the great masters of blues, B.B. King and Jimmy Hendrix. There was a touch of Eric Clapton and the Stones as well. The music drew them in and made them want to stay longer. John ordered another bottle of wine. Jessica stated, "We'll make this one last longer. It doesn't look good for a country's religious leader to be over indulging." John exclaimed, "They know this is our honeymoon! You're right though. We're always in the public eye. We must be good examples. We'll only have one more glass full." Jessica responded, "Yes, we must sip it slowly. I want to hear more about your government. How does it work?"

John explained, "Right now I have emergency powers. I can decide most things for myself. Once things get back to normal, I'll be sharing power with the Congress and Senate. They propose bills and I pass most of them. I veto any bills that seem too poorly thought out. There's a give and take and sharing of power. I have a cabinet with leaders from the various branches of the government. They keep me advised about what they want or recommend. I, in turn, give them guidance. Our military has three branches which are led by the Joint Chiefs of Staff. I'm their boss." Jessica asked, "Who were you talking to that sent the two teams of agents?" John explained, "That was the Secretary of State." He's my most trusted friend and ally. He handles secret missions. Most of the functioning of his agency is on a need to know basis, so I don't talk about it." Jessica said, "But I'm your wife!" John went on, "Even though most of our enemies are now gone, I need to follow the rules of our country. Everything but the Central Intelligence Agency and Homeland Security is open for you to read about and hear about. Some projects of the C.I.A. and Homeland Security will involve you. Then you will be fully briefed. After our honeymoon is over, I hope you'll come with me to Iron Mountain and join me in a meeting with the Joint Chiefs of Staff and the cabinet. You'll be invited to help all of us plan the future development of the new hybrid planet. We'll be working quite closely together on everything."

Jessica sighed, "I'm glad to hear you say that. I want to work with America. It's unfortunate that the nations of the old earth couldn't have worked more profitably with America. There were always wars and fighting. As I told you before, I read quite a bit in our ancient history books. America was always fighting to keep other nations free. All American's got for their efforts was trouble. The French were ungrateful for being freed from the Nazi invaders. Countries which became rich selling oil to America, became her worst enemies. Iraq, Iran, Sudan, North Vietnam and North Korea were all enemies at one time or another. Windfall war profits often gave America a bad name, but millions of Americans died to help people stay free from tyranny and outside oppression."

John declared, "I can tell you've done some homework. It was a relief when we lost all our enemies after the splitting of earth. Some of our best allies were destroyed as well though. It was a tragic occurrence. I don't think anyone imagined that the earth would split and separate. There had been so many earth quakes and exceedingly violent volcanic eruptions, though, I guess people should have started to suspect that atomic blasts were causing problems with the tectonic plates. The North Koreans had the fusion bomb and fully intended to use it. We had focused much of our surveillance activities on keeping track of what they were doing with that bomb. We knew right when they launched theirs. Our fusion bomb missile was launched automatically when they launched theirs. We detonated ours when it got close to their incoming missile over the Atlantic Ocean. Even though both bombs exploded in mid air, it was still enough of a shock wave to split the earth apart. The pressure on the Pacific Ocean was severe enough that it pushed the surrounding continents apart violently. That separation opened up the magma layer of earth, which increased the explosion when much of the ocean was instantly turned to steam by the heat."

Jessica stated, "It's a wonder that more of my people weren't killed!" John sighed, "Most of the surface people were killed. I'd like to tell you more about my thoughts on North Koreans, but this isn't the place. When we get back to the room I'll go into it." Jessica sipped her wine as she looked into John's eyes. They were the eyes of a man who had seen plenty of trouble. They were warm and friendly eyes. She liked the way he could still be a fun loving person, even when there was trouble afoot. John was looking back into her eyes and enjoying her youthfulness. He thought about how much responsibility she had, and yet how carefree she seemed. He stated, "You must know how to effectively delegate authority. You seem so carefree." Jessica laughed, "I spend most of my time reading the Bible and praying. There's no time for me to be involved directly with every detail of state affairs. I pick my people carefully and let them do their jobs. It works out fine. We've had no wars to complicate things. Our biggest worries are about where to place the next entertainment center, or where to build our next tunnel."

John exclaimed, "Yes, war can take up lots of time and energy. After finding the food cave your mother left for us at the Panama Canal, we used your technology to build more food caves like it. We didn't have your advanced tunneling machines, so it took us longer than it would have taken your people. Since the splitting of earth, our Iron Mountain population has grown rapidly. Unlike your country, with a billion plus people, we only have about twenty thousand people. I'm hoping you'll help us build our own advanced tunneling machines. That seems to be the biggest key to your success." Jessica admitted, "Yes, without them, we wouldn't have been able to expand our population nearly as much. Our culture depends heavily on them."

Jessica started playing footsy with John under the table. The wine was starting to affect her. John took a lighter tack, "Do you enjoy sailing?" Jessica looked a little embarrassed, "That's one thing we haven't developed. Our artificial oceans are a little too small for that, and we'd have to make artificial wind. Where do you sail? The world's oceans have been split in half. The water has turned to steam and ended up as snow on the north and south poles." John explained, "We have the Great Lakes. We can do some sailing there after the lake thaws." Jessica responded, "I'd like that. Seeing a large lake like that would be refreshing. Are there fish in it?" John answered, "Yes, it's full of fish. There are perch, salmon, pike and bass, just to name a few. Would you like to fish with me?" Jessica sighed, "That would be wonderful. I want to taste some of the fish I catch. What about the atmosphere?" John explained, "We'll take some emergency oxygen tanks with us. If the wind blows in a low atmosphere condition, we can put on the oxygen."

Jessica asked, "What do you think we should do about the atmosphere?" John answered, "I agree with you. The best way to make plenty of oxygen is with trees. We need to create good soil on Mars and then plant it with trees." Jessica said, "If we make plenty of metals, we can build a surface tunnel system, as I mentioned to you before. It should be made with a framework of metal, and the top should be made of clear material so people can view the sky." John responded, "I like that idea. We could build entertainment centers every fifty miles or so. They would help keep the people content." Jessica smiled, "And we need to build many residential units with sleeping quarters that have clear domes for night sky viewing. Let's make sure every family has a telescope! We'll keep night time outdoor lighting to a minimum, so viewing of the night sky won't be hampered by that kind of light." John said, "You think of everything." He put his arm around her and kissed her ear. She turned and kissed him on the lips. He could sense her passion as her tongue teased his.

Jessica asked, "Why don't we go back to the suite now. I could use a back rub." John sighed, "I agree. I long for your touch. It's been a long day." They walked hand in hand back to their suite. Their guards stayed close by. When they got there, John switched on the steam sauna and they took a long steam bath together. They gave each other back rubs and kissed frequently. Their passions were strong and they didn't wait to get in bed. The sauna filled with their passionate sighs. They kept making love for hours after they turned the steam room temperature down a bit. They were hot enough the way it was, without too much steam.

They spent the whole week going from the bed to the steam room. They never tired of each other and the fun things they had found to do together. They stopped from time to time for a few hours to discuss the atmosphere and the new tunnels to be built. Jessica explained, "We have technology for creating fertile soil that is effective. We heat and sterilize the ingredients and use automated material transfer and mixing equipment. I can have my people increase our production a hundred fold or more. We can have the Mars portion of Mirth covered with quality soil in a shorter time than you might imagine." John smiled as she danced in front of him in one of his favorite negligees. Finally at midnight, she decided she'd better let him get some rest. They cuddled romantically all night and slept the deep sleep of those who are content and fully sated with pleasure. After several more days of displaying their intense affection for each other, the couple was ready to travel to Iron Mountain. As they rode the electric train to America, the American surveillance teams were hard at work.

Chapter Five

Surveillance

The ten men working on placing listening devices were doing their work at a wide variety of locations along the rail line that headed towards the South Pole. Each of the men worked closely with his translator and tried diligently to learn the new language of the North Koreans.

Don Meyers and Deb Sanders were with Shawn Lui at one of the southern most locations, interrogating a rail worker. They gave him a permission slip from Jessica, explaining that he should drink with them and try to answer their questions. In return he would receive the rest of the day off with pay. His drink would include the truth serum, which would help reduce his inhibitions about giving out information about fellow North Koreans. It was dangerous to inform on one's countrymen. This subjects name was Tang Du. He was twenty-six years old and an intelligent man. He asked many questions. "Why are you here? Have I done something wrong? Are you sure your note is legitimate?" After he drank with them, he relaxed and became more agreeable. He bravely complimented Deb on her good looks, "You have a nice figure Deb. I think I like you very much." He put his arm around her and sat close, as Don asked the questions. "How long have you worked here?" he asked. Tang responded, "Six years.

This is the only job I've ever had. I'm always here. I never miss a day." Don continued, "Have you seen any large crates or open drilling machines go past here in the last two years?" Tang laughed, "I see many machines. Maybe six machines. Someone is making many tunnels or big caves. I've heard of a man called Dr. Li. I think he's using the machines. He raises morels. There is always demand for more morels. All tunnel people eat morels. They good fried in butter! I eat them too." Don asked, "When was the last time you saw a tunnel machine go by?" Tang laughed some more and squeezed Deb, "Two months ago was the last time. Dr. Li is a scientist. He's highly respected. I'm sure he wouldn't do anything wrong. He raises more morels than any other place. I'm sure he was tunneling for more growing space. What do you think he is doing?" Tang was getting a little alarmed. They gave him several more drinks and Deb massaged his neck. He grew happy again. They had him drink enough truth serum that he would forget what they had been asking him about. Just to be sure of no complications, they sent him on a year long vacation to the Bahamas. They asked Shawn Lui to keep an eye on him until they could find someone else to help watch him. They loaded him on the next north bound train.

Deb stated, "We certainly hit pay dirt this time. We need to find Dr. Li and question him." Don responded, "It does sound like he might know about what's going on with the drilling machines. We still don't know if he's involved in any sort of plot. Possibly he just likes to avoid red tape and delays. He knew how to get the machines and he may have just taken them to avoid paper work." Deb said, "I wish we hadn't sent Shawn Lui away. We could use her input on this. Let's go to Dr. Li's morel farm. One of our surveillance team members is probably still there with his interpreter. We can use her to help us." Don said, "I like that idea. I'll call the next train and have it stop for us." He used his Xanadu radio, on a nonscrambled frequency, to call the train and ask to be picked up.

They were given a private car at their request. They called John and Jessica and filled them in on what was happening. John spoke with Don. Don said, "We uncovered valuable information about the tunnel machines. They went to a man named Dr. Li and the southern most morel raising laboratory. We don't know yet whether he's up to no good. He may have just wanted to save time, by taking the machines without going through the proper channels. He has a reputation for producing large quantities of morels. It's possible he's just expanding his legitimate operation. Over?" John answered, "I read you. I want you to go to the lab as soon as I can get two of my body guards down there to back you up. I don't want you going in there alone. On the other hand, we don't want to alarm Dr. Li. If he's up to no good, we want to find out about it. We must not send him into hiding. Do you copy?" Don stated, "I copy. We'll wait for the guards at the southern most recreation center. We'll get rooms and wait for them there. Is that acceptable? Over." John said, "That sounds fine. They should be there in less than twenty-four hours. Report back to me as soon as more develops. I may start some troop movements now, just in case they're needed. Over." Don stated, "That's a 10-4. Over and out." He turned off the radio and poured himself a drink from the deluxe car's wet bar. It was mango juice and rum. He stated, "These fruit drinks grow on you. Do you want one?" Deb answered, "Sure. Why not? We'll be off duty for awhile now." Don mixed up another drink. They sat across from each other at a table and sipped their drinks.

Deb asked, "What have they had you doing at Iron Mountain lately? I haven't seen you since the last C.I.A operatives convention. Don explained, "I've been working on marksmanship. The new Beretta they've issued is more reliable than the Walther PPK was. I have to get used to the feel of the new gun. What about you? Deb said, "I've been working with that gun too. I like it. It's lighter and fits in my handbag nicely. I've been working on linguistics, mostly. Don stated, "They've had me working on that too. I never thought I'd need it. Now I wish I'd studied harder." Deb responded, "We had no way of knowing what to expect from the future. We were just floating through space, way out of orbit. I didn't know if my skills would ever be needed again." Don said, "That's just what I mean. Who could have guessed we'd land on Mars and find ourselves investigating North Koreans?"

Deb mixed them a couple more drinks and stated, "You must be a little tense after that interrogation and talking to the President. Let me massage your feet." She passed him a drink and took off his shoes and socks. They moved over to a soft couch that was along the other wall. John took off her shoes and they rubbed each others feet. John said, "I was beginning to think you were all business until now. Why the change? Deb explained, "We've made progress. I feel like we deserve a little break. I'm sure John and Jessica are impressed with the quick results. Don't you think we deserve a little reward?" Don smiled and said, "What sort of reward do you have in mind?"

He rubbed her toes as he looked into her eyes. Deb replied, "I think we should enjoy this time together and get to know each other better, as long as we don't let it get in the way of the mission." Don lightly tickled her foot. She squirmed and pulled away, "Don't. Please, I'm too ticklish! Just massage. What part of Iron Mountain did you grow up in?" Don replied, "I lived with my parents in one of the western agricultural caves. My father was a biologist. He monitored the soil conditions and controlled threats to the crops, like fungus and insects. Where were you located?" Deb responded, "I was in the eastern side of Iron Mountain. My parents were both astronomers. They helped keep track of what was happening to earth after the split. I'm quite proud of them. What do you do for recreation?" Don responded, "I play ping pong and practice shooting with rifles and pistols. What do you do for recreation?" Deb replied, "I like pistols and rifles too. I prefer swimming to ping pong, but I'm not too bad at ping pong. Do you swim?" Don answered, "Sure I swim. It's part of our training as you know. I'd like to do some scuba diving if we ever get the atmosphere fixed so it's a possibility. There are supposed to be some interesting ancient ship wrecks in the Great Lakes." Deb said, "I'm sure we'll have good atmosphere in ten years or so. Our best scientists will be working on it. I want you to show me those wrecks. Now that we know each other, I think we should stay in touch after the mission. They may ask us to work on other missions together."

Don exclaimed, "We have to live through this mission first of all." Deb frowned, "Do you think this mission is that dangerous?" Don continued, "We need to be prepared for the worst. This Dr. Li could be leading some people in an attempt to take over, or he may be a nihilist with plans for destroying us all. When the desire to avenge wrongs done to their relatives takes over, I've got an idea that these people can become less than practical." Deb stated, "You told the president that Dr. Li could be legitimately expanding his morel operation." Don explained, "There was no reason to alarm them yet and spoil their honeymoon. When we find out what Dr. Li is up to, we'll notify John and Jessica right away." Deb sighed, "I hope he is just expanding his morel growing facilities, but that doesn't explain the warning of the dying man, Jessica spoke of. He warned her of trouble with the North Koreans in the tunnels." Don replied, "Yes, I thought of that. That's why I'm pretty sure Dr. Li is up to no good."

Don got up and poured them a couple more fruit drinks with vodka. When he brought them over to the sofa he said, "We'll have to try to spot where the tunneling machines were unloaded without drawing too much attention to ourselves. I'm sure they've concealed the entrance to their secret operations areas, if there are any. If there is no secret operation, they'll be proud to show us their new enlarged morel growing facility." Deb stated, "That makes sense. If there is no new facility, we'll start looking for hidden passageways or elevators." Don said, "Precisely. We'll use the badges Jessica gave us to gain access to the morel lab at night when there's no one to guide us away from the point of access to the hidden operations."

Deb asked, "Would you like a back rub. I think we've covered about all there is to think about with relation to the mission tomorrow. Let's just relax." Don agreed, "I'd like that." He laid on his belly and let her massage his back. She was quite thorough and professional in her handling of him. It was so relaxing he almost fell asleep.

Soon they were at the southern most recreation center. They booked their rooms, and then went to the nearest dining area. It was part of a large casino. They were seated at a table with a view of a giant screen T.V. which presented a view of the surface of the South Pole. Jessica's mother had ordered the cameras placed there when the earth split apart. They had been used for keeping an eye on the position of their half of earth in relation to the rest of the solar system. Now that earth was back into a stable orbit, some of the cameras were being used for entertainment purposes. Penguins had been released to their natural habitats. Polar bears were introduced as well, even though they had previously been present only at the North Pole. The large crowd in the dining room was watching the screen with fascination as the penguins played and slid into the icy water.

The waitress arrived in just a short time. She said, "My name is Becky. I'll be your waitress. Would you each like to select something from the wine list?" Deb responded, "No, I feel like having a Brandy Alexander. Don chimed in, "I'll have one too. I haven't had any ice cream for quite a while."

Becky asked, "Would you like to place your order now?" Don explained, "We'll need a few minutes to decide." Becky stated, "That's fine. Take all the time you need. I'll be back with your drinks in a few minutes." Deb was a shapely young woman with shiny long black hair. She was average in height with dark brown eyes. She had on a white mini skirt with white fur trim around the bottom edge. It was part of the polar motif of the restaurant. Don couldn't help but notice how attractive she was as she waltzed away. Deb frowned slightly, "Does she do something for you, Don?" Don laughed, "She's good looking. No one would deny that. I was just enjoying the outfit she has on. It goes with this place well." Deb responded, "And her bare shapely legs aren't the main attraction, then?"

Don responded tactfully, "Actually, I'm looking forward to seeing you in the swimming pool this evening. Did you bring your suit?" Deb smiled, "That's nice of you to say. I always pack my swim suit. Remember? I love swimming." Don responded, "Don't worry, I remember everything you said. Your mom and dad are astronomers and you're quite proud of them." Deb said, "So you were listening. I'm pleased. You'll be pleased to learn that my suit is small and revealing. I think it's tasteful though. If you like women in mini skirts, I have some short skirts with me. Do you think I should wear one tomorrow?" Don smiled, "I'd like that. You could help provide some distraction that would keep the laboratory workers from watching to see what I'm looking for. I'll appreciate it too of course. You have an exquisite figure. Pant suits don't do you justice."

The Brandy Alexanders came. Becky asked, "Have you decided on your meal?" Don nodded for Deb to go first. She said, "I'll take escargot and morels with buttered bread. A salad with cherry tomatoes, egg and blue cheese dressing." Don explained, "I'll take the raw oysters and the rest will be the same as she ordered." Becky asked, "Would either of you like and appetizer?" Deb said, "Not for me, thank you." Don shook his head no. Becky trotted off in her fetching little mini skirt. Don felt Deb's bare foot tickling his leg. He pulled off his shoes and engaged in some footsy with her.

Suddenly everyone gasped involuntarily as red drops of blood splattered across the Television screen. One of the polar bears had just snatched up a penguin and was ruthlessly shaking it to death in its jaws. The management jumped on the intercom to calm the viewers, "As you know, polar bears must eat. This is only normal behavior for them. There are plenty of penguins. A technician will soon switch us to a different camera." The screen went black and in a minute there was a new view of other penguins playing in a bay not too far from where the first camera was.

Don sighed, "I hope that's the last blood we'll be seeing on this mission." Deb responded, "I agree. That's enough blood for one trip." Their food came and they enjoyed the meal while some of their favorite jazz tunes were being played softly over the sound system. Deb said, "Jessica warned us about being sure to get separate rooms, but I wish I knew more about the customs down here. Should we even go to each other's rooms?" Don said softly, "We can ask Becky. She's a nice young woman. She'll tell us." Deb responded, "That's fine, just don't embarrass me." Don caught Becky's eye and signaled for her to come over. Becky came right over. "What can I do for you?" Don said softly, "Without letting others know what we're talking about, can you tell me if it's acceptable, in the residences, for a single woman to be in her boyfriend's room?" Becky said softly, "As long as she doesn't stay past midnight it's fine. Few people would notice if it was later by a few hours. It just depends on how concerned you are about your reputation. If you aren't from around here, it probably won't be of too much concern for you. Our people want to discourage immorality. If you're in love, no one will be too upset about long times spent together." Don said, "Thanks for the information. We'll try to be discrete about our time together." Deb stated, "That was fine. I wasn't too embarrassed. So who comes to whose room this evening?" Don said, "I would like to talk a little more about the mission. Let's meet at your room right after our swim." Deb smiled, "I like that idea." She traced his calf and ankles some more with her toes.

After the meal, they went to their own rooms and got dressed for the pool. Don was indeed pleased to see how alluring Deb looked in her small white bikini. He swam back and forth with her in the pool for a long time. The artificial lighting was starting to dim in order to simulate evening. The pool was refreshingly cool. As they stepped out of the pool, Debs white suit didn't leave much unrevealed. Her attractive firm breasts could be seen rather clearly through the wet white cloth of her suit. Don didn't want other people to be embarrassed, so he suggested, "Why don't we go to your room now. There's much we need to discuss." Deb smiled knowingly, "I agree. Let's have a long chat in private."

They walked to her room and entered the outer kitchen. Deb asked, "Do you want some coffee? They have the kitchen furnished with most things people might want. She opened the freezer, "Look, they even have ice cream in here." Don said, "You already had ice cream tonight. You want more already?" Deb responded, "We swam over a mile. We deserve some more ice cream. She put coffee cups in the microwave and started dipping up ice cream. Soon they were sipping coffee and eating ice cream. Deb said, "See what I like to do?" She put a spoon full of ice cream in her coffee. Don responded, "That looks like a good idea." He put a big spoon full of the vanilla ice cream in his coffee. "This way we can drink it faster and get down to important things." Deb smiled, "What important things are you talking about?" Don said, "I want to talk more about the mission, but we're right next to outside windows here. The bedroom would be a better place to talk." They finished the ice cream and coffee and walked to the bedroom.

When they got to the bedroom, they both gasped in amazement. It was the largest bedroom they had seen. There was a gas fireplace next to the bed. The walls were done in wall paper with images of trees. It looked like they were in the middle of a forest. John started the fireplace and said, "We'd better get out of these wet suits." Deb frowned, "Are you trying to get me stark naked this quick. I don't want you thinking I'm loose!" Don asked, "Well what would you suggest? I can see right through that suit, anyway. I promise to be a perfect gentleman." Deb laughed, "Nice try. I've got an extra bath robe you can wear." She went to her suit case and pulled it out. She tossed it to him. Then she took off her suit and put on the other bath robe. Don watched her closely as she stripped. She laughed, "I thought you said you had already seen my nakedness in the suit." Don responded, "Well, I was just comparing in my mind, the difference between suit nakedness and stark nakedness. I think I like you either way."

Deb smiled, "That's nice, now what did you want to talk to me about?" Don took her hand and led her to the masonry ledge in front of the fireplace. They sat there and warmed themselves. Don said softly, "I'm not a womanizer. If I was, I would have fed you more liquor at the restaurant. I want us to really get to know each other on this trip. I hope that after our mission is over, we can start spending lots of time together back in America, or on other missions. Deb stated, "I was hoping you felt that way, Don. I also want us to spend time together." Don continued, "This mission is more dangerous than I've alluded to, so far. If we get too close to the North Korean tunnelers, they won't hesitate to shoot us. I'm almost sure they would have developed guns by now. They aren't stupid. I suspect they may be building an atomic or fusion bomb. If they want revenge, that would be the way to go. They can't shoot a billion people in Jessica's country. She could close off the tunnels and keep them out of Xanadu. If we find Dr. Li, we won't be able to stop him with a couple bodyguards. We'll have to send for reinforcements. If we don't find him, we'll have to keep looking. We can't let him vent his desires for revenge on the entire population of mankind."

Deb asked, "What if one of us is killed?" Don said, "Try not to think about it. If one of us survives, at least there will be good memories of the time we had together. We need to make plans just as though nothing will happen to us. I like to think of us retiring together. When they get the atmosphere fixed, we could go to the Great Lakes and do some boating and swimming." Deb laughed, "I'd like that. We could travel all over. I love to see new things." They discussed their possible future together for a long time, there in front of the fire place. Finally they turned off the light. Deb found a bottle of lotion in her suit case. They took turns rubbing lotion on each other in sensuous ways till they emptied the bottle and it got to be midnight. They were both still flushed with excitement, but forced themselves to say good night. Don climbed into his swim suit and gave Deb one final kiss before he returned to his own room.

In the morning they went to the train station and told the clerk to have the guards escorted to their breakfast table if they arrived. They went to the same restaurant they had been to for supper. They ordered the breakfast special of waffles and eggs with sausage. Don reached over and took Debs hand and whispered, "I enjoyed being with you last night. We can stop by here on the way back. I'm sure they have body lotion for sell here. We can start a little earlier instead of swimming so long." Deb laughed and whispered back, "You've got it all planned. I like that. I don't mind losing a little swim time for more massage from those strong hands of yours! You know how to drive me nuts. I tingled all over!" Don rested his left hand on her knee as she sat to his left at the table. He started to move it up towards the mini skirt she was wearing. She pulled his ear and whispered, "People will be watching. Behave yourself!" Don frowned and put both hands on the table. "Very well. I'll wait till tonight. You're worth waiting for."

The food arrived and they both prayed silently for the food. Several people around them were watching them, and approved of their praying. They were starting to fit in to the new society. They ate their food eagerly and chatted about the few buildings they had taken time to look at on the way to the restaurant. Don stated, "The buildings are like the ones in Xanadu, only they aren't as big." Deb said, "Yes, the cave here doesn't have such a high ceiling. They had to keep the buildings shorter. They used lots of bricks and stone. I suppose they didn't want to use up their trees for housing." Don commented, "They used Roman arches. I suppose that's appropriate for this igloo setting. I hope breakfast doesn't include watching penguins being torn to pieces, like at supper." Deb moaned, "You and me both. They should put those bears back in their cages!"

Just then the guards arrived. Don introduced himself and Deb. The guards only used their first names, which were Burt and Dave. Both men were tall and muscular. They had dark short hair and sunglasses. They looked a little like twins. Don said, "I'll get the waitress if either of you are hungry." Burt smiled, "I could use a little breakfast." Dave said, "Yes, I'm hungry." Don waived for the waitress to come. She came right away and got the men's orders. Burt was a little darker skinned than Dave. That was how Don decided to tell them apart. Burt said softly, "We were only told to come down here. We don't know what the plan is. You'll have to brief us." Don explained, "We'll have a private rail car for the trip to the morel caves. I'll explain everything when we get on the train. For now, just enjoy your food and have a look around the resort. Our train leaves at 10:00 o'clock this morning. Be here a little early, so we're sure not to miss the train. Let's synchronize our watches. It's now 8:31 A.M. He held his watch out so they could correct their watches.

Dave exclaimed, "They certainly are friendly down here. We each got back massages from nice young women, and they chatted and drank with us during the whole trip." Don explained, "I'm sure Jessica ordered V.I.P. treatment for both of you." The meals arrived and the men ate and chatted some more about the train and the young women. When they finished their meals, the guards went to see more of the recreation center. Don and Deb went sight seeing as well. The place wasn't nearly as wide and spread out and Xanadu, but it was still impressive. There were several casinos, with different themes. One was built like a pyramid. One looked like a circus tent and another was a giant igloo. There were dozens of massage parlors and fitness clubs with wet and dry saunas. There were gift shops and snack shops. At the north end of town was an artificial lake with white sand and tanning lights. They didn't get to see everything. In no time at all, it was time to board the train. At ten till ten, the guards arrived at the station and met Deb and Don.

Right at ten, the train pulled up and stopped. They were signaled to their car, by the conductor. The train only loaded a couple other people and took off minutes later. They were told, by the conductor, that the trip would take one hour. He left as soon as he had given them that information. Don started briefing the men right away. He stated, "The train will wait for us, in case we need to make a quick get away. We are trying to find where some tunneling machines have gone. A man named Dr. Li, is in charge of morel growing at the laboratory we are going to. If we find no new morel growing areas and the tunnel machines are gone, we'll know that Dr. Li is up to some kind of secret initiative. Keep your eyes open. If that's the case, we'll be looking for the access point to Dr. Li's secret world. There must be some elevator or hidden tunnel which he uses to get from the secret world to this world. We're just looking for that port of entry now. If we find it, we'll return with reinforcements. We'll all stay in radio contact, but maintain radio silence except for emergencies. We'll keep our ear phones in place at all times. If we click the microphone several times, you'll know we can't speak right then. Dave will stay on the train to retreat and call for reinforcements if we get into serious trouble and can't make it back. Burt will cover our backs as Deb and I talk to people. We should be in and out of there in just a few hours at the most. If Dr. Li is there and shows us the tunnel machines and the new growing areas, we'll be done in less than an hour. Is that clear?"

Burt stated, "That's clear enough." Dave asked, "How far do you want me to retreat? Don explained, "Take the train back to the entertainment center and wait for the reinforcements. They should be here in less than twenty-four hours. I'm sure the President is working up a contingency plan even as we speak. Dave stated, "He did say he'd have us covered."

They rode quietly the rest of the trip. No one touched any alcohol. They just drank the fruit juices and water. When they arrived, Burt led the way to the entrance. They all showed their passes and were allowed to enter. A short male tour guide met them as they entered and introduced himself as Ty Po. The guide had black hair and looked like he was North Korean. Don asked him, "Where is Dr. Li?" The young guide stated, "Dr. Li is in a lengthy meeting today. He'll be busy till 6:00 o'clock this evening. Why do you want to see Dr. Li?" Don explained, "We need to know if he has any extra tunnel machines which can be used to explore Mars. We need all the machines we can get." Ty smiled, "I'll leave you to look around for a few minutes while I check with Dr. Li." The guide hurried away and went to his office. He called Dr. Li. When Dr. Li answered, the guide explained, "There are some people here looking for tunneling machines. They say they need them to explore Mars. What should I do?" Dr. Li stated, "Tell them I have become quite ill and have had to cancel all meetings today. Tell them I'll talk with them on the telephone tomorrow. Stall them. I need time to make final preparations here." The guide went back to his visitors and explained the situation, "Dr. Li has become ill. He will call you tomorrow or as soon as he is well enough. I think it was sushi. The fish must not have been fresh enough. He is terribly ill. I'm sorry to disappoint you."

Don stated, "That's not a problem. If you don't mind, we'd like to look around some more at your operation." Ty smiled and stated, "You can look around as much as you like. I'll be happy to answer your questions." He couldn't take his eyes off the lovely Deb in her mini skirt. While Deb talked to Ty, Don went looking for a hidden opening. It was obvious they were hiding something. There were no new caves to be seen. All the ceilings were covered with moss. Don could see on the floor where some train rails had been at one time. There was new cement hiding what was sure to be the old rails. Don followed the cement to the far end of the caves, where the cement disappeared under deeper dirt. There was a service elevator hidden behind endless stacks of wooden skids. Don thought, *This must be where they took the tunneling machines to their secret location.*

He had learned enough for today. He would return with reinforcements. He strode briskly away from the elevator and rejoined the group. Ty was still fascinated with Deb and barely noticed when Don returned. Don said, "Well I guess we'll be leaving. Thank you for your time. We'll give Dr. Li a call in a couple days when he's feeling better." He shook Ty's hand and then they walked back to the train and left.

Don called the President at once. "Mr. President. We have completed our initial mission. They are hiding the machines. There are no new morel caves. I've located the elevator they've used to move the machines to a different level. I need the reinforcements to help search for hostile forces. Over?" John answered, "I'll have three hundred fully armed men down there in five hours. They're just now arrived in Xanadu. I'll send them on through. They're already fully briefed. I brought them down, just in case you needed them. Do you read?" Don answered, "I read you loud and clear. Over and out." The radio became silent. Don said, "We'll wait at the recreation center for the train load of troops. Then we'll come right back and search for the hidden tunnels."

Five hours later, the troops arrived at the recreation center. Don and Deb led them to Dr. Li's morel growing facility, on hour further down the tracks. They were allowed entrance with no resistance. Don led them to the elevator he had found on his previous visit. The troops quickly moved the skids that were hiding the elevator and making it inaccessible. Quickly, Don, Deb and fifty of the troops took the giant elevator to the lower level. The men's guns were pointed and ready when the elevator opened. To there surprise, only a man in a white lab coat was waiting for them when the door opened. He said, "Welcome. I've been expecting you. My name is Dr. Li. I knew that eventually I might have to explain why I took the ten tunneling machines. As you see. They are all right here." He pointed in the direction of a long row of tunneling machines. "I have them poised and ready to make some new morel caves. I'm just waiting on the trained operators to arrive. When I took the machines, I didn't realize they were so complicated. I didn't want to waste time getting the required permissions for the machines. People are pressuring me for more morels. I like to keep my customers satisfied."

Don asked, "Do you mind if we have a look around?" Dr. Li stated, "I don't mind at all. Please don't mix up my paper work. That's all I ask. I try to keep good records of my work." Don and Deb went to some filing cabinets they saw along one wall and searched for anything subversive. All they found were personnel records and records of morel growing transactions. Deb explained, "We're sorry to have troubled you. Everything here looks to be in order. We came because of reports of trouble or unrest. How many workers do you currently have?" Dr. Li answered, "I now have five hundred workers including the clerical and administrative people." Deb continued, "Do the workers seem content?" Dr. Li smiled, "My people love to work. They are happy with life here. Don't listen to rumors about us. Everyone is content here." Don stated, "We'd like to examine the walls of this area if you don't mind." Dr. Li laughed, "Feel free to look at the walls. We aren't hiding anything." Don and ten of the troops examined the walls for secret tunnel openings. They found nothing. Don came back to Dr. Li and asked, "Why is the large elevator hidden by skids?" Dr. Li explained, "We only use that elevator when there is a large item like the tunneling machines to bring down. We have a separate personnel elevator." Don asked, "Why did you build this lower level?" Dr. Li explained, "We needed to keep the moisture away from our records. Also, our geologist advised us to dig at this deeper level so as to find more suitable rock that would support wider caves."

Don asked Deb to walk with him across the room. When they were far enough away, he spoke softly to Deb, "Do you think he's telling the truth?" Deb answered, "Everything he says is logical. There isn't much more we can do here now. We'll have to tell the President and Jessica that it was a false alarm. I think we should do some follow up checks on Dr. Li, though, just to be safe." Don said, "I agree. Let's take the troops back to the recreation area. They deserve a little break after their long trip down here. I'll get orders from the President for them to take a day or two of leave time down here. The cultural learning will be valuable for them."

Don and Deb walked back to Dr. Li. Don said, "We're sorry to have troubled you. We'll leave you in peace now." Dr. Li stated, "It was a pleasure meeting all of you. We seldom receive visitors down here. It's always a pleasure to meet people from a different culture. I'm sure Jessica has made the right decision in cooperating with your country. Come again sometime, if it fits into your schedule." Don said, "Thank you. Dr. Li. You do a great service, raising morels. They are a wonderful food."

They all got back on the elevator and returned to the surface. When they were back on the train, Don called the President. "Mr. President, this is Don. It appears to have been a false alarm. All the tunneling machines are just sitting there. He says he has no one to operate them yet. He's planning to expand the morel facility. Deb thinks we should check on him from time to time. Over?" John answered, "We'll keep checking on him from time to time. Jessica says the troops can stay at the recreation center down there for a couple days. Tell them everything's paid for. Do you read me?" Don stated, "I read you. I'll keep the troops at the recreation center for a couple days. Is there anything else?" John said, "That's all for now. Thanks for the update. Over and out."

Back in Dr. Li's lower laboratory his assistant came up to him and said, "Our observer says the troops have passed the five hundred mile marker." Dr. Li stated, "Good. They probably won't bother us again for awhile. It was lucky I brought these worn out tunneling machines back to the lab. My engineers have duplicated them in sufficient numbers that we can have our culture on Mars fully operational in just a couple months. There are over fifty tunneling machines working day and night. In a few months we can start bringing in more workers who are loyal to our ancestors. We don't want to leave any of our loyal people behind when we destroy earth." The assistant asked, "Are there any new orders?" Dr. Li explained, "No. We continue as planned. Everything is going just as I wish it to."

In another hour and a half, the troops were back at the southern most recreation center. There were enough rooms to accommodate them all, and soon they were enjoying the restaurants and entertainments that were to be found there.

Chapter Six

Jessica Visits Iron Mountain

John and Jessica were on their way to Iron Mountain to meet with the Joint Chiefs of Staff and the cabinet,and to allow Jessica to see the facility. Don and Deb were given some vacation time, at their request. They spent several months seeing the underground cities and resort areas.

When John and Jessica arrived at Iron Mountain, secretary of state, Warren Anglemeyer was there to greet them as soon as they left the tunnel. He was a stocky man with white hair, in his early sixties. He stated, "Welcome back Mr. President and Mrs. President." John responded, "Thank you, Warren. You can address us informally since we're in private." Warren asked, "So the rebellion was a rumor?" John responded, "Don't tell anyone, but we still have some misgivings about how things are going at the South Pole. We'll make periodic checks to see that things aren't getting out of hand. It appears that Dr. Li is a little too independent about how he obtains what he wants. There doesn't seem to be any immediate threat to Jessica's government or us." Warren said, "That's good to hear. Will you meet with the joint chiefs of staff and the cabinet tomorrow?" John explained, "Yes, I'd like to have Jessica join us. She has input with regards to the atmosphere and development of the new planet." Warren responded, "Good. I've been hoping we'd get going on those two items of business. Jessica, it's good to have such a lovely and intelligent woman helping us with matters of import. Will you be able to stay long?"

Jessica responded, "John and I will be shuttling back and forth between my country and yours. We call my country The Cave. I know that sounds primitive, but we're actually quite an advanced civilization. Our initial founder, Dr. Exeeto, named the subterranean world over eleven hundred years ago. We have kept the name in honor of him." Warren said, "I hope you'll tell me all about your country. Have you eaten lunch yet?" Jessica explained, "Yes, we ate on the train. I wouldn't mind some fruit drinks, if you have them." Warren said proudly, "Our food caves are doing well with citrus products. I think we can find some fruit drinks at my quarters, if you'll both accept my invitation to join me there." John said, "Lead the way. We're completely at your disposal."

They took an electric cart to Warren's quarters. He lived in one of the executive suites, not far from John's suite. John and Jessica were introduced to Warren's wife, Laura. She was short and thin, with short curly gray hair. She brought them all fruit drinks and some crackers with cheese. John stated, "I'll have my secretary call the Joint Chiefs of Staff and the cabinet, and have them meet me in my suite at 2:00 o'clock tomorrow. We can develop many new initiatives and really get things moving. Jessica's country has a billion residents. I'm sure we can recruit some crews from there to help us with our reconstruction efforts. We'll have to work out some method of cooperation on financial matters. They don't use money. Everything is socialized. The government provides food, housing, heating, education. Jessica doesn't want her people bringing gold and rubies out of The Cave. We'll need to provide everything for her people who come here to work. I don't think it will be a problem."

Jessica explained, "We are terribly concerned with the plight of poor people. We don't have poor people. We don't want any people to be made poor. I'll only allow my people to come here if they are well cared for." Warren stated, "That's only reasonable. Our Bible says that one should never muzzle the mouth of the ox that treads out the grain." Jessica laughed, "We have that same Bible. My country is mostly Christian. Some of the North Koreans refuse to convert and cling to their ancestor worshipping. However, they are a small minority of under a hundred thousand people. I'll keep them happy growing morels in the south. I'll send my more technically trained people to help you. I want us to start making transparent surface tunnels which will allow people to see the surface world even before we succeed in creating more atmosphere." Warren responded, "That sounds like a worthy project. Our western states have plenty of sand that can be used for making the glass windows. We have the technology for making the glass shatter proof."

John explained, "The metal frameworks will help us use all the steel and aluminum which we produce. I want our steel and aluminum mills to operate to full capacity. We'll need to build added facilities to meet the high demand for steel and aluminum." Jessica said, "The gases from the metal manufacturing process, specifically the burning of coal, will create more carbon dioxide. The carbon dioxide will later be converted to oxygen by the trees we'll soon be planting. My people know how to create fertile soil in large quantities. I hope to have Mars planted to trees in short order."

Warren exclaimed, "You certainly are a can do person, Jessica. I admire your determination. What other plans do you have?" Jessica continued, "My people are big on recreation centers. We love comedians. I would like the tunnels to lead to recreation centers all over the entire planet. I'd like to see live entertainment with comedians at each center." Warren asked, "What sort of comedy to your people like?" Jessica explained, "Some of our most successful comedians do Bible monologues. They tell accurate Bible stories and then point out various ways in which our world is funny. They point out the foibles of mankind and how often we stubbornly resist the will of God. My favorite comedian is Jim Benny. He named himself after one of America's top comedians from the past, Jack Benny. He play's the violin like Jack Benny did. I have a video disc with me of one of his performances. Would you like to see it?" Warren exclaimed, "I'd love to see it." Jessica pulled out her lap top computer and inserted the memory stick. They watched with amusement as Jim played the slightly sour notes on his violin.

Jim then went into his monologue, "When the Hebrew people were wandering about in the desert, looking for the promised land, they were fed on manna which came from heaven every morning and evening. It could not be stored. They were dependent on God each day for their food. After some time they got tired of the flavor and texture of the manna. It was like a sweet light bread of some kind. I'm not sure exactly how it tasted. They complained bitterly about the boring food. God listened patiently to their complaints and started sending them small birds, called quails, to eat. These birds satisfied the Hebrew people for some time. Remember, they wandered for forty years in the desert before they found the promised land of milk and honey. They started complaining about the diet of quail. God was vexed exceedingly that they were looking a gift horse in the mouth. Here he was, making sure they were fed, and all they could do was complain. Next he sent them poisonous snakes to bite their legs and ankles. The people were punished for a long time by these venomous snakes. So we should learn from this. Don't complain about your food. If you're paying the bill, maybe you can complain. If God is feeding you, eat what he prepares for you and don't complain. I eat morels fried in butter every morning. I never get tired of them. They grow everywhere here in the tunnels and caves. God is feeding us. Of course we have plenty of variety in our foods now. The point is, we shouldn't take God for granted. He doesn't want us to be overly concerned about food. He wants us to think and pray for wisdom, which he says is more valuable than rubies or fine silver.

Possibly at times your job becomes boring. Don't complain bitterly about the job. Be glad you have a job. Try to do the best job you can do even though it isn't glorious. Look at the job as a vital part of our society, just as each part of the human body is vital. Look at the anus. It isn't glamorous. Where would you be without one, though? Look at the waxy ear canal, always getting plugged with orange wax. Without one or two of them, you couldn't hear well.

If you're a lowly security guard and things often get boring, remember, you're protecting people. Even if you never stop a dangerous situation from expanding, you are always there, protecting. Read Proverbs and look for wisdom. Don't argue with fools. A foolish man will hate you if you try to instruct him. If you instruct a wise man, he will love you for it and he will become wiser yet. Don't throw your pearls before swine. They will turn and rend you to pieces. If people hate sound Biblical instruction, let them be. They will find their reward."

Jim started playing his violin, which signaled the end of that session. Jessica turned off the lap top. She asked, "See what our monologues are like?" Warren exclaimed, "That was quite a bit like our Sunday morning sermons. I think our people would like to experience your so called comedians. They certainly pick interesting topics. I don't know my old testament as well as I should. This was a learning experience." Jessica said, "I have dozens of these videos. If you want to duplicate them it would be fine." Warren asked, "Are there copyright laws in your country?" Jessica explained, "Our comedians want as many people as possible to hear them. They are our most highly paid people. They have gold, rubies and long vacations. They don't need to get money every time someone copies their routines." John explained, "It's just another little difference in our cultures. I'll have copies sent to all our entertainment centers." Jessica smiled, "My comedians will be honored."

Warren asked, "Do you think we should start tunneling into the depths of Mars?" Jessica responded, "Once we have the atmosphere improved and enough trees planted, then it might be good to tunnel into Mars. If a large meteor would happen to hit the surface of Mirth and possibly destroy the earth section, it would be good to have the Mars portion of Mirth developed to assure the continuation of mankind's existence. Also, my people are always interested in finding more gold and rubies. They are the status symbols of our culture. There is nothing to spend them on. They give us a feeling of happiness like your people used to feel when they had a powerful shiny muscle car in the garage. I've read about them in our ancient history books. The corvette was one of the most prized cars. People waxed it, looked at it, but rarely drove it very far. They didn't want to wear it out. Am I correct?" John laughed, "Yes, your research into our history is accurate."

Jessica continued, "People, in ancient times drove fast and recklessly, often losing their lives trying to get from point A to point B. That seems like foolishness. I think we should find the plans for the corvette and other great cars. We should build millions of them and drive them around slowly. They would create wonderful green house gases which would help warm the planet which is now in a deeper and colder orbit. We need green house gases. Everyone must have a classic car and all the free gasoline they want. Of course this will have to wait until the atmosphere is thickened enough for us to breath outside the tunnels." Warren exclaimed, "Americans are going to love you, Jessica. That's the kind of talk they like to hear."

Jessica responded, "I think I'll enjoy riding around your country in a muscle car. I've heard the scenery is wonderful. You have tall mountains and some of the largest lakes in the world. I want to see everything!" John said, "I have some cameras positioned in many places around the country. You can get some nice views of America right from my suite." Jessica exclaimed, "That will be great! I'm looking forward to that." John said, "I'd like to show you some of Iron Mountain first.

They said their good-bys to Warren and his wife, and John led Jessica to the missile control room. John explained, "This is where we launched our intercontinental ballistic missiles. We built Iron Mountain so we'd be able to launch a counter attack even if we took a direct hit from an atomic bomb right here at the mountain." Jessica responded, "It must have been terrible, worrying all the time about the end of the world as they knew it. I hope we can live a more relaxed and fun filled existence."

John took her with an electric cart to the growing caves. John stated, "We've made lots of progress in growing larger quantities of food. However, we've only just recently started growing large numbers of trees to help keep the oxygen supply ample. Always in the past we were dependent on electrolysis. We had to split water into hydrogen and oxygen in order to have enough oxygen. With the help of your tunneling technology, we should be able to expand our food and oxygen production greatly." Jessica smiled, "We'll give you all the tunneling machines you want. Just promise not to devote all your time to improving Iron Mountain. We need to develop the whole planet." John laughed, "That's fine Jessica. Save the speech on development of the planet for the Joint Chiefs of Staff and the cabinet. Also, I want you to address all of Iron Mountain. I want everyone to hear your ideas on development of the planet. The idea about everyone having a car to drive around will be a great morale booster."

They drove their cart through cave after cave of growing vegetables and trees. There were sheep wandering amongst the trees keeping the weeds and grass under control. Bald eagles were nesting in the jagged ledges of the cave walls. Rabbits were everywhere for them to feed on. Jessica asked, "What is that bird with the white head?" John smiled and spoke proudly, "Those are our bald eagles. They are the national bird. They are symbols of courage. We wanted to be sure they survived the atomic warfare. The eagle's image is on most of our currency." Jessica exclaimed, "You have a proud and aggressive nation. I've read in our history books about the many wars your country has engaged in down through the years. Your brave men sacrificed their lives to stop Hitler from killing all the Jews and from taking control of the entire world. America was often at war, but not because of a desire to control the world. You wanted God's will to be done. You wanted free elections for the nations of the world. You wanted to stop genocide and tyranny. You gave jobs to much of the world.

Good intentions, however couldn't save you from the attacks of Satan. The evil nations of the world were constantly at work against you. North Korea was giving atomic bombs to all her friends, to be used against you. Man's evil nature made sure that war would be never ending. It's unfortunate that Great Britain was on the wrong side of the Atlantic when the earth split. They were a good friendly nation and didn't deserve to be eliminated." John exclaimed, "Yes, they were a brave people. The Irish too were brave, and the Scottish people. They'll all have a place in heaven, though, if their hearts were right and they took Jesus as their savior." Jessica responded, "Yes, you can call on God as Jehovah all your life, but if you don't believe in Jesus as the messiah, you won't have eternal life. Jesus is the key. He is essential."

John asked, "I wonder why our half of earth was allowed to survive. What purpose does God have for us now?" Jessica responded, "I think we've been given a second chance. We may have a planet where there's no war. We can have a planet where there are no poor. Everyone can be well cared for." John sighed, "I hope you're right."

They stopped for awhile and walked through the trees. John apologized, "I'm sorry about all the sheep droppings. We don't do much strolling through the trees here." Jessica laughed, "Don't worry. I brought plenty of shoes with me. They stopped under a large hackberry tree and held each other while they looked into each other's eyes. John was fascinated by how green Jessica's eyes were. He asked, "Were your mother's eyes green too?" Jessica smiled, "Yes, it's common for the women in my family to have green eyes and red hair." John said softly, "Your eyes are gentle and attractive. I'm glad we were able to get together." Jessica leaned in closer to John and kissed him gently on the lips. They held each other for a long time under the tree. Jessica whispered, "No matter what happens, I'll always love you. You came into my life like a brave knight and brushed away my fears. I know you can help me maintain peace. I was terribly worried about the North Koreans. Now I know they'll stay under control." John whispered, "Don't worry about a thing. Your people love you and respect your abilities. The North Koreans are the only trouble makers. I'll send Don and Deb back down there to check on things every couple months. I trust them completely." Jessica responded, "They seem quite competent. I trust them too." They grew silent and kissed gently as the eagles cried in the background.

Finally Jessica asked, "Can you show me your steel mills? I've heard that American's are good at making steel." John smiled proudly, "Yes, our ability to make lots of steel quickly is what allowed us to win the war against Hitler. We made so many tanks and ships that he was overwhelmed. Of course the Russians made large quantities of tanks too, that were used against Hitler. Hitler made the biggest and most powerful tanks, but he was overwhelmed by numbers." Jessica exclaimed, "You certainly know your ancient history. I thought I was the only one on earth who is so caught up with history. I always say, if you can't learn from the past, you're doomed to repeat it." John laughed, "Those sound like wise words. Somewhere in Proverbs it says, in effect, 'If you keep company with wise men you become wise, but if you keep company with fools you become a fool.'" Jessica laughed, "Oh yes, I like that Proverb."

They drove to the steel mill. It was a hot noisy place and people were everywhere, working at a brisk pace. John handed Jessica a pair of deep violet colored glasses to wear. He said, "These will protect your eyes from the brilliant light of the molten steel." Jessica put on the glasses. She watched as the huge steel ladle poured its contents into the waiting rectangular molds. Sparks flew everywhere as the overhead crane adjusted the pour position to avoid waste. They drove their cart further down along the mill and saw ingots coming out of a furnace. The rectangular cubed ingots were white hot and even where they stood the heat was terrific. They traveled on to the plate mill, where the hot ingots were rolled out into thin sheets.

John explained, "You probably use electricity to heat the steel, so it's easier to conceal your operation. We haven't been in hiding, like The Cave has been, so we simply vent our smoke to the surface." Jessica responded, "Yes, we use electricity to heat the steel and ore. It makes sense for you to vent as you do. We'll be adding many new mills. I hope you can teach us how you have built these mills. They'll help us create more atmosphere." John stated, "We'll be glad to send you as many advisors as you like." They walked through the mills and John explained everything to Jessica. Jessica asked, "Would you show me the astronomical observatory?" John responded,

"Certainly, it's at the very top of Iron Mountain." They drove their cart to the elevator and took it to the top floor. In the observatory room, there was no telescope. One wall was covered with large monitor screens.

John explained, "In order for Iron Mountain to be bomb proof, we had to build the telescope outside of the mountain. We operate the telescope by remote control. The only way to reach the telescope to do repairs is to use a helicopter." Jessica exclaimed, "That's quite interesting. Can I see something?" John said, "We'll need to wait till tonight. There's too much light right now for good viewing." John offered, "Why don't we go to my suite now. You can see the views I have from my remote cameras." Jessica answered, "I'd like that. I can put on some fresh shoes."

They rode the electric cart to John's suite. The dining room and living room had the walls covered with screens that gave live coverage of various places in America. John explained, "This is one of my favorite views. It's of the Grand Canyon. The cameras have solar batteries, so they operate without maintenance for many years. They transmit their signals with a laser beam which is aimed at our receiving dish on top of the mountain. A backup atomic battery helps keep up the power supply necessary to operate the laser." They watched the view of the Grand Canyon together. Jessica exclaimed, "I've never seen anything so panoramic and grandiose. It makes my tunnel existence seem so confined and restricted." John said, "I want to walk in the Grand Canyon and throw some small stones off the edge." Jessica stated, "I'll go with you. We can drive our vette." John smiled, "I like that idea."

He used his remote to turn on another screen. The view was of the Great Lakes. He asked, "Have you seen snow before?" Jessica responded, "Only on the South Pole." John explained, "Lake Michigan appears to be covered completely with snow and ice. It's April and usually there's little snow at all. Lake Michigan rarely ever used to ice over completely. Our deeper orbit has made the weather of our earth portion turn noticeably colder." Jessica responded, "I agree. The ice on the lake would seem to prove that."

John clicked the remote and another screen became active. This screen depicted a moving view of the ground. There was scrub brush and an occasional jack rabbit. Then the camera would swoop up over a mountain and then back out over the plains. Jessica asked, "How do you get that view?" John explained, "It's a drone plane that operates on atomic batteries and electricity. We keep it circling Iron Mountain to alert us if anyone is approaching." Jessica asked incredulously, "Do you really think there are survivors out there?" John explained, "Even though it seems highly unlikely, we can't afford to let down our defenses. We believe in staying informed."

There were several cameras which offered views of the American borders. The Pacific coast cameras reminded them that the major oceans had lost much of their water. The shoreline was full of shallow pools of water, where there had been recessions in the ocean floor. Most of the water from the oceans had poured over the broken edges of earth and had been turned to steam by the geothermal heat which was on the newly exposed center of earth. That steam quickly turned to snow as earth's new orbit caused it to become colder. The snow was deposited mainly at the North and South Poles. It wasn't quite a new ice age, but the snow on the poles was over a hundred feet deeper and the snow fields expanded much further towards the equator. The coastal cameras documented the increased snow fall.

One Atlantic coast camera was focused on New York. It was clear that not one sky scraper had survived the fusion bombs as they exploded over the Atlantic. The city appeared to be nothing but a pile of rubble. John stated, "The broken cities are an embarrassment to us. We'd like to remove them as soon as possible. The skyscrapers will no longer be needed. We can salvage quite a bit of steel from the cities along the coast line. Both fusion bombs were exploded over the Atlantic, so the Pacific coast cities weren't damaged as badly. We can probably use some of the buildings on that coast line. We don't have cameras on Detroit, Chicago or many of the other major cities. I think we may be able to resume automobile production in Detroit without too much in the way of repairs being necessary. Most private homes are ruined by now, but the factories were made to last longer."

Jessica said reassuringly, "Don't feel you have to apologize for the way things are. We can get everything looking good again. I have a billion people at my disposal, and they all want to be helpful. They like a challenge. We'll clean up the mess and move ahead." John hugged her and responded, "I like your can do attitude. We'll make a good team. Now let's order in some food and relax for awhile. You'll have a long day tomorrow. There's the meeting with the Joint Chiefs of Staff and the cabinet, and the address to the nation. You'll need some rest."

They took a long steamy shower together. Jessica made sure John was immaculately clean. She loved running her soapy hands over his body. They held each other in the flow of hot water and looked closely into each other's eyes. John reminded Jessica, "You need your rest. I don't want you yawning during your address." Jessica smiled, "As soon as the address is done, we're coming right back here to make up for what we didn't do tonight." John laughed, "Agreed! Let's get our robes on. The food will be here soon." They put on their bath robes and let the caterer in with the food. It was lobster and shrimp with stewed vegetables cooked in butter and garlic. They said a prayer of thanks for the food and then ate heartily. As they ate, they looked at each other with amorous thoughts. They played footsy under the table as they professed their undying love for each other.

After about an hour of sweet talk and drinking coffee together, Jessica said, "I hate to be overly concerned about this, but your suite looks a little too much like a command center. All these monitors of the outside are important, I'm sure, but we need a living room that allows us to forget the troubled state of the outside world." John explained, "I should have given you a tour of the place. Come with me." He led her into an adjoining room. There was a large stone fireplace with real wooden logs stacked beside it. The whole room was done after the fashion of a log cabin. There was a white polar bear rug in front of the fireplace. There was a large couch on the left side of the fireplace and some stuffed rocking chairs at various places around the fireplace. John explained, "This is where I spend most of my spare time. I like to think and work on my laptop, in front of the crackling fire." Jessica responded, "This is more to my liking." There were rustic paintings on the walls and tapestries with deer and moose images on them. The tables and chairs were made of pine limbs with the bark left on and covered with heavy layers of varnish.

John built the fire by lighting a pile of wood pellets with lighter fluid and then piling on small limbs and finely split wood. The pine wood ignited rapidly. John added some bigger hackberry logs. Jessica stated, "I'll have some nice dry oak logs shipped up here. I know you haven't had time to grow big oak trees like we have. The hackberry is excellent wood and it grows much faster than oak. Oak is better though. I want us to have the best for this room." John laughed, "I was hoping you wouldn't notice the lack of quality hardwood here. We used it all up years ago. You're well informed on firewood. I'll appreciate some of your dry oak wood."

As the fire got warmer they sat on the couch working on their laptops. Finally they got done working, and undressed each other completely and turned off the lights. They took turns lying on the polar bear rug while the other spread lotion all over their body. Then they took turns lying on top of each other while they kissed tenderly and passionately. The orange and yellow flames traced their bodies as they kissed. They fell asleep in each other's arms with an Indian blanket pulled over them.

In the morning, they slept in till 8:00 o'clock A.M. Since they had restrained themselves from consummation the night before, they looked refreshed and rested. They were still tingling with desire for each other. Jessica said, "I can't wait to meet the Joint Chiefs of Staff and the cabinet. How much power do they have?" John explained, "I'm their boss, but I always consult with them. They represent the various branches of the military, the Secretary of State and other important cabinets. They keep me informed, and I usually try to keep them happy by giving them what I feel they need." Jessica explained, "I operate in a similar fashion, but I only meet on an as needed basis with my leaders. We don't all meet at once."

John said, "They'll be excited about your new ideas. We've been a little discouraged here about the almost impossible task of rebuilding America. We've been playing a waiting game. The loss of the oceans gave a death blow to our navy. We only have a hand full of ships in the remaining shallow waters of the Atlantic and Pacific. They can't reach many ports because of the shallow water. Those ships are spending all their time mapping out the current depths of the oceans. My best geologists are saying that the cooling edges of the earth will expand and rise up as they cool. This will allow the oceans to refill to a certain extent. They will most likely never be as full as they once were. We'll need to build piers that go out many miles to reach the ships. Until then we can only access them with helicopters and shallow running barges. We may be able to dig channels once we examine the ecological effects of such actions."

Jessica exclaimed, "I never thought about how terrible the loss of ocean water would be to your navy. It might be a hundred year project to build levies along the broken edge of the world to hold back the water. We need to do it though. Building these levies should be our highest priority. They need to be in place before we initiate global warming, or we'll lose most of our water from the polar caps onto the surface of mars. The surface of the bottom side of earth will be cool enough soon, that instead of turning the ocean spill off water to steam, the spill off water will run out onto Mars and be trapped where it can't be easily accessed, between earth and Mars. We don't want the earth portion of Mirth to look like a place of drastically drained oceans. I think we have enough snow to refill them when it melts." John sighed, "That type of thinking will make my Secretary of the Navy happy. He's usually on the winning side of decision making. He has lots of support from the other members. If you win him over, you'll have the rest of them in your back pocket."

Jessica stated, "I'll start out by explaining the vast capability of The Cave to move rock and dirt. Our tunneling machines and rail systems can move an entire mountain in about a month. Without that knowledge of our capability, they will think I'm crazy to suggest building a rock and dirt levy around the entire world. I'll also mention that I have a billion people at my disposal, who are highly trained and well motivated. As I said before they love a challenge."

Jessica spent the next hour writing out her outline for the speech to the nation. They made sandwiches and had coleslaw for lunch, as they compared notes on what to say at the meeting. John explained, "I don't think we should mention the classic cars driving around. It's a little too fanciful. I love the idea, but save that for the address to the nation, and mention that it's a long term goal." Jessica responded, "Good idea. I want your key leaders to take me seriously. I won't get too futuristic. I'll stick to short term goals with them, for the most part.

I think I should explain our economic differences. Our economies will have to operate on the basis of gifting. We will donate our services. In return we want assurances that people won't attempt to alter our economy. No gold or rubies will leave my country. No cash or credit cards will come into my country. Everyone needs to understand that." John laughed, "Don't get defensive! Just explain how things are in a scientific unemotional manner. My people will understand. Please don't lecture them about the poor. We have no poor anymore. It's ancient history." Jessica smiled, "I'll not mention it. Since you're my husband, though, I must mention that I suspect you have some greedy people here at Iron Mountain. Some people want more and more. More power and wealth." John exclaimed, "Do you think you married a wimp? If someone gets out of line, I'll stomp them. We have what we call trust busting measures here. We don't allow any one man to wield too much power. I'm thinking of appointing you as special White House whistle blower. If you see someone you don't like and think they should be investigated, we'll look into it. I'm not a puppet or a lame duck President. I represent the people."

Jessica squeezed his hand and said, "I sensed your power when I first met you. That's part of why I married you. That, and the excellent back rubs you give." They both laughed. "Will you push for some legislation to prevent poverty in the future, after we've passed from Mirth?" John exclaimed, "That's an interesting request. I'll let you write it up and present it to me. We'll discuss it together and come up with something that might fly. I'll send a draft to our religious leaders and try to work up a grass roots call for the legislation. I think the idea will sell best if we present it as mandatory full employment with a minimum wage which ensures that people will live well above the poverty level. That fits within the democratic concepts we're used to hearing. It won't alarm our stock holders. Try to avoid catch phrases like redistribution of wealth, heavy taxes for the wealthy or socialism. I want to be reelected. This is my first term, and we have legalized a third term because of the traumatic nature of our current times."

Jessica looked a little peeved, "I love you, John, and you have a tender heart, but if you're so concerned about your countries stock holders, you'll never prevent poverty. You're on the right track with the phrase 'mandatory full employment'. People with nothing to do, is an invitation for Satan to move in and cause trouble. There will always be people who are not profitable. They can't keep up. They aren't smart enough to avoid mistakes and injuries. Such people can only sell soft drinks or weed gardens. They aren't profitable. What does your society do with people who can't help with the profit margin of a company?" John explained, "We have charities that help such people. Our people, who are kind hearted, give money to the charities and the charities feed the poor people. Jessica asked, "What about the people who have their heat turned off because they can't pay the bill?" John blushed a little. "That is embarrassing. How did you find out about all this?" Jessica explained, "It's all in the history books. What ever you do goes down in someone's history book. The Chinese history books are full of the reports of how poor people have suffered at the hands of greedy companies." John answered, "Individual states had programs to help the poor keep their homes heated. It's regrettable that some people suffered and were thrown out of their homes. Charities aren't perfect. Our Salvation Army was one of our best charitable organizations for feeding people. It had a Christian message and fed millions of people."

Jessica asked, "Do you have any literature on your Salvation Army. Does it still exist?" John explained, "It still exists, but there are no poor people. The Salvation Army did much to alleviate suffering during the last years of the world as they knew it. Most of the volunteers died with the people they served, when the fusion bombs went off. There is still a group of people who keep the books. They still have a fair amount of money set aside to help people with, if such people would again come to exist." Jessica said, "I'd like to meet with them after my address to the nation. Can you arrange it?" John sighed, "If it will make you happy, I'll arrange it. After that meeting, I hope you won't rock the boat too much. Big companies aren't the bad guys. Don't set yourself against people and organizations when they're just trying to be aggressive. That's the American way. We channel everyone's aggression and make it work for us. Greed feeds peoples adrenal glands and makes them do their best." Jessica said soothingly, "I won't try to interfere with your way of doing business, even though I find it quite flawed. I just want to set up a trust for the Salvation Army. My country is bursting at the seams with wealth. We'll bankroll the care for the poor, since it seems to be an insurmountable task for your culture. Your population will explode when we break back onto Mirth's surface. You'll have lots of low paid workers and people too old to work. We'll feed them. It's the Jesus thing to do. We want riches in heaven. Riches on earth don't give lasting pleasure. People jump from one toy to another longing for a good feeling. The good feeling would come if they would spend some money helping other people solve their problems. Pay someone's heat bill. Feed an old person who spent all their money on high priced medications." John exclaimed, "You aren't going to give your high priced medication lecture, are you?" Jessica laughed, "Don't worry, I'm not a commie sympathizer. I believe in motivating people with rewards that are meaningful to them. My people love gold. Your people love cars and boats. I love boats too. I hope you'll take me for a boat ride on a big yacht soon. We don't have yachts, only small power boats for skiing. Don't worry, we like nice things. We love vacations on sandy beaches. Part of the reason I'm so concerned about the oceans, is that I want to go sailing with you. Promise me we can spend plenty of time sailing together."

John promised, "We can sail as much as you like. Just promise to skinny dip with me when the Pacific is warm enough." John got on the phone and set up the meeting of the Salvation Army with Jessica. They were delighted to hear from the President that they would be receiving almost unlimited funding as long as there was life on Mirth.

Jessica read up on the Salvation Army, while John prepared his notes for the meeting. He also planned on saying a few things before and after Jessica's address to the nation. They drank fruit drinks and chatted as they got ready for the meeting. John's aid set up the conference room table with drinking glasses and coffee cups. He brought in coffee carafes and pitchers of ice water. John and Jessica went to the pine room with the fireplace and waited for the guests to arrive.

The people were punctual and the meeting started right on time. John started things off by going around the table and introducing each member of the Joint Chiefs of Staff and the cabinet. John started to his left, "Jessica, this is our Secretary of the Navy, James Hesston." Hesston nodded. John said, "Next, we have Warren Anglemeyer, whom you've met." Warren nodded. "Next is Phillip Bradley, our Secretary of the Army." Phillip nodded. "Next to him is our Secretary of the Air Force, Alexander Schrock." Alexander nodded. "Next is Beverly Pilmore, the Secretary of the Treasury." Beverly nodded. John went clear around the table and introduced the rest of the cabinet. Then he addressed them, "My new wife Jessica, the leader of the tunneling country called The Cave, would like to address you." They all applauded.

Jessica went to the front of the table and gave them a winning smile. "First of all, I'd like to say that your President is an exceedingly handsome man." They all laughed and smiled. Jessica continued, "Our countries have operated in isolation from each other for many years. I'd like to assure you that we are a deeply Christian nation with goals similar to your own. Our economic systems are quite different, but that shouldn't interfere with the way we work together. We operate on a gold standard. The gold is given to our people as a status symbol for great frugality or achievement. Our highest status symbol is the ruby. It is given for outstanding long term meritorious service. I have explained to President Miller that no gold or rubies are to ever leave my country. We do not wish to barter them or trade with them.

My country has over a billion well trained and eager people who want to give their services to rebuild the world. We will work in cooperation with you on rebuilding America and on developing our new planet. Your President and I have discussed the extremely high importance of restoring our oceans to their former glory." James Hesston jolted in his chair as though shot by a gun, but he kept his face calm. Jessica noticed his reaction and continued, "I know it sounds like a preposterous proposal of attempting the impossible, but I'd like to inform you that my culture has developed tunneling machines capable of moving this entire mountain in just a couple months. Our rail systems can move material faster than you may have ever thought possible. Our trains move at a thousand miles per hour. I'm proposing that my people and yours work together to build a levy of rock and dirt that will seal off the oceans from the broken edge of earth. This can be accomplished in about seven years. Then we can concentrate on warming our new planet, which John and I have called Mirth. This warming will be accomplished by increasing the use of fossil fuels in steel making. I would like us to build a system of tunnels out across the surface of Mars that will allow recreational viewing of the night sky. My people have been in tunnels and caves for eleven hundred years. We long to see the sky." There was a round of applause. Jessica continued, "The burning of fossil fuels will create atmosphere and warm the planet. As the ice caps melt, the oceans will be filled back to near capacity." At this, James Hesston brightened. He smiled and asked, "What do you see as the future role of the navy, once the oceans are back to normal?" Jessica said, "Be prepared. We can never know what the future may bring. Satan is still active here. We will never be free of him until God decides the time has come. As long as peace seems to be with us, the navy can serve to transport personnel and materials around the oceans. Of course training will continue, to make sure we are prepared for any threats which might arise." James responded, "I like the way you think. You'll be a big help to John in the years ahead." Everyone applauded.

John stepped up to the front of the table and took over for Jessica, "Jessica has generously offered to set up a trust fund to assure that in the future there are never any poor people in our country. She is the religious leader as well as political leader of her country. Her Biblical understanding causes her to be appalled by the thought of poverty. In her country there are no poor people and everyone has a job. I think that is highly commendable, and I appreciate her concern for our future people." There was a round of applause. John continued, "Jessica has a hidden agenda. Her concern for the oceans is partially motivated by her love for sailing. She wants to sail with me on the oceans." There was a round of applause. Everyone stood up and applauded along with James Hesston who was beside himself with happiness and excitement. John added, "We weren't going to unveil this plan yet, but since you're such a receptive audience, let me include this. We have a priority for reopening Detroit and other automobile manufacturing cites. We think that classic cars like corvettes and jaguars should be back on the streets as soon as possible. These will be valuable rewards for our good workers and they will help burn fossil fuels. We'll be offering inexpensive cars to everyone who wants one and all the free gasoline they care to use. It will make for lots of happy people. I know I want my name on the bill when the next election comes up." There was loud applause and everyone stood up again.

"Jessica will be addressing the nation as soon as this meeting is over to let all our people know what you now know. It will be basically the same address. That's all I have. You can talk with us individually now for twenty minutes before we go for the public address." They all talked about how America and The Cave could cooperate. Everyone was interested in hearing more about how The Cave functioned as a country.

John took Jessica to his office, where the camera crew was set up. Jessica explained on camera to the America people, what her hopes and dreams were for the new planet, which she publicly named, Mirth. After the address, Jessica answered phoned in questions for about thirty minutes. Finally John finished with a statement about the use of troops at the South Pole. He said, "There appears to be no threat to peace at this time. We will be keeping a close eye on the situation. There is nothing to worry about. If you would like to volunteer for the levy building project, please send a letter to your project manager so that plans can be made to fill your current position. Because of the urgency of the levy project, all volunteers will receive double pay during their entire tour of duty. Please remember that population growth is important now. Spend lots of quality time with your marriage partner." John waved to the audience and the camera was turned off.

Jessica called Deb and Don at their Cave resort. Don answered, "Yes, Jessica. This is Don." Jessica explained, "I need you to show us where those ten tunnel machines are. We need them right away. Meet us at my suite. I'll have my aid let you in. You can stay there till I arrive. I'm not sure John can come with me. I haven't consulted with him yet. Over?" Don stated, "We'll be there waiting for you. Over and out."

Jessica asked John, "Can you come with me? John answered, "I need to stay here and organize things for a day. Then I'll join you. Promise me something." Jessica asked, "What?" John said, "Don't go to Dr. Li's lab without enough muscle. I don't want you kidnapped or killed. Dr. Li is a suspect. You don't want to be around him. Why don't you let Deb and Don take some of the troops back to get the machines. You'll need some engineers too. Don said the tracks have been cemented over. It won't be easy getting those machines out of there. You'll need to take ten flat cars down there to load them onto." Jessica said, "Thanks, John. I forgot that Dr. Li might be dangerous. Those machines will be a little tricky to load. I'll just brief Don and Deb and send the right people with them. I have quite a bit to do at Xanadu."

Jessica met with the Salvation Army people and encouraged them about their mission. She praised them for all the people they had helped and asked them to be sure that people had warm homes in addition to having enough food to eat. She told them about how wealthy her country was and that she would establish a trust with plenty of money for their future projects.

Chapter Seven

A New Encounter with Dr. Li

John took Jessica to the train and they kissed goodbye. John said, "I'll come down and see you tomorrow morning. I'll get on the train tonight when my work is done here." Jessica smiled and hugged him, "I'll have the sauna nice and steamy for your arrival, and some of your favorite wine." Jessica left him and boarded the train. John went back to his work of arranging new work crews to get the latest projects underway. He wanted to impress his new wife with how quickly America could get things done.

Once Jessica was back in her suite with Don and Deb, she called for some of her best engineers to move the tunneling machines and check them out. Don called General Hershberger, who was in charge of the three hundred troops at the South Pole recreation center. Don said, "We need your troops to go with us once more to Dr. Li's morel laboratory. We need those ten tunneling machines right away. You need to be there in case there's trouble." General Hershberger responded, "I'll have the men ready. When will you be here?" Don explained, "Our engineers should be here in an hour, and then we'll be at your location in five more hours. It's six o'clock A.M. now. We should be there by noon. Over?" General Hershberger said, "Over and out."

An hour later, all the engineers had arrived and they were briefed by Jessica. They headed out with Deb and Don for the South Pole recreation center. Once at the center the troops quickly boarded the train and they all headed for Dr. Li's laboratory. Don said, "Look, they're expecting us. They must have spies along the tracks with radios." There were several workers at the gate waiting for the train. As the troops got off the train, the workers looked worried. Don told them, "We need to see Dr. Li right away. No delays this time." The worker who had spoken to them before was there. Ty said, "Dr. Li isn't here. He didn't say where he went." Don explained, "We need the tunneling machines right away. We aren't waiting for him to return. Let us into the lower lab right away." Ty responded, "He will be angry with me, but I'll do as you say. Come with me."

They followed him to the elevator and took fifty of the troops with them and the engineers to the lower level. The engineers went to the tunneling machines and looked them over. One of them reported to Don, "Those machines have been used hard. They're worn out and will have to be refitted with new cutting teeth. We can have it done in about a week, but I thought you should know how worn they are. We never wear them down this completely in normal use." Don said, "So Dr. Li has been doing quite a bit of tunneling, and he didn't want to tell us about it. That's interesting." Deb stated, "Let's give this lab a more thorough going over. There has to be a secret tunnel."

One of the engineers said, "I think I can be of assistance. I brought my ultrasonic scanner along to test the machines for cracks in the metal. If I adjust the intensity of the scanning beam, we can look through the walls of this cave. He turned some dials and the hand held machine gave off a few squeals and then calmed down. He walked slowly around the outer edge of the laboratory and pointed the machine at the wall while he watched the display screen. He stopped right behind the tunneling machines. He pointed proudly to the display screen. There, before their eyes, on the screen, was the outline of a large square doorway. Don asked, "How do we gain access?" The engineer explained, "Dr. Li probably has a remote controller hidden somewhere. It would look like the controller for a television set. Let's check in his office." Don had one of the army men shoot open the locked office door. They went in and found the controller in Dr. Li's desk drawer. When they pushed the open button, a massive rumbling announced the sliding in and away of the tunnel door. It had been a perfect fit, impossible to detect with the naked eye.

Don explained, "I think Deb and I should go in alone. If they've set up some sort of revenge on the rest of the world, we need to catch them unawares, before they can execute their plan. Watch all the workers and make sure they don't make any calls to Dr. Li. If we aren't back in twenty-four hours, come in after us. Be prepared for the worst. General, you'd better call the President for reinforcements. Have him send everyone he's got." General Hershberger called the President as Deb and Don climbed on an electric cart and disappeared into the tunnel.

About five miles down the tunnel they came to the first cave. The cave was full of armed guards who were guarding two tall stainless steel cylinders which were forty feet wide and at least that tall. The guards immediately pointed their guns at Don and Deb and took them captive. Deb asked, "Where are you taking us?" One of the guards explained, "We are taking you to see Dr. Li. You wanted to see him didn't you?" Deb made no response. They were loaded onto a high speed train with eight guards to watch over them. All the guards had their guns pointed at them. There was no use trying to escape at that point.

In about an hour, they arrived at Dr. Li's central laboratory. The large cave was brightly lit with white fluorescent lighting. Dr. Li was working with some wires at the far end of the room. He had the guards keep Don and Deb at a distance. Dr. Li explained, "Since you were clever enough to find my tunnel, I'm sure you were clever enough to have backup troops follow you after a certain amount of time. That's why I've moved my time schedule ahead. My fusion bombs will send earth on its merry way into the sun just like my ancestors were sent there by America. I'm afraid that I made my timing device a little too intricate. In my desire to make it tamper proof, I made it difficult for me to reset. You surprised me by finding my tunnel so soon. I truly thought I was rid of you for a few months at least. My operations can get by with fewer people. I have everything here that I need to continue as a new civilization. I had hoped to take much of The Cave's gold and rubies with me, but I'm sure I can find plenty of that right here on Mars. Who needs those little trinkets?"

Don asked, "Why don't you use your bomb as an extortion device? You could demand all the gold and rubies in return for not blasting the earth into the sun." With your finger on the trigger of the bomb, you'd be the most powerful person on the planet!" Dr. Li laughed, "I like your logic, but it's obvious you're trying to buy some time. Jessica and the American President would start tunneling immediately into Mars in an attempt to find the bombs and disarm them. I'm not after power or wealth. I'm after revenge, and I shall have it. Just as soon as I can figure out which wires to connect. This is almost as complicated as a washing machine. Do you know anything about wiring?" Don laughed, "You don't actually expect me to help you, do you?" Dr. Li explained, "Without you, I'll figure it out sooner or later. If you help, I'll keep you alive. I like your sense of humor. The woman with you is attractive. You can have her as your mate if you help."

Don explained, "I can't resist a challenge. There won't be anyone left to punish me. Is it O.K. with you dear?" He turned to Deb and winked. She took her cue. "Sure dear.

Help the man out. He's in charge now and we have nothing to lose." Don stepped over to the far wall where Dr. Li was struggling with the wires. Dr. Li stepped back and smiled, "You are a practical man. I admire a man who knows about wiring. Everything is color coded. I think there's a loose ground wire somewhere. The bomb should be exploding, even as we speak." Don picked up a wire cutter and eagerly started cutting every wire he could lay his hands on. Dr. Li was alarmed and screeched at the guard. The guard hit Don in the back of the head with his rifle and dragged him away. He was thrown in a confinement cell. Deb was taken back to the fusion bombs and handcuffed to one of them. All the guards left her. They knew the bombs were about to go off. Dr. Li worked most of the night on the wiring for the bombs, and couldn't get them to go off. Finally he went to sleep in his chair right there at the control panel.

Don regained consciousness soon after he was thrown into the confinement room. He used his laser watch to cut through the bolt of the door. He surprised the sleeping guard and strangled him with the hidden wire in his watch. Don took the guard's gun and found Dr. Li. Dr. Li wasn't so brave with a gun pointed at him. He told Don how to disarm the bombs directly, on sight. It was a delicate operation and not too likely to succeed. Dr. Li explained, "The fusion bomb is actually a large mass of weapons grade plutonium surrounded on both sides by a regular atom bomb. Both atom bombs must go off simultaneously in order to adequately compress the large mass of fusionable material." Dr. Li was obviously proud of his knowledge. He seemed to temporarily forget his ancestors as he described the bomb to Don. Don realized that and played it to his advantage, "You are obviously a true genius by all measures of the term. You will be moved to head of all sciences if this succeeds. Your people will be given places of honor and full apologies will be made to your ancestors." Dr. Li smiled, "Had I know that Americans could be so reasonable, I might have been less harsh in my plans for punishment. You simply cut the wires to the top of these two cylinders at the same time. That is the only way to bypass the tamper proof system. Only I knew about this. It was a fool proof system. I hate to see it disarmed, but I long to face new challenges. If you say my people will be honored I believe you. We have to work in perfect timing. If we're off more then a tenth of a second, the timer will be activated which assures detonation in one hour. Why am I helping you?" Don said, "Most of your people are still on earth. You will be their hero if you let them live and bring honor to them." Don knew if he didn't really convince Dr. Li, he would intentionally throw off the timing of their wire cutting." Don said, "I will personally see to it that you get eleven rubies for your decision to forgive earth and let us make it up to your ancestors. Your ancestors will smile from beyond the grave when they hear that one of their people is the world's most respected scientist and he has brought great honor to his people." Dr. Li exclaimed, "I know you are being honest. I will help. Let's cut these wires." They did a three numbered count down and then cut in perfect timing. The bomb was defused!

Dr. Li exclaimed, "I'd better release your attractive assistant!" John explained, "She's another agent. Not my assistant." Dr. Li responded, "Yes, I understand. She is worthy of my respect. I'll radio my new plan to my subordinates. They worship me. They'll go along with any plan I come up with. How do you propose to get me out of hot water with your President and Jessica?"

Don explained, "I'll forget to mention the bombs, if you let Deb stay here and supervise the depositing of all bomb materials on the surface of Mars where I can monitor them. Deb will report back to me every ten minutes until the mission is accomplished. Once that is done, I'll mention what a brilliant scientist you are and how you took initiative to develop Mars into a gigantic morel growing facility. I'm sure you'll be put in charge of developing the entire planet. I'll also arrange for you to keep all the gold you find. Jessica is a terribly generous person. She'll want you to have plenty of gold. If you don't find any, we'll ship you a few tons. The Cave has a surplus of gold. She'll make up for the shortages your people have experienced in the past. We need all the Mars materials you dig out of the tunnels. We're repairing the oceans. By supplying us with all that fill material, I'm sure your people will be given more gold than they can fit under their beds."

Dr. Li smiled, "I'll send you more fill and rubble than you can possibly imagine. Don't forget to call your troops off. We don't want them charging in here spewing bullets everywhere, do we?" Don exclaimed, "You're right. We have an agreement, then?" Dr. Li extended his hand. They shook hands. Don called General Hershberger, "Everything is fine here. Send the troops back to the entertainment center. Dr. Li is expanding the morel growing facility. Everything is normal." Dr. Li exclaimed, "I can't thank you enough for working with me. I know you're taking a risk. You can trust me. I know my ancestors are satisfied now. You have restored honor to my people. We are at peace."

Don took the electric cart back to the Dr. Li laboratory on earth. He rode back to the entertainment center with the troops and stayed there till the bombs were dismantled. Deb joined him then and they enjoyed each other's company while they waited for another mission.

Jessica was so delighted when she heard about Dr. Li's initiatives on Mars, that she sent several tons of gold to Dr. Li. She went with John to personally present the eleven rubies to Dr. Li. He was invited to the next ruby watching ceremony. This delighted him more than he could express. Dr. Li was put in charge of jettisoning all fusionable materials from the new planet. His rocket launching system reestablished the presence of satellites orbiting Mirth. The rubble from Mars helped shore up the oceans. John and Jessica spent much of their time sailing in the Pacific. They had many wonderful children who were obedient and honored their parents. The classic cars were manufactured in large numbers and contributed to the necessary global warming. Jessica's tunnels were made all over Mars and earth. The Cave manufactured enough quality soil to allow the spread of forests all over the surface of Mars. The oxygen levels became normal and people could enjoy walking around without oxygen masks. Dr. Li and his people started watching more of Jessica's comedians. Everyone had a good sense of humor. They drove their cars slowly and there were no traffic jams. Road rage was something they read about in the history books and couldn't really imagine.

Satan was thoroughly upset by the way things were going. He said to his most favored assistant, as he viewed the new planet from outer space, "Soon they'll over populate. Then I'll be back. People will start cutting more trees than they plant. That's my favorite trick. I love to encourage people to be fools!"

The End

The Autobiography of Mark Lee Masters

The Autobiography of Mark Lee Masters

For those who are interested, my given name is Jonathan Lee Miller. I wanted to include that in my autobiography so my relatives won't think I'm trying to disown them by using a pseudonym. My wife likes for me to use the pseudonym. She doesn't approve of some of my writing. For those who read this book, the secret is out.

My most interesting relative is my mother's father. His name was Howard A. Bosler. I always called him Grandpa Bosler. He was a medical doctor who was a general practitioner and a surgeon. That's rare now days. Most doctors specialize. He went to Nigeria, Africa, as a missionary doctor for the Church of the Brethren. He hadn't even received the results of his medical exams when he arrived in Africa. He worked for twenty years in Nigeria before he returned to Waterford, Indiana to carry on a private practice for many years. He worked at Beatty Memorial Hospital for eight years as part of his plan to reduce stress. He always had a little trouble with his heart. Grandpa spent four years working as a doctor in Puerto Rico. He spent his last working years as an emergency room doctor at Goshen Hospital, in Goshen, Indiana.

When grandpa got to Nigeria, the Mennonites had already been there for many years. Their doctor had gotten sick from being bitten by a mosquito that carried sleeping sickness. That doctor later died of his illness. Grandpa found the same type of mosquitoes in the house he was to live in. He always wore long sleeve shirts and used mosquito netting. He and my grandma, Edith Bosler, never came down with the illness. He treated many cases of leprosy and some of the types were contagious. He said that he never knew which cases were contagious. The Smoker Craft Corporation management was friendly to him. They are in New Paris, Indiana. John Smoker was in charge of the corporation then. They sent grandpa a large powerful generator and two high quality hunting guns. My grandpa did quite a bit of hunting while he was in Africa. He hunted ducks on Lake Victoria and shot crocodiles on the local rivers. He had a special way of shooting the crocodiles so they would be good mounting specimens. He could shoot the gun so precisely that the bullet would go in one eye and come out the other eye. He often did this for visitors from England and the States. Where ever he went with his jeep, he would accidentally run over lots of animals. The Nigerian natives would feed themselves and their families on these animals. They considered grandpa to be a great hunter. Grandma Edith said that when she cooked chickens she gave the internal organs to local people who would cook these and eat them. Nothing was wasted. In later years, my grandparents were always concerned that I shouldn't waste any food. We never filleted fish. We always cut the fins off and skinned the whole fish without the head. That way we were conserving the meat which was on the ribs. That meat was good and sweet. I learned to like it best of all. Grandma said that she had to be careful with her money. People were so poor, they would be driven to steal if the opportunity arose. She had a pump organ which she played for church services. I used to play songs on it when I was young.

Grandpa was glad to receive the generator that Smoker Craft sent him. It allowed him to do surgeries at night. It was cooler at night and sometimes the patients needed the surgery immediately. One of the female assistants which grandpa had trained would hold a urinal for him so that he could relieve his bladder during long surgeries. I'm not sure why he told me about that. He had to sharpen his own scalpels. They had to boil rubber gloves since they didn't have enough of them. Grandpa did many eye surgeries to correct crossed eyes. He was proud of his ability to shorten one of the muscles just the right amount so both eyes would be able to look the way they should.

Grandpa had several motorcycles while he was in Nigeria. Once, when he was driving at night, he hit a wash out in the road and broke his leg. He had to drive a long way with a broken leg. At times he would have to hire locals to use their dugout canoes to carry his motorcycle across flooded steams and rivers. When my mother was about to be born, he had to carry my grandmother four hundred miles in a motorcycle side car to another doctor so the birth could take place. My mother, Esther Gene Miller, lived for four years in Nigeria. She had to be sent home because of an undiagnosed illness. It turned out that she had malaria. She went to school in Indiana and only saw her parents when they came home on leave. My father, Rex W. Miller, proposed to her when her parents were still in Africa.

Grandpa showed me many before and after pictures of patients he did surgeries on. The patients had tumors that were as big as the patient was. He said it was difficult to shut off all the large veins that connected the patient to their tumor. If patients were inoperable and were likely to die, grandpa would assign them to the village witch doctor. The witch doctor became known as the doctor of death. Most people wanted to be treated by my grandpa.

Grandpa truly loved the Nigerian people. He paid for the medical education of five Nigerians. He used to always give five thousand dollars per year to the NAACP. (National Association for the Advancement of Colored People.) The FBI investigated him for being so generous to them. He loved black people. He asked me to always be nice to black people. When he worked at Beatty Hospital, half of the workers were black people. They liked him quite a bit.

While in Africa, grandpa found that there were many leopards prowling around at night eating the people's goats. He baited the goats with poison and killed several leopards. He said he was afraid they might start eating some of the children. He gave me two of the leopard skins before he died. One of them has a full skull with artificial eyes. It looks realistic and frightening. Grandpa and my grandma made me promise to walk on the skins with my bare feet as they had always done. One of the skins is worn from all this walking upon it. They thought they would be able to watch me from heaven when they died and see what I was doing. They also thought they would be able to help me from heaven.

Grandpa loved to fish. From the time I was eight or nine years old, he went fishing with me every weekend. There was a house trailer which he kept on Pine Lake near Marcellus, Michigan. That's where we did most of our fishing. We caught many bluegill, bass and crappy. I loved to swim in that lake with my aunt Cynthia, my mother's younger sister. Cynthia married a mean crazy man whom she met at Manfest College. (Name of college changed to protect me from law suits.) He beat her and her daughter, April. He finally left them and April was raised by my older brother, Kevin. Cynthia married several times unsuccessfully, but is now married to a nice man and lives in Elkhart, Indiana.

April just got a good job in an upscale clothing store. She dresses elegantly for the customers. April is a wonderful lady who is a devout Christian. She is single and always seems to be happy and has a vibrant personality.

Grandpa loved to ice fish. He had an ice house that was big enough for five or six people. It was heavy. He used to let me drive his car on the ice. I did "kitties" with it. Spinning around and around in circles. It was his second car and only cost about eight hundred dollars. He wasn't worried about me breaking it. I remember it clearly. It was a big thrill for me. He loved seeing me having so much fun. Grandpa sometimes would fish for pike from a house he owned at 302 River Vista Drive. He would leave the pole propped up against something and sit in the house waiting for a bite.

Once he took us all on a trip to Canada fishing. His wife's brother, Les Gump, owned a charter fishing business on Lake Superior. I was twelve years old when we went fishing there on Chapawana Bay. I wrote about those days of fishing in detail in my Book entitled *Fishing for Almost Anything that Moves*. I changed the names of my relatives a little. I didn't mention grandpa in the book, only my aunt and uncle who owned the fishing business. I changed their names from Gump to Gamp. In the book, the actions and fun on the trip are all recorded faithfully in line with what actually happened. I had two of my fictitious characters as the visiting fishermen instead of me and my relatives. A cousin, Dave, went on the real fishing trip. My older brother and father went, and my grandpa. We caught 101, twelve inch long perch the first day and a four foot long northern pike. We ate quite a few of those fish for supper. Then we fished for pike along the lakeside where the road came up close to it. In my book I told how uncle Les caused Aunt Erma to lose a big pike that was on her line. Next we fished for rainbow trout in a mountain lake. We caught seven trout. My father kept catching this painted turtle over and over again. I had fun on the trip lighting fire crackers. I had a home made cannon which I had made out of pipe and a hinge attached to a piece of plywood. I used it to fire rocks out over the lake. That fishing trip was the most memorable time of my life. It was a wonderful experience.

When I was at Goshen College, I was sent to Costa Rica for studies in Spanish language and for intercultural experience. I was working towards an interdisciplinary degree with Biology emphasis and Psychology and Sociology minors. When I arrived at the Costa Rican airport in San Jose, I was surprised that no one was there to pick us up. We had gotten there a day early and surprised our group leaders. Two other male students and I walked down the main street of the town until we got tired of walking. I saw a place that had a room for rent. I paid the rent and we spent the night in a tawdry looking room with a dingy looking bathroom. There were giant cockroaches all over that night. They crawled on some of the students. The next day, we located our group and got started on the planned adventure. We were each driven to a host family where we were not allowed to speak any English. The family would provide most of our meals and help us with the language studies. I stayed six weeks in a mountain village seven miles from San Jose, which is the capital of Costa Rica. We went on side trips to various locations around Costa Rica. I visited a small communist settlement. I was blind folded on the trip there, since I was not too sympathetic to communism. I wanted to see the settlement though. It was just a collection of small shacks on the mountain side. There wasn't much of interest to see there. We went to a language seminar in one location where they sometimes train CIA operatives in Spanish language. They were good teachers. I learned a few things there. The learning of Spanish on location was a painful and tough experience. I always felt dumb for not knowing how to speak properly. I received an "A" though, for the Spanish part of my studies. I still remember the language fairly well. During the last six weeks of my stay in Costa Rica, I planted trees in a tree nursery just outside the mountain town of Turrialba. The family I stayed with were devout Christians and very kind to me. I almost wanted to stay with them for several years, but I longed for the States immensely. The mosquitoes bothered me the whole time I was in the country. Few people use screens to keep them out of the house. I had to wear repellant the entire time I was there. In Turrialba, they let me read the Bible in the Spanish language at church one Sunday. I love to read to people. They said I did a good job.

I must have planted over forty thousand trees in the tree nursery. The agency that ran the nursery was called The Department of Stakes and Posts. They encouraged local farmers to plant pine trees for stakes and fence posts. They promoted the raising of eucalyptus trees for the making of telephone poles which they hoped to sell to Honduras. The chemical treatment plant for the posts and stakes was given to the Costa Ricans by the United States of America. I toured the treatment plant. They pressure treated the wood with a cyanide solution that would keep away insects for over twenty years.

I worked with a heavy old peasant woman. She never spoke, and I never learned her name. I gave her a Bible, just before I left. I was told that it was too expensive of a gift. People would think I was in love with her. She was more homely than I can express effectively. I can't believe people would think I was in love with her. She was earning twenty-five cents per hour. She and I mixed dirt with fertilizer and insect killer. Then we filled thousands of small plastic black bags with the mixture. After we had four foot wide rows of the bags in ten forty foot long rows, we started poking a hole in the dirt of each bag with a stick. In each hole we placed a baby Honduran pine tree that was only two inches tall. We packed the dirt tightly around each tree. The seeds for the special fast growing Honduran pines cost four hundred dollars per pound. They had to be smuggled in. There were laws against the transfer of the pines or their seeds. I helped load eight inch tall trees onto farmer's trucks. The farmers paid four cents per tree. Once, while I was lifting a crate of trees about ten fire ants started biting me on the hand. I washed them off quickly. The poison from them made me dizzy.

One local environmentalist told me he didn't like the planting of pine trees. He said the country needed the original forest with wide leafed trees that would catch the fog from the ocean and help keep moisture on the land. I'd like to see the country stay full of trees. I love trees. I've been thinking of starting an agency to promote the planting of trees and creating forests in countries where they've cut all the trees for fuel. It's hard to keep people from cutting all the trees, when they need the fuel desperately for cooking. I think the Mennonite Central Committee has done some things with planting trees. I may check to see what they are doing. The National Arbor Society is doing good things as well. I'd like to see our nation's criminal population put to work planting trees all over our entire country. We could send teams of tree planters all around the world. It would be an excellent good will gesture.

When I returned to America, I was delighted to be home. It was only about a year later that I got married to my wife, Nancy Miller. We've been married for twenty-three years. Our children, Chris and Mark are married now and have children of their own. Chris has three boys, and Mark has a boy and a girl. I love to give all my grandchildren coins. I liked getting coins from my grandfathers. Both of my grandparents me coins. It's a family tradition. My father's father, grandpa Everett Miller, liked to throw a big bag of coins on the floor at Christmas time and let all the children pick them up. We all liked grabbing the coins. It helped us to learn that coins were valuable. It may have been a little primitive, but it was fun. My Grandpa Bosler didn't give me coins so often, but when he did, they were silver dollars. I kept them for twenty years, and then gave them to my youngest brother for Christmas one year. He kept them for ten or more years and then sold them. I especially prize the 1899 silver dollars, since my Grandpa Bosler often mentioned that he was born on that year.

In 1985 I returned to Goshen College to add an English major to my degree. The first degree had been finished in 1981, before I was married. I secretly wanted the education to help me learn to write books. I knew I had to act like I wanted to teach, or no one would have gone along with my returning to college. To be in the English department as a major, you had to profess that you wanted to teach. It was during this second time at Goshen College that I traveled to Ireland. The trip was for studying linguistics and for visiting poets. We visited the dead poet, William Butler Yeates at his tomb. We visited a living poet, named Peter Fallon, on his family farm north of Dublin about fifty miles. I enjoyed meeting Peter. He was proud of his farm and gladly showed us around. There was a mysterious tunnel there, that went on for a long way and led to an underground cavern. I didn't go in at first because I have claustrophobia. Finally I couldn't bear missing out, and ventured in alone with no light. It was scary, but I found the group about fifty feet down the tunnel. Peter didn't know what the tunnel or cavern were for. I speculated that it had been for hiding from Vikings. Peter didn't think the Vikings had come this far from the shores.

Peter and his wife fed us a brunch on their yard. I asked him for a copy of one of his books. He gave each of us a copy. They were small books of poetry which he used to sell in Dublin on his bicycle. He took us to his cousin's house which was a large brick mansion they used for a bed and breakfast. We were fed sumptuous meals there. They used the best crystal for us. All ten of us sat at a big table to eat. I had gone hungry the previous four weeks in Dublin. The currency exchange had made an unfavorable change and our money didn't go very far. I lived on one candy bar and a quart of milk per day. Professor Fisher and his wife took me to a nice restaurant meal one day. They regretted that the meals couldn't be furnished every day. While at the restaurant I enjoyed the local cuisine and beverage.

On one occasion, early in the five week trip, I was standing on a pier with my camera bag hanging from my shoulder. A Middle Eastern man sneaked up on me with a knife and cut one of the straps of my camera bag without me even seeing him. Professor Fisher was a little alarmed about the occurrence until I told him I had arranged for the man to cut the bag. He was one of the students on the trip. I was just trying to have interesting things happen to tell about later. I still have that camera bag. The man who cut it was a good friend. I always remember him when I look at the camera bag. I didn't really need that extra strap anyway.

About ten years ago, Peter Fallon came to the United States. I was glad to see him again. I gave him a hat from my father. He was pleased to receive a hat that was actually like the ones farmers wear here in America. When I get enough money for the postage, I'm going to send Peter a couple of the books I've written.

The stay with Peter's cousin was the best part of the trip to Ireland. Peter showed us where some of the inspirations for his poetry came from. There was a barn with a mow full of antiques. David offered to take me fishing. I don't know why I didn't go. I helped him fix his car instead. The battery terminal was corroded. Once we got the car going, he and his wife and I went to a pub out in the country and had some lemonade. It was the best lemonade I had ever tasted. The local people were friendly and happy. Definitely a time to remember.

I will continue writing till I die. I don't want to be just a "flash in the pan" as some people say, of authors who only write a book or two. I'm working on my sixth book. It's a mystery book that starts with a huge boat explosion on the first page. As they say, "Sink the hook". I try to get the reader hooked on the first page. I didn't do that with my third book. The Mary Thresher book started out too slowly. Several test readers complained about so much written about a parrot. I liked the parrot. A parrot worked for Walt Disney, why not me? That taught me to have real excitement on the first page. Readers expect that. Publishers expect that.

My best friend died of muscular dystrophy a month ago. It made me start thinking about death. I want to be cremated and have my ashes spread over the deepest waters of Lake Michigan. I don't want the ashes to wash up to shore right away. I would like an eternal web site that plugs my books and tells a little about me. It could include a picture of me holding up a fish. Fishing has been my favorite pass time. I was talking to one of my good friends today on the phone. I told him I'd like to start an internet cemetery. There would be a web page where relatives and the curious could click onto a picture of the cemetery where the person is buried. There would be a nice picture of a tombstone that could be computer generated if the person didn't want to spend the money on a real tombstone. The obituary would be included and a short biography. Biography lovers would have a field day at such a site. I would charge about a hundred dollars for each site. I think I could make a living at that. Other people would start to imitate my work, but I would still have a large clientele. If I have a real tombstone, I'd like it to be interactive. People could choose between several buttons and get a tape of my voice telling them about my books, about my life, my favorite Bible passages. I could make money selling tombstones like that. I am an entrepreneur if nothing else.

I'm getting into coin collecting. I dream about gold and silver. I collect new and old coins. I hope to have a reserve of wealth to draw on this way. I tend to spend money as fast as I make it. By spending all extra money on coins, I will have money when I need it. I'm also contributing to a pension fund. I hope to live well when I retire. I've never enjoyed the work I do for a living. It's tragic that I've spent so much of my life doing things I don't like doing. I'm just not smart enough to get a good job. I've worked at factories most of my life. I'm just a simple person with a creative mind. I like writing. I feel the happiest when I'm writing. Today I went to a fishing store called Lunkers in Edwardsburg, Michigan. A friend went with me, and we had dinner there. I told the waitress about my latest book and gave her my card. She was supportive and said she would buy the book. That made my day. That is the kind of thing that keeps an author going. Next year, I hope to have enough money to publish this autobiography in a collection of five of my books.

I want to find a publisher that really knows how to sell books and get them to publish the Mary Thresher book again. I haven't been successful at selling very many of them. I don't have enough money to buy twenty-five books so I can have a book signing. It takes money to promote books. I just don't have enough now. I only sent to about twelve publishers on the first two books. I don't think I sent Mary Thresher to any place but Xlibris, my print on demand publisher. With them, you have to pay for your own promotion work. I don't think I'll do that. I'll keep looking for other publishers to promote my books on a large scale. That won't cost me much, other than postage.

There are two miracles that have happened in my life. Back in 1975, I was doing a voluntary service assignment in Stratford, Ontario, when I decided to pray to God to heal a wart that was on my wedding ring finger. Of course I had no wedding ring. I was divorced in 1974 from my first wife. I had gotten the wart first of all on my smallest finger. I had it burned off by my doctor. The wart migrated to the next finger the following year. The wart had been on the tip of the smallest finger. Next, it was above the nail of the ring finger. I couldn't easily have it removed from there. The very week that I prayed for God to heal it, the wart disappeared and never came back.

The second miracle involved an angel. I had a bulge on my left wrist's tendon sheath. It had been there for over ten years. I got it from following the orders of a sadistic straw boss at a steel mill where I had been working. He ordered me to load a five gallon bucket full of steel plates and carry them up a stairs. I did what I was told to do, but the bulge formed right away from that feat of strength. The bucket had probably weighed around two hundred pounds. In 1985, I was asleep when I think a partially woke up. There was an angel in white attire standing by the side of my bed. I didn't notice if the angel was male or female, but it reached out its hand and touched the bump on my wrist. Something popped, but there was no pain. I fell back asleep, and woke in the morning still remembering the angel. I discovered that the bump was gone. That bump had been painful and I had at times tried to get rid of it. I even hit it with a hammer once. That hurt quite a bit, and I never did it again. To this day I am exceedingly grateful to God for sending the angel to heal my wrist.

I'm doing my favorite cooking thing tonight. I'm barbequing chicken with my old Smoker/Miller family recipe. The sauce is a mixture of vinegar and brown sugar with pepper, salt, garlic salt and Worcestershire sauce. There is a quarter stick of margarine that I sometimes use. It tends to cause more flare ups of the grill, so I often leave that out. I'm including the recipe here:

Smoker and Miller Family Barbequed Chicken Recipe

1 cup white vinegar
2 quarts water
1-2 tablespoons salt
¼ stick margarine
1-2 tablespoons garlic salt
¼ teaspoon Worcestershire sauce
¼ teaspoon black pepper
2/3 cup brown sugar, or sweeten to taste. (Enough sugar to counter the sour taste of the vinegar.)

Bring to a boil and then apply liberally to the meat as it is cooking. Most commonly used on chicken, but this sauce will work on beef as well. Soak the pieces of chicken in the basting solution often. Sometimes I boil the chicken in the solution for three minutes before I put the pieces on the grill. I then pour the basting solution on the chicken with a coffee cup. Have water handy in a quart container. The margarine makes the fire flare up and threaten to burn the chicken.

Cook time: Usually it takes 1 hour and 15 minutes to get the chicken done all the way through. Add about 15 to 30 minutes more for winter cooking. Cut into some thick pieces and look for red uncooked meat. Cook until the meat looks thoroughly cooked, even at the joints. Remember, a good cook never strays far from the grill. Fat from the chicken can quickly cause a big fire that will destroy all of the chicken. You don't want to lay a big egg at the most important barbeque of the summer.

I also have a good pecan pie recipe that my mother always used. My wife uses it now. It makes pecan pie possible that is better than any you have ever tasted. I cook the pies myself sometimes. I can make excellent pecan pies. It's a family tradition. My mother always took pecan pies to the family reunions that took place on Syracuse Lake during the sixties and seventies. There were usually eighty relatives that showed up for the occasion. We would water ski and fish together. I had several beautiful female cousins that were fun to sun bath with. I had fun throwing baseball with my cousins Eddie and Doug Smoker. Doug was the first one to loan me a fly rod to practice with. I'm not the worlds greatest even now, forty years later. Doug and I used to throw crab apples at each other. It was lots of fun. He is now the Vice President of Smoker Craft boats. They make a great line of reasonably priced boats. I bought one of their seventeen foot canoes thirty years ago. I put it through some rough waters, but it's still in great shape. I worked for Smoker Boats quite a bit down through the years. First of all, I was their night watchman for a year in 1975. I discovered a paint resin fire one night, and saved the company a lot of money. Later, in 1977, I drove truck for the company. I delivered pontoon boats and other types of boats to Pennsylvania, Alabama, North Carolina, Illinois, and Ohio. I loved driving truck, but I finally decided to go for more money working for Fairmont Homes as a fork lift driver. Doug Smoker had been my boss during my work as truck driver for Smoker Craft. He was great as a boss. He was always understanding and kind, even though I made a few mistakes.

When I worked at Fairmont Homes, I worked about fifty-six hours per week. I had so much extra money, that I started buying an ounce of gold bullion every couple weeks. I had studied the price of gold from the Wall Street Journal microfilm files at the Goshen College library. The price had gone up 33% per year from 1967 to 1978. I decided it was a good investment. Three months after I bought my three ounces, the price of gold went from $180 per ounce, to $214 per ounce. I decided to sell two of my ounces and took a quick profit. A couple months later, the price of gold skyrocketed to $800 per ounce. The day of the peak, I couldn't get the bank that had sold me the gold on the phone. The next day, they answered and I sold my last bar of gold for $500. It was my biggest success with the stock market. I also played my cards right by selling all my stock right before the recession of 2000. I decided to pay bills with the money. Many people lost half of the equity that was in stocks during that recession. They are slowly getting some of it back.

My advice to people is, always pay cash for what you buy. Don't borrow money unless it's an absolute necessity. Tithe 10% and put 10% into savings or investments. If you start at around 30 years old and invest 10% of your net income, you will almost certainly be able to retire early and have a more enjoyable life. I certainly don't enjoy needing to work in a factory till I'm 63 years old. It would be much nicer to retire this year. I love fishing and writing. I could easily spend all my time doing those two things now that I'm 57 years old. Some people love their work and will never quite their jobs. I love having good work, but I wish I had been more responsible with money early in my life. I could be retired now.

I recommend for people who want to save money, to buy cars with 30,000 miles or a little more on them. Drive the car till it has 180,000 miles on it, or till it becomes a maintenance problem. If the transmission goes out, trade it. Repaired transmissions often don't last long and you'll end up fixing it again and again. I like Toyotas and General Motors cars. Honda engines last a long time, but exhaust parts are terribly high priced. I had a Honda Accord which I paid $500 dollars for. When the two foot exhaust pipe went bad, that was flexible and fed off the exhaust manifold, I paid $440 for that small section of exhaust. No more Hondas for me. The electric window went bad and the timing belt failed. I sold the car after one year for $60. It wouldn't even run anymore. I hated that car.

I loved my Ford Thunderbird. I kept that car for 13 years. It never needed anything but brakes and exhaust. I got the complete exhaust replaced for under $300. I paid $13,000 for it. That's only $1,000 per year. It got 27 miles per gallon and was a V-8 luxury car.

My first car was a 1940 Hudson. I drove it from the time I was fourteen years old. I used to drive it on the road illegally. I only drove it to the neighbor's. Someone must have reported me to the police. The police warned me to keep it at home till I was a legal driver.

My first job was for a Goshen doctor named, Dr. Charles Gorham. He had me plant pine trees and hardwoods in a woods he owned that was east of Goshen four miles on College Avenue. He also had a forty acre pasture which he bought from a neighboring farmer. He had me plant that to trees as well. Some of the pine trees are now 35 feet tall. I'm quite proud of those trees. I was 15 years old when I worked for him. I planted trees all summer and watered them. The doctor later sold the pasture back to the farmer. Doc Gorham died young in a car wreck. His car hit a tree as he was speeding home to investigate a prowler. There was a pistol found in his lap. He had a car wreck when I was working for him. He had been trying to shave with his electric razor while he drove the car. He only broke his arm during that accident. He was always coming out and offering to help me weed his tree nursery. He would crawl around on his hands and knees pulling out weeds with a cast on one arm. He always said that he wished he had been a forester instead of a doctor. I inherited his love of planting trees. I often order oak trees from the state forestry service and plant them at the local park or on my father's farm. You aren't supposed to use state trees for landscaping. They don't want to compete with private tree nurseries. You are allowed to create nature areas in your yard. That's what I have. The trees are close enough together to form a cluster that is a habitat for squirrels.

Squirrels are my friends. My mother had a business selling squirrel corn. It made her enough money that she was able to loan me money when I was in trouble. That was often. My mother was generous with her money. My father is generous too. I hope that when I'm out of debt, that I won't need to ask anyone for money ever again.

When I was eight, my parents started giving me money for doing chores, and I got money for my birthday. By the time I was ten, I had started putting money into a bank account at Salem Bank, in New Paris. I would ride my bicycle one mile to town and deposit money. I loved to watch the account grow. By the time I was 15 years old, I had \$500 in the account. I loaned my father the \$500. He paid me 10% interest. I had mowed quite a few yards and did lots of chores to get that \$500. It disappeared in no time when I got to college. When everyone discovered that I wasn't going to be a doctor, and didn't know what I wanted to be for sure, I lost financial support from the family. After 1 ½ years at Manfest College I was out of funds. Manfest had been a terrible experience. Other students had mistreated me violently with severe hazing. I still have a great dislike for that College. In later years, I went to Goshen College where they had no hazing. Hazing, for those who are not familiar with them, are when older students do embarrassing and mean things to the freshmen. The men are the hardest hit. I had alcohol poured on my genitals after having my clothes ripped off by the upper classmen. I'll admit that one student got expelled for that, but I still feel that Manfest is too lenient with students about hazing. My younger brother went to Manfest seven years after I first went there. He too was hazed. He was forced to yell out a dorm window that he was a homosexual, which he is not. He begged my father to let him come home. He had been a straight "A" student in high school and had hoped to become a doctor. I would recommend that all parents investigate what types of hazing are practiced at the school where they are thinking of sending their boy. It could be the difference between his success or failure.

It would be good if federal funding were withheld from schools which allow hazing to go on. The school could control it if they had enough resolve. All they need to do is expel all students involved in perpetrating it. It would rapidly become a thing of the past. There have been public reports of hazing that involved homosexual rape and electrocution of freshmen. It isn't cute anymore. I never thought it was cute.

By stark contrast to such schools, you have Goshen College, where students are fully occupied with learning. I went to Goshen College for four years, and I was impressed with how much the students studied. The courses were interesting and challenging. I fully recommend Goshen College. They have excellent pottery courses and a full sized swimming pool. Their library is well supplied with books and the food there is excellent. They are quite helpful about coming up with loans and grants to help with funding.

My problem, when I was first in college at Manfest College, was that the funding plans all required a major contribution from the parents of the student. My father wouldn't contribute, so I had to go to work and quit school. My Grandpa Bosler, coaxed me to come work with him at Beatty Memorial Hospital. I volunteered for alternative service at Beatty and worked there for two years to fulfill my service obligation to the government. There was a lottery then. It was 1970 and I didn't want to get drafted. If I did, I would have no control over where they sent me. When you volunteered, the government allowed you to pick where you wanted to work. I would find out later that my number would have never been called. I wouldn't have had to do any service assignment at all. I enjoyed the time at Beatty. I had a sexy girlfriend that I was happy with for one summer. I had been quite inexperienced with women until I met her. I found out towards the end of the summer that she was seeing other guys. That was a little deflating, but I forgave her and continued seeing her. She married a lawyer at the end of the summer. She had told me, from the beginning, that was her plan, so I wasn't too upset when she left me. She was a cute girl who was a life guard. She loved to swim. I used her appearance as a model for my characters Mary Thresher and Jessica, in the book *Dr. Exeeto*.

My first book was a murder mystery entitled *Who's got a Taste for Killing*. I loved writing that book. The first part of it included scenes from Venice, Florida where I vacationed with my family and grandparents back in 1964. I had a girl friend whom I met on the beach down there. Some of the scenes described in the first chapter of my first book came from that vacation and the memories of my girlfriend there. In the book I allowed myself to have the week with my girlfriend turn out the way I would have liked it to turn out. In reality, after that one week, I never saw or heard from the girlfriend again. I can't remember her name, but I remember she was a catholic cheer leader. I used to enjoy watching her do her stretching exercises. She was incredibly beautiful. We did quite a bit of kissing. That was all. It was the first that I had done any kissing with a girlfriend. I had never had a girl friend before. She and I sunbathed together and talked quite a bit. She invited me to her parent's bungalow, which made it into the book. I never went fishing with her family like the book says. There was no fishing for me at that time.

My second book was entitled, *Fishing for Almost Anything that Moves*. I enjoyed writing that book. It allowed me to include actual fishing trips I've been on. It included a fishing trip to Canada that I went on when I was twelve years old. The book included many scenes of older fishermen being doted on by young beautiful Mexican women. That was a fantasy which I enjoyed entertaining often while I wrote the book. Finally I realized that I had taken the characters too far into sin. I labeled the book as "Rated R" on the front cover so I wouldn't be guilty of corrupting people who normally wouldn't read such material. I decided to have the characters meet terrible deaths. This was a tactic which Cecil B. Demill used in one of his movies. He had shown a woman's bare breasts while she bathed. The movie had been about a civilization that was decadent and immoral. To sooth the ruffled feathers of the censors, he had all the people meet with terrible punishment. I decided if it worked for him, it might work for me too.

My third book was entitled, *Mary Thresher In Search of Sunken Treasures*. I think it is my best accomplishment so far. I pushed hard to keep the plot interesting. Most readers like the book. Men tend to enjoy the book about fishing, the best. I had enough characters in the Mary Thresher book, that I ran into a little trouble keeping their hair colors right. I had to go through the whole book and check for that. I hope I caught everything. I'm afraid that I rushed into publishing the book. I didn't have any good help with proof reading. I did all the proof reading myself. When the finished book came to me to read, I found some mistakes right away. At that time I met a good proof reader who helped me locate six mistakes that I hadn't found on my own. Luckily only four copies of that version are in print. I made thirty corrections to the second version of the book. It cost me $185 to make those corrections. If I hadn't been using print on demand publishing, there would have been thousands of books with all those mistakes in them. I'll be more careful with future books. I have another proof reader now. She is good and works for a reasonable price. I hope I don't lose her. I've changed proof readers four times now. One died. One was too critical of my writing. My wife didn't have enough time. One proofreader was the girlfriend of a room mate of a friend of mine. He divorced his wife and no longer sees the girl. The woman I now use is a girlfriend of one of my best friends. She has started to publish some of her own poetry. I've never met her. My friend met her at work. I hope to meet her soon. She has helped me greatly. I'm sending her a copy of my fishing book as a reward for her work on my first book.

When I write, I write rapidly and make many mistakes that go unnoticed by me. I'm not a total genius. I like to think I have some creative genius, but my proof reading skills are only slowly improving.

I went to the Union, Michigan Plum Cemetery today to visit the grave site of Bruce Elliott. He was my best friend since I was six years old. He died of muscular dystrophy recently. I'm thinking about being buried in Goshen when I die. There's a plot at Violett Cemetery in Goshen for me, which my Grandfather Bosler bought for the family. The plot is on Maple Road. It's a boulevard that goes through the center of the cemetery. I want my pen name listed under my given name on my tomb stone. I want my books listed with a short one sentence description of each one. I might even include a picture of me in my easy chair working at my laptop computer. I've been seeing some tombstones with nice pictures etched into them.

In 1975 I went to Stratford, Ontario to work for a year for the Mennonite Board of Missions. I had been reading the Bible for several hours per night when I was a night watchman the previous year. It made me want to do something good, like the Bible said we should. I was a religious counselor in Stratford. I worked with teenage kids who had no parents to raise them. I operated out of an old YMCA building in the center of Stratford. I had only three kids to work with, but they kept me busy. We played many games of basketball during that year. The building had its own built in basketball court. I got good at long shots. Once I made two shots in a row from about sixty feet out. I also once made twenty free throws in a row without missing. I had my canoe with me and took the kids canoeing on the Avon River. I attended three Shakespearian plays at the Avon Theater. At another theater, I saw *The Importance of Being Ernest*.

I met some Canadians who were good guitarists. John Neilson showed me some important practice exercises and chords for the guitar. At the time I had a nice Gibson Hummingbird guitar. It had excellent sound, but it was a little hard to play. It got cracked by one of the kids there, and I sold it a couple years later. I now have a Dove acoustic/electric guitar. It's easy to play, but I don't play often.

There was a donut shop right next door to the YMCA building. I went there often with friends. I had some free time on my hands, and I used it to make a potter's wheel out of an old washing machine. I made a couple nice pots on it. There was a woman who came to the building sometimes to see us. She was a social worker for one of the boys. I got to know her and she invited me to her house several times. She asked me if I could fix the horn on her car. I didn't know how to do it properly, but at the time I'd tackle about any job. I ran a new wire to the horn from the battery and installed a house door bell button on the console. She liked the repair job, even though she at times, would hit the button accidentally with her knee. She talked to her plants often. She told me they talked to her too. I thought it was strange, indeed. A doctor had been dating her. I advised her to marry him. It sounded good to me for her to marry him after she told me all about their times together. I also tuned pianos for people while I was in Stratford. I only tuned about four pianos. I put my best effort into it. I later gave Bruce Elliott my tuning tools. I don't tune pianos any more.

I played some soccer while I was in Stratford and also played ice hockey. I love to ice skate. I still do a little ice skating once and a while. I snow ski too. There was no snow skiing in Stratford however. I had a free day once when I went ice fishing about sixty miles from Stratford at a reservoir. I didn't catch any fish, but I enjoyed myself. The ice was about a foot thick. It took me forever to drill a hole in the ice. I got cold quickly and was glad to get back to the V.S. unit. The voluntary service unit was an old cozy house with lots of rooms. I didn't date more than one of the local girls in Stratford. I had a girl friend from the States who came to see me every month. We broke up after about six months, and I had no girl friend the rest of the time there.

The funding for the teenage center ran out after about half a year. I volunteered to work at a private home that cared for three homeless teens. Two were sisters who were Indians. I talked to one of the girls about Jesus, and she decided to be a Christian. I cooked for the family of ten people for half a year. I was glad when it was time to go back to the states. I got a little bored at the cook job.

When I returned to the States, I took some courses at Goshen College in 1978. I didn't do to well. I had trouble sleeping. There were nightmares about my first wife and how terrible she had been. I spent a year working as a diesel mechanic and then I worked for a year and one half as a motorcycle mechanic. I returned to Goshen College and finished my degree in 1981. After graduation I lived on our family's farm in the original 1860 farm house which had belonged to my father's grandfather and his family. It was my great grandfather who homesteaded the Miller farm. He didn't like cutting fire wood. His wife would tell him to go to the woods and cut some wood. He would walk out to the woods and go through the woods and into town where he would talk with the other men. His wife never had dried fire wood. It was always green and freshly cut. Her husband never cut any ahead. He just cut enough to barely keep her happy. One of his sons was Orb Miller, my uncle. Orb was the hunter. He provided most of the meat for the family table. I hunted with Orb a few times when he was in his eighties. He was still a good shot then. We were out squirrel hunting once when I saw a crow in the top of the tree we were sitting under. I pulled back both hammers on the double barrel shotgun I was using, and aimed carefully. I pulled one of the hammers, and both barrels went off. It killed the crow and almost knocked me to the ground. Orb said, "I guess that's the end of squirrel hunting today." He didn't sound angry. He just knew that I'd scared away all the squirrels. Orb was a Mason. He warned me that if he attempted to go into a church the roof would probably cave in. He was trying to say that he felt his being a Mason, hindered his standing with the church, I think.

My Grandpa Everett taught Sunday school for many years. I learned my first Bible stories from him. Everett loved to raise apples. I'm following that family tradition and raising apple trees. I was allowed to have hard cider even when I was young. I helped prune the trees. My father usually sprayed the trees. I also mowed the yard for $2.50. It was a difficult yard to mow. There were many trees to mow around. I liked mowing my Aunt Nett's yard better. I got $2.50 for it, and it was much smaller. My Grandpa Bosler's yard was the best to mow. He spoiled me by paying $7.50 for his house and the yard at his doctor's office combined. He let me use his riding mower. There was lots of trim work, but I loved mowing that yard. I always got a good meal with the deal too.

Everett used to have me help him pick stocks when I was about nine years old. I made some good lucky choices at first. Then I caused him to loose a big sum of money once. He never had me help after that. He was good with the stock market and made money from trading rare coins too. He was the Elkhart County Commissioner during the sixties. His name is on a bridge over Turkey Creek on County Road 146. It is right next to the house I grew up in.

When I was eight or nine, I did quite a bit of swimming in Turkey Creek. We had a rope which we used to allow us to swing out over the water and drop in. As we went out across the water we would yell "Yaba daba doooo!" as though we were the comic character Fred Flintstone. Even the neighborhood adult men would occasionally use the rope and it became a big celebration.

My father had seven and a half acres by Turkey Creek. We raised sheep and I had a pony for one summer. I spent most summers after 1962 hunting sparrows. I loved to shoot them with my 22 caliber rifle. I still have that rifle. I got so accurate with it that I could put one bullet right on top of another at ten yards distance. I demonstrated it for Glen Eisenhower once. He couldn't believe it and dug the bullets out with his knife to prove to himself whether I had done it or not. Glen died out west after years of running a gun shop in New Paris. He was found under his truck. People thought maybe the wolves had come and scared him to death at night. I sold a pistol to him once. It was a 22 caliber Ruger. My brother Dana had sold it to me. He didn't like it that I turned around and sold it. I don't know why it bothered him.

There is plenty of depression in my family tree. Down through the years there have been several suicides. Sometimes depression is found in quite creative people like Vincent Van Gogh. I think Ernest Hemmingway was manic depressive. Don't quote me on that. He shot himself with a shotgun when he was sixty-one years old. He had terrible health though. He just didn't want to be a vegetable. You can tell by his eyes that he had trouble with depression. I loved his book, *The Old Man and the Sea*. He wrote it when he was fifty-four years old. Hemmingway said that authors should avoid liquor when they're writing. I just had some barbequed chicken and a beer. I think I'll write a little more before the beer takes effect.

I've been reading much literature about rare coins. The object is to buy the rarest coin in the best condition one can afford. I currently only have one gold coin. It's an 1860 liberty head 2 ½ dollar piece. I love the coin and wish I had more gold coins. I'm quite short on money for the next three weeks. I've been tempted to sell some coins to help me through this tight time. I should be doing well for the rest of my life. I have an attitude now for saving money. I plan on having cash available for emergencies. The coin collection is not only a hobby, it's back up emergency money. I found a roll of uncirculated new California quarters at the Chiphone credit union in Middlebury last week. They didn't charge me any surcharge for them. I was delighted. I have one two dollar bill with a 1976 date on it, in my Bible. I put the bill at my favorite Bible passage of II Kings Chapter two, verses twenty-three and twenty-four. The bald prophet Elisha is being taunted by over forty-two children on the outskirts of a city. They are saying "Go up oh bald. Go up oh bald." He became upset about it and called on God to punish the children. God sent two she bears which "tare" forty-two of the children. "Tare" means the bears tore the children. It doesn't mean they were killed. Many of the children got away. There might have been a hundred children taunting the man. One of my good friends thinks it's inconsistent of God to have a bear attack children when he sent his Son to tell people to turn the other cheek. He isn't bald. He has nice long full black hair. What does he know? I'm bald. I'd love to have a bear bite people who make fun of me. That same friend said, "God only made a few perfect heads. The rest he covered with hair." It's interesting to talk with Paul. I call him every week. He shingled ten percent of my house twenty-three years ago. I paid him $150. I didn't know at the time what a good deal that was. Now the contractors want over $4,000 to do the house and garage. Paul hurt his back a couple years ago on a construction job. He tried to go back to work, but hurt his back again. His doctor told him he'd need to retire because his insurance wouldn't cover his back anymore. Not since he's been warned not to work. Paul retired at 64 years old. He's nine years older than I am. I'd like to be retired too. I guess I'll just have to keep on working for awhile longer. Paul loves to discuss religion. He studies Hebrew and Greek to attempt to find the true original meanings of Bible verses. I don't go in for all that, but it's fun to talk to Paul.

In 1981, I went with Bruce Elliott to Colorado to see Garden of the Gods. I borrowed my brother Dana's Toyota Celica for the trip. He didn't think I was serious when I asked for it. He must have not even heard me. When we returned, we found that he had reported it stolen. I had some fast explaining to do. Bruce and I hiked in the Grand Canyon. He tried to exit going up the wrong side, and ended up staying in the Canyon depths for the night. He said he slept on a picnic table. I waited for him at the top. We drove the car right through the middle of a giant sequoia tree. Then we went to Grand Junction where four different states meet at one point.

We made our way south into Arizona. There was a small store by the side of the road where we stopped to look at everything. It was the only thing out there in the desert. I bought a piece of Zunni pottery. The older more authentic pottery was more expensive and I was running out of money. We drove over a hundred miles per hour through most of Texas. There wasn't any surveillance there. You could see for fifty miles in any direction. I kept an eye out for police in helicopters while Bruce drove. We made it back to Indiana in no time at all.

When I returned to Indiana, I worked at the Goshen Kendall's Honda shop for the rest of the summer. One day a fellow mechanic was working on adjusting the valves of a Honda 900. He dropped a disc shaped shim down into the engine. He was getting ready to tear down the engine, when I stopped him. I told him to hold on. I had him drain the oil from the engine and then I got out my magnet that was on a telescoping handle. I turned the magnet to a position that formed a 90 degree angle. Inserting the magnet just into the drain plug hole, I slowly rotated it a full 360 degrees. When I pulled the magnet out, the shim was attached to the magnet. The mechanic was so happy that he bought me a steak dinner. We took the rest of the day off and went right to the restaurant.

I enjoyed the work at the Honda shop more than any other work. I was able to out figure the boss one day. He was a shrewd businessman, and the shop foreman was amazed that I was able to out maneuver him on a business deal. I offered to bring in three loads of fill dirt in trade for two new crash helmets that were state of the art. They looked quite sporty. I brought the three loads of dirt. It was more like sand. I dug the sand out of my father's pond. It was still wet. I didn't actually plan on defrauding the boss. I just never thought about how there wasn't much clay in the sand. The helmets were worth about a hundred dollars. I sold one of them and kept the other one. The boss never complained about the sand. He wanted me to be a salesman for him. I liked the mechanic work too much and turned him down. I wish now that I'd done the sales work. I think I would have liked it.

I was instrumental in closing Beatty Memorial Hospital. It was a terribly depressing place. I thought it would be better for people to be cared for in regular hospitals close to their relatives. I called the governor and explained my plan. The governor came and visited the hospital and then he turned it into a Juvenile corrections facility. I spent three years working in the Beatty Memorial Hospital School. I was a teacher's aid. They always referred to me as a teacher. I had a class of four to five students. They were slow learners and made little progress under my tutelage. I taught them Greek Mythology with programmed readers and we worked on phonics quite a bit. I also taught swimming. I was the best swimmer in the school. We went to the Laporte YMCA every Wednesday. I remember that one day I was training a 16 year old blond girl to swim, and her bikini top fell off. That was quite embarrassing. She was good looking, but as slow as molasses. She always worked hard at her studies.

One of our students could balance on his head and spin in circles at the same time. They were trying to get him to stop doing it. I was amazed by his skill. I sometimes took the students fishing at the hospital's fish pond. One day the boat tipped over and we all fell in. Luckily the water wasn't deep. We all made it back to the unit safely.

I'm an independent voter. I split my voting between Democrats and Republicans. I'm not sure which party will help the economy the most. I vote for Democrats if I've heard something good about them. I know that Indiana went deeply in debt after our last Democratic governor got done with things. Democrats tend to get us into more wars than Republicans. The Democratic president John F. Kennedy got us into Vietnam. Of course President Bush got us into Afghanistan and Iraq. I think we had to do something about terrorists in those countries, but I'm against spending American tax dollars to rebuild those countries. If we turn every country we attack into a utopia, every country in the world will want to start a war with us. All so they can take tax dollars out of wage earner's pockets. Let me keep the money I earn. If we have a war, win it and get out. Let the terrorists rebuild their country. Someone can do it other than me and my fellow tax payers. Eighty billion dollars is what President Bush wanted to spend on rebuilding Iraq. Leave it like it is. Use the money to get our homeless off the streets. Build some quality roads without chuck holes. Build some quality housing for our poor people. Eliminate poverty in America.

We need to watch war profiteering closely. If big money people find they can make a killing from war profits, we will always be at war. I know I'm a little cynical, but money is what makes things happen in the world. The flow of money needs to be watched closely. If we allow too many crooked politicians to bleed the country dry, we may end up in another depression. Before the depression of the thirties, there were rich tycoons who manipulated the stock market and caused millions to loose their shirts. It hurt the whole country. Rich people know how to get richer. The people with a little less inside trader knowledge are the ones who lose their money. The key is to imitate the moves of such people, but get out just before they do.

One of my favorite coin dealers told me that it's smart to invest in Carson City silver dollars. I have about twelve silver dollars, but none of them are rare. I only have a couple rare coins. They are an 1864 two cent piece and an 1852 large penny. They are only worth $20 each. They aren't remarkably rare. Just mildly rare. I've been buying rolls of nickels at the bank. I go through them and look for old coins. Last week I found a 1939 nickel that's worth about forty cents. I love that kind of find. It's fun to get something for nothing. I buy rolls of dimes too and go through them. I save everything that's from the sixties. I'm saving all the nice unscratched dimes that I get in change from purchases. I don't think they will become valuable unless my relatives keep them for a hundred years. I just like dimes. They remind me of the seventy Mercury dimes I foolishly cashed in when I was a teenager. I wanted the paper money for my college fund. I sure wish I had those Mercury dimes now. They're worth about four dollars each. I also took my father's collection of silver half dollars and quarters and cashed them in. He didn't get mad, because he knew I wanted the money for college. I still feel guilty about taking his silver. I offered to pay him back this year, but he can't remember the coins at all. I'll do something nice for him to make up for that silver I took. I don't want to have to explain that when I get to the pearly gates. I can hear it now. "You stole twenty-five dollars worth of your own father's silver coins? You can go to Hellllllll!" I don't want to go through that. I always ask for forgiveness for my sins, but how do you get rid of guilt for doing something like that?

I used to be pretty greedy. I loved money more than anything. I loved my mother about as much as money. She was a doting mother. She always made tea and toast for me. When I was young, we played Scrabble every week. We played with an open dictionary. That caused me to do much dictionary reading. It's a good way to get your children to learn new words. I also studied the Word Power section of the Reader's Digest. The neighbors liked to take those vocabulary tests too. They were the Hoovers. Russell Hoover was the inspiration for my air conditioning business. I operated that business for ten years.

Lack of tariffs and "free trade" helps to create an economic climate where American workers will have to work frantically to compete with third world countries for jobs. I thought "free trade" was a good idea at first. It isn't good for American workers. I wish I was working with a union. Without a union, workers are at the total mercy of employers. I worked with a union at Bethlehem Steel. I got more respect there. You didn't get as much brow beating in that company.

My grandchildren are coming over Sunday for the afternoon. I'm going to give them each two half dollars. That's all I can afford this week. I love to give them coins. I can see that they get excited about receiving them. If my sons and their wives agree, I may start this Christmas with the old family tradition that my grandfather Everett started of pouring a bag of change on the carpet and letting the kids gather it up and keep the money. It's exciting, but I don't want to do it if the kid's parents think it's too primitive. My youngest son has said that he wants he children to grow up not being too greedy. He likes to be generous and not worry too much about having an expensive house or car. I don't want to go against his desires for training the children. I sure enjoyed picking up those coins when I was young, but I think I'm a little too greedy. I like giving money to the church, and I like to be generous with the poor, but I sure love to look at gold and silver coins.

I love to read about treasure hunting in the ocean too. That's what inspired my book, *Mary Thresher In Search of Sunken Treasures*. I love to write about treasure hunting and I love to read about it too. This month's issue of *Coinage* magazine told about two big finds of sunken treasure. Each one gave the hunters a wealth of gold and silver that was equal to around $100,000,000. I wouldn't mind actually finding that much gold and silver. I dream about it often. Sometimes when I'm asleep I'm seeing gold coins before my eyes. It's my favorite dream. I love gold.

I keep a back pack in the back seat of my car at all times. If I die unexpectedly in the car, I'm going to take the back pack with me to heaven. The streets are paved with gold up there, and I'm going to pull a couple of the gold bricks loose and put them in my back pack. I told my dad of my plan. He said that I might get kicked out for that. I hope I can resist the temptation. Maybe I'll just content myself with polishing the streets and admiring the gold. God will think I'm being tidy and keeping the streets looking nice. I might get some special commendation. Maybe they'll give me some extra large and bright white wings. I long to be in heaven. I know my friend Bruce has got it made. He doesn't have to work. He probably gets to sit around the camp fire every night and listen to stories. That was what he and I did when he was alive. We had campfires down by my father's fish pond on his farm. We discussed religion and reminisced about the good old days. Bruce loved to tend the fire. It was never perfect enough for him. He was always poking at the fire. We drank beer and listened to music from the early sixties. Jesus loved to cook fish on an open fire. The Bible tells about how he had fish cooking for his disciples once when they returned from fishing. I suppose he and Bruce are cooking fish around the evening fire in heaven. Probably once and awhile Jesus even turns some water into wine and the evening gets a little more verbose than usual. I can't wait to get there to join them. I'll just have to wait. I'm starting to have some heart pain once and awhile at work. I may be joining them sooner than I think. I get real happy when my heart starts hurting. I start thinking, "Maybe today's the day!" No more work. Just fun in heaven! My mother's there, my brother's there. All my grandparents are there. I can't see much point in sticking around here on earth forever. I do enjoy seeing my grandchildren. They're fun to watch. They take delight in simple things. If I don't die from over work, I hope I can live to take my grandchildren fishing. I want to get some pictures of them with their first fish.

There are some short bits of history from my family members that I should share. Once when my grandmother Edith Bosler was young, she was driving a horse and buggy and stopped suddenly. The horse and buggy following them couldn't stop in time and the head of the horse behind them came right through the back of the buggy.

Many years ago in Churubusco, Indiana where my Grandpa Bosler grew up, he and his brothers were moving a hay wagon down a hill towards the barn. The wagon got away from them and rolled right through the barn busting out a wall. On another day Grandpa Bosler was riding a horse when his brother jumped out from behind a bush and frightened the horse. It rose up on its hind feet and threw grandpa onto the ground. He was a teenager at the time. He played dead and forced his brothers to carry him clear to the farm house. Once in the bed, he started laughing and showed them that he had played a trick on them.

My father and his sisters used to get whippings often with apple tree branches that were small and thin. When they got in trouble they were forced to go out and cut the switches that were to be used to whip them. It's no wonder my father was a little strict with us. When he got older, he was allowed to drive the family car. Once as he was turning south, to leave New Paris he had too much speed and rolled the car over. By then they were more lenient with him. It only damaged the door a little.

One day when I was about nine, I decided to start throwing apples at my Grandpa Everett's bird house. I must have thrown about thirty apples. I didn't know that each of the apples I threw knocked down about four or five good apples from a tree under the bird house. I was impressed that grandpa didn't get mad about it. I suppose he knew we could make apple cider from the apples I knocked down. When I was a teenager he would tell me with mischief in his eye, that grandma still liked to prime the pump. I knew he was talking about sex. He had a great sense of humor.

Let me tell you a little about what movies I like. I especially like the 2001 Space Odyssey movie, produced by Stanley Kubrick. Arthur C. Clark wrote the screen play. That movie is out in space anyway. If you're spaced out too when you watch it, there is a unique experience to be had. I've watched that movie about forty times. I never get tired of it. Stanley Kubrick was a total genius. I wish I could have met him. I first saw the Space Odyssey at a theater in Laporte, Indiana. I was really feeling good at the time. It was 1970, in the winter. That was a beautiful movie indeed.

I love to watch a movie I have of Claudia Witt skating at the 1984 Olympics when she was sixteen years old. She was at her best then. She was totally inspired. She wore a black leather jacket with hundreds of small mirrors all over it. Her legs, her smile, she was too much. I love to watch the Winter Olympics. Skiing, bobsledding skating. Nancy likes to watch it with me. I have most of the James Bond movies. I'm starting to collect Ian Flemming books.

I have many large plants in my house. I have a bamboo palm that reaches the ceiling. I need to fertilize it soon.

That's my favorite plant. When I first married Nancy, she had no plants. She said they all died for her. I showed her how to plant them in big pots and keep them near the windows. We've had nice plants ever since.

We have good police protection in New Paris. The only thing that gets robbed is the Church of the Brethren next door. People keep stealing the sound equipment from the church every year. They do it around Halloween time. I think they must be Satanic. Maybe they're just on drugs. I wish the police would catch them. I think the church needs a burglar alarm system or surveillance cameras. I think a burglar alarm system would be the best. People in church don't want to be on camera. They keep the church locked, but these people know how to get the doors to open. Maybe they are hiding inside the church and opening it from the inside.

New Paris is adding on a housing addition east of town. We also have a new grade school. It cost $25,000,000 and is costing me $500 per year in higher property tax. I hope the housing addition doesn't bring in a lot of trouble making people. It could change the nature of the whole town if 250 new homes are filled with troublesome people. Maybe some of them will buy my books. I guess growth isn't that bad. They'll all have to pay taxes too. They will cause the size of the sewage treatment plant to double. My father had to sell part of his farm so they could have the treatment plant. He lost nine acres. He says it smells pretty bad sometimes, when they are stirring the sewage. The Chinese use human waste as fertilizer on their fields. We should learn from them. Here I am talking about human waste again. I'll try to change the subject.

This summer I plan on spending more time swimming than I have in the past. Last year, for my birthday, my father gave me a set of swim fins with a snorkel and mask. I plan on getting good with the snorkel. In 2009 I plan to go to Key West and snorkel with Nancy. I want to see the maritime museum that has gold artifacts retrieved from the Gulf of Mexico. There is a large gold chalice which I have to see. I've never been to Key West. I wrote about it in my last book. I want to see if my description of the place was at all accurate. I just pulled my description out of my imagination, but maybe I was imagining it just as it is. I hope to find some gold coins on the beaches like the characters in my book did. It'll be fun to visit the house where Ernest Hemmingway lived while he was there. He had a favorite bar there too. I'll have to have a beer there. I wish Hemmingway was still alive. I'd love to talk with him. He had an interesting life. It's easier to have an interesting life when you have plenty of money. His father was a doctor. They had money, I'm sure. I loaned a copy of a book by the granddaughter of Ernest's brother, to my youngest son. I hope he returns it. I liked that book. It told about his life in Cuba. He took his boat and helped look for enemy submarines in the area. He tried to armor plate his boat, but the steel made the boat too heavy. Hemmingway had a Thompson submachine gun which he kept on his boat. He liked to shoot sharks with it. He also had a .22 caliber pistol which he accidentally shot himself in the leg with once, while trying to shoot a shark. All these things are in the book. If I don't get it back I'll have to buy another one. I also have Hemmingway's short stories and a paperback version of *The Old Man and the Sea.* Hemmingway liked drink and guns. He was a man after my own heart. I've read *A Farewell to Arms* and most of his short stories.

I was on my way home from the tax man's house today when I got a flat tire. It was 5:00 P.M. and most of the stores were closed. I walked a block north to The Electric Brew coffee house and used their phone to call the AAA motor club. I had no jack in my trunk. I always count on the motor club. While making my call, I noticed they were having Jazz music that night at the coffee house. I met the tow truck about an hour later, and he towed me to

Wal-Mart. Wal-Mart fixed the flat right away. I went home and helped Nancy get ready for Easter. The grandchildren are coming over Sunday. I filled fifty plastic Easter eggs with candy and two dimes in each egg. I love to give the kids coins. It's what I like best. When I finished the egg work, I went shopping for car jacks to keep in the cars. I didn't buy one, I just wanted to know where I could get one when I get the money. I stopped at The Electric Brew coffee shop and listened to the last piece the band was playing. I love the eight foot by eight foot painting on the north wall of planet earth as viewed from outer space. I'd like a painting like that for in my office.

In an hour it'll be Easter Sunday. I think I'll go to church with Nancy. I always stay up till four in the morning writing. That makes it hard to wake up in the morning for church. Working second shift keeps me on a strange schedule. I'm always going to Wal-Mart at 2:00 A.M. in the morning after I get off work. At least I never need to wait in line at that time of night.

The second young woman that I ever did much kissing with was named Annett. (Fictitious name) I was seventeen at the time. She was much older. She was twenty-one. I took her to my Grandpa Everett's cottage on Syracuse Lake and took along a record player with seven Tijuana Brass Albums. We had a fire in the fire place and it was late spring. The windows were open and a cool breeze danced across the room. We played those seven albums about three times, when she finally made me quit playing them. We must have kissed for three or four hours. I was trembling all over with excitement. Finally she insisted that we go home. I was in love with her, but when I went to her house to visit her, I found she had an older boy friend there. It was a shock to find I wasn't the only man in her life. It would be a pattern that would repeat itself throughout the first half of my life.

After Annett, I started dating many different girls without getting attached to any of them. I had learned that making out was just for fun. It didn't mean you were getting serious or planning on getting married. My parents didn't approve of that philosophy, but they didn't tell me. My father only mentioned it last year. He only dated girls if he was seriously considering the possibility of marrying them.

You may be wondering why I don't mention my first wife much. I used to talk about her some. One of the people I talked about her to, contacted her about what I said. I found myself being threatened by her father. Out of a desire for peace and harmony, I won't mention her. I will say that she was a true genius. She only had flaws in the social areas of her life. She won a National Science Foundation Grant when she was in high school. She had successfully explained the presence of a pair of twin craters that were on the moon, I think. Her father helped her build a large telescope during high school. They lived in Utah, so the viewing was good. He was a genius as well and had a distinguished work history. I used to fish with him.

During the time I worked at Beatty Hospital, starting in 1970, I belonged to a jug band at Valporaiso University. I played trumpet, fiddle and mandolin. I only had one girl friend from Valpo. She was exceedingly thin and played the flute. We never got serious or anything. We only dated a short time. Shortly after her, I got married for the first time. After three years, we got a divorce and I've never heard from that wife since. I told her I wanted it that way.

I waited eight years before I married again. I did little dating during that time. I just drank lots of beer and played poker with my friends. I didn't do much working at factories then. I just helped my father on his farm in the spring. I don't know why I didn't write then. I didn't have a good typewriter then. I didn't even know how to use a computer. I was always worried about privacy. I didn't want to write things down and have people read what I had written without my permission. I kept all my thoughts in my head. It was when I attended Goshen College that I was exposed to lots of good literature. I started to know how good plots were constructed. Most of the courses I took required papers. I did quite a bit of writing for those courses. It built up my confidence.

Don't ask me why I waited fourteen years after graduation to start writing. Something in me took time to grow. I think when I turned fifty, I realized that I had to start writing right then, or I would lose my abilities before I got any books written. I couldn't put it off any longer. The thought of dying without having written any books, scared me. Being an author meant much to me. I wanted to quit just talking about being an author. I knew it was time to put up or shut up. Once I started writing my first book, I loved the way it made me feel. I felt excited every night. I couldn't wait to get off work so I could write some more pages to my book. On weekends, I'd write fifteen pages almost nonstop. I'd stay up all night writing. My secret is that I drink lots of Folgers instant coffee. After my first book, I started taking Ritalin for depression. It almost doubled my productivity. That did a lot to relieve my depression.

Without coffee, my blood doesn't circulate well enough and my mind stays lazy. All I think about then, is whether or not I have enough beer in the frig. My mind without coffee just sits contentedly and watches television. I love The History Channel on cable television. I canceled the cable television in order to save some money. I've gotten much more writing done now that the television isn't such a tempting use of my time.

Soon I'll start advertising and pushing the books more. I'll have book signings with plenty of books available. Right now I only have two. One is going to the Goshen College Library. It's *Mary Thresher In Search of Sunken*

Treasures. The other one I'll sell to someone. Then I'll order two more books. I'll never become a well known author at this rate. It takes money to do it. I'll have more money next year. Then I'll publish my first collection of books. I have five books to put in the first collection book. Three of the books aren't previously published. That will bring my total of published books up to seven.

I hope my wife and I can have some nice romantic vacations together soon. We spent one night at the Oakwood Inn, in Syracuse, Indiana. That was about five years ago. I had to reserve the room three months in advance. It was one of two special rooms that had a giant hot tub big enough for ten people. It had a view of Wawasee Lake too. The food at the Oakwood was delicious. They have some attractive inlaid wood around the edge of the floor in their library. There is a player grand piano in the lobby. It's a nice elegant place to stay. In the winter, when I went, the price was only $150 for one night.

We've been to Mackinac Island. That was about eight years ago. It was fun riding the horse drawn wagon around the Island. They don't allow cars. Everyone travels by bicycle or by horse. The guide, who gave a talking tour of the island from the driver's seat of the horse drawn wagon, was entertaining to say the least. He would mumble, I'm sure intentionally, at times so that you had no chance of making out what he was saying. It was funny. We bought some clothes on the island. I brought back a hat and a coffee mug. I took a picture of a light house, which I later framed.

Our latest anniversary holiday was in New Buffalo, Michigan. We stayed at the Grand Hotel. Once again, we saved money by going in the winter. The room was only $99 for one night. During the summer it's more than twice as expensive. There was a nice quaint restaurant in the basement that had a wall of glass that looked out over Lake Michigan. I think some recent construction has made the view less spectacular. The food was great and the service exceptional. The price included some free wine or milk and cookies. We passed up the offer. The room had a giant king sized or larger, bed. There was a gas fireplace right beside the bed and there was a small Jacuzzi in the bathroom. We stayed on the fourth floor, which I'm sure still provides a good view of the lake. The fireplace quickly makes the room too hot, but you can open the sliding glass door to the small balcony and cool off the room enough so you don't mind the heat from the fireplace.

There is an interesting bar in New Buffalo called Casey's Bar & Grill. The prices are geared to people who don't mind spending a little money. I usually go there by myself and just eat the hot wings appetizer and one beer. The beer is $4 per glass. There is a nice rustic atmosphere in the bar and in the summer you can see lots of wealthy people in there. I try not to stare at them. I always wear my diamond ring when I go there so I'll fit in better. The waitress made me wait a long time for everything. You get the best service if you sit at the bar. Their coffee is delicious and only costs $1.75. You get plenty of free refills.

One of my dreams is to have a 28 or 31 foot power cruiser when I retire. I'll keep it there in New Buffalo. The prices for boat storage and care are reasonable. I've been checking around and comparing prices. It's more expensive to keep a boat on Lake Wawasee than it is to keep one at New Buffalo. The total price for a 25 foot cruiser for a year is about $2,000 at New Buffalo. I'm not sure about that price, but it's close. That includes winterizing and keeping the boat in a heated building. It also includes the price of the summer docking rental. I often go to New Buffalo to look at the people with their boats. I even go in winter and look at the boats when they are on dry dock.

There is good fishing at New Buffalo. It isn't as good as in Grand Haven though. Grand Haven is where I often fish for lake trout and Coho salmon. I go with Captain

Bill who charters with a 31 foot boat he rents, called the Thunder Duck. Fishing doesn't get much better than when you're fishing with Bill. He has a golden Labrador that always goes along with him. Bill usually finds plenty of fish for me. I've taken several groups of friends out with him. One year there were four of us, and each of us had a twenty pounder or two and several twelves.

Bill cleans all the fish for you. Last year I had to cancel out. The other people I had lined up to go along fizzled out. The price is currently $480 for four people. It includes a sandwich and cold pop. You can go in the morning or the afternoon. The morning is the best time to get lots of fish. I like to fish around August 10th each year. That's when the Coho start to bite, and the weather is usually good then. I fished with Bill once in June, and the strong wind drove us off the water. My younger brother, Jeff was along. The seven foot waves had him perpetually heaving his cookies out the back of the boat. He won't go along anymore. I caught a twelve pound Coho in those waves. It was the only fish we got. We asked Bill to take us back for Jeff's sake. We weren't charged for the short trip. We went back in August and had good fishing. That was about ten years ago. It's been five or six years since I've gone fishing with Bill. I'm planning to go again soon.

I wouldn't mind catching some walleye on Lake Erie sometime. I've checked out the pricing. The cost is quite a bit higher than with Captain Bill. Five people can fish there for about $560 for the day. I want to try it someday. One of my neighbors takes his own boat there often. I may not go after all. I prefer big boats with a head. I don't like having to pee in a can or bottle. That's what happened on Lake Superior once. The captain of the charter boat was too cheap to let me use the head. He didn't want to have to pump it out. At least he only charged me $60 for the charter. I only caught one lake trout. It was a nice one though. It weighed twelve pounds. The city I fished in was Marquette, Michigan. It was hard for me to remember the name. On that vacation, I told Nancy I was going on a fishing vacation for five days. She wasn't listening to me and when she discovered I was gone, she put out an all points bulletin on me. The police were looking for me the whole time. I had been camping at Deer Park in the Upper Peninsula. I was driving at night from the shower area back to my primitive camp site where my tent was waiting. I had a big black bear run across my path as I neared my camp site. I packed up the tent and headed out right away. I didn't want some bear around my tent. I did some fishing and then returned to my wife who was wondering where I was.

I wish more people would write about their lives. My mother always talked about doing some writing. Her father talked about recording his experiences in Africa. He was too shy of the microphone. My mother waited too late to start writing. Even if a person doesn't write as well as Hemmingway or Agatha Christi, it's fun to write. It allows you to get things off your mind. I'd like to live in Ireland. They have great reverence for writers. I don't know why that is. People there love to read. Books are expensive, and many people there don't have much money. I'm the type of person too, who will spend his last dollar on a good book. I want a book on Jamaica right now. It costs $21 plus tax. I have $27 dollars right now. I'm still tempted to get that book. I'll try to force myself to wait till two weeks from now when I have more money. I'll have to drive to Mishawaka to get the book at Borders Book Store.

For those of you who will never read my second book, *Fishing for Almost Anything that Moves,* I think I'll give a little more detail about the family fishing trip to Canada which I incorporated into the book. I was twelve when we went on the trip. My older brother, Kevin, went along. My cousin, Dave, was there. Grandpa Bosler and my dad completed the group that went. We took two boats with us. One was a sixteen foot aluminum fishing boat, and the other was a twelve foot boat. The twelve foot boat made a good cover for the other boat. The first night we camped in Canada, there was a hail storm that tore up the tent. We had to sleep in the car. That experience didn't make it into the book. Next we arrived at Thessalon, Ontario. I went into a store and asked if they sold fire crackers. The owner said indignantly, "We don't sell fire crackers in Thessalon." I can hear those words to this day. The old man was quite shocked that I was asking for firecrackers. What he didn't know was that I had hundreds of them out in the car. I was just worried that I'd run low. I had bought them in Tennessee on the way back from Florida a couple years before. Finally we made it to Chippawanna Bay where my Uncle Les and Aunt Erma had their log cabin and fishing charter business. In those days money went farther. They had purchased the land and built two log cabins, plus a boat garage for only $4,000. Their boat was an old wooden 25 foot cruiser with twin 60 horsepower outboards. The first day out fishing, we caught 101 twelve inch long perch and a four foot northern pike. I caught a seagull with a dead fish tied to my fish line. I released the sea gull unharmed. It bit me on my thumb. Aunt Erma cooked up the perch that night and we had a wonderful feast. Next we went pike fishing along the coastline of Lake Superior. We didn't fish long till Erma got a big one on. It was taking out line so fast, that Les tried to adjust the tension and got his finger caught in the line and broke it off. Erma got so mad about it that it ruined the rest of the day.

The next day, we climbed a mountain carrying the smallest boat, and fished on a small lake. We caught seven rainbow trout that were about a foot long. Grandpa Bosler and Dave were fishing from a log raft that was a little water logged. It floated about a foot under the water. Dave saw a leach swimming up to grandpa's leg and warned him about it. It alarmed grandpa so much that he fell in the water. He was rescued by Uncle Les in the small aluminum boat. Grandpa couldn't make it into the boat all the way and was rowed back to shore with his hind end hanging out of the boat in the water. They had been fishing in their underwear. It was quite a site to see.

I went swimming in Lake Superior a little too long and caught a cold. The last day at the lodge, it rained. We all sat around the stove and told stories. When we ran out of stories, we all took turns arm wrestling each other. It was great fun.

I had some larger fire crackers that got me into trouble. I put one in the mouth of a dead fish and blew off its head. I still don't know why the adults got so upset about that. That was the end of the firecracker displays. I hated having to leave them alone the rest of the trip.

Well, it's Easter morning and I've been writing all night. I've written thirty-six pages of six hundred words each this weekend. It's a new record for me. I guess when you start to get older, and you know you could die any time, you get desperate to write everything down. It's like a futile attempt at immortality. Just because you have your life written down in a book doesn't mean it will be read by anyone. Just because you have a real nice tombstone, doesn't mean anyone will like it that much or learn anything from the wise sayings you had carved on the stone. "All we like grass, do wither away." The hairs on my face keep coming out closer to my eyes. The hair on my arms is growing thicker. My body is producing all kinds of testosterone in one last futile attempt to have eternity. It wants more children. Children are a mild form of immortality. They don't last forever, but they keep your memory alive for awhile after you're gone. You won't know whether you're forgotten or not anyway. I hope that when I'm in heaven, I won't have to look down on earth and fret about all the bad things that are happening. It would be nice to be able to keep my mind on the fun going on up there. It's hard to imagine what heaven will actually be like. All I know is there will be streets paved with gold. I know I mentioned the gold streets before, but that's what I always think of when I think of heaven. I don't understand why I love gold so much. When I stare at it, I just feel warm all over. Especially if it's my gold. Silver is wonderful too, but not as fine as gold. I won't starve myself or Nancy, but I'm going to start building up the biggest hoard of gold which I possibly can. Don't tell anyone that I'm saying this. I don't want robbers coming around to my house. I know only upright people bother to read books. Especially autobiographies. They probably have their own pile of gold already.

If a person can learn from the mistakes of others, and learn from the successes of others, there is no reason why an intelligent and healthy person can't amass some wealth. Let me reiterate some of the points I've made so far in this book. I may make some new points as well. A person should not trade cars too often. Avoid borrowing money that carries an interest fee. Don't borrow money at all, unless it is low interest money and you are going to use is for investing in such a way that you will end up with a profit. Don't pay off a six percent home loan early, if you could leave it in a 401k where it's earning eighteen percent. Don't think you have to have everything you want. Let your needs become wants. Realize what you don't really need. Eat at home as much as possible. Eat plenty of cereal and milk. Both of them are inexpensive foods. Don't get accustomed to eating in expensive restaurants. Eat at cheap fast food places, but watch the calories and the grease. Research cars before you buy one. Buy ones like Buick LeSabre that have a good history of not having many things go wrong with them. Some of the big V-8 cars get better gas mileage than the compact cars. Do your research before you buy. I love my Saturn. It's been a good car, but everyone is telling me how many new ones are in junk yards. Many people have problems with them. I like the plastic, no rust, side panels. Too bad the hood rusts. Don't buy Hondas. The replacement parts will put you in the poor house. That's only my opinion. I don't want to get sued by some car manufacturer for having an opinion, learned opinion that it is. Don't lease cars. You may get a lower payment, but you don't get the pleasure of spending half of your life with no car payment. It's twice as expensive. Cars are the biggest expense you will likely suffer in your life. The house is a good investment and makes money for you. The cars only lose money. Try your best to minimize that lose. Buy cars with 30,000 miles on them and drive them at least ten years. If it's a good car to start with, you'll save money this way.

Don't go on too many far away vacations that cost thousands of dollars. Once and a while is fine if you can afford it. Save that for your retirement years. When you're young, put ten percent at least, of your income into investments for retirement. You don't want to need to work past the age of fifty. Work is not as much fun when you start getting old. By planning ahead and saving lots of money, you can afford to retire early.

Pick a good Christian person to marry. That is one of the most, if not the most, important decisions of your life. If you don't choose wisely you will be in for lots of unhappiness. Emphasize early in the dating process that you want a loyal spouse. You don't want adultery to be part of your life. Make sure you don't marry someone who is all about getting what they want. Marry a caring sharing person.

Watch your children closely so no harm comes to them. You never know who might be a pervert. Bring up your children in the faith and they will not depart from it. I was paraphrasing from the Bible. Feed your children plenty of milk. It makes them bigger and more powerful. That will help them be successful. Let children earn money at home early. Nine years old isn't too young to start learning the pleasure of building up a nice savings account. Spell out to your teenagers how credit cards and high interest loans can doom them and make them life long paupers. No one can make it through life with seventeen credit cards dragging them down. I used to have seventeen credit cards. Not a good idea. If you can't control your own spending, get friends to help you control yourself. Ask them for advice about how much of what type of things you should buy. If your spouse and a friend both agree with you to buy something, it's probably a good thing to do. Don't shop for groceries when you're hungry. You'll buy too much, and much of it will go bad in the frig. Don't fill a freezer with tons of meat that you can't use in time and have to throw out. If you like to fish, don't let fish go bad in the freezer. Eat those fish right away or soon after you catch them. Don't keep more fish than you can eat. Let someone else catch some too.

Plant trees where ever possible. Be one of the people making this a better planet. Don't spend too much on clothing. I wear the same blue jeans for fifteen years. Keep your weight the same so you aren't constantly buying new wardrobes. If you tithe on your income, God will bless you. You will be more conservative with your spending and do better in life. Be generous to the poor. God notices things like that. The thing that impresses God the most, in my opinion, is faith. Pray for more faith in God and in miracles. God will do miracles for you if you pray to him in faith. I don't know why everyone with faith isn't healed of illness. That's a tough one. Be knowledgeable about the Book of Job in the Bible. God wants people who will praise him even when the chips are down. He doesn't need a bunch of robots that are forced to praise him. That wouldn't give him much pleasure. If everyone had wonderful lives, sure they would be likely to praise God. Satan gets real upset when he sees people who have it rough, but they keep on loving God and wanting to please him.

Don't send your son to a school where they will beat him and humiliate him. Hazing is not cute. It is the work of Satan. Do careful research about schools before you allow your son or daughter to go there.

Don't attend séances and don't get involved in Halloween. Stay away from Satan and he can't hurt you. Stay under God's protection. Witches are real, and many of them would like to hurt you. Avoid such people.

Be generous with your children. The book of Matthew says, "If your son asks for a fish, would you give him a serpent?" "If your son asks for a loaf of bread would you give him a stone?" We know how to give good gifts to our children. God knows how to give good gifts to us.

Those are some of my favorite Bible verses. I always used to refer to them when I was asking my father for a loan. He has helped me quite a bit. I will in turn be generous with my children and grandchildren.

My favorite book of the Bible is Matthew. I love the Sermon on the Mount. I read it often. The story of Jesus talking with the centurion and then healing his servant. I'll include the story here: "And when Jesus was entered into Capernaum, there came unto him a centurion, beseeching him, and saying, Lord, my servant lieth at home sick of the palsy, grievously tormented. And Jesus saith unto him, I will come and heal him. The centurion answered and said, Lord, I am not worthy that thou shouldest come under my roof: but speak the word only, and my servant shall be healed. For I am a man under authority, having soldiers under me: and I say to this man, Go, and he goeth; and to another Come, and he cometh; and to my servant, Do this, and he doeth it. When Jesus heard it, he marveled, and said to them that followed, Verily I say unto you, That many shall come from the east and west, and shall sit down with Abraham, and Isaac, and Jacob, in the kingdom of heaven. But the children of the kingdom shall be cast out into outer darkness: there shall be weeping and gnashing of teeth." I love this passage because it shows that Jesus had room in his heart for gentiles. He loved those who had great faith regardless of whether they were gentiles or Jews. He was sent first and foremost to save the Jews, because of the promises God had made to some of the Jewish forefathers. I'm not up on all those promises. I know that the Jews were God's favorite people at the time Jesus came to earth. I'm not sure what plan God has for the Jews now. I'm just glad that people like the centurion proved to Jesus that gentiles were worth saving too.

I was so tired this morning from staying up all night writing, that I set my alarm clock wrong. I missed the Easter service. Nancy gave me a recap on what the sermon included. She lectured me that I won't be spending the whole day writing. She has five hundred things for us to do before our guests arrive. She also says I can't use the phone. She says I use it too much. Nancy seems to love controlling me. I don't know why this is. I'll do a few chores. Maybe then she'll let me write some more. I was looking forward to this long weekend all week. I wanted to get this autobiography well on its way to completion. It's still short.

Don't use lots of credit cards and get into trouble financially. Just control your wants and keep your spending under control. I had a boss at work who often told me about his financial problems. His wife constantly spent them into a hole. She charged up the home phone to $900. It had to be disconnected. Then she charged up a cell phone to $500. He can't control her. She is impulsive and doesn't care about him. She's only thinking about how she wants to talk on the phone. I love the phone too, but I try to keep the long distance bill down to around $25 per month. We're being gouged for $74 per month on our local phone service. I might as well use that all the time. I'm paying for it. They charge businesses a fortune for phone service. My friend, the boss, used to fish with me. Then he got fired for missing too many days. I haven't heard from him since.

My whole life I've been kissing other people's butts and doing what other people want me to do. During my retirement years, I'll do what I want to do. It'll be nice to stay up late at night writing, without needing to worry about having enough energy for work the next day. I won't need to put up with annoying people in the work place. I won't need to drive as much either. Road crowding is getting to be a big problem here in Elkhart county. I'm looking forward to a life with less stress involved in it. I'll spend much of my time traveling, fishing and working to promote tree planting around the world.

I just called the phone weather report. They said it would be up to 60 degrees Monday. I heard at Wal-Mart that it would be up to 74 degrees by Wednesday. I'm going to celebrate by going Muskie fishing on Tippicanoe Lake. The Indiana State record Muskie was caught on Little Tippicanoe Lake a couple years ago. I'd like to be the next record holder. I sold my electric trolling motor last year, but I think I can do a good job of trolling with the 10 horse power outboard I have. I need to find someone to run the motor for me. My old fishing pal Bruce is dead now. I'll need a replacement. I know I can find someone to go along. I don't really mind going alone, but I'll have a better chance of catching something if I have some help running that motor. It doesn't want to keep a straight course. I keep tightening the steering, but the boat likes to go in circles. I'll try some bluegill fishing down at my dad's fish pond on the farm too. It might still be a little early for bluegill. At least I can watch the bass swimming around. There are lots of bass in there. This summer, I may try fishing some new lakes in Michigan which I haven't tried before.

My grandchildren left a few hours ago. I got plenty of pictures of them finding Easter eggs all around the house. They knew there was candy and two dimes in each egg. Before the Easter egg hunt they asked if they could go to the basement and see my safe again. They love the fact that I have a secret code which they must not know about. They close their eyes and stand back while I dial the combination. When I got the safe open they lined up and asked if I had anything for them. I was pleased that they had learned what the safe held for them. I gave them each a half dollar coin. Then I told them about the money in the Easter eggs and that they would need to divide it up equally after they found all the eggs.

During my vacation this summer or even before that, I'll get serious about writing my next book. I'm working so much overtime now, that I can't feel too inspired. I can't believe how much I wrote this weekend on my autobiography. I also made the changes my proof reader recommended on my first book. That book is one hundred and thirty-five pages long. It's my shortest book.

It would be nice to sell lots of books. I may try to peddle a little more violence. That's what really sells in America. Everyone wants to read about someone's arm being shot off. Kids especially delight in reading of, or viewing on X-box, the decapitation of people with swords. During the end times there will be plenty of that. I suppose it doesn't hurt to get used to it. That way people won't go into shock when it actually starts to happen.

America doesn't like people reading about sex. The British prefer for their people to read about sex. They abhor violence. I should pursue selling my "R" rated fishing book to the British. I might become a best selling author there.

Last Sunday, the grandchildren lined up at the safe to see if I had anything in there for them. They know there is always at least one coin in there for them. My granddaughter asked if they could all have gold coins. It took me by surprise. I said I wasn't that rich yet. It didn't occur to me that she was talking about the Sacagawea dollars I'd given them a couple weeks ago. I've got about fifteen nice shiny ones that aren't too scratched up. I'll have to give them each one the next time they're here. Nancy said, "Now you've started something." She's right. They'll always expect a coin or two. I like giving them something to look forward to. I hope some day soon, I can start reading my books to them. The Mary Thresher book is great for children. I offered one to the Goshen College Library today. I have to wait for them to evaluate it to see if they want it. I already donated one to the Goshen Public Library. The librarian said she would read it to the children. I wrote the book in such a way that it is fun for adults and for children. I tried to include layers of meaning. The experiences of Mary in the desert with her grandfather and with the Jade Goddess are prime examples. The adult reader will read more into the various substances used by Mary than a child would. The children won't be so interested in the desert. They'll think Mary is just learning about medicines. They'll be most interested in the treasure hunting and the discovery of large amounts of gold and gems. That is what I was hoping to excite the young people with. The older people will be more interested in the romantic sections, possibly. I hope to write more stories that are for adults and children.

I guess spring is actually here. I called the phone number for the short term weather report and it said tomorrow is supposed to get up into the low seventies. I'm glad it also said there will be thunderstorms. Otherwise I'd feel like not going to work and enjoying the day outdoors. I absolutely can't miss more days of work.

When I was in the seventh grade, I decided I'd like to be in the band. Most of the students had started when they were in the fifth grade. I excelled at trumpet. I never had an extraordinary range of notes. That is, I couldn't hit real high notes, but I played on key. I had perfect pitch. The piano tuner noticed it when he tuned my piano. I was real fussy about how he tuned the highest notes. I started playing piano when I was nine. I took lessons for four years. By my sophomore year, I had taken the first chair position in coronet. I usually played the coronet, but sometimes I took in my grandfather's silver plated trumpet. Grandpa Everett used to play in the Elkhart County Band. My father used to whistle with that band. Whistling was more revered in those days. It isn't done much now. I played first chair coronet for three years. I almost lost my position once to the second chair coronet player who challenged me. I just barely beat him. He was a good player. Whenever you thought you could play better than the person ahead of you, you could challenge them. That meant there would be a contest where you would both play a section of music the band director selected. He would listen with his back to the two players. He would then announce his decision as to whether the first player of the second player had won. It was stressful to do those challenges, but I did quite a few of them. I was driven to be the best. Some day's I would practice the coronet for five hours per day. I usually practiced at least one or two hours per day.

I've had about forty jobs in my life. When I start to get bored with a job, or when I start having trouble with a supervisor, I go to a different job. A few times I've been laid off because of no work, but most of the time I've quit the job to return to school, or I've just wanted a change. My schooling was spread out over eighteen years. I attended college first in 1968. I went to Manfest and then Hamline University. In 1973 I attended Purdue for one and a half years. In 1978 I took a few courses at Goshen College. I first graduated from Goshen College in 1981. I took my last major from Goshen College in 1986. I always enjoyed my courses. Learning is fun for me. All together I attended college for five and a half years.

Today I received word from Goshen College Library that my Mary Thresher book has been accepted into the Mennonite Historical Library. It will be kept there forever. I was greatly pleased to hear the good news. It will be a form of immortality for me. It won't compete with heaven, but it is a pleasant occurrence by any stretch of the imagination. I may donate some money to the Historical Library. They will have to wait until my finances improve. It won't be too long of a wait. Things are starting to get a little better.

I barbequed some chicken with my family recipe today. Don't worry, I haven't forgotten that I promised to include my family's pecan pie recipe. I'll find it soon. I just need to consult Nancy about it. I promised my dad two of the chicken thighs that I barbequed. He likes chicken too. He said he put a couple hundred sun fish in the farm's fish pond today. Then he fed them some fish pellets that he bought. Dad loves to feed the fish. It's fun for him to see his relatives catching some fish from that pond. He doesn't like it when some people get permission to fish and then catch all the big ones. It's fine to take a dozen, but don't get greedy and take forty every day till their all gone. He doesn't let people keep the bass. That way they get bigger and they're more fun to catch and release.

I gave both of my living brothers copies of the family barbequed chicken recipe. My youngest brother, Jeff, seemed rather interested in it. My older brother, Kevin, only likes to grill hamburgers. He doesn't like to spend the time that chicken requires. I gave my dad two pieces of chicken that I barbequed yesterday. He gave me nine frozen pieces of chicken and some brown sugar. I barbequed those pieces of chicken right away. It was a sunny day and I liked being out barbequing.

When I was in Costa Rica planting trees in Turrialba, I saw a line of leaf cutter ants working on some small cocoa trees that were planted in the nursery. I didn't know that I should report it. When I finally did mention it, all the leaves were gone from the trees. There were about twenty of them. I rarely went to the office of the Posts and Stakes Department where I worked. I kept busy pulling weeds out of the trees. I reported a snake once that had lunged forward in a ditch as I walked by. It was five or six feet long and was colored dark blue or black. I thought it was a Fere de Lance, the most poisonous snake in Costa Rica. The workers for the Posts and Stakes Department all went out with four foot long machetes and killed the snake. I thought they had to be brave to go looking for such a poisonous snake. If it bites a person and there is no antivenom close at hand, the flesh is dissolved down to the bone. It's not a pretty sight. I saw pictures of bite victims at a snake farm not far from San Jose. People usually get bitten on the arms or legs. The bites can be fatal. The Cobra that was displayed for us, was unusually aggressive. When it looked at me, shivers went up and down my spine. I consider myself fearless, but that snake had an affect on me. I'll never forget it. The man who handled it was quick as lightning with his hands. Once he did get one drop of the venom on the out side of his skin. He took the serum right away, but the venom managed to dissolve away the tip of his little finger.

When I was around twelve years old, I would go to our fish pond and find young garter snakes that were around two feet long. They were friendly and I could hold three of them at a time. I would take them to show my mother. I just wanted to show off how brave I was. She didn't appreciate these displays. Once I was holding a garter snake that wasn't real friendly. I let its head get out from between my fingers a little too far and it quickly turned its neck and opened its mouth to bite me. In a quick reflex motion, I threw the snake way up in the air. That was the closest I ever came to getting bit. My neighbor, Dave

Hoover who is an English professor now, liked handling snakes too. He got bitten by a water snake once. They aren't poisonous, but it made him a little sick because of the nervous strain of being bitten. I wish he had time to read my Mary Thesher book. I'm sure he'd like it. He's a busy man now. He's in charge of twelve new professors who are teaching six hundred English majors. He and I had a gang when I was ten years old. We had home made pipes that we would smoke weeds from the woods with. The weeds didn't get us high or anything. We also smoked corn silk. A few years later, we started removing tobacco from discarded cigarettes we found along the road. We would put the tobacco in our pipes and smoke it. Dave got caught for doing that, by his parents. We were told we could only smoke corn silk.

The gang we formed was called the Turkey Creek Gang. We wrote letters of loyalty in milk on paper and then scorched the paper over fire. After a year or two, we accepted a new member named Bruce Elliott. He was eager to join the gang. We made him chew on a dandelion stem as his initiation. They have a terrible taste. He was glad to get into the gang. We never did violent things or broke the law. We camped together on Turkey Creek. Once we stayed out for three days. We ran low on food and tried making French toast by frying bread in bacon grease. It tasted terrible. We made chairs and a table out of split logs. We cut the logs from an old thorn tree. The owner later told us not to cut down any more trees. We kept a camp fire going the whole three days. That's what I like about camping in Indiana. You can always have a camp fire. In the Upper Peninsula, of Michigan, there are often camp fire bans, because of dry weather. Forest fires are a threat up there.

I know I have to stop buying everything I want. I need to spend less on transportation. I need to trade cars less often. I won't buy cars or a boat until I have the money to pay for them in cash. I'll resist the temptation to put too much of my money into a boat before I can actually afford it. I've learned that I won't be happy with owning many things. I'll be happy when I've saved a big chunk of money. I'll be happy when my investments grow. If they fall I won't let it kill me. I know that money is only a tool for helping people with. I'll keep working even though I don't like my job. I haven't liked my jobs for thirty-five years. What's new about that? I'll control my beer consumption. One beer a night is enough. Beer can consume much of a person's income. I'm thankful I never got into cigarettes. They're expensive. One thing I'll continue to do is drive around more than is necessary. I like seeing the country. I grew up in the country, but I've been forced to live in town. I don't like being around lots of people. I like the solitude of the country.

Older people like myself aren't likely to do too well in trailer factories. They make people run here and run there. The pace is truly frantic. When I was young, I got along well in the trailer factories. Everyone liked me. I won't go back to them now. They always lay most of their people off after the spring and early summer are over.

In a couple days I'm going to ask the boss to put down that I want my vacation as soon as I qualify for it. June tenth is my hire date. That's when I qualify for two more weeks of vacation. I can't wait to have that much time to write.

I'm a would be philanthropist. I'd like to help lots of people if I had the money. My Grandpa Bosler was a philanthropist. He gave money to students who wanted to be doctors. He gave money to colleges and to Goshen Hospital. I'm not sure what all he gave his money to, but he gave most of it away even while he was alive. I suppose that people who give money to their children are also philanthropists. They're just keeping it in the family. I think fathers and mothers should keep things equal with their children. Don't give one child five percent of what you give the other child. Keep it fifty fifty. Why make children feel less loved than their brothers and sisters. I am equal in my giving to my children and grandchildren. I don't give all my money to charities and leave my children without anything. My Grandpa Bosler gave me money to finish my college work at Goshen College. He asked me once if I wanted him to give the college money. I said no, because I thought it would look like I was trying to curry favor. I'll give them money when my ship comes in. I love the college for the good training they gave me. I called one of my favorite professors from Goshen College, to tell him about the book I had given to the Mennonite Historical Library. I invited him to give it a read. The professors were always willing to meet individually with students to help them with whatever the students needed help with. I asked for more help than most students. I was nearer the age of the professors and felt kindly towards them. I tried not to make a pest of myself, but I was like a human sponge and soaked up everything I could get out of them about being a writer.

When I was seventeen years old, back in 1967, I used to sing in a swing choir at school. It was fun to wear a white diner jacket and dance with beautiful girls that I was fond of. My senior year, I grew tired of the swing choir. None of them seemed to like my new moustache. I grew it the summer of 1967. I had to shave it before I went back to school in 1968. After I graduated, I always wore the moustache. Some employers would ask if I minded shaving it. I would always say that I thought it was my own business. When I first attended college, at Manfest, back in 1969; I was asked to shave my beard if I wanted to stay as a music major. I decide to change my major to psychology. Later I found that there wasn't actually a psychology major offered. I had to have a teaching major with social studies certification. It didn't matter too much anyway, because I was destined to leave college many times before I would finally graduate.

When I got half way through writing this book, the memories from the past started pouring out from distant recesses of my mind. Things I thought I would never think of again came back to be noted down. I started wondering if it was about time for me to die. They say that just before you die, your whole life passes quickly before you. I wonder if that's actually true. I've never heard a dying person tell me that was happening to them. I've watched quite a few people die. I worked in a nursing home for six years. I used to wash up the dead bodies before the undertaker would arrive to take them to the morgue. I would train new workers, who were usually young women, to wash the bodies. They would often get emotional about it. I was always happy when I was washing up a dead person. I would think about how lucky they were to be dead. It reminded me that some day my troubles would be over.

I just got back from Lake Wawasee, in Syracuse, Indiana. I was watching the sunset, lovers making out on a blanket by the water, boats on the water, children playing in the park. It was an interesting evening. I was writing with my laptop in the passenger's seat of my Saturn passenger car. I accidentally let a mosquito into the cab. Now I am at home working on the laptop in the car again. The mosquito came and hovered at the computer screen. I smashed it between my hands. In one of Hemmingway's books, his character named Nick, burned a mosquito with a match. The mosquito was in his tent. That was Hemmingway's realism. He included little things that were just like real life. In his book, *The Old Man and the Sea,* he even included a passage where the old man is relieving his bladder while still fighting the monster fish he had on the line. I agree with Hemmingway that real life details are important. I've never studied "Realism" to know exactly what that school of writing believes in. I'm just going from what the name implies. Someone told me that Hemmingway had been trained in "Realism". I hope I'm not completely off the ball. I'll have to do some studying of the topic. I need more Hemmingway books. I have his short stories, but I need some books by him on Africa. I wrote a little about Africa in this autobiography. Hemmingway and I have some things in common. We both have written about fishing. I'm not a successful big game hunter yet. I have dressed out some road kill deer. I shot one deer. I suppose that does make me a successful big game hunter. Not as amazing as Hemmingway, but I'm sure I took just a much pleasure in the kill. I never kill what I can't eat. There is an exception. I like to shoot sparrows. I shoot male English sparrows. The females are too hard to distinguish from song sparrows. Song sparrows have beautiful songs and are not to be shot. English sparrows build dirty shabby nests everywhere. There are too many of them. Then make deposits on everyone's cars. I know that God knows when each sparrow falls, but I still don't like sparrows. I shoot them on the fly with a 12 gauge shot gun, or I stalk them and shoot them where they roost with a .22 caliber rifle. I used to be a good enough shot to shoot their little heads right off. I know that sounds a bit sadistic, but it actually is the most humane way to kill them. A body shot leaves them flopping around in pain for a long time before they die.

I have found that if I'm having great trouble with writer's block and feel there is no use trying to write something better than I ever have before, I just sit down and drink a can of cold Miller Lite. It has just enough alcohol to remove inhibition, but not so much as to make one tired or sluggish. Then after the beer, I drink two cups of real strong coffee. That causes the creative urges to take over and before you know it I'm writing up a storm. Last week I was starting to wonder if I would write any more books. I felt I could do no better than my Mary Thresher book. Now I'm on my way to the fourth book. At the same time I'm still working on my autobiography.

We had snow this weekend. I was afraid it would kill the apple and pear blossoms, but Sunday it warmed up a little and the blossoms seem to be fine. My biggest yellow delicious tree doesn't have many blossoms yet. I hope more show up in a week or two. I'd hate to not be able to make apple cider this year. Last year I had twelve gallons. I still have one gallon in the freezer. I think I'll get it out this week. Last year was a good year for apples. Most of my trees cycle. One good year and then a year with few apples. I suppose I should fertilize the trees. That way they wouldn't cycle so much. The fertilizer would make it so I would need to prune them more. I don't know what to do. I'll have to think about it. My yard is full of moles. All the neighbors are using high dollar insect and grub killer on their yards, so all the moles come to my house. I'll need to fight back. Nancy is complaining about it being hard to mow because the moles are so bad. I asked Khalaf Mashhour to pick up some grub killer for me. He said he was going to buy some more too. This whole week is going to be cold. I hope it gets warm then and stays warm. I don't want a real hot summer. I don't like sweating. Just warm enough so it'll be nice for fishing and swimming.

The most wonderful thing happened to me today. I got fired from the terrible factory job I had. Now I'm free to find a job which I like. Luckily I have a little extra money to live on while I look for the next job. I only have about three hundred dollars, so I'll have to find a job soon. I applied for two jobs today. One was for a retail store where they need someone in sales or warehouse work. I prefer the sales work. I'm too old and decrepit for lots of heavy lifting. The other job I applied for was a maintenance job. Tomorrow I'll apply for a security officer job. I'd like that one the best. I'm sure there will be plenty of people applying for it. I have two years of experience in night watchman work. I'd better not call it that. That's the way I listed it on my resume. I hope it doesn't cost me the job.

I've been barbequing chicken out in the cold night's wind. There was even a little rain. Chicken is inexpensive and helps us stretch our grocery dollars. The chicken, cooked with my old family recipe, is one of our favorites. We never get tired of it. That reminds me. I still haven't included the pecan pie recipe which I promised. I'm sure I'll find that recipe soon. Don't give up!

I was day dreaming a while ago about hiking in the mountains with only my original copies of my books on floppy disc. I stopped at a log cabin and asked if they had a computer and some floppy discs. They just happened to have some. I copied off about forty copies of my books on floppy discs and paid the family for the discs and computer use. Then I hiked all over the mountain, selling my books to other campers and hikers. It was a nice day dream. I always love it when I can sell a book that I've written. It makes me feel good all over.

Friday I have to pick up my last pay check at the cabinet factory. I sure hope they don't lecture me or try to make me feel bad. I have to turn in my ID badge. I've always had direct deposit with my check. I don't know which way this last check will be. The human relations woman asked me to pick up my check. Maybe she just assumed that I didn't have direct deposit. I don't like that woman. She wasn't at all understanding about my situation. She impressed me as being a company goon. I'm not letting anyone push me into a heart attack. I'm going to find a nice job this time. No more sweat shops for me. If I can't find a job in couple weeks, I'll just have to do more fishing and writing.

I just switched my font from Times Roman to Book Antigua. It instantly added fifteen pages to the length of this book. That was a neat trick. I like the Book Antigua font better because the letters are thicker and easier to read. If I'm printing books from my computer, it takes a little more ink, but it's worth it. The writing looks a little nicer.

I'm clear out of books. I gave one to both Goshen College Historical Library and to the Goshen Public Library. I sold one this week. I don't have any more. I suppose I can order two of the Mary Thresher books. I'll wait till I get a job to order any more of the fishing books.

I need to buy a fishing license Friday when I get my check. This weekend I might do a little Muskie fishing on Little Tippecanoe Lake. I have a nice rubber rainbow trout minnow imitation. I like the idea of not needing to use the large expensive live minnows. I hate torturing those minnows by putting a hook in their back. Even if that's the way to really catch some Muskies, I prefer the artificial bait. If I absolutely can't get one on artificial bait, then I might try a live minnow.

My friend, Joe Myers, just informed me that his mother has a toll free number for her phone. Now I can call him without it costing me a cent. Joe and I are planning on fishing in my dad's fish pond Sunday. Neither of us wants to buy a fishing license. The fishing is better in my dad's pond than anywhere else. The bluegill are a little small this year I hear, but there are plenty of bass in the pond.

I like taking my boat to Wawasee Lake because the waves sometimes challenge my small fourteen foot boat. When that happens, I stay on the far western end of a bay on the north end of the lake. I can't remember what they call that bay. I think they just call it "The Slip". There's a channel there that leads to the "Frog Tavern". That way I'm not too far from some beer when I'm fishing. I don't like to drink in the boat. If I do, I'm always needing to get rid of the processed beer. I don't like going in a can. It just isn't civilized. That's why I want a nice big thirty-one foot boat with a head. That's the civilized way to fish. The problem with a big boat is, you can't get into the shallow water where the bluegill are. I guess I'll keep my small boat too. That way I can either catch lots of bluegill in the small boat, or I can drink lots of beer in the big boat. I'll hire someone to be the designated driver. I sure don't want to run over another boat. That's what happened a few years ago on Wawasee Lake. A guy got drunk and ran his big cruiser right over a small fishing boat and killed the fisherman. That's why they don't allow drinking and boating anymore in Indiana.

It's a good thing I had the laptop in my car last night. The house blew up from a gas explosion. The bricks are all over the street. There's nothing left of my house. There are police cars everywhere. The fire truck is here. Luckily nobody was hurt.

The house didn't actually blow up. I was lighting the gas stove front burner and it flashed a little. See how I can exaggerate. I was just trying to create a little more excitement with this autobiography. I bought some fish worms today at the Travel Tender bait shop. He has the freshest bait. I don't like to buy worms when there is mold growing on top of the dirt. The big stores that try to sell bait, don't sell the bait fast enough. That's when you get mold growing on the dirt. I'm going to do a little bluegill fishing Friday. Today I just slept most of the day. I couldn't sleep well last night. It doesn't look like my weed killer is working on the chick weed in the back yard. The weed killer sat in the garage all winter and was frozen. I think that's why it isn't working.

I think viruses are promoted by some of the big computer manufacturers. They force many people to buy new computers. The viruses might have been the idea of small time hackers in the first place, but I think they are being promoted now by big money. There's big money is selling the latest anti-virus software. If people would quite spreading viruses all over the place, big money people would start to lose money. I think it's wise to buy inexpensive computers. That way it doesn't hurt your budget so much to buy a new one whenever you get too many viruses. I want a new desk top that has a built in CD burner. They only cost around six hundred dollars these days. I paid sixteen hundred dollars for my first computer back in 1991. I kept it for eight years. It was an IBM. Its memory is in a different language than the current Compaq Presario I have. I've had the Compaq for six years. It still works pretty well.

The internet is a pain, much of the time. You can't get any good maps. They are all primitive. Everyone wants to sell maps. That's why they won't let you get good ones off the internet. I was able to get quite a bit of information about Jamaica off the internet, but I couldn't get any nice close up pictures of the plant life. I know they have palm trees, but that's about all. When I get paid tomorrow, I'm going to the Borders book store and buy a travel book on Jamaica. That's the best way I can think of to learn about the island. I might stop by the public library and look it up in an encyclopedia.

I wish I had another book case in the house. I'd like one in the dining room. I have a book case in the basement, but I rarely use it. My most frequently used books are lying on the floor next to my easy chair. That isn't good for them.

I just got a packet of flyers with beautiful pictures of yachts on them. The various manufacturers want to know which ones I'm interested in. I mailed off the post card where I circled my selections. I picked the most stylish yachts of course. I need to become more informed on these yachts. I'll be picking one out in a couple years. I need one that can be used for fishing, but still offers exquisite styling and good fuel economy. I listed that I also wanted to be informed about financing for boats. I need a ten to fifteen year old yacht. I want one with good motors, but I won't be putting lots of miles on the boat. I'll be cruising and trolling for about a hundred miles per year. Even an older engine should be able to keep up with that, if it was properly cared for. Smoker Craft makes good boats. They make 28 foot pontoon boats. I could ask them to build me a combination fishing boat and house boat on 28 foot pontoons. That would be more in my price range.

I went over by Albion today to visit my friend, Joe. He bought me a pork chop dinner with mashed potatoes and sweet corn. It was a delicious meal. The restaurant was overlooking a lake. It was a combination restaurant and bar. We drank some beer and a couple hours after supper had some hot wings. The meals were only six dollars each. There was a fire place and there were stuffed fish all over the walls. The place was called the Wonder Inn. I'd like to go back sometime. The owner and his wife talked to me. They were nice people. The place is on Skinner Lake, which is two and a half miles east of Albion on highway eight. Sunday afternoon till eight at night is the time to get the supper special. I don't know what the prices are like during the rest of the week.

Not all the fish on the walls were caught on Skinner Lake. Some of the bigger fish were caught on Wawasee Lake. One of the fish, on the wall, was a large piranha. I had heard a few years ago that a piranha had been caught on Wawasee Lake. This might have been the one. The beer was only a dollar twenty-five per bottle. That's a nice price. Joe bought the beer. He's a generous guy. I loaned him a couple hundred dollars a few years ago. He was thanking me for it today. I couldn't even remember it. I guess my memory actually is fading.

Monday I'm going to apply at some more places. I'm going to try to find out from a friend who works in a bank, how much the banks pay to people who are just starting out.

I know of a building maintenance position that pays from eight to nine dollars per hour. I'll apply for that job. I'll call the security company and remind them that I want their job. I need to practice shooting my 45 caliber pistol. I usually shoot fifty rounds per session. The box of shells costs ten dollars. I can't afford to practice too often. I don't actually want the building maintenance job when it only pays eight dollars per hour. The work is too dirty and dangerous for that little money. I would gladly do it for thirteen dollars per hour. I prefer the job at Meijer. That would be clean work.

I need to go to sleep now, but I drank more cups of coffee than I can remember at Joe's place. I wanted to be wide awake for the long drive home. I made it home fine, but now I'm not sleepy. When I can't sleep I often go eat some berry berry cobbler with ice cream at Steak n Shake. It often gives me indigestion, but it sure tastes good. I can't justify spending too much money that way. I need to save every dime I can until I get another job. My wife is pressuring me to buy health insurance while I'm looking for a job. I'm pretty sure I can't afford that. The only time I've ever gotten injured in the last thirty years was from lifting a hundred pound chunk of steel at a factory. That caused a rupture operation that cost four thousand dollars. Since I won't be working for anyone, how will I get injured? I'm a very defensive driver. I don't get into car accidents. I think I'll be fine with no insurance for a little while. I don't think I'll be without a job for long.

It's May 3, 2005 and I just got a new job. I'm a professional security officer. Tomorrow I go to pick up my uniforms and Thursday will be my first day on the job. I'll be stationed at a company in Elkhart, Indiana. I'll be monitoring who comes into the building and I'll help people find places in the building. I also will need to do some driving and watching parking lots. I'll get paid every two weeks. I have to pay quite a bit for my health package, but it includes dental and eye care. This will be the job I'll stay at till I retire. I know I'm going to like this job. I won't be carrying a gun, but I'll have a radio. I know I can call the police if there's any trouble. The boss seems like a nice guy. He'll be nice to work with. This kind of laid back job should leave me with plenty of energy to write and to go fishing. I feel like my prayers have been answered. When I was in that last factory, I felt like I was going through hell. I think I'm entering what they call the golden years. I might be a little too young for that, but things certainly are becoming more golden.

I picked up my uniforms for the new job today. I had to pass a urine test, which I did without much effort. I signed about one million forms. I'm looking forward to my first day on the job tomorrow. I'm taking a small note book so I can write down various training information. I don't want to have to rely totally on my memory. It's a good thing I shaved off my beard before I applied for this job. They don't like beards. The job manual says you have to get permission before you can grow a beard. The manual also said that I can't miss many days of work. I'm setting a goal of never missing a day of work.

I have the weekend off. I'm going to do some pistol practice and then do a little fishing. There is a remote possibility that I might be called upon to carry a gun for the job. There isn't a big chance, but it's possible. I need to be a good shot with the pistol.

I like my new job. There's quite a bit to learn. It's a complicated job. There's much to remember. It doesn't wear you out like a factory job. I know I'll like it even more when I know how to deal with all the phone calls I need to answer and redirect. The phone rings much of the time. If I leave for thirty minutes to make patrols, the phone says that I've missed ten phone calls while I was away.

Tomorrow I'm going mushroom hunting with my friend, Tom Myers. I met an avid mushroom hunter at my store where I buy beer. He said that from May 1st to May sixth, he found hundreds of gray mushrooms. His name was Eric. He said that most people say you start finding yellow mushrooms on Mother's Day, May eighth. He said we'll need a rain to get the mushrooms to come up. They often grow under apple trees. I love to fry morels in butter on a cast iron skillet. I roll them in flower and then fry them. Morels are one of the best foods that exist. They're almost as good as my barbequed chicken. Tom and I will be hunting the yellow morels in Michigan. They are somewhere off Highway 40, I think. I don't dare give away Tom's favorite mushroom hunting spot. One of the bosses I had at the cabinet factory said there are many mushrooms to be found about fifteen miles north of Cadillac Michigan. You have to know someone who lives there that will let you hunt on their property. There is some public land. When I retire, I'll go up there and try to make friends with some local land owners up there. I remember last year the morels were selling for twenty dollars per pound in Goshen. I heard that this year they will be higher.

My chicken is starting to get done on the grill. I'm going to finish it in the oven at 350 degrees for an hour. That way I'll know it's done all the way through. Nancy loves the chicken I make. I traded my 2 ½ dollar gold coin today for sixty-three dollars cash and three old coins. All together I got one hundred and thirty-six dollars for the gold coin. I can't believe I was trying to sell it for one hundred dollars this week. I went to a coin shop in Goshen, and the owner would only give me a hundred dollars for it. I couldn't believe my ears when the owner of the shop in Bristol, Indiana said he would give me a hundred and twenty-five cash or one hundred and thirty-six with trades. I traded for an 1803 large penny, an 1822 large penny and an 1858 Flying Eagle penny. I like having a large variety of coins in my collection. I only have about one hundred and fifty dollars in the collection now. I sold most of my silver last month. I use coins to get me through emergencies. I can't seem to save cash very well. I spend it as fast as I get it. If I buy rare coins, I tend to hold on to them unless I need the money desperately. I've missed nine days of work from losing my old job, so I needed some cash from the coin collection. If it weren't for the coin collection I'd be in a jam. I use my gun collection in a similar fashion. It's like a bank. It preserves my money. I only sell a gun if I need money desperately.

I'm going to find that pecan pie recipe soon. I know that my readers are getting impatient for the recipe. I think I have it in the desk top computer upstairs. I have my barbequed chicken in the oven now. It's finishing cooking there. It doesn't hurt the flavor to cook the chicken for an hour in the oven. You need to put a cup of the basting sauce in the bottom of the pan so the chicken won't dry out. It doesn't hurt to cover the pan with foil or a lid. I just leave it open. When it's cooked, I let it cool down and then put the chicken in freezer bags and place it in the refrigerator till I'm ready to eat it.

I have quite a bit on my mind right now. I'm trying to memorize all the things I need to know to do my new job as a security officer. I'll probably do this job for twenty years. I might get a little bored at times, but I won't quit. I'll spend time at work thinking about how to make my latest book better. I can read the Bible at work after eight in the evening, when the phone stops ringing so much. I'll enjoy going to the 7-11 store for a sandwich during my lunch break. You can get a sandwich for $2.00 there. That's a good price. I can hardly afford to bring one from home for that much. At least those sandwiches will give me a little variety. I soon get tired of my own sandwiches. I'll snack on cheese sticks and apples. I like apples and oranges. I need to buy a small satchel to keep my pills and books in. Then I could put ice in my lunch box and keep barbequed chicken in there. I never get tired of barbequed chicken.

Once I get this new job learned well, I'm sure my mind will return to writing my next book. Well, I'm starting to get tired. It's almost time to take the chicken out of the oven. Then I'll go to bed when I get the chicken in the frig.

I was tired last night and didn't dip the chicken in the sauce often enough. The chicken doesn't have as much flavor as I'd like. At least I got it well cooked. My friend Tom and I went mushroom hunting today. We went to a state woods that is close to Swiss Valley ski lodge. We didn't find any mushrooms, but I got some valuable information about the mushrooms from another mushroom hunter who we ran into in the woods. He was a young and friendly person. He showed us where he sometimes finds mushrooms in the woods. He said to look near some pine trees in the woods. There's a trail from the ski lodge parking lot that leads right to the pine trees. If you walk south along the pine trees to a dry stream bed, you may find mushrooms on the sides of the stream bed. The informative young man had seven or eight small gray morels in his plastic bag. He probably had so many good places which he knew about, that he could afford to be helpful to some people like us. It's supposed to rain tonight and tomorrow. That should bring up the morels. I'll go back to the Swiss Valley woods next Thursday. There should be some morels big enough to see by then. Our young informative mushroom hunter had a children's rake with him for pushing the foliage aside to make it easier to see morels.

I found myself wishing that I'd brought a bottle of water with me. The hills in the woods were steep and I felt my heart pounding in my chest. My father wants to go with me Thursday. I warned him that the hills are rough on the heart. I'll take him along. We'll just have to take our time. It was great to be out in the woods. I don't do enough hiking. I have a nice backpack and plenty of camping gear. I'll start hiking more now that I have an easy job. I'll need the exercise.

Tom and I walked for about forty minutes without coming to the end of the woods. I think I might be more correct to call it a forest. There have to be hundreds of acres of trees in that forest. I can't wait to explore it more. There were many dead elm trees in the forest. Some were standing, while others were lying on the ground. Tom thought that morels tend to grow around elm and birch trees. He also thinks they grow around apple and pear trees. I think during dry times like we've had this spring, you'll do better if you look where water is. Go to low areas where the soil is moist. The helpful morel hunter said he found his morels on the side of a ditch that ran along the road. As we left to go home, I saw a man searching the ditch for morels. The trouble with that type of search is that everyone else is looking there every day. I like the idea of searching wooded areas, especially areas that are far enough from the road that not many people will be searching there.

I forgot to mention, there were thousands of flowers out today. They were white and lavender colored. Many areas were blanketed solid with flowers. It was a sight to behold. I need to find some flyers from the DNR which tell where all the public campgrounds and forests are in Michigan. I have a strong urge to go hiking and camping now that I've been in the big woods this year. Since I couldn't find any morels, I decided to eat an orange mushroom that I found growing at the base of a tree. I sat leaning up against that dead elm tree and munched on that mushroom. Soon a little leprechaun came up to me and gave me a tour of the woods. We walked to the source of the stream bed that I mentioned earlier. He led me to a pile of stones. He rolled some of the stones away and showed me a pot of gold. He said I could have it all for a day, but then I had to return it. I ran my hands over the gold and enjoyed its glitter in the sun light. I filled my pockets and ran around the woods laughing and enjoying the weight of my new found wealth. As the sun started to set, I returned to the stone pile and put the gold back. The meal of the mushroom had worn off and the leprechaun was gone. In a half hour the gold disappeared. Then I realized that gold is just temporary. You can't take it with you to heaven. I had known that before, but this made it more real. Of course the whole thing wasn't real. I never ate a mushroom. I was just trying to tell a tall tale.

I want to have a pile of gold some day. I will first be generous with the poor and tithe like I should. The money that's left over, I'll use to build up a nice pile of gold. It will be nice to fall back on in case my car's engine falls apart. There is always another reason that comes along why a person needs a little money. If you try to keep piles of paper money, you are more likely to spend it as you go. The pile of gold becomes a friend to you. You like to look at it. You don't want to spend it unless it's absolutely necessary. Luckily, my friend Tom loaned me twenty bucks today, or I would have needed to cash in another coin from my collection. It's hard to go two weeks with no income. I used the money to buy some groceries. My future pile of gold will make it so I won't have to borrow money from Tom any more. I don't like borrowing from people. I try to keep some money stored away in case of emergencies. I've had plenty of trouble finding enough money in the last ten years. I know things will get better.

In 1977 I started to build a cabin of slab wood out in the twenty acre woods on my father's farm. I started a chimney of field stone and built a roof with an upstairs room. Then someone cut up all the slab wood for firewood and the project came to a halt. I found out that the person who cut up the slabwood was my wife's first husband, Waldo Gaby. When I found out it was him, I didn't complain. I knew Waldo. I must have sensed that he would die soon of a heart attack, leaving his wife and children for me to take care of. Waldo had a great sense of humor. My father's parents liked him quite a bit. It was my father's mother who told me I might want to marry Waldo's widow. My grandmother said that Nancy's piano playing would be a blessing to me through my entire life. That was Grandma Mayme. She always wished I would do better at sticking with a job and amounting to something. At least I followed her advice and got a nice wife for myself.

I think I'll do well for myself now that I have a pleasant security job. The pay isn't real high, but I know I've learned to control my spending. That's the important thing. I can always moonlight a little if I find that I want to buy something I can't afford. But I'll wait till I have the cash in hand before I buy things. No installment payments or credit cards. I don't want to go on cruises too often. Some day, though, I would like to take a cruise to Montego Bay, Jamaica. That is one place I would love to see. I love the security of the United States. I don't have much desire to go where I might get bombed or taken hostage. I wouldn't mind seeing Rome and England. Vacations can easily end up costing you more than you planned. I'll probably get a package tour where everything is included. That way I'll know how much I'm going to spend.

The nicest thing about fishing is seeing the fish come out of the water. There is always a surprise about how big the fish is or what kind of fish it is. I don't enjoy cleaning fish. I don't mind cutting off the head of the fish. I don't like cutting the fins off. The thick fins are difficult to cut through. I've spent around a hundred dollars buying various knives trying to find the best kind. The best one I bought only cost about four dollars and was made in Finland. It's short and flexible. It holds an edge. I use it for cutting fat off my chicken parts before I barbeque them. I don't mind running fish through my fish skinner. You just turn a crank and it pulls the skin off the fish. I don't like filleting fish. It seems to waste too much meat. You have to have a big fish in order to have much meat left after you fillet it. I suppose I just need a little more practice so I can save more of the meat when I fillet. Nancy will only eat fish that are filleted. I prefer the fish that still have the rib cage on. I don't mind picking the bones out so I can eat the rib cage meat. That's some of the tastiest meat on the fish.

My youngest brother used to like to catch all the biggest bluegill out of the pond and then chuckle to himself when he saw me down there catching little ones all the time. He's stopped doing that, but his friends have taken over the practice. They take home forty big bluegill per day until the big ones are all gone. They are hogs. It makes my dad mad. He pays to stock the pond and then my brother's friends take all the fish. That's why I usually fish somewhere else. I don't like being in competition with my brother's friends. Tippecanoe is where I like to go. Not too many people fish that lake. I don't have to worry about big luxury boats running me over. I know where I can get some big bluegill there. I fish the channels around the lilly pads. I usually take some ice and a cooler with me. If I keep the fish on ice, they'll stay nice even if I keep fishing for five or six hours. Fish in a bucket of water will die and get stiff. I never clean a fish if it's gotten all stiff. I think they might have gotten too much bacteria growth by then.

My job went quite well today. I'm learning how to use the phone to page people and transfer calls. The day shift officer that I replace each day likes to collect coins like I do. He's going to bring some coins to work tomorrow. I'll take some of my collection in to show him. He's a nice guy. The officer who replaces me each night is quiet and all business. He just comes in and says I can leave. There is little discussion. I just oblige him by going home.

The time went quickly tonight. The workers often have family and friends who feel they must talk to the worker even though he is at work. It's almost comical, but some of the problems are indeed serious. One friend wanted to warn a worker that someone was waiting at his home with a big knife and wanted to kill him. I thought that was a little unusual.

It's Thursday, May 12, 2005, and I'm getting better at using the phone. I'm giving out traffic tickets and doing my patrols. I think I'll be able to do this job till I retire. I'm starting to know who is authorized to pick up paychecks. I had a few unauthorized people picking up checks. I reported them to my boss. I can handle minor frustrations like that. Some people with egos just want to pick up checks like they're a foreman when they actually aren't. They'll soon learn that I'm not the kind of person you want to mess with that way. I report everyone who is up to mischief. I always cover myself, by reporting everything that is suspicious. I used the two million candle power spot light tonight as I did my drive patrol. That powerful light helps quite a bit. It penetrates the dark spots where people could be hiding. I have an ear infection and it's making me too tired to do much writing. I hope to make more progress soon on my next book.

My wife saw me for the first time in my security officer coat and hat. She got a twinkle in her eye. I could tell she liked the uniform. I've noticed that some of the young women I work with seem to think I'm a nice guy. I think it must be the uniform. When I'm in jeans and a flannel shirt, women don't take a second look at me. Monday I'm going to get the owner to give me a new jacket and some better pants. I want to look my best. I know the owner wants me to look good too. The women want me to look good. Everyone wants me to look good.

I need to write to President Bush about some things. I'm sure I can come up with some ways to make this country better. Why not have criminals planting trees all over the country. We need people other than criminals planting trees. A group like The National Arbor Society needs to be formed that is more aggressive at getting the whole world covered with trees. I want thousands of acres of trees to be planted every day all over the world. I'll name the new tree planting group: Tree Planters of Planet Earth. Maybe another name could be: Global Tree Promotion, or make the word Green mean something. The last two letters could mean "Every Nation" I prefer three letter slogans like ABC. PTE= Plant The Earth PTN= Plant Trees Now TTT= Trees, Trees,Trees

Cover the Denuded Planet = CDP
Mark Lee Masters Tree Society
Tree Society of Planet Earth
Brotherhood of Tree Planters
Brothers and Sisters for a Greener World
Aggressive Forestry Society
Restorative Forestry Club
Restorative Forestry Club International
Forest Reclamation Club International (I like this one!)
Forest Reclamation International FRI (I like this one too!)

I'm enjoying some new readers here at Accra Pac. Everyone likes the Mary Thresher book. I'm not promoting the other books now. I can't wait to get money to publish my first book, *Who's Got a Taste for Killing?*. It's painful to tell people about that book, but have no copies to sell them. I currently only have two loaner copies of my Mary Thresher book. I hope to order some more copies soon.

I certainly am tired of working every day for a month! I need the money, but I'll be glad when next weekend comes and I have the weekend off. I have plenty of extra time at work, but there are interruptions. I need to be in my easy chair to write comfortably. I still need to work some more on the plans for my next book. I have the opening pages done, but I need to do more research on the fishes of the area and on the topography. I'll write about one area and then when it's time to move to the next area, I'll research that area. That way I won't forget too much of what I've done in the way of research. My memory seems to be getting a little shorter. I hope I can make the next book almost as good as the Mary Thresher book. I sense though, that Mary Thresher may very well be my best book. I have to maintain my momentum anyway. Writing, and thinking I am doing good work, is what keeps me feeling positive about life. Without the writing I would probably get depressed and discouraged.

A couple days ago I ordered two more copies of the Mary Thresher book. I have one of them sold already. A young man who is on work release said he would like to buy one of my books. He works with me at Accra Pac. He said he likes working with an author. He wants to help me out. The book will give him something to do while he's in jail. The wife of one of the line mechanics is an author. She wants to read my book too. I think she'll buy the other copy that I've ordered. One quality control worker is reading a loaned copy of the book. He's slow getting the book read, but he said that it's a good book.

The Mary Thresher book has too much witchcraft in it for powerful Christian organizations to want to back it. It has too much straightforward Christian evangelism in it for the Harry Potter crowd to want to back it. It's too full of real life. People's lives are often full of both good and evil. The Mary Thresher book is truthful. It says the evil leads people to hell. Jesus leads people to heaven. The twenty or so readers I have found, love the book. Who will have enough guts to back this good book? I need to send a letter with my description of the assets of the book to some powerful people who might be able to get the book moving. Oprah Winfrey or President Bush's wife. I need more copies of the book to do this. I'll start working on the letter soon.

I completed a promotional letter for the Mary Thresher book. I took a copy to Wal-Mart and posted it. I'll send a copy with one of my books to the President's wife. I'll have to get her name and address. I'll order a couple more books as soon as I can. I don't think I should send the book to Oprah unless she expresses an interest based on my promotional letter. I'll concentrate on Oprah first. I'll go to the internet and see if I can get her address.

The internet was discouraging. I found the Oprah web site, but when I tried to go to the book club, the computer seized up. Maybe the internet is overloaded on a Saturday night. I'll try tomorrow. I wish I'd had a little less coffee this evening. I don't feel sleepy at all, and it's after one o'clock at night. I'm too tired to work on the book, but not tired enough to go to bed. I guess I'll just brain storm a little about what should go into the next book. I think I'll leave witchcraft out of it all together. I'll have fishing and scuba diving at many Caribbean locations. The main characters will all be generous to the poor and they will all be Christians. The captain will have the book of Job explained to him as an explanation for why his Christian good family was killed in the hurricane. He will come to understand that God needs people who will praise him even when the chips are down. He doesn't want a bunch of robots who must praise him. He wants people who of their own free will praise him just because he is God. No praise for gifts and blessings. Praise because of love for him. This way I get to send out the message that I was going to send in the next Mary Thresher book.

The speeches about the book of Job will take place when the main characters are starving and thirsty on a desert island where they are marooned by a hurricane. The story of Job is revisited when the fishing party is saved and they get back more than they had lost. There are two boats, two movie cameras, more children and much more money. A Christian psychic helps locate the general area of the search for the captain and his fishermen. It's a boat load of environmentalists who actually save them and scold them for burning a tire as a signal fire. While they were on the island, their stocks soared. When they returned, they were all millionaires. This will be the parallel to how Job ended up with more livestock, children and houses.

I still don't feel like starting again on the book. I want to learn more about Montego Bay. I went to Barnes and Noble and glanced through some of the travel books. What I need is a topographical map and a road map. I need the names of streets. I need to know where the high spots and cliffs are. I need to know if there are any cliffs. I could bluff it through, but I'd prefer to be accurate. Ian Flemming wrote about a castle on the beach in Japan that didn't actually exist. I'll do as much research as I can about Montego Bay and the rest of the Caribbean, then I'll have to just go ahead with my writing.

I visited the Violett Cemetery today once again. I've been going there quite a bit. I'm trying to decide if the stone I contracted for is actually the one I find most pleasing. I don't see much gold or white lettering. Sometimes it's hard to read the lettering on the stones. I'd like gold lettering if it would last. I wonder what gold lettering would be made of. It's frustrating to not have the money to pay for the stone I've contracted for. Actually I've just asked for an estimate. I haven't signed any contract. I'm using black polished granite. I might change to a dark gray. I saw one stone that was like the stone in 2001 A Space Odyssey. I was not thrilled with the author's verses on the stone. I don't know if I could do better though. I think it helped me decide that I might use a verse from Shakespeare, "When I compare my state with . . ." I'm not sure of the title. It would be good on a stone. I'm going to work on something similar now.

One's stature and earthly goods will not endure,
When God your heavenly spirit doth require.
The power of Jesus covers all our sins.
His love will lift us up and take us higher.
By Mark Lee Masters

Di Vinci and Michelangelo would inspire
Mankind to know perfection in their art.
Yet somehow we descend a slippery gyre,
Towards doom, our best attempt is but a start.
My hope is that the cycle is complete.
No lower will we go into the mire.
May renaissance occur on every street.
Creative minds must once more set a fire.
Regardless of our current lowly state,
I've tried to entertain with humble pen.
When I am laid below the earth, in state,
May people read my titles once again.
A simple story sometimes is the best
In heaven now I'll live to tell the rest.

By Mark Lee Masters
Inspired by William Butler Yeates

The previous sonnet may go on the back of my tombstone. I read Yeates's *Under Ben Bulben* just before I wrote this. The word gyre came from the poem. The idea of man's culture going through cycles of excellence and then poor quality was partly my own idea and partly learned from Yeates. All one has to do, is look at the history of art, to see that the idea is true. Nothing currently being done is as good as the Renaissance work. Stanley Kubrick was a genius in producing films. His 2001 A Space Odyssey was an excellent film. He would be an exception to the decline of excellent work.

When in disgrace with fortune and men's eyes . . . is my favorite sonnet by Shakespeare. I think it stands out as his best sonnet. I've read all 152 of his sonnets. Most of them don't come close to the quality of the one I just referred to. I can't decide whether to put it on the back of my tombstone, or to put my own poem on the back. I may put them both there. That would tend to highlight how inferior I am to Shakespeare. But isn't everyone inferior to him?

It's regrettable that few people read books compared to twenty years ago. Many people have been lured into videos. Even if people want to read, the books are priced too high for many people today. I'm still thinking of having my books printed in the Philippines or in China so I can make them available to people with less money.

I feel good about writing a sonnet today. I hadn't written one for fifteen years. Subject matter is everything when writing sonnets. If you write of love, the state of man or death, you have a chance of writing something profound. I take solace in the fact that most of Shakespeare's sonnets were a little boring. I wrote about eighty poems back in the early 1980's. They were a little boring. I still have them in the memory of my first computer. There is a problem with converting them to the new computer languages. I don't feel like typing them all off the old computer. Maybe when I retire, that will seem like a worthwhile use of my time. Poetry is sometimes popular because it carries a political theme that is popular. I haven't written political poems. There might be money in doing that. I think I'll stick to writing about fishing. The fishing story that also carries the story of Job is a worthy undertaking, I think. It might be a better book than Mary Thresher. I think it was a bad idea to try to have a book that would lure in the Harry Potter readers and then explain the evil of witchcraft to them. By having too much witchcraft in the book, it alienates the Christian reader. The heavy Christian theme at the end of the book alienates the witchcraft lover. I have a book that alienates most readers. I think many readers have liked the book. People like surprises. People think the book is a witchcraft book, and then they are surprised to find it is a Christian book. The next book will have no witchcraft in it. It doesn't pay to try to sell a book with lots of witchcraft in it to Christians. Some Christians are open minded enough to read the witchcraft part of the book, but most are too turned off by it. I've read a Harry Potter book. I admit that it was interesting. I just don't like the message that witchcraft is just fine, and witches live happily ever after.

I wrote another sonnet. This one I also tentatively plan to have put on the back of my tombstone. My wife was appalled when she read it. She thinks that I think too much about death.

With no vast gift to drive me on to fame,
I worked with simple thoughts which came to mind.
Small words oft graced the pages as they came,
To fill my books, leaving pretense behind.
My coffers were not filled with grand reward,
For verse that titilates the yearning ear.
No terse satire cut like a two edged sword,
Cutting deep and causing all to fear.
A story teller can do naught but say,
The words which muses whisper in his ear.
At times a word or two from God will play,
Upon his mind and make the vague come clear.
Now from the grave I've gone to heaven above,
With all my dearest friends I leave my love.

I was thinking about the trip to Ireland I made in the spring on 1986. I remember there were about ten students on the trip. I was studying linguistics in addition to the literature studies we were embarked upon. For some reason the first thing I remember was when we went out in a field near the farm of Peter Fallon. We came to a small hill with some boulders at the top. When we got to the boulders, we saw that some carvings had been made on some of the stones. There was a large spider portrayed. I told the other students that I thought the spider meant that the person who carved it was a witch. The stones had been a meeting place for witches. There was also a circle carved in the stone. I thought that might have meant sun worship. I can't remember what all I said about the spider cult, but I know that I probably created a long shaggy dog story about what the witches did in those days. They used the threat of curses to get the local people to give them food. I'm pretty sure they did that. They experimented with herbs and weeds to find powerful medicines. Most people probably wished the witches would stay away, but when they were desperate for a cure, they would go call the witch.

That day at the cairne, where the stones were carved, I did more talking than at any other time on the trip. I wrote some poems while I was in Ireland and I kept a brief journal. It was a wonderful experience. Everyone should spend some time in Ireland.

I am starting to feel like bringing this book to its conclusion. I've promised all along that I'd include my pecan pie recipe. Here it is.

The award winning pecan pie recipe of Esther Gene Miller,
the mother of Jonathan Lee Miller.
AKA Mark Lee Masters.

Two 9" Pecan Pies

Five extra large eggs or six large eggs.
One and 1/3 cups sugar.
Two thirds teaspoon salt.
Two thirds cup butter.
Two cups dark corn syrup (Or one cup light and one cup dark.)
Two cups pecans.

Bake at 375 degrees for 40 minutes. Reduce heat to 300 degrees for 10 minutes.

Pastry:

One quarter teaspoon salt
One and one third cup Crisco
Two cups flour
Eight tablespoons water
Use standard procedures for combining ingredients to make the crust.
Prebake crusts for 4-5 minutes in oven preheated to 375 degrees.

More About the Author

Mark Masters graduated from Goshen College in the spring of 1986. He had written poetry all his life, but it was Goshen College that encouraged him to write longer works. The faculty of the English department encouraged him to follow his lifelong yearning to write books. His first copyrighted book was *Fishing with a Young Nymph.* He finished that book in April of year 2000. Over the next three years, he developed the detective story version of that book, which he titled *Who's Got a Taste for Killing*? *Fishing For Almost Anything That Moves* was his next book. It was full of fishing action. Fishing action will likely play a part in most of his books. Mark often goes on charter fishing trips to Lake Michigan. He can often be seen fishing the small lakes around his home town. He learned to love fishing from his grandfather on his mother's side of the family. His grandfather was a medical doctor who fished to relax. Mark still loves to relax by fishing. He also loves to eat fish. Bluegill are his favorites.

When Mark retires from the various jobs that he does to earn cash, he longs to go bonefishing in the Caribbean. With a great love for the scenic beauty of the tropics, there is a tendency for him to choose tropical settings for his books. He thinks the readers should be given some time to imagine themselves in the tropics. He gives them a chance to do this with his vivid descriptions of tropical settings. Not everyone can afford to go to the Caribbean or to Tahiti, but they can buy a book that will take them there. The reader can enjoy the fun of being there without having to tip everyone who carries a bag or brings a drink.

Mark's third book was entitled *Mary Thresher In Search of Sunken Treasures.* That book was action/adventure. He feels it is his best book to date. Mark has traveled to Costa Rica where he stayed for three months studying the language. He later stayed in Ireland where he also studied the language and made friends with the poet Peter Fallon. Mark spent a full year in Canada back in 1975. He worked with young people there as a Christian counselor. He was born in 1950, on March 1st. He hopes to come out with a new book every couple years. He enjoys fishing books, Agatha Christi, and Earnest Hemingway for leisure time reading. His fouth book was *Dr. Exeeto,* followed four months later by the sequel entitled *Mirth.* His sixth book is entitled *The Mark Lee Masters Collection Vol. I.*

The End

Printed in the USA
CPSIA information can be obtained
at www.ICGtesting.com
LVHW052140070923
757597LV00029B/138